Pr...
Smoke a...

BARBARA MICHAELS

SMOKE AND MIRRORS

BERKLEY BOOKS, NEW YORK

This Berkley book contains the complete text
of the original hardcover edition. It has been
completely reset in a typeface designed
for easy reading and was printed from new film.

SMOKE AND MIRRORS

A Berkley Book / published by arrangement with
the author

PRINTING HISTORY
Simon & Schuster edition published 1989
Berkley edition / January 1990

ISBN: 0-425-11911-4

To Grace Peterson

One of the great ladies of the book
 business
And my dear friend

"Politics are almost as exciting as war, and quite as dangerous. In war you can only be killed once, but in politics many times."

—Winston Churchill,
Remarks (1920)

"You have all the characteristics of a popular politician: a horrible voice, bad breeding, and a vulgar manner."

—Aristophanes,
The Knights (424 B.C.)

"Politics is still the greatest and the most honorable adventure."

—John Buchan, Lord Tweedsmuir,
Pilgrim's Way (1940)

PROLOGUE

THEY CAME *to him every night. They never moved; they never spoke. They just stood there, by the side of the bed, their grave dark eyes fixed on his face. One of the smaller ones clung for support to its mother's skirt. The smallest of them lay cradled in her arms.*

She didn't look at all the way he remembered her. She looked old—scant graying hair, wrinkled cheeks—the way she might have looked if she had lived out her natural life, prematurely aged by poverty and hard work. He had never seen . . . the others. (Don't use the words, don't even think them: the little ones, the children.) The images he saw bore no resemblance to reality, they had shaped themselves from the dark ectoplasm of guilty nightmare. But those cobweb forms were stronger than sleeping pills or liquor or any of the other means by which he had sought oblivion. Shadow shapes, stronger than steel or stone. There was no way he could prevent them from coming.

Every night he lay paralyzed and helpless, waiting for it

to happen. It was always the same, and oddly beautiful—a bright ruffle of gold around the hem of her ragged skirt. That was when he woke, sweating and struggling for breath and thanking God for sparing him the final horror. But the night breeze seemed to carry a faint, grisly scent, and there was always the fear that one night he might not wake in time.

Chapter One

THE FACE was thirty feet high. Dark hair crowned it, like a hillside streaked with snow. The yard-long lips curved gently, with just the hint of a smile. The eyes were mesmerizing, not only because of their size; by some trick of setting they seemed to stare straight at the viewer, demanding his attention.

Erin turned the wheel slightly; she had been drifting dangerously close to the shoulder of the road. The billboards must be new. She had not noticed them before. They should have been hard to miss; but the eyes and their complex interconnections with brain and nervous system have a disconcerting habit of seeing only what concerns them. Until recently Erin had had only the mildest interest in politics, much less a local Senate race.

She wondered who had designed the advertisement, if that was the right word. But it was just that, an ad designed to sell a product—in this case not so much a person as a carefully packaged image. Rippling folds of red and white framed the giant face, stars floated on an azure background. The printed message, in glaring crimson, was short and simple: ROSEMARY WHITE MARSHALL FOR U.S. SENATE. No doubt the anonymous designer had calculated to the letter how many syllables an average reader could absorb while approaching the billboard at so many miles per hour.

Traffic was heavy, as it always was, even on Saturday. The Virginia suburbs of Washington had expanded rapidly over the past decade; housing developments, huge office complexes, and gargantuan shopping centers funneled tens of thousands of cars daily onto the highways. The traffic issue was a hot one in local politics, with one candidate pointing out the increased prosperity such growth had brought and another pandering to the fury of frustrated commuters who spent hours inching along the crowded roads on their way to and from work. Not until after she had passed the Dulles Airport exit was Erin able to relax at the wheel of her borrowed car. Traffic patterns and routes were unfamiliar to her, and she had not been behind the wheel of a car for almost a year. Fran, who liked to cultivate an impression of carefree affability, was in actual fact extremely selfish about her property, and the car was a prized possession. Only a very special occasion—and one from which, Erin thought uncharitably, Fran hoped to profit—had prompted her generosity on this occasion.

Fran was Erin's roommate, and at times her pet peeve. A friend . . . well, they certainly had not been friends in high school. It was not a question of active dislike back then, just of paths that seldom crossed. Their senior-class yearbook entries made their differing life-styles explicit. Fran's toothy grin appeared on every other page; as a cheerleader, member of the debating society and a dozen other clubs, as "most popular" and "most likely to succeed Joan Rivers." There were four pictures of Erin, in addition to the official senior photo. She had been editor of the literary magazine, a library aide, a member of the choir, and winner of the award for highest senior-class average grade. When they ran into one another at their class reunion five years later, they both had to squint surreptitiously at one another's name tags. It was pure accident that they had started talking.

Or so Erin believed at the time. To Fran, there were no such things as accidents. It was Fate—Karma—that had brought them together. It was Meant to Be. Fran had a way of encouraging people to talk—one of the reasons why she had been voted "most popular"—and Erin had been in a particularly vulnerable state of mind that day. She had talked, all right—spilled her guts, in fact—and Fran had made the right responses: sympathy for the recent death of Erin's father, interest in her plans, helpful suggestions.

"Suggestions" was probably too weak a word. As soon as Erin mentioned that she was thinking of moving to a larger city, where jobs in her field were easier to find, Fran began babbling about Karma. What a coincidence! Her roommate had just left and she was looking for someone to share her apartment in the Washington suburbs. It was a Sign, that was what it was. New York? You're crazy love, do you know what a one-room hovel in Manhattan would set you back? Do you have any idea what they pay editorial assistants? And talk about your mean streets—you'd be mugged or raped, or both, within a day. Listen, sweetie, there are thousands of magazines and newsletters and house organs published in D.C. . . .

Erin finally got a word in. "Thousands?"

Fran grinned and ran a careless hand through her fashionably tousled hair. "Hundreds, at least. Honestly, Erin, this is too perfect. I mean, you have to get out of this hick town. You said your mother is all set, living with your aunt and sharing expenses, but you can't stay there, you'll go crazy with two old ladies bitching at you all the time about cleaning your room and getting home by midnight."

Erin was feeling guilty and disloyal for complaining about her aunt's nagging and her mother's helplessness, but Fran's shrewd assessment struck a nerve; her lips curled, and Fran was quick to exploit her emotions. "They can't help it," she said kindly. "You know mothers. But that's no way for you to live. We can have a great time. And I know we'd get along. Just look at us, we're exact opposites. We complement one another perfectly. Yin and Yang, Laurel and Hardy. I'm Scorpio, you're Aquarius—''

"Gemini," Erin said.

"What? Oh." Fran dismissed this minor error with a wave of her hand. "Same thing."

The more Erin thought about the idea, the more it appealed to her. She had only dim memories of the years she had lived in Virginia, but the memories were all happy ones. She told Fran she'd think about it and let her know; and when she got home to face her aunt's probing questions about where she had been and why she was so late and how many beers she had drunk, the decision was made. It pleased everyone. Her aunt wasn't quite rude enough to say so, but her first, unguarded reaction to the news made it very evident that she would be delighted to see the last of Erin. Even her mother adjusted to the idea more readily than Erin had expected—so readily that Erin felt a little hurt.

"Well, but darling, you'd have to leave home sometime, everyone does, and at least you won't be alone—I know Mrs. Blenkinsop slightly, she was on the Library Committee with me, and she seems very pleasant, I'm sure her daughter must be a suitable companion for you—of course I would rather you were going to a home of your own, but you'll surely meet someone soon, there are lots of nice young journalists and congressmen in Washington."

Erin saw no reason to correct the numerous misapprehensions in this naive speech. Her mother was right about one thing—at least she wouldn't be alone. The transition to independence would be eased by someone who knew the ropes, the shortcuts, the pitfalls to be avoided. There were advantages for Fran too. She had found the ideal roommate—one who was too meek to complain or criticize.

On the whole they got on better than one might have expected. Fran had been right about how different they were, even in appearance. Fran was short and dark and rounded; Erin was six inches taller, with strawberry-blond hair and, in her opinion, a figure embarrassingly flat fore and aft. (She got no sympathy from well-rounded Fran about that.) Fran dressed in clothes she fished out of bins at Goodwill and local thrift shops; Erin's blouses, pants, and skirts were color-coordinated, and she never appeared in public with a button missing or a hem that sagged. Erin's room was immaculate; Fran's was a cheerful confusion of discarded garments, magazines, and newspapers heaped onto the perpetually unmade bed. Fran had dozens of friends; after almost a year in Washington, Erin had made none.

Fran couldn't understand it. "I can't figure you out, Erin. Is it insecurity or conceit that keeps you from opening up to people? You don't go anyplace or do anything—"

"That's not true."

"Well, maybe it's a slight exaggeration." Fran studied Erin with a speculative look the latter had come to loathe; she knew it often heralded one of Fran's forays into amateur psychoanalysis. "I guess losing your dad was traumatic," Fran mused. "According to that article I read last week, the death of a parent rates nine and a half on a scale of ten, and you were always his little girl—"

"Shut up, Fran," Erin said.

Fran was not offended. "At least you're learning to talk back. Must be my good influence."

Erin had to admit Fran was correct. What she could not admit, even to herself, was that Fran's offhand comment about her father had also struck home. She still dreamed about him several times a week, and often woke crying.

Her job was a disappointment. Fran had helped her find it, on the staff of the newsletter of a national merchandising organization. Erin had not minded starting out in a secretarial position, but after months of typing and filing and making coffee, with no prospect of the promotion she had been promised, she began to feel put upon. Fran listened sympathetically if impatiently to her complaints. "If it bores you, quit. There are other jobs; hell, there's always McDonald's. That bastard isn't going to promote you, not if he can find a man for the job, he's nothing but a goddamn chauvinist. Look what happened last month with the associate-editor job. You said the guy who got it had only been there six weeks."

"He does have a wife and a couple of children," Erin said. "He needs the money more than—"

"Jesus H. Christ! If you insist on walking around bent over, somebody is going to accept the invitation and kick you in the butt."

"I don't want to sound like some strident women's libber—"

"No, you're going to go on being one of those mealy-mouthed 'please-kick-me-because-I'm-a-woman' types."

When she was passed over the second time—for yet another man—Erin didn't mention it to Fran, but stored-up resentment boiled within her all week, and by Saturday night she was in a very sour mood.

For a wonder Fran was not going out, or entertaining friends. Erin knew what that meant, and as they settled down in front of the TV, she wondered what masochistic impulse kept her from excusing herself and retiring to her room with a book. Fran was a news freak. She could sit unblinking and absorbed through endless repetitions of the same information, including the weather. First came the local news, then the network news, followed in due course by the late-night news— one program at ten and another at eleven. On weekends the program was varied slightly by the addition of a number of talk shows and public-information broadcasts, not to mention political specials, of which there were an inordinate number during the fall of this particular election year.

Fran settled down with a tray that held a huge bowl of chili, accompanied by chunks of cheese and half a box of saltines. She was always trying to diet, but on Saturday night before the tube she didn't even try. "I need all my strength to yell at Novak," she explained.

Fran yelled at all of them—Novak, Sidey, McLaughlin, Will. She even yelled at Sam Donaldson, her idol, when she thought he wasn't forceful enough. Once, during one of Fran's verbal attacks on Morton Kondracke, Erin had been moved to protest. "They can't hear you, you know. Why do you waste all that energy?"

Fran wiped her perspiring brow. "It relieves my pent-up rage. Oh, hell, Kondracke, you limp wimp, why don't you tell him he's a carbuncle on the backside of journalism?"

At first Fran couldn't believe Erin failed to share her passion. "Not interested in politics? What the hell do you mean? How can anybody not be interested in politics? These people are running your life. Don't you care what they think—what they do?"

"They never say what they think and they never do what they say they're going to do," Erin said. "What's the point?"

"Huh," said Fran, for once at a loss for words.

Despite her lack of interest, Erin couldn't help absorbing some information. Washington was a political town. It was a trite truism, one to which she would have acquiesced without giving it much thought; but she had never really comprehended what it meant until she had moved to the area. There was only one subject that interested metropolitan Washington more than politics, and that was the Redskins. Mercifully Fran wasn't a football fan. Erin would have seriously considered moving out if she had been forced to watch football as well as political discussions.

Fran polished off her chili and trotted into the kitchen to prepare the next course. Erin slumped lower in her chair and pushed the salad around her plate. She had spent all morning cleaning the apartment; it wasn't her turn to do it, but things had gotten to such a state she couldn't stand it any longer. Then she had accompanied Fran to a newly opened thrift shop in Alexandria. The store had lived up to its principles by failing to install air-conditioning, and the internal temperature had been in the high nineties. Erin was tired. She wanted to sit and stare mindlessly at something that required absolutely no effort, physical or mental. There was a forties' musical on cable, and Channel 4 had a comedy sitcom about two guys and two girls who shared an apartment, an abandoned baby, and a cute chimpanzee. But the TV was Fran's, and Fran picked the programs, and Fran had chosen to watch a debate on one of the public-broadcasting stations. The District of Columbia had no voting representation in Congress—as its residents were constantly pointing out—but the suburbs of the city were in both Maryland and Virginia, so the congressional races in those states concerned a large percentage of the viewing audience.

Fran returned with a huge bowl of popcorn just as trumpets heralded the celebration of the democratic process. She thrust the bowl at Erin.

"Here. Eat up and pay attention. You'll be voting for some of these characters—Virginia Tenth District congressional race, and a senator."

Erin saw no reason to mention that she hadn't registered to vote. Fran seemed fairly calm at the moment; why stir her up? The popcorn was excellent, a little too salty, but dripping with butter. When Fran went off her diet she went all the way.

Erin reached for her mending and let her mind drift away from the TV as she concentrated on making the stitches neat and tiny. The object was a black lace dress she had rescued from a carton of miscellany at the thrift shop. Fran insisted on dragging her along on her cheapie shopping trips; she had that variety of enthusiastic self-confidence that tries to impose its tastes on unwary friends. Usually Erin managed to resist the two-dollar sweaters ("Real cashmere—those stains under the arms will wash out") and the limp, out-of-style skirts. The stains never did wash out, and the skirts could never be remodeled or mended or revived. But the dress had caught her eye, torn and crumpled as it was, because it was obviously of good quality, and the rents were mendable by someone with her skill at sewing. Besides, it only cost five dollars. The expensive wardrobe her father had given her was beginning to wear out, and she certainly couldn't afford to replace it. Might as well get used to thrift shops and Sears instead of designer labels.

Fran nudged her. "This is it. The Senate race. Are you watching?"

"Yes," Erin said absently.

The encounter wasn't a debate in the formal sense; a moderator asked questions, which the opponents answered. Erin rather liked the looks of Senator Bennett, the Republican incumbent, but she knew better than to express her views, for Fran's opinion of the gentleman and all his works was outspokenly profane. He was a fine-looking man with a profile that resembled one of the more high-minded Roman emperors. Though he had obviously been schooled in public speaking, enough remained of the soft Virginia accent to make his slow, deep voice very easy on the ear.

His opponent was a congresswoman making her first bid for the Senate. The fact that she was a woman would have been enough to win the loyalty of Fran, a self-proclaimed and defiant feminist. Erin had another, more personal reason for being interested in Rosemary White Marshall. She let her sewing fall to her lap and watched.

Marshall was in her early fifties and, Erin thought, she looked every day of it. Her eyes were her best feature, large, dark, and wide-set, but makeup didn't hide the fan of fine wrinkles at the corners of her lids or the deeper lines bracketing her mouth. When she smiled, which she did frequently, the lines curved into softer shapes, but her face was that of an affectionate grandma, not a mover and shaker of world events. Who, after all, would want a senator with dimples? Her soft pink suit and the ruffles framing her chin increased the grandmotherly image; she wore no jewelry except pearl earrings and a wide gold wedding band.

I'd have recognized her, Erin thought. She's changed a lot, but the resemblance is there.

At first Bennett dominated the debate; his booming voice sounded forceful and confident next to Marshall's soft alto. He took the offensive, reminding the audience of the worthy causes he had supported and the admirable legislation he had introduced. Among the latter was a day-care bill; and all at once, Marshall, who had been smiling and dimpling at the camera, interrupted.

"Now that's just so sweet," she said loudly.

The inappropriate comment caught Bennett off guard. His brief second of hesitation gave Marshall her chance. Her smile continued to dazzle, but it had turned predatory, lips curled back, teeth bared: Grandma transformed into the wolf.

"So sweet of Senator Bennett and his friends to jump onto the bandwagon. Better late than never, one presumes, but I only wish they had chosen to take this stand five years ago, when I introduced a child-care bill in the House. The companion bill in the Senate was defeated, thanks in large part to the tireless filibustering of Senator Bennett here. He was all in favor of six-hundred-dollar toilet seats for the Defense Department, but supporting the needs of America's children—oh, no, that would have been a waste of taxpayers' money! Now, five years later, child care is a national disaster, so desperate that even my myopic opponent has been forced to take notice. Ten and a half million children under six who are cared for by people other than their parents! Neglect, child abuse, physical and emotional torture. . . ."

Bennett couldn't defend himself, she never gave him a chance; the soft but surprisingly incisive voice went on and on, barely pausing for breath. The questioner had to interrupt her to explain that they were out of time, whereupon she apologized, with the prettiest smile imaginable. "I just get carried away when I think about children being in danger. As a mother and grandmother . . ."

Fran was beside herself. "Isn't she great?"

"She dresses nicely," Erin said. "That soft pink—"

"Oh, for God's sake, I wasn't talking about her looks! Didn't you hear what she said? She ran rings around that old fart Bennett. He's the most reactionary, bigoted—"

"How could you tell? I didn't hear him commit himself to anything except God, motherhood, and a strong national defense."

"Hell, everybody's in favor of a strong defense. Marshall has fought Pentagon waste and overspending for years. Bennett gets hundreds of thousands in campaign contributions from military contractors; you think he's about to bite the hands that feed him by questioning their bills?"

"I think a person's appearance is very important," Erin said, reaching for her sewing.

"If you aren't the most . . ." Fran stopped and then went on, grudgingly, "You're right, actually. Politics is more appearance than substance these days. You can bet her staff has calculated every nuance, down to the diameter of her earrings. I guess the results must appeal to the greatest number of potential voters, but I'd like to see her show a little more pizzazz—funky earrings, a plunging neckline."

"I don't know anything about politics, but I know enough about clothes—and about people—to know that would be disastrous. She's not a young girl. Older women should dress conservatively, like ladies. I admit that pink is a little bland. With her coloring she could wear more vivid shades—turquoise or bright coral. It would come over better on television too, I'll bet."

"Maybe you ought to write and tell her all about it," Fran said sarcastically. Her fingers scraped the bottom of the bowl, gathering the last stray kernels.

"Maybe I will," Erin said. Sometimes Fran's superior manner rankled. "Mother's been nagging me about getting in touch with her."

If she hoped to impress Fran, she succeeded. The latter's eager questions made it easy for her to appear cool about the relationship—which wasn't, in her private opinion, worth bragging about. Her mother and Rosemary White had once been close friends; "but it was years ago—they were in college together." The correspondence had deteriorated into little more than an exchange of Christmas cards and family photos, but Rosemary had written a lovely letter of condolence after the death of Erin's father.

"Written? In her own hand?" Fran asked breathlessly.

"You don't type condolence letters."

"I do. When I write them at all." Fran considered the matter. "My God, this is exciting Why didn't you tell me you knew her?"

"I don't. And I don't understand why you're so thrilled. She's just another politician. Washington is full of them."

"She's not just another politician. She's a comer. No question about it. With a little luck she could be the first woman President. Not now—maybe in ten years. If she wins this fall . . ."

"According to McLaughlin and Novak, she hasn't a prayer," Erin said. "All the commentators I've heard seem to favor the other candidate, Mr. Bennett."

"Popularly known as Buzz the Buzzard," said Fran. "You haven't read the latest polls, I guess. It's true that when she first agreed to run, nobody gave her a chance. Bennett's entrenched, he's been in the Senate for fifteen years. But after the flap about him and that girl . . ."

"I heard about it," Erin admitted. "But I didn't think it would make much difference. Everybody seems to be doing it."

Fran grinned. "You're more cynical than I thought. No, honey, everybody isn't doing it, and the ones that do do it are careful not to get caught. Buzz got caught with his pants all the way down to his ankles, and he'd been so damned self-righteous about his moral virtues that it hit him harder than it would have hit someone else. Then there's his wife. She's very popular with his constituents—the sweetest little old honeypie you'd ever want to meet. . . . Oh, hell, let's not talk about that, let's talk about Rosemary. She's my idol—"

"I thought your idol was Sam Donaldson."

"It's his eyebrows," Fran said dreamily. "They do something to me."

Erin had no comment to make on this but she wouldn't have been allowed to make it in any case. Fran sat bolt upright. "Hey. Hey! There's your answer!"

"Answer to what?"

"Your job problem. The campaign is heating up and she's still the underdog; she'll want all the people she can get. Why don't you ask her to hire you?"

"Her? Who?" Erin stuttered. "Her? You must be crazy. Why should she give me a job? I don't know anything about politics, or running a campaign, or—"

"You could give her advice on how to dress," Fran said, grinning. "No, but seriously. You're a crackerjack typist, and not entirely devoid of brains. That combination is rarer than you might suppose."

"Yes, but—"

So in the end—as she might have expected—she wrote the letter. Withstanding Fran's manic enthusiasm was like trying to remain stationary in a gale-force wind. Erin could do it— but only when the wind wasn't blowing in the direction she wanted to go anyhow. Not that she agreed with Fran's tirades about gender discrimination, but passing her over in favor of a less qualified applicant, male or female, just wasn't fair. The job was a dead end; high time she faced the fact. And it had been rather exciting to see Rosemary Marshall, after all the stories she had heard from her mother. Actually running for the Senate . . . The job, supposing she could get it, had to be more interesting than what she was doing.

The answer took a week to reach her. It sounded as if it had been written by an aide—cool, rather businesslike—but it did not propose a business appointment. Instead, she was invited to lunch the following Saturday. Directions to Rosemary's home near Middleburg were included. Fran was thrilled at this evidence of friendly interest. She had even made the ultimate sacrifice of offering the loan of her car, pointing out that it would be almost impossible to get to Middleburg any other way. Erin had accepted with thanks, and tolerated with relative good humor Fran's frenetic attempts to decide what she should wear; but she wasn't convinced the invitation was a good omen. She had not asked for friendship, she had applied for a job. This might be a way of turning down the application without overt rudeness to the offspring of an old friend.

She would soon know. The road had narrowed and the tight-packed dwellings of suburbia had dwindled to isolated houses. She was in the country now.

From time to time she caught glimpses of the distant mountains. That was what they called them here, mountains; a westerner would have laughed at the idea of using that word to describe the tree-covered, gentle mounds of the Blue Ridge. In the bright morning light they were more green than blue, with a few patches of pale color to break the monotony—soft yellow and muted orange, the beginning of the autumn change. It was late September, and unusually hot for that time of year. At least that was what Washingtonians claimed. They were, as Erin had learned, given to exaggeration.

Gilbert's Corners, where Routes 50 and 15 intersected, boasted a stop light and little else. Four miles to Middleburg. Seized by a sudden attack of stage fright, Erin pulled off the road. She didn't have to refresh her memory of the route she had been directed to take; she had memorized it. Instead she twisted sideways and looked into the rearview mirror.

It was too small to give her an overall view of her anxious

face. She started at the top and worked down. Frown lines
scarring her forehead—smooth them out, relax. Narrowed
gray-green eyes—open wide, look interested and optimistic.
There was nothing she could do about her nose. It was hopelessly plebeian, snubbed and freckled like a plover's egg. Not
that she had ever seen a plover's egg, but that was the conventional literary image. . . . She stretched her mouth and
stroked on additional lip gloss. Her hair was her biggest problem; both fine and thick, its reddish-blond waves refused to
stay confined in a neat coil. I should have had it cut, she
thought, and reached for the pins. A glance at the clock on
the dashboard warned her against that move; better to be on
time and slightly disheveled than late—and probably just as
disheveled. Short of a coat of varnish, there was no way she
could confine the floating wisps. In the humid heat, hair spray
turned sticky and gluey. Erin's tailored wool suit was uncomfortable as well as somewhat inappropriate, but she had had
little choice; her summer-weight clothing was hopelessly out
of style, or too casual. The pale-green classic suit had lived
up to the saleslady's claim, and Erin was determined to look
professional. Fran had hooted at the suit, the white blouse
with its soft bow at the throat, and the simple pumps—''You
look like little Miss Manners''—but Erin had remained ob-
durate.

A chorus of whistles and howls from a passing pickup
brought the frown back to her face. Chauvinist rednecks . . .
Realizing what she had thought, she was surprised at herself.
She'd been listening to Fran yelling about men too much. Nor
was ''redneck'' a good choice, the young men were potential
voters, and for all she knew, they could be Harvard Ph.D.s.

She waited until another truck had passed—did everyone
in rural Virginia drive rusty-blue pickups?—before pulling
back onto the road. Soon she was in the outskirts of Middleburg. Handsome dignified houses, set back from the road,
low stone or white-painted fences preserving their privacy.
Then the town itself—elegant shops, eighteenth-century
houses and inns. She made a left turn and was soon in the
country again; white fences outlined rolling pastureland where
horses grazed on grass yellowed by the summer heat. Occa-

sionally the chimneys and rooflines of mansions could be seen over the trees that enclosed them in smug aloofness. Fran had given her a crash course on the notables of the Middleburg area: actors and football players, publishers and presidents. John F. Kennedy had spent only a single weekend at his retreat at Wexford before the fatal trip to Dallas; the estate had passed through several hands before Reagan stayed there during the presidential campaign of 1980. The region's most glamorous resident had been Elizabeth Taylor, when she shared the heart, hand, and home of Senator John Warner. Taylor had gone on to greener pastures, but another of Hollywood's not-so-youthful glamour queens had recently moved in to replace her on the local scene, if not in the hearts of her fans and those who had found her outspoken comments on the political world enormously refreshing.

Erin drove slowly, watching for the turn. She found it, though not without difficulty; there was no sign except for a small country-road marker. The new road was well maintained and fairly straight, but it was barely wide enough for two cars. She met only one vehicle—sure enough, another pickup.

The first sign of habitation appeared as a break in the tangled vegetation to the left, marked by a pair of stone pillars. It couldn't be the Marshall place; according to the directions she had received, it was on the right-hand side, and there was still another mile to go. The people who lived out this way certainly cherished their privacy. The clustering greenery lining the road appeared to be impenetrable.

As soon as she had received the invitation, Erin had begun cramming on the subject of politics in general and Rosemary White Marshall in particular. Even Fran had been impressed at her industry, though her compliment might have been phrased more politely: "The one thing you do know is how to study."

The Marshalls didn't have as much money as some of the other residents of the area, but their social and political lineage was impeccable. There had been a Marshall in state or national politics for almost two hundred years, and Rosemary's husband Edward had held the House seat to which she succeeded upon his death—the so-called "widow's game," which until recently had been a woman's easiest entry into politics. The Marshalls were aristocrats of Ole Virginny, but Ed Marshall had married beneath him; Rosemary's father had been a postal clerk from Arlington, her grandfather, a laborer. These biological details were stressed in her campaign literature; the monied, old-boy network might be useful in raising funds and collecting favors, but the average voter was more impressed by a picture of Granddad in overalls, brandishing a hammer.

Erin glanced at the odometer. Almost there. Another break in the underbrush, this time on the right. This must be it. As she had been promised, the gate was open. It was no impressive construction of wrought iron between massive gateposts, but a simple wooden farm gate. Beyond was the driveway, graveled but not paved, with ominous ruts and potholes breaking its surface. The house was a good quarter mile from the gate. Erin stopped and stared.

She had expected a stately mansion, along the lines of Twelve Oaks or Tara—a white-pillared monument to the Old South set in green velvet lawns, or a graceful gem of Federal architecture like Monticello. The house was big enough, and white enough, but there wasn't a pillar to be seen, and the wings and additions that shot out from it, apparently at random, robbed it of any claim to architectural purity. To the south and east of the grounds the land rose in an enclosing semicircle of heavily wooded hills. The land to the north was open field, sloping down to a little river—a run, as they called them here. No blooded horses cropped the pasture; the fields had gone wild, Queen Anne's lace and burdock and the blue of wild gentian mingling with knee-high grass.

Erin took her foot off the brake and proceeded at a cautious crawl. The driveway really was a disgrace. The closer she got to the house, the more evidences she saw of—not neglect exactly, but certainly not the impeccable maintenance one would have expected to find in an estate with the imposing name of Fairweather. The house needed a coat of paint. The lawn had been cut but not raked; a series of flower gardens to the left of the driveway, running to the edge of the pines, were weedy and carelessly tended. The bright profusion of blooms seemed to consist mainly of zinnias, petunias, and marigolds—the cheapest, most easily maintained of all annuals.

So maybe the Marshalls weren't rich. Money was the manure of politics, according to Fran, and a campaign could do nasty things to a candidate's cash flow, especially if he or she was running against a popular, well-funded incumbent. A thirty-second TV spot cost more, and was more important, than a coat of paint.

The drive divided as she neared the house. The left-hand portion, narrower and even more rutted, led toward a clutter of outbuildings. Erin took the right-hand turn, which circled the house and ended in a sunbaked stretch of bare ground. She pulled up beside one of the cars parked there and turned off the engine.

It was no wonder she had received no coherent impression of the house; what she had seen before was only one side of it. This was the front, the formal entrance, but the adjective was screamingly inappropriate for what she beheld: Victorian Gothic at its best, or worst, with the wonderful indifference to coherence that had marked some of the more entertaining examples of the genre. A stately tower, with a shingled cupola; a long porch or veranda, stretching all the way across the front and curving giddily around the corner; windows of all shapes and sizes, some perfectly ordinary rectangles, others arched and framed in gingerbread. It might have looked impressive if the material had been stone, but white clapboard just didn't do the job. The bits and pieces of furniture scattered the length of the veranda were an eclectic blend of rickety wicker and modern plastic. There was even a porch swing, hanging from rusted chains. The cushions on sofas, chairs, and swing matched only in the degree to which the varied fabrics had faded. And most of the cushioned surfaces were occupied, though not by people. The motionless mounds appeared to be cats—of all sizes, colors, and shapes. At least a dozen of them.

Even in the few moments she had sat there, the interior of the car had warmed up considerably. She rolled the window down, but only a cautious two inches. Fran might be thrilled at pointing out a stain on the upholstery as having been made by one of Rosemary Marshall's cats. On the other hand, she might not.

Through the opened window Erin heard a sound she had not been aware of earlier, and her hand stopped on its way to the handle of the door. If it wasn't the furious baying of a gigantic hound, that was certainly what it sounded like. Not one hound—two or more. None of the cats had so much as flicked a whisker; it was probably safe to assume the dogs were chained or caged. Probably . . .

As she hesitated, the front door opened and a man came out onto the porch. (Though surely they called it a veranda in Ole Virginny?) He shouted at the top of his lungs, "Knock it off, will you? I heard you!"

The dogs stopped barking, so Erin deduced the remarks had not been directed at her. She got out of the car and walked toward the house. The newcomer trotted down the stairs and met her with a broad smile and an outstretched hand.

"Didn't anybody warn you about the dogs? It's okay, they're locked up."

Her modest two-inch heels raised her to a height of five-nine, only a little shorter than he. Her eyes were level with the tip of his nose—a particularly fine-cut, narrow nose, she couldn't help noticing. Fran would have noticed his eyebrows—thick, dark, splendidly arched. Any female with functioning eyesight would have noticed his build; his jeans fit like a second skin over lean hips and thighs, and his thin blue cotton shirt clung to shoulders that were almost disproportionately broad. His sleeves had been rolled to the elbows, baring muscular brown forearms, and the hand he extended was crisscrossed by scratches, presumably feline in origin.

"Hey, don't you listen to the weather forecast? Take off your jacket, why don't you, you must be roasting."

The hand, which she had mistakenly believed she was supposed to shake, had actually touched her shoulder before she stepped back, her face stiffening. "No, thank you. I'm quite comfortable."

"Oh, come on. You don't have to impress us, we're a casual lot—"

"So I observe."

He was a very good-looking man, with thick, unruly dark hair and brown eyes fringed by curling lashes. It was obvious that he was only too well aware of the effect those eyelashes— and his other attributes—made on impressionable females. Instead of being intimidated by her frosty tone, he grinned even more broadly.

"Okay, melt if you want. I was just trying—"

"I believe Mrs. Marshall is expecting me. My name is Erin Hartsock."

"I believe she is," the other agreed. "How do you do, Ms. Hartsock? Or do you prefer Miss?"

"As a matter of fact—"

"My name is Nick McDermott. I prefer Nick." He seized her limp hand and pumped it vigorously, continuing to hold it as he started for the house. His grip was firm enough so that Erin would have had to struggle to free herself. She had no intention of doing so, it would have been undignified, but she raged inwardly as she trotted to keep up with his long strides. From his confident manner she assumed he must be someone important, someone she dare not risk offending, but she resented him all the more because he looked so cool and comfortable in his shirtsleeves while her blouse was sticking to her perspiring body.

He led her up the stairs and across the porch, stepping over and around sprawled cats with practiced unconcern. The cats were equally unconcerned; one rolled over onto its back and stretched lazily, but none of the others stirred.

Nick opened a screened door and motioned her inside. The interior of the house was dark and shady, and cooler than the out-of-doors, but it was obviously not air-conditioned. At first, eyes blinded by the transition from bright sunlight to cool gloom, she could make out very few details. There were no windows in the vestibule; the only light came from the door behind her. Matching doors on either side were closed; a third door, straight ahead, opened onto a long hallway. Here a ceiling fixture glowed softly, showing stairs on the left and more closed doors on the right. "Offices," Nick said, gesturing but not pausing. "We go this way. . . ."

Past the stairs, straight down the hall, to another door, of heavy oak shining with varnish. He threw it open.

Light at last—floods of sunlight from wide windows on two adjoining walls. An ancient window air conditioner, clacking and grumbling, lowered the temperature somewhat. It was a big room, high-ceilinged and paneled in dark wood; and the furnishings suggested that it served a variety of functions. Sofas, tables, and chairs formed a social "grouping" in front of a massive brick-and-marble fireplace; one end of the room contained office equipment: filing cabinets, a desk, tables covered with books and papers; the other end had been fitted up as a dining area. The long table held cups, some used, some clean; boxes of sugar and artificial sweetener; plastic stirrers; and the oversized coffee maker without which, as Erin was to learn, no political campaign could function. Built-in bookcases flanked the fireplace; the shelves were piled high, not only with books but with office supplies, magazines, and . . . knitting bags? Yes, unquestionably knitting bags; one had tipped over onto its side and spilled a tangle of bright-red yarn onto the shelf.

Erin was always nervous when she had to meet a group of strangers; she had developed a cowardly habit of focusing on some inanimate object or piece of furniture instead of meeting eyes that might be critical or curious or unwelcoming. On this occasion she found herself stupidly wondering how the yarn had got into such a tangle. Perhaps one of the cats . . .

She gave herself a mental slap and forced herself to concentrate on the people in the room. If things worked out as she hoped, these were the men and women she would be working with—or for. Her chances of getting the job weren't very good if she stood gawking like a shy teenager.

There were three of them: an older man, balding and incredibly rumpled, wearing horn-rimmed glasses that looked too small for his broad, heavy-featured face; a woman, whose graying brown hair was coiled into a heavy bun at the back of her neck; and a young black man.

The latter appeared to be about the same age as her guide, in his late twenties or early thirties, but he was taller and more slightly built. His aquiline features and precisely shaped mouth were as attractive as Nick's. but more refined. The word "patrician" came to Erin's mind; if he had worn ruffles at his throat and a sword at his side he might have posed for a portrait of a Gentleman of Aristocratic Lineage. His attire was just as formal, if more contemporary—a well-cut three-piece suit and a carefully knotted tie.

". . . Joe Esler, campaign manager and Grand High Monkey-Monk," Nick was saying. The older man hoisted his posterior an inch off the seat of his chair and nodded at her. "And Jeff Ross, our legal counsel. At least that's his official title; like all the rest of us, he does a little bit of everything. He's also Joe's aide, assistant, and intellectual superior."

Joe chuckled, and Jeff allowed himself a tight, brief smile. With a start of chagrin Erin realized she had missed hearing the older woman's name while she dithered about yarn. When would she ever learn . . .

"And then there's me," said a voice from the far end of the room. "Or, more properly, 'I.' Unfortunately, grammatical precision sounds pompous and incorrect, accustomed as we have become to the vulgarities of common usage."

A man rose from behind one of the desks. He was so tall, and he moved so deliberately, that it seemed to take him forever to get all the way up to his full height. It was no wonder he had blended into the furniture; he was all one color, a faded grayish buff, from his close-cropped hair to his khaki pants. His glasses had gold rims; a toothbrush mustache of the same shade as his hair blended with the bookish pallor of his face.

"Hello. I'm Will."

"Sorry," Nick exclaimed. "I didn't see you."

"People don't," Will murmured.

"It's your own fault, Will," the woman said in a brisk, no-nonsense voice. "You must learn to assert yourself if you want to be noticed. Please sit down, Erin. Rosemary will be here in a few minutes, she's on the telephone."

She was knitting as she spoke; a virtuoso performance, for

the pattern was complex and she kept her eyes fixed on Erin as the wool looped unhesitatingly over and under the needles. So she was the knitter—and a fanatical one, if she had several projects underway at the same time. The afghan on which she was working was a fisherman's knit in pale-cream wool, with a complex cable pattern.

"I hope you had no difficulty following my directions?" she asked.

Erin shook her head. "No, ma'am."

It had been years since she had called anyone "ma'am." Her use of it now was unplanned and spontaneous, perhaps because this woman conjured up images of stern schoolteachers and Victorian governesses. She was big-boned and heavyset, and dressed with a sobriety that suggested a uniform: white shirtwaist blouse, brown tweed skirt, and flat-heeled walking shoes. The courtesy was well received; the woman's stiff features relaxed, and she nodded pleasantly. "That's good. I'm glad you have your own car."

"It isn't mine, actually," Erin admitted. "My roommate lent me hers."

"Oh, really? Dear me. That presents a difficulty. There is no way of getting here by public transportation, you know. And you must understand that we really can't afford to hire additional staff. We depend to a large extent on volunteers. Running a political campaign is very expensive, especially when—"

"For God's sake, Kay, Rosemary is the one who makes the decisions about hiring," Joe growled. "Get off the girl's back. Relax, kid, you aren't on trial. How about a drink?"

Kay didn't bother to conceal her annoyance; she frowned at Joe, and Nick, glancing from one to the other, burst into rapid speech. "Good idea. What'll it be, Erin? Sherry, Chablis, beer, gin, bourbon? Normally we're a sober lot, but Saturday is supposed to be our day off."

"Just a soft drink, if you have it," Erin said cautiously.

Kay nodded approvingly. "Very sensible. Nick is joking, of course. During this stage of the campaign we work seven days a week. And although some people claim they are not affected by alcohol, I am convinced it lowers one's efficiency.''

The criticism was obviously aimed at Joe, whose glass was filled to the brim with a dark amber liquid. Erin would have been willing to bet it wasn't sherry.

Joe's only response was to raise the glass to his lips and take a long swallow. Kay continued to glower, Jeff stared at his own glass, which appeared to contain tonic or mineral water, and Nick whistled loudly and tunelessly as he rummaged through a miscellaneous collection of bottles in a cabinet behind the table. Erin could feel the tension in the air. It was only to be expected, she supposed. These people were the inner circle, those responsible for the day-by-day running of the campaign; to a large extent success or failure depended on their efforts. The older woman—Kay—must be Rosemary's personal secretary, or perhaps her aide. Not only was there tension between them, there was a measurable degree of jealousy as they jockeyed for position and influence.

Nick handed her a glass. ''Behold the Star Chamber,'' he said. For a startled moment Erin wondered if she had spoken aloud, his comment matched her thoughts so closely. ''The powers behind the throne, the Cardinals Richelieu, the *éminences grises*. Except me. I'm nobody. They let me hang around because I do the chores nobody else wants to do. Polish shoes, de-flea dogs, scrub floors—''

''Wrong,'' said Joe, with a rumble of laughter. ''We let him hang around because he's so goddamned handsome. Gives the girls a thrill. Right, Kay?''

''Don't tease the boy, Joe,'' Kay said gravely. ''Nick is one of our dedicated volunteers, Erin. He acts as media consultant, speech writer—''

''And court jester.'' Jeff spoke for the first time. He may have meant it as a joke, but he didn't smile, and the look Nick gave him was visibly devoid of amusement.

''He keeps our spirits up,'' Kay said, with another of her decisive little nods. ''That's very important.''

Nick did find this amusing; he rolled his eyes and grinned at Erin. She couldn't decide whether Kay was unaware of the nuances, or determined to pretend they did not exist.

The door behind her opened. Erin didn't have to turn to
know who had entered; Rosemary Marshall's presence was
mirrored on the faces of the men who faced her, in very
different but equally visible ways. A heightened awareness, a
stiffening of pose—and something more, a kind of reflected
glow.

Erin turned in time to see her hostess lunge forward.
"Goddamn it! Catch him, Joe, Nick—somebody—"

"He" was a cat, though at first Erin saw only a mottled
blur, heading at full speed for the nearest place of concealment—the sofa. After being flushed out from under it he ric-
ocheted around the room, from the mantel to the back of Joe's
chair, to the table, and then beneath it. She joined in the
chase—the peremptory voice had been as compelling as a
direct order—and it was she who fished the cat out from under the tablecloth. As soon as he realized he was fairly caught
he melted, hanging limp from her hands and giving her a
look of pained reproach. He appeared to be a tabby of indeterminate age and considerable bulk. Opening massive jaws
and displaying a set of sharp white fangs, he emitted a small
soprano mew of protest.

"Give him to me," said Nick, red-faced with exercise and
laughter. "He's shedding on you. He does it on purpose."

Deliberately or not, the cat had left fuzzy souvenirs all over
her palms and fingers. Erin dusted them off as Nick cradled
the animal in his arms.

"Out." Rosemary gestured vigorously. "Get him out,
Nick. Damn the creature, he lurks like Dracula. I didn't see
him until he was on his way through the door."

The ice had definitely been broken. Rosemary was laughing and even Jeff's austere face had softened into a half-smile.

The first thing that struck Erin was the distinguished congresswoman's size. Somehow she had gotten the impression
that Marshall was much taller. In the flesh she appeared almost diminutive, a scant inch over five feet tall, and her informal clothes made her look even tinier. She wore faded,
baggy jeans, a man's shirt that flapped loosely over generous
hips, and a pair of dirty sneakers. Her hair had been pulled
back into a ponytail, and a smudge of ink marked her chin.

Erin knew she was staring, rudely and openly. She couldn't help it. The contrast between the sophisticated candidate and this sloppy specimen, dressed like a street person and swearing like a farmhand, was too much for her. Rosemary was quite accustomed to being stared at. She smiled—the practiced candidate's smile Erin had seen on the tube—and said, "You're Erin, of course. You look so much like your mother."

Erin began, "People say I look more like—"

"Not the way she is now; the way she looked in college. Oh, Lord. I don't know whether that makes me feel eighteen again, or a hundred and eighteen."

For a moment she appeared to be about to embrace Erin, but she changed her mind and stepped back. "You'll want to wash your hands. God knows what rubbish bin that damned animal has been rooting in."

"I'll show her." Kay put her knitting aside. "And Rosemary—please watch your language. Someday one of those words will slip out during a speech or a debate—"

"A little 'damn' never hurt anybody," Rosemary said defiantly. "Oh, well, I suppose you're right. You always are."

A door near the long table opened onto a passageway that led to a butler's pantry and kitchen, with a half-bath next to the latter. Erin emerged from the bathroom in time to meet Kay coming from the kitchen with a large cut-glass bowl of shrimp salad. She asked if she could help.

"Thank you, but I have everything under control. We wait on ourselves weekends; Rosemary prefers it that way. You go and sit down."

Rosemary had taken Kay's place on the sofa, as well as her knitting. She wasn't as skillful as Kay; she had to watch her hands, but it didn't keep her from talking.

"I won't appear on the same platform with that sleazeball, Joe; no way. Tell him thanks but no thanks. Be tactful, as only you can be. . . ."

Seeing Erin she broke off and motioned at the place beside her. Joe wasn't willing to abandon the topic, however.

"Damn it, Rosie, you need his endorsement. Those union votes—"

"You're out of touch with modern politics, Joe," Rosemary interrupted. "Unions don't vote as blocs—if they ever did. The last election . . . " She dropped the knitting and snapped her fingers. "Will?"

Will had blended back into the scenery. An apparently disembodied voice replied promptly, "Split all the way down the line from President to county council. Rosemary got sixty-one percent last time."

"Thanks, Will." Rosemary snapped her fingers again. "I love doing that," she murmured.

"Power mad," said the distant voice of Will.

"Talk about being out of touch with political reality!" said Joe, who had not appreciated Rosemary's criticism. "Last election you were the incumbent in a district you've owned for over a decade. This is the Senate, dammit. Buzz Bennett owns that seat the way you own yours."

"Never mind that now," Rosemary said firmly. "We have a guest, and I'm sure political strategy bores her. How is your mother, Erin?"

But it was impossible in that house and that time to keep off the subject of politics. They served themselves from the dishes Kay had placed on the table—shrimp salad, hot rolls, iced tea—and before long Joe had returned to the forbidden subject. "So maybe he can't deliver the votes he thinks he can; we can use his organization and his people, for canvassing, direct mailings—"

"His idea of a direct mailing is a quick and dirty," Rosemary retorted, biting into a roll with a ferocity that implied she would have preferred to sink her teeth in someone's jugular. "Even if I'd stoop to those tactics, they do more harm than good."

Erin found herself on one of the wide, cushioned window seats, with Nick beside her. "All this is so much Greek to you, I suppose," he said.

Torn between resentment at his patronizing tone and genuine curiosity, Erin yielded to the latter. "What's a quick and dirty?"

"Something that accuses the other candidate of a charge that is either false or impossible to refute. Even if he can prove it's a lie, the damage is done; people remember the accusation longer than the refutation.''

"Oh.''

"You didn't tell me you knew Rosemary way back when.''

"It was my mother who knew her.''

"Before you were born?''

"Well—before and after. We lived in Richmond until I was two.''

"And then you moved to—''

"Indianapolis.''

"I thought the accent was midwestern,'' Nick said. "So you haven't seen Rosemary since?''

"No.'' It was beginning to sound, and feel, like an interrogation.

"Nobody ever tells me anything, but I get the impression this isn't a purely social call. Kay was right, you know; our cash flow is a muddy trickle. If you're looking for a job—''

"I don't know that that's any of your business, Mr. McDermott.''

"Nick. It could be my business I wear a lot of different hats; you might end up working for me if you—''

"Excuse me.'' Erin rose. "I'm going to have a little more salad.''

After helping herself, she went to join the others. The job wasn't so important to her that she was willing to be quizzed by a lowly volunteer, how ever many hats he wore. He had no right to pry into her background. Hadn't Joe said it was Rosemary who would make the decision?

She looked at Rosemary—feet on the coffee table, hair straggling—and hoped her feelings about this peculiar interview didn't show on her face. It was so wildly different from the way she had pictured it—a stately mansion, a handsomely furnished office, Rosemary rising with quiet dignity from behind a mahogany desk, wearing something elegant and tailored. . . . Surely this was not a typical political campaign, or a typical candidate. Why did Rosemary allow these people, her subordinates, to treat her the way they did? Well, not Nick or Jeff, they were polite enough, but even they didn't demonstrate the deference a congresswoman ought to command, and the other pair were downright rude at times.

Kay was the next one to engage Erin in a private conversation—not difficult, since the argument between Joe and Rosemary had risen in volume and the others were listening, putting a word in now and then when they could make themselves heard. Kay's questions were even more searching than Nick's had been, but this time Erin felt she could not refuse to answer. She wasn't sure of Kay's precise position, but the older woman obviously held a high-level job. Perhaps Rosemary had deputized her to conduct the job interview.

Erin had barely begun to describe her background when Kay surprised her by saying, "I knew your father, years ago, when he handled some of Congressman Marshall's legal work. We were sorry to hear of his death. Cancer, wasn't it?"

"Yes. I didn't realize you—"

"You yourself have had no legal training?"

"No. I majored in English."

"No experience in the law? Not even in your father's office—part-time, perhaps?"

"I did work for him one summer." Erin realized that legal experience would have been a plus, but honesty compelled her to continue. "It was just routine. Typing and filing."

"I see." Kay's eyes dropped to her work. She executed a series of complex stitches and then looked at Erin. "What made you decide to leave Indianapolis? I would have thought your mother would want you near her, especially now."

The not-so-implicit criticism put Erin on the defensive. "She's living with my aunt. There was . . . there wasn't as much money as we had thought. We had to sell the house, and Aunt Ann was living alone, she never married, and she was glad to have Mother, they've always been close. I didn't feel . . . They didn't really need me. . . ."

Kay's gaze was cool and unwavering. A wave of resentment filled Erin, not so much against Kay as against herself. It did not occur to her—then—that the questions had no real bearing on her qualifications for a job. She only knew she was telling Kay far more than she needed to know, and when she went on her voice was brusque to the point of rudeness.

"I need the money—for myself and for Mother. I thought I could earn more here."

"I see." Kay's voice matched hers. "But why Washington? Why not Chicago, New York?"

It was another question that had no short, simple answer. Erin explained about Fran and the apartment and the job opportunities; Kay listened with an expression that suggested none of it made any sense or answered the question. "I suppose," Erin said finally, "it was partly because the area wasn't entirely strange to me. It was years ago that I lived in Virginia, but I liked it, and—and . . ."

She stammered into silence as she realized the other voices had stopped and that they were all looking at her. Rosemary frowned.

"All right, Kay," she said. "If you don't mind, I'll talk to Erin myself."

The others took the hint. Jeff was the first to leave, after a coolly courteous "Nice to have met you, Miss Hartsock." Joe's comment was more friendly: "See you around, kid." Nick followed him out, with no more than a nod at Erin. She wondered if she had offended him, and decided she didn't care if she had. Kay remained firmly planted in her seat until Rosemary asked pointedly about some letters that had to go out that day; then she moved slowly, stopping to look back at Rosemary as if she were hoping to be asked to remain.

When the door closed after Kay, Erin expected Rosemary to begin questioning her. Instead she turned and called loudly, "We give you leave to depart, Will."

Erin had forgotten he was there. He rose slowly, fixing Rosemary with a critical stare. "Now it's the royal 'we.' I do urge you to consider what you are about to do, Miss Hartsock. It's dangerous enough to get involved with this gang of rampant individualists, but a boss suffering from delusions of grandeur—"

"Go away, Will," Rosemary said

Will winked solemnly at Erin and ambled out.

Ten minutes later Erin left the house. There was no one in sight, except for the scattered cats. Two kittens—a tabby and a gray-and-white—were chasing a leaf, but the rest were asleep, forming furry puddles on the chairs or sprawled in drowsy stupor across the worn floor.

The car was as hot as an oven. Erin took off her jacket and then—after a wary glance to make sure no one was looking—struggled out of her panty hose.

Thus refreshed, she was able to think more clearly. It had happened so fast she felt a little dazed. A series of rapid-fire questions from Rosemary—none of them personal, all of them relating to her experience, expectations, and salary requirements—had relieved her of any need to explain or elaborate. Nor had Rosemary deliberated over her decision.

"I can't offer you any more than you are presently earning, and I certainly can't promise you job security. I'm not even sure at this point precisely what I will ask you to do. It depends to a certain extent on you—your interest, your willingness to turn your hand to whatever may be asked of you. To an even larger extent, however, your job depends on factors over which none of us has any control. The only thing I can promise you is that you won't be bored. If you are willing to take a chance—"

Erin had committed the social solecism of interrupting in her eagerness to accept.

As she sat mopping her perspiring face she wondered why she had been so eager. Rosemary was unquestionably an attraction; she had been charming and friendly, even insisting Erin call her by her first name. It was exciting to be on first-name terms with someone you had seen on television. But was that ephemeral reward worth the risk of finding herself unemployed after only a few weeks or months? What would happen to Rosemary's staff if she lost the election? Rosemary would be out of a job too. She had given up her House seat in order to run for the Senate.

I must have lost my mind, Erin thought. At least I could have told her I wanted to consider it for a day or two. . . . And then a sudden, uncharacteristic burst of recklessness overwhelmed her. Why the hell should I consider it? Fran is always telling me I'm too chicken, too conservative. Why not take a chance for once? I'm young and healthy and capable. I can find another job if I have to; there's always McDonald's!

And if Rosemary does lose, I won't be the only one looking for work. They'll all be unemployed, including her.

She put the car in gear and turned the air-conditioning on full blast. It made enough noise to drown out the sounds that were coming from the house, but she glanced into the rearview mirror in time to see Kay come running out onto the porch, with a speed that contrasted sharply with her usual deliberate movements. Erin stopped the car. But apparently Kay didn't want her; the older woman came to a halt at the top of the stairs and stood gazing, but she didn't motion or call.

After a moment Erin drove on. She had forgotten the incident by the time she reached the highway.

Chapter
Two

ERIN STARED at the letter in disgust. It had been written on coarse brown paper torn off a grocery bag and the ball-point pen had scored deeply into the rough surface.

"Problem?"

She looked up to see Nick standing by her desk. He was usually around; she had been working for a week, and so far he hadn't missed a day. She was not vain enough to suppose that she was the attraction. The office, just outside the District in Arlington, was Rosemary's headquarters, the space having been donated—like so many other things—by an admiring constituent who hadn't been able to rent the store anyway. It had the look of all temporary offices: paint hastily applied, wires and extension cords running every which way, cheap hired desks and office chairs. From the walls Rosemary Marshall's face looked down in endless repetition, surrounded by draped red-white-and-blue bunting. The acoustics were terrible: phones shrilling, word processors humming, typewriters clicking, blended into a dull roar of sound.

For once she didn't mind Nick's assumption of authority. Wordlessly she handed him the paper. He scanned it in a glance, his lips curling.

"Cute. Can't spell very well, can he?"

"He knows the two essential four-letter words."

"Probably from seeing them scrawled on walls." Nick dropped the letter and dusted his fingers fastidiously. "File it under *S*, as usual."

"*S* for 'sicko'?" Erin placed the letter in the designated basket. Incoming letters were sorted by type: contributions, requests for help or for information, complaints, and so on. Since Rosemary was both candidate and, until the end of her term, congresswoman as well, it was not always easy to determine into which category a particular letter might belong, but Rosemary was insistent on keeping them separate. Letters that dealt with constituents' problems were forwarded to her office on the Hill, and that office in turn sent campaign mail to Arlington. Erin had been given the sorting job only that morning. It was a step up from typing lists, for it required some discrimination—and, as she had already learned, one could not be too squeamish.

"Or 'shit,' " Nick said. There were half a dozen other sheets of paper in the *S* file; he picked one up and began to read it. His face was as mobile as an actor's; eyebrows, lips, and cheek muscles twitched in sympathy with his emotions.

"Why does she keep them?" Erin asked.

"What would you do with them?"

"Throw them away. Burn them—"

"Oh, everybody gets letters like these," Nick said absently. Then he realized what he had said, and laughed. "All public figures, I mean. They develop a certain thickening of the skin. But crap like this can't be ignored. There are a lot of loonies in the world, and thanks to the NRA, too many of 'em own guns."

"But surely no one would—" She broke off, not needing Nick's quizzical sidelong glance to tell her she was being naive. People would; people had.

She shivered and Nick looked at her. "Maybe you'd rather do something else."

"Of course not! I can handle it. You're the one who's making a big thing of it!"

Nick pretended to cower. "Please don't hit me, lady, I was just trying to be a little gent. I keep forgetting you feminists don't like it."

"I am not a feminist. I hate that word."

"Why? What's wrong with being a feminist? High bloody time you were, isn't it?"

"I do not want to discuss the subject," Erin said frostily.

"Right, right. Nothing to discuss. Self-evident. Anything you say. No, but seriously—I wasn't trying to put you down; I encountered a couple of equally foul offerings when I was sorting mail, and I'm not too proud to admit they made me sick at my stomach."

The confession made Erin feel a good deal more kindly toward him. "You sorted mail?"

"Lady, I've tackled most everything," Nick said in a John Wayne drawl. "I wasn't always the big shot you see today. Only one year ago I was as insignificant and humble as you; a mere cipher in the majestic numbers of politics, a cog in the bureaucratic wheel. . . . "

"Then you must have something more important to do," Erin said, unable to refrain from smiling.

"My day wouldn't be complete without a quick glance through the shit file," Nick said. "This guy doesn't know his Bible very well. The number of the beast is 666—no way you can get Rosemary's name to fit that—and said beast is specifically designated as male."

The letter he held was almost a manuscript—eight single-space typewritten pages. "It was incoherent throughout," Erin said. "Why are the religious-fundamentalist people down on her?"

"She's against prayer in the schools and public funding for private schools. Both hot issues in rural Virginia." Nick tossed the letter aside. "That one wasn't so bad. 'Whore of Babylon' seems to be the strongest epithet. What's this?"

It was the last letter in the basket—typed, like the one he had discarded, but containing only two lines. Erin glanced at it.

"I wasn't quite sure what to do with it. At first I thought it might be from some undetected criminal, asking for reassurance; but it's not a question, is it?"

The message was short and simple. "There is no statute of limitations for murder."

Nick departed somewhat abruptly, taking the S file with him. He mumbled something that sounded like "right to life," and Erin puzzled over it briefly, wondering if some new in phrase had replaced "see you around" and "so long." Then the light dawned. Of course, that must be the meaning of the ambiguous letter—another way of calling Rosemary Marshall a baby killer, a favorite epithet of right-to-lifers.

She had worked her way through most of the letters when one of the volunteers brought the morning delivery, and an involuntary moan escaped her when she saw the bulk of it. The other girl's smile was not untouched with malice; Erin was one of the few in the office who was getting paid, and she knew she was an object of envy.

Steeling herself, she returned to the attack. There were no more anonymous outpourings in the first dozen envelopes, only a letter written more in sorrow than in anger that wanted to know why Rosemary didn't find herself some nice fella and settle down, instead of chasing around the state doing stuff "wemin" wasn't meant to do. After brief consideration, Erin decided not to consign it to the S file. "Mrs. Dick Milhauser" had signed her name, and she didn't sound threatening. Was there, Erin wondered, a form letter for such impertinent and irrelevant inquiries?

As she studied it, the door of an inner office opened and Joe ambled out. From the corner of his mouth a cigar emerged at a jaunty, FDR angle. He stopped by Erin's desk, removed the cigar, looked around as if searching for an ashtray, found none—there were "No Smoking" signs all over the office—and put it back in his mouth.

"Let's go out for coffee."

"There's a coffee maker back there." Erin started to rise. "Would you like me to—"

"I said 'out.' " Joe took her arm and led her to the door,

giving her barely time to snatch her purse from where it hung over the back of her chair.

That should do it, Erin thought. The people who had been sucking up to her would increase the suction; the ones who resented her would have even greater cause. If Rosemary Marshall was the White Goddess of the volunteers, Joe was her High Priest, and although he was matey enough with the others, cracking jokes and slapping backs and bottoms, such a sign of favor to an individual was rare.

The coffee shop down the street was crowded, since it was getting on toward lunchtime. The place was popular with Rosemary's supporters, being convenient to headquarters; they were easy to identify, since they all sported huge "Marshall for Senator" buttons. Joe stopped by a table occupied by a pair of them. "You guys through?" he asked.

By a strange coincidence, they were just going. Joe pulled out a chair. Catching Erin's critical eye, he gave her a broad grin. "When you've got it, flaunt it."

"What's *it*?" Erin asked.

Joe looked down at his stomach and brushed cigar ashes off the bulge of his shirt. His tie was beyond such first aid; the stains appeared to be coffee. "It ain't my good looks," he admitted.

Erin laughed. Elbows planted on the table, forehead gleaming with perspiration, he nevertheless had a certain charm. He must have been a good-looking man once, she thought, with the unconscious condescension of youth. Before he let himself go.

Joe planted his cigar in an ashtray. "Do you mind my smoking?" he asked, in a voice whose suddenly cultured accents fell oddly on her ear.

"No, that's okay. My father smoked cigars. I like the smell."

"Rosemary told me about him. Was he ill long?"

"It was lung cancer," Erin said.

She looked at his cigar, and Joe acknowledged the unspoken lecture with a grimace. "Yeah. We always assume it will happen to the other guy. I'm sorry. Must have been tough—for you and your mother both."

"Tougher for Dad," Erin said, reaching for the cup the waitress had brought. She was reluctant to break down in public, though the sympathy in Joe's voice had touched depths of grief she had believed were decently buried. But she found herself talking freely, describing her father's anger—"Why me, God?"—and her mother's collapse into teary helplessness. "She's angry too—angry with Dad for dying—but she can't admit it."

Joe nodded. "That's a normal reaction. I suppose he handled all the financial matters. That's a heavy load to have dumped on you without warning or advance preparation."

"There was time. He tried to go over things with her, once he realized . . . But she couldn't handle it. Most of it fell to me. That sounds disgustingly self-pitying, doesn't it? But it was a shock to find out there was so little money left. No savings, no annuity, only a minimal amount of insurance. Mother still refuses to accept the fact that her life-style has to change, we'd always lived comfortably—too comfortably, I realize now. We had to sell the house, there was a huge mortgage—and both cars. . . . Oh, you don't want to listen to this. I'm sorry."

"No sweat, honey. Is your mother all right financially? Rosemary wouldn't want—"

Erin felt her cheeks flame. "Please don't say anything to Mrs. Marshall! We're fine—we really are—and I wouldn't want her to think . . . Promise you won't."

"Okay, I promise. But she has her little ways of finding things out. If you need any advice—legal or financial—remember I'm not as stupid as I look."

Joe frowned, but not at her; turning, she saw Jeff threading his way through the tables toward them.

"I might have known I'd find you feeding here," he said, taking one of the empty chairs and putting his briefcase under it. "Hi, Erin. How are things going?"

Except for occasional glimpses as he passed in and out of the office, Erin had not seen him since their first meeting at the house in Middleburg. He was dressed with the same formality as before, but the smile that warmed his sharp features made him look like a different man—a much more attractive one. Erin was too dazzled to do more than murmur a reply and smile back at him. He had even remembered her name.

"When did you get back?" Joe asked.

"A couple of hours ago. Rosemary was exhausted; I persuaded her to rest this morning, she's got a speech later, and then that fund-raiser this evening."

Erin knew that Rosemary had been on a tour of southern Virginia, making a dozen speeches in two days. According to the polls she was in good shape in the northern counties, but she was still far behind her opponent in the rural areas. "How did it go?" she asked.

"Not bad." Jeff's tone was the same he had used with Joe—equal to equal, without condescension. "Nobody's better at working the shopping malls and the grocery stores. By the time she gets through exchanging recipes with the old ladies and telling the young ones how to handle diaper rash—"

"Never mind the diaper rash," Joe grunted. "What about that direct-mail list we were promised?"

Jeff glanced at Erin. She reached for her purse. "I'd better get back—"

"It's okay," Jeff said, with another dazzling smile. "I wasn't being cagey, I just didn't know how much of this boring stuff you'd want to hear." He summoned a waitress with a wave of his hand. "Have you had lunch? Joe lives on coffee and Danish, it would never occur to him to offer you food fit for humans."

"Hey, it is lunchtime, isn't it?" Joe glanced at the watch strapped to his hairy wrist. "Make mine a double cheeseburger and fries. Erin?"

Lunch with the two top men in Rosemary's campaign was too heady an invitation to refuse. Fran would be green with envy. . . . Though admittedly the Columbia Café didn't sound as impressive as Duke Zeibert's or one of the other restaurants favored by top politicians. As she ate a decidedly wilted chef's salad, Erin comforted herself with the knowledge that she was already more savvy about politics than her starry-eyed roommate. This was what it was about, in reality—too much coffee and too little time, conversations about money and mailing lists and little old ladies in shopping malls. No glamour, just plain hard work.

The conversation that ensued wasn't boring, though some of it was incomprehensible. Key wards and swing wards, maxing out, hard money versus soft money. . . . During a brief lull in the talk when Joe had bitten off a larger bite of cheeseburger than was easily manageable, she ventured a question. "What does that mean—to go where the ducks are?"

Joe's cheeks still bulged, so it was Jeff who answered. "That's just one of those colorful phrases old-time political hacks like Joe enjoy using. Don't waste valuable time and money in areas that are unwinnable, or that you're already sure of."

"Oh. You mean, concentrate on swing wards." Jeff's eyes shone with what she took to be amusement; she added, "Did I say something stupid? I thought a swing ward—"

"I wasn't laughing," Jeff protested, and then proceeded to do just that. "I apologize, Erin; it's just that you sound so knowledgeable, and you look . . . well, you don't look like a politician. Most of 'em look like Joe."

Joe, still speechless, rolled his eyes in sardonic commentary. Jeff went on, "You've got the idea. A swing ward, as you obviously know, is one that can go either way and that therefore may pay off in terms of votes for your candidate if you play it right. The ones you go after are those with a large number of non-registered and uncommitted voters. It's unlikely you can get a die-hard, longtime Democrat or Republican to change his commitment unless your candidate does something brilliant or the other guy does something abysmally stupid."

Joe's Adam's apple bulged alarmingly as he swallowed. "Like old Buzz's fling with his floozie. God bless him. . . . Let's get back, time's a-wasting."

Snatching up the check, he headed for the cash register. Jeff helped Erin out of her chair. "When Joe's finished, everybody's finished," he murmured.

*   *

THE WORKDAY was drawing to a close, and Erin was tallying the checks that had come in the mail, when a burst of hilarity from the other end of the room made her look up. It was Nick again, going through his daily routine of entertaining the troops. The overwhelming majority of them were female, which might have had something to do with Nick's dedication. Most of the volunteers seemed very young to someone who had reached the advanced age of twenty-three; but there was a sizable sprinkling of middle-aged women among them, and to give Nick his due, he was as popular with the senior citizens as with the girls. He was particularly attentive to one white-haired old lady who lost no opportunity of proclaiming her age: "Eighty-four last birthday, and still with it!" She leaned heavily on a cane when she walked, but she never missed a day, and her vocabulary would have made a truck driver blush.

Watching Mrs. Watson flirt outrageously with Nick, who responded in kind, Erin wondered why there were so few men among the volunteers. Many women worked these days, and children kept others homebound, but the proportion was still out of balance. Was it because of Rosemary Marshall's strong support for so-called women's issues? That might have been a factor, but from what she had learned, the same thing was true of other candidates, including those who thought a graceful compliment was to tell women that without them men would still be walking around in skin suits. Perhaps the true explanation was that women, unlike men, were accustomed to working without pay. Funny that the idea had never occurred to her before, even after watching her mother and her mother's friends provide free labor for most of the charitable, cultural and social services of the town.

She grinned as she watched Nick plant a smacking kiss on Mrs. Watson's cheek and dodge the playful swipe of her cane. He might resent the term "court jester," but she was beginning to understand that it was an important job. Volunteers were a vital part of a campaign, especially one as poorly financed as Rosemary's. Keeping up morale could make a difference; and Nick did it superbly. It wasn't all calculation on his part, either. He was obviously delighted by the spunky old lady. When he came toward Erin she greeted him with a smile so warm he blinked.

"Hi," he said.

"Hello again. Sorry, I have no more goodies for you. This afternoon's mail was astonishingly unperverse."

"Please don't think I am attracted to you only by your collection of obscenities," Nick said.

"Oh, no. I assumed it was my efficiency, intelligence, and graciousness."

"Graciousness?" Nick hoisted a hip onto the edge of the desk and considered her thoughtfully. "You probably have bushels of it, but you haven't dumped much on me. Why don't you like me?"

"I don't even know you," Erin protested, taken aback by the blunt question.

"That's easily remedied. I'm available. Lunch, dinner, breakfast. . . . Tonight's out, though, I have to work. Unless . . ." His face brightened. "Hey, that's an idea. Want to go to a football game?"

"I thought you said you had to work."

"I do. I'm covering the game."

"You're a reporter?" Nick nodded. "But the Redskins aren't playing tonight—or are they? I don't follow sports closely."

"You're absolutely right," Nick said seriously. "The Redskins are not playing tonight. And if they were, I would not be attending the game. About the only way to get tickets to regular season games is to inherit them. As for covering the game—who do you think I work for?"

The gleam of sardonic amusement in his eyes told Erin her first assumption was undoubtedly wrong. "Not the *Post*?"

"The Washington *Post* is one of the country's major newspapers," Nick said. "I should be so lucky. You behold before you the sports editor of the Loudon County *Daily Sentinel*. At least I was as of this morning. My boss isn't too happy about my political activities."

"Conflict of interest?" Erin hazarded.

Nick shook his head. "Not exactly. It would be hard, even

for me, to insert a political opinion into a story about a high school football game. It's a question of time. Working two full-time jobs is taking its toll. Especially," he added in a lighter tone, "of my social life. So how about going to the game with me? You can point out the niceties I might miss. I'll even buy you dinner. The affair is being catered by the ladies of the Boosters Club and some of 'em bake a great apple pie."

"Thanks, but no thanks. I hate football."

"Oh, come on. This isn't your ordinary boring major-league game. The Vikings are playing their arch rivals, the Demons of St. Joseph's Academy. It will be the thriller of the year. The Vikes are really up for this one, they got knocked out of the play-offs last year by St. Joe's. And"—he paused for effect—"during the time-outs I'll tell you everything you ever wanted to know about politics. Including the definition of a swing district."

"Jeff told you? I suppose I asked him some dumb questions, but I didn't think he would laugh at me behind my back."

"Oh, hey, it wasn't like that. Everybody knows you haven't had any political experience, you made no secret of that; he wasn't making fun of you, he was impressed by your intelligence and quickness to learn. . . ." Nick broke off. "What am I doing defending a rival?" he demanded dramatically. "Never mind Jeff, I'm just as knowledgeable as he is, and I'm almost as good-looking. I can teach you a lot, baby. What do you say?"

"Well . . ." Erin told herself it would be foolish to refuse. Keeping on good terms with coworkers was only common sense. Nick could be irritating, bossy, chauvinist (that word again!), but he did have his moments. "Why not?"

Nick dropped to one knee, snatched her hand, and raised it to his lips. "Thank you. Thank you! The gracious enthusiasm of your response overwhelms me. You have made my day. Your ineffable condescension—"

"Oh, get up! I have to finish adding up these checks."

"I go, but I will return. In half an hour?"

"Okay."

Erin went back to work, fully aware of the curious, amused, and frankly envious stares that had been focused on them. She couldn't help wondering about the reason for his persistence. Nick might be one of those men whose interest is piqued by a woman's indifference, but he would never be hard up for female companionship—not around campaign headquarters, at any rate. Talk about your ready-made harems. . . . And surely it was not a coincidence that she had been favored, that same day, by attention from both Joe and Jeff. Rosemary must have passed the word: "Give the kid a pat on the head, I can't be bothered."

Rosemary made her appearance shortly before five-thirty. She looked like Her Majesty paying a flying visit to the workhouse, swathed in rainbow chiffon, white-gloved to the elbow, glittering with jewelry. The man who was with her wore tails and carried a top hat and stick. His brown hair, worn in a vaguely old-fashioned style, with a dip or wave on one side, showed not a trace of gray, and his sharp-cut features would have been attractive if the curve of his long thin lips had not resembled a perpetual sneer instead of a smile. He surveyed the cluttered room and the motley assortment of volunteers with an air of looking down, not from his actual height of six-two or -three, but from the lofty peaks of Olympus. There was something vaguely familiar about him, but Erin couldn't remember where she had seen him.

Looking like a daintily dressed doll next to her tall escort ("Send no money now, the Fund will bill you only $79.98 per month"), Rosemary made the rounds, smiling impartially on all and addressing an occasional greeting to a favored and flattered worker. Erin received the greatest mark of favor—a full pause, an outstretched hand, and a friendly "How is it going?"

"Fine," Erin answered. "Some of the letters are—uh—very interesting."

Rosemary's escort laughed. "Is that what you've been doing, you unfortunate infant? My commiseration. You may find them interesting now, but I assure you, the maudlin outpourings of the illiterate public will soon pall."

He reached for the *S* basket. Erin wasn't surprised that he

had selected that one; his low, murmurous laugh had given
her the necessary clue to his identity. Philips Laurence, com-
mentator, columnist, and moderator of a television talk show,
and the man for whom Fran reserved her choicest epithets.
He called himself a neoconservative; Fran called him, among
other things, a Fascist reactionary. What on earth was he
doing with Rosemary Marshall, when he opposed almost
every issue she supported?

"Your love of the common man is notorious, Philips,"
Rosemary said. "Didn't your mother ever teach you it's rude
to read other people's mail? If you dare quote any of those
letters—"

"Hate mail isn't worth quoting," Laurence said lazily.
"Most consist of a nice derangement of epithets and a singular paucity of imagination." He tossed the letters carelessly onto the desk.

They fluttered and fell in a disorderly pile; Erin made a
grab for a sheet of paper that was about to slide off the desk.
Rosemary bent over to study one of the papers more closely.

"There is no statute of limitations . . . " she began.
"Good God. What's that all about?"

"Nick said something about right-to-lifers," Erin offered.

"I suppose that's it." Rosemary grimaced.

"My poor darling." Laurence put his arm around her.
"You're too sensitive. The effusions of clods like this writer
aren't worth your notice. Philips will get rid of the nasty
thing." Using only the tips of his fingers, he folded the letter
and tucked it into his pocket. "See? All gone."

"Throw it in the wastebasket," Rosemary said shortly.

"And contaminate the office? I'll find a handy trash can
outside."

"Philips, you can be a real pain in the posterior sometimes," Rosemary snapped. "Stop treating me like a frail
little southern lady."

"But, darling, you are."

"Like hell I am. Where's Joe? I told him to be ready at
five-thirty."

The office door opened and Joe emerged. He looked mildly
exasperated, probably because someone had forced him to

stop working and get dressed up. The results were splendid; he wore a tuxedo that fit him reasonably well, he was freshly shaved, brushed, and combed; there was not even a cigar in evidence. Nick followed him out. Catching Erin's eye, he went through an extravagant pantomime, clasping his hands and fixing an adoring gaze on Joe's back, then wiping his brow and staggering, as if to suggest that the effort of producing the resplendent effect had worn him out.

Rosemary's lips quivered, but she kept her face straight. "Very nice, Joe. You really can look like a gent when you try."

Joe came to a dead stop and fixed a stony glare on her escort. "What the hell is he doing here?"

"Now, Joe—"

"It's all right, Rosemary," Laurence said gently. "I'm well accustomed to Joe's diamond-in-the-rough manners. Sorry to spoil your evening, old chap, but I'm attending this function too."

"So long as you paid," Joe grunted. "Come on, Rosemary, shake a leg."

Instead of offering his arm he grabbed hers and towed her toward the door at a pace that made her break into an undignified trot. Laurence followed, smoothing his gloves onto his fingers with voluptuous care. He was smiling smugly, as well he might; his cool control had made Joe look like an ill-bred boor. Surely there was something stronger than political antipathy there. . . .

Nick joined her at her desk, but continued to glower at Laurence's retreating form until the door closed behind it. How much of *his* antipathy was personal? Erin wondered. His dedication to Rosemary and/or the causes she supported was obviously intense, but there was more to it than that; he looked like an overprotective father who harbored the direst suspicions about his daughter's date.

"Talk about your unholy alliances," he muttered.

"You mean Rosemary and Mr. Laurence?"

"Who else? Haven't you read his column—watched his show?"

"Uh . . . occasionally. I gather he's a trifle conservative."

"He's so right-wing he'll drive all the way around the block rather than make a left turn. You didn't see today's column, where he said the homeless should thank God they're freezing on the streets of an American city instead of living in a one-room apartment in Moscow?"

"He didn't say that."

"Oh yes, he did." Nick glowered even more darkly. "I can't believe people take that jackass seriously. And I can't figure out why he's supporting Rosemary. I guess it's like they say—politics makes for strange bedfellows."

"Or the reverse?"

It took him a few seconds to understand what she meant. "Good God, no!" he exclaimed indignantly. "At least . . . I hope to hell not."

"Why? She's a woman, not a two-dimensional campaign poster."

"Well, yeah, sure, I guess. . . ." The idea seemed never to have occurred to him. "But not . . . Look, Erin, it's nothing like that. You don't understand the way these things work in Washington. You can call somebody a Comsymp and a lecherous cretin in public—Laurence has done it—and invite him out for a drink afterward, and he'll say, sure, why not? It has to be that way. If politicians took insults personally, there'd be bleeding bodies all over Capitol Hill."

"I don't think I'd be so detached," Erin admitted.

"I'm not very good at it myself. I hate people who have the goddamn gall to disagree with me!"

Erin laughed and after a moment Nick's scowl faded into a sheepish grin. "Which is why I'm an enthusiastic volunteer instead of an up-and-coming political reporter. Ah well, I'm learning; I haven't slugged Laurence yet, and believe me, that has required considerable self-control. My car's over there. . . . Damn. Another parking ticket."

"At least they didn't tow you."

"There is that. Wait a minute. The door sticks some. . . ."

The door looked as if it were about to fall off. The car was an ancient Dodge whose original green had faded to a dusty indeterminate gray. Nick wrenched the door open, helped

Erin in, and, after a prolonged struggle, managed to shut it again.

The drive was hair-raising, in every sense of the word. The window on Erin's side wouldn't close. Nick was apologetic. "The part costs sixty bucks, and that doesn't include labor. I meant to look for it in a junkyard, but I haven't had time. . . . Oh, hey, sorry about that. The catch on the door to the glove compartment doesn't hold very well. . . ."

Perched on a sagging bench in the bleachers, watching the Vikings devastate their hapless opponents from St. Joe's, Erin realized with some surprise that she was enjoying herself. Her supper had consisted of a country ham sandwich and a Coke; the portly person seated next to her was the father of the Vikings' quarterback, and whenever he bounded to his feet to cheer a completed pass, the plank seat slapped Erin's posterior. But the night air was cool and crisp, the ham sandwich was excellent, and the portly person's enthusiasm was rather touching. Nick kept running back and forth from the seat beside her—to the bench, to the trailer manned by the mothers of the Boosters Club.

During halftime she joined him on the sidelines, at his request. Among the people to whom he introduced her, with transparent pride, was a sports reporter from a local TV station. "What are you doing out here?" Nick asked. "Thought you'd been promoted to news reporting."

"Dave called in sick," the round-faced youth explained morosely. "You know how it is. Listen, you got any openings for a media man in the campaign?"

"We haven't got any openings, period. Here." Nick reached in his pocket. "Have a button."

The youth allowed Nick to pin the campaign button to his shirt. "Keep me in mind, okay?"

"Yeah, sure, old buddy. Gotta run now; Erin is dying to meet some of the players."

"I'm not, you know," Erin remarked, as he led her away.

"Never pass up an opportunity to do some work for your candidate," Nick said. "Some of the players are eighteen and they all have relatives who vote—or should. Smile and look pretty—that won't be hard—and tell them all how wonderful Rosemary Marshall is.''

Most of the players were too concerned with the game to listen to Nick's political lecture. Those who did promised him—leering amiably at Erin all the while—that, sure, they'd vote for Marshall, why the hell not? Only one objected. He was an extremely large eighteen-year-old, who would have made two of Nick. Instead of being intimidated by the bulk looming over him, Nick fell on him like a piranha on a whale. "How can you vote for a man who helped promote Virginia's massive resistance to integration when he was in the state legislature and who said, as recently as 1984, that he had no regrets about doing it?''

The large young man was no match for Nick in rhetoric; when it dawned on him that he was losing the argument, he cocked an enormous fist and Erin prudently retreated behind one of the other players, a rangy black youth who had been introduced as the star tight end. He was pleased to see her, but showed no desire to prevent the imminent annihilation of Nick; in fact, he and the other players cheered the debaters on. Erin was relieved when the coach finally intervened with a firm "Knock it off, you guys. We got a game to play. Carson, don't waste your energy. Get the hell outta here, Nick, what's the idea of bugging my guys?''

"They're ahead twenty-one to zip," Nick reminded him. "Great job, Coach; how about an interview?''

"Later, maybe. Get lost.''

"Right." Nick seized the ham-sized fist of his antagonist and shook it vigorously. "Great talking to you, bro. That's what this country is all about, right? Honest disagreement and discussion, the heart of democracy. You just think over what I said—''

Erin took him firmly by the arm and led him away. They were followed by the jeers and cheers of the players.

"Why do you do that?" she demanded.

"Do what?''

"Argue with people like that boy. His mind, what there is of it, is made up. You're supposed to go where the ducks are, aren't you?''

Nick stopped, and in full view of all the spectators, under the glaring lights, seized her in a fervent embrace. "You're awfully cute," he said.

Up to that point Erin had found his exuberance entertaining. Why the compliment roused such sudden, violent annoyance she could not have said; a few weeks ago she would have accepted it with a modest simper. Instead she jabbed her elbow into Nick's midsection and snapped, "Don't patronize me!"

"I didn't. I wouldn't! If you want to tell me I'm the sexiest man you've ever met, go right ahead; I won't take offense."

"Oh, yeah?"

"Yeah. I said you were cute and you are cute, by God. I didn't say, and didn't mean, that you were not also intelligent, capable, worthy of respect—"

"You implied as much. That's what 'cute' means to men like you. Cute and dumb."

"Not true." Infuriatingly Nick's lips curved into a smile. "Hey, have you been reading Rosemary's speeches?"

"I can take offense at rudeness without help from Rosemary."

"Sure you can," Nick said. "But listen, you ought to read the one she gave a couple of years ago when she spoke in support of her day-care bill. I'll get you a copy. Though it loses something in the mere reading; Rosemary's a great speaker, and she's improving all the time. Even television doesn't capture her quality completely. Tell you what, next time she gives a major speech maybe you'd like . . . ."

It was difficult to quarrel with a man who blandly ignored your complaints and launched into a lecture. Erin let him escort her to her seat in the bleachers.

As soon as the second half started he was off again, after presenting her with a piece of apple pie. The pie lived up to his praise, but the paper plate on which it reposed wasn't very sturdy, and the gyrations of the quarterback's adoring dad sent trickles of sticky amber juice cascading onto Erin's skirt. Philosophically licking her fingers, she was seized by a fit of the giggles, as she remembered Fran's envious comments. "Politics is the most glamorous business in the world.

Mixing with the rich and famous—gorgeous clothes, beautiful people, caviar and champagne . . . ''

Caviar and champagne . . . Well, there was something to be said for limp chef's salad and homemade apple pie too. It all depends on the ambience, and the company.

*   *

BY THE FOLLOWING morning her opinion of Nick had undergone another switch, back to the negative side. He had accepted her invitation to come in for a cup of coffee and had stayed till 2 A.M. arguing politics with Fran. She would like to have believed he had lingered in the hope that Fran would go tactfully to bed and leave them alone, but she had already learned enough about Nick to recognize the hope was delusory. Nick would rather argue than eat, or sleep, or . . . anything else.

She could cheerfully have murdered Fran, who had committed the unforgivable sin of being bright-eyed, alert, and witty while she sat like a lump of suet. She couldn't have gotten a word in even if she had had anything intelligent to contribute; Fran and Nick were a perfect match in loquacity and detailed knowledge of political issues. They agreed on practically everything, including the dazzling wonderfulness of Rosemary Marshall. And after Nick had left—remarking calmly that he still had a story to write—Fran had raved on and on about him. ''Talk about your fringe benefits! Of course, if you're really crazy about the guy I wouldn't dream of horning in, but after all, you just met him. . . .''

The unspoken assumption being that if Fran wanted him, she could get him.

Erin pushed the stack of mail aside and stood up, avoiding the eagle eye of Mrs. Patterson, the office manager. Patterson was a soured virgin of ninety-seven (Nick's description) who clearly believed Erin was badly hung over after a night of sinful dissipation. To hell with Patterson; she needed coffee.

The coffee urn and accompanying amenities—which included a soft-drink machine and an unpredictable selection of doughnuts and pastries—were concealed behind a screen at the back of the room. Erin filled a cup and stood by the

table as she sipped; she was in no hurry to return to her desk
where she would be overlooked by Mrs. Patterson's critical
eye. All at once she heard her own name, uttered in tones
that rose distinctly over the usual background noises.

"Erin! Where the hell has she gotten to?"

Erin made haste to present herself. There was no mistaking
Joe's bass roar.

"I was just getting a cup of coffee," she began.

Joe slung his coat jacket over one shoulder and wrenched
at his tie. His face looked as if he had shaved in the dark or
a thick fog; patches of unattended bristles marked his jutting
chin. "Bring it to my office, I want to talk to you. Get me a
cup too. Cream and sugar." Without waiting for an answer
he swung on his heel and stamped toward his office.

Erin's hands were unsteady as she filled the cup according
to his specifications. The milk looked a little peculiar; she
hoped it hadn't gone sour, Joe was obviously in a foul mood
already. Had she done something to anger him, or committed
some ghastly blunder with the mail? In spite of Joe's kindness
to her she was a little afraid of him; she had seen him reduce
one of the typists to tears for committing a minor error.

The office door stood open. Joe was speaking on the phone,
and Jeff stood by the desk. Joe gestured to Erin to close the
door; while she was trying to work out the logistics of obey-
ing his order while holding a Styrofoam cup in either hand,
Jeff came to her assistance. She thanked him, and murmured
an apology. "I didn't know you were here. Would you like
some coffee?"

"No, thanks. Haven't you heard that fetching coffee for
the boss is a feminist issue?"

The edge in his voice surprised Erin and increased her
nervousness. She racked her brain trying to remember
whether she had said something to Nick that might have
sounded critical of Rosemary, the issues, the world in general. . . .

Joe slammed the telephone into the cradle. "We're trans-
ferring you to home base," he said. "Kay managed to mash
her hand last night—the right hand, of course—she can't type,
or tie Rosie's hair ribbons, or whatever the hell else she does.

Better get out there as fast as you can; Kay's in one of her states.''

Erin felt as if the hinges on her jaw had given way. "I don't understand," she gasped.

"What don't you understand? English?"

"You mean . . . Do you want me to go to Middleburg?"

"For Christ's sake!" Joe bellowed.

"Cool it, Joe." Jeff smiled encouragingly at Erin. "Give her a chance to assimilate it."

"So what's to assimilate? Most people would consider this the biggest break of their lives."

"No doubt she is speechless with joy," Jeff said sarcastically. "People like to be asked, Joe. Asked, not told."

The expression on Joe's face as he considered this astonishing idea was almost comical. "That's not it," Erin said quickly. "Of course I'll go. I just wondered why—"

"I told you, Kay's crippled herself. Caught her hand in the car door, for God's sake. Broke a couple of fingers. Do you want to go, or don't you?"

"Of course. I'll leave right away. Should I tell Mrs. Patterson, or—"

She stopped; Joe's face was crimson, and he looked as if he were about to explode with exasperation. Initiative, Erin told herself; display a little initiative, woman. When a man like Joe gave an order, he expected the orderee to work out the details. Such as how she was going to get to Middleburg without a car.

"Yes, sir," she snapped. "Right away, sir."

She didn't hear Jeff follow; he walked like a leopard. But his hand reached the knob before hers, and after he had ushered her out he said in a low voice, "Don't mind Joe, he's in a bad mood. Things are a little tense all around."

"He talks as if the poor woman broke her hand on purpose," Erin muttered.

"Things are a little tense," Jeff repeated. "I'll explain to Mrs. Patterson. You'd better go home first and pack a bag in case they want you to stay overnight."

"Thanks," Erin said gratefully. His quiet, calm manner

was as helpful as the practical suggestions Joe hadn't bothered to offer. "Is there . . . I suppose there's a bus?"

"To Middleburg?" His elegantly shaped eyebrows shot up.
"Oh, that's right, I remember you said you didn't own a car.
No problem. I'll drive you. I have to go out there anyway.
Why don't you go home and pack, and I'll pick you up in
. . . say an hour and a half?"

The office was in Falls Church, only twenty minutes away
from the apartment, but by the time she had waited for the
bus and walked the distance on either end, she had very little
time to spare. She made it, just barely, running breathlessly
out the door only seconds before Jeff arrived. He acknowledged her promptness with an approving smile, and got out
to take her overnight bag and stow it in the backseat. The
contrast between his immaculately tended though modest Camaro, and the wreck Nick drove was ludicrous. The backseat
of Nick's car looked like a traveling office, heaped with boxes
of campaign literature, newspapers, and miscellaneous debris. Jeff's contained only his briefcase. Even the car keys
reflected the personality of their owners. Nick's chain held
over a dozen keys, held together by twists of plastic ties; Jeff's
key ring was a polished curve of heavy silver in the form of
a stylized fish.

"That's good-looking," Erin said, indicating the orna-
ment.

"Thanks." Jeff wasn't the man to waste time on meaningless courtesies, especially when, as seemed apparent from his
frowning look, he was preoccupied with more important matters. Erin waited until the lines on his forehead had smoothed
out before she ventured to speak again.

"Can I ask a question?"

"Sure. Sorry if I sounded a little brusque. I was thinking
about a sentence in a speech I'm working on for Rosemary."

"I thought Nick was the official speechwriter."

"There is no official speechwriter," Jeff snapped. He gave
her a rueful sidelong smile. "There I go again. Sometimes
the way this campaign is being run gets to me. We all have
official titles, but they don't mean anything, except in Joe's
case—and a campaign manager is supposed to be a jack-of-

all-trades, in charge of everything. Not that political campaigns are ever models of organization, I've heard the process described as lurching from one crisis to the next. But this one . . ."

He shook his head. "As for the speechwriting, we all take a shot at it. Rosemary reworks every word herself, but she's very good about listening to other ideas. So feel free, if the urge strikes you, to become the next Schlesinger."

"I wouldn't dare."

"Why not? Erlichman began as a baggage handler for Nixon's 1960 campaign—though that may not be a career you'd care to emulate. And I know of one political writer who was writing speeches for Robert Kennedy two days after he began work as a junior-grade assistant. But you wanted to ask me something. What was it?"

"You've already answered it," Erin said. "I was going to ask whether things were always this frantic."

Jeff seemed quite at ease, now that he had let off a little steam. "Actually, they get worse," he said, smiling. "The closer we get to election day, the more frantic the pace. A lot of people who go into that voting booth make up their minds, or change them, at the last minute. The polls are increasingly accurate in predicting the outcome—some would say they affect the outcome—but there are always the famous exceptions. Something can happen at the last minute to change the whole picture."

"Like Rosemary's secretary breaking her hand?"

"Oh, that. A minor contretemps. Kay doesn't like to admit it, but she can be replaced."

"But why by me?"

"That's the question I thought you were going to ask," Jeff said. He was silent for a moment. It was not a pause of uncertainty, but of someone coolly considering all the pros and cons before issuing a statement. Then he said, "I don't ordinarily gossip about people, but you're being tossed into the thick of this situation, so you have a right to know some of the problems you'll be facing. Kay is Rosemary's secretary. Period. She's had the job for years, and by all accounts she has handled it well. Lately, though, she's aspired to giddier heights—aide, executive assistant. And that job she cannot handle.''

''Why not?''

''It's hard to explain. And,'' Jeff added, in a burst of unexpected candor, ''it makes me feel like a petty-minded lout to criticize Kay; I'm fond of her, and she's always been nice to me. But she just doesn't have it. The imagination, the political savvy, the subtlety . . . Oh, hell, I have to say it— the brains. She can't accept that, of course. But it makes things very awkward, especially when Kay tries to usurp the functions of the office she doesn't hold. She's always snipping at Joe, which doesn't improve his inequable temper. If Rosemary weren't such a sentimental sucker she'd retire Kay and give the job to someone younger and more flexible.''

''Kay seemed perfectly competent the day I met her,'' Erin said. What she didn't say, because it was not her place to do so, was that Kay had been a little too competent, too quick to assume authority. She hadn't even asked the right questions.

''She's not senile,'' Jeff said. ''I didn't mean to imply that. But she's slowing down; it's become more apparent even in the past few days. Being personal secretary to a person like Rosemary involves more than typing and filing. You have to be tactful, quick to react in a crisis, a generally soothing influence. Kay's performance this morning, when she realized she was temporarily out of commission, was indicative. She carried on like a maniac; Rosemary had to soothe her, instead of the other way around. She wouldn't shut up until Joe agreed to send you out to the house.''

''Then this was Kay's idea?''

''I guess so,'' Jeff said disinterestedly. ''But it was okay with Rosemary; she said something about keeping it in the family. As I said, she's a sucker for sentimental relationships. If I were you, I'd be careful not to complain about Kay to Rosemary, no matter what dumb thing she does. Rosemary isn't stupid, she won't blame you for goofing if it isn't your fault, but she'll like you better if you take the 'full-responsibility' route.''

"Thanks," Erin said gloomily. "I don't get it, though. Why would Kay want me, of all people?"

"Oh, that's obvious, I should think. She doesn't consider you a threat. Some of the other secretaries could replace her. You—forgive me—you couldn't. Not with your lack of experience. Don't get any grand ideas about your job, you're just another pair of hands—Kay's hands—doing exactly what she tells you to do."

Chapter
Three

IF ERIN HAD entertained any remaining illusions about her promotion, they would have been stripped away by the manner in which Kay received her. She and Jeff had barely gotten out of the car when Kay rushed out of the house and down the porch steps. She stumbled on the steps; Jeff, who had apparently feared just such an accident, dropped Erin's bag and leapt forward to catch the older woman.

"What're you trying to do, break a leg to match your hand?" he asked, setting her back on her feet.

Kay looked ten years older than she had the previous Saturday. Her hair had been bundled into an untidy wad at the back of her head, her face was sunken, and her eyes looked odd and unfocused. Her right arm had been strapped to her body, probably to keep her from waving it in agitated gestures.

"What took you so long? The work is piling up. I can't even . . . " She brushed a lock of straggling hair from her face and then pressed her hand to her forehead. "Those darned pills are too strong, I feel funny. I didn't want to take them, but Rosemary insisted.''

"Well, of course you have to take them," Jeff said easily. "If you'd let me drive you to the hospital last night, after it happened, instead of waiting till this morning—"

"I thought it was only bruised." Kay's lips turned down like those of a sulky child. "Don't just stand there, Jeff, Rosemary wants to see you right away. You're late."

"We came as fast as we could. I suggested Erin pack a suitcase."

"I should hope so. This isn't any nine-to-five job, she'll be staying. I've had a room prepared for her. I suppose I'd better show her, but she'll have to get right to work. Hurry, both of you."

She turned back to the stairs, holding the rail with her good hand. Jeff gave Erin a meaningful glance and followed Kay, ready to steady her if she stumbled again. Once inside, he disappeared into the office and Kay fussily directed Erin to the stairs. Erin wondered what on earth she would do if Kay fell. Drop the suitcase, grab the rail, and hope for the best, she supposed; Kay outweighed her by at least fifty pounds.

Fortunately she was not called upon to put her plan into effect. Kay's steps were slow but firm; she paused to catch her breath on the landing, and then proceeded up another flight of stairs to the third floor. "Here we are," she panted, opening a door. "This will be your room."

Erin's image stared back at her from a mirror opposite the door. If she had come into the room at night and seen the reflection, she probably would have yelled and backed out again; the streaked worn surface distorted her features hideously, and patches of silver had worn off, giving her face a leprous look. The mirror and the dresser to which it was attached stood between two windows. They were dormers; the roof slanted sharply down on that side of the room. A braided rug covered part of the worn floor. The narrow single bed was part of a suite, matching the dresser and a chest of drawers; it had once been pretty furniture, with an inlaid design of formalized flowers and leaves, but some of the inlay had fallen out and the veneer was flaking.

Kay dropped heavily onto the bed, producing a squawk of rusting springs that boded ill for the future sleeper. She pressed her hand to her heaving chest and waited for her breathing to slow, while Erin examined her new quarters. There wasn't much left to examine—a big, ugly wardrobe on the wall to her right, a few chairs, and a closed door in the left-hand wall. Life was certainly strange, she thought philosophically. Here she was, translated in less than a day from her small apartment to the dwellings of the rich and famous. But this wasn't exactly the setting she had pictured.

"My room is next door," Kay said. "We'll be sharing the bath, it's across the hall. I hope you don't mind being way up here; the stairs are no problem for a young thing like you, and it will be convenient for me to have you close by, in case I need help dressing."

So she was expected to act as Kay's maid, as well as her office assistant. Jeff had tried to warn her, and Erin knew she had no legitimate cause for complaint. Hadn't Rosemary stressed flexibility and willingness to lend a hand? Erin didn't mind performing personal services for other people, she had done a great deal of it for her mother, who took a certain rueful pride in her own lack of domestic talent. Erin had been glad to sew on buttons, arrange hair, carry trays, and smooth pillows when her mother took to her bed with a cold or flu.

She couldn't object to assisting an elderly woman, her superior in rank, who was temporarily incapacitated. Nobody had promised her a rose garden—or anything else. She was lucky to be getting a salary, and she suspected she owed that to the streak of sentimentality in Rosemary that Jeff had stressed. She ought to be grateful—but the situation was depressingly reminiscent of the one that had characterized her other job.

She reminded herself that Kay really did need her help, and that she ought to understand. She had broken her wrist once, in high school, when an overenthusiastic teammate had whacked her with a hockey stick, and she remembered all too well how madddeningly helpless one could be with an arm out of commission. Even such simple tasks as tying a shoelace became impossible. She wondered, though, why

such a kindly person as Rosemary Marshall would expect an
older woman to climb two flights of steep, narrow stairs.

Kay seemed to read her mind. "Rosemary wanted me to
move down to the second floor," she said defensively. "She's
been after me to do that for years. But we're short on staff—
as always—and the guest rooms ought to be kept ready for
important visitors. I'm perfectly capable of climbing a few
stairs."

"Of course." Erin put her suitcase down. Adjust, she told
herself. Be flexible. And for God's sake, try to be cheerful
about it. "But it's hard to do some things with only one arm.
Like fixing your hair. Would you like me to see whether I
can't anchor your chignon a little more securely? It seems to
be coming loose."

"We ought to get right to work."

"It will only take a minute. I'm very good at doing people's hair—honestly. Why don't you sit here, in front of the
mirror? Then you can tell me if I do something wrong."

The idea obviously appealed to Kay; after only a little per-
suasion, she went to get her comb and brush. She didn't invite Erin into her room, but she left the door open, and Erin
could see it had been furnished with a degree of comfort and
ruffled charm that made her room look even shabbier. Which
was only as it should be, of course. Quite obviously hers was
seldom if ever occupied; the days of big, live-in household
staffs were long past. If anything, Kay's room was overcrowded and overdecorated, but that was a question of personal taste. Maybe she enjoyed her aerie at the top of the
house and preferred the privacy it afforded. What did she do
up here, all alone by herself—entertain gentlemen friends who
ascended to her window by means of a rope ladder? Indulge
in orgies of pot smoking or Scotch? Erin smiled to herself.
If there were orgies of any kind, they probably featured choc-
olate bars and dirty books—though Kay's definition of the
latter, she supposed, would be more PG than X-rated.

She placed one of the straight chairs in front of the dresser,
and Kay sat down. After taking out pins and combs Erin
began to brush the long, graying hair, deliberately prolonging

the process as she saw the lines in Kay's face fade and soften. "My, that feels good," Kay said dreamily.

"Do you always wear your hair in a bun?" Erin asked. "I mean, a chignon?"

Kay's shoulders heaved with silent laughter. " 'Bun' is the right word, honey. I get fancied up for special occasions—I know what's proper—but the good old common bun is the real me."

Her voice was a little slurred, and her eyes were drowsy and unfocused. Finally Erin stopped brushing and began to twist the heavy hair into a neat coil. In another minute Kay would topple gently off the chair; she was already listing visibly to one side.

"How does that look?" she asked.

Kay opened one eye and contemplated her reflection. " 'Most as neat as I could do it myself. Rosie tried, but she just ain't no good at it. . . ." And then, in a loud angry voice that made Erin jump, she said, "Goddamn this lousy hand anyhow!"

Erin's fingers fumbled as she stared in shocked disbelief. She had heard that people under the influence of analgesics or anesthesia sometimes came out with uncharacteristic, even obscene, remarks, but the change in Kay's accent and vocabulary was so dramatic as to be almost frightening.

"Just one damn thing after another," Kay muttered. "They say things allus come in threes, but I swear to God there's been so many. . . . Like she was cursed or somethin'. She'd say that was crazy, but I dunno, seems like it ain't natural somehow. . . . So many accidents . . ."

"What on earth are you talking about, Kay?"

The speaker had come unobserved and unheard; her voice startled Erin so that the hairpin she was holding stabbed into Kay's scalp.

"I'm so sorry," Erin exclaimed "Did I hurt you?"

"My fault," Rosemary said. "I shouldn't have crept up on you. Kay, how do you feel?"

Kay did not turn. From the direction of her gaze Erin realized she was looking at Rosemary's reflection in the mirror, as Rosemary was looking at hers.

"What was I talking about?" Kay asked. "I was half asleep. . . . "

"You were talking a lot of nonsense," Rosemary said.

"She was fixing my hair," Kay muttered.

"And very nice it looks too. Thank you, Erin, that was kind. Perhaps you can persuade her to rest, and let you take over. She's out of her head from those pills, she isn't used to them."

The suggestion that anyone could take over Kay's work acted like a shot in the arm. Her slumped shoulders straightened and when she spoke it was in the well-bred, unaccented voice Erin had heard before. "Don't be silly, Rosemary; I'm quite all right. I won't take so many of the pills next time. I can't rest, I have to show Erin what to do."

"There's no reasoning with you," Rosemary said. She put an affectionate hand on her old friend's shoulder. It was a gentle touch, it couldn't possibly have jarred the injured hand; it must have been the expectation of pain that made Kay cringe away.

*   *

KAY WAS CRISPLY businesslike as she showed Erin around. The change in her manner was so extreme Erin almost fancied she must have imagined that brief, frightening metamorphosis.

The former library had been converted into offices. Makeshift partitions divided it into one large room and several smaller cubicles, and the flat, featureless surface of the newer walls looked odd compared with the dark wooden paneling and casemented windows of the older ones. Kay had her own cubicle, as did Joe, when he was there. Rosemary's office had not been altered, it was a pleasant room next to the library, with deep window seats and a fireplace. The furnishings were old and somewhat masculine in character—leather chairs, engravings of animals and birds on the walls, a dark geometric print covering cushions and windows.

"This was Congressman Marshall's office," Kay explained in a hushed voice. It was an odd way of putting it, Erin thought; the use of the past tense told her that Kay was referring, not to Rosemary, but to her husband. "It's just as it was in his time. Nothing has been changed, not even the curtains. Oh, they've been replaced, of course, fabric fades so badly in sunlight. But it's the same print."

She closed the door quietly, as upon a shrine.

She went on to explain that although it was convenient for Rosemary to maintain an office in her home, the practice had certain disadvantages. "Especially when, as in this case, we are running a campaign from here. It's a rather unusual arrangement, in fact, but Rosemary prefers it that way, and thanks to telecommunications and computer hookups we can keep in touch with our workers elsewhere. Rosemary has several offices in her district, like the one in Arlington; in other cities where offices have been opened for the Democratic presidential campaign, we share the space and the personnel to some extent, but of course the presidential race gets most of the money and almost all the press. Rosemary refuses to let her office on the Hill be used for campaign practices, she's made a big point of refusing to use taxpayers' money for that purpose, and it certainly does go over well with the voters."

She introduced Erin to the office workers. There were only four of them—and Erin couldn't help noticing the balance; two men, two women; two blacks, two whites. She made a conscious effort to remember their names. Jan Berger, a stocky, sober-faced blond boy who didn't look a day over sixteen; Anita Valdez, raven-haired and conspicuously plain, with a long thin nose like a heron's beak; Jackson Price, who looked like an ebony version of the linebacker who had engaged in political dispute with Nick, except for his shrewd dark eyes; and Christie Johnson, office manager and political aide—titles she was careful to emphasize when she acknowledged the introduction. Christie was several inches taller than Erin and made rather a point of looking down on her. She was also devastatingly attractive, with features as chiseled as those of a Benin bronze head, and a lean athlete's figure. She wore tight designer jeans and a shirt that might as well have had a designer's name on the pocket; it was cunningly cut to look both sexy and businesslike. All the workers except Christie were part-time volunteers, political-science and government majors from various universities who were earning credits as well as practical experience, and whose training made them more valuable than the average enthusiastic amateur. Christie was the only true professional; as Erin was to learn, she had been one of Rosemary's aides on the Hill. Obviously Christie wasn't afraid of taking a chance, but on the other hand, she had little to lose. If the campaign was successful, she would have taken a giant step up the ladder, ending as aide to a senator rather than a representative.

Kay took Erin into her own cubicle and put her to work. By late afternoon she was hard-pressed to hold on to her sympathy for the invalid. Kay's increasing discomfort, as the medication wore off, was discernible in her tense muscles and tight lips, but surely, Erin thought, pain couldn't be entirely responsible for her alarming lack of organization. Erin barely had time to finish one task before Kay told her to stop doing it and do something else. Though she was familiar with several different kinds of computers, Kay's was new to her, and Kay's instructions only confused her more. If Kay was testing her ability to perform under pressure, she wasn't doing very well. But she felt sure that wasn't the reason for Kay's brusque manner. Circumstances had forced Kay to open her private files to a stranger, and admit someone else into the world of sensitive information she had taken pride in handling herself. She had to do it, but she resented the necessity, and her innocent assistant, bitterly.

Rosemary finally came to the rescue, appearing in the doorway to announce it was quitting time. "Five o'clock, you poor wage-slaves."

"Since when has five o'clock been quitting time in this office?" Kay demanded. "I want Erin to finish typing these memos, and then she can—"

"Never mind the memos." Rosemary reached over Erin's shoulder and punched the break key. Kay let out a gasp of outrage.

"Now you've lost that one. Honestly, Rosemary!"

"I haven't lost it, it's somewhere in the metal innards of that contraption. And if I have, so what?" Rosemary looked tired, her nose shiny as a mirror and her lipstick blurred.

"Close up shop, I said. Erin hasn't even had time to unpack, and I need you to help me. I have to get dressed."

This time she had taken the right approach. "Oh, the fundraiser," Kay said. "Yes, you'd better hurry."

"Another one?" Erin asked incredulously.

"One of many." Rosemary leaned against the desk and passed a grubby hand over her face "The curse of the candidate. The food is boring, the company is boring, the speeches are boring. But without them we couldn't operate. I don't get a lot from the PACs. . . You do know what a PAC is, don't you?"

"Yes, of course." Mercifully, that was one of the political terms she did know. "Political Action Committees. They were set up by various groups—business. labor, special interests such as education, conservation, animal welfare—"

"Don't forget women," Rosemary interrupted, her lip curling. "It drives me crazy to hear women referred to as a special-interest group, but it's common usage. Half the goddamn population of the country . . . All right, Kay, all right, no more cussing. Your definition is technically correct, Erin, but in actual fact PACs were set up to get around the laws limiting the amount of individual campaign contributions. If I could afford it I'd refuse to take PAC money, even from organizations whose aims I would ordinarily support . . . Kay, what the hell are you doing? I don't have much time."

"I have to lock up," Kay said. "There are important papers in my desk, you know. It wouldn't do to leave them lying around."

Rosemary's hands clenched, but she said nothing, only watched in stoic silence as Kay fumbled with keys and locks.

"But aren't PAC contributions limited too?" Erin asked.

"Yes—by federal law. But some states have no reporting requirement, and others allow contributions over the federal limit. In theory this money is supposed to be used only to benefit local candidates and parties, but a lot of it is diverted out of state. Oh, it's too complicated to explain in a few minutes; ask Joe to explain the difference between hard and soft money. Or Nick; he adores showing off his expertise to attractive young women. Kay, if you don't stop, I swear I'll go to the Sheraton looking like this.''

Erin followed at a modest distance; but when she would have continued up the stairs to the third floor Kay stopped her with a sharp question. "Where are you going? I'll need you to do some pressing.''

"We didn't hire her to be a maid of all work, Kay," Rosemary protested.

"You didn't hire me as a maid, either. I'm not ashamed to help out in any way I can, and neither should Erin be.''

"I'm not. Anything I can do, of course.''

She wasn't sorry to have a chance to see Rosemary's private quarters, and possibly—dream on, she told herself—make a few modest suggestions about clothes. Rosemary's request for Kay's assistance might have been a tactful means of getting her secretary away from her desk and onto her bed for the rest she needed, but if Kay was her adviser on wardrobe and makeup, Erin could understand why Rosemary looked a little dowdy.

Rosemary's bedroom wasn't really a letdown, or a surprise. Erin had grown accustomed to the casual life-style and organized chaos that characterized both the candidate and the campaign. The room had been beautifully decorated and furnished with fine antiques, dominated by a mahogany highboy and canopied bed. The color scheme was blue and white, restful if unimaginative. But the clutter was indescribable. Papers covered every flat surface, books lay in untidy heaps; a television set glared from one corner and an IBM Selectric on a table by the window proved that Rosemary shared her generation's suspicion of word processors.

Adjoining the bedroom was a dressing room, with clothes hanging from open racks and shoes neatly aligned. It contained an ironing board and sewing supplies—everything needed to keep a wardrobe in repair. To Erin it seemed beautifully organized, but Kay began apologizing for its condition. "I just don't know what I'm going to do, things are in such a mess, and the girls don't know how to take care of them—"

Rosemary cut her short. "I'm going to take a quick shower. Stop fussing, Kay, everything looks fine. Pick out a dress. The aqua or the rose, I think."

When she came out of the adjoining bathroom, modestly wrapped in a cotton robe, Erin was passing the iron carefully over a smooth stretch of rosy-pink silk, while Kay breathed anxiously down the back of her neck and asked for the fifth time if she was sure she hadn't set the iron too high.

"It's fine, great, perfect," Rosemary said impatiently. "Leave it, Erin. Kay, you go lie down on my bed. You can supervise this massive undertaking and we'll carry out your orders. Erin, would you get the jewelry boxes? They're in the second drawer of the wardrobe. What do you think, Kay— the pearls or the gold earrings and necklace?"

Kay settled herself and watched complacently as Erin trotted back and forth, helping Rosemary into her dress, hanging up the robe, locating the jewelry and carrying it to the dressing table where Rosemary sat. As the boxes were opened and their glittering contents displayed, Erin wondered where Rosemary kept her good jewelry, and why she wasn't wearing any of it. These ornaments were all fake—faux, to be more elegant—although they were expensive and in excellent taste. The pearls, on which Kay decided (against Erin's judgment), were obviously cultured.

She helped Rosemary fasten the clasp and watched while she inserted the matching earrings with quick, impatient fingers.

"You've torn a nail," she said hesitantly.

"Oh, shit, so I have." Rosemary glanced guiltily in the mirror. "Sorry, Kay, it just slipped out. . . ." But Kay's eyes had closed and she made no comment. Rosemary let out a little breath of relief. "Is she asleep?"

"I think so."

"Good." Rosemary picked at the broken nail.

"Don't do that," Erin exclaimed involuntarily. "Oh, I'm sorry, I didn't mean to sound . . . Would you let me?"

"With pleasure." She held out her hand. "Do you really like to do this sort of thing?" she asked curiously, as Erin carefully trimmed the mutilated nail. "Or are you just being polite? You don't have to—do it, or be polite about it. I'm quite accustomed to looking after myself. And," she added with a smile, "I get the impression, from the way you've been looking at me, that you don't think I do it very well."

"You always look nice," Erin murmured.

"Nice, she says." Rosemary leaned back in her chair and ran her fingers through her hair. She had taken out the pins that held it in its regal, upswept coiffure, and it stood out around her face like Medusa's snakes. "Nice is, I'm afraid, the safest option for a lady candidate. Nice and neat and well-groomed. I wish television had never been invented. I spend more time thinking about how I look than what I'm going to say; the damned political process has become a beauty contest." Then she burst out laughing, muting the sound into a rich chuckle in deference to the sleeper. "Erin, you have the most transparent face. I know exactly what you're thinking: if that woman doesn't stop pawing at her hair, I'm going to scream! Just hand me that brush, will you please?"

She was easily persuaded to let Erin do the brushing and pin the thick, heavy locks into a becoming shape. "You look lovely," Erin said, when the job was done. "You really do."

Rosemary glanced casually into the mirror. "Rich but not gaudy? But not too rich, nobody will give me money if I look prosperous. Thanks, Erin. I'd better run; Joe will be here any minute and patience is not one of his virtues." She reached for the lacy stole Erin had laid out for her and then paused, glancing at the sleeping woman. "Maybe I ought to wake her and help her into her own bed."

"Would you like me to stay with her?" Erin asked.

"Would you? That is kind. I'm afraid she may be disoriented—from the pain and the medication—when she wakes. She could fall, or stumble. . . ." Rosemary bit her lip. "Poor Kay, she's hating this, that's why she's so brusque and impatient. I hope you weren't offended by the way she spoke to you. It's not like her, she's usually not so—so peremptory."

Erin rather doubted that; but if Rosemary allowed her secretary to scold her like a naughty child, she, Erin, was in no position to complain.

"Honestly, I don't mind a bit. I only hope I can help out.

This is all new to me, but I'll do my best, and it's all so—so interesting.''

The speech sounded stilted and too, too sweet, but apparently Rosemary didn't think so; she reached out and touched Erin's cheek in a gesture as affectionate as it was unexpected. "You're a darling. Your mother said you were, but naturally I assumed she was a little prejudiced. . . . I was wrong. Just relax, take it easy. I'll send someone up to relieve you soon."

Her departure left the room feeling strangely empty. Erin was beginning to understand, not only why Rosemary was a successful politician, but why she commanded such devotion from her staff. How much of that charm had been calculated? It was alarmingly effective. In less than an hour Rosemary had managed to make her feel as if she really were one of the family—an intimate friend, a confidante. Yet what had she really said? Nothing Erin didn't know, or could not easily have surmised. A graceful apology some self-deprecating humor, a few casual compliments—and that quick, warm touch on the cheek.

She glanced at Kay, whose mouth had dropped open. From it came a series of sounds that the dignified secretary would indignantly disavow if anyone had accused her of snoring. Erin grinned. Kay's efforts equaled those of her father, and he had been a champion snorer, audible through a closed bedroom door.

She looked around the room wondering how to occupy herself for the next . . . however long it might be. There was no dearth of things to do: a television set, countless books and papers, and even one of the ubiquitous knitting bags on the blanket chest at the foot of the bed. A folded afghan lay beside it. Erin unfolded it and placed it carefully over the sleeper.

She wandered to the window, feeling like Cinderella as she saw Rosemary sweep down the porch steps on Joe's arm. I have to hand it to her, Erin thought admiringly; when she's in her public persona, she can make even that insipid pink dress look regal. The car was a limousine—hired for the occasion, one presumed. The uniformed driver helped them in, got behind the wheel, and the long black vehicle moved smoothly away. As smoothly as it could, considering the condition of the driveway.

The gray-blue shadow of the house lengthened as Kay continued to snore. Christie emerged into view, got into her car, and drove off. There were several other cars in the parking areas, including Nick's unmistakable old Dodge.

Erin didn't want to turn on the TV, for fear of waking Kay, but as the dusk deepened she ventured to switch on a lamp and, greatly daring, to investigate some of the papers lying around. Newspaper clippings and magazine articles, lists of contributors, notes for speeches . . . She recognized Nick's vigorous sprawling hand, and a neat, precise script that could only be Jeff's—if the theories of orthographers were indeed correct. His ideas were as ordered and as passionless as his handwriting, Erin thought, as she read. A good point, the one he had made about verification of nuclear testing, but there must be a more emphatic way of phrasing it. . . .

She was absorbed in the notes when there was a gentle tap on the door. Opening it, Erin put her finger to her lips, but the newcomer—Jeff—only smiled, and said in a normal speaking voice, "Whew, what a racket! I had no idea she snored like that. Sorry to have left you on duty so long; I was talking to a particularly long-winded constituent." He glanced at the papers she had left on the table beside her chair, and his smile broadened. "Couldn't you find anything better to read? You must have been desperately bored."

"Oh, I'm so sorry—maybe I shouldn't have looked at them—"

Jeff's smile shut down behind tight-set lips. "For God's sake, Erin, stop apologizing for everything! You have a perfect right to read any garbage you find lying out in the open. If I had anything to hide . . ." He stopped, and then said lightly, "You sure don't need me yelling at you, do you? Let's get something to eat. I'm grumpy and I'll bet you're starved as well as bored."

"What about Kay?"

"Time she got up anyway." Jeff bent over Kay and called her name.

He had to repeat it several times before she stirred and

groaned. "Oh, dear . . . What? Who is it? I was resting my eyes. . . . Where's Rosemary?"

"Long gone." Jeff put his arm around her and helped her to sit up. "Supper is ready; do you want to come downstairs, or shall I bring you a tray in your room?"

"Of course I'll come down." Kay yawned widely. Her eyes slid sideways, with an unpleasant suggestion of slyness. She gestured to Jeff, who bent obediently so she could whisper in his ear. "Who's that?" she hissed. "What's she doing here?"

Jeff's brows drew together, but he mastered his surprise and said calmly, "You know Erin. You asked me to bring her here to help you—"

"You don't have to tell me who she is. She's Roy Hartsock's little girl. I dreamed about her. The strangest dream . . . You shouldn't have let me sleep so long. I never take naps."

She swung her feet onto the floor and stood up. Jeff tried to take her arm, but she shook him off. "I wish you'd stop treating me like an invalid. I'm just a little groggy from sleep, that's all. Perfectly normal. No, wait, Jeff, I have to clean up this mess before I go downstairs. Rosemary's room—"

"I'll do it," Erin said. "You go ahead."

She had already picked up after Rosemary; there was nothing left to do but smooth the rumpled spread and fold the afghan, but she was glad of a few moments alone. What was the matter with everyone? First Jeff's outburst, so uncharacteristic of him, even though he had apologized with the grace only he could employ; then Kay's memory lapse. There had to be something seriously wrong with her. Maybe, Erin thought more optimistically, it was only the medication she was taking. Sometimes drugs affected people in odd, unexpected ways.

When she left the room she heard Kay's voice from the hall below. It was as brisk and peremptory as ever. Whatever the cause of her confusion, the spells didn't last long.

The commons room, as she had learned to call it, was deserted except for Jeff and Kay, who had entered just before her. The door to the kitchen was open; Erin heard voices, first Nick's, raised in poignant protest, followed by a woman's rich laughter.

"Is Nick still here?" Kay asked, lowering herself carefully onto the sofa.

"Is the Pope Catholic?" Jeff's tone was caustic. "He's always here when it's time to eat."

Kay reached for the knitting bag, and then made a sound that, in another woman, would have shaped itself into a hearty "damn." "This is driving me crazy. I can't even . . . Erin, do you know how to knit?"

Erin decided it was time to draw the line. Politely but firmly she said, "I used to, but I've forgotten everything except the basic stitches. I certainly couldn't do anything as complicated as that."

"This is a very simple pattern," Kay insisted. "That's why I selected it; we all work on it from time to time. Rosemary agrees with me that it's relaxing and therapeutic."

Jeff came to the rescue. "Cut it out, Kay. Since when has knitting been one of the job requirements around here? We *don't* all work on the cursed thing. Erin, you should have heard Joe when Kay suggested he learn to knit. Come to think of it, I'm glad you didn't hear him. Susceptible as I am to her charm, I too have thus far resisted the opportunity to broaden my skills. In fact, the only sucker in the crowd is—voilà, he comes."

"Hard upon his hour," Nick agreed. "What am I being accused of now? Ah, my adored one." He rushed at Kay. "I would have been at your side and wakened you with a kiss, but this jealous swine prevented me. How are you feeling, gorgeous?"

Kay's tight lips curved into a smile. "Don't you dare touch me, Nick. You don't know your own strength; it's like being hugged by a gorilla."

Arms ostentatiously behind him, Nick leaned over her and gave her a delicate peck on the cheek. "Only your fragile condition keeps me from crushing you in a passionate embrace. Hi, Erin."

"Hi."

"Now, what's the problem?" Nick went on. "The famous—the notorious—knitting! Allow me to step into the breach. Untainted as I am by the slightest tinge of male chauvinism, I had no hesitation at adding this skill to the others for which I am so highly commended.''

Jeff said something rude under his breath and retreated to a chair, where he picked up the newspaper and hid behind it. Nick grabbed the knitting bag with such ardor that balls of wool rolled in all directions. Kay exclaimed, ''Oh, Nick, be careful. You've ripped out that last row—''

''No problem, love.'' Nick began clumsily to pick up the dropped stitches. He hammed it up, eyes crossed and tongue protruding in fierce concentration as he crooned an absurd litany of inappropriate terms. ''Hook one, skip one, knit some, drop one . . . oops. . . .''

The appearance of the cook carrying a covered casserole put an end to Nick's performance. She was a middle-aged black woman, with the round, comfortable figure that becomes a chef.

''You shouldn't have stayed so late, Sarah,'' Kay said. ''We could have managed.''

''I figured that with you not feeling so good I should do a little extra.''

''That was very kind, and I'm sure Miss Rosemary will appreciate it. Run along, now; I'm sure you must have something else to do this evening. Sarah is very active in her church,'' Kay added, glancing at Erin. ''This is Miss Hartsock, Sarah.''

Everything she had said grated just a little; even the studied pleasantness of her voice was the tone of a lady of the manor to a servant. Nothing that any reasonable person could possibly object to, but . . . The introduction was the last straw. Erin stood up. ''My name is Erin,'' she said clearly. ''Please let me help, Sarah; I should have offered before.''

''It's all done, honey, thanks just the same. Nick, you gonna bring in those plates, or aren't you finished messing up that poor old afghan?''

Nick squashed the knitting back into the bag. ''You cut me to the quick, madam. I will carry your plates, or anything else your little heart desires, but note that I do it with my spirits crushed and my ego deflated.''

"That'll be the day," Jeff said, as Nick followed the cook toward the kitchen.

Supper was a simple meal—a spaghetti casserole and a tossed salad, with a plate of rich homemade brownies for dessert. Nick was the only one who ate with any appetite; and even he ate left-handed while he scribbled on a pad of paper.

"How does this sound?" he asked through a mouthful of salad. " 'The citizens of Virginia deserve a representative who is not only honest but honorable; whose personal life is as unblemished as her political record.' "

"Aren't you being too subtle?" Jeff asked, with a twist of his well-cut lips. "Why don't you just run the famous photo of Buzz emerging from the motel room, next to a shot of Rosemary with her granddaughter?"

"Negative campaigning tends to backfire," Kay said seriously.

"I'm not suggesting she keep referring to 'my opponent the adulterer,' " Nick argued. "But that little error really hurt old Buzz, in the districts where he has the strongest support. We don't want the voters to forget it. They have short memories."

"They aren't likely to forget it, with Miz Marylou turning up at every rally looking as if her li'l ol' heart was broken," Jeff said.

"Yeah, that's the truth, isn't it?" Nick agreed. "If I were Buzz, I'd lock her in her room and tell the press she has a bad case of flu. It's the duty of every good political wife to play the loyal long-suffering spouse, but Miz Marylou looks more suffering than loyal."

"Poor thing," Kay murmured. "She's worked so hard for him, and she was so in love. I remember their wedding. When she looked up at him and said, 'I will,' her face just glowed."

"Do you know her?" Erin asked.

"Oh, yes. When you've been in politics as long as I have, you get to know everybody—especially in your own part of the country. She's some distant relation of Eddy's—Congressman Marshall's—I believe.''

''The good old First Families of Virginia,'' Jeff murmured.

There was a brief, rather uncomfortable pause. Then Nick said, ''Oh, well. If he can't see how she's hurting him, I'm sure not the boy to point it out. 'Personal and professional integrity . . .' ''

After they had finished eating, he and Erin cleared the table, while Jeff settled down with a stack of computer print-outs. Kay turned on one of the television sets—there were three of them in the room—and Jeff looked up. ''Oh, no, Kay—not one of your glitz, glamour, and sleaze shows! I hate that garbage.''

''There's not much else I can do.'' Kay said sulkily. ''Unless Erin needs me to help her finish those memos she was typing—''

A joint grumble of protest from the men stopped her. ''Lay off the lady, Kay,'' Jeff said. ''She's been hard at it all day.''

''Right,'' Nick agreed. ''She needs a break. Come on, Erin, let's take a walk.''

''It's pitch-black dark out,'' Kay objected.

''But the moon is full,'' Nick intoned in a sepulchral voice. ''You wouldn't want her to miss seeing me turn into a were-wolf.''

Kay laughed and made no further objections. Erin would have accepted an invitation from a genuine werewolf—anything to get out of the house for a while. She accompanied Nick through the kitchen and into an enclosed glassed-in porch. The windows were opaque with darkness; not only was the promised moon missing, but not a star was visible.

''Damn, nobody turned on the lights,'' Nick muttered. ''Wait a minute. . . .'' A battery of floodlights came on, bathing the area in garish brilliance. Erin could see only a wide stretch of grass bisected by a brick walkway that stretched off into the dark.

Nick collapsed heavily onto the steps. ''Whew. I hope you didn't mind my pressing invitation; I had a feeling you needed to get away from Kay.''

"You were right." Seeing his drooping shoulders and general air of collapse, she asked, "I expect you're tired, after your late night."

"Nah, I'm used to that. What wears me out is being so relentlessly, tirelessly funny all the time." Erin laughed, but Nick only shook his head gloomily. "Jeff was right, that's my most useful role—court jester. All those massive egos in constant conflict generate a lot of tension. I make 'em laugh. Ha, ha."

"But you do lots of things," Erin said. "Wasn't that a major speech you were working on at supper?"

Nick straightened up and beamed at her. "I love a little sympathy and appreciation. That wasn't a speech, but it was major—a mail-out we're preparing. You're absolutely right, you wonderful woman, they couldn't get along without me. Jack-of-all-trades and master of none. . . . I'd better go and see what Sam is up to. He's supposed to be in charge of security around here. If you want a hearty laugh, wait till you meet our security guard."

"Everything seems so casual," Erin said as they walked along the brick path. "I expected—oh, I don't know; a guard at the gate, and someone at the house to check IDs and screen visitors."

"That's not Rosemary's style. Her accessibility is one of the reasons why she's so popular with her constituents, and this relaxed, seemingly casual life-style goes over very well. 'See, she can't get her lawn mowed either, or afford a new coat of paint on the house.' Which," Nick added, "is in fact the case. And there's really no need for tight security. She gets lunatic letters, like the ones you saw, but no more than other representatives, and a really effective security system would cost— Careful, the bricks are uneven back here. There's a gate. . . . Well, at least the old coot has switched on the lights in the stableyard."

There were three lights, one on a post in the middle of a paved area, the other two on buildings that ran in parallel rows flanking it. Those on the right appeared to be garages or workbuildings; a row of smaller, separate structures on the left-hand side looked like cottages. As they approached these,

a door opened and a man's figure appeared, silhouetted
against the glow inside. A rattle of what sounded like automatic rifle fire made Erin start.

"Hey, Sam, don't shoot," Nick bellowed. "It's me."

"Nick?" The quavering voice was that of an old man.
"What you doin' out in the dark? You lucky I didn't shoot
you at that."

"Don't worry, he doesn't have a gun," Nick murmured.
"That was the TV you heard. We're just taking a walk, Sam.
Nice night."

"Nice night, my foot. Too hot. And it's comin' on to
storm. Who's that you got with you?"

Nick performed the introductions. Sam was completely
bald, and apparently very nearsighted; he thrust his withered
face so close to Erin's that she could feel his breath. He
greeted her with old-fashioned courtesy: "Welcome, young
lady," he added, "you may's well let them dogs out, Nick. I
was just gonna do it, but so long as you're here. . . ."

"Okay. Get back to your cops and robbers, Sam."

The old man retreated and slammed the door.

"See what I mean?" Nick asked.

"He's sweet."

"Sure he's sweet. And so decrepit a faint breeze would
bowl him over. Another one of Rosemary's sentimental at-
tachments; he's been with the family for a million years and
she thinks his feelings would be hurt if she hired somebody
to assist him. Here, take my hand, it's pretty dark back this
way."

The dogs were penned in a run behind the garage. The
first sight of them made Erin cling more tightly to Nick's
hand; a pillar lamp cast a dim glow and made the huge bodies
hurling themselves at the chain-link fence look formidable.

"You aren't afraid of dogs, are you?" Nick asked casually,
opening the gate.

After slobbering messily over Erin, from her face to her
feet, the dogs gamboled off, baying wildly.

"Retrievers," Nick sneered, wiping his wet forearm on
his shirt. "They are the most useless excuses for watchdogs
I've ever seen. I suggested Dobermans—"

"They sounded fierce." One of the dogs was running around in circles, baying like the hound of the Baskervilles.

"That's all they do. Look at that furry idiot, chasing his own tail. Thinks he's a cat."

"Don't they chase the cats?"

"They chase the cats? It's the other way around."

He led her across the dew-wet grass to a bench in the shadow of a group of white pines. When they sat down, one of the dogs joined them, collapsing onto Erin's foot. The white hairs of his muzzle glimmered palely, and she bent down to pat his head.

"He's old, isn't he?"

"Ten years old. This is Samson. The other one is Tiny. He's four, but he's mentally retarded. Thinks he's a puppy."

Head down, tail thrashing, Tiny followed some arcane unseen path across the lawn.

As the panting breath of the old dog quieted, other sounds became audible—small, sly rustles of movement made sinister by one's inability to identify their causes. As her eyes continued to adjust to the darkness Erin began to see shapes moving noiselessly from the shadows. The cats were on the prowl.

One pale fuzzy shape strolled toward the dog. Tiny welcomed it with a sharp bark and pounced, then yelped and backed off, pawing at his nose. The cat walked away as leisurely as it had approached.

"It's very . . . peaceful," Erin said. The word wasn't entirely appropriate. Bathed in the merciless glare that showed all the imperfections of flaking paint and splintered trim, the house looked like a tiny island of life besieged and about to be overwhelmed by towering walls of darkness. Clouds massed like attacking armies overhead and along the horizon.

"Sure is," Nick said, not hearing the note of uncertainty in her voice. "Rosemary is lucky her home is so close to D.C.; she doesn't have to maintain two residences. It's a long commute, though."

"Is this her husband's family home?"

"Yes. Ed Marshall's family used to own half Virginia, but they lost everything in the War Between The States except a town house in Richmond and this place. It was just a farm then; a brief period of questionable prosperity (there were nasty rumors about illegal investments) resulted in the architectural abortion you see before you "

"You know a lot about the Marshalls."

"I should. My aunt was the Marshalls' housekeeper till she retired some years ago. How do you think I got my foot in the door?"

"I thought you were a volunteer. Anybody can volunteer, can't they?"

"Sure. I assure you it wasn't my family connections that got me my present munificent salary of zero a year. What it got me was noticed, so that when I did come through in a clutch situation, people were watching."

"What did you do, rescue Rosemary from a mad dog?"

Nick chuckled. "You'll never guess. I won my spurs baby-sitting."

"What?"

"You heard me. The Lord works in mysterious ways. . . . They came for a visit last spring—Rosemary's daughter and her husband, and the kid. Kevin and I hit it off right away, he's an antique car buff and a fiery liberal. Elizabeth—the little girl—reminds me of Rosemary, she's funny and spunky and cute as a tick. I like kids, and being creatures of rare discernment, they adore me. Before they left I was 'Uncle Nick,' and the most popular guy on the block."

Erin was about to express incredulity when she remembered that she had won a friendly smile and a pat on the cheek by offering to baby-sit Kay.

"I guess it can happen," she said doubtfully.

"Take my word for it. Of course," Nick added modestly, "I was doing a superb job in every other way. I was also one of the first to volunteer, way back before the primary, when nobody gave her a prayer. They thought she was crazy to give up a sure House seat for a long shot. The local party supported her opponent in the primary—a well-heeled, well-connected realtor who suffered from delusions of grandeur. We beat the pants off the sucker, but it took Buzz's half-witted performance to make people sit up and take notice.

We're on a roll now, contributions picking up, endorsements from some key people, but it's still up for grabs.''

''Baby-sitting aside, I can see why you're so highly esteemed,'' Erin said. ''To jump feet first the way you did, into what looked like a hopeless cause—''

''I wasn't doing anything important anyway. The truth is, I'm what you might call a late bloomer. I screwed around with a lot of things—a little PR work, courses in business administration, before I decided to follow in the footsteps of Edward R. Murrow and Dan Rather. It didn't take me long to realize that that path was a bit crowded—a regular traffic jam. As a matter of fact, I quit my job today.''

''Your job at the paper? Why? Too many high school football games?''

''Too little time. The next few weeks are crucial. Rosemary hasn't got the financial backing Buzz commands; he had raised a million bucks by the middle of the summer. He can afford to pay a big staff, and a team of expensive media consultants. Rosemary has me.''

''But Nick, that's really . . . What are you going to live on?''

''Oh, I'll get by. And don't get the wrong idea about how noble I am. This is a gamble, but if it pays off I'm in the catbird seat. Even if we lose, I'm making useful contacts and—I hope—impressing them with my brilliance and dedication.''

The branches over them swayed in a sudden gust of wind. ''Storm's about to break,'' Nick muttered. ''I hope Rosemary doesn't stay in town too late, these roads can be murder when they're flooded.''

The comment was more revealing than he realized, and Erin thought she knew the real reason for the dedication he boasted about. Only a fool would have hitched his career to a star as low in the sky as Rosemary's had been, and Nick was no fool. He was undoubtedly an idealist, but sympathy for the causes Rosemary supported wasn't the reason either. It was Rosemary herself who had won him over. A young man's platonic devotion to an older woman whose profession (if not her face and figure) was the quintessence of glamour.

Shades of the Round Table and the ideals of chivalry . . . She liked him all the better for it, though Nick would have scoffed if she had compared him with Sir Lancelot—and maybe that wasn't the most appropriate comparison, come to think of it. There were all those rumors about Lancelot and Guinevere.

A fat, warm raindrop splashed on the back of her hand. "We'd better go in," Nick said.

"I haven't seen you turn into a werewolf," Erin protested. "No moon."

There was a moon, though; Erin saw it over her left shoulder as they crossed the lawn toward the house. The clouds closed over it again even as she looked: a monstrous, swollen globe of tarnished silver, with a single shadow of dead branch piercing it like a spear through a knight's shield.

*   *

LATE THE FOLLOWING morning Erin snatched a moment to call Fran. "I won't talk long," she began. "I know your boss doesn't like you to get personal calls—"

"Never mind him," Fran cut in. "I've been dying to hear from you. Tell me everything!"

"There isn't much to tell."

"Oh, for God's sake! You're there, right in her house—have you seen her? What's she doing? What are *you* doing?"

Erin was tempted to tell her, if only to shatter Fran's illusions about politics, which now seemed to her hopelessly naive and infantile. She had spent a restless night with the connecting door between her room and Kay's ajar, listening to the snores and groans and squeaking springs as the older woman tossed and turned. Kay hadn't settled down until almost dawn, but she had been up and raring to go shortly after seven. Erin had helped her dress, arranged her hair, made both beds, dusted and swept. She had not seen Rosemary at all that day.

She managed to cut into Fran's raptures long enough to explain why she had called. "I'm going to try to get a ride in this evening so I can pick up some more clothes. I'm not sure when, everyone is so busy—"

''No problem. I'll bring you whatever you need. I'd love to.''

Erin didn't doubt that. Her need was an answer to prayer. If it hadn't happened, Fran would have found some other excuse to come for a visit.

''What do you want? The black lace formal, of course. What else?''

Erin pictured herself making Kay's bed in black lace and ruffles. ''Never mind the formal. I need everyday clothes—jeans, tops, underwear. . . . What am I saying? You can't come, Fran. I can't invite you, not without asking permission. . . .''

She might as well have protested to the wind. Fran assured her she didn't need directions, she knew the way, and then hung up without so much as a good-bye.

Erin went in search of Kay, who was no more inclined to listen to her than Fran had been. When she finally got her point across, the old woman thought for a moment and then nodded. ''I suppose that would be best. I can't see any other way of arranging it. You should have brought more than an overnight bag. Didn't Joe explain the situation? Well, never mind, there's no sense in crying over spilt milk. Tell your friend to come ahead, there's no one here who can drive you, and no extra car to lend you. Except mine . . . but I really can't spare you today.''

Erin had already heard a few jokes about Kay's precious Mercedes, for which she had been saving all her life, and which she refused to entrust to anyone else. ''She ought to lend it to you, since she can't drive right now,'' Nick had remarked at breakfast, when Erin explained her problem. ''But she won't even let me behind the wheel—can you imagine that, superb driver that I am? I wish I could take you, but I have to go to Richmond and I don't know when I'll be back.''

The others had also scattered on various errands, which left Erin to the tender mercies of Kay. The older woman seemed sharper, in every sense of the word—efficient and in control as well as sharp-tongued and critical. Though Erin was the chief victim, the other workers also felt the brunt of Kay's disapproval, and during the brief lunch break—sand-

wiches and coffee in the commons room—Jan muttered sourly.
"The old witch is in a foul mood today."

"Sssh." Christie gave him a warning look. Kay had gone
to the kitchen to talk to Sarah about supper—and, Erin
thought, to get *her* back up too. There was no way Kay could
have overheard the complaint; it was the presence of an outsider, Erin, that had prompted Christie's warning.

"She's probably in a lot of pain " said Jackson.

"I'll bet she's not taking those pills," Anita said shrewdly.
"She was so out of it yesterday—" She broke off as the distinctive click of Kay's heels sounded along the passageway.

Erin knew they all shared her hope that Kay would rest
after lunch, but none of them had the nerve to suggest it, and
Kay went doggedly on, wearing herself out and driving everybody crazy. The afternoon crawled by, with no end in
sight; she would be through for the day when Kay released
her, and not before. She was taking notes on voter break-
downs, by age, gender, and occupation, when Christie poked
her head in the door.

"Excuse me. Erin, are you expecting company by any
chance? There's someone at the door asking for you."

Her curt, critical tone was another reminder that Erin was
the new kid on the block, and no more popular with Rosemary's possessively adoring staff than she deserved to be. The
others were beginning to unbend a little—Jackson had even
asked her whether she wanted sugar in her coffee at lunch—
but Christie remained aloof. Once Erin would have assumed,
smugly and simplemindedly, that Christie was just jealous of
the attention Jeff and Nick were lavishing on another woman.
She knew better now. People like Christie were more interested in power than in passion or popularity. But how could
Christie possibly believe that she, Erin, was any threat to her
ambitions? In training, experience, and education, if not in
actual talent, her qualifications were so inferior to Christie's
it was laughable.

Fran had not been invited in. Erin found her sitting on the
porch steps with a cat on her lap and several others nudging
for attention. Animals adored Fran, probably because she

didn't particularly care for them. But these were Rosemary Marshall's cats, and therefore worthy of attention.

She jumped to her feet at the sight of Erin, spilling the lap-sitter ignominiously onto the ground. "Hi. Is she here?"

Erin didn't have to ask who "she" was, nor did she feel obliged to answer. Eyeing the two big suitcases, she exclaimed, "What did you do, pack everything I own?"

"It's better to have too much than not enough. You never know what will come up, and you have to be prepared."

Fran had to be pushed toward the stairs; she eyed the closed doors longingly and asked question after question. "Which is her office? Is Nick here? What a great portrait! Do you suppose it's her husband?" Even the sight of Erin's unpretentious room didn't dim her enthusiasm. "Imagine being right here, in her own house," she exclaimed.

"Servants' quarters."

"Listen, kid, I'd sleep in a closet." She opened the adjoining door. "Is this her room? It's just the way I expected it would look!"

"Frilly and feminine and pink?" Erin inquired sarcastically. "Get the hell out of there, Fran; that isn't Rosemary's room, it belongs to her secretary, and you have no business prying."

"Oh." Fran closed the door. "Where is *her* room?"

"Never mind, you aren't going to see it. This isn't the historic-homes tour."

Feeling like a sheepdog herding a recalcitrant ewe, she escorted Fran down the stairs and headed her off when she tried to turn into the second-floor corridor. Kay was waiting at the foot of the stairs.

"Oh, there you are," she said. "I couldn't think where you'd gotten to."

Erin had no choice but to introduce Fran, adding, "You remember, I told you she had volunteered to bring my clothes."

"Certainly I remember. How do you do, Fran." She bestowed a gracious smile on the potential voter and apologized for not offering her hand.

"Oh, gosh, that's a terrific shame," Fran exclaimed. "Erin said you'd had an accident, but I didn't realize how bad it was. Gosh, that's just terrible. Especially right now, with the campaign heating up and you so important to Rosemary . . . Oh, gee, I should call her Mrs. Marshall, but honestly, I'm such an admirer of hers, I feel as if she's a friend, you know? I just wish there was something I could do to help.''

The performance was so outrageously saccharine, Erin expected Kay to be as revolted by it as she was. Kay only smiled more warmly; of course she couldn't know that "gee" and "golly" were foreign to Fran's normal vocabulary.

"You're very kind. I presume you're one of our volunteers?''

Caught flat-footed, Fran looked her interrogator straight in the eye and lied. "Yes, ma'am. But if there's anything I can do for you personally—I mean, I can imagine how awful it must be for you, your hand and all. . . .''

Feeling her self-control about to give way, Erin said firmly, "Thanks, Fran, I appreciate your help. I know you're in a hurry to get back, so—''

"Oh, no, I haven't a thing to do this evening,'' Fran assured her.

Erin glowered at her, and Kay said pleasantly, "We certainly can't let you make that long drive back to town without at least offering you some refreshment. It's about that time, I believe.''

It was exactly that time, a little after five-thirty. Fran must have left work early in order to arrive at the conventional cocktail hour. She probably thinks we sit around swilling sherry and Chablis every afternoon, Erin thought disgustedly. She didn't quite have the nerve to appear at suppertime. . . .

But she managed to stay for the meal, such as it was. The intimate little dinner of the previous evening had been an aberration; Sarah's usual custom was to provide a cold buffet, in order to accommodate the unpredictable schedules and increasing work load. People wandered in and helped themselves to the covered dishes of salads and cold cuts, and expelled cats that had invaded the room—when they could catch them. From five to eight, and sometimes later, there was usually someone in the room eating and/or drinking.

It was exactly the casual ambience in which Fran shone. Though visibly disappointed not to find Rosemary, and to learn that she was not likely to return for several hours, she flattered the women, flirted with the men, and kept at a safe distance from Kay, who was inclined to ask embarrassing questions about her fictitious volunteer work.

It only required one look at Will to tell her he wasn't worth cultivating. After mumbling a vague greeting and fussing nervously with his glasses he sank back into obscurity behind his desk.

Erin was praying Fran would get bored and go home when Nick's appearance put an end to that hope. In Erin's opinion his greeting was far more enthusiastic than their brief acquaintance justified. Before long they were engaged in an animated discussion, and a couple of the others had joined them. Only Christie remained aloof; arms folded, eyes calculating, she watched the laughing, chattering group with a cynical smile. Erin was forced to sit with Kay, who couldn't manage her food with only her left hand; cutting Kay's cold turkey into ladylike bites, she watched her roommate winning all hearts and tried to think of reasons why she shouldn't kill her.

Fran lingered up to, but not quite beyond, the point of rudeness. The others had drifted away, and Nick was beginning to drop hints about work that awaited him before she gave up.

"I guess I'd better be going," she said to Kay. "I know how busy all you people must be, and I just want to thank you for letting me stay. I'll never forget this."

Erin leaped to her feet. "I'll walk you to the car."

"Talk about how to speed the parting guest," Fran said as soon as the door had closed behind them. "You could have let me go on being sweet and winsome for a few more minutes; that gorgeous man might have offered to see me to the door."

"That," said Erin, "was the most disgusting demonstration of bullshitting I've ever seen."

"Oooh!" Fran clapped her hand to her heart. "How shocking. You said a dirty word! What's come over Miss Prim and Proper? Once away from my restraining influence—"

Erin kicked the screen door open and propelled Fran out with more force than was strictly necessary. Recovering from the burst of giggles that had interrupted her last sentence, Fran went on, "You're a fine one to talk. Sitting there sweet as pie cutting up the old lady's food and looking demure. What kind of an act is that?"

"It's no act," Erin said slowly. "At least it wasn't, once upon a time. . . ."

"That's true. Sweetness and light come naturally to you. Well, maybe someday you'll grow up. Listen, kid, there's something I want to talk to you about. A proposition you can't refuse—"

This time the interruption came from one of the cats, whom Fran had attempted to push aside with her foot. The animal retaliated with a snarl and a swipe of a clawed paw. Fran swore and clutched her ankle.

"I haven't time to talk now," Erin said, noting that the cat in question was a lean, gray tom. She must remember to give him a piece of chicken later. . . .

"No, this isn't the time or place," Fran agreed. "I'll call you. We'll have lunch." She got in the car and turned the key; Erin's reply, a vigorous negative, was lost in the roar of the engine. Fran put her head out the window.

"What did you say?"

"Never mind. Good-bye, Fran."

"Say rather au revoir," Fran retorted, grinning. "You haven't seen the last of me. I have only begun to fight."

"I suggest you start by signing on as a volunteer," Erin said sarcastically. "A post-dated finding, so to speak."

Fran only laughed heartily. "I had already planned to be at local headquarters first thing Saturday morning. Bye, bye, sweetie."

When Erin returned to the house she found Nick at the door, about to evict a cat. He held the door for her, then eased the intruder out. "Fran gone?" he asked.

"Yes."

"She's quite a character," Nick said admiringly.

"Yes."

"Did you get those clothes and things you wanted?"

"Yes." The repeated monosyllables sounded childish and sullen. She added, "Fran brought them. That's why she was here."

"Oh. I wondered."

"Oh, I see. You wondered. You assumed, I suppose, that I had the nerve to invite a friend to someone else's house for purely social purposes?"

"What the hell is the matter with you? A person asks a simple question or makes a harmless remark. . . ."

He stopped, obviously expecting an apology or an explanation, but Erin was in no mood for either. She found it hard to admit to herself, much less to Nick, how sharply Fran's assessment of her character, or lack thereof, had stung.

"Oh well, that's okay," Nick said, after a prolonged pause. "I understand. It's been a long day for you. Kay isn't the easiest person in the world to get along with, even when she's in a good mood. Come on, let's sit down and swing for a while. Nothing like an old-fashioned porch swing to induce a gentle, relaxed frame of mind, possibly even conducive to a touch of equally old-fashioned and respectable dalliance."

It wasn't so much the fact that he took her agreement for granted, coolly seizing her arm and pulling her toward the swing; it was a number of irritations, from his unfortunate choice of words like "old-fashioned" and "respectable" to the insulting assumption that all she needed to put her in a better humor was a little kissing and fondling.

"I have to go in," Erin said, pulling away. "Go and—and swing yourself."

Nick followed her without further comment; he appeared to be more perplexed than angered, and she really didn't blame him for failing to understand her reaction. She was just beginning to understand it herself.

When she entered the commons room she saw Jeff sitting next to Kay, listening to her with the grave, courteous attention he always showed her.

"I didn't know you were back," Nick remarked. "How long have you been here?"

"I arrived about an hour ago. Hearing sounds of uncouth revelry coming from this room, I went straight to the office."

"The way you avoid harmless social activities is just plain unhealthy," Nick declared, throwing himself into a chair. "All work and no play makes Jeff a dull boy. I thought you were going straight home from the Hill."

"What is this, an inquisition?" Jeff demanded, frowning. "I brought those reports out for Rosemary to look over."

Nick cowered, covering his head with his arms. "Sorry, sorry, boss, sorry. I was just making conversation."

"Huh." Jeff relaxed. "Hello, Erin. I'd have greeted you properly if this clod hadn't started yakking. I was just telling Kay about the Buzzard's latest gaffe."

"I heard about it." Nick rubbed his hands together with an evil smile. "I've already started composing responses."

"What was it?" Erin asked.

Jeff chuckled. "You won't believe this. He was making a speech this afternoon in Warrenton, and after a lot of stupid remarks about giving the ladies the respect and admiration that is their due, he said, 'But we don't want to see a senator in hot pants, now do we?' "

"How vulgar," Kay murmured.

"Vulgar? It's beautiful!" Nick exclaimed. "He actually said 'hot pants'? Oh, boy, oh, boy—"

"You can't do it, Nick," Jeff warned.

"I don't have to. The phrase itself is enough. What speech-writer came up with that gem?"

"It's outdated," Erin said critically.

"It's also plagiarized." Will's head appeared over the stack of papers like that of a wary rabbit emerging from its hole. "Spiro Agnew said that about Abzug, back in 1972. Or was it 1971?"

"Who cares?" Nick demanded gleefully. "You mean we can get him on plagiarism as well as sexism, vulgarity, and remarks degrading to women?"

"I do think a statement might be justified," Will said mildly.

"You're damn right, Will." Nick reached for a pad of paper.

The statement didn't go together as quickly as it ought to have done because of the suggestions, some from Will, most from Nick, that reduced all of them except Kay to helpless laughter. "I can't see why you find it so amusing," she de-

clared indignantly, after a particularly unprintable idea of
Nick's that made even Jeff whoop with unseemly laughter.
"Senator Bennett ought to be ashamed of himself. Rosemary
never wore hot pants in her life, and she certainly wouldn't
be ill-bred enough to wear them to the Senate."

"Exactly." Jeff wiped the tears from his eyes and patted
her hand. "That's exactly what we're going to do, Kay—make
him ashamed of himself."

"Maybe he's trying to imply that he's so uninterested in
women he doesn't even notice what they're wearing," Erin
said. "Or not wearing."

"Oh, Lord, it is tempting, isn't it?" Jeff shook his head.
"Can't do it without being coarse, though."

"What about something like 'Senator Bennett's contempt
for women extends even to their attire,' " Erin suggested.
" 'As the quintessential symbol of sexism in fashion . . .' "

"That's not bad." Nick began scribbling. "Go on, Erin,
keep talking."

They were still hard at work when the frantic barking of the
dogs announced the arrival of Rosemary. She looked tired and
irritable; Joe, who had accompanied her, tossed his coat in the
general direction of a chair and loosened his tie before proceeding with what was obviously a continuing argument.

"I tell you, I don't trust him. He's got something up his
sleeve, or he wouldn't be playing footsie with you. Why is
he giving you all this support?"

"I can think of several possibilities," Rosemary said. She
batted her eyelashes and simpered.

Joe replied with a single emphatic word that made Kay turn
to him in indignant reproof. "Oh, shut up, Kay," he snarled,
before she could speak.

Rosemary's flirtatious smirk turned to a scowl. "Watch
your damn mouth, Joe," she snapped, taking the seat next to
Kay and putting an arm around her. "I don't trust Philips
any more than you do, but it's just possible that I know him
a little better. He's perfectly dependable where his own self-
interest is involved. He's had it in for Buzz Bennett ever since
Buzz did that ghastly takeoff on him at the Press Club Dinner.
I know, everybody is supposed to be a good sport about those

things, but Philips—well, let's face it, Philips is not a good sport, and that was a particularly devastating imitation.''

Joe's eyes gleamed with reminiscent pleasure. ''Yeah. I loved every second of that routine Of course old Buzz never wrote it himself—''

''No, he hired that young man from Boston U—the one whose Nixon record sold so well. That's not the point, nor does it matter *why* Philips is so supportive. I can use his support and I will, as long as it lasts—which, given Philips's reputation, may not be very long. You may not like it, Joe, and I certainly don't, but the brutal truth is that political analysts like Philips do affect public opinion. They don't exactly distort the facts, but by careful selection and interpretation they can make a saint look like Jack the Ripper and turn a catastrophe into a triumph.''

''Not to mention the equally brutal fact that a lot of idiots believe everything they read in the paper,'' Joe agreed sourly. ''Okay, okay. You're right, I'm wrong. But you know something? I don't hate many people in this business, but I really do hate that son of a bitch.''

''You amaze me,'' Rosemary exclaimed, and the last of the tension dissolved as they all laughed at Joe's look of surprise.

''Did you hear about Buzz's latest?'' Nick asked.

''Yeah, it was on the late news, ' Joe answered, reaching for a cigar. ''We heard it in the car coming home.''

''We've been working on a statement,'' Jeff said.

''Good. Let's hear what you've got.''

''Hold on a minute,'' Rosemary begged, sagging against the cushions. ''Or ten, or maybe even fifteen? I need to unwind before we go back to work. I haven't even had a chance to ask Kay how she's feeling, or say hello to Erin. Hello, Erin. Kay, how's the hand?''

Kay began to talk, recounting in laborious detail all the problems that had arisen that day, and how she had handled them. Rosemary listened patiently, her eyes half closed.

''Anything to eat around here?'' Joe asked. ''I'm starved; don't know why it is, but I never seem to get any food at those damn receptions.''

''It's because you talk all the time.'' Nick said.

The same was probably true for Rosemary, Erin realized. She followed Joe to the kitchen, where she found Will filling a plate with cold turkey and salad.

"Hey, leave some for me," Joe said. "You've been noshing all evening."

"This is for Rosemary," Will said. "I don't suppose she got anything to eat at that bash, she never does."

"How should I know? I'm not her mama," Joe grunted.

"Would she like coffee?" Erin asked, as Joe dived head-first into the refrigerator and began rummaging.

"A glass of milk, I think," Will answered. "Much more healthful."

Rosemary accepted the food with a smile of thanks and began to eat, slowly at first and then with increasing appetite. "Thanks, Will. That was just what I needed. Five more minutes, Joe, and I'm all yours—you lucky devil."

"Not that damned knitting," Joe grumbled, as she reached for the bag.

"Two rows, Joe."

She reached into the knitting bag and then recoiled with a muffled cry, jerking her hand out of the bag and dislodging an object that fell to the floor at her feet. "God! What is it?"

At first Erin thought, as Rosemary must have done, that the small, shapeless bundle was a mouse or some other creature. But it didn't move; it lay where it had fallen until Nick gingerly picked it up.

"It's just a bundle of rags," he announced, relieved. "No, wait a sec. It looks like . . ." He turned it over and held it up, and its true character became apparent: a shapeless body wrapped in dusty cloth, a crude painted face, strands of black yarn for hair. . . .

"It's a doll," Nick said in a puzzled voice. "Cinderella? It's covered with ashes."

Like the others, Kay had leaned forward to stare at the thing. Nobody noticed what was happening until she slid to the floor in a dead faint.

Chapter
Four

"SON OF A BITCH!" Joe snatched the cigar from his mouth and hurled it across the room. "Down four points!"

The cigar landed on a pile of newspapers. Erin pounced like a cat, only to find that the disgusting object was thoroughly dead.

The others hadn't turned a collective hair. "I wish you wouldn't be so confounded dramatic," Jeff said crossly. He plucked the computer printouts from his superior's clenched fist and smoothed them out. "There's a three-point margin of error and you know we anticipated a slight drop; the last poll was taken right after Bennett's escapade hit the fan. He was bound to bounce back."

"Goddamn stupid voters," Joe grumbled. "Memories like sieves and brains like mush."

"I thought we weren't supposed to refer to voters that way," Nick said.

"You aren't. I can say anything I want." But Joe sounded less irate; he took a sip of coffee and recovered the printouts from Jeff. "Could be worse," he admitted, perusing them. "Allowing for the margin of error . . ."

Erin had had another bad night. Kay had made light of her collapse: "Faint? Nonsense, I just lost my balance. So stupid of me. . . ." But Erin had felt she ought to leave the door open again, and although Kay had slept like a rock, thanks to the sleeping pill Rosemary insisted upon, she had snored mercilessly. Erin had crept downstairs at daybreak to find Nick and Jeff hunched over the table in the commons room plotting their counterattack on Bennett. She had ignored Nick's unsubtle hints about breakfast, but hunger finally drove her to the kitchen and it seemed rude to cook for herself and not the others. Joe turned up shortly afterward, so she made bacon and eggs for him too.

"Yeah, it's about what we expected," he said finally. "Southside and the upper Valley. Bennett country. We'll have to make another swing south. Danville, Martinsville, Harrisonburg, Roanoke . . ."

"The TV spots are due to start next week," Nick said.

"Should have been this week."

"You know why it wasn't this week." Nick was on the defensive. "We didn't have the money. Then Rosemary objected to the format—"

"Okay, okay," Joe grunted.

Realizing she was unneeded and probably unwanted, Erin stacked the dishes and went upstairs to see if she could do anything for Kay. She found Kay up and looking for trouble. Her hair straggled down her back and she had thrown a robe around her shoulders. "There you are," she snapped. "I couldn't think where you'd got to."

The criticism and its corollary—that she should have stayed in her room awaiting Kay's commands—was infuriating, but Erin bit back the reply that had sprung to her lips. She mustn't let newly aroused sensibilities affect her judgment. Kay wasn't Nick; Kay could, and probably would, get her fired if she talked back. It was not until that moment that Erin realized, with genuine amazement, how desperately she wanted to keep her job. It involved unpleasant duties like waiting on Kay and putting up with her rudeness, but it also included times like that exhilarating hour the night before, when they had huddled around the table laughing themselves silly and plotting the downfall of Buzz Bennett.

"I brought you some coffee," she said stiffly.

"Oh." Kay had the decency to look embarrassed. "Sorry I snapped at you; I just hate being dependent on other people. I can't even do my hair by myself, and my room is a mess, and there's such a lot of work to do. . . ."

Erin couldn't help thinking that it would have been easier to keep the room tidy if Kay had not been so addicted to little ruffled pillows and framed photographs and countless china, glass, and stuffed ornaments. At her suggestion Kay sat down at the dressing table and sipped her coffee while she straightened the room. Kay watched her every move and made helpful suggestions. "That cushion with the cat on it goes on the chaise, not the chair. Just push that picture of Mr. Kennedy a little to the right—no, I mean the left. . . . You'd better strip the bed and remake it. I didn't do a very neat job."

After she had brushed and arranged Kay's hair, Kay graciously dismissed her, and Erin made her escape. The others were hard at work on a tall stack of Sunday newspapers. Knowing she lacked the knowledge to assist in selecting pertinent articles and editorials, she stole the comic sections and retreated to Will's desk. An interlude with "Doonesbury" and "Bloom County" refreshed her. When Kay appeared, she was able to ask, quite pleasantly, what the other woman wanted for breakfast. She knew Kay was about to ask, or order, her to prepare something, and it gave her a small sense of satisfaction to play volunteer instead of servant.

Kay ordered a soft-boiled egg— 'Exactly four minutes, Erin, I can't stand runny eggs—" and added, "Rosemary just has juice and coffee and a piece of toast. You might see if there are any of those muffins of Sarah's left. Warm them in the oven, the microwave makes them soggy."

It wasn't only the way she said it, it was what she said! Erin was washing dishes, amid a violent splashing of suds, when Jeff came to the kitchen in search of more coffee.

"Hey, you don't have to do that," he exclaimed. 'Just stack them. Or, if you want to be truly noble and acquire

Sarah's heartfelt thanks, rinse them and put them in the dishwasher.''

"I wouldn't leave a mess like this for Sarah," Erin said.

Jeff put his hand on her shoulder. "I don't know what we did to deserve you. Everything is in such a state of chaos around here, we don't say thanks as often as we should, but believe me, we do appreciate what you're doing—and you."

His warm fingers moved to the curve between her neck and shoulder. "Mmmm," Erin murmured. "That's nice."

"You're all tensed up." His other hand found the corresponding muscles on her left shoulder and moved in slow rhythm. "Relax. There. How's that?"

"Lovely."

She was sorry when he took his hands away—for reasons she was in no mood to analyze. When he stepped back away from her she felt oddly chilled.

"Have you ever considered running for office yourself?" she asked, smiling at him over her shoulder.

"Who, me? I've got better sense."

The brief intimacy was gone and neither of them tried to recapture it. Erin thought he looked a little self-conscious. Afraid she would mistake his kindness for something else?

"I'll bring the coffee when it's ready," she said.

"Thanks."

She made fresh coffee and carried the pot into the commons room just as Rosemary entered. She was wearing a demure dark-navy print dress with a lace collar, a navy hat with a veil, and white gloves.

"What's that in aid of?" Joe asked. "You don't have to get all gussied up for me."

"I had someone a little higher up in mind," Rosemary said, rolling her eyes heavenward. "It's Sunday, in case you've forgotten. I'm going to church."

"Church? Church!" Joe's voice rose. "For Christ's sake, Rosie—"

"Precisely," Rosemary agreed. She stripped off her gloves. "Is there any . . . Oh, thanks, Erin. I hope these louts thanked you properly for feeding them—if it was you, which I assume it was, since Joe can't cook and Jeff won't eat unless someone shoves a plate in front of him, and Nick's culinary talents run to omelettes bulging with unseemly vegetables.''

Her attempt to distract Joe didn't work. "You can't go to church," he bellowed. "Have you seen the latest polls? We need to plan another series of speeches—"

"Later."

"Not later, now. There isn't time—"

"Goddamn it, Joe!" Rosemary slammed the empty juice glass down on the table. "Don't tell me what I can and can't do! I missed last week and the week before—"

"So what?"

"So what about my image?" Rosemary's voice was higher in pitch, but even more penetrating than Joe's. "You're always bellyaching about images. It's important—"

"Not as important as that five-point drop—"

"Four," Jeff murmured.

Erin was the only one who heard him. Rosemary's cheeks were crimson with rage; she looked magnificent, like a miniature Medea. The argument climaxed in a ringing crash as Rosemary picked up the empty juice glass and heaved it into the fireplace.

Silence fell like a pall.

"Well, for God's sake," Joe said. "If you feel that strongly about it, why didn't you say so?"

Rosemary told him to do something that was anatomically impossible. Kay gasped, Joe hooted with laughter, and everybody relaxed.

Rosemary caught Erin's eye. "Excuse my language," she said primly.

"I'll—uh—make toast," Erin muttered, and fled.

Nick followed her to the kitchen. "Are you okay?" he asked.

"What kind of prude do you think I am?" Erin demanded.

"A cute, adorable, innocent kind of prude." He slipped his arms around her and kissed her on the ear.

"Stop that!"

"It's okay," Nick mumbled into her neck. "I'm listening. If somebody comes—"

"I don't care about that." She wriggled away from him

and stood at bay, her back to the counter. "I mean, I do care about having people catch me behaving like an adolescent jerk, but that wasn't— How dare you talk to me that way?"

Nick flung his arms wide and looked hurt. "What did I say?"

"Cute, innocent, adorable . . ."

"Ah." Nick tugged thoughtfully at a lock of hair. "Sexism again. And who was it, a short while ago, who yelled when I said she was a feminist? Make up your mind."

"How about you making up your mind? One minute you talk to me like a human being, you expect some evidence of intelligence—and the next minute you're grunting into my ear and calling me cute."

Nick considered the speech. "You may have a point."

"Huh?"

"Don't look so surprised. I am not impervious to reason, or so damned arrogant I can't admit I was wrong."

"Oh. Well . . ."

"It's true I haven't got my emotions straight on this liberation bit," Nick continued. "I mean, injustice to anybody—black, white, or purple; male, female, or other—gets my blood boiling. But when it comes to personal relationships I seem to have trouble figuring out how to behave. Vive la différence, right? Maybe my problem lies in—"

"Oh, Nick, knock it off. I don't want to discuss your psychological problems, I want to make sure Rosemary eats something. And you're standing in front of the toaster."

Nick turned, plucked the toast from the slots, and reached for the butter. "You looked so shocked," he said, chuckling, "when Rosemary pitched the glass into the fireplace. You better get used to scenes like that. She has a quick temper, and Joe gets her madder, faster, than anybody else."

"I don't blame her. It wasn't so much what he said—though that was bad enough—bossy, arrogant man!—it was his tone of voice."

"He's noted for it," Nick said. "He's been fired by more candidates than any other guy in the business. He's brilliant, but he gets people's backs up. Do you want to go to church?"

The abrupt change of subject caught Erin by surprise. "Not especially."

"The church is worth seeing. It's an historic building that Ed Marshall helped to restore and reconsecrate. He's buried in the cemetery there."

"Oh, really? Is it the traditional family burial ground?"

"I don't think so." Obviously Nick had never given the matter much thought and didn't intend to do so now. He added, "Rosemary tries to go every week. Makes a great impression on the voters."

"Don't you people ever do anything without calculating its effect on the voters?"

"Rosemary's reasons for going to church are her own business," Nick said. "But sometimes good politics simply consists of doing the right thing. Did you ever think of that?"

"No."

"Think about it then. Honest to God, Erin, a person can get too cynical!"

"Sez who? Does she visit her husband's grave?"

"I don't know. Why don't you come along and find out?"

"Maybe I will. I'll ask Kay if it's all right."

Kay pondered the question as solemnly as if she had been asked to pronounce on some issue vital to national policy, but Rosemary interrupted her discussion with Joe long enough to nod approval. "A sweet innocent young girl will add a nice touch, won't she, Joe? 'Rosemary Marshall Helps American Youth Find Jesus. . . .' "

"Smart ass," Joe said amiably.

Suspecting that Rosemary's remark had been intended as a tactful hint as well as a dig at Joe, Erin selected a demure Laura Ashley print with a high neck and long sleeves. In lieu of a hat—an article of clothing she did not possess—she pinned a black satin bow onto her head. When she joined the other women on the porch, Kay looked her over from head to foot (low-heeled plain black pumps) and indicated she would pass. "I don't suppose you have a handkerchief. Young women never seem to carry handkerchiefs. Here, I brought an extra."

She always has to find something to correct, Erin thought,

accepting the linen square. But this time Kay's criticism didn't irritate her; it was reminiscent of all the grandmas and maiden aunts she had ever met, more amusing than annoying.

Nick, looking immensely dignified in a three-piece gray suit, drove up in one of the cars and got out to help the women in. Kay and Rosemary sat in the back; Erin joined Nick in the front seat. The car was an Oldsmobile—nothing flashy like a Cadillac or Lincoln, Erin thought cynically. Image, always the image.

Nick drove impeccably, back straight, both hands on the wheel, eyes front. When he spoke it was out of the corner of his mouth. "You look terrific. That's a pretty dress—if you don't mind my sounding like a sexist pig."

"If you don't know the difference between an acceptable compliment and a sexist remark, you'd better start learning," Erin retorted in the same undertone. "You look adorable yourself. I rather thought you'd appear in a chauffeur's uniform, though."

"Heaven forfend," Nick said piously. "We're just folks, we don't go in for fancy touches like that. Did you ever hear the story about the jar of caviar that defeated an incumbent senator from North Carolina? His opponent waved it at the voters and bellowed, 'Cam eats Red Russian fish eggs that cost two dollars! (Weren't those the good old days?) Do you want a senator who's too high and mighty to eat good old North Carolina hen eggs?' "

Erin's laughter was echoed by Rosemary's; leaning forward, the congresswoman said, "Tell her about Vic Meyers, Nick."

"Who was he?" Erin asked. "Should I know?"

"Not really," Nick said. "He ran for mayor of Seattle back in 1932. But he carried on the wildest political campaign of all time. He used to drive around town on a beer wagon, making speeches at street corners; once a wheel came off, and Vic fell out of the wagon, along with two kegs of beer. Whereupon he yelled, 'Drink is my downfall; vive le downfall!' "

"I'd love to do something like that," Rosemary said wistfully. "Tell her about the Gandhi stunt, Nick."

"No time, we're almost there," Nick said. "It wouldn't look right for us to arrive at church howling with laughter."

The church was as attractive as Nick had promised, and under ordinary circumstances Erin would have admired the rural setting, the simple dignity of the small red brick building and slender white spire, and the quiet graveyard sheltered by overhanging boughs of oak and maple and pine. As they made the turn and the church came into view, Nick let out an exclamation. "Something's happened. Rosemary, did you—"

"No. Stop here, Nick."

He had no choice. The crowd at the gate had spilled out into the drive and a van with prominent blue lettering blocked the way. Almost as prominent, in the forefront of the spectators, was a young man carrying a video camera with a portapak slung over his shoulder.

Nick leapt out of the car and ran around to the opposite side in a noble but futile effort to interpose himself between Rosemary and the camera. After only the briefest of pauses she had let herself out; a candidate couldn't enjoy the luxury of avoiding cameras, even when she had no idea of what was happening. Erin didn't know either, but she hurried to join Rosemary. Something about the atmosphere—the looks on the faces of the spectators, the agitated bleats of the tall, stooped man who appeared to be the minister—made her suspect that Rosemary was going to need all the support she could get.

"What's the idea, Paul?" Nick demanded.

The cameraman was the TV reporter Erin had met at the football game, back on his regular straight news beat. He twisted agilely around Nick and pointed the camera at Rosemary. "Mrs. Marshall, have you heard—"

The minister pushed him aside. "Oh, Mrs. Marshall, I am so very sorry! I wouldn't for the world have allowed—"

Cameraman, pastor, and Nick gyrated in a bizarre dance, babbling in counterpoint, until Rosemary said crisply, "It's all right, Nick—Mr. Jones. Young man, I'll be happy to answer questions later, but you'll have to wait until after the service. This is a church, not a political rally."

"Yes, ma'am, sorry, ma'am, but I guess you don't know." His voice took on its professional tone. "This is Paul Dubermann for Channel 22. Mrs. Marshall, the cemetery here was vandalized last night, and your husband's grave was the main target. Would you mind telling our viewers . . ."

For a moment no one moved. Then Nick lunged at camera and cameraman.

"Nick!" Rosemary's voice stopped him as if he had run into a wall. She held out an imperious hand. "Give me your arm, please. Mr. Jones?"

With Nick on one side and the pastor on the other, she walked toward the cemetery. It made an effective tableau—the small woman between her two tall escorts—but Erin felt sure Rosemary was restraining Nick, not leaning on him for support. The cameraman trotted alongside; the watchers, murmuring sympathetically, fell back to let them through.

It wasn't until Erin started to follow that she realized Kay stood frozen, her face as gray and rigid as the granite markers in the grassy graveyard. She touched the older woman's arm. "Are you all right?"

"What?" Kay turned a ghastly face to her. "Oh my God. . . . Did he say—desecrated?"

"Why don't you get back in the car, Kay? There's no need for you to see—"

"No. No. Rosemary will need me."

Erin made no further attempt to dissuade her, but she wished Kay weren't so determined to be helpful. It wouldn't help Rosemary if she collapsed or had hysterics—a distinct possiblity if the images conjured up by the word Kay had repeated turned out to be accurate. Coffins dragged out of the earth, broken bodies, scattered bones. . . . She felt her stomach twist at the idea, and it would be much worse for Kay than for her. Kay had clearly idolized Edward Marshall. . . .

To move from the side of the church toward the brick wall behind the graveyard was to move forward in time—from the worn marble slabs of the late eighteenth century to the ornate monuments of the mid-nineteenth, and finally to the simple granite markers of the recent past. The place was beautifully tended; the grass was trimmed, the flowers fresh. None of the stones was tilted or fallen. The black blotch on one grave stood out like blasphemy made visible.

Only blackened cinders and charred sticks remained of what had been burned. Smoke had stained the pale-gray stone, like dark fingers clawing at the name of Edward Marshall; a deformed, palm-shaped blotch covered the modest epitaph that described him as beloved husband, devoted father, and loyal servant of Virginia.

Kay's breath caught in a harsh hiss when she saw the grave, but Erin sensed her relief. Bad as it was, this was not the horror she had feared.

As they joined the others, Erin heard Mr. Jones say, ". . . no idea, until this—this—this person arrived a few minutes ago. Had I but known, I would certainly have warned you—"

"Yes, that's quite all right," Rosemary said. "Please don't distress yourself, Mr. Jones. No permanent damage appears to have been made."

The cameraman edged cautiously closer to Rosemary. "Would you care to make a statement?"

"There is very little one can say." Rosemary faced the camera. "Except to express pity for the person who could do such a terrible thing. I hope the police find him and give him the help he obviously needs."

She started to turn away, but the tireless tracker of news was not ready to give up. "Do you think there is a political motive behind this?"

"Certainly not," Rosemary said sharply. "The perpetrator is obviously mentally ill."

"What do you think—"

"You'll have to excuse me," Rosemary interrupted. She raised a gloved hand to hide her eyes. "This has been—this has come as quite a shock, surely you understand. . . . I've already kept the other worshipers waiting too long. Mr. Jones, may I. . . ."

The pastor moved to her side; as his body hid her, briefly, from the camera, she turned a dry-eyed, furious glare on Nick and whispered, "Cool it, Nick. Why don't you take Kay home and come back for me?"

"I'm staying," Kay said quietly.

Rosemary's lips shaped a word she dared not utter. "Erin," she said, with a meaningful look at Nick.

"Yes, ma'am," said Erin.

The two older women moved toward the church, escorted by the pastor. The cameraman's attempt to follow them was thwarted by Nick, who placed a large, heavy hand over the camera lens.

"Go right ahead," said the prospective victim, baring his teeth. "A little violence always films well."

"Son of a . . . gun," said Nick. "Okay, Erin, unhand me, I'm not going to do anything either of us would regret. Where'd you get this, Paul?"

"Get what?"

"You know what I mean. You must have gotten a tip from someone. Who, when, how? Come on, pal," he added with a smile that convinced neither of his listeners. "Fair exchange. I don't break your nose, you tell me what I want to know."

"You guessed it," the other admitted. Rosemary had disappeared; he lowered the camera from his shoulder. "Anonymous phone call, about half an hour ago."

"This isn't big enough for the nets, of course." Clearly Nick didn't believe that himself.

The other man grinned. "You've got to be kidding."

"Yeah. Who called—man or woman?"

Dubermann hesitated, and Nick abandoned threats for reasoned argument. "Come on, old buddy, you've got the story. Man or woman?"

Dubermann shrugged. "Oh, well, why not? Man."

"Accent?"

"Local redneck, replete with ain'ts and—er—four-letter adjectives," the other said, with a glance at Erin. "Sounded authentic, but you never know."

"No, sir, you shore don't, 'cause it ain't all that goddamn hard to fake," said Nick caustically. "Well. Thanks. Lay off her, will you? You've got plenty already."

Dubermann smiled sweetly.

He was persuaded not to turn on the camera while Nick

poked distastefully in the burned rubbish. "I already looked," Dubermann said. "Looks like sticks and leaves and stuff like that; no significant remains."

"The cops won't thank you for messing up the evidence," Nick muttered, messing it still more. "You have called them, haven't you?"

"No time. I barely made it myself."

"Yeah, sure. Half the fun of this business is being the one to break the news to the victim. Why don't you go find a phone and break it to the police?"

"What, leave the scene of the crime?"

"Hey, it is a crime, isn't it?" Nick exclaimed sarcastically. "I have an excuse for failing to report it—I'm escorting the distraught widow. What's yours?"

"Hmmm. Guess I'd better. Don't do anything newsworthy till I get back."

He loped off, hugging the camera.

With the van gone, Nick was able to park directly in front of the gate. He and Erin sat at the back of the church rather than parade down the aisle to the front pew where Rosemary sat with Kay. The church was almost full. A touching demonstration of piety, or an example of the public's interest in celebrities? Rosemary often attended services, and perhaps there had been time for the news to spread, locally at least. . . . With such thoughts to preoccupy her, Erin didn't derive much spiritual benefit from the service. Mr. Jones was not at his best, whatever that might have been. He cut the congregation's responses off more than once and rushed through his sermon in a rapid mumble.

Rosemary was forced to run a gauntlet on her way through the vestibule. The people who stopped her to express their indignation and sympathy were all friends and neighbors, with the kindest of motives, but it obviously cost Rosemary considerable effort to linger. As soon as she decently could, she made for the door. When she saw who was waiting outside, she stopped with a muffled exclamation and yanked her veil down over her face. Not only had Dubermann returned to his post, camera at the ready, but two uniformed police officers were with him.

"Lean on me and look frail," Nick muttered.

In what might have passed for modified mourning, face veiled and head bowed, Rosemary looked like a new-made widow instead of a woman who had received a minor, if unpleasant, shock. The effect on the policemen was exactly what Nick had hoped; they readily agreed to his suggestion that they come to the house later instead of subjecting Rosemary to the torment of a public inquisition, and by escorting her to her car they frustrated Dubermann's further efforts at photography and interrogation.

Once in the car and underway, Rosemary pulled off her hat and sank back against the cushions. "God," she muttered.

Kay patted her hand. "As soon as we get home you go up and lie down. I'll talk to the police—"

"No, you won't," Rosemary snapped. "Oh, Lord, Lord, Lord! Wait till Joe hears about this."

The rest of the drive passed in silence. After they had passed through the gates, Nick stopped the car.

"I'll close them and put up the chain. The boys of the press should be along pretty soon."

"Surely not," Erin exclaimed.

Rosemary's voice was dry and controlled. "When Jim Wright pushed Fauntroy around the Capitol in a wheelbarrow after losing a bet on a Redskins-Dallas game, he got full network coverage. Sunday is a slow news day. They'll be here."

*   *

ERIN HAD BELIEVED she was growing accustomed to the bizarre life-style of a candidate for public office, but the remainder of the afternoon showed her she had a thing or two yet to learn. The press did show up—all the Washington television stations, plus newspaper and press services. Nick had not barred the gates to keep them out, as she had innocently supposed, but only to sift the news people from ordinary curiosity seekers. The press was welcomed in, served food and drink—mostly the latter—and entertained by Nick and

Jeff, while Rosemary, closeted in conference with Joe and Will, prepared a statement.

Erin was kept busy serving drinks and making sandwiches. She expected to pass unnoticed, but she was foolish enough to tell the truth when a reporter asked her if she had been at the church. Instantly she found herself besieged, and was only rescued by the appearance of Rosemary, poised and cool, wearing a smile that contained exactly the proper blend of friendly welcome and pained distress.

The hounds and the cameras converged on Rosemary; Erin didn't need Nick's scowl and peremptory gesture to know this was her opportunity to escape. She locked herself in the bathroom next to the kitchen and cowered there until she heard Nick's voice.

"It's okay, they're gone."

When she emerged, the hallway was empty. She found Nick in the commons room, hands on his hips, staring disgustedly at the wreckage—empty glasses, crumbs, crumpled napkins, scraps of paper, cigarette butts and ashes.

"Why do we bother with these slobs?" he demanded.

The question was obviously rhetorical, and Erin didn't bother to answer it. "I'm sorry," she began.

"What for?" Nick yanked his tie off and stuck it in his pocket.

"For talking to that reporter. I should have kept out of the way, but he started asking me questions and it seemed rude not to answer—"

"Oh, that. You couldn't have done anything else. Have you ever been on television before?"

"They won't use that! I didn't say anything important—"

"None of us did. None of us ever does. But you're a helluva lot prettier than Kay and I."

He picked up a glass, looked helplessly around the room, and put it back on the table.

"I'll clean up," Erin said. "You probably have something more important to do."

"I should get in there," Nick muttered, gesturing in the direction of Rosemary's office. "If you're sure you don't mind—"

"No, I don't mind. But, Nick—"

"Hmmm?" He was already at the door.

"Never mind, you're busy."

"We'll talk later," Nick said, and went out.

As she washed glasses and emptied ashtrays and vacuumed the carpet, Erin's mind was free to wander, and the tracks her thoughts followed were not strewn with roses. The physical disorder was only a pale reflection of the emotional invasion that had taken place. An hour's work, and all signs of the former would be obliterated (except for a few rings on the coffee table—hadn't the press ever heard of coasters?). The other, deeper intrusion left worse scars, and it had no limits. Nothing in a candidate's past was sacrosanct or private, not any more. Ancient infidelities, misdemeanors, and even simple errors of judgment—all had been dragged into the light of day, discussed and dissected, served up as the butt of humor and of sermonizing.

Not that Rosemary's misfortune fell into any of those categories; she was a victim, not a villainess. In fact, the incident would probably win sympathy for her, if it was handled properly. And Rosemary knew how to handle it. She was a past master at making the most of "free media," as opposed to the political advertising she couldn't afford to buy. The object was to get your name and face before the public, as often and as prominently and as cheaply as possible. This particular story would have been a candidate's dream, except for its grisly associations. . . .

The idea that struck Erin was so ugly she stopped short, letting go of the vacuum handle. Surely not. Surely no one—not even Joe, who had been heard to say that no trick was too underhanded, no publicity stunt too low . . .

The vacuum cleaner buzzed angrily, and she began pushing again. No. Rosemary wouldn't tolerate anything so disgusting as desecrating her husband's grave.

Then who had done it, and for what unimaginable reason? Rosemary had denied there could be a political motive. Naturally she would; they all played that game. "I am certain my opponent would never stoop. . . ." In this case she was probably right. Bennett was too seasoned a campaigner not to know such a trick would only rebound to Rosemary's advantage.

The perpetrator had to be some anonymous lunatic. That was the only sensible explanation.

She didn't stop working until the room was spotless and the papers had been neatly stacked. The rest of the afternoon dragged. She was afraid to leave the house, for fear some enterprising newsman might be lurking; the sight of the knitting bags made her shudder, as she remembered the ugly little doll.

There was another bizarre incident. Two of them, seemingly pointless, apparently meaningless, in twenty-four hours? They seemed to have nothing in common, though, except their very lack of purpose. The only result of the first episode had been Kay's fainting spell, and she had denied there was any causal relationship, had insisted a child must have hidden the little bundle of rags in her yarn. Children, playing games. . . . Sam's grandchildren visited him occasionally; Mary Ann, one of the cleaning women, had a little girl. Possible, but unconvincing. Yet the alternatives were literally unimaginable. She couldn't think of any.

It was late in the day when the others began to drift in, Rosemary and Joe from her office, Kay from her room, Jeff from wherever he had been, and Nick from outside. He was in shirtsleeves, tieless and windblown; his flushed face and quick breathing suggested he had been working off the frustrations of the day in violent physical exercise. It wasn't until he went to the television that Erin realized why they had come together. On Sunday the news began at six, an hour later than was the case on weekdays.

Nick switched on all four sets. An old movie on one channel, football games on two of the others, golf on the fourth.

"Not on yet," Nick announced unnecessarily.

"What's the score?" Joe planted himself in front of one of the sets. A pile of writhing bodies broke up into individual players mouthing obscenities at each other and the referee.

"Dunno." Nick didn't have to ask which game he was concerned about. "They're playing in San Diego, aren't they? Damn!" A score had flashed on the screen. "Down by ten."

Rosemary had collapsed onto the couch. She had changed into slacks and an oversized white shirt, and her lipstick had worn off, except for a rim of red around her full lower lip. "Who's the good fairy who cleaned up the mess?" she asked.

"Had to be Erin," said Jeff, smiling. "I think she deserves a drink, don't you?"

"We all do," Joe announced, eyes glued to the screen. "Damn it, Gibbs, what kind of call is that, running the ball on third and five?"

"He made it," Nick said. "First down."

"Still a stupid call."

Nick passed out cans of beer to everyone but Kay, who accepted sherry. The 'Skins tied it up with a last-minute field goal, and the game went into overtime. But nobody watched. The six-o'clock news had begun on Channels 5 and 7.

Erin had hoped and believed Nick's judgment was in error; she gasped with surprise when her own face appeared on the nineteen-inch screen. The sound of her voice made her wince, and the content of what she had said made her cringe, but when she murmured distressfully Nick only laughed, and Joe said approvingly, "Cute as a tick and sweet as sugar. Adds a nice—" At that point Rosemary hit him with a rolled-up newspaper, and he shut up.

"Well," Joe said, when it was all over. "Not bad. Pretty good, in fact. You can't—"

"If you say, 'You can't buy publicity like that,' I'll scream," Rosemary said through clenched teeth.

"I wasn't going to say that."

"Then what . . . Oh, never mind. Erin, you handled yourself very well. You have real talent for this sort of thing. Though I'm not sure that's a compliment."

"I'll take it as such," Erin said with a smile. How could she have suspected Rosemary of setting up such a disgusting story? She added, "Watching you, I realize how much I have yet to learn. You were superb."

"She should be, she's the pro" was Joe's comment.

"I liked that touch about offering a reward," said Jeff.

"Joe's idea," Rosemary said briefly. "Is anyone else hungry? I could eat a horse on the hoof."

"I'll go and see—" Erin started to get up. Rosemary waved her back into her chair.

"You've done more than your share already. Why don't we send out for pizza or Chinese or something?"

After some wrangling they decided on Chinese, and Nick called the restaurant to place the order. As soon as he put it down, the phone rang. It was a private line, never used for business purposes, and when Nick heard the voice on the other end he looked both surprised and annoyed. "It's for you," he said, handing the phone to Erin.

"You looked great on TV," Fran said. "How does it feel to be a celebrity?"

"How did you get this number?" Erin demanded. "It's private and unlisted."

"Oh, I copied the number when I was there," Fran said without shame. "Don't worry, I won't bug you, but this is an unusual occasion. I mean, what an awful thing! How is she? What do you think. . . ."

Erin was painfully conscious of the listeners as Fran rambled on. Rosemary had picked up a paper and was politely pretending to read it, but Joe and Nick stared in critical silence. Finally she cut Fran off with a brusque "That's crazy, Fran. I have to hang up now. Don't call me, I'll call you. Good-bye."

Obviously an apology was called for, but it infuriated her to have to make it on behalf of Fran, who wasn't in the least repentant.

"I'm sorry about that. It was my roommate, the one who was here yesterday. I'll warn her about using that number again. She's such a fan of Rosemary's—"

"Not your fault," Nick said. "What's crazy?"

"I beg your pardon?"

"You said, 'That's crazy.' "

"Oh, that." Erin laughed. "She thinks we—you—have a poltergeist."

"Poltergeist?" Kay repeated blankly.

Evidently she was the only one who didn't know what the word meant. "Doesn't fit," Joe said, masticating his cigar. Nick grinned and shook his head. Rosemary frowned and shook her head. Jeff rolled his eyes in sardonic, silent commentary; and from Will's lair in the corner came a soft, pedantic voice that made Erin turn and stare. How long had Will been there? She hadn't seen him come in.

"The word means 'racketing spirit' in German. Phenomena include objects flying around the room without visible means of locomotion, fires starting without apparent cause, raps and knocks, furniture moving—"

"Doesn't fit," Joe repeated. "The fire in the graveyard was caused by a weirdo with a match. And nobody except us knows about . . ." His eyes focused on Erin.

She knew she was suspected of something, but she didn't understand what it could be until Nick spoke up in her defense.

"Don't glare at Erin, Joe. I was the one who told Fran about the other fires. I don't even remember how the subject came up, but I didn't think it was important."

"Were there other fires?" Erin asked.

"Two," Jeff said. "Nothing major. The first one occurred—when was it, Nick? A week ago, Saturday, I think. A wastebasket. We thought it was started by one of Joe's filthy cigars."

"It wasn't," Joe said. "But it wasn't a goddamn poltergeist either. Your roommate sounds a little loony, kiddo."

There was a general murmur of agreement. Then Jeff said, "Actually, the great majority of the poltergeist cases that have come under investigation were proved to have been caused by human agents. Children playing tricks."

"Correct," said Will. "The little dears were incredibly skilled at sleight of hand. Like any good stage magician, they knew how to distract the audience's attention from what they were doing—pointing with one hand while they used the other to tug on a thread or strike a match."

"Kids," Joe muttered. "Can't stand 'em myself."

"Not always kids," Jeff said. "Sometimes the perpetrator was an adolescent or young adult. Emotionally disturbed, of course."

The silence that followed was distinctly uncomfortable.

Erin had the feeling that they were all carefully not looking at her.

Then Nick said briskly, "I'll go pick up the food. Want to come along for the ride, Erin?"

The dogs were out. They fell on Erin with howls of rapture, and when Nick opened the car door, Tiny shoved past him and climbed into the passenger seat. He had to be hauled out, protesting vehemently, and he made another attempt, this time on the driver's side, when Nick got out to open the gate. After he had closed the gate both dogs sat in the drive baying dismally as they drove away.

The dogs' antics amused Erin, but not enough to make her forget what was on her mind. She was trying to think how to introduce the subject—and whether to mention it at all—when Nick said suddenly, "Damn that bastard Joe. Did you see him leer when I asked you to come with me?"

"I didn't notice."

"Maybe I'm too self-conscious. But I'm getting tired of all the jokes about me and the women on the staff, and what a stud I am—or think I am. I mean, hell, this is a job. I'm not about to risk my professional status by fooling around."

Distracted though she was, Erin couldn't let that pass. "Then you'd better stop grabbing people and nuzzling them on the ear."

"That was precisely the incident to which I was indirectly referring," Nick said, with freezing dignity. "Fear not, it won't happen again."

"Oh?"

"No. From now on you'll have to eat your heart out and soak your lonely pillow with tears of remorse, unless, of course, you come groveling to me and plead with me to reconsider."

"Nick, can't you ever be serious?"

"Admit it," Nick said, laughter lightening his voice. "I'm not so bad. You could probably learn to like me if you gave yourself half a chance."

"Mmmm."

"What's the matter?"

"What? Sorry, I was thinking about something else."

"I noticed. What is it? Tell Uncle Nick."

"You'll think I'm paranoid."

"Maybe, maybe not. You'll never know unless you spit it out."

"They think I'm the poltergeist."

"Who thinks?"

"Don't tell me it didn't occur to you."

"No," Nick said. "It didn't."

The moon had not yet risen; the only light came from the car's headlights casting twin spears of brightness through the dark. Erin shivered, and Nick said, "You should have brought a sweater. My heater doesn't work too well; I was going to replace it, but—"

"You don't have to change the subject. I need to talk about it. Face it, Nick; I was here a week ago Saturday. Was that the first time anything odd happened?"

"Are you kidding? Odd is the norm in this business." After a moment he went on, "Put it out of your mind, Erin. Last night's fire couldn't have anything to do with the others. The cemetery isn't guarded, any one of a million people could have done the job. You read, every now and then, about some weird cult holding ceremonies in a cemetery—"

"By itself it doesn't mean anything." Erin was determined to play devil's advocate. "But add it to the other things. That awful little doll, for instance. Why won't anyone talk about it? A child didn't put it in the knitting bag; I've seen kids around, but they don't come in the house."

"What other explanation can there be?"

"I don't know. 'Too many accidents.' That's what she said. Kay. Not to me, it was as if she were talking to herself."

"Kay said that?" Nick came to an abrupt stop as an octagonal red sign loomed up ahead. His outflung arm caught Erin painfully across the chest, and she let out a yelp. "You didn't have to do that! I had my seat belt fastened!"

"Well, see, my seat belts aren't exactly. . . . Sorry about that. I was thinking about what you said, and forgot about the stop sign. The traffic cops around here lie in wait for me, I swear they do. I sure don't want to be stopped tonight after drinking that beer. Can't you see the headlines? 'Marshall Aide Ticketed for DWI, Beautiful Redheaded Passenger Unable to Walk Straight Line. . . . ' "

Erin thought he was trying to change the subject, but after they had turned onto the highway and were proceeding at a discreet speed toward town, he said, " 'Too many accidents.' I suppose you could call the wastebasket fire an accident; the other one was in the stableyard, day before yesterday. Another accident, but a minor one—no damage done, just a pile of dried weeds. The only serious accident that's happened recently was Kay's, when she hurt her hand. From her point of view that was one too many, I guess."

"She sounded really strange, Nick," Erin insisted. "It was the day I moved in. Day before yesterday. 'Too many accidents,' and something about things coming in threes . . . She was out of it, groggy with painkillers, it was like her mind was somewhere else. Off in outer space, or wandering in the past—"

"Oh, no," Nick exclaimed. "No, that's too far out."

"What are you talking about?"

"Too far out," Nick repeated. "But . . . that's how he died, you know. Edward Marshall, Rosemary's husband. An accident. He was cleaning his gun. '

Chapter
Five

WHEN NICK SLOWED to turn into the driveway the gate stood wide open and one of the dogs—the older of the pair—lay in the middle of the road.

"Damn it," Nick exploded, coming to a crashing halt. "Who opened that gate? Samson—Samson! If he's hit—"

"He's just resting," Erin said with relief, as the old dog got lazily to his feet and ambled toward them.

"Sure, right on the road. Really intelligent animals. . . ." He got out of the car. "Inside, Samson. Move it, you furry moron. I suppose that stupid Tiny is halfway to Richmond by now."

His shout produced a crashing in the underbrush across the road, and then Tiny himself, delighted to find a friend. He hurled himself at Nick; after considerable discussion and exercise Nick got him inside the gate, the car inside the gate, and the gate closed.

"Somebody must have come after we left," he said as they

proceeded along the drive at a cautious crawl, while both dogs hurled themselves merrily at the wheels.

"More reporters?" Erin asked.

"I doubt it. My profession isn't noted for its manners, but trespass is against the law. There's only one person I can think of who would barge in without an invitation and not bother to close the gate. . . . Yep. That's his car."

Presumably he knew; Erin recognized the Mercedes insignia, but the sober dark-blue vehicle looked very much like the one that belonged to Kay.

Philips Laurence's arrival must have preceded their own by only a few minutes. He was still on his feet and in full verbal spate when they walked into the room.

". . . saw it on the evening news. Naturally I hurried right over. Why didn't you call me?"

"It would have been a waste of time, wouldn't it?" Rosemary said. "You just said you were at the races this afternoon. Thank you, Nick, Erin—put the cartons on the table and we'll help ourselves."

Reminded of their presence, and his manners, Laurence turned his peculiar smile on Erin. "Ah, the ingenue You performed charmingly, my dear. Hello, Nick."

Nick's brusque response did nothing to lighten the atmosphere, which was stiff with interwoven currents of hostility. Joe's scowl would have soured milk, and Jeff, his head bent over his work, fairly radiated dislike. There was no sound or movement from Will's corner.

"I'll get plates and silverware," Erin said, and retreated to the kitchen.

When she came back, Laurence had arranged himself before the fireplace, one arm resting on the mantel. He looked like an advertisement from *Country Life* or *The Pink Sheet*. His coat was not pink, but it had been cut by a master tailor; riding breeches and polished boots, scarf and narrow gold stockpin completed an ensemble which should have looked affected, but which did not. He wore it with such splendid self-confidence that he could have walked down the meanest streets of Washington at midnight and not appeared improperly dressed.

Laurence was talking again—or perhaps he was still talking.

". . . crack down on these blasphemous local cults. One can't permit such things to go unpunished. You remember the case in Maryland when a group of young degenerates disinterred the body of a child and used its—"

"Never mind, Philips," Rosemary said, her face twisting in disgust.

"Yeah, for God's sake," Joe exclaimed. "You trying to spoil my appetite? Sorry we can't ask you to stay, we only ordered for seven—not knowing you were about to honor us with a visit."

Laurence responded to this demonstration of bad manners with a raised eyebrow and a knowing smile; Kay roused herself to make the proper response.

"I'm sure there's plenty, if you would care to join us, Philips. Chinese food, you know; they always send so much. . . . I'm not especially hungry."

"I am," said Joe.

His rudeness was wasted effort; Laurence simply ignored him and went on lecturing. Not only did he dominate the conversation, but he wielded his chopsticks with a skill that infuriated Nick; the latter's attempts to imitate it only succeeded in flipping sticky wads of food all over the room. Laurence was maddeningly tolerant, even when a blob of rice landed on his immaculate knee. "You're trying too hard, young fellow. One's grasp must be delicate and flexible, responsive to the slightest muscular effort. . . ."

Laurence's admirers considered him a modern Renaissance man, astonishingly well versed in all subjects. His enemies, who were legion, insisted that the information he spouted so glibly had been fed to him by a cadre of aides and had been memorized instead of assimilated. That evening he treated his listeners to a lecture on the subject of superstition. They were too tired or too courteous or—in Erin's case, too morbidly fascinated—to interrupt him.

"Some claim that these blasphemous ceremonies go back to prehistoric times, and that the masked, horned god became

the Black Goat of the Sabbat, the incarnate god of evil. I
remember seeing at Lascaux—''

This was too much for Will, who roused himself long
enough to murmur, ''What a memory you've got, Philips.
The caves were closed to visitors in 1963.''

''To the ordinary tourist, yes,'' Laurence replied smoothly.
''M. Benedict, the curator, was kind enough to show me
around in 1986.''

Erin, who was watching Will, saw his lips shape a word
that looked like ''Liar,'' preceded by a colorful adjective;
but he chose not to speak aloud, and Laurence went on.

''As I was saying . . . Whatever the origins—and I myself
refuse to dignify these perversions by the name of religion—
as satanism exists today it is evil, pure and simple.'' He
smiled gently at Erin. ''The word disturbs you, doesn't it? It
isn't the fault of your generation that words such as good and
evil, right and wrong make you more uncomfortable than the
easy obscenities. In this case you can blame it on your elders
and be entirely correct. The so-called science of psychiatry—
an oxymoron if ever there was one—has attempted to deny
the reality of spiritual sin—''

''Bullshit,'' Nick said suddenly. ' We're afraid of words
like good and evil because they're too subjective. Hitler
thought the Jews were evil. Torquemada burned heretics alive
in the name of God. The witch-hunters of Salem believed
they were serving the good—''

''Ah, yes, the classic examples,'' Laurence said. ''My
young friend, you are heading blindly into a logical impasse.
Do you consider the rape of children a morally neutral activity?''

''Of course not,'' Nick said. ''But—''

''Do you believe that a few years in a comfortable mental
institution is fitting punishment for a man who molests in-
fants?''

''Hell, no; burn him alive,'' Joe shouted. ''Are you
running for Pope, Laurence, or are you just trying to be disgusting?''

Philips passed his hand over his waving, suspiciously brown
hair. ''I'm sorry if I offend the faint of heart, but it appears

to me you may have a very practical need to consider these matters. They are disgusting; I couldn't agree more. Are you too squeamish to consider them dispassionately and arrive at the inevitable conclusion?''

"No, I guess I'm just too stupid," Joe said. "What conclusion, professor?''

"That someone with a corrupt soul—call it a sick mind, if that makes you feel better—has selected Rosemary as the object of his hatred. The desecration of her husband's grave, the poppet in the knitting bag—''

"The what?" Kay exclaimed.

"Such a charming word for that malignant object," Laurence said. "You may be more familiar with it in its classical manifestation, an image of wax or clay which is used in homeopathic magic to inflict harm on the person it represents. A variety of materials can be used, of course; certain North American Indian tribes simply sketched the outline of the human figure in sand or ashes and then stabbed it, thereby, they believed, injuring the body of the enemy. You'll find a full discussion in *The Golden Bough*."

"Oh no, I won't," said Joe, heaving himself out of his chair. "Is there any more mo shu pork?" He kept up a loud monologue as he rummaged among the white paper containers. "If nobody else wants this egg roll, I may as well finish it. . . . Kay, don't you have a doctor's appointment tomorrow? Who's going to drive you? Somebody ate all the chow mein. . . . You ought to get some sleep, Rosemary, we've got a breakfast meeting tomorrow.''

Laurence laughed. "*Sufficit*, Joe. You've made your point. Good night, Rosemary. I wanted to discuss something with you, but it's obvious I won't be allowed to carry on a sensible conversation this evening. Young Nick—Jeff—Kay, my dear lady, you do look exhausted—my apologies. . . .''

He stopped in front of Erin and stood looking down at her. Then he placed the palm of his hand on her cheek and tilted her head back so that he was looking deep into her eyes. It was a gesture as offensively intimate as an embrace, and it was much more painful than it appeared; his fingers pressed into her skin and his thumb dug into the sensitive spot at the juncture of throat and chin. *"À bientôt,"* he said, and sauntered out of the room.

Erin raised her hands to her flaming cheeks. She didn't believe for a moment that Laurence's gesture had been sensual, or even affectionate; his eyes had been as cold as pebbles and he wasn't the sort of man who would make such a blatant approach. What his reasons might have been she could not imagine; but it wasn't long before she found out.

Joe's voice was ominously calm. "Who told him about the goddamn doll?"

Erin's breath caught. There had only been seven of them present that evening, the inner circle and one outsider—herself. Laurence's gesture of intimacy had been delicately designed to suggest that there was a bond between them, and she knew she looked as guilty as a murderer caught with the smoking gun in his hand.

The room was still, Rosemary's soft voice echoed like a shout. "I did."

She opened the box on the table and took out a cigarette. It was the first time Erin had seen her smoke; deliberately she struck a match, lit the cigarette and inhaled deeply. "I did. Is there any reason why I shouldn't have?"

"Well, for one thing it apparently prompted that asinine lecture we just sat through," Joe grumbled. "What the hell made you do it?"

Rosemary exhaled a cloud of smoke that veiled her face like fog. "I just happened to mention it in the course of conversation. It was a meaningless, mildly amusing story, nothing more."

"Amusing?" Joe repeated incredulously.

"That's right," Kay said. "Leave Rosemary alone, Joe, she's had a horrible day."

For a moment no one spoke. Then Nick said, "I'll go down and close the gate. His lordship won't bother."

"Never mind, I'll do it on my way out." Joe got heavily to his feet. "Coming, Jeff?"

"Ready when you are." Jeff gathered his papers and put them in his briefcase.

Rosemary's confession had restored Erin to favor. Joe threw

her a friendly " 'Night, kid," and Jeff smiled. Rosemary and Kay left the room together, the former remarking, "I'll help Kay get into her jammies, Erin; you've done more than your share today."

Erin caught Nick's eye. He shook his head; after the two women had left, he said in a low voice, "That was a tactful request for privacy. I guess they have some things to talk about."

"So do I," Erin said.

Nick began piling dirty plates and empty cartons onto a tray, his back to her. "Why did he do that?" she demanded. "You didn't believe—"

"Just stirring up trouble," Nick answered, without turning around. "Typical Laurence tactic. Divide and conquer."

"It worked, didn't it? You did believe I was the one who told him. That I'm a spy, an informer—"

"Now listen, Erin—"

"You did." Erin picked up the loaded tray and started toward the kitchen. "All of you believed it. If Rosemary hadn't spoken up—"

"Goddamn it!" Nick ran after her. She slammed the tray down on the kitchen table; the towers of empty food cartons tottered and spilled. "You're getting egg foo yung all over the floor," Nick exclaimed.

"So, too bad. I'll clean it up. That's what I'm here for, washing dishes and being the scapegoat."

Nick rolled his eyes, took a deep, quivering breath and began to count. ". . . nine, ten. Okay. Would you just listen to me for a minute? How about a friendly cup of coffee?"

"I have to clean up this mess."

"I'll clean it up. Sit down! I mean, *please* sit down."

She sat with folded arms, glowering, while he picked up the spilled cartons and made coffee. Then he took the chair across from her at the table.

"This way of life isn't easy to understand," he began, "but you'd better try, because things are going to get worse before they get better. Everybody is short on sleep, uptight, on the defensive. Right now Rosemary's chances of winning this race are anyone's guess. She's still behind in the polls, but she's moving up; and in these last crucial weeks some unexpected incident could make all the difference—even a careless statement, by Rosemary or Buzz.

"Buzz knows he's in trouble. He'd give what's left of his mean little soul to get something on Rosemary. The media people are always looking for a scoop, and dirt makes more interesting reading than positive news. You could pick up a nice piece of change from a number of sources if you had inside information on campaign strategy, or damaging information."

"Is there anything like that to be found?" Erin asked coldly.

"No. Our campaign strategy is about as subtle as a bulldozer, and as for damaging information . . . One of the things that attracted me to Rosemary is the fact that except for the unfortunate accident of birth that made her female, she's a picture-perfect candidate. Not too old, not too young, easy on the eyes but certainly not glamorous; good speaking voice, excellent debater—and clean as a whistle. There is literally nothing in her background that could hurt her. Devoted wife, mother, grandmother; honor student; she never gets drunk, never plays around, she even quit smoking a few years back. When the great marijuana issue arose a few years ago, some reporters asked her if she'd ever indulged, and her answer was 'No, bourbon has always been good enough for me.' ''

"Wasn't that rather flippant?" Erin was in a mood to be critical.

"It was the way she said it." Nick's face had relaxed into a half-smile. "And the fact that she never drinks in public except for an occasional glass of wine. It reduced the whole business to nonsense. Oh, well, never mind that. What I'm getting at is that political spies aren't unheard of. The fact that Reagan had Carter's notes before their big debate, and knew in advance exactly what Carter was going to say, helped him enormously. It needn't be anything as underhanded as passing on strategically important information; a slip of the tongue could hurt, and people like Laurence are skilled at setting up traps for the unwary. I know you didn't tell him

about that damned poppet; but you might have, in all innocence, without realizing it could hurt.''

"How could it?"

"I can't imagine how," Nick admitted, frowning. "It doesn't
make sense, not even to Philips Laurence; his performance tonight was designed to annoy and stir up dissension and mistrust.
But I didn't fall for it, Erin. Honest. Even if Rosemary hadn't
'fessed up, I wouldn't have suspected you.''

"Why not? I'm the logical suspect—the outsider, the
stranger in your midst. How do you know I wouldn't sell
Rosemary out for cold cash?''

"My dear girl, you are talking to an experienced, hard-
headed, cynical political analyst," Nick exclaimed. "Do you
think I could be taken in by a pretty face, a gorgeous figure,
a pair of big green eyes?''

"Could you?''

"You're damned right I could." Nick planted both elbows
on the table and gazed at her soulfully. "Take me in. Please?''

"There you go again," Erin exclaimed. "Look, Nick, I
don't mind you lecturing me or even correcting me; you know
a lot more about this insane business of politics than I do,
and I want to learn. How often do I have to repeat this? How
many times do I have to tell you I only want to be treated
like—''

"Now who's lecturing?''

"Me. And you had it coming. Maybe you weren't trying
to be condescending, maybe you wanted to change the subject. Is that it? If you . . . Where are you going? Don't you
dare walk out on me in the middle of a discussion.''

"I'm just going to wash the dishes," Nick said, suiting the
action to the words. "It's a dirty trick to leave them for Sarah.
No, I do not want you to help me, I want you to sit tight and
talk to me. What's your point?''

She much preferred this tone to his flattery. "My point is
that although you may not suspect me of pulling these tricks,
someone else obviously does.''

"Laurence?''

"You saw it. That long, rambling lecture of his also had a
point, and he drove it home when he—when he touched me

in that offensive way. The disturbed adolescent, trying to cause trouble and gain attention—''

"Wait a minute." Nick turned, his hands dripping water. "Laurence didn't say that, Jeff did. Or Will—I forget which. And you sure as hell are no adolescent."

"But if I had done those things it would be because I was mentally disturbed," Erin argued. "Not because I was in league with the powers of evil."

Nick's eyes widened. "Hold it. I think I see what you're driving at, but if you will forgive me for saying so, your oratorical style is somewhat lacking in coherence. Nobody in his right mind could suppose—''

"That I had sold myself to the devil. That's what I said! Don't be so obtuse, Nick. Laurence isn't stupid. If there is something sinister about the fires, I am, as I pointed out, the obvious suspect. All that talk of his about black magic was just to cover up the fact that he can't think of a sensible motive. He loves showing off and sounding theatrical, he knows as well as we do that people don't . . . people . . .''

Her voice faltered as she saw the look on Nick's face.

"But they do, though," he said slowly. "Don't they?"

"Yes." Erin's eyes fell. "I guess some people do. I've read about cases in the newspaper—''

"I've read about them in *The Golden Bough*, as a matter of fact. Did you notice the way he tossed off the name, as if it were some esoteric work none of us illiterate slobs had ever heard of? I don't know why that bastard affects me the way he does; usually I'm pretty good with a snappy comeback, but I was still trying to think of one when he pulled that stunt on you."

"You're grinding your teeth," Erin said. "And getting off the subject."

"Ain't it the truth. Point is, it's barely conceivable that some religious fanatic or dabbler in black magic is trying to put a hex on Rosemary."

"No, that's not the point. The point is, so what? I haven't read *The Golden Bough*, but I've heard Fran talk about such people—she's into spiritualism and astrology and that sort of thing—and they are as harmless as they are crazy. They can stick pins in waxen images all they want, they aren't going to hurt anyone that way. By the way—were there any pins in that doll?''

''No. Not that I noticed.'' Nick placed the last of the plates in the rack to drain and dried his hands.

''Damn it, Erin, I don't even want to think about this. It's disgusting, frightening, and far-out.''

''You'll have to excuse my biased viewpoint, but I find the idea of a wandering lunatic more attractive than the possibility that one of us—me, for instance—is responsible.''

''I see what you mean. What about Laurence? It would be just like him to focus suspicion on an innocent party in order to divert it from himself. I've never trusted the bastard. It's completely out of character for him to support Rosemary. He despises everything she stands for.''

''Maybe he's in love with her.''

''That's the accepted theory.'' Nick looked dubious. ''As a self-appointed expert on the romantic passion, I can't see him as an infatuated lover. He was Ed Marshall's friend originally, and I suppose it's barely possible that he has a few decent feelings under that cynical facade—old loyalties, sentimental memories of boyhood days. . . .''

''Why not? He can't be all bad. Nobody is.''

''Bless your sweet little heart. I hope you can hang on to that idea. How about more coffee?''

''No, thanks. It's late and I'm tired. Don't you ever go home?''

''I am home. I've moved into the overseer's shack, next to Sam's quarters.''

''You gave up your apartment?''

''Had to, couldn't afford it. It was no problem; the furniture was rented too. I'll be on the spot from now on, so feel free to lean out your window and scream for help if the occasion arises.''

''I fondly hope no such occasion does arise.'' But she felt a sense of relief, all the same, to know that the isolated household of women now had an able-bodied man on the premises. Sam was too old and too deaf to be of much use in case . . . In case of what? she asked herself. I sound like some feeble-witted antifeminist.

Nick hung the dishtowel neatly on the rack and came toward her. "How about a friendly good-night kiss to take the nasty taste out of my mouth and send me rejoicing to the pallet in my hovel, among the lowest and meanest of the humble servants of the mighty?"

"Not on your life." Erin ducked as he swooped upon her, arms extravagantly outstretched. "I wouldn't want to be responsible for making you break your sworn word."

"Not ready to grovel yet? Oh, well, I'll wait." He blew her a kiss from the door. "Sleep well."

Somewhat to her surprise, Erin did.

Chapter Six

CONTRARY TO popular opinion, the Congress of the United States does not usually take four-day weekends. It is true, however, that in even-numbered years members try not to schedule important debates or roll calls on Mondays and Fridays during the autumn. One third of the Senate seats and all those of the House go up for grabs every two years, and members who aren't campaigning one time will be another. A little consideration for others makes life easier all around.

Rosemary was luckier than many of her colleagues because her home base was so close to Washington. Candidates from the West Coast spent precious hours commuting and almost as much recovering from jet lag.

By nine o'clock on Monday morning Rosemary had left the house, driven by Nick. Where they were going and what their schedule was Erin didn't know; no one had bothered to inform her. Of course she had no right to expect them to do so, but the more her involvement and expertise increased, the more she resented the routine chores she would once have accepted without question. Politics was addictive. It was also a lot less difficult to comprehend than she had supposed—complicated, maddeningly unpredictable (which only added to its fascination), but not intellectually daunting. Despite the fact that many of the processes could be reduced to charts and numbers, it was more of an art than a science—the art, some might say, of manipulating people's minds. But it wasn't that simple. The techniques of political manipulation were pretty crude, in fact, and the most consoling thing about them was that they didn't always work. Why did a candidate's populist message bring him an overwhelming victory in one state primary, and bomb everywhere else? Why was a group of voters bewitched by a candidate who offered them nothing but platitudes and a practiced actor's smile, when they turned thumbs down on another man with precisely the same attributes?

There was another, more personal reason for her let-down feeling that morning. In the cold light of day some of the ideas she had raised the night before seemed frivolous and unreal. But Nick had raised another fear, and this one was not for herself. She cared about Rosemary. She cared about all of them, in different ways. Kay was a pain, of course, but Erin was becoming accustomed to her foibles; they bothered her far less than they had at first. Even Christie seemed to be mellowing a little. The only person she didn't know much about, the real enigma of the group, was Will. Who the devil was he, anyway, and what did he do when he wasn't wandering in and out of the house? He treated Rosemary like a casual older brother, and she teased and criticized him—and obviously depended on his advice.

During lunch break she asked Jackson about him. Jackson seemed surprised that she didn't know. "He's the research honcho. Teaches history at Charlottesville. He's kind of weird—almost like a caricature of your absentminded-professor type—but he's a nice-enough guy."

He didn't know how Will and Rosemary came to be acquainted. Nor, obviously, did he care.

As luck would have it, Erin was still in the commons room finishing her lunch when Kay came looking for her. Kay could make her feel guilty just by looking at her, and her look now was distinctly critical. Brusquely and without preamble she informed Erin that she would have to drive her to the doctor. "My appointment is at one, so if you're quite finished eating . . ."

Knowing how reluctant Kay was to have anyone else driving the car, Erin wondered whether this was a signal honor or the reverse. The wink and grin Jackson gave her, behind Kay's back, made her suspect it was an honor nobody wanted.

She backed the Mercedes out of the garage with her foot quivering on the gas pedal. Kay sat rigid as a poker, tense with anxiety. "I wouldn't have asked you," she muttered, "but the mail is picking up and you're the only one who . . . Watch out for that rut—and don't hit the cat, do you see him?"

Not only had Erin seen the cat, it was a good ten feet off the driveway, squatting in the grass. In an effort to distract Kay's attention from her driving, she said, "Rosemary seems to be very fond of cats. How many are there?"

"Fifteen or twenty, I guess. There's a tree branch down— you'd better go around it. . . . It was Congressman Marshall who loved cats, actually. Rosemary doesn't really care. . . . You're a little too far to the right, Erin, you're going to scrape the fence. What was I saying?"

"I don't know," Erin said under her breath. She got through the gate safely and negotiated the turn.

"Oh, the cats. Rosemary is fond of animals, of course, but she doesn't care about them as much as Edward— Congressman Marshall—did. Their presence is a tribute to his memory, one might say."

Like Edward Marshall's office? For some reason Erin didn't find the idea as touching as she ought to have done. It made her think of Queen Victoria's morbid obsession with the relics of her dear dead Albert—having his clothes laid out every evening, sleeping with his nightshirt clutched in her arms.

The distraction didn't serve for long; Kay was soon pointing out fallen leaves, twigs, and pebbles, and warning her to watch out for them. It was a beautiful autumn day, with a brisk breeze sending clouds scampering across the blue bowl of the sky. The road was walled with tapestries of living color—scarlet and crimson and amber, the deepening gold of maple leaves. It would have been a pleasant drive if Kay had kept quiet.

Erin made it to Middleburg without damage, except to her nerves, and stopped at the blinking light in the middle of town. Flanking the intersection were the two handsome old stone structures that housed Middleburg's most popular restaurant-inns. The one on the left boasted a terrace that ran the length of the house; tables and chairs provided al-fresco dining, but on this cool day only a few fresh-air enthusiasts lingered over coffee and dessert.

"Turn left, Erin," Kay ordered.

"Right. I mean—yes, I know. There's a car coming."

"Park wherever you can find a space. There's one there. . . . No, it's next to a fire hydrant. The parking lot is down the street, but if you can find something closer. . . . It's a pity this town has become so . . . Look at that woman, did you ever see such a sight? Why anyone with a rear end like hers would wear stretch pants . . . Oh."

Her voice changed so dramatically that Erin had to look. It was not the unfortunate woman's rump that had affected Kay, however. The cause of her surprise was not hard to find. Posed and poised, halfway down the steps that led to the terrace of the restaurant, he had obviously seen them too.

"I wonder what Philips is doing here," Kay said.

"Having lunch, I suppose." Erin turned and proceeded at a decorous crawl, looking for a place to park. "Doesn't he live around here?"

"No, he lives in Maryland—Chevy Chase. There's a spot."

It wasn't the space Erin would have chosen for her first try at parallel parking someone's cherished Mercedes, and the fact that Philips was walking toward them, watching interestedly, didn't help. It took her two tries, but she finally made it without scraping the curb. As soon as she turned off the key, Laurence opened Kay's door.

"What a pleasant surprise," he said, smiling wickedly.

Kay accepted the hand he offered with a look that was

almost coquettish. It occurred to Erin that Kay was the only one of Rosemary's entourage who had never indicated dislike or disapproval of Laurence. Was it possible . . .

"Surprise, my foot," Kay said. "What are you up to, Philips?"

"Waiting for you, of course." He raised her hand to his lips.

Grudgingly Erin admitted he was one of the few men she knew who could carry off such a gesture. And he certainly knew how to dress. Ordinarily she paid little attention to men's clothing, but Laurence's was spectacularly suited to his public persona and his lean, trim figure. He would have been a good-looking man except for those cold, knowing eyes and the cynical twist of his lips. The fresh breeze had not dislodged a single lock of his hair. Erin smiled to herself as she remembered Nick's comment: "He doesn't go to a barber; his hairdresser comes to him, if you please. The same guy who does Reagan's hair—you noticed it's the same style, didn't you?"

"I had a luncheon appointment with a friend," Philips went on, retaining his hold on Kay's hand.

Her smile almost matched his in cynicism. "A useful sort of friend, I presume?"

"You wound me to the heart!" He dropped her hand to press his over the organ in question. "I lingered in the hope of seeing you. I had hoped for a little private chat."

"Oh, indeed? Well, I haven't time now, Philips. My appointment is at one."

"Yes, I know." Again they exchanged knowing smiles—almost, Erin thought, like lovers who couldn't be bothered to conceal their liaison. "Afterward, then. Come, I'll escort you to the door."

She took his arm. Erin followed; for once she didn't mind being overlooked. But when they reached the doctor's office Laurence took possession of her with the cool aplomb of an arresting officer. "I'll show Erin the sights of Middleburg, such as they are. We'll be back in half an hour."

Erin got out one word—"But"—before she was interrupted. "I need your assistance in selecting a gift—for a lady. You can't refuse, my dear."

Laurence's glance at Kay implied she was the lady in question. Her faint frown disappeared. "I'll wait for you here," she said, turning into the office. "Don't be long."

Outflanked and outmaneuvered, Erin had no choice but to go with him. Like Joe, she wondered what he was up to. Was he planning to apologize for his performance the night before? An apology was certainly called for, but she doubted Philips Laurence was the man to make it.

Laurence's face was well known because of his television appearances; people stared and pointed, and one woman stopped him to ask for his autograph.

He made quite a performance of it, murmuring compliments and deprecating remarks; but as they walked away, leaving the fan in a state of gaping adoration, he said, "I've seen sheep with more intelligent faces."

Erin said nothing, but her reaction would have been clear to a less perceptive student of human nature than Laurence. With a sidelong smile he said, "You think I'm a twenty-four-carat son of a bitch, don't you? Well, you're mistaken. It's only twenty-two carats." While she was trying to decide whether to respond—and what to say—he went on, in quite a different voice, "Do you like to shop?"

Another loaded question. If she refused to accept the stereo-typed female role, she was letting him manipulate her into a flat-out lie.

"I do," Laurence said, without waiting for an answer. "The truth is, there's not much else to do in Middleburg. Oh, we have our tedious historic buildings and our boring quaint inns, and I could lead you up and down the streets spouting data. . . . For instance, did you know Middleburg got its name because it is halfway between Alexandria and Winchester? Do you care? Does it matter? I mean, for God's sake, who ever goes to Winchester?"

"People," Erin said.

"Doubtless." He hadn't heard her; he took it for granted she wouldn't say anything worth listening to. "But the real tourist sights—the house where the Reagans lived during the

1980 campaign, the sumptuous mansion of Senator Warner and his much more famous wife, Elizabeth Taylor—aren't in town. So the inhabitants shop, the tourists shop, and everybody hopes that one of the famous names will shop. We have here kitchen shops with names like Cozy Cupboard and the Gingham Goose; craft shops with names like the Calico Cat and Country Cozy; innumerable restaurants, cafés, pubs, and the like; and clothing shops where you can buy the same garments you would find in D.C., but for twice the price. They all have names such as—''

He waved her gallantly into the door of a shop called the Sly Fox. ''It's the hunt scene, of course,'' Laurence went on. ''So tacky.''

''Don't you hunt?'' Erin asked. ''You look as if you would.''

''Ouch.'' He grinned at her. ''I deserved that, I suppose. No, my dear, I do not hunt. Oscar Wilde said it best—''

'' 'The unspeakable in pursuit of the inedible.' ''

''Just as I thought; you are adequately educated as well as beautiful. Go on, browse to your heart's content.''

Erin turned to a rack of blouses. ''What size is she?''

She had hoped to catch him off-guard, but he was too skilled at subterfuge—or perhaps he had only spoken the simple truth. ''Your height, but considerably broader. One hesitates to use the word 'fat' of a lady. . . . About her size.'' He indicated the hovering saleswoman. It was a gratuitously cruel remark, and the woman's smile wavered.

Erin had expected the prices would be high, but the first tag she examined made her wince. Two hundred and ten dollars for a plain linen blouse?

Laurence flipped through a rack of robes and nightgowns. ''Frightful,'' he said loudly. ''Do you see anything that would melt a woman's heart, Erin? No? You have excellent taste. Let's try elsewhere.''

They were followed out of the shop by two other customers and—Erin felt sure—the silent curses of the saleslady. As they emerged onto the street a breeze caught at her hair and lifted it like a bright banner; a scattering of golden leaves from a nearby tree sprinkled her head, and Laurence stopped short.

"Exquisite," he breathed. "No, don't brush them off, they suit you better than gold or gems. You're a pretty thing, Erin. Not beautiful, I lied when I said that. Not sweetly pretty, either. Pretty . . ."

The questionable compliment didn't offend Erin, perhaps because it sounded not only genuine but genuinely impersonal. He might have been talking about a statue or a painting.

"Why do you do things like that?" she demanded.

Laurence knew exactly what she meant. He laughed. "My dear, I must maintain my image. My public expects it. Think of the pleasure that women will derive from telling their friends that Philips Laurence is as rude and unpleasant as he is reported to be. What about a sweater? One can never have too many sweaters."

He stopped before a display window. Soft swirls of cashmere had been strewn with seeming carelessness over cardboard logs and paper sprays of bright-colored leaves. The colors glowed like autumn—forest green, deep gold, rusty red.

"There's nothing like cashmere," Erin said dryly.

Some of the labels were familiar—Braemar, Pendleton—and the clothes were country casual. One table was heaped with hand-knit and embroidered sweaters which the obsequious salesman assured them were one of a kind. Erin believed him; someone with a charming sense of humor had designed the patterns of marching cats with separate, swinging yarn tails, foxes sneering at panting hounds, horses engaging in inappropriate contortions, elephants trooping in solemn parade.

"Elephants sell well in this bastion of conservatism," Philips remarked, playing with the dangling trunks of the animals in question. "No donkeys? I fear Kay would never stand for the insignia of the other party. Do you think she'd like the cats?"

"They're absolutely adorable, but I can't imagine Kay wearing anything like this," Erin said. "What about a scarf?"

None of the scarves suited Laurence's refined tastes, so they left without buying anything and headed back toward the doctor's office. Bright leaves swirled and danced in the freshening wind; on the hillsides beyond, the colors of the trees burned like flames.

Laurence said unexpectedly, " 'The scarlet of the maples Can shake me like a cry Of bugles going by.' " Then he added coolly, "I memorized that piece of sentimental trash in prep school. What a pity one can't purge one's mind of childish enthusiasms."

"Isn't it just as childish to cultivate a veneer of false sophistication?"

Laurence stared at her in surprise and then burst out laughing. It was the first spontaneous demonstration of genuine amusement she had seen him display, and it warmed his austere features amazingly.

"I've heard that particular put-down before, but no one has expressed it quite so effectively," he said. "I suppose it's the contrast of your ingenuous face and your cutting words. So you do think I'm a twenty-four-carat bastard, and a hypocrite to boot? You needn't be afraid of offending me by speaking the truth."

"I'm not afraid." The statement was true. "Liking" was too strong a word for her new feeling of Philips Laurence; it would be more accurate to call it an absence of positive antipathy.

"No, I can see you aren't. Let me confess something to you, since you read me so accurately. I am genuinely and sincerely anxious to see Rosemary win this election. I'm sure the entourage has speculated about my motives?"

"Not to the exclusion of all other subjects," Erin said, in a fair imitation of Laurence's drawl.

It won her another burst of laughter. "Oh, excellent. I know they've been wondering, and suspecting me of subtly sinister designs; but they're wrong. I've known Rosemary ever since she was Ed Marshall's shy little bride. She's come a long way since then. I differ with her on many issues, but I have enormous respect for the passion and integrity with which she pursues her goals." The speech flowed so fluently that it sounded like a quote from one of his columns; but the next sentence did not. "I'll do anything I can to help her win."

"I believe you. But why? Are you . . ." Erin stopped. "None of my business."

"Am I in love with her? I've asked myself that same question, and I'm damned if I know the answer." His even voice roughened, as if with anger. Then he laughed lightly. "She has her own peculiar charm, does Rosemary. You must have felt it."

"She's very nice," Erin said.

"Ah, you haven't yet succumbed. You will. Everyone does. Even Buzz Bennett . . . Let's run in here for a moment, I can't return to Kay empty-handed."

The store was a food shop, featuring expensive gourmet goodies. Laurence wasted no time looking around; he picked up a handful of tiny gold boxes with the name of a well-known candy manufacturer, and paid cash for them.

"If you want to ingratiate yourself with Kay, this is the way to go," he said, pocketing his change.

"Godiva chocolates? Poor as I am, I think I could spring for something a little larger in size," Erin said.

"Ah, but that's the point," Laurence said cheerfully. "Kay has a deplorable tendency to pig out—isn't that the phrase?—on chocolates, and an even more deplorable tendency to gain weight. These little dainties contain only two pieces, just enough to satisfy her sweet tooth without making her feel guilty about devouring the entire box. We feed them to her one box at a time."

Kay seemed to appreciate the minuscule offering, and Laurence's broad hint that it was a token of a finer gift to come. But Erin's hunch that she, not Kay, had been his real quarry, was confirmed by the conversation that followed, over cups of tea in the Hungry Hound Café. Laurence said nothing new or confidential, he only reaffirmed his desire to help Rosemary, and his concern for how her health would stand up to the stress of the campaign. When Kay said it was time they were getting back, he didn't try to detain them.

Kay had obviously enjoyed herself. She looked like a different woman when she came out of the doctor's office, and Erin suspected that the new, lighter bandage was only part of the reason. She had applied fresh makeup, and loosened strands of hair so that they curled softly around her face. For the first part of the return trip she was silent, not even commenting when Erin wriggled the car out of the parking space, which had been constricted by a newcomer who had pulled up behind her.

I wonder if I'll ever understand people, Erin thought. Just when I think I've got someone figured out, they turn into an entirely different individual. Like the two-headed god Janus of Roman mythology, but even more complex; a dozen personalities instead of two, layer upon layer of masks. Maybe I'm the one who's naive, to suppose people are so simplistic. Or are these people more accustomed to concealment—two-faced in the slang sense of the word?

If someone had asked her to justify her conviction that Kay and Philips had once been lovers she could not have pointed to a single piece of evidence. It was more an atmosphere, a vague feeling. For the past few days Kay had been moping around the house, looking like an old woman. Now she looked her true age—and she wasn't that old. No older than Laurence, at any rate.

Kay sat up straighter. "Watch out for that branch," she said sharply.

"I see it." Erin smiled. Kay was herself again.

As soon as they walked into the office they knew something had happened. The clerks were all clustered around the door of the inner office; none of them actually had his or her ear pressed to the door, but that would not have been necessary since the raised voices could have been heard at a considerable distance.

"If you have nothing to do I can find work for all of you," Kay said loudly.

One by one they sidled back to their desks. Only Christie remained, facing her superior. "They're at it again," she said.

"I can hear that," Kay said caustically. She put her handbag down on the nearest desk. "Rosemary isn't back, is she?"

"No. It's the triumvirate. Sounds as if Joe and Nick are doing most of the yelling." Christie's smile was broad and unashamed.

Kay marched to the door and opened it. The voices stopped abruptly, but resumed as soon as she had closed it after her.

"What's going on?" Erin asked.

Christie had been more affable recently, perhaps because Erin's humble station had become so apparent. Christie didn't wash dishes or brush hair. She didn't even bring coffee to other people; they brought it to her.

Now her eyes sparkled with excitement. "There's a rumor going around that Joe was the one who leaked the story about Buzz Bennett and the Shady Lane Motel. Set him up."

Erin's face betrayed her bewilderment, and Christie was happy to display her superior knowledge. "Look, the *Times* had to get a tip from somebody; how else would they know exactly when Buzz and his floozie were going to be there? I mean, did you see that photo? They caught him in his under-wear, and her right behind him, wearing even less."

Erin hadn't given the matter any thought, but she hated to admit she was as innocent as Christie thought her. "I assumed the floozie—the girl—was the one who tipped off the photographers."

"Sure, she was part of it. Got her cute little bod right out there where the cameras could catch every curve. She was paid to perform—by the same person who called the paper."

"Well, suppose that person was Joe." Erin argued. "It's a rotten, low-down trick, but all's fair in—"

The door exploded outward and Nick emerged. His face was crimson. Joe's voice followed him: "Get the hell back in here!"

Nick's reply was emphatic and of the variety that would, in earlier times, have been considered unprintable. A mild ripple of amusement ran through the avid listeners. Nick's glazed eyes focused on Christie and Erin. "Excuse me, la-dies," he snarled, and stormed out of the room.

"Wow," Christie said appreciatively. "He's really pissed, isn't he? Go on after him, and see if you can find out what's going on."

"I really don't think—"

"Oh, for God's sake, don't be such a self-righteous prig."
Christie gave her a shove.

Erin expected to find Nick in the kitchen; he had a thing
going with Sarah, the cook, and often retreated to the comfort
of motherly sympathy and muffins when things got too much
for him. Nick wasn't there. Sarah was staring at the back
door, which still vibrated from the fury of his exit.

"He's gonna break that door one of these days," Sarah
said critically. "What's the matter with him this time?"

"I was just about to ask you the same thing."

"He didn't stop to talk," Sarah said. "Just came roaring
through like a cyclone and slammed out the door."

She went back to rolling out pie crust, and Erin said,
"Men! They can be so childish sometimes."

"So can women, honey."

"Got me there," Erin admitted. "Okay. I won't be childish; I'll go after him and see if I can calm him down."

"Good idea. He's gonna do himself an injury someday,
banging around the way he does when he gets mad." She
glanced at Erin, her eyes twinkling. "He's not so bad, you
know—for a man."

As Erin crossed the stableyard the dogs howled a welcome,
but she didn't stop to chat. In the pasture below the house
she saw a lonely figure running wildly in circles.

By the time she reached him the circles had decreased in
diameter and the run had slowed to a jog. He rolled his eyes
in her direction but did not stop.

"Say it," he wheezed as he passed her.

"Say what?"

She had to wait for the answer until he came around again.
"Childish. Me."

"Oh, Nick. . . ." On the next round she caught hold of
him with both hands. He had taken off his coat and loosened
his tie; his blue shirt showed dark patches of sweat.

"The wind is chilly," she scolded, reaching for the jacket
he had flung carelessly onto a rock outcropping. "Sit down.
Put this on. You'll catch cold."

She suited the action to the words, draping the garment

over his shoulders and tugging at him until he sat down beside
her. Nick grinned. "I love being mothered. Do it some
more."

"You don't need a mother, you need a kick in the rear.
What are you doing out here, running around in circles like
a mad dog?"

"Working off steam," Nick replied. His breathing was still
quick and his cheeks were flushed with exercise, but his voice
was calm. "More socially acceptable than punching your boss
in the nose, don't you think? Do you know what that louse
accused me of?"

"Setting Senator Bennett up for a photo opportunity?
They're saying he was the one who did it."

"Who says? Oh, the kids in the office?" Nick swabbed his
wet forehead with his sleeve. "That shows you how rumors
get started. They were half-right. I accused him, he accused
me. The story is all over town. I heard it from one source,
he got it from another. He was steaming when he arrived and
I was in no mood to take any crap from anybody. Jeff kept
trying to play peacemaker and both of us turned on
him. . . ." A reluctant smile twitched his lips. "That's what
usually happens to peacemakers."

"Explain it to me." Erin shifted position. The rock was
not the most comfortable of seats. "I thought politicians did
this sort of thing all the time. Why the high moral indignation?"

"You sure do have a low opinion of us, don't you?" Nick
shook his head sadly. "Wish I could say it was undeserved.
But in this case it is. Oh, I admit I'd have been sorely tempted
if the information had come my way. Buzz has flaunted his
sexual peccadilloes for years, and believe me, some of them
were pretty vile. But aside from the fact that the idea makes
me sick, it's simply bad politics. If you're caught, and chances
are you will be, there's a backlash of sympathy for the victim.
Americans hate a snitch. Remember back in grade school,
when 'tattletale' was the worst name anyone could call you?"

"I can recall a few that were worse," Erin said wryly.

"So can I, now that you mention it. But you know what I
mean. It's a stupid, dangerous attitude; there are times when

you are morally obligated to blow the whistle on someone, friend or foe, to prevent serious trouble. But I sure didn't see it that way in my salad days, and most Americans still feel that betrayal is worse than the crime itself. Remember Chambers and Alger Hiss?'' He was silent for a moment; then he said slowly, ''I guess I shouldn't have sounded off to Joe. He's too smart to pull a stunt like that—at least he's too smart to be caught. But it really burned me when he suggested I was the one who did it.''

''What you resented, in fact, was not the insult to your integrity but the implication that you had made a stupid mistake.''

''I should resent *that*,'' Nick said. ''Actually, I think I do resent it.''

''Weren't you the one who suggested I was hopelessly naive about politics? I'm learning. It's not a very pleasant process.''

''You got it.'' He slid off the flat surface of the rock and propped his head back against it, knees drawn up and head tilted back. ''I admit the whole business seems pretty trivial on a day like this.''

From where they sat they could see the valley fields stretching down toward the stream and its rich green-and-gold boundary of trees. The summer crops had been garnered in; amber stubble of cornstalks, yellowing close-cropped hay glowed in the sunlight. Across the stream, figures moved slowly across a velvety square of pasture: white and bay and chestnut brown, graceful and remote as horses in a Persian miniature.

Nick uncoiled himself and stood up. ''Therapy complete. I'd better go back and grovel to Joe. Then maybe we can figure out how to handle this latest mess.''

He offered his hand to Erin and pulled her to her feet. As they started up the hill he said casually, ''I hear you went shopping with Laurence today. Lucky girl.''

''How on earth did you find that out? We just got back half an hour ago.''

''Kay mentioned it.'' He added with a grin, ''She had to outshout both me and Joe to get a word in, but she managed.

What she actually said was that you had had a long talk with the lout, singly and together, and that he hadn't mentioned the rumor, which he, of all people, should have heard.''

"She's got a point." Erin stumbled over a rock concealed by the long grass; Nick's hand was quick to steady her. "If it's all over town, he must have heard it. He didn't say anything. Unless . . ."

"Unless what?"

"I'm starting to find sly innuendos in a simple good morning,'' Erin grumbled. ''But he did emphasize his willingness to do anything he could to help Rosemary. Could that have been a subtle way of warning us this was about to break? Oh no, that's too silly."

"It's not silly, but it's a little obscure even for Laurence."

"I wondered at the time why he was so insistent about it,'' Erin mused. "Could he have meant it as a warning to me personally? 'I'll do anything I can to help Rosemary win, and you'd better not get in my way?' "

"Nah. That is silly. Unless you are a political Mata Hari in disguise—a very good disguise—you have no connection with any of these people. And you don't know a setup from a place setting."

"But I'm learning," Erin said again. The words left a sour taste in her mouth.

She still had a lot to learn, though, as she was soon to discover. Rosemary had returned, tired and cross after a long day of meetings and luncheon speeches—''Concerned Mothers for Nuclear Disarmament'' and ''Future Farmers of America, Northern Virginia Chapter '' Erin was at her typewriter when Rosemary entered the office; her expression was so formidable that only Christie would have dared to speak to her.

"How did it go, Rosemary?"

"I expect to suffer from indigestion the rest of my life." Rosemary didn't stop; she went on to the inner office.

"She's heard it too," Christie muttered. "By the way, somebody delivered a package for you. It's on the table in the hall."

"For me? I didn't buy anything."

"Oh, really? Then it must be a present."

As Erin started out of the room someone said, "Make sure it's not ticking before you open it."

The package was not ticking. It was wrapped in glittery bronze paper stamped with little figures of running foxes, and tied with an elaborate medley of gold, russet, and green ribbons. It may have been the foxes that touched off a quiver of premonition; instead of taking the parcel to her room Erin attacked it immediately, ripping off the paper and opening the box. Inside was the sweater she had admired that afternoon. Blue cats, green cats, rosy-pink cats marched across the creamy white wool. The tiny gems in the embroidered collars winked and twinkled, and the cats' tails—some braided, some wisps of fluffy angora—swung as she held the sweater out at arms' length. The price tag had been removed, but she remembered the figure. Three hundred and ten dollars. Middleburg shops had a peculiar penchant for those extra ten dollars.

Shaken by a blend of fury, bewilderment, and shame, she didn't hear the footsteps, or realize she was not alone until Jeff said, "Very pretty. Just your colors, too."

Erin whirled around. Jeff wasn't the only one who had crept up on her; Joe and Nick were with him. Christie had wasted no time spreading the word. Or it might have been one of the others, someone who recognized the distinctive wrapping paper and wondered how a humble typist/maid-of-all-work could afford to shop at such an expensive boutique.

She waved the sweater defiantly. "Take a good look. I'm sending it back, right this minute. There's some mistake."

"No, I don't think so," Joe said. He took the cigar out of his mouth, studied it as if wondering where it had come from, and tossed it into a Sèvres bowl. "I don't think it was a mistake."

"Is there a card?" Nick's voice sounded strained.

"No," Erin said.

"Hardly necessary, is it?" Jeff caught the garment as Erin flung it away. "Not that a mere male like me would know, but I gather the price on this is about the same as the yearly income of a Third World peasant. Kay said Laurence had taken you shopping. He assumes we have enough intelligence to put two and two together, but not enough to recognize this as another of his dirty little tricks. '

Erin turned to him. "Then you don't believe—"

"Believe, hell. I *know* you aren't conspiring with Philips Laurence."

Slumped against the wall, hairy arms folded, Joe emitted a hoarse Humphrey Bogart chuckle. "Don't be simple, sweetheart. If you were spying for Philips he wouldn't pay you off so publicly. Besides, he doesn't need a snitch inside the organization. He's got Rosemary."

*   *

ERIN REWRAPPED the sweater in plain brown paper and addressed it to Laurence in care of the newspaper that carried his column.

The suggestion had come from Jeff: "A public slap in the face—much more effective than sending it to his home address."

"I dunno," Nick said doubtfully. "I mean, it's certainly more effective, but it could be dangerous. Laurence doesn't like being publicly humiliated."

"Too bad," Erin growled. She handed the parcel to Jeff, and gave him her most caressing smile. He had jumped to her defense with a speed and certainty that made Nick's failure to do so a double affront. Come to think of it, Nick still hadn't . . . She put both hands on Jeff's broad shoulders. "Thanks, Jeff. For everything."

Jeff blinked as if in surprise, but looked pleased. "Hey, you don't owe me. I wish I could . . . It's the least . . ."

"Good gracious me, you've got the poor chap all in a swit," Nick said caustically. "Come off it, Jeff. That aw-shucks, little-boy routine is pretty corny, don't you think?"

Jeff's expression did not change. Slowly and gently he moved away from Erin's touch and started to turn. It was the way he moved that warned her, smooth and controlled as a snake coiling before it struck. She caught at his arm.

"Jeff, don't. Nick, what are you trying to do, start trouble? Seems to me there's enough of it around here already."

The two men eyed one another challengingly. Nick was the first to back off, though he obviously hated doing it. "I was out of line," he mumbled. "Sorry. Can't imagine what got into me."

"Can't you?" Jeff's tight muscles relaxed; he even smiled faintly. "Think about it—buddy. I hate to tear myself away from one of you, but if you'll excuse me. . . . By some miracle there is no fund-raiser, speech, meeting, or conference scheduled for this evening, and I intend to make the most of what may be my last night off before the election. I am going home. If I can remember where it is."

He walked away, leaving Nick looking, and obviously feeling, foolish in the extreme. As soon as the door closed, Nick began, "Listen, Erin, I didn't mean—"

"Yes, you did! I've never been so disgusted in my life. How could you be so rude to Jeff?"

"Well, dammit, you didn't have to fall all over him!"

"I expressed my appreciation for his thoughtfulness and his trust. He spoke up for me. Unlike some people I could mention."

"Jesus Christ, how often do I have to tell you—"

"Oftener than you have. You stood there with your mouth hanging open, looking glum—"

"Glum! That was my introspective look. I was trying to figure out why Philips L. has gone to such lengths to get you in trouble. A flunky like you should be beneath his notice—"

Erin was so furious she couldn't speak. Instead she let out a wordless shriek that stopped Nick in midsentence and gave her time to catch her breath. "You've really outdone yourself, Nick McDermott! I never thought even you could get so many insults and nasty insinuations into a single speech. If you don't leave, I'll—I'll—"

"Oh, shit," Nick said gloomily. "I can't win. Go on, hit me. It'll make you feel better." He offered a tanned cheek.

"I wouldn't give you the satisfaction." Erin turned on her heel and stamped up the stairs.

Once in her room she flung herself on the bed and contemplated the iniquities of Nick while she pounded the pillow with both fists. She was still pounding when she heard some-one giggle, and realized, with astonishment, that the sound came from her own throat.

But it *was* funny. A tempest in a teapot, the result of strained nerves and Nick's unfortunate habit of moving his mouth without consulting his brain or his heart. He had them both, intelligence and compassion, and he had another talent, that of stirring people up. I enjoyed that, Erin thought dis-believingly. A good straight fight, the kind I've always shied away from.

You've come a long way, baby.

*   *

ERIN WAS LOOKING forward to an evening off too, though she had no idea what she wanted to do with it until she learned that her assumption has been erroneous. "I want to wash my hair," she bleated, as Joe handed her a thick report that had to be retyped. "And read and write to my mother and—"

"Life is tough all over, kid," said Joe.

Kay was more sympathetic than Erin had expected; the euphoria of her trip to Middleburg still lingered. "I'm sorry I can't help you, Erin. If I hadn't been so clumsy . . . I never imagined it would be as bad as this " She looked resentfully at her bandaged hand. "The fingers are healing nicely, but there's still something wrong with the thumb. You wouldn't think a little thing like a thumb could be so important."

"Ask any anthropologist," Joe said. He picked up his briefcase and stalked out.

"Goodness, he's in a bad mood," Kay muttered. "And Rosemary is even worse."

"I suppose this business about the leak has upset them."

"Oh, that." Kay shrugged. "None of us had anything to do with it, so they can't prove we did. Let's have a bite of supper and then get started on that report."

Supper was the usual buffet arrangement, with people wan-dering in and out as their schedules allowed. Kay allowed no lingering over coffee; they went straight to her office, and it was almost ten before she leaned back in her chair with a sigh and allowed as how she was getting too tired to think sensibly. "Just finish that last letter, Erin," she said. "Leave them and the report on Rosemary's desk. And turn off the lights when you leave."

"Yes, ma'am. Thank you, ma'am."

The sarcasm was lost on Kay. Just as well, Erin reflected guiltily, as she watched the older woman make her slow way to the door. Why should she resent Kay, when she had everything Kay wanted and was rapidly losing—youth, competence, a healthy body and a future limited only by what she could do with it?

With any luck she would still have time to wash her hair. Might as well dash off a note to her mother right now, while she was at the typewriter. She could claim, with perfect truth, that she was too busy to write a long, chatty letter. The cheerful remarks she had imagined herself writing—humorous stories about the funny things that happened during the political campaign—didn't seem appropriate. "Funny things" was right. Not the sort of funny things a depressed widow would find amusing.

She finished the last letter and the note. "Don't worry, Mom, I'm a little tired, but so is everyone else; and the job is fascinating. I had no idea . . ." Lucky her mother couldn't see her face as she fought her way out of one Freudian tangle after another. ". . . no idea how complicated politics is." Of all the stupid remarks! Doggedly she continued, "Everyone has been so kind to me . . ." Especially Philips Laurence. ". . . and I'm learning a lot." Such as how to return a bribe and avoid nosy reporters. She yanked the paper out of the machine and signed it. "Your loving daughter." Well, that was a simple statement of truth, at any rate.

Writing the string of evasions had exhausted her. She gathered up the report and the letters she had typed and went to Rosemary's office. The room was quite dark; shrubbery outside the windows obscured what little light came from moon and stars. She didn't realize someone else was there until she turned on the light and saw a form huddled forlornly in the window seat, half concealed by the long draperies.

Instantly and reflexively her hand reversed the switch, but

the image had burned itself onto her vision. Rosemary was wearing her favorite at-home costume of oversized shirt and faded jeans, and her feet were bare. Somehow the pale, dusty toes looked even more pathetic than the clear evidence of tears.

"It's all right. You can turn the light on." Rosemary's voice gave nothing away.

"I didn't know you were here."

"Why should you? I must have startled you as much as you startled me." A softer, kindlier light went on; Rosemary had reached out to turn on a standing lamp. "Kay shouldn't have kept you working so late."

Since the damage was done, Erin crossed to the desk and put the papers down. "I don't mind. I mean, she was working too. I mean . . . I'm on my way to bed right now."

She carefully avoided looking at Rosemary. "Sit down for a minute," the latter said quietly. " Unless you're too tired."

"Oh, no. But I don't want—"

"I know you don't. But I'd like to tell you why I'm blubbering here in the dark."

"You don't have to explain anything to me."

"You are the only person around here I don't have to explain myself to," Rosemary said with surprising vehemence. "Maybe that's why I'd like to. I get so tired of putting on an act—being cool and unruffled when I feel like screaming, pretending to be cheerful when I'm depressed, exhibiting a stiff upper lip when I want to cower in a corner. I have a feeling you know about that."

The words woke to aching life a nerve she had thought atrophied by now. She nodded mutely, remembering her mother's endless tears. She had wept for her husband's pain and for his loss; she had also wept for her loneliness and her fear of the future. There had been no room in that watery flood for Erin's grief.

Rosemary shifted position, edging forward so that the shadow of the draperies no longer hid her face. She was not one of those women who weep prettily (if any such really exist). Her nose was red, her eyes were swollen, and blotchy patches of pink marked her cheeks. "At least you had a noble cause for grief," she said, with a faint smile. "Do you know what I was bawling about? Today is my granddaughter's birthday. She's four. That's an important year, you know. She's a big girl now. That's what she said. It's the first birthday of hers I have missed. I always made it before, even if I had to fly out in the morning and back the same night.''

Erin's eyes went to the photograph on the desk. It had been reproduced in one of Rosemary's publicity flyers: a formal photographic sitting that had gone awry and, as a consequence, had produced a uniquely charming picture. The little girl, perched on her mother's lap, had turned at the last minute to say something to her grandmother, who was seated on the couch beside her. The child's smile, and Rosemary's delighted, doting grin intensified the resemblance between them to an uncanny degree; they had the same turned-up nose and wide mouth, the same dimple, the same determined chin. Rosemary's daughter was laughing, and the young man standing behind the couch leaned forward, arms spread as if to include the three generations of womenfolk in a warm embrace. Erin had never seen such an outpouring of love and affection captured on film. It was no wonder Joe had insisted on using the picture, over—Erin had heard—Rosemary's objections.

''She's adorable,'' Erin said. ''I don't blame you for feeling sad. Why didn't you just say the hell with it, and go?''

Rosemary drew her knees up and circled them with her arms. ''It wasn't only a question of time, though God knows we're short on that. I hate—'' She made a fist and brought it down on the padded cushion. ''I *hate* using my kids as political symbols. It degrades the whole relationship. Kevin, my son-in-law, is one of those rare people. . . . It really was a case of not losing a daughter but gaining a son. I love them all, all three, so much. . . . Can't you see the press releases Joe would have sent out, if I had decided to go? 'Lo-o-o-ove is more important than politics,' says adoring grandmother.''

''He wouldn't do that,'' Erin exclaimed.

''Like hell he wouldn't. He'd have me walk naked down Pennsylvania Avenue if he thought it was worth a dozen votes.'' A sudden spontaneous burst of laughter lit her face. ''Fortunately, he knows it would have precisely the opposite effect. Sheer aesthetic horror would send hundreds of voters emigrating to Canada. Joe is furious with me because I refuse to drag the kids to fund-raisers and bake sales. I don't want them involved. Especially since . . ." She broke off and frowned at her toes.

"Why don't you fire him?" Erin asked. "Or is that a stupid question?"

"Not only is it a damned good question, it's one I've asked myself over and over." Rosemary's frown deepened. "It wouldn't be the first time Joe has been booted out in the middle of a campaign. He's abrasive, outspoken, rude—and the best in the business. Don't tell him I said so—his ego is inflated enough already—but I was enormously pleased and flattered when he offered to work for me. And the very qualities that have cost him at least three jobs, and that drive me up the wall, are the qualities that make me value him. I need him all the more because everything else about what I'm doing is unreal. Sometimes I get the feeling that Rosemary Marshall exists only as a campaign poster and a series of platitudes mouthed over and over; that if you stripped the image away there wouldn't be anybody there."

"It sounds . . . awful." The word was weak and inadequate, but Erin couldn't think of a better one. "Is it worth it?"

"That's another question I keep asking myself. But I know the answer. Maybe." Rosemary laughed mirthlessly. "I could say I wouldn't put myself through this torture if I didn't believe it was worth it, but that wouldn't be strictly accurate. Sometimes people do things out of habit, without ever questioning their motives. 'Because it's there.' I believe I can do some good; but every psychopath in history has believed that, from Alexander to Joe McCarthy. Of course they were wrong and I'm right. . . ." Rosemary's chin rested on her raised knees. "Do you know what my favorite fantasy is?" she said dreamily. "I imagine myself running a real, honest, genuine campaign—the kind that never existed, at any time in history. I'd get up there to make a speech looking just the way I do now—baggy jeans, bulging hips, no makeup—and I'd tell it like it is. I'd tell the audience that Buzz Bennett is a slimy

old lecher who has cheated on his long-suffering wife for
forty years—and I'd go on to say that that doesn't matter as
much as the fact that Buzz would sell his vote for a champagne breakfast or a token to the local whorehouse. I'd talk
about the issues. I wouldn't try to win votes by equivocating
or lying or avoiding questions.

"I'd cry if I felt like crying. Candidates for public office
aren't allowed to shed tears in public, you know. Remember
what happened to Ed Muskie? No, I suppose you don't; you're
too young. But even Pat Schroeder's supporters criticized her
when she broke down after announcing she wouldn't run for
president.''

"President Reagan used to cry," Erin said.

"Oh, Reagan." Rosemary dismissed the President with a
flip of her hand. "He can get away with anything, I don't
know how he does it; it is the ultimate triumph of image over
reality. Or charisma—defined as 'I don't know what the hell
it is, but I wish I had it.' ''

"Some people think you do."

"I hope not. I'd prefer to think my appeal is to reason
rather than emotion. I'm kidding myself, of course. I have to
tailor every speech to my audience, avoid issues that might
offend. Joe doesn't want me to talk about women's issues.
Women's issues, for God's sake!''

She broke off, with a snort of rage; and Erin said, " 'We're
not a special-interest group! What's so special about our interest? We're your mothers, your sisters, your daughters, your
wives. We care for your children and ours; we tend your
aging parents and our own. We work in the factories and the
hospitals, in the farmyards and in the shops and in the schools.
We pay taxes. We don't pay as much as you do because we
don't earn as much, even at the same job; but in what ways
do our interests differ from yours? Don't all human beings
want the same things? Don't you want peace and freedom—
clean air to breathe and unpolluted water to drink? Do you
care less about your children's safety and happiness than we
do? Don't call us a special-interest group; and don't tell us
that if it weren't for us you'd still be wearing skins and wield-

ing clubs. Do you think so little of yourselves and so nar-
rowly of our abilities?' "

She couldn't remember the rest of it.

Rosemary lifted her head. "That's the speech I made in
support of the day-care bill."

"I know. I've been doing some reading." Erin added apol-
ogetically, "I didn't know much about politics when I came
here, so I thought I had better try to catch up."

"But you memorized it!"

"I didn't intend to. I guess it just sort of stuck in my
mind."

"I see." After a moment she swung her feet to the floor
and stood up. "Damn, I'm stiff as a board. Never curl up in
a corner to brood when you're over fifty, Erin. Oh, by the
way—Jeff let it slip that his birthday is next week. We're
going to have a surprise party—nothing fancy, just a cake and
some silly presents."

"That's nice," Erin said, smiling. Rosemary really seemed
to be looking forward to the event; her eyes sparkled and the
traces of tears were almost gone.

"Tell Nick, and warn him not to give it away." Rosemary
wandered over to the desk and glanced at the letters. "Funny
hats," she murmured, "and balloons. And those things—
what do you call them—that you blow into, and a paper strip
uncurls."

"And we all sing 'Happy Birthday.' "

"Of course. The rest of us will have to bellow, to drown
Joe's voice. He's tone-deaf and croaks like a frog."

"I'll do my best. Well—good night."

"Good night."

But as she turned toward the door Rosemary said, " Erin?"

"Yes?"

"You asked me a question a while ago: 'Is it worth it?' I
think you just answered that question. Yes, it is. Thank you."

The trained debater's voice dismissed her even as it left her
speechless with gratified embarrassment. When she turned to
close the door, Rosemary had seated herself at the desk and
was reading the letters, her head propped on her hand.

As she climbed the stairs, Erin's mind was a welter of

confused thoughts. That's what she meant, it must have been—you, the young, the future, you make it all worthwhile by your caring. What a cliché. . . . But she put it awfully well. Hard to resist that kind of flattery. . . . "She has a peculiar kind of charm," Laurence had said. "You haven't felt it yet—but you will."

Now she knew what he meant. Not charm, something stronger. More like magic.

Chapter
Seven

AFTER LISTENING to her mother endlessly bemoaning her poverty, Erin had believed no one could be more concerned with money, or the lack thereof. She had been mistaken. Money—and the lack thereof—was a constant source of anxiety to Rosemary's staff. There just wasn't enough.

Erin had read about the unending debate on campaign financing; she decided it was like the weather—everybody complained about it, but nobody did anything about it. A few people, including Rosemary, had tried, but bills limiting contributions, personal expenditures, and paid advertising had a strange habit of dying in committee or being emasculated by amendments.

Over $211 million spent on Senate races, almost $239 million on the House. Add the cost of presidential campaigns and state races, and the total became horrifying—and the implications even more so. The candidate with the most money didn't always win, but he had an edge that was difficult, if not impossible, to overcome.

Television was one of the reasons why the cost of a campaign had increased so astronomically. TV spots were the most effective method of reaching large numbers of voters. They were also one of the most expensive. (The United States was one of the few Western democratic nations to allow paid commercial political advertising; Rosemary's attempt to introduce a bill forbidding this pleasant and lucrative activity hadn't even made it to committee.) The cost of a single thirty-second spot on a local station in New York City was over $8,000. New York was the most expensive market in the country, but D.C. wasn't far behind; and since most of Virginia picked up the Washington stations, Joe had insisted they buy time on "Eyewitness News" and the others. They had saved the major effort for the final weeks of the campaign, and Rosemary had reluctantly agreed to hire a professional media firm to produce the spot. She remarked that she didn't know where the hell the money was going to come from; and Nick, trying to hide his resentment at being supplanted, said sourly that he didn't either.

"Listen, it's no criticism of you, Nick," Joe insisted. "You've done a great job. You just don't have the technical equipment—special effects, and all that jazz."

Nobody mentioned specific figures, but Erin's reading had given her some idea of the amounts involved. Fifty thousand up front, plus 15 percent of the buy (the total amount spent on radio and TV time). Or $75,000 clear. Both figures were real, from real campaigns, covering the cost of production only, not the cost of air time.

Joe had high hopes for a reception–fund-raiser that was to be given that weekend by one of Rosemary's supporters. One thousand a head was the asking price, as Joe crudely put it. He obviously hoped for more, and nobody was vulgar enough to ask how he planned to get around the laws limiting campaign contributions. There were ways. Even Erin knew that now.

The reception was being hosted by a Hollywood actress whose enthusiasm for liberal causes was as notorious as her habit of acquiring and discarding husbands. (When asked why she bothered to marry the gentlemen in question, whose tenure usually averaged less than a year, she replied that she was just an old-fashioned girl.) Her current spouse owned a beautiful mansion near Leesburg that was considered one of the showplaces of the old South, but the attraction was not so much the house and its collection of valuable antiques as the guest list, which glittered with big names from the show-biz world. Entertainment was to be provided by a famous concert pianist and the hottest new rock group, whose lead singer was one of the lady's exes.

It had never occurred to Erin that she would be asked to attend. She had taken a certain malicious pleasure in informing Fran of that fact, when her roommate called with the transparent hope of wangling an invitation, or, more accurately, a free ticket.

Fran wasn't convinced. "What do you mean, you aren't going? My God, you've got no more imagination than a goldfish. Can't you think of some way—"

"I could poison Kay," Erin said. "Was that what you had in mind? Sorry, Fran, that wouldn't do it. Anyway, I'm not interested in going."

"Now that," said Fran, "has to be a flat-out lie. Honest to God, Erin, I can't believe you. I know you aren't exactly the most forceful person in the world, but there you are, in a position where you could do yourself and your friends a lot of favors—"

"Friends like you?" Erin inquired softly.

"You wouldn't have had the nerve to write Rosemary if I hadn't pushed you."

There was too much truth in that for Erin to deny it, even if Fran had given her time to do so. "You owe me," Fran insisted. "I'd kill to go to that party. Get to work on it."

"No," Erin said.

"I have a couple of other ideas I want to discuss with you. Like, you could ask Rosemary . . . What did you say?"

"I said no. No party, no pressure, no whatever you were going to propose. I don't owe you a damn thing, Fran, especially if it means betraying the confidence Rosemary has in me. Such as it is."

"Why, Erin, I wouldn't do anything to hurt Rosemary, you

ought to know me better than that.'' Fran's voice changed. She knew when she had gone too far. ''I was only going to suggest . . .''

She went on and on. Erin finally hung up on her. She despised herself as much as she despised Fran; how could she have been such a spineless wimp as to let Fran push her around and put her down? Even more infuriating was the fact that Fran's eagerness had forced her to admit to herself that she had been lying when she said she didn't care about going.

Late Friday afternoon she left the office for a much-needed break. After pacing along the driveway to relax her stiff muscles, she sat down on the porch steps, where she was promptly submerged in cats. The beautiful fall weather held; a haze of warmth veiled the far-off hills, and sunlight freshened the colors of the massed chrysanthemums in the flower beds by the porch. They blazed gloriously—golden yellow, snowy white, all shades of russet and rust and cinnamon. Her fingers buried in the soft fur of the feline who had been first onto her lap, Erin was enjoying a complete absence of coherent thought when Nick came around the corner of the house.

He shifted a cat and sat down beside her. ''I thought you'd be upstairs primping. Don't Newman and Redford deserve your best?''

Erin stared. ''Who?''

The question was meaningless in itself; it led to an agitated (on Erin's part), amused (on Nick's) exchange of query and response, and finally Erin let herself be convinced that Rosemary really did expect her to attend the party.

''She told me to keep a fatherly eye on you,'' said Nick clinching the argument. ''Now don't tell me you don't have anything to wear, that's such a tired old cliché.''

''But I don't—nothing suitable. The only formal dress I brought with me is one I bought in a thrift shop because it was only five bucks. Every other woman there will be wearing gowns they bought from Neiman Marcus and Saks and Garfinckel's. . . . I'll bet none of them have even heard of Second Time Around!''

Nick dismissed this argument with a shrug. ''So what? You

don't have to go if you don't want to, but think what you'll be missing."

"Redford and Newman," Erin murmured.

"Not to mention me in tails."

"That might make it all worthwhile."

"Rented, I hardly need add." Nick stretched his legs out and leaned back, bracing himself on his elbows. "Our youth and beauty will overcome any minor disadvantages of previously owned attire. We'll make those tired, paunchy, dissipated millionaires look sick."

Two cats climbed onto his outstretched legs. Erin added the one she had been holding and retired, leaving him up to his navel in fur.

Rosemary was on the Hill and wasn't expected back till evening; when Erin located Kay, she put the question rather tentatively. Kay frowned.

"I hadn't heard anything about it. But if Nick says so, I expect he's right. I had hoped you would be able to help me with my hair. . . ."

"It looks lovely," Erin said. She had chauffeured Kay to the hairdresser earlier in the afternoon. "But of course I'll be glad to help any way I can."

"Thank you." Kay's voice was cool. "I have a few things to finish up here. Did you type those memos?"

Chastened, Erin went to her desk. Obviously Kay didn't approve of her going. So what? she thought defiantly, echoing Nick. She worked steadily until Kay came out of her office and summoned her with a curt "Leave the rest of them."

If she hadn't known she was being unfair, Erin would have suspected that Kay deliberately prolonged the process of dressing in order to shorten the time Erin could spend on herself. Kay tried on three different dresses before settling on the one Erin knew she had bought especially for the occasion.

It was not until she asked whether she should offer her assistance to Rosemary that she got an inkling of the real cause for Kay's ill humor. "She doesn't need either of us," Kay said with a short laugh. "She's got Raymond."

She pronounced it in the French fashion, with the accent on the last syllable and an exaggerated, drawn-out vowel.

Seeing Erin's blank look, she explained, ''He's a hairdresser and makeup 'artiste,' as he calls himself. *The* hairdresser; does the Vice President's wife, and all the other la-di-da types. Silly business, if you ask me, but Joe said this was an important occasion and only the best was good enough. Personally I can't stand the man; silly, affected creature. . . . There's Hoboken or Brooklyn under that fake French accent of his, or I miss my guess.''

''I suppose this is a special occasion,'' Erin said.

Kay sniffed. ''I think Rosemary will just end up looking ridiculous. Her own natural style is good enough for anybody.''

Another prolonged period of fussing and indecision over jewelry, shoes, an evening wrap followed, before Kay finally dismissed Erin and suggested that she had better make haste or they would have to go without her.

The fear of being late made Erin clumsier than usual, and her hair seemed to have acquired an agitated life of its own; it clung crackling to her fingers and fought every attempt to confine it in a roll or a chignon. The dress, a simple sheath of black lace over a slim underslip, could have done with a quick pressing, but Erin was afraid to take the time to look for an iron. The long tight sleeves were modest enough, but she tugged anxiously at the low-cut neckline, wondering if she was showing too much skin. She was putting on earrings, long dangles of jet and crystal, when she heard Kay's door open; with a last despairing look in the mirror she stepped into her black pumps, snatched up her knit stole and black evening bag, and bolted.

Kay didn't turn, though she must have heard Erin behind her on the stairs. Kay reached the landing and turned toward Rosemary's room just as the door of the room opened and a man came out. It could only be Raymond himself—tall and impossibly thin, a neat black short-cropped beard enlarging a jawline that without its aid would have jutted not at all. His vaguely vacuous expression hardened when he caught sight of Kay. He stopped short with a theatrical start. The two acolytes who had followed him out of the room pulled up short and stood quivering as they juggled the boxes and bags that presumably contained Raymond's tools. It would have been funny if the two girls had not been so visibly terrified, and if Raymond's faint smile had succeeded in concealing his dislike of the woman who passed him with only a brusque nod in response to his *"Bon soir, madame."*

Raymond glared at Kay's back and stuck out a long red tongue. Turning, he saw Erin, who had been watching in fascination. His distorted features relaxed and he swept down on her, cooing. "Ah, *la pauvre petite belle!* Do you attend upon the dragon? She is beyond help; even I, Raymond, can do little for her; but you, *si belle, si charmante. . . ."*

His hand swooped out, gathered Erin's loose hair and gave it a painful twist. She was too startled to protest, nor could she move without hurting herself.

Raymond snapped his fingers. One of the girls rushed to him, the bag she carried already open, her hand fumbling inside. Like a surgeon awaiting the service of an operating-room nurse, Raymond accepted the hairpins the girl slapped into his open palm, and in a few daring movements had fixed the twisted coil to Erin's head.

The girls broke into a soprano duet of admiration. Raymond smiled complacently. *"Oui, oui, c'est admirable.* I could do more, *vous comprenez,* had I the time. For you, *ma chérie,* there is no charge."

He passed on, trailed by his entourage. Erin raised a careful hand to her aching head. The pins felt as if they had been stabbed directly into her skull, but she was afraid to loosen them for fear Raymond would turn and see the sacrilege.

Rosemary emerged from her room. "Has he gone?" she asked in a stage whisper.

Erin nodded dumbly.

"He's a dreadful little man," Rosemary said. "But Joe insisted. . . . My dear, how pretty you look. I like your hair that way." Something in Erin's petrified look betrayed the truth. She began to laugh. "Don't tell me. Did Raymond . . ."

"In about thirty seconds," Erin said. "Snap, snap, swoop, pounce. . . . I'm afraid to move. Does it look awful?"

Rosemary was whooping with laughter. "If you could see your face. . . . It looks divine, *ma chérie.* Oh, dear, I mustn't laugh or my makeup will run. Every damned grain of mascara cost—''

"Here." Kay, who had followed her, produced a lace-trimmed handkerchief. She wasn't laughing. "Wipe your eyes, Rosemary. Personally, I can't see what's so funny."

"You didn't see Erin's face." Rosemary accepted the handkerchief and dabbed carefully at her eyes. "Admit it, Kay, she looks adorable, with her hair that way. Raymond may be a pompous poseur, but he knows his stuff. That's one of his favorite tricks, Erin—leaping on some unsuspecting female and transforming her with a single twist of the wrist."

"Hmph," Kay said.

"He did a wonderful job with you," Erin said.

The white streaks in Rosemary's hair lifted like wings, their contrast to the surrounding darkness subtly enhanced and shining. Upon closer examination Erin realized they really did shine; tiny flecks of glitter sparkled with the slightest movement. Bouffant puffs of black chiffon framed Rosemary's shoulders and throat; the dress itself was dramatically simple, a straight fall of satin that followed the curves of waist and hips before flaring to the floor.

"You ain't seen nothing yet," said Rosemary. With a snap of her wrist she unfurled a huge ostrich-feather fan whose soft rosy-pink color matched her lipstick. "Ta dah!"

Kay sighed loudly. "Rosemary—"

"Oh, don't be such an old poop, Kay," Rosemary said. "I look sensational and you know it. I don't look like me, but I look sensational. My face feels like a plaster mask and my girdle is killing me; if I can stand it for a few hours, you can stand looking at me."

Flapping the fan vigorously, she marched forward. "Let's do a Raymond. Fall in, please, ladies."

Kay's expression softened as her eyes followed the parading little figure. "You do look lovely," she called out; turning to Erin she added, "But I like Rosemary better the way she usually looks. This is so—so artificial."

Erin was inclined to agree; but she wondered whether Kay was referring to Rosemary au naturel, in ragged sneakers and flapping shirt, or the smooth, smiling candidate. The latter image was, in its own way, just as artificial.

Joe was waiting for them downstairs. Circling Rosemary, who posed with the fan held behind her head and her hips seductively tilted, he grunted approval. "Good. Just control yourself, and don't get cute. Where's your coat?"

"The mink is in storage," Rosemary purred. "The sable needed glazing—"

Joe slapped her on the rump. "Cool it, I said. No horsing around tonight, okay?"

"You're no fun," Rosemary said sulkily. She rubbed her hip. "That hurt."

"It'll hurt a lot more if you sound off to a contributor. Where the hell is Jeff? We should have left five minutes ago."

"I'll see if he's in the commons room," Erin offered. She didn't really care where Jeff was, or whether they were late. What she wanted was a mirror. She had a desperate, almost compulsive need to see what Raymond had done to her hair before she appeared in public.

She hadn't expected to find anyone in the room. She started and gasped when she heard the rustle of paper, like a mouse scuttling for safety. Then Will's face appeared over the barricade of his heaped desk. He adjusted his glasses, studied her thoughtfully, and then remarked, " 'Oh, she doth make the candles to burn bright.' Or, as Joe might say, you look sharp, kiddo."

"Thanks, Will, I was just . . ." A glance into the mirror over the fireplace told her the compliment was not misplaced. She couldn't see the back of her head, turn and twist as she might, but the general effect was chic as well as becoming.

Watching her pirouette, Will chuckled. "Take my word for it, or you'll have a stiff neck in the morning. Are they ready to leave?"

"I guess so. Aren't you going?"

Will glanced down at his wrinkled shirt and rolled-up sleeves. "Like this? I'm a research analyst, my dear, not a gigolo. Give this to Rosemary, will you?" He held out a sheaf of papers.

"You really should go and wish her good luck. She looks marvelous."

Will considered the suggestion, head tilted and lips pursed. "No doubt that would be the proper thing to do. Not that I necessarily endorse all forms of meaningless social courtesy, when they interfere with—"

Joe's roar sounded as if he were in the room with them. "Jeff! Son of a bitch, where have you been? Goddamn it all, now Erin's disappeared!"

Will grinned and rose to his feet. "I'll accompany you, if only to provide a buffer. I don't know what Joe's complaining about, there's plenty of time."

"I guess this is a big deal," Erin said, following him to the door. "Everybody seems high-strung tonight."

"Not me," Will said, throwing the door open and bowing her through. "Sometimes I think my massive, unconquerable calm is the only thing that keeps this covey of lunatics from . . . Yes, Joe, I mean you. Lunatic in chief."

Joe glowered at him. "Aren't you going?"

"Obviously not," Will said in a resigned voice.

"Oh. Well, did you finish that research I asked for?"

"Of course." Will handed him the papers. "I can't understand why you wanted it, but here it is. Much more important is the other data, summing up Bennett's contributions from various PACs and interest groups and equating them with his votes during the past six years."

"You carry scholarly detachment to the point of stupidity," Joe grunted, shuffling through the papers. "These people don't give a damn about Bennett's voting record, they want to see charm, glamour, and glibness. Oh—here it is. Rosie, we'll go over it in the car. Your hostess's foibles, hobbies, weaknesses. Things to talk about, things not to talk about. Don't mention anybody named Oscar, she never got one. She's becoming a little sensitive about husbands and divorce. Collects Meissen, antique dolls, stuffed teddy bears. . . ."

Rosemary took the sheet of paper from him. Her eyes were fixed on Will, who was studying her thoughtfully, arms folded, forehead corrugated. "Well, Will?"

"It's all there," Will said abstractedly. "Frivolous nonsense, in my opinion, but Joe wanted—"

"That isn't what I meant," said Rosemary, her voice dangerously quiet.

"Ah." Will nodded. "It is conventional, I believe, to reassure an individual—I would say a woman, but then I would be accused of rampant sexism—who is about to make a public appearance that his or her physical appearance meets some undefined and abstract definition of acceptability. Indeed, by the conventions of the society in which you are about to plunge, I feel certain you pass the test."

Rosemary stamped her foot. "Will, you are really a number-one pain in the—"

"Rosemary!" Kay exclaimed.

"You look lovely," Will said hastily.

"Too late." Rosemary furled her fan and tapped him rather emphatically on the nose. "Take that, you cad. Have a wonderful time with your facts and figures while we swill down champagne and devour imported caviar and mingle with movers and shakers. We'll bring you a doggy bag. Well, Joe, weren't you the one who was yelling about being late?"

She sauntered toward the door, swinging her hips and humming. " 'Oh, what a time I had with Minnie the Moocher—' "

"Cut that out," Joe shouted, following her.

The screen door slammed. As if on cue, Nick appeared from the shadows under the stairs, where he had been lurking. Erin and Will inspected him in silence. His hand went nervously to his white tie.

"Struck dumb with admiration?" he suggested hopefully.

"You look gorgeous." Erin advanced on him. "Except for that waving lock that has fallen across your alabaster brow—"

"Leave my lock alone, it's part of the effect. How's the suit fit?"

Men, Erin thought with amusement. They were much vainer than women. . . . No, that was sexist. Just as vain. She offered further compliments and reassurances, demurely received Nick's in exchange, and then said, "I take it I'm going with you."

"Oh, right." Nick fished a set of keys from his pocket. "And in style. We get the Olds; Jeff is driving Kay's car."

"Ho, ho," said Will without humor. "What's that going to do to the image, having Jeff play chauffeur?"

"Couldn't be helped," said Nick. "Kay refused to let Joe get behind the wheel of her precious. My name wasn't even mentioned."

"Run along then," Will said. "Have fun and drive carefully."

"And have her home by midnight," Nick chanted. "By the way, Will, you scored a real zip on that last one. Haven't you learned anything about women from me?"

"Have her home by midnight," Will said.

"Yes, Pop."

But after they had left the house they heard Will's voice again. "Nick."

"What?"

Light was fading and the hall behind Will was dark. They could see him only dimly, his form blurred to ghostly indefinition by the screen.

"Tell Rosemary not to bother with the doggy bag. I have to go back to Charlottesville tonight."

"Okay."

"Nick?"

"Yes, what?" Nick demanded impatiently.

"Watch out for her. Rosemary. She's in an odd mood tonight. Fey."

The indistinct shape faded from sight.

Nick drove smoothly and competently, if a little faster than the growing darkness and narrow road made expedient. "Damn Will," he grumbled. "I planned to pull off the road and spend a few minutes nibbling on your ear. You look delicious. And, of course, outstandingly intelligent, competent and well informed."

Erin was too excited to be critical.

"Dislodge one lock of this fancy hairdo and I'll run a

bobby pin into you," she said amiably. "Why do you suppose Will was worried about Rosemary?"

"She was in a giddy mood," Nick said thoughtfully. "But that's not unusual; she hates formal affairs like this one, and often lets off some steam beforehand. Nothing to worry about, she's too much of a pro to ham it up in public."

"That word he used . . ."

"Fey?"

"Yes."

"Showing off his vocabulary," Nick said, amusement coloring his voice. "It just means excited, wild."

"Now who's showing off?" Erin demanded. "I know what it means, and it means more than just excited. 'Doomed' was the original meaning. Disturbed by a premonition of approaching death."

"Oh, shit!" The car swerved. "You're a nice cheerful date, I must say. If you can't think of anything nice to say to people, keep quiet."

Nick was graciously pleased to accept Erin's apology, and for the rest of the drive they talked about less ominous subjects: Nick's frustration in not being able to rent a gibus—one of the folding top hats, which he had always yearned to play with—and the foibles of their hostess. Joe was one hundred percent right about the importance of that issue, Nick said, adding the sweeping and probably unfair generalization that people in show business were paranoid, unduly sensitive, and arrogant. "Especially this female. Her IQ and her bust measurement are roughly the same. The latest kick is the collection of dolls, so be sure you admire them if she shows them off, which she probably will, because her interest is not so much in the objects themselves as the hope that other people will desire them and envy her for possessing them."

"I'd rather see her jewels. Like that diamond necklace that's supposed to have belonged to Marie Antoinette, and the Chavez emerald."

"My dear, naive creature, you'll be lucky if she says anything other than 'Good evening, dahling,' to you. Neither of us is important enough to rate her attention."

Darkness was complete by the time they reached their des-

tination and when Nick turned into the driveway Erin let out
a low whistle. "This is more like it," she said appreciatively.

The tall wrought-iron gates were closed and the security
guard checked not only the engraved invitation, but Nick's
driver's license before crossing their names off a list and waving them through. The house was lit like a stage set; every
window glowed, and strategically placed spots and lanterns
made the scene bright as day. The theatrical effect was heightened by the architecture itself—Twelve Oaks in all its pillared
purity and pride of place. "Ah 'spect Miz Melly's waitin' for
us down by the barbecue pit," Erin murmured. Nick chortled
appreciatively. "Wait'll you see our hostess. Miz Scarlett
thirty years later."

Nick had caught up with the Mercedes a few miles back,
it was directly ahead of them as they proceeded at a decorous
pace along the drive. Uniformed attendants pounced as soon
as they stopped moving; Nick handed over the car keys and
took Erin's arm. She was disgusted to discover that her palms
were wet with nervous excitement, and she clung to Nick as
they climbed the stairs. The dress was a little too long and
she had not had time to shorten it.

Kay and Jeff preceded them; Rosemary, disdaining Joe's
arm—if indeed he had thought to offer it—seemed to be managing both skirts and fan with practiced grace. As she reached
the top of the stairs the door opened; without breaking step
she swept into the house, and Erin heard a shriek of feminine
delight. "Rosemary, dahling! You look absolutely divine!"

Rosemary's reply was almost as shrill. "Dahling! So divine of you to do this. . . ."

Nick gave a strangled gasp of laughter, and Erin found that
she was suddenly no longer nervous. "Stop it," she hissed,
pinching his quivering arm.

If she hadn't known better, she would have supposed the
front door opened directly into the living room. The vestibule
was twice the size of a normal parlor and looked like the
entrance to a museum. The only color breaking the icy whiteness of marble floors and walls were the enormous bouquets
in niches at either side of the door. A cut-glass chandelier
and wall sconces of crystal and silver bleached the whiteness

to a purity that dazzled the eyes. She handed her humble stole
to a maid, and watched Nick's chagrin at having nothing to
give up—alas for the gibus—and then turned toward the open
double doors beyond. Rosemary was passing through the entrance affectionately intertwined with another woman whose
arm was around her waist. Erin assumed the figure in the
clinging beaded silver gown was her hostess; she had thought
that Juliet MacArthur was a brunette, but this woman's hair
was scarlet. Not red, as in Titian-haired, but scarlet, as in
Little Red Riding Hood's cloak.

The drawing room appeared to be approximately the size
of the Hall of Mirrors at Versailles, and it was only one of
the apartments open to the guests, who spilled out into the
corridors and onto the terrace. The greedier ones clustered
in the room where an ostentatious buffet had been spread
along a twenty-foot stretch of damask. Nick had to identify
some of the opulent dishes for Erin, and a few baffled even
him. "Too small for grouse, too boneless for quail. . . . Lark?
Nightingale?" The finishing touch, which sent Erin into a fit
of reprehensible giggles, was an ice-sculpture centerpiece
featuring the ship (of state, one surmised), a covey or bevy
of eagles, and a bust of Rosemary. It had begun to melt;
water dripped off the eagles' beaks and Rosemary's nose.

There were a lot of people. Erin started counting, but gave
it up when she realized she was enumerating as Joe might
have done: "One thousand, two thousand . . ." Were spouses
included in the price, she wondered? There were a number
of non-paying guests, of course; people like herself and Nick,
a few journalists, and the performers. The pianist had been
isolated in a small (twenty feet by thirty) room. Erin hoped
he was taking advantage of the opportunity to get in some
practice, since nobody stayed to listen to him. The rock
group, on the terrace, was doing better. A few people gyrated
in approximate time to the music.

At first she was too dazzled by the glitter and the noise,
by fabulous gowns and glamorous surroundings, to take much
notice of details, but as the evening went on the novelty wore
off and she began to view the proceedings with an increasingly cynical eye. Nick stayed close by her side; she appre-

ciated his courtesy, but sensed that he was as ill at ease as she, out of his element and not caring much for the new one. It wasn't until their hostess sidled up to them that she realized Nick had been seriously in error about one thing. Juliet didn't consider *him* unworthy of her attention.

"Rosemary says you're her media adviser," she said. "Isn't that just wonderful."

"Uh—yes, it is," said Nick. "And this is Ms.—"

"Lovely you could come," murmured the actress, her eyes considering and dismissing Erin in a single glance. "Why don't you come and tell me all about your job, Mr.— Oh, I just can't remember all those names; you don't mind if I call you Nick, do you?"

She drew him away. Erin turned for consolation to the caviar, but it wasn't long before Nick returned, perspiring visibly.

"That was a very succinct lecture," Erin remarked, viewing his distress with mean satisfaction.

"I was rescued by the president of GM or the managing director of Amalgamated Chemicals or some such notable." Nick mopped his bow. "Geez. She had just invited me to come look at her dollhouses."

"Is that what she calls them?"

Nick grinned. "I don't know what she calls them, but I've already had a good look."

Before long they were joined by Jeff, looking superb in a tuxedo that fit much better than Nick's rented white tie and tails. He carried a glass of champagne in either hand. Presenting one to Erin, he remarked in a low voice whose sarcasm contrasted with his fixed, pleasant smile, "Might as well drink up. Unfortunately this seems to be a very successful affair; we won't get out of here for at least another hour."

"Aren't you having *fun*?" Nick inquired.

"I endure. Anyhow, we look damned effective together, don't you think? Not only because we're young and beautiful, but as a token of Rosemary's campaign. A black, a woman, and your good old standard Anglo-Saxon male Protestant."

"Too bad I'm not gay," Nick said cheerfully.

"Too bad *I'm* not. It's so economical to double up on your token representation."

Nick refused to take offense. "You're in a cruddy mood, even for you. Has anything gone wrong?"

"Quite the reverse." Jeff drained his glass. Erin realized he had had a little too much to drink; it didn't show in his voice or his manner, only in a careful consciousness of incapacity. "Quite a successful affair."

"Don't run off," Nick said. "You're such a delightful companion this evening."

"Up yours too, pal." Jeff glanced at Erin. "Sorry, Erin. This sort of thing"—his gesture took in the ostentatious house, the rich food, the overdressed, overfed people—"gets my l'il ole liberal hackles up."

"*À la lanterne,*" Erin suggested, smiling up into his face.

"*À bas les aristos,*" Jeff agreed. "I'd better get back to work. Hang in there."

He walked off, steps steady, shoulders straight. "Maybe we should circulate more," Erin suggested.

"Not much we can do," Nick said. "Unless you want to let a rich industrialist pinch your bottom and offer you wealth undreamed of, which you will of course contribute to the Cause."

"From the way some of these aging females are drooling at you, you're more likely to collect than I am," Erin retorted. "Not to mention a few of the . . . Oh. Oh, Lord!"

"What's the matter?"

"When did he get here?"

"Who?" But it didn't take Nick long to locate the source of Erin's perturbation. He was several inches taller than the people around him, and he was staring straight at Erin. His narrow lips twisted when he realized she had seen him, and he raised his glass in a mock salute.

"Laurence," Nick muttered.

"He's coming over here." Erin clutched Nick's arm. "Don't leave me."

"Fear not, timid beauty, I will defend you to the death. Against what, if you don't mind my asking?"

"He must have gotten the sweater."

"So? Don't let him put you on the defensive; he's the one in the wrong, not you."

Laurence took his time approaching them, stopping to address smiles and greetings to various people. A casual observer might not have known Erin was his goal until he stood before her.

"What a nice little frock. A sweater wouldn't have been appropriate anyway, would it?"

The bland insolence of his voice brought a rush of anger that destroyed the last vestige of Erin's nervousness. "I don't take bribes," she said bluntly.

The columnist's eyes narrowed. "I should have known you'd misunderstand. You're a novice at this game and I fear your friends aren't much more experienced than you."

This was obviously directed at Nick, who resented it as fiercely as Laurence had known he would; his face darkened, but before he could retort, Laurence went on smoothly, "Contrary to what you may have heard about me, I have a generous heart. I like giving presents to deserving inferiors. If I had been trying to bribe you, dear girl, I'd have sent diamonds, not knitwear. Keep in mind; I won't charge you for the advice. And do try not to lose your sense of proportion. Ask yourself the essential question before you leap to conclusions. Have you anything I'd be willing to pay for?"

He started to turn away, but Erin was too angry to let him have the last word. "And you might ask yourself, Mr. Laurence, whether you have anything that could possibly interest any normal decent person. I wouldn't grab a rope you threw me if I were going down for the third time."

The color rushed to Laurence's face, and then drained away, leaving him as white as his stiff shirtfront. He turned on his heel and walked away.

Impulsively Erin started to follow. Nick wrapped a long arm around her waist and held her back.

"Let me go," she snarled. "I wasn't finished. That cowardly bastard hasn't even got the guts to stand and take it. I'm going to tell him—"

"Please don't," Nick said in an oddly muffled voice. "I couldn't stand it. Will you marry me?"

"What?" She stared at him and realized he was shaking all over with laughter he could barely contain.

"That was the most beautiful thing I've ever seen in my life," Nick stuttered. "And to think the first time I met you you were too prim and proper to take off your jacket. . . . You don't have to marry me if you don't want to, just let me adore you from afar."

"I'll add your application to the others," Erin said. It was a rare and unexpected pleasure to have Nick cool her temper instead of inflame it.

"Forget him," Nick said, sobering. "He isn't worth your trouble. Where's Rosemary got to, do you suppose?"

"I haven't seen her for quite a while. There's Joe, looking like a thundercloud."

"More like a tornado," Nick said. "I hope nothing has gone wrong. I'd better talk to him."

Joe stood alone; his dour expression would have frightened off anyone bent on casual conversation. The evening had taken its toll on him and his attire. His high forehead glistened with perspiration and a stain on his shirtfront had been dimmed, but not obliterated, by hasty first aid. The offending splash appeared to have had a tomato base.

He acknowledged their presence with a deeper scowl and a muttered word that might have been a greeting. "What's up?" Nick asked. "If we're not collecting, we may as well go home."

The attempt at wit was not well received. "We're collecting. No thanks to you two; every time I see you, you're stuck together like Siamese twins. Why aren't you mingling?"

"Rosemary is the star," Nick said. "We are only faint spots of light in the firmament, undetectable except by a high-powered telescope."

"Rosemary!" Joe gritted his teeth. "I knew she was in a weird mood, but she's so damned bullheaded, nobody can stop her when she. . . . Look at her. Just look at her making an ass of herself!"

Rosemary's petite size and the fact that she was always surrounded by people made her hard to locate. Following Joe's gesture, Erin recognized . . . the fan. Opened to its full size, it covered the lower half of Rosemary's face. Her eyes were fixed on the man who leaned toward her, talking and smiling so emphatically his jowls quivered. The light reflected dazzlingly from the silver streaks in Rosemary's hair and the hairless dome of her admirer's head.

"Look at her," Joe repeated. "Smirking and flirting and coming on to that lascivious old—"

"Lascivious!" Nick laughed. "A four-syllable word, no less. Who is he?"

The name Joe mentioned meant nothing to Erin, but it impressed Nick. "One of the *Fortune* Five Hundred," he murmured. "What's the problem, Joe? That's what she's here for, isn't it—to charm the cash out of those bulging pockets?"

"She's hamming it up. Making fun of him."

"He's too dumb and too horny to catch on," Nick said, his smile broadening as he watched One of the *Fortune* Five Hundred trying to look over the fan and down the front of Rosemary's dress.

"That's what I'm afraid of," said Joe, and departed without further comment.

He detached Rosemary from her admirer with brusque efficiency; leaving the hopeful one gaping. Rosemary didn't appreciate his interference. Her smile never wavered, but the purportedly playful tap of her fan on Joe's cheek produced a wince clearly visible to the fascinated observers across the room. They exchanged glances.

"Warm in here, isn't it?" Nick said.

"That looked like jealousy," Erin exclaimed. "Pure, naked jealousy. Do you think Joe—"

"Please don't say it," Nick begged. "I can't stand it."

"Why shouldn't he be in love with her? Isn't she entitled to some personal happiness? She needs someone who cares for her as a woman, not a political robot—"

"The last thing she needs is a campaign manager who's so besotted he can't think straight."

"Politics and love don't mix?"

"Well, I wouldn't necessarily insist on that. . . . How about a little more champagne?"

"I've had enough. I'm saying stupid things." Erin dabbed

delicately at her upper lip with the handkerchief Kay had insisted on giving her.

"A breath of fresh air, perhaps?" Nick suggested. "You won't need your scarf; the terrace is heated."

"The terrace is what?"

"Electric coils under the flagstones. I read about it in some magazine."

They threaded their way through the crowd, which seemed to have increased. The celebrities, including Rosemary, were surrounded; a flourish of the fan betrayed her presence and suggested Joe's lecture hadn't had much effect. Erin caught a glimpse of Jeff in deep discussion with a tall slender female swathed in emerald-green taffeta—the Style editor of the *Post*, according to Nick.

Electric coils notwithstanding, the terrace was cooler than the drawing room, and the fresh breeze felt good on Erin's feverish cheeks. People were seated at the tables scattered along the expanse of flagstones. A woman who had been pointed out to Erin as the wife of an influential Democratic senator looked deep into the eyes of a man who was not the influential senator; at another table a group of men had their heads together in a discussion whose intensity appeared to be financial rather than romantic. It was a good place for a private conversation. The musicians were making such a din that Nick had to yell in order to be heard.

"Let's get out of this!"

A glare of blue-white light drew them along a winding path that ended in another flagstoned terrace fronting the swimming pool. It was enormous, heart-shaped, and of course heated. Erin was not surprised at any of these features; what did surprise her was the extremely artificial and pricey scent that permeated the air. Juliet must have dumped a couple of gallons of Musky Lust into the water.

Farther along the terrace a rumba band, ruffled from wrists to waists, performed while laughing couples made rough stabs at the intricate steps. There were murals along the sides and bottom of the pool; dolphins, mermaids, Father Neptune complete with beard and trident, and other interesting accoutrements. Erin gasped. "That man—there—he hasn't got on any—"

"Neither does she," said Nick, indicating the second of the two intertwined bodies. Slowly, hieratically, the writhing forms sank toward the bottom of the pool.

"They'll drown!"

"No such luck," Nick said. "How about a refreshing dip?"

"No such luck."

"My dear young woman, I was not proposing anything improper. I'm sure those engaging little cabanas are fully equipped with bathing attire in every possible size and shape."

Erin supposed the structures in question were cabanas. What they looked like was a row of ancient Roman houses, with terra-cotta facades and red-tiled roofs. She stared at them incredulously.

"She had them copied from the ruins of Ostia," Nick said. "But I understand the murals on the inside walls are from Pompeii. You know the ones I mean."

"Oh, those murals. I've heard about them." In fact she had seen a set of purportedly bootlegged postcards. Italian guides made a big deal of showing the paintings of Pompeii's whorehouse only to men, but it was said that a bribe—even a modest bribe—would remove their moral principles.

"Heard about them? If you haven't seen them—"

"No." Erin resisted his attempt to draw her toward the restored ruins. "God, this is disgusting. It's not that I object to orgies per se, but a political fund-raiser. . . . And for Rosemary!"

"It's not that I object to orgies or to any means of raising dough; I just hate tacky orgies," Nick said laughing. "Let's take a turn in the garden. 'Where every prospect pleases, And only man is vile.' "

The gardens of Magnolia Hill were famous, tended lovingly for generations. The lighting, it was safe to assume, had been added by Juliet. But even the garish spots and clusters of colored lanterns could not destroy the classic elegance of the landscaping. The waxy white magnolia blossoms were

long since gone, but the glossy leaves glimmered with a more
austere beauty; azaleas and rhododendrons formed masses of
soft foliage; and the fall flowers put on a brave show. There
were shadowy alcoves along the winding, carefully mani-
cured paths. As they moved farther from the house the music
faded, allowing them to hear softer sounds—rustles and muted
laughter and heavy breathing. They had to go some distance
before they found a bench that was unoccupied, probably
because it was brightly illumined by overhanging lanterns.

The garden it faced had been laid out in formal French
style, with angular strips of low plantings outlining squares
and circles of earth. A few roses still struggled to bloom; the
circular pool in the center of the bed was as still as a dark
mirror.

The lanterns were red, yellow, and blue—bright red, yellow, and blue. They turned Nick's face into a bizarre patch-
work of color. Erin knew hers must look just as odd, but
Nick didn't seem to notice. "Are you cold?" he asked softly.
She shook her head, but Nick took off his jacket and draped
it around her shoulders. She leaned against the warmth of his
arm and shoulder; when his other hand touched her cheek
and turned her face toward his she protested.

"We're absolutely spotlighted, Nick. Anyone can see—"

"So what?"

The distant beat of the music was drowned out by the rush
of blood in her veins as his lips found hers, gently at first,
then with growing insistence. Her arms went around him,
hands moving slowly across the hard muscles of his back
until they found a resting place, and she felt his response in
the pressure of his mouth and the rhythm of his pulse.

She had forgotten about the lanterns overhead and the possibility of being observed. It was Nick who ended the kiss
with a final soft touch on her parted lips. He guided her head
into the curve of his shoulder and rested his cheek against
her hair.

It was all very sweet and harmless and romantic, and Nick's
kisses aroused her in a way she had never experienced, not
with such intensity. There was no reason why she should have
felt a gradual, rising unease. It might have been the soft

sounds in the trees behind them: sounds that could have been wind, or night animals . . . or something else. The sensation was as difficult to define as it was increasingly peremptory. Erin stirred, and Nick's arms tightened.

"No," she said reluctantly. "Let's go back, it must be late."

"Not that late." His fingers curled around her cheek and turned her face toward his. The warmth of his breath brushed her mouth.

"No, don't. Nick, please."

"What's the matter?"

"Your forehead is blue."

Nick chuckled softly. "Yours is red. It looks wonderful. You look wonderful. You taste wonderful—like strawberries, and roses, and—"

"Nick." She knew now what the trouble was. "Somebody is watching us. I can feel them—eyes, staring, leering. . . ."

"Oh, for God's sake!" Nick let her go so abruptly that she swayed backward. He jumped to his feet. "If you don't want me to kiss you, just say so. You don't have to invent horror stories to turn me off."

He loomed over her, arms crossed, face set in a scowl. Erin scowled back. "One of these days, Nick McDermott, you are going to believe me when I tell you something. It will probably be the same day hell freezes over. Until then . . ."

"I get it. Sure, I get it! I don't need a brick wall to fall on me!" Nick raised his arms in an appeal to the starry heavens. "Women!" he told them.

"Men!" Erin shouted after his retreating form. There was no reply.

As soon as he was out of sight, the discomfort she had forgotten in her anger fell on her with the force of an avalanche. She started up and turned, scanning the clustered shadows. There was no sign of life or of movement, but she knew IT was still there, watching and waiting. She said weakly, "Nick?"

No answer. He really had gone, gone and left her alone in this place of murky shadows and lurid lights. . . . At that moment the lights flickered and went out.

Erin picked up her skirts and ran. Never mind common sense, never mind dignity; the fear that gripped her was primitive and primeval, as reasonless as it was compelling. She wasn't even surprised when something long and dark snaked out of a shrub alongside the path and wrapped around her throat.

The hand that clamped over her mouth as she was dragged into the shrubbery was a little slow. She got out one shrill cry before her breath was cut off, not only by the fingers squeezing her face but by the arm pressed against her throat. She kicked and squirmed and tried to bite. When the deadly grip suddenly released her she thought for a moment that her struggles had succeeded. Then she heard him.

"Erin? Where the hell are you? Erin, answer me. . . . Oh, damn!"

He had fallen over her feet, which were stretched across the path.

The ensuing interval was a wild fumbling in the dark that ended with both of them kneeling, their arms around one another. Nick's conversation consisted solely of profanity and self-recrimination. "I never should have gone off like that . . . damn it, damn it, oh, shit, are you all right? Oh, damn it to hell!"

Finally they composed themselves, and still embracing, staggered along the path until they found light. Nick stopped, held her off at arm's length, and inspected her.

"No blood," he said, his voice wavering. "Are you . . ."

"I'm not hurt. Just shook up. What about my dress? It's torn, isn't it? I can feel a breeze down my back."

"Never mind your goddamn dress. I should be kicked from here to Florida and back. Leaving you alone with this place full of drunks and dirty old men—"

"Dirty old . . . Oh. Are you suggesting—"

"I'm not suggesting anything, I'm too busy despising myself." Nick groaned and smote himself heavily on the brow. "And after you told me, begged me—you said there was somebody there. . . . How about if I lie down and you jump on me a few times? Then we'll go over to the pool and I'll quietly drown myself while you watch."

"Don't go to all that trouble just for me," Erin said.

He grabbed her, holding her so tightly she squeaked in protest. "I've never been as glad to see anyone as I was to see you," she admitted. "But my dress—"

"Women," Nick said, grinning sheepishly. "Turn around and let's have a look. Hmmm. Seems to be a slit or a hole or something down the back. Very sexy. However, you might care to resume my coat until you can wend your way to the ladies' room and make repairs."

"Your coat! I had it. . . . It must be back there in the bushes."

"I'll go look. You wait here." It was evident from Nick's expression that he hoped to find something besides his coat in the bushes, but Erin refused to be left behind, and Nick didn't argue with her. He was doomed to disappointment; the coat was there, crumpled and dusty, but there was no sign of anyone.

Nick held her hand tightly as they retraced their steps. He was silent, having used up his stock of expletives, and Erin was absorbed in her thoughts. No doubt Nick was right, her attacker must have been one of Juliet's guests, too drunk to know what he was doing or too drunk to care. But there had been nothing even remotely sexual about that hard grip. She couldn't even be certain that it had been a man's arm and hand.

The majority of the guests had left but a few remained— the serious eaters and drinkers, and the journalists, hanging grimly on for fear of missing some titillating news item. They had some reason to hope for a damaging statement or embarrassing display; a goodly number of those present were far from sober, including the hostess, who was notorious for her after-hours performances.

The latter clung limpetlike to Rosemary. "You can't leave yet, dahling, I haven't had a chance to talk to you. Now that those other boring people have gone home, we could . . . dance, maybe? Or have a good old-fashioned sing-along. Where's that damned piano player?"

"Things appear to be getting out of hand," said Erin, as the distinguished actress lifted the damask tablecloth and bent to peer under it—looking for the vanished pianist. "Where's Joe?"

"He's given up," Nick said, indicating the weary figure propped against a bookcase. From Joe's expression of satisfaction Erin deduced that the take had been even better than he had hoped.

"Poor Rosemary," she said. "She looks exhausted."

Nick squared his shoulders and straightened his tie. " 'Once more into the breach, dear friends. . . .' "

The distraction proved effective, though it took the famous thespian a few seconds to recognize Nick. The contact lenses she wore to intensify the color of her famous sapphire-blue eyes seemed to be irritating them.

He succeeded in distracting her from Rosemary, but not from her determination to prolong the life of the party. "Dolls," she murmured, gazing into Nick's eyes.

"Uh," said Nick. "I don't think—"

"No, honey, you're right. Dollhouses. That was it. I was gonna show you my . . . Hey, Rosie! You haven't seen my collection." Her coordination was better than it appeared. Without loosing her hold on Nick she made a grab for Rosemary, who was edging away. "Come on. We'll all go see my collection!"

Nick went with Juliet—it was that or have the sleeve of his rented suit ripped off. Erin joined Rosemary, who had waved away a proffered tray filled with brimming glasses. Rosemary's cheeks had a grayish tinge and her smile was as rigid as concrete.

"You must be ready to lie down and die," Erin said.

Rosemary studied her thoughtfully. Erin was suddenly conscious of her disheveled state—smeared lipstick, tumbled hair, and, most damning of all, Nick's jacket, which she still wore because she had not had a chance to examine the damage to her dress. That Rosemary observed these phenomena was obvious; that she misinterpreted them became clear when she tactfully refrained from comment.

"On the whole, I think I'd rather kill Juliet," she said. "Oh, well, such are the vicissitudes of politics. Maybe she'll pass out on the dolls."

It was a long walk, down crossing corridors, to the rooms where Juliet kept her collection. The rooms were unlocked but not undefended. A guard had been posted in the corridor. He saluted Juliet respectfully; she paid no more attention to him than if he had been a suit of armor.

No doubt the dolls were beautiful, rare, and expensive. Erin was too tired to give them more than a passing glance, or pay much attention to their hostess's lecture. Juliet admitted she couldn't remember all the names, but she knew what each had cost, down to the last penny.

Most of the dolls were in glass cases, along with various accessories—clothing, doll furniture, and so on. In the center of the room, on long tables arranged in an open square, were a number of dollhouses. They ranged from an elaborately detailed Victorian mansion inhabited by a large family of blank-faced dolls to a reproduction of a Tudor cottage with a real thatched roof and an attached garden of tiny dried flowers. Erin stood swaying gently, her eyes half-closed, until a voice murmured, "You appear as animated and as charming as these dolls. I'm about to escape; I presume if I offered to drive you home, you'd mistake my intentions again."

Erin forced her eyes open and looked up at him. "Mr. Laurence, if this is your idea of an amusing game, get someone else to play with you. And if it's supposed to count as an apology for your boorishness, don't trouble yourself."

A faint but perceptible flush stained Laurence's high cheekbones. "I deserved that," he said with unexpected humility. "If you'd just give me a chance to explain why I behaved so badly . . ." He broke off with a hiss of annoyance. "Joe, as I live and breathe. Have you no tact? Didn't you observe I was trying to make my peace with a justly offended lady?"

"Is that what you were doing?" Joe yawned till his jaw cracked. "Do me a favor and work on turning Juliet off. I can't stand this much longer. Dolls, for Christ's sake!"

"Juliet is one of those unfortunate individuals who can't endure her own company," Laurence replied. "Small wonder; no one else can endure it for long. Very well, old chap, since you ask me, I'll see what can be done."

But Rosemary had taken matters into her own hands. Erin observed the technique admiringly; it consisted of talking without drawing breath or allowing the other person to get a word in, while moving inexorably toward the exit. "Dahling Juliet, it's been so unbelievable, I cannot tell you; I'll call, write, bless you; come along, Erin, everyone, it's been so-o-o-o-o stupefying. . . ."

She glided out of the room, followed by her hostess. Joe let out a sigh of relief. "Thank God. Hurry up, Erin, before Rosie has to stop for breath."

They were in the vestibule collecting coats and wraps when they heard the hoarse shouts and the pound of heavy running feet.

Joe swore long and loud, but they had no choice but to retrace their steps. One could hardly desert the ship without at least asking what had caused the alarm.

They were in time to catch one quick, unforgettable glimpse of the disaster. The cottage was burning, with a miniature fury as delicate as the flaming flowers in its garden. A golden lacework of fire covered the thatched roof. One of the doll-dwellers, dressed in flowered farthingale and tiny ruff, lay face down across the threshold as if it had fallen in a futile attempt to escape. Then the guard ran in with a fire extinguisher and a fountain of white foam buried the ruins.

Chapter Eight

BY THE TIME Erin finally got to bed she was so tired she thought she could sleep through a hurricane. But some part of her mind must have remained alert and on watch; when the sounds from the adjoining room began, she woke instantly.

Every limb felt as if it were encased in iron, and for a while she argued sleepily with the warning mental voice. "It's just Kay going to the bathroom, she doesn't need me. . . ." But the footsteps didn't cross the hall, they passed her door and went on. "She can't sleep, she's going down for a book or a glass of milk. . . ." The silent sentry didn't believe that either. There was something about the footsteps. . . . They were too loud, they clicked emphatically, with no consideration for other sleepers in the house.

Erin struggled out of bed and ran to the door. She had opened her window and the night air was chilly, but she didn't stop to put on robe or slippers. Kay's footsteps, still unmuted, made it clear that she was heading for one of the rooms on the second floor. Erin followed. The light on the landing, which was left burning at night, showed her that Rosemary's door stood wide open, though the room itself was dark.

Erin's alarmed imagination boiled with theories she would have been ashamed to voice aloud. But surely there was something wrong. No one would waken a weary friend except in a dire emergency, and if Kay were bent on a private conference she wouldn't make so much noise, or leave the door ajar.

Noiseless, on bare feet, she crept toward the door, not entirely certain of what she intended to do. As she stood in brief hesitation, a light went on within; and in its glow Erin beheld an eerie sight: Kay, standing at the foot of the bed, perfectly perpendicular and totally unconscious. Her staring eyes looked past Rosemary at some vision only she could see, and her hands fumbled across the blankets like those of a blind woman.

Rosemary's face was crumpled and sallow. The muscles in her throat contracted as she swallowed. "Kay," she said hoarsely. "What is it?"

Kay's hearing was as distorted as her vision. She did not respond. Bending stiffly, she raised the ruffled flounce and looked under the bed. Then she straightened, crossed the room, and went into the closet.

"I'm sorry," Erin whispered from the doorway. "I heard her moving around, and there was something odd. . . . She's sleepwalking, isn't she?"

"It would seem so." Rosemary showed no surprise at seeing her.

"Has she done this before?"

Rosemary shook her head. "Not for years. . . ." She started violently. A voice—obviously Kay's, but eerily unlike her normal tones—echoed from the depths of the closet.

"Nobody. Nobody here. Have to make sure. Where else? . . . The dressing room? Have to look. Make sure he is all right. . . ."

Rosemary threw back the covers. Her nightgown was an astonishingly flimsy feminine concoction of ruffles and lace and ribbons, but she didn't seem to be aware of the cold.

Kay was groping among the garments hanging on the racks. She had not turned on the light, and Erin shivered with a chill that had nothing to do with the temperature of the room. Could a sleepwalker see in the dark? Impossible. There was nothing supernatural about the phenomenon, it was a purely explicable, if not exactly normal, aberration. . . .

"It's all right, Kay," Rosemary said quietly. "There's no one here."

She had to repeat the reassurances over and over before they penetrated Kay's sleeping and obsessed mind, but when Rosemary finally took her gently by the arm she went along, docile as a child. Between them they got her up the stairs and into bed. The moment she lay down, her eyes closed and she began to snore.

Rosemary let out a long, shaken breath. "She'll be all right now. Try to get some sleep."

"But what if she—"

"She won't. At least . . ." Rosemary fell silent; every strained muscle in her face mirrored her thoughts as she grappled with the problem, considering alternatives, and decided on a course of action.

"I'll lock her door," she said finally. "If she wakes before I can unlock it—well, that can't be helped, I'll have to tell her anyway. . . . Take action to prevent this from happening again. Perhaps you had better lock the connecting door as well. Don't worry, it's extremely unlikely that she would repeat the performance twice in one night. I'd appreciate it if you didn't mention this, not even to Kay. I'll tell her she woke me when she came into my room and that I got her into bed without disturbing anyone. She'd be distressed and humiliated to think anyone else knew about her weakness, as she would view it."

She had it all figured out. "I'll do whatever you want," Erin said.

Rosemary put an affectionate hand on her arm and exclaimed, "Good heavens, child, you're cold as ice. Hop back into bed. Don't give this another thought, it's not your responsibility."

Whose then? Erin wondered, as she curled up under the

covers and tried to defrost her frozen feet. Rosemary's, of course. How long had it been since Kay stopped being a prop on which Rosemary could lean and started to become just another burden? Days—or years? Jeff had mentioned Kay's increasing inefficiency, but that was only part of the problem. Kay was devoted and dedicated to someone—but that someone wasn't Rosemary. The single revealing pronoun that had slipped from her subconscious gave her true feelings away. "He" could only be Edward Marshall—long dead, but still the object of her fanatical concern. Erin could only wonder that she had been so slow to recognize the truth. Kay never referred to Rosemary by the title she had won; "congressman" was reserved for Edward. And whose idea had it been to preserve his office like a shrine?

It must have been sheer hell to live like that, Erin thought drowsily. To be, not just the shadow of your predecessor, but the shadow of a ghost.

She fell asleep before she could decide what, if anything, she could do about the situation. The sentry went off duty; she didn't wake until sunlight stroked her closed eyelids.

Her first thought was for the occupant of the adjoining room. Jumping out of bed, she went to the connecting door and turned the key.

Kay's room was unoccupied. The bed was neatly made. Rosemary had been as good as her word.

From the strength of the sunlight Erin realized it must be late morning. Her watch had stopped; she had forgotten to wind it the night before. She put on jeans and a sweatshirt emblazoned with "Rosemary White Marshall for Senator" and ran downstairs.

There was no one in the commons room—not even Will. Erin remembered he had said something about having to go to Charlottesville. She was filling a cup from the coffee urn when Christie came in. "Good morning, Cinderella. Or should it be Sleeping Beauty?"

The tone was less provocative than the words, however, and Christie went on, "I guess you're entitled to sleep in. What happened last night? I tried to worm it out of Jeff, but you know him, he just primped his mouth and looked stern."

She splashed coffee into a cup and sat down next to Erin.
The latter took her time about answering. If she had learned
one thing since she started working for Rosemary, it was to
think before she spoke. Not that she always succeeded in
following the rule. . . .

The brilliant scarlet and mustard-yellow stripes of Christie's skirt made her eyes ache. Christie also wore a sweatshirt,
they were standard issue, but she had added a few strands of
bright beads and shoved the sleeves up to her elbows. On
her, the baggy garment looked like a designer creation.

With an effort Erin forced her memory back past the sleepwalking episode—which Christie couldn't possibly know
about—to the reception. How much did Christie know—how
much should she be told? Was she only curious about the
life-style of the rich and notorious, or had she heard of the
evening's blazing conclusion?

"It was a great place to visit, but I wouldn't want to live
there," she said cautiously.

"Then you're crazy. Who was there? Did you talk to Juliet? What was she wearing? How was the food? Did you get
to meet Paul Newman and Stevie Cortlandt?"

"Stevie . . . oh, the singer. I didn't get to meet anybody,"
Erin admitted regretfully. "The famous names were surrounded all evening."

Christie didn't bother to conceal her contempt. "Why
didn't you walk right up and introduce yourself? I can't imagine being in the same room with Robert Redford and not
having the gumption to meet him."

"It was a rather—confused evening," Erin said humbly.
Knowing Christie wouldn't give up until she had squeezed
some vicarious excitement out of the event, she launched into
a description of the buffet, Juliet's gown, and the guest list.
"I gather it was a success financially," she added. "At least
Joe implied it was."

"Yeah, he is even talking about hiring a direct-mail company. How was Nick?"

"Haven't you seen him?"

"No. He left you a message."

"With you?"

"How could he leave a message with me when I didn't see him?"

Erin bit back a sharp retort. She didn't blame Christie for resenting her evening out; in Christie's place she would have felt the same. Passing over a highly placed worker in favor of a newcomer still wet behind the ears wasn't just or kind. It was not the first time Erin had wondered why she was so extraordinarily favored.

"He left a note," Christie said, rising. "It's on your desk. You do remember where your desk is?"

That didn't deserve a reply either. Erin followed Christie into the office, where she found Nick's note lying on her desk blotter. It was brief and to the point: "Had to go out, see you lunchtime. We need to talk."

An emphatic black slash underlined "need." Erin slipped the note into her pocket. She "needed" to talk to Nick too. They had barely spoken on the drive home.

She worked steadily until twelve. Nick hadn't shown up, so she went looking for him and found him in the commons room browsing among the cold cuts. On the table next to him was a fat green-eyed calico cat devouring a piece of salami.

Another tribute to the memory of Edward Marshall. . . . Erin picked the cat up and carried it out, the salami still dangling from its mouth. When she returned, Nick looked at her sourly. "If you are quite finished playing with the kitties," he began.

"They aren't supposed to be in here, much less eating off the plates. Are you too hung over to notice such minor details?"

"I am not hung over."

"Preoccupied, then. Your note was somewhat peremptory—"

Nick cleared his throat loudly and gestured. "You haven't said hello to Will."

"I didn't see him. Hello, Will."

"Hello," said Will.

"I thought you were in Charlottesville."

There was no answer from Will; by his standards none was required, since it was obvious he wasn't in Charlottesville.

"He just got back," Nick said. "Want to go for a walk?"

"I haven't had lunch."

"Oh." Nick slapped a piece of ham between two pieces of bread and handed it to her. "Here."

"Thanks," Erin said. There were other things she might have said—yearned to say, in fact—but Nick didn't give her the opportunity. "Nice day for a picnic," he mumbled, nudging her toward the door.

It was a nice day. Jackson and Jan had taken advantage of the sunshine and were sitting on the porch eating their sandwiches. Instead of lingering to talk as he usually did, Nick replied to their greetings with an abstracted wave and kept walking.

He had made it clear that he wanted a private conversation, so Erin waited till they were some distance from the house before she spoke. "Has something happened?"

"Has something happened?" Nick directed his query to the unheeding sky, arms flung wide in appeal. "Listen to the woman! You saw what happened. Too many things have happened. Doesn't anyone but me wonder why they're happening and who is making them happen?"

Erin came to a stop. "Nick, if you want to talk, I'll listen. I can't concoct sensible answers to incoherent cries of woe. Let's sit down. This isn't much of a lunch, but I want to eat it."

Nick stared. "My God, you sounded just like Rosemary. Aren't you going to yell at me for treating you like an object?"

"No, but I may throw something. There's a lot to be said for Rosemary's methods. She seems to get more respect from you guys than I do."

"I'm sorry. I lay awake half the night brooding about this, and I've got to get it off my chest before I explode."

Two cats joined them on the bench under the pines—one gray Persian, one tabby of questionable ancestry—and Erin fed them bits of the sandwich while Nick sat in silence scowling at his dusty shoes. Finally she said, "For a man who threatened to explode if he wasn't allowed to talk, you aren't being very vocal."

"I'm trying to find a good lead." Nick ran his fingers through his hair. "How does this grab you? 'What lunatic has been setting all the goddamn fires?' "

"Too wordy. If there is such a word as 'wordy.' "

Nick wasn't listening. "Politics is a weird business and a lot of weird things can happen during a campaign. Hate mail, demonstrations, even assault and battery. But I've never heard of anything like this. Taken singly, the incidents are meaningless and nonthreatening. When you add them up. . . . And please don't utter the word 'coincidence.' "

"I wasn't going to. You seem to have forgotten that we discussed this same subject a week ago. You were the skeptic then. You laughed at me when I suggested—"

"Laugh! I did not." Erin fixed him with a steady stare. After a moment Nick's eyes dropped. "Anyhow, things were different then. The fire last night was one coincidence too many."

"He's slow but he's sure," Erin informed one of the cats, who opened its mouth as if to reply but yawned instead. "Why don't you admit it, Nick? You didn't want to see a pattern in these incidents because it was Laurence who proposed the theory."

"Er—never mind that. Laurence's theory is off the wall, Erin. Even in sensational fiction it's against the rules to make the criminal a homicidal maniac."

Erin protested. "Don't use that word. Nobody has been killed, or even hurt."

"Not yet."

The dry sandwich stuck in Erin's throat. She divided the rest of it between the drooling cats.

"These incidents are not the work of a lunatic, homicidal or otherwise," Nick went on. "The first two fires could have been accidental. The third, in the cemetery, was no accident; but its significance, insofar as Rosemary is concerned, was questionable. Any anonymous loony could have done it, for any one of a hundred reasons. Last night . . . That could have been an accident too. The material of that dollhouse was highly flammable and there were a lot of drunks wandering around brandishing cigars and cigarettes. But that makes four fires in a row, four in less than two weeks, and all of them connected in one way or another with Rosemary. There's a recurrent theme, isn't there?''

"You're forgetting something," Erin said reluctantly. "The doll, or poppet, or whatever you want to call it."

"I hadn't forgotten. I was waiting for you to bring it up. Same theme, Erin. It was smeared with ashes."

Erin sighed. "Fire again."

"Yeah."

"What about the attack on me last night?"

"Obviously I considered that. But it doesn't fit the theme. Unless there was something you forgot to mention."

"No lighted matches or smell of smoke," Erin said wryly. "I guess it was just your common garden-variety rapist. That's a relief, in a way; I'd rather not be part of your pattern. But Nick, what's the point of it all? Without some logical connection—some common, underlying motive—the incidents don't fit together. Are they meant to be threats—warnings of worse to come? Like, for instance, setting fire to the house?''

"I don't think so. It would be too difficult to start a fire that could cause serious damage, much less bodily harm. There are smoke detectors in every room, people coming and going all day, the dogs patrolling at night. It seems more likely to me that the fires aren't portents of future events, but reminders of a past event."

Erin felt a cowardly sense of relief. She and Kay would be most vulnerable to an attack by fire; the rooms on the second floor had wide windows and a relatively easy drop into thick shrubbery below.

"That's ingenious," she said. "Rosemary's past, you mean?"

"She's the focus," Nick insisted. "Maybe I'm unduly influenced by the political angle, but that's the nightmare of every campaign staff—the fear that the candidate has something nasty lurking in the closet, disclosure of which could wreck his chances. Rosemary has run for office before, but those were shoo-ins, virtually uncontested races. This is different. This could lead . . . all the way to the top. Buzz Bennett isn't the only one who would pay any price to get something damaging on Rosemary.''

"Agreed. But Nick, if Bennett knew about the skeleton in the closet, he wouldn't play cat and mouse, he'd just leak it to the press. Wouldn't he?''

"I would think so. I've been over this again and again, and I can't make sense of it either But I'll be damned if I'm going to sit here like a toad on a rock and wait for the next fire.''

"Have you discussed this with anyone else?''

"Who, for instance?'' He turned to face her, his eyes narrowed and his lips tight. "You're too intelligent to miss the logical conclusion, Erin; you just don't want to admit it. The arsonist isn't an outsider. It has to be one of us.''

Erin was unable to produce a convincing counterargument. Not only had she reached the same conclusion, she had carried it one step farther; to an unbiased observer, she must be high on the list of suspects, if not at the top.

Luckily for her, Nick was not unbiased. She saw no point in mentioning this little aberration, since it would only have hurt his feelings; and anyway, he could undoubtedly come up with a convincing rationalization for his naive trust in her.

She edged closer to him and he responded at once, draping his arm around her shoulders and smiling as cheerfully as if the ominous scenario he had produced were only a plot for a novel he planned to write. If she had cheered him, he had done the same for her; bad as it was, his theory wasn't as grisly as some of the ones that had occurred to her.

"Do you suppose Rosemary knows?'' she asked.

"Well, she'd have to, wouldn't she? She hasn't given anything away, but that's only to be expected; these days a politician has to cultivate a poker face and outperform Gielgud. But did you see her face last night when we burst into the room and saw the blazing dollhouse?''

"No.''

"I did. All I can say is, I'm glad she's never had occasion to look at me that way. Now it's not Rosemary's style to remain passive; sooner or later, she'll act—confront her adversary, if she knows who it is, or take steps to find out, if she doesn't. That's why I decided to get you in on this. I can't be with her all the time—''

"Wait a minute." Erin stiffened. "You don't mean . . . spy on her? On Rosemary?"

"I wouldn't exactly put it like that. . . ."

"I would." She moved away from him, to the farthest end of the bench. It was depressing to discover the real reason why Nick had confided in her—not blind, doting trust, but brutal necessity. And the idea of spying sickened her. "Maybe I should get one of those Groucho Marx masks with a big nose and a mustache," she added bitingly.

"You look ridiculous when you're mad," Nick said, grinning.

"Why don't you say I'm cute when I'm mad, and be thoroughly offensive? If a man took offense at your behavior, you wouldn't tell him he was cute—''

"He wouldn't *be* cute. Okay, I'm sorry. Look, Erin, I don't like the idea any better than you do, but it has to be done. For her own good.''

"I'll bet that's what the boys in the CIA tell themselves," Erin grumbled; but when he put his arm around her and pulled her back to his side she didn't resist. "It's impossible, Nick. Aside from the moral issue, how are you going to keep up with Rosemary's activities? She's always on the go these days.''

"Ah, but most of her activities are public," Nick said. "It's her private time that interests me, and God knows she has little of that. I'm not suggesting you should listen at doors or anything like that, just keep an eye on her, and try to let me know if she makes an attempt to sneak off on her own. That would be significant; she almost always has someone with her during the day, Joe or Jeff or Kay.''

"All right, I'll try. But it's a far-out chance, Nick.''

"Admitted. There is one other thing we could do.''

"Like what?''

"Try a little detective work on our own." He was so obviously pleased at the idea, Erin knew better than to laugh. She fixed a bright, interested look on her face, and Nick went on with mounting enthusiasm, "We'll start with the theory that these incidents refer to something in the past involving Rosemary and maybe her husband. It couldn't have happened recently or someone would have dug it up. Nor could it have occurred more than thirty years ago, because it would be irrelevant."

"Not necessarily. I've seen so-called exposés about college careers of candidates—something as seemingly trivial as cheating on an exam."

Nick's answer was a triumph of inverted logic. "Right. So most likely the Marshall name was never mentioned in connection with this unknown event—"

"Then how the hell do you expect to identify it?"

"Ouch." Nick rubbed his ear. "You don't have to yell."

"Sorry. But you really are . . . Let me try that again. You said yourself that the press and political opponents would love to get something on Rosemary. If skilled investigators haven't found this mysterious crime, how do you think you're going to succeed?"

"We have a clue they don't have," Nick said. "Fire. This has something to do with a fire, not just a little backyard bonfire but something serious. Arson, perhaps. It may have been serious enough to rate newspaper coverage, at least in the local rags. The Marshalls have lived in Virginia since prehistoric times; we won't have to check every newspaper in the country, just those in the state."

"Oh, great. That shouldn't take more than a month."

Nick glanced at his watch and then jumped up. "I've got to go. Is there any way you can get to a library in the next few days?"

To call Nick single-minded was to understate the case. None of her reasoned arguments had had the slightest effect, or dimmed his manic enthusiasm one whit. She shook her head. "I don't have a car, remember?"

"Maybe you could ask Kay. . . . No, I guess that won't work. Okay, I think I can get away Friday. Ask for the day off. In the meantime—watch Rosemary. I'm late. Gotta run."

He planted a quick, forceful kiss on her mouth, hugged her till her ribs creaked, and dashed off.

Erin stood watching him. She was reminded of an antique

movie advertisement for a now-forgotten film—"Will She Kill
Him or Kiss Him?" She didn't really want to kill him—not
more than once or twice a day, at any rate. His volatile personality took a little getting used to, but really, his outbursts
and subsequent apologies were easier to live with than days
of sulking. As for kissing him . . . Nobody was perfect, especially Nick, but in that particular area he came very close.

The next few days passed quietly, insofar as mysterious
fires were concerned. In every other way they were chaotic.
With Election Day almost upon them, the pace began to pick
up, though Erin would not have believed it to be possible.
Sunday was a working day like any other; no mention was
made of going to church. At least Kay was sleeping through
the night. The bottle of sleeping pills Erin found on her bedside table when she tidied the room might have had something to do with that. Rosemary indulged her old friend and
secretary in a lot of ways, but she could put her foot down
when she had to.

Erin could almost have wished Kay's nights had been more
disturbed; rested and refreshed, the older woman had plenty
of energy during the day, and she kept the others hopping.
Between her household duties and her office chores Erin
barely had time to snatch food at irregular intervals, and Kay's
temper was so short she drove the entire office staff to the
verge of revolution. Yet no one wanted to complain to Rosemary, who had more than enough on her mind as it was. She
was on the go from morning till night, and claimed to be so
full of coffee, tea, and other liquids that she sloshed when
she walked.

"I just wish people wouldn't insist on feeding me," she
groaned. "It can't be because I look undernourished. I can
hardly fasten this skirt." She demonstrated, trying to insert
a finger into the waistband.

"Food is a traditional symbol of hospitality and of approval," Will explained seriously. "The psychological implications of offering and accepting sustenance—"

"Don't use that word in my presence, Will," Rosemary
said.

Will smiled gently. "Which one? Psychological or implications?"

"Both. Either. None of the above. I'm so sick of jargon."

Passing through the commons room on her way from the kitchen, Erin overheard the last part of the conversation. Rosemary gave her a severe look. "You aren't going to offer me that cup, are you? I don't care what's in it, I don't want it."

"It's for Kay," Erin explained. "She's working on that speech, and she wanted—"

"Working? It's almost midnight. Tell her . . . No, I'll tell her myself. Give me that cup and go to bed."

When Rosemary used that tone, nobody argued with her— except possibly Joe. Erin handed over the coffee. "Oh, great," Rosemary muttered, inspecting the dark liquid. "I don't suppose it's decaffeinated? No, I thought not. That woman . . . She is sleeping, isn't she? No more alarms and excursions?"

She had not lowered her voice. Erin glanced at Will, who had turned his back and bent his head over his papers. "No," she said. "I mean—yes, she's sleeping through the night."

"Good. I told you not to worry about it. You aren't, are you?"

"No."

"Any problems? Anything you want to unload?"

"Nothing," Erin said firmly. "Everything is just fine."

"Liar." Rosemary rose on tiptoe and gave her a quick kiss on the cheek. "Nice, kind, thoughtful liar. Good night, Erin."

The kiss burned like the conventional coals of fire. I can't spy on her, Erin thought, as she beat a hasty retreat. Not even for her own good. Damn Nick anyway. He had gotten her all stirred up and worried, and then disappeared; she hadn't set eyes on him for days. Just like a man . . .

She was awakened at what felt like the crack of dawn by Kay's knock and call: "It's after seven, Erin. Rise and shine."

Rise and shine indeed. It was a phrase Erin particularly loathed, having heard it only too often from her aunt. Nothing else was shining. Fog pressed at the window like a huge gray face, an accidental arrangement of branches without forming slitted eyes and a sullen slash of mouth.

Erin pulled the blanket up over her head. But it was no use; Kay's tone had been of the variety that might be characterized as pleasant but firm.

Sarah's placid, cheerful face and one of Sarah's excellent breakfasts improved her spirits a little, but from then on things went from better to worse. Rosemary was in a bad mood; Joe, never one to take criticism amiably, snapped back at her when she took exception to something he had said; and even Jeff was glum and silent.

The general malaise came to a head later that morning, during a strategy meeting in Rosemary's office. The raised voices and sound of fists pounding furniture were audible in the outer office. Finally the door burst open and Rosemary came out. Her face was crimson with fury. She was followed not by Joe but by his voice which would have carried clear to Middleburg: "Get your butt back in here! We haven't decided—"

"Oh yes, we have!" Whirling around, Rosemary delivered the defiance at top pitch. "I'm not going to do it, and that's final! Who the hell do you think you are?"

A crash from within the office was probably Joe's chair going over. He appeared in the doorway waving his cigar. "I'm the stupid ass who's trying to run this campaign, that's who! I must have been crazy to take on the job. If I can't get the slightest degree of cooperation from you—"

Jeff's anxious face appeared at Joe's shoulder. "Hey, Joe, calm down. Rosemary, why don't you come in and sit down and we'll have a nice quiet discussion—"

This conciliatory speech was drowned out by Joe and Rosemary yelling at once. Rosemary ended the discussion by groping blindly for the nearest loose object on the nearest desk and pitching it straight at Joe.

The results were horrendous. The coffee mug had been half full, but the amount of brown liquid that spattered wall and floor looked like a gallon. Rosemary's aim wasn't too good—or perhaps it was excellent. The cup hit the wall next to the door and shattered, sending fragments flying.

Joe's head came back into view. "Now that you've got that out of your system, come back in here," he said mildly.

"No." Rosemary's voice was just as calm. "I said I won't, and I won't. I'm going upstairs for a while. Leave me alone."

"You're supposed to be on the Hill at two—" Joe began.

Jeff cleared his throat. "We've got a meeting at noon, Joe. In D.C. Maybe we ought to postpone this. The weather is bad and if we don't get started pretty soon. . . ."

"Oh, all right," Joe said ungraciously. "Maybe Rosemary will be through sulking by the time we get back. Honest to God, talk about childish, irrational behavior—"

Jeff reached around him and pulled the door shut.

Rosemary swept the room with a long, sober survey. "Joe is right. That was a childish, rude performance, and I apologize to all of you." Then a broad smile spread across her face. "But, by gosh, it sure felt good!"

She knew how to play an audience. Erin felt her lips stretching into an answering grin, the same look that transformed all the other faces. "Christie, I've made a mess of your office and disgraced myself," Rosemary went on. "I'm afraid you aren't going to respect me in the morning."

She could have spattered the office with Joe's blood and Christie wouldn't have said a word. She murmured a bemused disclaimer. Rosemary gave her an affectionate pat on the back and announced, "I am going into seclusion to meditate on my sins—and maybe get a little work done. See you all later."

She had scarcely left the room when the door of the inner office opened and Nick slithered out. He came straight to Erin. "I need you to help me with something."

"What?"

His back to the others, Nick made a hideous face. What he was trying to convey Erin did not know, but the effect was so grotesque she decided she had better not ask any more questions. He hadn't even answered the first one.

She followed him into the hall. "This is it," Nick hissed theatrically. "Hurry up!"

The hall was quiet and gloomy. There was no one in sight. "This is what?" Erin demanded. "Hurry up where?"

"Jesus H. Christ, do I have to spell everything out?" Nick waved his arms wildly but kept his voice low. "This is a setup. She picked that fight deliberately, to get some time to herself. We have to be ready to follow her."

"It's raining," Erin protested, as he towed her toward the door. "Why can't we wait inside?"

"Because there are five different ways out of this house, and also because when you are trailing someone the idea is to keep them from noticing that that's what you're doing. Here—take this."

He snatched a garment at random from the coats hanging on the hall tree and flung it at her.

Nick's car was parked by the front door, along with several others. Erin struggled into the coat; from its length and its brilliant crimson color, she deduced it must belong to Christie, and she hoped devoutly that that wronged woman would not decide to leave the house before they returned.

Nick fought his usual battle with the recalcitrant car door, finally got it closed, and slid behind the wheel.

"Hunker down," he ordered.

"She couldn't see me if I were outlined in neon," Erin said crossly. "The windows are all fogged up. How long do we have to sit here before you admit you're wrong? Rosemary isn't going anywhere."

"This is the first chance she's had to get away since the last fire," Nick replied, squinting through the rain-streaked windshield. "And that argument was a fake. I know Rosemary; she and Joe are always yelling at each other, but she never walks out on a fight."

"What was the argument about?"

"Joe wanted her to plan a series of speeches and visits to the southwest. That's Bennett country, and we're down in the polls in that part of the state. She said there wasn't time—"

"That's true, isn't it? Her schedule is impossible already."

"There's always time for what has to be done," Nick said. "Then she said— Hey, look! Was I right or was I right? Squat down!"

The figure he had indicated had emerged from one of the side doors and was walking quickly toward the garage. It wore a nondescript flapping raincoat and carried an umbrella; but the brassy gold of its hair was visible even through the falling rain.

"That's not Rosemary. It must be one of the girls who—"

"That's Rosemary. Haven't you ever heard of wigs? I recognize her walk." The keys were already in the ignition; his fingers played with them but did not turn them. "Hunker—"

"Shut up."

Before long they heard the sound of a motor, and a vehicle came into sight. It was the old pickup truck; through the window Erin saw a glint of brassy hair. The driver's head did not turn as the truck passed them and lurched along the rutted driveway, sending sprays of water from under the wheels.

Nick turned the key. The engine whined and coughed and died. "Goddamn battery," he muttered. The truck reached the gate, paused briefly, and turned left. Nick swore and pounded the dash with his left fist; the engine caught, stuttered, and settled to an uneasy roar.

Erin was thrown forward, then back, as Nick went in hot pursuit. His natural resiliency had asserted itself and he was beaming with satisfaction. "We can't follow too close anyhow," he explained. "I should have taken one of the other cars, I guess, but there wasn't time to borrow . . . Oops, sorry, you'd better buckle the seat belt, I may have to make some quick stops and turns."

Erin rubbed her forehead. It had contacted the windshield rather forcibly when Nick hit a large-sized pothole. He continued to drive with more panache than care until they caught sight of the pickup a few hundred yards ahead. Rosemary—if it was Rosemary—was driving under the speed limit, keeping carefully in her lane and slowing on every curve. Rain had soaked the fallen leaves into slippery masses and visibility was poor; but Nick, characteristically, found another interpretation for the other driver's caution.

"She doesn't want to get stopped by a cop," he muttered. "Wonder where she's going?"

"Home, I shouldn't wonder. If that's one of the maids—"

"It is not one of the maids, none of 'em have hair that color. Nobody has hair that color. . . . They wouldn't take the truck, it belongs to the estate."

"Maybe they—she—got permission to borrow it. Maybe she's going home to get lunch for her husband, or on an errand for Sarah."

"You have a very vivid imagination," said Nick, banging on the windshield in an ineffectual effort to speed up the wipers, which seemed to suffer from the same lassitude that affected all the other parts of the car.

"*I* have a vivid imagination? If that's Rosemary, why didn't she use her own car? Or Kay's?"

"Obviously because she doesn't want to be recognized," Nick said smugly. "Sam won't even notice the truck is missing; he's deaf as a post and right now he's absorbed in his soaps. No reason for him to go out on a day like this."

Ominous noises from under the dash implied that the heater had been turned on, but the air blasting Erin's legs was ice cold. She turned the collar of the coat up and shivered.

Her own theory received a blow when they passed through Middleburg without stopping and headed east on Route 50. Most of the kitchen workers were local people, and 50 was the most direct route to Washington. Nick grunted with satisfaction as the pickup increased its speed. "I knew it. She's meeting someone. If she turns north at the crossroads, she could be going to Leesburg."

The pickup turned south, onto Route 15. "Not Leesburg," Nick muttered. "The Virginia suburbs? Route 15 to 66, I'll bet. She should have stayed on 50."

There was a good deal of traffic; Nick let several other vehicles get between them and their quarry. The wipers wheezed and stuttered.

Some distance ahead a stoplight glowed green, where a state route intersected the highway. Without signaling, the truck moved into the left lane, catching Nick by surprise. He stamped on the brake. "Now where the hell is she going? Come on, one of you guys, get in that left lane, I don't want to be right behind her. . . ."

The truck had to wait for oncoming traffic to clear. The

light turned yellow and it completed its turn, followed, illegally, by the car behind it. Nick pulled into the left lane and sat quivering with frustration while the pickup disappeared into the distance. "That is Route 234. Maybe she's going to take 29 east to Fairfax. Unless she spotted us and is trying to lose us. . . . Damn! She's going to do it, too, if I don't get moving!"

He made an illegal turn on the red; the car veered sickeningly as the balding tires skidded on wet pavement.

"Nick, for God's sake," Erin groaned.

"It's okay, I'm a good driver," Nick assured her. Water rose in a mighty spray as the car roared through a puddle.

After a frenzied mile or so they caught up with the pickup, whose driver was proceeding at a sedate pace. Nick grunted with satisfaction and slowed down. In good weather it would have been a pleasant drive, for the road wound and curved through the countryside, and the fall foliage was muted by mist into soft pale shades of umber and topaz, like a time-faded tapestry. Gradually the rain slackened to a drizzle and the sky brightened.

Nick paid no attention to the scenery or the weather, he was still theorizing. "Wherever she's going, it's this side of the Beltway. Fairfax, maybe, or west Falls Church. She'll have to turn on 29."

She didn't. A stoplight marked the intersection. Instead of turning, the pickup crossed the highway.

"Manassas," Nick said blankly. "She's heading for Manassas. Why would anyone want to go there?"

Erin huddled into the folds of the coat. The question was obviously rhetorical, so she didn't answer it, though she could think of a number of reasons why a number of people might want to go to Manassas. It contained as many potential voters as any other town of its size in Virginia, and it was large enough to rate a temporary Democratic campaign office. However, she was becoming a reluctant convert to Nick's theory. A worker on a legitimate errand to local headquarters would take his or her car, not Sam's pickup.

The imminence of the town was announced by the usual sprawl of commercial clutter—gas stations, fast-food chains, motels. Traffic had thickened; there were several other vehicles between them and the truck when it made a sudden turn into a small shopping center and pulled into a parking place next to a fast-food restaurant with a familiar arch. Nick followed suit, picking a spot from which he could see but not easily be seen. The driver got out of the truck and trotted toward the restaurant. She was not carrying an umbrella, but she had tied a brown scarf over her brassy curls.

By this time Erin was thoroughly infected with the thrill of the chase. Height, shape, and walk were definitely Rosemary's and the choice of a rendezvous was unexceptionable if her aim was to pass unrecognized. No one would expect to see Rosemary Marshall lunching in a McDonald's on the outskirts of a town forty miles from home, and the chance of accidentally encountering a colleague was almost nonexistent.

"Now what?" she asked.

"We can't go in," Nick said. "She'd see us for sure. Are you hungry?"

"Not especially. Are you?"

"I'm always hungry. Have you got any money?"

"Not a cent. You dragged me out of the house before I could get my purse."

Nick shifted position and dragged a worn wallet out of his hip pocket. It bulged, but not with cash; sorting through a motley collection of business cards, scribbled notes, and receipts, Nick finally located a few bills. "Seven bucks. Hey, not bad. What would you like?"

"Just coffee. You said we couldn't go in—"

"We are about to make use of that marvelous modern invention, the drive-in window. And, not so incidentally, case the joint as we do so."

The front and side of the restaurant had large windows. Heedless of the fine drizzle, Nick rolled his own window down and peered intently as they glided slowly past. "I don't see her, do you?"

"No. Wait—there she is, on the other side. I recognize the scarf."

"Where? Oh—yeah." Nick's voice rose in a howl of triumph. "Who's a genius? There's someone at the same table. A woman. Do you recognize her?"

"She's got one of those plastic rain hats shielding her face. You're going to hit that post. . . ."

The car swerved and managed to avoid the post. Nick drove on around the restaurant and turned into the drive-in lane. He was ingenuously delighted to learn there was a special on hamburgers and ordered three, with fries and coffee, receiving a jingle of change in return. Then they went around again, with little more success; both women were leaning forward, heads together, and Rosemary's scarf hid the face of her companion. Nick backed into a parking place near the door of the restaurant and turned off the ignition.

Nick ate two of the hamburgers and all the french fries, munching vigorously without taking his eyes off the door of the restaurant. Erin found she was hungry after all and accepted the other hamburger. It was lunchtime; the door of the restaurant kept opening and closing as customers crowded in. A few came out. Nick had barely finished eating when Rosemary appeared. Without pausing or looking around, she walked to the truck and got in.

It was unquestionably Rosemary, though Erin wouldn't have recognized her if she had not been expecting to see her. A thick layer of bright-red lipstick had altered the shape of her mouth, and mascara practically dripped from her lashes. She looked like an aging but optimistic go-go dancer, and the brilliant red mouth wore a wide familiar smile.

"There she is," Erin exclaimed. "Aren't you going to follow her?"

The truck backed out of its place and jolted toward the exit. Nick shook his head. "I know where she's going. Home. She has to be at her office on the Hill at two, and if she doesn't drive like a bat she won't make it. It's the other one I'm interested in. Come on, lady, come on; I haven't got all day."

Another five minutes passed before he got his wish, and at first Erin wasn't certain the plump little woman who came out was their quarry. A couple of other women had worn the cheap, ubiquitous plastic rain hat and she had seen only the shoulders of a tan coat, the commonest variety of bad-weather clothing. This woman had a round, healthy pink face and pink-tinted glasses. Masses of fluffy white hair had been flattened by the plastic cap.

Nick let out a startled exclamation. "My God! It can't be!"

"Who? Who?"

"Don't you recognize her?"

"She looks vaguely familiar."

"It's her all right," Nick said, neglecting grammar in his excitement.

The woman trotted across the parking lot and got into a long, sleek black car—a Cadillac. "Yep," Nick said. "She favors Cadillacs. Jesus, look at that! They tell stories all over the state about her driving. When the word goes out that she's on the road, everybody stays home."

The big car shot forward in a series of jerks and starts, skimmed a post, forced the driver of an oncoming Camaro into a wild sideways swerve, and turned into the line of traffic on the highway without pausing or signaling. Horns blared.

"That's her," Nick repeated.

"Who, damn it?"

Nick turned to face her. His face was awed. "That, my dear, was Miz Marylou. The much-loved, loyal wife of our incumbent senator, Bill the Buzzard Bennett."

Chapter
Nine

THE DISCOVERY stupefied Nick so completely that he didn't even swear when his car refused to start. Calmly extracting a set of jumper cables from the trunk, he talked a boy in a car almost as decrepit as his into assisting in the restoration of power and presented him with a campaign button as a thank-you gift. Not until they were back on the road heading home did he condescend to discuss the matter, and with less than the exuberance Erin would have expected. She was the one who peppered him with questions and speculations.

"I suppose they've known each other for years, haven't they? Would you say they were friends? Because if they are, then it would be a little difficult for them to get together, with things as they are. Maybe they have a mutual godchild or friend who's in trouble, and they wanted to confer."

"That's stupid."

"You think everything has a political orientation. It doesn't, you know; there are some people in this world who go right on sleeping and eating and worrying about the mortgage without giving a damn whether Rosemary Marshall wins an election. There are matters of greater importance—" Her voice rose to a shriek as Nick cut across Route 29 on the last split second of the yellow.

"Sorry," Nick said. "If I stop, the damn engine may conk out for good. The battery is shot."

"Why don't you buy a new one?"

"Can't afford it,"

"Oh. Maybe if you asked Rosemary—"

"No!" Nick added less vehemently, "It was my decision to quit my job, she didn't ask me to. I'll make out all right. Rosemary has done enough for me already—and believe me, she doesn't have any money to spare. Do you know how much it costs to run a political campaign these days?"

"Yes, I know. If I've heard that once, I've heard it a hundred times."

"I'm sorry I yelled," Nick said. "Don't say anything. . . . I mean, *please* don't say anything to Rosemary about my cash flow. Or about following her."

"Oh, all right."

"I don't know how to figure this," Nick muttered, scowling at the streaked windshield. "Is it a side issue, or is it connected with the other business? It has to be! Supposing Miz Marylou found out Buzz is paying somebody to harass Rosemary. . . ."

"Would she betray her own husband?"

"Hard to say. She's known for her good works and general saintliness; Buzz's constituents adore her, she's been one of his biggest assets. She's stuck to him through thick and thin and forty years of adultery. I mean, hell, everybody knew what he was up to, the Shady Lane Motel deal only made it public. It couldn't have come as a shock to her unless she's as stupid as she is noble."

"It might have been the last straw."

"Yeah, I suppose. You never know what will tip someone over the edge."

They were approaching the stoplight at the intersection of 234 and 15. Erin braced herself and involuntarily closed her eyes. They made it through on the green, with only a little skid.

"Something else could have been the last straw for Miz Marylou," Nick said. "If she's the saint everyone believes her to be, she wouldn't stand by with folded hands if Buzz were planning something that goes beyond the normal dirty tricks of politics—something criminal or life-threatening. She'd warn the intended victim, wouldn't she?"

The conversation went downhill from there. Erin argued that even if Nick's surmise was true, Rosemary had now been fully informed about the danger. "Forewarned is forearmed," she insisted.

"Don't throw that tired old cliché at me," Nick snarled, hunching over the wheel. "Women always seem to think they've solved a problem by quoting a proverb."

"And men are always making wild generalizations," Erin snarled back.

"Like that one?"

Neither spoke again until they reached the house. Patches of blue sky were visible to the west through rents in the clouds, and the sun burst through, sending sparks winking from wet branches and waking the autumn colors to dazzling brilliance.

"What did you get for Jeff?" Nick asked.

Erin was still sulking and his sudden cheerfulness annoyed her. "Why should I get something for Jeff?"

"There's a birthday party today, isn't there?"

"Oh, damn, I forgot. What time is the party?"

"Around six, I think." Nick glanced at his watch. "I'd offer to drive you to town, but I'm already late. Tell you what, you can go halves with me. I spent more than I could afford."

"How much?"

"It'll cost you fifteen bucks."

"No wonder you're broke. What is it?"

"You have to see it to appreciate it fully." Nick grinned. "Take my word, it's sensational. What do you say?"

"Oh, all right. I suppose you want me to pay you now."

"That's okay. I trust you." He opened the screen door. A cat walked out, stopped directly in their path, studied the weather, and decided it would pass. It stood there, tail erect and twitching, and Erin preceded Nick inside. He headed for the commons room with a casual "See you later."

Nick had an admirable if irritating ability to forget all about an argument once it was over. It was a habit almost essential to anyone involved in politics. Erin wished she could do it. Not that it was easy to stay angry with Nick. He was such a cheerful character. His penniless state didn't seem to bother him, and he was generous to a fault. Imagine spending thirty dollars on a present for someone who was not a close friend, when he couldn't afford a new battery for his car.

Christie was at her desk when Erin entered the office. She stopped working long enough to skewer Erin a cool stare but didn't speak, so Erin decided she was in bad odor for taking a long lunch hour, but that the theft of the coat had not been discovered. She settled down at her own desk, but found it hard to concentrate. It was difficult to think of a reason why Rosemary and her archenemy's wife would put their heads together in private. There were a lot of holes in Nick's theory; if Erin hadn't been so annoyed with him, she would have pointed them out. She was quite willing to believe that a politician might consider winning an election a sufficient motive for murder—but only if he believed he had no chance of winning otherwise. Bennett was still ahead. Possessing even more than the average politician's share of ego, he surely must be convinced he would win. If he knew something that would damage Rosemary's chances, he would publicize the fact, not kill the opponent.

None of it made sense, not even political sense, which was only distantly related to the real world. Erin was relieved when Kay called her into her office and gave her a pile of papers to be copied and mailed out.

She saw nothing of Rosemary until late afternoon. The sight of her, smiling and composed and elegantly garbed in a softly tailored wool suit, was so at variance with the brassy-haired conspirator and the mug-throwing virago, Erin could only stare.

Rosemary greeted the group with a cheerful "Another day, another vote for the right—sorry, make that left." She stopped at Erin's desk; the latter braced herself. There was no reason why she should feel guilty, but she had an irrational feeling that her knowledge was printed on her face.

"How are you at blowing up balloons?" Rosemary asked in a conspiratorial whisper.

"It's one of my prized skills."

"Go help Nick with the decorations, then. I'll keep Jeff occupied."

She looked as if she had nothing on her mind but surprising her aide. Humming under her breath, she went on her way.

Erin found Nick hard at work, aided and abetted by Will. Sarah stood in the doorway, hands on her hips and a broad smile on her face, watching Will drape crepe-paper streamers from the chandelier. "That's enough," she called. "Save some for the table."

"This goes on the table." Nick roped the plastic envelope from a gaudy paper tablecloth covered with cavorting bears dressed in party clothes and a glaring HAPPY BEARTHDAY in bright red.

"Rosemary sent me to blow up balloons," Erin said.

"The balloons are my province." Will said, removing a package of them from a brown paper bag. His expression was as solemn as ever. "I happen to have an extremely capable set of lungs. I don't waste my breath shouting idle threats and insults at other people, the way the rest of these neurotics do, so I have more to give to balloons."

"How are you going to hang them up?" Nick asked.

Will looked blank. "I don't know. Scotch tape?"

"You can't put tape on a balloon. How about if we tie a piece of string around each one? Sarah, got any string?"

"There's a ball of it in the drawer beside the sink. You put that back when you're through with it, and my scissors too!"

Leaving the balloons to the two self-appointed experts, Erin spread the cloth on the table, laid out napkins and paper plates, and went to help Sarah in the kitchen. The cake was a masterpiece that deserved the hearty praise she heaped on it: a huge angel food piled with whipped cream and filled with strawberries. She sneaked a sandwich from under the damp cloth that covered the plate and took a bite. "Mmmmm, that's wonderful. Tuna—but what else?"

"A smidge of that Dijon mustard and sour cream, along with the mayonnaise."

"You went to a lot of trouble, Sarah."

"Rosemary said to, but I would've anyhow. I get the feeling that boy don't have much family life, or if he does, it's the wrong kind. He never talks about his folks."

"Maybe he's an orphan. Or just a very private person. I haven't heard anybody talk about family, it's all politics around here."

"They talk to me," Sarah said.

Erin paused with another sandwich halfway to her mouth and considered Sarah's placid face and round, comfortable figure. "Yes," she said. "I can see why they would."

"It's the kitchen, honey," Sarah said. "Not me. People come in for a cup of coffee or a snack, and sit down, and put their elbows on the table; and there I am, stirring something on the stove or mixing batter—it's like being back home with your mama, you know what I mean?"

"You're an archetypal figure," Erin said.

Sarah gave a rich laugh. "If you say so, honey."

"You know what it means. Don't kid me."

"Sure, I know. I just don't hold with fancy words. Hear too many of 'em around here all the time." She took another plate from the refrigerator and filled in the empty spaces Erin had left. "Have some more, Erin, there's plenty. Then tell me how many candles."

"Gosh, I don't know. I'll ask Nick."

Nick knew. According to Rosemary, Jeff was thirty-one. Erin retreated to the kitchen to report, adding, "You should see what those two characters are doing to that room. They've got crepe paper hanging from every hook; it looks like a jungle."

"Good to see 'em enjoying themselves," Sarah said. "Everybody needs a little break. Things have been pretty tense around here lately."

"You noticed it too?"

"It's natural, I guess." Sarah brooded over the cake, her

face unusually serious. "Means a lot—this election. High time we had somebody like Rosemary up there in the Senate. She stands for—well, for a lot of things. Here, Erin, open that jar of nuts and put 'em in a bowl."

"Could that be why Rosemary decided to throw Jeff a party? To give people a chance to relax and be silly?"

She expected Sarah would deny this and claim Rosemary's reason was purely altruistic; but Sarah's answer had more than a touch of ambiguity. "She usually has a couple of reasons for doing what she does."

The other guests straggled in over the course of the next half hour. By six o'clock they were all present, stealing sandwiches, laughing and talking, and making rude remarks about the decor. Nick defended his work heatedly; Will simply blinked and remarked that the detractors obviously lacked the barest rudiments of artistic taste.

Nick was enjoying himself. His face beamed, and his eyes shone as he rushed around the room, rearranging his balloons, listening at the door to see if Jeff was coming, distributing party hats and noisemakers. His suggestion that they all hide behind sofas and draperies and jump out shouting "Surprise" was unanimously hooted down, but when Jeff came in, following Rosemary and followed by Joe, the chorus of "Happy Birthday" was heartfelt, if somewhat ragged.

Jeff registered the proper emotions—surprise, pleasure, embarrassment, appreciation—but Erin suspected he had not been completely unwitting. There had been a dozen people in on the secret; perhaps one of them had let something slip. At any rate, Jeff's pleasure seemed to be genuine. He let Nick put a cardboard party hat on his head, and when Sarah carried in the cake ablaze with candles, he directed the chorus of "Happy Birthday," beating time with his tin noisemaker.

The sight of the stack of brightly wrapped gifts obviously disconcerted him. "Whose idea was this?" he demanded. "I didn't expect . . . You shouldn't have done this, Rosemary."

"What makes you think it was her idea?" Joe asked in an injured tone. "I am known all over Washington for my benevolence, my constant care for others, my—"

A chorus of jeers and laughter drowned him out. Christie handed Jeff a glass of wine. "You'd better wait till you see the gifts before you start thanking people."

"I guess that's right." Jeff smiled. "I shudder to think what Nick's idea of an appropriate gift might be."

"You wound me to the heart," Nick exclaimed, clapping his hand to his chest. "Since you're so suspicious, you can open mine first. It's from me and Erin, actually; we expect a groveling apology when you see what it is."

Erin still had no idea what was in the box; she braced herself, hoping Nick had not selected anything too vulgar. The gift was certainly vulgar, though not in the sense she had feared. It was a cheap copy of a British barrister's wig, curls, queue, and all. Jeff's amusement and delight were unfeigned; he clapped it onto his head and wore it while he opened the remainder of the gifts.

Most of them were funny or friendly or both: a box of homemade cookies from one of the girls in the office, a five-foot-long scarf from another ("considering you get paid about the same as Bob Cratchit"), a hideous plaster kitten with oversized eyes, and so on. Joe's offering was different: a leather wallet and matching key case, of rich and obviously expensive morocco. "I noticed you'd lost your key chain," Joe grunted, when Jeff turned to him in speechless surprise. "Anybody else want something to drink besides me?"

He wandered off before Jeff could say anything, and Rosemary shook her head. "Don't thank him, he doesn't know how to accept graciously."

She had saved her own gift for last. The others crowded around, laughing and conjecturing, while Jeff undid the pretty wrappings and opened the plain white box. His face went absolutely rigid, a carving in mahogany.

"It's an antique," he said in an odd, strained voice. "A family heirloom. You can't. . . ."

"It's no heirloom," Rosemary said casually. "My dad loved it, though; it was the only thing he never hocked."

"Your father's?" Jeff's clenched fingers relaxed; carefully he placed the box on the table. "I can't take this."

"Sure you can. There's a chain too." Rosemary lifted the

watch and draped the chain across Jeff's flat stomach. "Now I ask you—is that class or what? It goes with your three-piece suits and your image of aristocratic intellectuality."

Joe had joined the group, a glass of bourbon in his hand. "You may as well take it," he advised. "If you don't, the damn thing will keep turning up. In your soup, or your underwear drawer, or the glove compartment of your car."

Rosemary had replaced the watch and chain in the box. Jeff eyed it as if it were a snake coiled to strike. "Don't tell me your father would have wanted me to have it, Rosemary. I can't imagine. . . ."

"And you'd be right." Rosemary accepted the implicit challenge head-on, as if she refused to insult Jeff by pretending there was no problem. "My father was the biggest good-ol'-boy bigot in Virginia. The only reason he didn't join the Klan was because he was such a famous drunk they wouldn't take him."

"I can't imagine the Klan turning anybody down on those grounds," Nick said.

If he was trying to lighten the tension he failed. Jeff looked around the circle of sympathetic faces and then fixed an unsmiling stare on Rosemary. "I don't get it."

"I didn't want to embarrass you," Rosemary said quietly. "But if you insist, I'll make a speech. You gave up a good job to join a campaign that appeared to be doomed from the start. God knows I'm not paying you what you're worth, and if we lose, which is quite possible, you'll be out of a job. You've worked outrageous hours and put up with my tantrums and Joe's rudeness, and tried to keep the peace—"

Jeff stopped her with a brusque gesture and turned away, his face averted. After an aching pause Rosemary went on, "Don't make a big deal of it, Jeff. What the hell, it's not a family heirloom, Pop won it in a poker game. I should apologize for insulting you with a secondhand present. Look at it as a gift from one gambler to another. Or . . . as a token of esteem and affection from a friend."

The voice was the one she used in public, every inflection controlled and skilled. Erin had heard it before, mouthing the common catchwords of modern politics. Even so, she had a lump in her throat and two of the girls were frankly sniffing.

But the one who appeared most affected was Kay. She had participated in the festivities with the pained smile of some-one who is ill-adept at friendly foolishness; her gift had been appropriate and unimaginative—a handsome fountain pen. Like all the others, Erin had been focusing on Rosemary and Jeff during the little drama and she was caught by surprise when Kay suddenly rose and blundered out of the room. The silly party hat looked grotesque above her strained face and haunted eyes.

Chapter Ten

ERIN WENT TO BED early and dreamed she was trying to climb a tree whose upper branches burned like a giant torch. On the tip-top branch perched Miz Marylou; and though the flames curled all around her, her clothes didn't even smolder and the expression on her plump pink face, as she peered down at her would-be rescuer, was one of amused interest.

Erin found it hard to get back to sleep after that. As she turned and squirmed, trying to find a comfortable position, the disquieting ideas Nick had planted in her head took on new and more alarming dimensions.

Kay had returned to the commons rooms after only a few minutes, perfectly composed; she had made no reference then or later to her precipitate departure from the party. Erin might have supposed she had imagined the look of strain and horror if there had not been other evidence that something was bothering Kay.

If Rosemary knew the reason for the campaign of harassment, Kay surely must know too. The relationship between

the two women was much more complex than Erin had originally supposed; undercurrents of jealousy and resentment
blurred what had appeared to be a long-standing, easygoing
friendship. But the one thing the two undoubtedly had in
common was their familiarity with intimate details of Rosemary's life with Edward Marshall.

Kay must know why these things were happening. Either
she knew more than Rosemary, or she was less skilled at
concealment. Her reaction to the poppet. her sleepwalking
. . . What could have happened to upset her at the birthday
party? Something about the watch? Had it really belonged to
Edward, and not to Rosemary's father?

No, that was impossible. Erin didn't doubt that Rosemary
could lie like a trooper when she had to—she would never
have succeeded in politics without that skill—but not even
Rosemary would produce so flagrant a falsehood in the presence of someone who knew the truth. If the watch had been
Edward's, though, Kay's reaction would be understandable.
She would feel that Edward Marshall's possessions ought to
be preserved like holy relics, not given so casually to a mere
acquaintance.

Erin rolled over and pounded the pillow. The whole situation was impossible. Perhaps she and Nick were both losing
their minds. Infectious insanity . . . Nick was such a smooth
talker, he could hypnotize a listener into believing anything
he said.

She hadn't mentioned the sleepwalking incident to Nick.
Rosemary had asked her not to. It was a confidence not to
be violated lightly, especially since she couldn't see that it
added anything to their understanding of the problem. So Kay
was upset. Nick must know that; he had seen her collapse at
the sight of the poppet, he was fully aware of her relationship
with Edward and with Rosemary. Why hadn't he suggested
spying on Kay? What did he know that she didn't? What did
either of them know, in fact?

She finally did fall asleep, but the matter was still on her
mind when she woke next morning, and when she heard the
soft sounds from the next room she went at once to the door

and knocked. That was her job, after all, to be of assistance to Kay.

Kay was sitting on the edge of the bed. She had pulled the sheet around her, and her bra lay beside her on the bed.

Kay's modesty had surprised and annoyed Erin at first; it made the task of helping her dress doubly difficult. She was beginning to understand that a woman may not enjoy baring sagging breasts and lumpy thighs in the presence of a girl who is still some years away from those disasters, and now a certain degree of sympathy tempered her impatience.

"Let me help you with this," she said, picking up the brassiere. "It takes a contortionist to fasten one of the darned things, even with two good hands."

Kay turned her back and let the sheet fall. "Thank you," she said in a muffled voice. "I've been wearing the ones that fasten in the front, but my—my arthritis is bad this morning, and I couldn't reach. . . . Thank you. I guess I'll wear slacks today. Putting on panty hose is beyond me."

Erin knew better than to offer assistance with the last-named garment. Kay had been crimson with embarrassment the first and only time Erin had smoothed and shaken her into them.

"You look just fine in pants," she said tactfully, turning and plumping up a pillow while Kay got into the pants. "Can I . . ."

Kay submitted to having her blouse and pants buttoned up. "I hate depending on people," she grumbled.

"I don't blame you. Surely t won't be much longer, though."

"I hope not. My hand feels much better."

After Kay had gone downstairs, Erin made a whirlwind toilette and set to work straightening up the rooms. The maids—a fancy title for the two local girls who came in three days a week—had enough to do keeping the rooms on the lower floors clean. She stripped Kay's bed and wrapped the sheets around a bundle of her own clothes that needed washing.

When she entered the commons room with her armful of linens, she found Rosemary with Kay. Dressed for the day in one of her soft pastel suits, the congresswoman leaned forward at an acute angle to avoid dripping coffee on the immaculate white bow at her throat. "Good morning," she said. "What on earth is that?"

"Laundry," Erin said. "Is it okay if I use the machine?"

"Of course. But those look like sheets. You don't have to change the beds; ask Mary to do it."

Kay's lips pursed and she made clicking sounds of disapproval. "Now, Rosemary, you know I've always taken care of my own room. Those shiftless girls barely get through their work as it is. If you ask them to do something extra, they'll sulk and scamp the downstairs rooms. If I could do it myself—"

"I don't mind," Erin said quickly. She hoped to avert an explosion from Rosemary, whose countenance betrayed her annoyance, but she only succeeded in making matters worse.

"You interrupted me, Erin."

"I'm sorry—"

Rosemary banged her empty cup down on the table. At least she didn't throw it, though she looked as if she would have liked to. "For God's sake, Kay, don't pick on her! It's damned nice of her to do this dirty work; you should thank her instead of lecturing her about her manners!"

Kay did not reply. Eyes lowered, mouth a drooping curve, she radiated hurt feelings. Rosemary drew a long breath. "Sorry, Kay."

"That's quite all right, dear. Better you should shout at me than at a voter."

"Huh," said Rosemary. "We're all a bit edgy. Have you been taking those sleeping pills, Kay?"

"I don't believe in them." Kay's mouth set stubbornly.

"Honestly, Kay! The doctor said—"

"Excuse me," Erin said, and left them to it.

She stopped for a little gossip with Sarah and ended up sitting at the kitchen table pigging out on toast and homemade strawberry jam while she told Sarah how her mother used to make jam every summer—until this last year.

"I worry about her. She just sits around and mopes and feels sorry for herself, and my aunt is no help, she's five years older than Mother, and she loves to run other people's lives for them. She's babying mother instead of encouraging her to take control of her life.''

''That's not so easy to do when you've always had somebody to look after you,'' Sarah said soberly. ''There are a lot of women like your mama, Erin, and the men the age of your daddy, they wanted it to be that way.''

''You're absolutely right. He did everything for her—balanced the checkbook, took care of the cars, argued with repairmen—and kidded her about how sweet and inefficient she was. She ate it up, she'd giggle and smile at him. . . .''

''So she let him do it to her,'' Sarah said, passing the toast.

''She not only let him, she collaborated with him. She liked being . . .'' Erin's voice caught. ''Being a little girl. Daddy's little girl. Just like me. And I collaborated too, I loved it. Why did it take me so long to see. . . . Sarah, you're a witch. Or a closet psychoanalyst. How did you do that?''

''You're making an awful mess with that piece of toast,'' Sarah said. ''I didn't do nothing, you did it. Things boil around in your insides long enough, they finally have to come out.''

''Poor mother,'' Erin murmured. She had squeezed the toast in her clenched hand; absently she smoothed it out and took a bite. ''What's going to become of her? I should have seen it happening. I should have done something.''

''No, I doubt you could have, honey. Sounds like your mama's all right. She's got a roof over her head and enough to eat and somebody to look after her like your daddy did. There's plenty not so well off. You can't change her now. You can't really change anybody, you got to take them the way they are. All you can do is love them.''

Erin made a face, and Sarah laughed. ''Or hate them. Nothing wrong with some good healthy hate. Just don't waste any on your daddy. He didn't mean to do wrong. He didn't even know he was doing it.''

''You scare me sometimes,'' Erin said with a smile. ''You're right; for a while I almost did hate him, without realizing it. I've stopped dreaming about him.''

''That's a good sign.''

"I think so. And I know it's foolish to waste time regretting what might have been. But I wish I had been more forceful, and more aware those last months of his life. I might have made it easier for him if I had insisted on knowing more about his business affairs. There was something on his mind, I'm sure of it. But whenever I asked him a question, he'd just laugh and—and lie. He was going to be fine, he'd be on his feet again in no time, no need for me to worry my pretty little head; one of these days I'd find some nice young fellow who would take care of me. . . . Oh, damn it, Sarah, I'm dumping on you, like everybody else around here. Why don't you tell me to shut up?"

"I'll send you my bill," Sarah said placidly.

When Erin opened the kitchen door she saw Kay standing a short distance away. Her face was a trifle flushed, and there was something awkward about her pose, as if she had come to a sudden stop, or had stepped back instead of forward.

"Were you looking for me?" Erin asked.

"Yes. No. . . ." Kay's laugh had a strained note. "I've got so much on my mind I don't know what I'm saying. I came—I came to tell Sarah we are having extra people for supper. And I wanted . . . I wondered if you could do a few errands for me later. There's cleaning to be picked up, and a prescription to be filled. . . ."

"I can go now, if you like."

"No! That is . . . the cleaning won't be ready until after noon."

"Whenever you say."

"I'll talk to you later." Kay passed her and went into the kitchen.

Erin tried to remember exactly what she had said to Sarah. If Kay had been eavesdropping . . . But of course she hadn't, Kay wouldn't do such a thing, and anyway she wouldn't have heard anything important. Just family worries, some intensely personal, to be sure, but nothing she need be ashamed of.

It was slightly before noon when Kay called her into the inner office. "I'm leaving for a luncheon appointment," she said. "I'd like you to—"

"Drive you? I'd be glad to."

Kay's forehead creased. "That is a very exasperating habit, Erin. Please allow me to finish my own sentence."

"I'm sorry. I thought you wanted me to run some errands."

"I've changed my mind." She looked challengingly at Erin. Having been slapped down once, Erin was not about to venture an opinion, but Kay knew what she was thinking. "I am perfectly capable of driving," she said firmly. "What I want you to do is sit here and wait for a call I'm expecting. Actually, I don't believe it will come through today, but there is a possibility that Mr. . . ." She hesitated for a moment and then went on, "Mr. Brown will call earlier. Take notes of the information he gives you—"

"Shall I turn on the recorder?"

Kay's frown deepened. "I could do that if I wanted the information recorded. I said, take notes. On paper. Put them into this drawer, and close the drawer. It locks automatically."

"Yes, ma'am."

Kay reached for her suit jacket. Erin moved to help her.

"I apologize," Kay said, her face averted. "I didn't mean to snap at you."

"That's all right."

"I have a lot on my mind," Kay said, half to herself. "Make sure that drawer is locked after you close it, Erin. But as I said, it's unlikely the call will come through before I get back."

"I'll make sure."

Kay started for the door. Then she turned. "You understand, I'm sure, that this information is confidential. I don't want you to mention the call to anyone."

"I won't," Erin said shortly.

"Of course not." Kay forced a smile. "You're a good girl, Erin. I have every confidence in you. This information I'm expecting isn't important except—except to me. It's a—a personal matter. Don't even mention it to Rosemary. She has enough on her mind, and I don't want her worrying about my problems."

"Whatever you say."

After Kay had gone, closing the door carefully behind her, Erin allowed her face to relax. What was that all about? she wondered. Kay's compliments had been as unconvincing as her stammered explanation. She didn't have to explain an order; the very fact that she had done so suggested that there was something peculiar about this task. Erin had no doubt that the call was political in nature and that she had been selected to receive it because she was too ignorant to understand implications that would have been immediately apparent to Christie and the others. The idea only whetted her curiosity.

By one o'clock it seemed unlikely that her curiosity would be satisfied. That was when Nick found her, bursting into the office with an exasperated "What are you doing in here? I looked all over for you. Christie said—"

The phone chose that most inconvenient moment to ring. Erin's hand hovered over the instrument. Then she picked it up, said, "Hold, please," and covered the mouthpiece with her hand. Not only was Nick standing in the doorway, Christie was right behind him, remonstrating with him.

"Nick, you can't go in there; Kay said Erin wasn't to be disturbed till she—"

"Oh, for God's sake, what is this, the War Room at the Pentagon?"

"Five minutes," Erin said, hoping she was right.

The door slammed. Erin made a wry face. At least the caller didn't resent having to wait; from the earpiece came a mellifluous crooning. "Bringing in the sheaves . . . " Mr. Brown must be a member of a church choir.

"Hello," she said.

"Who's this?" asked a gruff male voice.

"Is this Mr. Brown?"

"Yes. Miss Goodrick?"

"This is her secretary," Erin said. "I was instructed to take down the information you have for her."

"She didn't say nothing about a secretary."

"She had to leave for an appointment, and she wasn't really expecting you to call until later."

"So I'm efficient. She told me—'

"See here, Mr. Brown. This number happens to be private and unlisted. Here I am, and there you are; how would I know your name unless Miss Goodrick had told me?'

A gruff chuckle vibrated against her ear. "Okay, sister, it's no skin off my nose anyhow. Got a pencil?"

"Go ahead."

It didn't take long. A few names, a few dates.

"That's all?" Erin asked.

"That's it. I'll send my bill. In a plain envelope like she said." Another hoarse chuckle, and then a click. Mr. Brown had hung up.

Erin looked at the sheet of paper in front of her. It told her nothing. Five first names—two male, three female—eight dates. As she studied them, a pattern began to emerge. Each name was followed by at least one date; these ranged in time from March 19, 1957 to December 10, 1966. All but two names had a second date following the first. And all the second dates were identical: July 4, 1967.

Birth and death? Juxtaposed pairs of dates almost demanded that interpretation, but the more Erin studied the figures, the less she liked it. If it was correct, the three people who had died were children; the youngest had been less than a year old. And surely three children wouldn't die on the same date of natural causes. Had they been members of the same family? No last names had been supplied. There had been two survivors; a boy, the firstborn, and a younger girl.

As she had been instructed, Erin put the paper into the drawer and slammed it shut. Kay's assumption had been correct, she had not the slightest idea what the information might mean. If Kay was engaged in some underhanded attempt to discredit Senator Bennett, she was glad she didn't understand.

She had only time to exchange a few words with Nick before he was off again; he invited her to come along for the ride, an invitation she was forced to refuse. "There's too much to do, Nick."

"Yeah, okay. I have to go to D.C. and I thought maybe . . ."

She knew what he meant, but she didn't say it either; they

were standing in the hall and there was too great a chance of being overheard. "I can't," she repeated, "Kay's not in the best of all possible moods these days, and if she came back and found me gone—"

"Okay, okay. But don't forget to ask her about Friday."

Kay returned a short time later. She had been gone for less than two hours, so obviously her appointment had not been in D.C. But of course she wouldn't risk driving that far, in heavy traffic, Erin thought idly.

To judge from Kay's expression, she had not enjoyed her outing. She darted a quick unsmiling glance at Erin, who was at her own desk, and hesitated for a moment, but went on without stopping. Erin half-rose and then sat down again. The situation was one Will would have considered self-explanatory; when Kay looked, she would find the notes of Mr. Brown's call, and would know why Erin had abandoned her post. She decided, however, that this might not be the best time to ask for a day off. She would wait until she could catch Kay in a better mood—if that eventuality ever occurred.

The opportunity did not arise until they stopped for supper, and before she had a chance to talk to Kay, the others began drifting in—Christie and Jan; Anita and Jackson; Joe, annoyed because Rosemary wasn't back from the Hill yet; and finally Rosemary herself, accompanied by Jeff and sputtering angrily over the defection of a colleague who had promised to support a bill she favored.

"Somebody got to him," she exclaimed, tossing her bag onto the couch. "He won't tell me who, or what he was offered in exchange, but I swear—"

"Never mind all that stuff," Joe interrupted.

"Stuff? What do you mean, stuff? That stuff is what I was elected to do, Joe."

The arrival of Nick broke up the argument. Erin tried to catch his eye, but he took a seat next to Rosemary and became intent on what she was saying. Erin joined Jeff at the table. He offered her the glass he had just filled.

"Have some Madeira, m' dear? It's Chablis, actually."

Erin shook her head. "I thought you didn't drink."

"I didn't used to." Jeff raised the glass to his lips.

"Bad day?"

"No worse than usual."

"You look exhausted. Have you had anything to eat? I'll bet you skipped lunch again. Have some cheese. Supper is almost ready."

She put a chunk of Brie on a cracker and held it out to him. Jeff smiled, and he accepted the tidbit. "Have I mentioned lately that it's very nice having you here?"

"You can't say it too often to suit me," Erin said cheerfully.

"You could return the compliment."

"Haven't I?" She handed him another cracker and watched soberly while he ate it. "I guess I haven't. This has turned out to be a fantastic experience for me, Jeff; a growing time, in a lot of different ways. But it's been difficult at times. You've made it much easier than it might have been. So often when I've been depressed or resentful or beleaguered, it was you who came to the rescue. You've defended me, encouraged me, taught me—"

"Hey, wait, this is embarrassing." Jeff actually did look embarrassed; his eyes avoided hers. "You make me sound like some kind of saint."

"No, actually I sound like one of Rosemary's early speech drafts," Erin said, laughing. "The kind she edits because, as she says, it oozes with sloppy sentimentality. But I meant it, Jeff."

"Thanks."

"Thank you. Have another cracker."

He laughed and accepted the offering. They stood nibbling and sipping in silence, comfortable in one another's company.

Night had fallen; the windows framed a sprinkle of stars, and the breeze carried the scent of burning leaves. The atmosphere had mellowed. Nick and Joe talked quietly, Rosemary was laughing over something Will had said. . . . Will? He must have been there all along; Erin hadn't seen him come in. His chameleonlike talent of blending with the background would have been very useful to a spy or undercover agent.

More likely, Erin thought charitably, it was simply the habit of a shy, reserved man.

The night was so still that the sound of gravel crunching under the wheels of a car carried distinctly to the two, who were standing near the window. Jeff turned to look.

"I wonder who that is."

"Kay said something about company for supper."

"News to me," Jeff said. "Maybe she meant Christie and Jan; she treats the office workers like outsiders. . . . Oh, no."

How he had deduced the identity of the newcomer Erin did not know. Perhaps it was the distinctive sound of the car's engine, or just the pricking of his thumbs.

Laurence didn't knock or ring the bell, he simply walked in. He stopped in the doorway looking them over like an actor counting the house, or a predator picking his prey from a herd of grazing deer. His eyes were as cold and opaque as those of a lion studying a potential kill, and Erin wondered how she could ever have felt the faintest stir of empathy for him.

She expected Jeff would speak, if only to warn the others their conversation was being overheard, but he seemed to be struck dumb. Kay was the next to see Laurence.

"Why, Philips," she exclaimed. "I didn't expect to see you this evening."

To Erin her surprise seemed exaggerated, but then so did the reactions of the others—Joe's unconcealed annoyance, Rosemary's forced civility. Laurence had that effect on people.

He greeted them with a casual flip of his hand and said coolly, "I knocked, but you were having such a jolly time you didn't hear. Please go on with what you were doing; I wanted to have a word with Rosemary, but I'm in no hurry, and I would hate to disturb such a pleasant gathering."

"I was just leaving," Christie murmured.

"Me, too." Jan edged toward the door.

Erin tried to join the exodus, but Laurence exclaimed, "Don't run away, Erin, or you'll force me to believe you are trying to avoid me. Oh, hello, Will, I didn't see you. Still hiding behind a stack of books?"

Will smiled vaguely and adjusted his glasses. Laurence's vulturine eye moved on to the next victim. "Nick, dear boy! You made quite an impression the other night; Juliet is still raving about your charms. Joe, how are you? You look a bit the worse for wear, old chap, you really ought to get more exercise, you know. And those cheap cigars aren't good for you. I speak only out of concern for your health, old fellow. With the campaign at such a crucial stage it would be a pity to lose you."

Rosemary put a firm hand on Joe's arm. "Would you care for something to drink, Philips?"

"Thank you, a glass of wine would be nice. No, don't get up, Rosemary. I'll help myself; or perhaps Jeff . . ."

He sauntered toward the table. Erin realized that this time he wasn't concentrating on her. If Jeff was aware of Laurence's speculative gaze he didn't show it; he poured the wine with a steady hand.

"Thank you." Laurence accepted the glass, his eyes never leaving Jeff's face. "I understand you celebrated your birthday recently, Jeff. I'm sorry I wasn't invited to the party, I'd like to have presented a small token of my esteem."

"It wasn't a formal affair," Jeff said quietly.

"No? I regret all the more having missed it then. I enjoy informal arrangements. And I love giving presents to deserving individuals."

He didn't look at Erin, but she knew the remark was directed at her. Nick had been right; Laurence would never forgive her for returning his gift so publicly. She was pleased to discover that she no longer cared what he did or said; she had a delightfully childish desire to put out her tongue, or thumb her nose.

"I've already had more than I deserve," Jeff said, with a glance at Rosemary.

"No, no, dear fellow. You deserve the best, and if you go on as you've begun, you will get what you deserve. Your future unquestionably lies in politics. I foresee a brilliant career." He lifted his glass in a toast.

Joe lit a cigar and blew a thick cloud of smoke in Laurence's direction. "I'm always suspicious of you when you're laying on the compliments, Laurence; are you trying to lure Jeff away from us?''

"Now why would I do a thing like that?'' Laurence asked innocently.

"Rumor has it that you have a few political aspirations yourself,'' Joe said. "Forget it, Laurence, or establish residence in another state. Sarbanes and Mikulski have got Maryland sewn up, and Montgomery County is solidly Democratic. You won't have a prayer.''

"I cannot imagine how these rumors start,'' Laurence said.

Rosemary's fingers beat an impatient tattoo on the edge of the table. "Come into my office, Philips,'' she said, rising. "These people have things to do. We can talk privately.''

"I had hoped to persuade you to have dinner with me,'' Laurence said. "I made reservations at the Red Fox, but if you prefer another restaurant . . .''

"No, that would be fine.'' Rosemary sounded less pleased than resigned; apparently she had decided it was easier to go along with Laurence's plan than get rid of him. "I can't take long, Philips. I have work to do this evening.''

"I'll make it worth your while,'' Laurence promised, smiling.

They went out together, Laurence's hand possessive on Rosemary's arm. "What do you suppose he's up to now?'' Joe demanded.

"We'll soon find out,'' Kay said. She had raised no objection to Rosemary's defection, but it was obvious she didn't approve.

Erin was the only one who heard Jeff's murmur. "Will we? I wonder.''

Chapter
Eleven

THERE WAS NO COMMENT from Nick, for the simple reason that he was no longer there. Erin turned in time to see the door close behind him. She took off in pursuit, heedless of the stares and amused speculation of the others.

Nick was at the front door. "Are you trying to avoid me, or what?" Erin demanded. "I haven't had a chance to talk to you for days. . . . Wait a minute. Where do you think you're going?"

Nick tried to shake her off. "Let me go or come with me. I'm going to lose them!"

The taillights of Laurence's car dimmed and brightened as he made his careful way along the rutted drive. Erin released her grip. "You're going to follow them? Nick, you are absolutely the most—"

"No time. Talk to you later."

He plunged out. Erin stood watching. The taillights had disappeared before Nick's balky engine finally caught; undaunted, he pulled a screeching turn and went in hot pursuit.

Torn between amusement and exasperation, Erin returned to face Kay's visible disapproval and Joe's jokes. "Never chase a man, kiddo, let them do the chasing. Especially when the man is Nick."

Will's head popped up over the books. "And above all, never take Joe's advice on matters of the heart. He doesn't have one."

Jeff's description of politics as stumbling from one crisis to the next became more apt with each passing day. Erin came downstairs the following morning to find a fresh domestic crisis awaiting her. Kay had fallen during the night and reinjured her hand; she and Rosemary were in the midst of a hot debate on the subject when Erin walked into the commons room. Her appearance ended the argument; Kay got up and walked out, leaving Rosemary flat.

"Oh, shit," said the latter, slamming her fist onto the table. "I'm sorry, Erin—"

"You know you don't have to apologize to me."

"Not for bad language, at any rate." Rosemary drew a long, steadying breath. "I shouldn't have lost my temper with her. She denies she was walking in her sleep, claims she was on her way to the bathroom when she fell."

"I didn't hear her," Erin said. "I should have been listening—"

"No, I'm guiltier than you, guiltier than you," Rosemary chanted. A haggard smile warmed her face. "Did you ever read *Pogo*? Remind me to lend you my collection sometime. She's trying to lay a guilt trip on me, says she was so groggy from the sleeping pills I made her take that she lost her balance. Which is a bunch of baloney—like your feeling that you ought to have been lying awake all night. In the next breath she insisted she had run out of sleeping pills. I think she flushed them down the john."

"Would you like me to take her to the doctor? I know you don't have time."

"I do like a person who makes practical suggestions," Rosemary said approvingly. "Unfortunately it won't work. Kay says she's fine, her hand just needs rest and time. And that old fake White—her doctor—is no damned help. I've already called him, he just said to refill the prescription for the pain medication and call him in a few days if it doesn't improve. I'll tell you what you could do, though—run into town and pick up the prescriptions. Sleeping pills and pain-killer. Would you mind?''

"Of course not. That is, if Kay will let me drive the car.''

"I'll make sure she does.'' Rosemary glanced at her watch. "Damn, I'm late. Thank you, Erin. I keep saying that—believe me, it's from the heart.''

It was shortly before noon when Kay called Erin into her office and handed over the car keys. She spoke about the errand as if it had been her idea; Erin was careful not to say anything that would indicate she knew better. Kay had a list of other errands as well: the cleaning that had never been picked up, a few groceries. She didn't look well; her face was gray under her heavy makeup.

It was a warm, bright day, with a brisk wind blowing the fallen leaves into multicolored clouds. Erin lingered to stroke a cat that came to rub itself against her leg. She wasn't look-ing forward to the drive. Accidents could occur even with the most skilled and careful of drivers, but she knew Kay would hold her personally accountable for any dent or scratch. Things like that always seemed to happen when you were using someone else's car. . . . She was tempted to ask Sam if she could borrow the pickup. She'd feel quite comfortable in that battered vehicle; nothing short of a major collision could worsen its condition.

Since she hadn't seen Nick's car parked out in front, she had assumed he was off somewhere. The car was in the stable-yard, and Nick was in it—literally, for the hood was up and only the lower half of his body was visible. He didn't hear her coming; when she greeted him, he started and he banged his head on the hood, which promptly collapsed on him.

"I'm so sorry,'' she exclaimed, helping him extract him-self from the metal jaws. "Are you hurt?''

Nick rubbed his head. "Happens all the time,'' he said cheerfully. "I should have propped it with something. Where are you off to?''

''Errands for Kay.'' She dangled the keys.

''How about a lift to town? I was trying to recharge the battery, but I'm afraid it's a hopeless cause. I'll have to buy a new one.''

''I thought you were broke.''

''I may be able to squeeze one more charge out of my Visa. Worth a try, anyway.''

He plucked the keys from her hand and led the way to the Mercedes. This high-handed maneuver would have prompted a caustic comment from Erin if she hadn't been glad to be relieved of the responsibility of driving. She allowed herself one mild warning: ''For God's sake, drive carefully, will you? Kay will kill me if anything happens to this car.''

''No, she'll kill me.'' Nick backed the car out and proceeded with exaggerated slowness down the driveway. ''Anything new to report?''

''About what?''

''Anything.''

''I don't know why you're asking me, you're the great detective. I presume Rosemary and Mr. Laurence went to the Red Fox last night, just as he said they would?''

''Uh-huh. Then home again, home again, jiggety-jog. Any comment?''

''No.''

''Good. Then I needn't mention that although tailing them turned out to be an idle exercise, I had no way of knowing that until I did it.''

''I can't argue with that,'' Erin said agreeably. ''Did you find out what he wanted to talk to Rosemary about?''

''Oh, that.'' Nick didn't stop at the end of the drive; after making the turn he put his foot down and the car picked up speed. ''He's invited her to appear on his show Sunday.''

''Firing Squad?''

''Hey, that's a good one,'' Nick said, with a sputter of laughter. ''Where'd you hear that?''

''It's Fran's name for it. She says Laurence is as bad as Buckley when it comes to snide comments and unanswerable questions—and since it's not taped, but live, a lot of his guests have had a rough time.''

"Shot down in flames, no survivors," Nick agreed. "Most of the guests are politicians, you'd think they would have learned how to lie and equivocate; but Laurence really knows how to needle people."

"That's why it's so popular, I suppose. It has all the ghoulish fascination of stock-car racing; the viewers hope someone will crash right in front of their eyes."

"A few people have. Remember the time he goaded Senator Willis into admitting he was gay?"

"Fran told me about it. Maybe it wouldn't be such a smart move for Rosemary to go on."

"That's what Joe says. He doesn't trust Laurence any farther than he can throw him, says he. But it's first-class exposure, free media to the max, and Rosemary says she'd be a fool to pass it up."

"He certainly seems to be an ardent fan of hers," Erin said doubtfully. "Slow down, Nick, this hill—"

"The trick," said Nick, over the squeal of tires, "is to get up enough speed going down so that you don't have to pump so much gas going up the next one. I dunno, though I'm like Joe, I don't trust the skunk. He may be fond of Rosemary, but he loves his precious self and his precious show more."

"Nick, the stop sign is there, just around the curve."

"Yes, darling, I know. If there's anything that gripes me more than a woman who is smarter than I am, it's a woman who tries to tell me . . ."

"What's the matter?" Erin asked.

Nick leaned forward, peering through the windshield. "Is that smoke?"

"Where?" Then she saw it. "Oh, God. It's coming from under the hood. The engine must be overheating. Stop, Nick."

Instead of stopping at the sign, Nick made an abrupt right turn onto the shoulder of the highway and slammed on the brakes. "That's not steam, that's smoke. Out. Get the hell out of the car."

There was no shoulder on the narrow road they had just left, no place to pull over without risking being rear-ended by another car coming around the curve. She understood his reason for turning, but she didn't understand his urgency, nor why, instead of opening the hood, he ran to the back of the car and unlocked the trunk. Not until she got out and saw that the vaporous extrusion was black, not the pale shade of steaming water.

Nick came running back, carrying a blanket. "Get the hell away from here," he yelled. "Move it!"

He had released the hood latch before he got out of the car. When he lifted the hood, a tongue of flame licked out at him; instead of drawing back he threw the blanket and himself onto the engine.

It had happened too quickly; Erin had no time to react to his orders, even if she had wanted to. When she saw him disappear under the hood, she ran—not away from the car, but toward Nick. "Get out of there," she screamed, tugging at his coattails. "Are you crazy? Let it blow up, let it burn!"

Nick said something. She didn't catch the words, she was screaming too loudly, using words she had never expected to hear from her own lips, calling him every name she could think of. Not until a pair of hands grabbed her by the waist and swung her aside did she realize another vehicle had stopped on the shoulder ahead of them. A pickup—of course. Rusty blue, of course. . . .

"It's okay, lady, you can stop yelling," said the Good Samaritan, a tall, towheaded youth in jeans and a visored cap. "He's got it out. You wanna dump dirt on it, buddy, just to make sure? I got a shovel in the back. . . ."

Erin staggered out of the way and sat down on the ground, while Nick and the other man evaluated the situation. For a while both of them had their heads together under the hood, and she bit her lip to keep from shrieking at them. After an amiable and hideously prolonged discussion, they nodded at one another, and Nick came toward Erin. "He's going to give us a lift back to the house. Are you okay?"

"Am I . . ." She took a long, steadying breath. "You stupid, bullheaded, thoughtless, arrogant, cocky . . . man!"

"Now that stung," Nick said, grinning from ear to ear. "Kindly select a less offensive epithet."

"You're all covered with soot!"

"And I have a blister on my thumb," said Nick. "Hold

on, honey, you can faint or do something interesting like that after we get home.''

"I am not going to faint!" She glared at him. "I am going to kill you. What do you mean by scaring me like that?''

"That's better. Here we go. . . . This is real nice of you, pal.''

The young man dropped them at the gate and brushed away their thanks with a casual "No sweat." Erin thought she was in perfect control of her emotions until Nick plucked the campaign button from his lapel and pressed it on the Good Samaritan. She collapsed onto the ground and laughed till she cried.

Nick sat down beside her and put a tentative arm around her.

"Don't touch me!" A hard shove emphasized the words.

"What are you mad at me for?" Nick demanded aggrievedly. "I didn't do anything."

"Except risk your stupid neck for a hunk of machinery, and push me out of the way like some doddering little old lady, and—"

"Oh, gee whiz, I apologize for all those terrible things."

"You could have been killed!"

"If I had let that car blow, Kay would have killed me."

"It's not funny! You never take me seriously. What's a rotten piece of machinery compared to death or serious injury?''

"There was no danger of that," Nick protested. "Luckily Kay had a blanket in the trunk. She read some newspaper article about keeping the car stocked with survival equipment; there's even a bag of kitty litter for icy conditions. . . .''

"Shut up! You're doing it again, talking down to me. Why won't you take me seriously?''

"I do, believe me I do. You scare the hell out of me when you act like this. I can't understand why you . . ." A new and apparently pleasing idea dawned and was reflected on his face. "Could it be that you're all shook up because you thought I might've been hurt? My mother used to scream at me when she—''

"You bastard!"

"Leave my mother out of this." There was nothing tentative about the hands that drew her into a hard embrace. He smelled of oil and smoke but Erin didn't care; it was an aroma as sweet as perfume to her. Not until much later did she realize that his lips were crusted with ashes, and that she had absorbed them into her mouth with the eagerness of someone participating in a ceremonial rite.

"We look kind of silly squatting here by the side of the road," Nick remarked some time later. "I know a pretty little spot back in the woods—"

"Certainly not. At least . . . not now. Talk to me."

Nick helped her to her feet. "About fires?"

"About this fire. What was it?"

Nick hesitated, but only for a moment.

"It looks as if one of the fuel-injection lines came loose."

"Fuel? You mean gas? But if gas was leaking, wouldn't we have smelled it?"

"No. That's the thing." Nick picked up a stone and began to draw in the dust. "See, the fuel-injection lines go into the fuel distributor—here. Gas doesn't flow through them until the fuel pump starts up. Then, if there's a loose connection, some of the gas will spurt out onto the engine, and when the temperature rises to a certain point, the gas will ignite."

"I see. Do I have to ask the next question?"

Nick sighed. "I wish I knew the next answer, Erin. If you ask a Mercedes dealer whether the line could work loose, he'll deny it with his last breath; but there's always a possibility of a faulty connection. A good mechanic will check things like that as a matter of routine when the car is serviced; and if I know Kay, it has been serviced regularly. We can find out when she had it in last, and we can ask the mechanic whether he checked the fuel connections. He will, of course, say he did."

"How hard would it be to loosen it?"

"All you'd need is a wrench and a couple of minutes—and the necessary know-how."

"So anyone could have done it."

"Not you." Nick produced a rather wan smile. "You aren't even sure gas is fuel."

Like Queen Victoria, Erin was not amused. "I wouldn't

have known how to do the job. But you don't know that I don't know.''

Nick rose lithely to his feet and helped her to rise. "Your syntax is a little confused, but I get your meaning. Anyone could have had what I am pleased to call the know-how. Even Kay, I suppose. You pick up odd bits of information here and there. Like, a mechanic might have pointed out that the connection was loose, and warned her always to have it checked.''

''Yes, let's not be sexist in selecting suspects. More to the point is why it was done.''

''That's obvious, isn't it?'' Nick kicked a pebble and watched it dribble off into the grass. "Another fire. Only this one could have been dangerous.''

''How dangerous? You said it wasn't.''

''I lied. Or let's say I exaggerated a trifle. To put it in the simplest possible terms—''

''In deference to my stupidity?''

''In deference to your charming ignorance of the internal combustion engine. If the driver kept his or her head, it is extremely unlikely that he or she could have been killed or seriously injured. If you see something boiling out from under the hood, your first impulse is to open it and find out what's going on. An inexperienced driver might assume, as you did, that the car had overheated. I knew that wasn't the case, but I thought—if I thought at all—that oil had slopped over onto the engine, or a rag or paper towel had been left inside. If I had known it was gas . . . Oh, I suppose I'd have done the same thing, most people would—try to put out the fire by smothering it. Opening the hood admits air, and that fans the flames, so you've got to move fast and hope the fire hasn't taken serious hold.''

''But you are an experienced driver,'' Erin said slowly. ''If I had been alone . . .''

''Don't think about it,'' Nick said gruffly.

''We have to think about it. What's the worst that could have happened?''

''The damned car could have blown up, that's the worst that could have happened!'' Nick shouted. They walked on in silence for a while, and then Nick said in a calmer voice,

"But not right away; long before that happened, even a moron would have taken alarm, and backed away. If you're thinking attempted murder, forget it. Not only was the method inefficient, but the perpetrator couldn't have known who would drive the car next. Up until this morning, Kay's hand was improving—"

"She did drive it," Erin said. "Yesterday."

"You've driven it recently," Nick pointed out. "So has Jeff. She'd lend it to Rosemary, I suppose."

"Or Will?"

"I don't know. Maybe."

"Joe?"

"He's the last person she'd allow behind the wheel of her precious," Nick said. "Next to last, I should say; I'm the ultimate. No, it has to be a piece of random malice, Erin, like all the others. Ask Kay if you can take tomorrow off."

The fire had shaken her nerve more than she had realized. At first she didn't understand what he was driving at. "Why?"

"You haven't had a day off since you started work, have you?"

"No, but I can hardly complain. Here I am mixing with the glamour guys and gals of politics, studying the inner workings of the greatest game on earth. It's all so—so stimulating."

"Isn't it, though. Nothing like being scorched periodically to add zest to life. . . . You've never visited the Hill, or had a power lunch. Yeah. That should work just fine. I think it's time our hardworking little novice got shown the sights of Washington. Duke Zeibert's for lunch, maybe."

"Nick—"

"Or The Monocle. It's not far from the Library of Congress."

*   *

KAY DIDN'T FAINT when they told her what had happened, but for a few alarmed seconds Erin thought she was going to. Her face turned a sickly shade of greenish white, and Nick had to help her into a chair. Her first coherent words were, "How bad is it?"

Nick crossed his fingers and lied like a rug. "Not bad, Kay. Really. It could have been a lot worse."

"Oh my God." Kay hid her face in her hands.

"It would have been a lot worse if Nick hadn't risked himself to put the fire out," Erin said. Kay hadn't even had the decency to ask if either of them had been hurt.

"I wasn't referring to the car," Kay said in a shaking voice. "Are you all right, Erin? When I think what could have happened . . ."

"Nothing happened," Erin said quickly, regretting her first assumption. "I'm fine."

"I have a blister on my thumb," Nick whined, holding the digit in question out for inspection. "Kiss it and make it well."

Kay's lips quivered; for a moment it was questionable as to whether she would laugh or cry, but Nick's foolery had the desired effect. "Well, thank goodness that's all," she said. "What were you doing with Erin, Nick? I am glad you were with her, and I'm very grateful to you for your quick thinking, but . . ."

"I hitched a ride," Nick said, looking as innocent as any saint.

"I see. Well, I'm grateful you did. I should never have asked Erin to drive that car."

"It wouldn't have mattered who was driving," Nick said. "It could have been you. Or me."

Kay shook her head. "That will be the day, young man. There aren't many people I'd trust with that car. . . ." Her voice trailed off and her face took on the blank, listening look of someone considering a new and not too pleasant idea. "Never mind. The important thing is that no one was hurt."

Nick went off to borrow the pickup and make arrangements for the Mercedes to be towed to a garage. He offered to do the errands while he was in town; when Erin handed over the list, he twisted his face into such hideous contortions she thought he was having a fit, until it dawned on her he was reminding her of what they had discussed earlier.

The color had returned to Kay's face, but she sat where Nick had placed her, hands limp and eyes abstracted. When

Erin asked if she could take the next day off, Kay nodded. "Yes, that will be quite all right."

Erin couldn't believe she had heard correctly. No argument, no discussion. "Are you sure?"

"Yes, why not? You deserve it; you've worked very hard and you've just had a very unpleasant experience. Run along now; I have things to do."

Nick returned with the cleaning and Kay's medicine, but without a battery. As he described it, the machine had emitted strident jeers of laughter when his credit card was inserted.

"I think mine might run to a battery," Erin offered. "Just as a loan, of course."

She wasn't sure how Nick would take the offer, and his first reaction was to stiffen and look haughty. Then he grinned sheepishly. "Save it. We may need it for something else."

"How are we going to get into town tomorrow?"

Nick waved an airy hand. "I'll think of something."

They ended up riding in with Joe, who had spent the night, as he was doing with increasing frequency. He and Rosemary had taken to working late; but according to Nick, fatigue wasn't the primary reason why Rosemary insisted on his staying over.

"Why, then?" Erin asked. "Do he and Rosemary have something going?"

Nick's brows drew together. "Have you got some kind of hang-up about Rosemary's sexual activities? First you had her hopping into bed with Laurence, now you're suggesting she and Joe—"

"Why, Nick, you're blushing," Erin said maliciously. "I didn't mean to shock you."

"I am not blushing!"

"But you're shocked. Yes, you are! Talk about hang-ups—you have a blind spot where Rosemary is concerned, and you're not the only one—you all do it, treat her like a piece of damp clay you can pummel into any shape you want." A poignant memory of Rosemary's lament on the night of her granddaughter's birthday came back to her, and she added with equal vehemence, "She's not a series of platitudes and a two-dimensional campaign poster, she's a human being, with human needs and, I daresay, a few human weaknesses."

"Okay, okay." Nick considered the idea. "So maybe you have a point. But Joe . . . He's not her type."

"How do you know?"

"I don't." Nick smiled reluctantly. "There's no accounting for tastes, as the old lady said when she kissed the pig."

"Cow."

"What?"

"When she kissed the . . . Oh, never mind, I don't think the comparison is very nice either way. Rosemary's private life is none of our business, so long as she's discreet about it. She seems to have been very discreet indeed, or you wouldn't be hanging on to this fantasy that she's as pure as Caesar's wife. You're probably right about one thing, though; she wouldn't carry on an affair with Joe here in her own house, under Kay's very nose."

"Kay's the worst offender, in your terms," Nick said. "She'd throw a fit if she thought Rosemary were betraying the sacred memory of Edward Marshall."

"So why does Rosemary insist Joe stay overnight?"

"What? Oh, that. It's just that Joe's drinking is getting a little heavy. She doesn't want him to have an accident, or get picked up for DWI. Listen, you're here at night, have you ever noticed—"

"Oh, grow up," Erin exclaimed.

Joe showed no ill effects when he appeared for breakfast. In fact, he was turned out with unusual smartness; suit pressed, shoes shined, shirt spotless. When Erin complimented him on his appearance he tugged self-consciously at his tie, a conservative paisley print on a dark background.

"Is this tie okay, do you think? Rosemary gave it to me; she says my others look like I'd closed my eyes and picked 'em off a rack at a discount outlet."

"It's perfect," Erin said. She caught Nick's eye. He blushed.

Joe dropped them at the Capitol. "How are you going to

get home?'' he asked, leaning across Erin to open the door for her—a mark of distinguished favor.

''Jeff said he'd pick us up at three, if we could be here on the dot,'' Nick answered.

''You'd damned well better be here on the dot. When Jeff says three, he means three, not three-oh-five or even three-oh-one.''

Nick grimaced. ''I know. He's in a foul mood lately, isn't he? Almost bit my head off when I asked him for a lift.''

''Wait a minute.'' Joe fumbled for his wallet. ''You better pick up a battery for that wreck of yours. Get Jeff to stop someplace on the way home.''

Nick stepped back, his hands behind him. ''No, thanks,'' he said stiffly.

''Don't be a goddamn jerk,'' Joe shouted. ''We need more vehicles. I'm renting yours for the campaign, okay? It's perfect for our humble, lower-middle-class image. So take the money and shut up.''

He dropped the bill at Nick's feet, slammed the car door and took off. Erin jumped on the money and caught it as it started to flutter away. It was a hundred-dollar bill.

Nick watched the car weave a path between the concrete barricades that had been set up in the hope of discouraging terrorists. ''He's in a *very* cheerful mood this morning, isn't he?''

Erin burst out laughing.

''What's so funny?'' Nick demanded.

''You. Are we going to stand here all morning?''

''Wait till he's out of sight. Turn around, admire the Capitol, and try to look impressed.''

That wasn't difficult. Erin had become accustomed to the sight of the massive dome crowning the city, but she had never taken the time to go sightseeing, and she was surprised at how light and well-balanced the building appeared at close range. The capitals of the Corinthian columns looked like frozen lace, and the lofty flights of marble stairs, one on either end and one in the center, raised the eye to the swelling curves of the dome.

''You've been inside, haven't you?'' Nick asked.

''No.''

"You haven't? I wish we had time for a real sightseeing tour of Washington. If I say it as shouldn't, you won't find a better guide. I'm hooked on this town. I used to spend all my spare time wandering the streets and poking into odd corners. I'll bet I'm one of the few people who can identify every single one of the statues."

"It is a beautiful city," Erin agreed. "Too bad about those barricades; trying to disguise them as planters didn't work very well."

"Life in the twentieth century," Nick said wryly. "Okay, he's gone; we can be on our way."

As they walked, Nick gave her a sample of his talents as a guide. "The Senate side of the Capitol is on the north, and the House is on the south, ahead of us. Those are the House office buildings across the street, facing the House side, as the Senate buildings face the Senate side. There are three House buildings—Cannon, Longworth, and Rayburn, the newest. Rosemary's office is there, in the Longworth Building."

"They're so big," Erin said, studying the long white marble facades that seemed to stretch for blocks.

"Well, there are over four hundred representatives. They all need offices, plus offices for secretaries and staff, meeting rooms, places to eat, restrooms. . . . As a matter of fact, this business of staff has gotten out of hand. Did you know that each congressman is allowed up to twenty-two staffers? Senators get more, depending on the population of the states they represent—as high as eighty in some cases. All salaries courtesy of the taxpayers."

"That seems reasonable. The more constituents, the more work, right?"

"It isn't the proportions, it's the sheer numbers. At last count there were 20,000 staffers serving the 535 members of Congress, and that doesn't include the staffs of legislative agencies. It's become a matter of prestige—how big your offices are, how many serfs you have attending upon your needs. Taxpayers' money shouldn't be spent puffing up the egos of their representatives. The worst part of it is, a lot of work the staffers do is either unnecessary or self-serving. One of the reasons why it has become so difficult to get legislation passed,

and accepted by the administration, is that the bills are packed
with special-interest provisions cooked up by staff representatives. The process is getting so complicated it can't work.''

''Very interesting.''

''Was I lecturing? Sorry, the subject gripes me. Of
course,'' Nick added with a grin, ''there has to be room on
Rosemary's staff for a few more worthy souls. Next year—
God willing and cross your fingers—Rosemary will be moving
a couple of blocks north, to one of the Senate office buildings. Now look over there—on the west lawn. See that big
oak tree? It's over a hundred years old. You've seen it on
television, it's where the correspondents do their stand-ups.
One of these days . . .''

'' 'This is Nick McDermott, reporting from Capitol
Hill.' ''

''Maybe. Or, 'This is Joe Schmoe, speaking with Senator
McDermott.' ''

''Is that what you want?''

''I'm not sure what I want right now. Just to be part of
this, somehow, some way.''

The gleaming white of the buildings, the emerald-green
lawns and brilliant fall foliage shone in the sunlight as if
freshly painted. But it wasn't only the beauty of the scene, it
was what it signified. The reality might be tarnished and
stained, but the vision somehow endured.

Nick tugged at her arm. ''Hurry up, let's make that light.''

''What's that big white building over there with the columns?''

Nick gave her a pitying look. ''That's the Supreme Court,
you sweet little hick. What have you been doing with your
time since you arrived in D.C.?''

''Not sightseeing.''

''Why not? People come from all over the country—the
world—to see this town.''

''I don't know. I wasn't much interested back then. And
it's no fun alone.''

''You poor abandoned child. Take a good look then, while
we're here.''

Erin squinted at the stately white building. ''What does the inscription read? 'Equal justice . . . under law.' Nice sentiment."

"That's what this is all about "- Nick gestured grandly. "At least that's what it's supposed to be about. Now this structure on your left, with the squatty green cupola, is the original Library of Congress, conveniently situated near the Capitol to make it easier for the legislators to improve their teeny little minds. That's the old building, named after Thomas Jefferson. There are two others—the Adams, over that way, and the newest, the Madison, where we're headed. You have to see the inside of the Jefferson, it's impressive as hell—long red curtains at the windows, paintings and marble floors and all that jazz. Maybe next time . . ."

The architecture of the Madison building was in striking contrast in that of its ornately adorned elder sibling. A stark cube of pale-gray marble, polished till it glistened, its entrance was lined with square unadorned columns of the same material. A number of redwood picnic tables added a pleasantly homely touch. Many were already occupied by students and tourists enjoying the fall weather.

Nick had obviously been there before. Without hesitation or questions, he led her past the guard and along a bare white corridor to a door labeled "Newspaper Room." After filling out a request form and handing it in at the Circulation Desk, they found a pair of empty places and sat down to wait for the microfilm to be delivered.

"You know how to operate these gizmos, don't you?" Nick spoke in a low voice, out of deference to the researchers occupying the other desks.

"Yes, I think so. Why did you ask for the Richmond newspaper?"

"Do I have to explain everything?"

"If you want my cooperation, you do. The main thrust of this enterprise is of course clear to me, but I cherished a forlorn hope that you had concocted some sensible way of carrying it out."

Nick gave her a pained look. "You had better pray we find what we're looking for in the Richmond paper, because if we don't, there are dozens of local rags we'll have to check. And

the Washington *Post*, which covers the Virginia suburbs.''
Erin groaned and Nick went on, "The Richmond paper is
the best bet for a couple of reasons. First, it's the biggest one
in the state. Second, the Marshalls lived in Richmond for ten
years, while Ed Marshall was in the state legislature. His
mother still lives there, in the family home.''

"His mother?''

"Most people have mothers.''

"Hard to be born without one,'' Erin agreed. "I didn't
know she was still alive.''

"She and Rosemary don't get along. She thought Eddie
Boy married beneath him. Point is, the Marshalls have Richmond connections. It seemed a logical place to start. So, if
you have no further objections . . .''

She had a number of them, but the arrival of the microfilm
put an end to the discussion. The sheer number of boxes was
daunting; Erin watched despondently as Nick divided them
into two stacks and shoved one at her.

He hadn't explained what she was to look for, and in a
way she was flattered by his assumption that she had sense
enough to figure it out for herself. The dates on the film she
had been given began with January 1, 1956, and ended with
1969. Nick had taken the lion's share; his presumably began
where hers left off, and went up to the present. The beginning
date was not as arbitrary as it might seem. In 1956, Rosemary
had been newly married. Nothing that had happened to her
before then would have much bearing on her career, which
was closely connected with that of her husband.

Erin sighed and extracted the first spool of film from the
box. It went faster than she had expected, once she got the
hang of it. Skip the sports section, the classified, the pages
devoted to entertainment and style, look for the key words:
"Fire, Blaze.'' They occurred only too often. "Two Children
Killed in Fire.'' "Blaze Destroys Warehouse.'' "Arson Suspected in Downtown Blaze.'' She had to read each of these
stories carefully, looking for anything that might connect them
with Rosemary, even indirectly. As she plowed doggedly on,
a pattern emerged, but not the one for which they were
searching. Most of the fires had occurred in low-rent dis-

tricts, and in winter. "Defective Space Heater Blamed for
Blaze in Apartment Building." "Police Suspect Child Playing with Matches Started Tenement Fire."

She had to stop every now and then to rest her eyes and
change the film. The third of these interludes coincided with
one of Nick's. They stared gloomily at one another over the
scattered boxes. "How far have you gotten?" Nick asked.

"Fifty-nine."

"That's pretty good."

"No, it's not. At that rate, it will take all day to finish this
lot, and how do we know we've even got the right time period? Or the right paper, or the right slant? Maybe the fires
have an entirely different meaning."

"I know." Nick knuckled his eyes. "It's so damned depressing. Did you notice how many kids are killed in fires?"

"That appears to be one of the hazards of poverty." Erin's
lips twisted. "There was no such thing as decent, cheap day
care—there still isn't—so single parents had the choice of
going on welfare or leaving the kids alone in the apartment.
I can't stand—"

She broke off. Nick said awkwardly, "Try not to let it get
to you. Can you stand a little more of it?"

"What? Oh, sure. It's okay."

The stories had affected her painfully, but that was not why
her breath had caught and her voice had stopped. After Nick
returned to his reader she sat staring at the lighted screen in
front of her, wondering why she had been so slow to make
the connection. Children, that was the catalytic word. Children killed in fires. . . . Kay's list of names, Mr. Brown's
list. Three children, three identical dates. And the poppet—
the doll. A child's toy.

She sorted through the boxes looking for the date. It was
an easy one to remember: July 4, 1967.

There was only one fire mentioned in the newspaper of that
date. Carelessly handled fireworks had started a small blaze
in a field, no harm done, no injury to man or beast. Erin was
about to relax when she realized an incident later in the day
might not have made that edition. She went on to July 5.

And there it was. Front page.

The name Marshall was not mentioned, but she knew she had found what they were looking for. The names had rooted themselves in her subconscious; they were instantly familiar. Raymond, the eldest; Mary Sue, Allen, Alice, Linda. And their mother, Josephine Wilson, age twenty-seven.

The police had gotten the names from the boy, Raymond. There was no other record; the family had been squatters, illegal residents of a building that had been condemned and was due to be demolished. The boy had tried to get back inside. . . .

Erin pulled back from the reader. "I found it," she said.

"What? Where? Let me see." They exchanged places. After he had read the story, Nick looked up with a puzzled frown. "There's nothing abut Rosemary in this."

"It's the one," Erin insisted. "It has to be. I'll explain in a minute. See if there's a follow-up. They said police were investigating. . . ."

Nick gave her a curious look, but did as she asked. After an interval he said, "Yeah, here it is. There was another body found—that of a man. Downstairs, in the room under the one where the family was staying. They think he was a bum, a wino, who passed out and let a cigarette fall into a pile of old newspapers. The weather was hot and dry, it hadn't rained for days. . . . Statement by an official of the company that owned the building. . . . Blah, blah, sad tragedy, blah, blah, said Mr. Roy—Roy. . . ." His voice trailed off.

"Well?" Erin said impatiently. "Roy what? Marshall?"

Nick raised his head and looked at her. His face was that of a stranger. "Not Marshall. Hartsock. Roy Hartsock, attorney-at-law. Your father?"

Chapter
Twelve

ERIN HAD ONLY the vaguest recollection of the succeeding half hour. She sat in a stupor while Nick finished the job with silent, tight-lipped efficiency. After he had collected the copies of the articles, he had to lift her bodily from the chair and lead her out.

It was not until they left the building and the fresh air brushed her hot face that she fully recovered her senses. One of the picnic tables had just been vacated; she dropped onto the bench with a thud that made her whole body vibrate.

"I didn't know," she mumbled. "I didn't. I really didn't."

Nick sat down beside her. He couldn't take his eyes off the pages he held—or else he was reluctant to look her in the eye.

"Then how did you know this was the right story?" he asked reasonably.

"I'll tell you. I was going to tell you. Just listen. . . ."

Her narrative was not a model of coherence but Nick had no trouble following it. "Brown," he repeated. "He didn't say who he was?"

"No. But it's obvious, isn't it? Kay hired him to find that information. Birth and death dates. He must be a private detective."

"So Kay knows about this."

"But I don't. I didn't. Nick, you've got to believe me!" She grabbed his lapels and tried to shake him. Nick sat like a rock, his eyes moving slowly over her face, feature by feature. Then he took her head between his hands and pressed his lips to hers.

When he raised his head she saw he was smiling. "Sure, I believe you. Whoops, there go the papers—grab them. . . ."

Erin let him chase the papers; she was so weak with relief she felt giddy. "Do you really, Nick? Not just because I kiss so well?"

"That doesn't hurt." Nick sat down again. "No, but seriously, as someone once said—you should have seen your face. If you were faking that wide-eyed horror you ought to try out for Arena Stage. And besides, if you had known about your father's involvement, you wouldn't have shown me the story."

"I can't believe it. I had no idea—"

"You're repeating yourself, love." Nick pushed a lock of hair away from his face; the breeze had stiffened. "I'm feeling somewhat bewildered myself. To be honest with you, and myself, I never really expected to find anything. The odds were so against it. It's like stumbling over a genuine dead body when you're playing cops and robbers. Why didn't you tell me about that phone call?"

"I didn't make the connection till now. There are so many underhanded, undercover things going on—I assumed it had to do with the campaign."

"Fair enough." Nick's eyes returned to the copies. "So what have we got? A tenement fire in which several members of a family were killed. They were there illegally. The building was owned by a corporation whose nominal head was your father. But we know the Marshalls were involved—"

"No, we don't. Not yet. Has it occurred to you, Nick, that this business might be aimed, not at Rosemary, but . . ." She swallowed. "At me? Unless there are earlier incidents of which I am unaware, the first fire happened the day I came to Middleburg for my job interview.''

"Jesus, I never thought of that.'' He thought about it, and Erin was guiltily pleased to observe that the possibility of a threat against her distressed him more than danger to Rosemary. Then his face cleared and he shook his head.

"I admit some of the incidents are ambiguous, like the one involving Kay's car; but except for you getting mauled at the fund-raiser—which I still believe was unrelated to the other things—nothing has been directed at you. Whereas the fire in the graveyard was a direct hit at the Marshalls—specifically Ed Marshall. I think he was the owner of that building. Your dad was just the owner of record, or whatever the term is.''

"Why should Marshall want to conceal the fact?''

Nick shrugged. "I don't know anything about corporate law, or finance, or any of that stuff. If I did, I'd be a rich entrepreneur instead of an impoverished journalist. There may not have been anything fishy about the corporation itself, but I can think of a lot of reasons why Marshall might not want his name on record. Tax evasion, maybe. And don't forget he was running for office. 'Slumlord' isn't a name politicians enjoy.''

"That's not good enough, Nick. I only read the first story; it said the police were investigating. What did they find?''

"The police always investigate fires,'' Nick began. Erin reached for the papers; he gave in with a sigh. "Okay, don't bother reading it, I'll tell you. The police found no sign of arson. They concluded the poor drunk downstairs started the fire. But it happened at a very convenient time for the owners of the building. It was heavily mortgaged and due to be demolished. It was also heavily insured.''

"I see.''

"Erin, honey, there's no evidence that your father had anything to do with that fire. He says in one of the stories that the corporation plans to set up a trust fund for the surviving children, even though there was no legal liability. They had ignored the 'Condemned' signs, broken through boarded-up windows, and sneaked in.''

"That sounds like a guilty conscience," Erin said dully.

"Any decent person would feel terrible about a thing like that, even if he hadn't been responsible."

"It was the year after the fire that Dad broke connections with the Marshalls and moved to Indianapolis," Erin said. "He never saw them again, never had anything to do with them, except for an occasional letter or card—and that was Mother's doing. . . ."

"Well, doesn't that suggest that if there was something fishy about the fire, your father didn't know about it beforehand? Maybe it was disgust and abhorrence that prompted him to break relations. Maybe it was just the way his career ball happened to bounce. Either way he's in the clear."

"Isn't there something called accessory after the fact?"

"Forget about your old man," Nick snapped. "Oh, hell, I know you can't, but at least try, for the moment, to concentrate on the issue at hand. Somebody knows about this incident and is holding it over Rosemary's head. Who?"

"Well, it isn't me. But . . . but—oh, Nick! Rosemary probably believes it is. Kay, too. I can hardly blame them. Look at the facts. I show up, out of the blue, asking for a job, and the very first time I set foot in the place there's an unexplained fire. I could have done everything that has been done—I was there. They made sure I was there, they invited me, so they could keep an eye on me—"

"Wait a minute, you're going too fast and too far. The only reason you were asked to move in was because Kay—"

"Yes, don't you see? That accident came at a very convenient time, didn't it? Kay is the only person who could have planned it. She deliberately injured her hand. Only it turned out to be more serious than she had expected, she only meant to bruise it."

"So Kay knows the whole story."

"Of course she knows. She worked for Mr. Marshall even before Rosemary came on the scene, she was his business assistant as well as a personal friend. And think of the time schedule, Nick. My father died over a year ago. He had plenty of time to straighten up his affairs, destroy any documents that might have incriminated the Marshalls—or hand them over to his heirs. I made good and sure everybody knew Mother was incapable of dealing with business matters; if Dad had passed the information on, it would have been to me.''

Nick nodded reluctantly. ''And the guilty parties would be only too ready to smell blackmail in everything you said or did.''

''Could something like that really damage Rosemary politically?''

''That would depend. How deeply was she involved? Was she an officer of the corporation—is her signature on the legal papers? Remember the flap about Ferraro's involvement in her husband's business, and what that did to her career. And this has sensitive side issues. The slumlord image wouldn't go over well, especially for a candidate who's made a big moral issue of supporting poverty programs and civil rights. Hypocrisy is the operative word, and a damned dangerous one in politics. Yes, I'd say Rosemary would go to some lengths to keep it under wraps.''

''Who's doing this, then? I swear, Nick—''

''I said I believed you. And what's more,'' Nick added thoughtfully, ''Rosemary and Kay aren't certain about you either. If they were, Kay wouldn't have bothered looking up those names. You want to talk about motives for harassment, the surviving members of that family have good cause to resent the Marshalls. Did you happen to notice—''

''I could hardly help noticing, it was right there in the paper.''

''Yeah. The Wilsons were black. If the oldest boy was ten in 1967, he'd be about the same age as . . .''

''Jeff,'' Erin murmured.

''Jeff came to work for Rosemary about a year ago. Gave up a good job, just as she said. When was it, exactly, that your father died?''

''May. It's been more than a year—almost eighteen months.''

''Let's assume the trust fund for the kids was set up,'' Nick said. ''Your father would have been the logical person to handle it; but the money had to come from Marshall, or from the corporation itself. They would take every possible precaution to keep Marshall's name out of it, but transactions of that sort can be traced, surely, by someone who knows the tricks of the trade.''

"A lawyer, for instance. And Jeff is a lawyer. Oh, damn." Erin bit her lip. "It looks bad, doesn't it? Jeff could be Raymond Wilson. He was born in 1957. . . . Nick! Raymond's birthday was in March! Nick, it can't be Jeff. We just celebrated his birthday, remember?''

"Hey, that's right!" Nick looked as relieved as she felt. "Are you sure about the month?"

"Pretty sure. We can find out."

"Do the same thing Brown did," Nick said excitedly. "I'll bet he just went to the courthouse and looked up birth and death certificates."

"We don't even have to do that. Mr. Brown is probably listed in the Richmond classifieds. I'll call him back, tell him I mislaid the data."

"Good thinking, Erin."

"I'm so glad," Erin said. "I don't want it to be Jeff."

"You don't want what to be Jeff?" inquired a mild voice.

Nick jumped a good two inches. Standing behind them, looking at them with a benevolent smile, was Will.

"If I ever saw guilt writ large upon a pair of human faces, I see it now," Will went on. "Don't worry, I won't tell Joe I found you canoodling instead of working."

"I've never canoodled in my life," Nick said, recovering himself. "Canoodled! Where do you find words like that? And don't tell me in the dictionary. We are not neglecting our duty, we've got the day off."

"Hell of a place to spend it," Will said.

"Uh—just part of the sightseeing tour. What are you doing here?"

Will raised his eyebrows. "I work here. Where do you suppose I get the information I give Rosemary?"

"I always thought you made it up," Nick said. "Well. I guess we'd better get moving, Erin, right? We've got to see the White House, the monuments, the . . . the . . . See you later, Will.''

Without moving or changing expression, Will somehow managed to look smaller. Abandoned, forlorn, lonely . . . "Join us for lunch?" Erin suggested. As soon as the words were out of her mouth she could have kicked herself—and so could Nick; he gave her a look of bitter reproach.

"I'm brown-bagging it." Will indicated his bulging, shabby briefcase. "I only brought one sandwich, but if you'd care to share it . . ."

"I wouldn't deprive you for the world," Nick assured him. "It's probably a peanut-butter sandwich, isn't it?"

"Why, yes. But you're more than welcome—"

"He lives on peanut butter," Nick explained. "Prolonged infantilism. No, thanks, Will. See you tonight?"

"Yes, indeed."

"You could have asked him for a ride home," Erin said, trotting to keep up with Nick's rapid strides. "If we miss Jeff—"

"We won't. Why'd you ask him to have lunch with us? We've got a lot of things to talk about."

"I don't know why. It was idiotic of me; the words just said themselves."

Nick's steps slowed. He looked back. "He's standing in front of the building watching us. You know, I wonder about Will. That absentminded professor shtick of his doesn't quite make it. Could he have been following us?"

"He has a logical reason for being there."

"Oh, yeah? There's a fairly decent library at the University of Virginia, and Charlottesville is only an hour from Richmond. Why does he have to come to Washington to work?"

"To be near Rosemary."

"Oh, God, you're not going to start that again, are you?"

"No, I was just suggesting one possibility. There are others."

"Indeed there are. He could be in on this, Erin. He and Rosemary go back a long way."

"So do a lot of other people and Rosemary. How long has she known Will?"

"Dunno. We're going to have to investigate the whole

crowd. Would your Visa run to a private eye's pay, do you suppose?''

''I don't suppose, I know. It wouldn't.''

''At least we can check on the surviving Wilson kids without too much effort,'' Nick said thoughtfully. ''Jeff's out; let's hope we can eliminate Christie and Jackson on the same grounds.''

''Jeff is only out if the arsonist is one of the Wilsons. There are other motives.''

''Damn, there you go again, being logical. And, what's worse, being right. Once you admit a political motive, the field is wide open. Three people certainly knew about the Richmond fire—Rosemary, Kay, your father. And one of *them* could have told others. Ed Marshall could have confessed, before he died. And if we managed to track this down, a trained investigator might well be able to do the same. This is the first really dirty campaign Rosemary's ever fought—the first one where she faced an opponent without scruples. It would be worth a lot to Buzz to get something on her.''

''But if he knows, why is he playing cat and mouse?''

''Yeah, well, I've been thinking about that. I doubt Buzz knows. What this looks like to me is a setup for blackmail. 'Pay me, in cash or in favors, or I'll take my information to Bennett.' When she balks, he lights another match.''

''Bennett's wife doesn't fit into that scenario.''

''I can't think of any way to make her fit,'' Nick admitted. ''So maybe the scenario is wrong. That meeting between Miz Marylou and Rosemary has to be connected with this somehow, there can't be two conspiracies going on.''

''Two? Why not six or seven? Washington is a city of conspiracies, big and small. Everybody's hiding something, everybody is up to something.''

''Now, now, don't exaggerate,'' Nick said. ''What you need is a little nourishment. And perhaps a drop of the cup that cheers and inebriates. Down this way.''

The building was of cream-colored brick, with dark-green shutters and a canopy of the same color. Window boxes held bright displays of crimson geraniums. Erin hung back, and Nick said, ''What's the matter? Aren't you hungry?''

"I am, actually. But Nick, isn't this place awfully expensive?"

Nick flung the door wide. "My dear, think no more of mundane matters. This is one of the few places in town where my credit is still good. At least I hope it is. . . . Please look impressed when the maitre d' greets me by name."

The maitre d' did greet him by name, and led the way to a table at the rear, behind a free-standing fireplace that occupied the center of the room.

"You notice I'm not important enough to rate a table where I can see and be seen," Nick explained.

"This is nice and secluded," Erin said politely. "Nick, was that Senator Kennedy?"

"Uh-huh. The guy with him is the majority leader. And that couple . . . I'll be damned. There's Philips Laurence. I wonder what he's doing here, this isn't his usual ambience."

"Who's that with him?"

"I don't know. Damnedest hat I ever saw, it's like a limp funnel." The deep-brimmed navy hat hid the woman's face, and most of her body was concealed by the table and by her companion. Nick twisted around to get a better look. Erin poked him.

"Don't stare, he'll see you. He's looking this way—"

"Oh, everybody stares in places like this. It isn't the food that brings people, it's the clientele. Damn, I think he's spotted us."

Laurence said something to his companion, rose, and came toward them. "Hello there," he said, smiling.

Nick gave a theatrical start. "Oh—hello, Mr. Laurence. I didn't see you. Would you care to join us?"

Laurence recognized this piece of bravado for what it was. His closed lips stretched wider. "What a lovely idea. Unfortunately, I'm lunching with someone else. Why don't *you* join *us*?"

"We haven't ordered yet and you're almost finished," Nick said.

"That's true. How clever of you to have observed that without seeing me."

There was nothing Nick could say to that, so he remained silent.

"I'd like to get your input on Rosemary's appearance on my show Sunday," Laurence went on.

"You got my input, such as it was, the other day," Nick said. "What's to say? It's your show, you have your own way of handling things."

Laurence tired of baiting him. "Quite. I understand; when you are entertaining a beautiful young lady, you don't want to share her. Enjoy your lunch, children."

"Smug son of a bitch," Nick said, glowering at Laurence's retreating back.

"Nick. That's—"

"I don't care if he does hear me. He is a smug SOB. Did I tell you about the meeting we had, to discuss Rosemary's appearance? He told me—"

"Nick, that's not what I was going to say. Just shut up and listen to me. That's your trouble, you know that? You never listen—"

The waiter glided up to ask if they were ready to order. Nick waved him away.

"Look at the menu," he growled.

"I'm looking at the woman with Mr. Laurence. Nick, it's Kay. That's what I was trying to tell you."

"The fish is good," Nick muttered. "Might as well . . . What?"

"Don't turn around."

"Why not?"

"Because if she had wanted us to know she was here, she would have waved or nodded or something."

Nick pretended to drop his menu. The performance wouldn't have deceived a child. "Are you sure?" he asked, straightening. "I can't tell."

"Yes, I'm sure. I got a better look when he was away from the table. Look at her hand—it's bandaged."

"Lunching with the enemy," Nick muttered. "And in disguise—"

"It's a pretty feeble disguise and a pretty public place for a secret meeting. And Mr. Laurence is an ally, not an enemy.''

"Hmmmm. So why doesn't she wave or something?"

"I don't know. I'll have a chef's salad," Erin added, as the waiter approached.

Nick insisted she look at the menu, and persuaded her to change her mind. Breast of Chicken Rosemary was too appropriate to resist. She paid no attention to the prolonged discussion about food and wine that ensued. She was watching Kay and Laurence—and thinking.

The Pandora's box she had unwittingly opened might yet contain a small sprite of Hope, but right now she couldn't find it. All she could see were the sins and mischiefs. The discovery had made clear a number of things she had vaguely wondered about—Rosemary's financial generosity to her, Kay's inappropriate questions during the purported job interview—and cast a cloud of doubt on others she hadn't considered. It was like a spotlight, distorting by its very brightness and casting of shadows. The conversation with Joe, in which he had expressed such a kindly interest in her and her father; Christie's antagonism; Laurence's dislike; Will's habit of turning up when she least expected him.

How many of these insights were real and how many were only distortions?

After Nick had dealt with the wine steward, enjoying every nuance of tasting and approving, he shook her out of her unhappy thoughts by demanding that she report on Kay and Laurence.

"They're still talking," Erin said. (And what about the innumerable combinations of people? Kay and Laurence, Jeff and Kay . . . Stop it, she told herself.) "Now she's handing him something. . . . The headwaiter is bringing the check. . . . Laurence is smiling in that patronizing way of his. . . . He's signing the check. Didn't even look at it."

"Adding up the bill is uncouth," Nick remarked. "Remind me not. . . . Now what?"

"Don't turn around! She's coming this way."

Kay's face was darkly shadowed by the drooping hat brim but a vagrant ray of light reflected from her eyeballs so that she seemed to be peering slyly out at them like a fox from its lair. Even her voice echoed oddly. "I didn't expect to see you two."

Nick had risen, napkin in hand. "Didn't Erin tell you I was going to show her the sights?"

"Oh, yes. It slipped my mind, I guess. Well—enjoy yourselves."

She walked toward the door, where Laurence was waiting.

"That was short and sweet," Nick said, sitting down and reaching for his wineglass. "I was too well-mannered to say so, but I wasn't expecting to see her either. I thought she was going to Norfolk with Rosemary."

"I'd love to have overheard that conversation," Erin said, watching Laurence gallantly usher Kay out the door.

"You wouldn't have heard anything interesting. If they have secrets to exchange they'll do it in Laurence's car, or on a park bench. Lunching together in a public place, openly and innocently, could be a cover-up for the real reason why they had to meet. But Kay sure as hell didn't think she would run into us. I'll bet she'd have tried to sneak out without speaking if Laurence hadn't convinced her she was bound to be recognized—"

"Stop it." Erin put her hands over her ears. "I feel as if I've wandered into a scenario about secret agents and the CIA. Their reason for meeting was probably quite innocent. I wouldn't be too surprised to learn that they had had an affair once upon a time, and perhaps the old flame still smolders. . . . Oh, damn. What's the use of speculating when we don't know what we're talking about?"

"That's all we can do—speculate. Hmmmm. That's an interesting idea. It hadn't occurred to me; but then I lack your fine insight into romantic matters. Laurence used to have something of a reputation along those lines. Seems to have reformed lately. AIDS has affected a lot of life-styles."

"It doesn't seem to have inhibited Senator Bennett."

"I refuse to discuss AIDS or Buzz Bennett," Nick declared. "Or anything else that might upset my stomach. Have some more wine."

By the time they finished the prolonged and expensive

meal, they had to hurry in order to meet Jeff. Nick had consumed most of the bottle of wine—"I'm not driving, and at these prices I'll be damned if I send any of it back"—and he called for the check with a flourish whose insouciance undoubtedly owed something to the alcohol. The waiter bent down and murmured something in his ear. The change in Nick's expression verged on the ludicrous.

"What is it?" Erin asked apprehensively, as the waiter glided away. "I've got some money, if there's any problem—"

Nick had to swallow twice before he could speak. "No problem. None at all. That bastard Laurence already paid it. Can you believe the chutzpah of that—"

"It was a nice gesture."

"Nice? Why is it that when Laurence offers me something, I want to snap at his hand like a mad dog?" Nick's lowering brows lifted and the corners of his mouth twitched. "If I'd known he was going to pick up the check I'd have had dessert."

A faint autumnal haze hung over the city, mellowing the afternoon sun. Nick sniffed the air appreciatively. "I suppose it's loaded with ozone and other yucky substances, but it smells good, doesn't it?"

"I keep thinking I smell smoke," Erin said.

Nick gave her a sharp look. "You do. Everybody's burning leaves this time of year. Don't let it get to you, Erin."

He left her no breath to answer, but took her arm and hurried her along. Even at the best pace they could set, they were a few minutes late. Jeff was waiting for them. He didn't look pleased.

"You know what the traffic on the bridge is like. I want to get the hell out of town before it starts."

"We were only three minutes late," Nick protested. "For me that's damned good. I wouldn't have done it for anybody but you, pal."

"I believe that." Jeff shifted into drive and slid the car deftly into the traffic. "But only because you know I won't wait for you. Punctuality isn't just a virtue, you know, it's a necessity in this business, especially for small-fry like you and me. One of these days you're going to cook your goose keeping some big shot waiting—"

"Okay, okay." Nick, in the backseat, stretched his legs out and relaxed. "What are you so grumpy about these days? Is something bugging you?"

"What's not to bug me? The polls are slipping, the paperwork is piling up, the flyer that should have gone out last week is still on your desk—"

"That's because the printer screwed up," Nick retorted. "Did you want me to send out the first lot, the ones that called Rosemary the candidate of the asses?"

"That's a rotten phrase anyway. Sounds like the Communist Manifesto."

Nick sat up. If looks could have killed, the glare he directed at the back of Jeff's neck would have felled him on the spot. "Oh, yeah? Well, for your information—"

"Boys, boys, don't fight." Erin mimicked Kay's prim voice. "We must all pull together and overcome these little difficulties."

The only response she got was a pair of grunts, one tenor and one baritone, but Nick leaned back and the tight line of Jeff's lips relaxed. In an effort to find a noncontroversial subject, Erin said, "I see you're using your new key case, Jeff. It's really good-looking."

"Yes." After a moment Jeff said awkwardly, "I—uh—I enjoyed the party. It was nice of you. Thanks."

"But you never wear your bee-you-tiful wig," Nick complained.

His high-pitched, whiny falsetto won a reluctant smile from Jeff. "I'm saving it for election day," he said.

"Good. We'll have a big drunken bash. We are going to win, you know."

"Yes," Jeff said. "We are."

Chapter Thirteen

KAY DID NOT refer to their meeting in town. In fact, if Erin had not known she was suffering from a tendency to find undercurrents where there were none, she would have suspected Kay deliberately kept her hopping from one task to another so she wouldn't have an opportunity to talk with anyone. It was almost eleven before Kay finally dismissed her. By that time the others had left. Rosemary was not expected back that night. She had gone directly to Charlottesville, where she was to make several appearances the following day.

Erin waited until Kay had gone upstairs before she headed for the commons room and the telephone. She didn't place the call until she had looked into every corner to make sure Will was not lurking.

Her mother was delighted to hear her voice, and brushed aside her apologies for calling so late. "It's cheaper after eleven, darling; there's no need to run up Rosemary's phone bill."

Getting her mother to talk about the good old days at U. Va. wasn't difficult. The hard part was turning the flood of nostalgia in the direction she wanted to go. She listened patiently to a long, rambling description of Rosemary's first meeting with the man she was to marry—a story she had heard dozens of times.

"She looked so sweet in that blue dress I loaned her. Her family was dirt-poor, you know, the poor girl didn't have hardly a stitch of decent clothes. Fortunately we wore the same size. She was a tiny little thing— Well, I was too, if you can believe it! She was going with some other boy, and I had a hard time persuading her to double-date with Edward and your daddy and me, but I knew she wouldn't be able to resist him. He had everything—good looks, money, a fine old family name. And he fell for her like a ton of bricks, if you know what I mean. Your daddy and Edward were fraternity brothers. . . ."

"Yes, I know. It's a pity you had to move away and break up a friendship. And a partnership—weren't Dad and Mr. Marshall partners?"

"Oh, no, honey, they were never in business together. Your daddy did some legal work for him, that was all. Yes, it was too bad, I hated to leave Richmond, but by that time Rosemary and Edward were living at Fairweather, and the offer was one your daddy just couldn't refuse. He never regretted it, I know. He was so happy in Indianapolis. We were both so happy. . . ."

Tears choked her voice; in the background Erin heard another voice, that of her aunt, demanding to know what Erin had said to make her poor mother cry.

She managed to get in one more question. Desperation made her frame it less subtly than she would have liked, but the word "fire" obviously struck no nerve with her mother. "Fire? At Fairweather? Oh, no, honey, there wasn't any such thing, not that I knew about. Nor at our house, I'd certainly remember that! Where did you get the idea? . . ."

"I must have got it wrong," Erin said quickly. "Mother, how are you feeling? Is your leg better?"

It was and it wasn't. The pills the doctor had prescribed helped some, but it still hurt when she walked too much. Erin listened, making sympathetic comments at appropriate intervals. That was the least she could do, listen sympathetically; but her heart sank as her mother kept referring to Ann's ideas and Ann's opinions and Ann's medical theories. I've got to get her out of there, she thought. But how? I can hardly support myself, much less another person, and I couldn't live with her, we'd drive each other crazy.

Finally her mother remembered Rosemary's phone bill. "It's been wonderful talking to you, darling."

"Me too, Mom. I love you."

After she had hung up she sat slumped in her chair for a long time, fighting discouragement. It appeared there was nothing she could do for anyone. She certainly hadn't learned anything that might help Rosemary.

The following day was a torment of mounting frustration. Kay was crankier than ever; the Richmond telephone directory had no listing for a Brown Detective Agency, and neither did the directories for D.C., northern Virginia, or the Maryland suburbs; Nick had left at dawn, to join Rosemary in Charlottesville and escort her through her schedule before driving her home. The idea of calling assorted detective agencies, starting with A-1 Investigative Services and going on through the alphabet, was too depressing to consider seriously, even if she had had time and privacy, which Kay made sure she did not. The state offices in Richmond were closed for the weekend, including the Bureau of Vital Statistics.

The appearance of Jeff, late in the afternoon, was a godsend. His affectionate, teasing manner with Kay amused her and distracted her attention from her victim. Joe came in shortly afterward and commandeered Erin's services with a peremptory firmness that left Kay no chance to object. As soon as he got her into his office he told her to sit down and put her feet up and keep quiet. "I figured you'd about had it with poor old Kay," he explained gruffly. "Read a dirty book or something. Relax."

However, he was unable to supply a dirty book, so Erin had to content herself with Elizabeth Drew's commentary on campaign financing—several years old, but unfortunately still only too apropos. Some of the figures quoted shocked her so much she ventured to disturb Joe with a request for verification.

Joe snorted. "Kiddo, it's worse now. A Senate seat today

costs three million bucks, give or take a few hundred thou. That means that if he wants to run again, a Senator has to raise ten thousand a week for six long years. Doesn't leave him much time to do his job, hmmm?''

"The best Congress money can buy," Erin said.

"Hey, that's not bad." Joe reached for a pen.

"It's not original. I read it somewhere. . . . In the *Post*, I think."

"So what's a little plagiarism?" Joe tossed the pen aside and picked up a cigar. "As for the cost of a presidential campaign these days . . ."

"I don't think I want to hear about it, I'm depressed enough already. It's funny," Erin added, "how little attention I've been paying to the Big One. I know it's more important than a Senate race, but . . ."

"Not to us," Joe said. "Oh, sure, the presidential race does affect others, including ours, but in my not so humble opinion it's a waste of time to worry about it, because the effect is so unpredictable. Local loyalties often supersede party affiliation. Look at Mac Mathias, and that seat in Maryland he owned for so long—a Republican in a solidly Democratic state. And this time we don't have to worry about those long Reagan coattails. George Bush is walking around in a . . . what do you call those cute little jackets like bellboys wear?''

"Those cute little jackets like bellboys wear."

"Smart-ass," Joe said, grinning. "You talk too much. I've got work to do."

Erin knew he had enjoyed the discussion. If he hadn't, he would have told her to shut up.

Thanks to Joe and Jeff—and Will, who had oozed imperceptibly into his corner at some point—the evening passed more pleasantly than she would have expected. They were all in the commons room watching the eleven-o'clock news when Rosemary came in, followed by Nick.

"How did it go?" Joe asked alertly.

Rosemary tossed her purse onto the couch and collapsed next to it. "Mediocre. I told you I couldn't compete with a football game, especially U. Va. and Maryland."

"Students." Joe dismissed the entire student body with a

flourish of his cigar. "I didn't expect much from that. Bunch of smug little yuppies."

"Rosemary, you look exhausted," Kay said. "Why don't you get ready for bed and I'll give you a back rub—"

She broke off, with a look of disgust. Rosemary laughed. "Not one-handed, darling."

"I keep forgetting," Kay muttered. "Erin, could you—"

"I don't need a back rub," Rosemary said. "Stop fussing, Kay."

"The Chamber of Commerce talk went great," Nick said, drifting toward the coffee maker. "Rosemary nailed them on waste in the defense budget—reeled off a long list of examples without even referring to her notes."

"We should have Charlottesville in the bag," Jeff said. "Albemarle County has gone Democratic in the last umpteen presidential elections, even the Reagan landslide. Our own polls show a comfortable lead."

"Yeah, right. I think we should concentrate on fringe areas now. Rosemary, I know you're sick of hearing this, but you have got to make another swing through the southwest—"

"Keep your shirt on, Joe," Rosemary said. "I'm making an appearance there next week. A coffee. Roanoke. Tuesday. How about that?"

"You didn't tell me." Joe's formidable eyebrows sloped into a V. "Why didn't you tell me?"

"Because I knew you'd try to set up a couple of dozen other appearances. I haven't time for that. I'm only doing this one because the subject is so important to me."

"What subject?" Joe demanded.

Rosemary's smile was seraphic. "Gun control."

"Gun—gun—gun control! Jesus Christ, Rosemary, are you out of your mind? There are five shotguns per household in that part of the state. Some of 'em have never tasted store-bought meat. What are you—why . . ."

It dawned on him that he was being set up, and he sputtered to a stop. Rosemary's dimple had put in an appearance, and Nick was grinning—though there was a touch of sheepishness in his expression. It was Will who caught Erin's attention, however. His silences had begun to fascinate her;

they were not simply an absence of speech, they varied in intensity and type and carried an astonishing variety of unspoken messages. Catching her curious gaze, he lowered one eyelid in a wink.

"You didn't ask who was sponsoring the coffee," Rosemary said.

"Okay," Joe said warily. "So I'm asking."

"Remember the story in last week's Roanoke paper, about the eight-year-old who shot and killed his little brother while he was playing with daddy's .45 Magnum?"

"There are stories like that all the time," Joe muttered. "How do you expect me to . . . Oh my God. Don't tell me. It isn't . . ."

"The mother," Rosemary said.

Erin gasped, and even Joe, the cynical old campaigner, looked shocked. But only for a split second.

"Did you set this up?" he demanded of Nick.

"Will suggested it," Nick said. "He found the clipping. We talked it over, and I made a quick trip to Roanoke the other day." He glanced at Erin and added defensively, "She suggested it. I swear she did. She talked. . . . Did she talk! Said the other women in the area, and a lot of the men, were sick of seeing kids getting blown away, sick of watching the NRA buy votes of congressmen whose constituents overwhelmingly favor some form of handgun control."

"Some of that was in the newspaper story," said Will in his soft voice. "The last part, as you probably realize, was Nick."

"Some of it was in the story, but believe me, it wasn't like actually hearing her." Nick's face was bleak. "It wasn't one of the happiest visits I've ever paid to a voter. I think it did her good, though. She . . . she broke down and cried, finally. All over my best tie."

"I had already written her a letter of condolence," Rosemary said. The dimple was long since gone and her voice had the note of crisp efficiency that often covered strong emotion. "I always write to the families in cases like that. That's one of Will's jobs, to find relevant stories. He didn't tell me what he and Nick were planning until after it had been arranged, but I approved wholeheartedly.''

"I guess even an old dog like me can learn something from beginners,'' Joe said handsomely. "Good work, guys. I suppose you've arranged for full media coverage, Nick? Hey—how about '20/20,' or 'Nightline?' I could call Koppel—''

"I already did. His assistant said he'd pass the idea on, but everybody has done the gun-control bit. The Washington stations are all sending crews, though.''

"Great.'' Joe rubbed his hands and beamed like Scrooge after his reformation.

"Pray for good weather,'' Will said. "She's arranged an open-air meeting, in the park.''

Joe looked doubtful. "She's arranging it? Listen, Nick, you better keep an eye on her. Tactfully, of course—like I'd do it. Amateurs don't know how—''

"She's no amateur,'' Nick said. "You haven't heard the kicker yet, Joe. Mrs. O'Malley happens to be the president of the County Right-to-Life Chapter. She's an old pro at organization; ran a couple of the marches on Washington.''

Joe seemed less bemused by this information than Nick himself. "People,'' he said with a shrug. "So now she's endorsing Rosemary? Fantastic! Great publicity!''

"It's not so surprising,'' Rosemary said. "She just decided that the right to life applies to children as well as fetuses.''

Erin was the first to say good night. As she had hoped he would, Nick followed her out of the room and caught up with her at the foot of the stairs.

"Are you mad at me?'' he asked.

"What about?''

"Taking advantage of that woman's personal tragedy for our own purposes. It may seem like a rotten thing to do, but—''

"Oh, that.'' Erin leaned wearily against the banister. "Either I'm becoming hardened to political reality, or I've learned that moral issues are seldom as simple as they seem. Does it bother you?''

"Yeah, some.'' Nick propped himself against the opposite wall, like a matching bookend. Even his eyelids sagged.

"God, I'm tired. Well, I'm glad you don't think any the less of me for being a lousy opportunist. You looked as if you had bitten into something spoiled."

"I did. Yesterday."

Nick began. "Moral issues aren't always—"

"This one is. Was my father a criminal or wasn't he? You can't get much simpler than that."

"It's a lot more complicated than that and you know it. The point is not whether your father was a crook. The point is that he's dead and buried." Erin gasped. Nick passed a weary hand over his mouth and then went on, "I'm too tired to think what I'm saying. I didn't put that very well. Look at it this way: Your father can't be hurt, he's out of it. But Rosemary . . ."

"Always Rosemary! All right, what about her? Not long ago you were all gung ho about saving her from scandal. What have you done for her lately?"

"You know what I've been doing. The campaign—"

"May come to a crashing halt if what you suspect is true."

"All right, all right. I know. But I can't take time off at this stage without arousing a lot of curiosity. Be fair, Erin, you haven't had time either. I'm sure Kay has had you on the run—"

"I found time to look through a couple of dozen phone books. Brown isn't listed."

"Brown. Oh, you mean that . . . I can't think what to do next, then."

"You can't think, or you prefer not to discuss it with me? My father is dead—and buried, as you so nicely put it—but I'm alive, and it would be naive of you to trust me. You just can't trust anybody these days, can you? Especially where something as important as Rosemary's career is concerned."

"You know that's not true. Erin . . ." He reached out for her.

The commons room door opened and Kay emerged, followed by Rosemary. Caught by surprise, Nick moved clumsily, tripping over his own feet and presenting a perfect picture of an awkward swain.

Kay frowned disapprovingly; Rosemary broke into a broad grin. Nick stepped aside to let them ascend the stairs. As

Rosemary passed him she muttered, "Carry on," and Nick turned red.

"I wish she wouldn't do that," he whispered, watching them disappear around the turn of the stairs.

"She was just kidding," Erin said. She added pointedly, "But I wasn't. I shouldn't have blown up the way I did, Nick. But everything I said was true. Maybe you have cause to question my motives; but you've got to do something, you can't just sit back and—"

"Nick! Goddamn it, where is that kid? Nick!"

Joe's voice was only slightly softened by the closed door. Nick groaned. "Talk about being caught between a rock and a hard place. . . ."

"Which am I?" Erin inquired sweetly.

"I refuse to answer on the usual grounds. Erin . . . Honey, darling, sweetie pie—give me a break, okay? I trust you, esteem and honor you. . . . Hell, I think I love you. I swear—"

"Nick!"

"Damn it! Just give me a little time, Erin. We'll talk later, I promise."

*   *

"LATER" TURNED OUT to be a stretch of three days. Nick spent a good deal of the time in Roanoke, "tactfully" helping to organize the gun-control rally. His brief visits to the house never coincided with Erin's free time.

No further incidents occurred, but Erin was always expecting something to happen and her nerves stretched tighter and tighter as the days passed. The smell of burning haunted her dreams. The smoke was actual and real; after the driest October in over twenty years, brush fires had broken out across the southeastern states. Weary fire fighters, their faces soot-blackened and drawn, appeared on the evening news broadcasts; weather forecasters reluctantly admitted there was no hope of rain in the immediate future. Police claimed that two of the largest blazes, one in western Virginia and one in South Carolina, were the result of arson. As far east as Baltimore and Washington the sun shone dimly through an overhanging haze of gray smoke.

"The fire won't come anywhere near here," Joe said, as they watched one such broadcast. "Just don't throw a lit cigarette away when you're walking in the woods."

Kay sniffed. "You're a fine one to talk. You and your cigars."

"Ah, but I don't walk in the woods," Joe said complacently.

"You don't walk anywhere," Kay snapped. "And you drink too much. You're a prime candidate for a heart attack, Joe."

Joe took the criticism good-humoredly. "At least I'm having a good time while I'm alive. Loosen up, Kay baby. There's no danger from those fires, they're miles away, and we may get rain by the end of the week."

Kay's hands moved restlessly, picking at the fabric of her skirt. Her favorite knitting bags were piled untidily on the bookshelves gathering dust. It was a pity she was unable to relieve the tension that stiffened her body and lined her face, Erin thought, reluctantly sympathetic. She suspected she knew why Kay was so sensitive to the mention of fire.

The only notable occurrence during Nick's absence was the change in Christie's attitude. She and Erin had been the only ones in the office Sunday afternoon; even Joe had taken time off to watch the Redskins play their longtime rivals from Dallas. His whoops of alternating triumph and rage, as the score fluctuated, could be heard even at a distance, and after one outburst Christie laughed and said, "That had to be an interception. You can almost tell what's happening on the field by the intensity of Joe's yell."

Erin wasn't sure how to react. Christie had made tentative overtures before, and then slapped her down when she responded. She leaned back in her chair and flexed her stiff fingers. "You sound like a fan yourself," she said. "Why aren't you watching the big game?"

"Not me, kid. I hate football. My ex–significant other used to be glued to the damned TV all weekend every weekend. Like a nice feminine female, I kept him company, worked hard to learn about his hobby. . . . Why are women such fools?"

"It's hard to break early training," Erin said. "Even if

you were brought up by a liberated mother—which I certainly was not—you're barraged by messages from other sources. Movies, TV, aunts and friends. Be nice, be kind, don't hurt people's feelings, no matter what they do to yours. . . ."

"He sure didn't do much for mine," Christie said sourly. "You should have seen me hauling beer and sandwiches at him and apologizing when there wasn't enough mayo on the bread. Apologizing when supper wasn't ready when he got home, apologizing for talking about my work instead of listening to him bitch about what a hard day he'd had. . . . I'm sorry, you don't want to hear this, it's so damned boring."

"If you feel like talking, I feel like listening. I think that's one area in which women have an edge over men; we can give each other support because we aren't ashamed to admit we make a mistake now and then."

Christie studied her expressionlessly for a moment. Then her lips parted in a flash of even white teeth.

"You a mind reader, or what?"

"Huh?"

"I was trying to work up to admitting I made a mistake with you. I took you for one of those sweet-faced ruffly-blouse-type females that was looking for a free meal ticket and a cushy job."

Erin winced. "I may have been heading in that direction." Then she added with a flash of temper, "But at least I didn't judge you, or anybody else, by some stupid stereotype."

Christie's eyes narrowed. Before she could reply, Erin went on hotly, "Did you think I was after your job? Oh, I see that amuses you; the very idea of a nobody like me undermining your position—"

"It's been done. By people less qualified than you, to people better qualified than I."

"Yes, I suppose so. That wasn't what I had in mind when I came here, Christie; I'll be damned if I know what I did want. But I know now: not necessarily your job, but one like it. I won't sneak in by the back door, I'll earn it fair and square. So watch out. From now on I'll be snapping at your heels."

Leaning against the desk, arms folded, Christie studied her without expression. Then her lips parted and she let out a whoop of uninhibited laughter. "Girl, I sure did you wrong. Fair enough; from now on it's a fight to the finish, no holds barred, but no hitting below the belt."

She held out a strong, slim hand and Erin grasped it. "We don't have to fight."

"Yeah, but we probably will. I'm competitive as hell, and apparently you are too. I'm all for a good honest fight now and then." She stretched, yawning, and Erin watched her lean grace with admiration not unmixed with envy.

"I think we're entitled to a break," Christie said. "I'm going for a run."

"Is that how you keep that gorgeous figure?"

Christie laughed, but looked pleased. "That's how I keep from going crazy in this madhouse. The conditions aren't ideal—there's no regular track, just a path through the woods—but it's sure relaxing. Do you run or jog or anything?"

Erin realized she had received an invitation. She said doubtfully, "I couldn't keep up with you, I'm really out of condition. And I don't have the right clothes."

"Nothing wrong with jeans and a sweatshirt. Let's see your shoes."

Erin stretched out a sneakered foot. Christie frowned. "Well, it doesn't matter, we'll just take it easy. That is—if you want to come."

To refuse might have weakened the tenuous new relationship. Besides, it offered a chance to ask questions. . . . Erin stood up, stretched. "Sounds like a great idea."

As they crossed the stableyard the not-too-muted sounds from Sam's cottage indicated that he was also glued to the big game. Fields and wooded hills dreamed in the hazy sunlight. Fallen leaves crackled dryly under their feet.

The path opened up between a stand of cypresses. It was in better condition than Erin had expected; when she commented on the relatively smooth surface, Christie said, "Thanks to Nick. You know the way he grabs hold of an idea and runs with it; I happened to mention it would be nice to have a place to run, and the next day he was out here with a rider mower. The weeds were waist-high! He even dug up a

roller someplace and ran it up and down.'' She bent to check
the laces on her shoes. "I kept him company when I could;
it was a pretty sight, I can tell you. Ever see Nick without a
shirt, and sweat gleaming on all those muscles?''

"No."

"Oh, really? There's a general impression—"

"It's wrong.'' After a brief hesitation Erin added, "Give
me a little more time.''

It was the right response. Christie laughed. "Good luck.
He's a sweet guy. Not my type, though. He's too intense. I
need somebody who can keep his cool.''

"Like Jeff?''

"From one extreme to the other.'' Christie's smile faded.
"There's something about Jeff . . I don't know, it's like he's
built a wall around himself a hundred feet high and two hundred feet thick. I'd like to be there if he ever tears it down,
but I haven't got the time or the energy to fight something as
strong as that. Ready? Watch your feet, the surface isn't as
smooth as it looks. You could sprain an ankle.''

She took her running seriously. The pace she set might
have been slow for her, but it left Erin gasping. When they
stopped for a brief rest she didn't have enough breath to ask
questions. Christie did all the talking; her breathing was
scarcely quicker than normal.

"I love this place,'' she said, the sweep of her arm indicating the panorama of meadow and forest stretching west-
ward, framed by the outline of the distant mountains. The
setting sun washed their slopes with apricot, and burned on
the tops of the trees behind them.

"You wouldn't think there was a house or a human being
for miles,'' Christie went on dreamily. "Even Fairweather is
hidden by the trees. If you come up here at twilight and sit
quietly, after a while you start hearing little rustles and movements in the grass. Once a doe walked right past me, not ten
feet away, with her fawn following—''

A sound like that of a dry branch cracking interrupted her.
Christie turned to look, shading her eyes with her hand.

"Was that a shot?'' Erin asked uneasily.

"Some jackass hunter,'' Christie said. "Deer season

doesn't start for another month, but there're always a few heroes who can't wait to start killing things."

Erin struggled to her feet. Her lungs still ached. "It sounded close."

"Sound carries a long way on a quiet day like this. He's not on Rosemary's land, at least not with her permission. We'd better start back, though, it's getting late. You don't mind if I go ahead, do you? You can't get lost, just follow the trail."

Erin dropped back onto the fallen tree trunk they had used as a bench. "I'll just rest a few more minutes."

Christie gave her a friendly slap on the back. "It gets easier with practice. You did fine for a beginner."

She took off, running with a grace and ease that made Erin feel eighty years old. Within moments she had disappeared among the trees.

As soon as she was out of sight, the strangeness began, as if her presence had held something sly and ugly at bay. Nothing in the landscape changed, but now it conjured up different images: loneliness instead of peace, isolation rather than solitude. The air was acrid with smoke, and the swollen, sullen sun sent long, blurred shadows sliding across the grass—shadows without definition or substance, like the thoughts in Erin's mind. She had reached a point where every statement, every look was distorted by her suspicions. Christie had been awfully anxious to make friends all of a sudden. And what had she said about Jeff. . . . "It's like he's built a wall a hundred feet high." Perhaps she had misremembered that vital date of birth, because she didn't want it to be Jeff. If he was the survivor of that tragic family, he had good reason to hide behind a wall of deception.

Was Nick avoiding her because he still entertained doubts about her, or for other reasons? He had personal and family connections with Rosemary that went back into the past; hadn't he said something about his aunt working for the Marshalls? A housekeeper had plenty of opportunities to discover the personal secrets of the people who employed her.

Erin jumped to her feet. The heavy dusk was making her morbid. Time she was getting back. She must be at least a mile from the house; the path had twisted and turned all the way. She should make better time going back, since it was downhill, but soon the sun would set, and considering her total ignorance of woodcraft, there was a distinct possibility that she might lose her way. She got to her feet. As she started toward the trees she heard a second, far-off echo of gunfire.

It was already dusky under the branches, but a long finger of sunlight kept her company for a short distance as she plodded through the fallen leaves. Then a turn in the path cut off the sunlight; shadows sprang at her like enemies from ambush. The leaves crackled under her feet as she broke into a trot. The distance seemed much longer than a mile, and it was with considerable relief that she emerged into the open and saw the roofs and chimneys of Fairweather below.

With the darkening woods behind her and an evening breeze dispelling some of the smoke, she felt rather foolish about her panic. That was what it had been, irrational terror, in the ancient sense of the word. The faint haze in the air only mellowed the pastoral beauty of pasture and field and clustered dwellings; she stood still, waiting for her breathing to slow and her weakened knees to regain their strength.

A rustle and snap of shaken branches behind her startled her, but at first she did not connect that sound with the other, the now familiar crack of a rifle. The next bullet came close enough to whine before it smacked into a tree trunk.

It was instinct rather than reason that sent Erin into headlong flight. She didn't stop running until she had reached the shelter of the stables.

A high-powered rifle could carry . . . how far? Miles, she believed. The hunter probably hadn't even known she was there. He had fired at some miserable animal, and missed. No one could have known she would walk in the woods that day.

But if someone had been out with a gun, hanging around in the hope of finding her out of doors . . . There were such things as telescopic sights.

No, and again no. That was too farfetched. Delusions of persecution, that was what she was developing.

And anyway, gunfire wasn't . . . fire.

*   *

IT IS A WELL-KNOWN FACT of life in Washington that the mood of the entire city is colored by the results of the Sunday football game. When the Redskins lose, especially to Dallas, eyes are downcast and voices are surly. When they win, even Monday morning can be endured.

Whether the 'Skins thrashing of their traditional rivals affected Joe's mood was unproved, but he was certainly in excellent spirits next morning. A meeting with the State Democratic Committee Monday afternoon proved to be the first crack in his good humor, but that wasn't unusual; he always managed to pick a fight with someone in that despised group. The final blow came at six o'clock, when Buzz Bennett's latest campaign plug was aired. Bennett had hired the most prestigious group in the country to produce the commercial, which lasted for a full three minutes, and they had earned their money; he kissed old ladies on their wrinkled cheeks and promised to introduce a bill doubling Social Security benefits; he hugged babies and promised their beaming parents he would make certain every child in Virginia had a chance to attend college, not to mention medical school; he stood stiffly at attention, hand pressed to his heaving chest, as a line of fighter planes shot across the cloud-strewn blue sky, and swore America would never bow the knee to tyranny. It was noticed by some that he conspicuously refrained form kissing, hugging, or even speaking to pretty girls. The overall effect—music, production, and Buzz's craggy, sincere face—was so skillfully calculated that Erin felt her throat tighten, even though she knew her response was as mindless and irresistible as the salivation of Pavlov's unfortunate dogs.

Joe was moved only to rage. "Why the hell isn't our new spot ready?" he roared, pounding on the table with both fists. "Where the hell is that lazy swine Nick?"

"You sent him to Roanoke," Will said. "He told you he couldn't—"

"We're shorthanded, that's the trouble," Joe snarled. "Short on people, short on money. It's Rosemary's fault. Goddamn prudish, overly fastidious broad—we could have got half a million more from PACs if she hadn't been so goddamn fussy. Where is she? Why isn't she here?''

"As you yourself told me not twenty minutes ago, she and Kay are dining with the Morgans," Will reminded him. "Probably trying to smooth over the insults you handed him this afternoon."

"If the man can't take honest criticism he doesn't deserve to be party chairman," Joe said, chewing on his cigar. "All I said was that if we depended on the support of the party we'd be dead in the water. What's wrong with that? When is Nick due back? I want to talk to him about lighting a fire under those media morons."

At midnight Nick still had not returned, and Erin decided to give up and go to bed. She was pleasantly tired after an afternoon walk—not run—in the woods. She had had to force herself to return to the scene of her panic, but the effort had been worthwhile; there had been no repetition of that odd, senseless fear, only peace and beauty. without so much as a distant echo of gunfire.

Rosemary and Kay had returned shortly after eleven. Both looked drawn and tired, and Rosemary lost no time in telling Joe what she thought of his performance earlier in the day. "Harry was seething. He said you called him an ignorant nincompoop."

"I did not. When have you ever heard me use a bland, innocuous word like 'nincompoop'?"

"I suppose he was too well-bred to repeat what you really said." Rosemary waved away the coffee Jeff offered her. "Thanks, Jeff dear, but I dare not insert another drop of liquid into this bloated body. And none for you, either, Kay," she added, turning to her secretary. "You hardly spoke a word this evening. That hand is giving you a lot of pain, isn't it? There must be something wrong. An infection, maybe? You're going to Dr. White tomorrow, and I don't want to hear any arguments."

"Not tomorrow," Kay said. "Tomorrow is Roanoke, remember?"

"Damn, I forgot. All right, Wednesday, then. Without fail. And take those sleeping pills tonight, do you hear?''

"I don't have any," Kay said.

"Surely you do," Erin exclaimed. "You gave me the prescription to be filled just last week. Nick picked it up for you, after the . . . after . . ."

Her voice faltered as Kay transfixed her with a furious scowl. She had spoken without thinking and without any intent except reassurance; why was Kay so angry?

"Good Lord," Rosemary exclaimed. "You haven't taken a whole bottle?"

"No, of course not," Kay said. "I do have them. I just didn't . . . I guess I forgot."

*   *

THE HOUSE SEEMED very empty next day. The inner circle had accompanied Rosemary to Roanoke; Christie was downtown, liaising, as the phrase went, with Democratic headquarters. As Erin typed the date on a letter she realized that election day was two weeks away. Two weeks to determine the outcome of Rosemary's bid for the Senate, and the futures of those who depended on her for jobs, patronage, support. Two weeks for her to find out the truth about her father. Assuming, of course, that the whole ugly business didn't blow up in their faces before then, wrecking Rosemary's reputation and career and the hopes of those who had supported her.

Erin wasn't even sure any longer what mattered more. Nick had been right; nothing could hurt her father now, though a disclosure of his complicity might have a devastating effect on her mother. But then her mother would probably just refuse to believe it. Erin wished she could do the same. She couldn't, and she could not share Nick's hope that nothing more would happen—that their theories had been wildly, melodramatically wrong, or that the unknown had, for reasons known only to himself, abandoned his campaign of intimidation.

It hadn't occurred to her before that she might search for clues in the house itself. The idea went against every moral principle she had learned. Besides, this was the first real opportunity she had had; there wasn't a soul around who would interrupt or interfere. It might also be her last chance.

One way or the other, win or lose, everything would come

to a crashing halt on November 8. Rosemary would finish out
her House term, a few office workers would clean up the
debris, financial and physical; but staff would be cut and Kay
would no longer need her assistance. Even if Rosemary won
and even if she offered Erin another job, that job would be
in Washington; the offices here had been set up especially for
the campaign. The others would disperse as well; she would
never again have as good a chance to watch them and question them, search. . . .

Hands idle on the keys of the word processor, she stared
into space and fought a battle with long-accepted values. What
she had said to Christie was only too true; women were
trained to be law-abiding, gentle, considerate of others. Ladies didn't pry. Neither, in fact, did gentlemen; that moral
maxim had no sexist overtones. Something Nick had quoted
came back to her; some government official, she had forgotten who, decrying the efforts to break foreign codes. "Gentlemen don't read one another's mail," he had loftily
proclaimed. A noble attitude like that one could lose a war,
cost thousands of lives. She could lose her own personal war
by following an equivalent ethical code. "Moral issues aren't
as simple as they seem." She had said that herself. It seemed
the most appropriate guide at this particular moment.

But where to look? Kay's office and Rosemary's were out of
the question; she couldn't spend the necessary amount of time
in either without one of the other workers' noticing. Besides,
damaging, secret information was more likely to be concealed
in one's private quarters. Too many people had access to the
offices, and some—Joe, for example—would consider no locked
drawer or safe out of bounds.

Rosemary's room, then. Or Kay's. Fine, Erin thought wryly.
Now if I only had the faintest idea what to look for. . . .

That wasn't the only problem, as she discovered when she
found herself in Kay's room. "The guilty flee where no man
pursueth," and they also quake in their boots or sneakers
even when no one is watching. She had taken the coward's
way out by going first to Kay's room. No one could climb the
bare, squeaking stairs or walk along the uncarpeted wooden
floor without her hearing them approach, and even if she was

found in the room, she had a valid excuse for being there. There was absolutely no reason why her hands should be icy and trembling, except her own guilty conscience.

She started by straightening up the room, plumping pillows—and feeling them to make certain nothing had been hidden inside—and remaking the bed. (Nothing under the mattress, nothing tucked in the springs, no locked box or briefcase under the bed.) Nothing under the rug, either. Lying flat on her stomach with the dusty stiffness over her head and shoulders, she swept the entire area with her hands, feeling at the same time for loose boards.

She had taken the precaution of arming herself, not with a weapon, but with a dustcloth. Next she tackled the mantel and the table, looking in every vase, opening every little box and jar. A crystalline tinkle of music broke out when she lifted the lid of a porcelain casket and her guilty start of alarm almost caused her to drop the fragile thing. She recognized the tune: "Tales from the Vienna Woods." A memento of a trip to Austria, or just one of Kay's collectibles? She seemed to collect everything—porcelain, pottery, crystal; stuffed cats, wooden owls; objets d'art and just plain junk. Erin's unsteady fingers tipped over an earring holder. It was of brass, in the shape of a cat with several tails, and couldn't be damaged, but the earrings flew in every direction and she had to crawl around before she found them all—and had to pray she had restored them to their original places.

The closet came next. She could always say she was checking to see if any garment needed mending or pressing. . . . Nothing in the pockets of coats and dresses, no betraying crackles or lumps in the linings. Nothing in the purses lined in a neat row on the shelf—navy, black, brown, white, beige— or the shoes, in a hanging holder. She got a chair and climbed on it to examine the topmost shelf. The boxes there contained hats, plus a few odds and ends of old accessories Kay seldom wore and couldn't bear to throw away.

The clock ticking on the mantel told her she had been away from her desk too long. Actually, it wasn't so much the clock as her own discomfort that urged her to complete the search or abandon it. Every quivering nerve argued for the second alternative, but she forced herself to continue. This might be her best, her only, opportunity. But the next part of the search was one she abhorred. Opening drawers seemed—was—an even greater violation of privacy than what she had done thus far.

Underwear, gloves, scarves, cosmetics. A paperback book, tucked under a pile of bras. Erin's compressed lips slipped into a half-smile at the sight of the title and the cover—an impossibly beautiful, artfully half-clothed female clasped in the ardent embrace of a handsome bare-chested hero. At least Kay's tastes were normal. This was just your average, acceptable bodice ripper. Poor prissy woman, why did she bother hiding it?

There were two more books of the same type in the drawer of the bedside table, along with three of the tiny gold boxes of candy Laurence had said were Kay's favorites. So Kay—poor Kay—hoarded chocolates as well as lurid novels. Erin flipped idly through the pages of one of the books, picturing Kay propped up in bed reveling in the passionate adventures of Raven, Countess of Woodbridge, as she munched raspberry creams. If Kay would just relax and admit her harmless weaknesses, laugh over them, enjoy them . . . There were several more of the little gold boxes, emptied of their contents, in the wastebasket.

On the top of the nightstand was an assortment of bottles—vitamins, aspirin, sedatives. The bottle labeled "Dalmane" was almost full.

Only one piece of furniture remained to be investigated—a low bookcase beneath the west window. Erin had put it off till last, almost hoping something would interrupt her search. In some ways books were more personal than souvenirs and accessories, even more personal than clothing. They were reflections, not of the body but of the mind and the heart. And the books people kept in their bedrooms were the most intimate of all—old favorites turned to for comfort when one was sick in bed with a cold, or wakeful during a long lonely night.

She recognized only a few of the titles. *Gone With the Wind*. . . . She might have expected that one, a whole generation of women must have yearned for Rhett Butler. Most of the other novels appeared to be old-fashioned historical romances; flipping quickly through the pages, she didn't see a single word that would have shocked the primmest censor. Kay had hidden the "dirty books" in her dresser drawer.

The majority of the books on the shelves were not novels. They were albums—some cheap plastic, some bound elegantly in leather. Photograph albums. And that too she might have expected.

She started with the last one and wasn't surprised to find that most of the clippings and photographs featured not Kay, but Rosemary. All of Kay's adult life had been lived vicariously, through someone else. She had no husband, no children, no life of her own.

The albums had been arranged in chronological order. Erin took out the one farthest to the left. Old family pictures, black and white originally but yellowing with age. One of the children might have been Kay, she couldn't tell. She returned it to the shelf and took out the next. School pictures, junior high and high school. The clothes had the archaic humor of past fashions not old enough to be quaint—bobby socks and saddle shoes, pleated skirts, baggy sweaters. Kay with her bike, her dog; standing in front of a narrow frame house. Erin didn't linger over these. Kay's youth was no business of hers.

She found the first pictures of Edward Marshall in the third album. Seated behind a desk, he had raised his head to smile at the camera, and the photograph was labeled in Kay's neat hand. "My new boss, Mr. Marshall, Virginia State Senator. An exciting job!"

Exclamation points proliferated thereafter. Mr. Marshall and his "sweet little bride" soon became "Edward" and "Rosemary," and family snapshots mingled with publicity pictures. "Rosemary and I making pancakes Sunday morning. Taken by Edward. We weren't very good cooks!" A coy "First pictures of the new baby" accompanied by a snapshot of Rosemary sprawled gracelessly in an easy chair; an arrow indicated her bulging maternity smock.

So by that time Kay was family friend as well as personal secretary. She had been with Marshall almost from the start of his political career. Most of the pictures were of him and Rosemary, of the baby, of the handsome mansion in Rich-

mond, of Fairweather. Several depicted Edward with his favorite cats—holding them, stroking them, dangling ribbons
for them to play with. Rosemary was also shown playing with
the cats. Her antipathy—or, more accurately, her indifference—must have developed after Edward's death.

Erin hurried through the other volumes. The search not
only made her uncomfortable, it had had another result she
had not anticipated—a profound if unwilling pity for Kay. No
wonder Kay was so fiercely devoted to Marshall's memory
and Rosemary's success. They were all she had.

All at once a familiar picture caught Erin's eye. She had
seen the same one in her mother's album. It had never interested her before; now she stared intently, as if she could will
the miniature faces to speak to her.

Her mother and father, Rosemary and Edward, and two
other people, dressed in evening clothes and standing beside
a limousine. Kay had labeled it, but the names of the third
pair struck no chord of memory. On their way to a ball at the
governor's mansion. . . . Her mother cherished that photograph, one of the few mementos of her participation in the
social life of the state capital.

At the end of the book, tucked into a pocket in the back
cover, she found a tattered business-sized envelope. Inside
were a few newspaper clippings, brown and frayed with age.
They were from the Richmond *Times-Dispatch* and they described a fire in an abandoned tenement. Tucked into the
envelope with them was a single sheet of paper. A list of
names and dates.

Chapter Fourteen

NICK CALLED shortly after four. He didn't have to tell her there were other people in the room with him; his formal tone and message made that clear. "Rosemary wants you to tell Sarah we'll be later than we expected—not to wait, just leave a casserole or something in the oven."

"How did it go?" Erin asked in the same tone. She was at her desk; the others made no pretense of not listening.

"Fantastic. Watch the six-o'clock news. We're leaving shortly, but it will take us at least two hours."

He rang off, and Erin turned to her audience. "He says it was fantastic; watch the six-o'clock news."

She went to the kitchen to pass on the message to the cook, who nodded as she tore lettuce into smaller pieces. "I figured that. My famous gourmet Chicken à la Sarah is in the fridge; I'll finish making the salad and then run along home in time for the news program. There's an apple pie too, you might want to warm it up before you serve it. Make sure Rosemary eats, mind."

Christie was just coming in the front door when Erin entered the hall. "Wooo, what a day," the tall girl groaned, running her hand over her tightly clustered curls. "Anything happen while I was gone?"

Erin passed on Nick's message. "That's great," Christie said. "Guess I'll stick around—catch the news here."

She gave Erin a sidelong look, and Erin said shortly, "You don't have to ask me—or even announce your intentions."

"My, my, aren't we touchy today. I just thought I'd be polite—seeing as how you're in loco housekeeper around here."

The hit was too close to home. Erin knew her face must have betrayed her, but Christie took guilt for resentment. "I told you we'd fight," she said.

"It takes two to fight. I'm not in the mood."

Christie laughed. "You're no fun. Want to go for a run? I need to stretch my legs. Been hunched over a desk or fighting city traffic the whole day."

"I guess not. I went out earlier."

She didn't tell Christie what had driven her out of the house—or why she had gone only a short distance before the stench of wood smoke sent her running back.

Christie sent the others home at five-thirty, though they obviously wouldn't have minded staying to watch the news. Erin went to the kitchen to check on the food situation and found, as she had expected, that Sarah had everything under control, including fresh-made coffee. She returned to the commons room to find Will adjusting the television.

"I thought you'd gone to Roanoke," she said.

"Not me. I don't make public appearances. Prefer my role as power behind the throne."

"But you weren't here—"

"Yes, I was. All day."

"I didn't see you."

Will lowered his voice to a sinister drone. "No one sees the Shadow. But the Shadow knows . . . ."

He knelt to adjust the controls of the VCR. Christie came in, saw what he was doing and nodded approval. "Good idea, Will. What are you going to do if it's on all the stations?"

"The best I can," said Will, inserting a blank tape.

Christie went to the kitchen and came back with a beer. "I deserve this," she announced, dropping heavily into a chair. "I don't know where the hell the committee finds these people. Half of them don't know what they're supposed to do and the other half don't do it."

She went on grumbling; Will responded with polite murmurs of sympathy, and Erin only half-listened. The slip of paper in the pocket of her jeans burned against her skin. She had copied the list of names before replacing it in the envelope and returning the album to its place. She was trying to figure out a subtle way of asking the date of Christie's birth when the news came on.

How much of the spectacle was due to Nick and how much to Mrs. O'Malley, Erin did not know, but it wasn't hard to understand why the event had rated such extensive media attention. The emotions of the crowd, most of them women and children, overwhelmed the small screen. The music was performed by massed church choirs, black and white joining in the old hymns: "Amazing Grace," "Abide with Me," "A Mighty Fortress Is Our God." And Rosemary—dressed not in black, but in a soft-gray print that made her the symbol of all grieving mothers, her eyes luminous with unshed tears. She began with a message of love and sympathy, but ended with a call to arms. "The time has come—the time is long past—to end the slaughter of the innocents. I'm not going to tell you that if I'm elected I'll make this my first priority. You know I will; you know I have. What I *am* telling you is that, win or lose, in the Senate of the United States or out of it, I will continue the fight till it's won—as a woman, as a citizen, as a mother!"

The choirs burst into "The Battle Hymn of the Republic," and the cameras panned to the audience—singing, swaying, faces streaked with tears.

The screen went black; Will switched channels in time to catch the same ending on another station. Christie turned to Erin. "You're crying," she said accusingly.

"So are you."

"Am I? Jee-sus! Is she fantastic, or what?"

"She is," Will agreed calmly. "But the setup couldn't have been more ideal. Any politician could have milked it, but Rosemary does it best because she—"

"Because she's a bigger ham than the rest of them?"

They hadn't heard her come in. She had left her coat in the hall and was still wearing the soft-gray dress, a grandmotherly ruffle of lace framing her face. Deep lines bracketed her level, unsmiling mouth.

"Because she really means it," Will said.

The brackets shivered, curved, disappeared. "Thanks," Rosemary said. "Hello, Christie—Erin."

"Where are the others?" Will asked.

Kay came in, followed by Jeff, who answered the question. "They're right behind us, unless that jalopy of Nick's broke down. Did you tape it?"

"Yes. Pretty impressive."

"We knocked 'em dead!" That was Joe, accompanied by the usual thick cloud of cigar smoke. "Sockerino!"

He tossed his topcoat over the back of the sofa. Kay clucked and carried it to the coat rack. Nick was the last to enter. Joe turned to him, beaming. "Good job, kid. I'm glad you listened to me and held off on our commercial. I want to incorporate some of that footage. Rosie, what do you— Hey, where are you going?"

Without speaking, Rosemary left the room. Joe started after her.

"No," Will said, his voice uncharacteristically sharp. "Leave her alone. She's going to call Jannie." Joe stared at him, and he added, "Her daughter—remember? She always calls Jannie when she's . . . Give her a break, Joe."

"I know who Jannie is," Joe grumbled. "Oh, well. Yeah. Now, Nick, as I was saying . . ."

Erin slipped out of the room and went to the kitchen. She had lit the oven and taken the casserole from the refrigerator when Nick came in.

"Need some help?"

"You can put the plates and the silver on the table. It will take twenty minutes or so to heat the casserole."

"Good. That will give Rosemary time to unwind." Nick

opened the cupboard doors. "Did you see her? Was that sensational, or what?"

"Sensational," Erin said.

Nick put the stack of plates down on the counter. "Something's bugging you. What happened?"

"I searched Kay's room this afternoon."

Nick crossed the room in two long strides and clapped his hand over her mouth. "Not so loud!"

Erin pried his fingers away. "Nobody's eavesdropping. They're all too full of their latest triumph. Including you. I found a set of those clippings—you know the ones I mean—hidden in an old photograph album. Along with the list of names. I was right about the boy. Jeff is in the clear."

"Wait a minute. I have to get my mind back on track, I've been so busy with other things. . . . Jeff's okay? Good. The clippings . . . That means she knows. She's always known."

"We assumed that," Erin said. "The search was wasted effort, actually. I didn't find out anything we didn't already know."

"Nothing happened while I was gone?" He lowered his voice to a conspiratorial whisper. "No fires?"

"The whole goddamn state is on fire," Erin snapped. "You can smell the smoke everywhere."

"Yeah, I know, but . . . You're mad at me, aren't you?"

Erin opened the oven door.

"Here, let me do that." Nick took the casserole from her. He put it in the oven, burned his hand on the rack, swore, and closed the door. "I'm sorry, Erin, honest. I'm still in a state of shock. I mean, I knew Rosemary was a pro, but after today . . . She had that crowd in the palm of her hand, it was pure magic, and she's got nowhere to go but up. We're going to win; I never really believed it till now. And after that—anything is possible."

His eyes were dazed by visions. Erin knew what he saw, heard the music that played in his inner ear. "Hail to the Chief"—brasses blaring, full military band. Even the secondhand echoes of it stirred her blood like bubbles in champagne, but it could not overcome her sense of foreboding.

She said harshly, "Not if someone is holding a dirty secret over Rosemary's head."

Nick came back to earth with a painful thud.

"But nothing has happened lately. Maybe it's over."

"It will never be over," Erin said. "Not for me. Not until I know what happened."

"Erin." He reached for her hand. She tried to pull it away, but he held on, closing hard, warm fingers over hers. "I know we can't just drop this business; I don't intend to. But insofar as your father is concerned, it's your personal problem. Either he had guilty knowledge of that fire, or he didn't. Nothing is going to change, except your perception of him."

"And that's not important?"

"Sure it is. But Rosemary's father was a lush and a bigot. My mom found Jesus a few years ago and now she sends every penny she earns to some slimy TV evangelist, and reads me long lectures about my sins every time I put my face in the door. She thinks Rosemary is an instrument of the devil because she refuses to fight abortion or condemn those dirty homosexuals."

"Is there a point to these rambling reminiscences?" Erin inquired.

"Oh, hell, you know what I'm driving at. You're responsible for yourself, not for anybody else—mother, father, brother, husband. Nobody's perfect—"

"Oh, Nick, what a stupid cliché!" She threw her arms around him and hugged him hard. "You always know just what to say, you silver-tongued devil, you."

The swinging door banged open. "Ha, caught you," Joe said cheerfully. "Can that wait till after supper? I'm starved."

"Twenty minutes," Erin said. "We were just about to—"

"I can see what you were just about to." Joe picked up a plate of rolls, popped one into his mouth and left, chuckling deep in his throat.

"Shit," Nick said, untangling himself. "This place is like Georgetown on Halloween. Look, honey, we'll keep at it. I promise. I just don't know what to do next."

"You don't have time to do anything. I understand. And

it's going to get worse before it gets better. I guess all we can do is wait.''

"I'll think of something," Nick promised. "I'd better put some food on the table before the rest of the crowd busts in here." He picked up a bowl of chips. "One good thing," he said with a grin. "If Rosemary makes it to the White House she'll be able to afford some servants."

He kicked the door open and passed through, balancing plates in one hand and the bowl of chips in the other. He was still on an emotional high, unable to believe anything could cloud the glorious future he envisioned. Erin wished she could believe in it—see herself opening the door of the Oval Office and telling the President (the President!) that the Prime Minister and the Premier were arriving at the East Portico. She lacked Nick's natural ebullience, his ability to bounce back from depression.

By the time the food was on the table, Rosemary was back. She had changed into her baggy jeans and campaign sweatshirt, but it wasn't the comfortable clothes that made her look twenty years younger.

"I think my granddaughter is a little confused about the election," she reported with a chuckle. "She wants to know when she can come visit me in the White House and meet Mr. Lincoln."

"Tell her to wait a few years," Joe grunted. "By that time she'll be old enough to settle for sleeping in Lincoln's bed."

Rosemary's performance had impressed even blasé Washington. The phones rang all evening with inquiries and messages of congratulation, and florists' vans made repeated visits. An arrangement of long-stemmed red roses moved Joe to a cynical comment. "That's a good omen; he never jumps on a bandwagon till it's at the finish line."

Most ostentatious of all the offerings was a basket of delicate, rare green-and-white orchids. Kay read the card first and handed it to Rosemary. Rosemary glanced at it and tossed it aside without comment. Later, when she was tidying the room, Erin found it and was unable to resist reading it. "To two beautiful women, and a bright future for both of them and their most faithful admirer." That was so typical of Lau-

rence, she thought, to include himself in the good wishes—
and not so typically tactful of him to include Kay. What was
the nature of the bond between that particular odd couple?
Erin was no longer certain that her original theory explained
the relationship. Former lovers could remain friends, but
Laurence didn't strike her as the sort of man who would
bother making, or keeping, a friend.

*   *

THIRTEEN DAYS to election. Everyone was counting down.
As she trotted around the house answering phones, helping
with mailings, and running errands, Erin wondered if anything short of a major conflagration would be noticed in the
general frenzy. Yet she couldn't dispel the feeling that something was going to happen; that the temporary lull was only
the calm before the storm.

Shortly before noon Jeff appeared, looking even more im-
passive than usual. He paused at Erin's desk to ask when Nick
and Joe were expected back.

"I think they said around two. They're finishing the commercial. Aren't you supposed to take Kay to the doctor?"

Since the accident Kay had not used the Mercedes or allowed anyone else to do so, though it was back from the shop
and the mechanic had assured them it was perfectly safe. He
couldn't understand how such a freak accident could have
happened. He had personally checked those connections when
the car was last serviced, only a few months earlier. It
wouldn't happen again, not in a million years. . . .

"I did," Jeff said. "I took her in, but she told me not to
wait. Said she had errands to do, and she'd call or get a ride
from someone."

He seemed to expect a response, though she couldn't think
why. "There's bound to be someone around who can go and
get her, Jeff. Don't worry about it."

"I'm not. I just . . ." Erin looked at him more closely and
saw the fine parallel lines between his brows. He leaned
closer. "She was acting kind of strange. Said some peculiar
things."

"Like what?"

Jeff hesitated. "Quoting Scripture. The word 'sin' kept recurring."

A trickle of cold touched Erin's spine. "That is odd. I've never heard Kay quote from the Bible."

"Suggest anything to you?"

"No."

"Well." Jeff straightened. "It isn't important, I guess. See you later."

The word had suggested something to her, though—a well-known phrase that had a grim, personal application. "The sins of the fathers . . ." With an effort, she forced herself to concentrate on her work. There were a lot of other mentions of that word in Holy Writ. She wished she had dared ask Jeff what Kay had actually said.

Later she got a call and recognized a voice she hadn't heard for some time. "Oh, hell, Fran. I'm sorry, but I can't tie up this line; we've had so many calls—"

"I know, I got busy signals all morning. Things are pretty lively around here, too."

"At the office?"

"No, I'm at Democratic headquarters in Arlington. I called in sick this morning. I figure I'm entitled to a few days off, and right now is when I'm really needed. Boy, you should see this place, Erin. That speech of Rosemary's yesterday—"

"I'll tell her you were impressed," Erin said. "I'm sure she'll appreciate it."

"Impressed? I was bawling so hard I got my popcorn all wet. How's that hunk of a manager?"

"I presume you're referring to Nick," Erin said, unable to repress a smile; the description certainly didn't fit Joe. "He's not the campaign manager, he's consultant for media affairs."

"Oh, right. He's doing a great job."

"I have to hang up," Erin said, knowing the usual polite evasions wouldn't work with Fran.

"What's his sign?"

"His what?"

"His sign. What's the matter, can't you hear me? My horoscope says a Libra will surprise me with a romantic gesture that could lead to a long-lasting affair.''

"Oh, his astrological sign. Honest to God, Fran, of all the idiotic questions!''

"Don't you know? I always ask guys, it's one of the first things—''

"No, I don't know. You really believe that nonsense?''

Fran giggled. "I believe it when it's something I want to believe. He's probably a Leo—or maybe Gemini. Libras are calm and well-balanced. Maybe that gorgeous Jeff—''

"Do you have anything sensible to say?'' Erin demanded. "If not, I'm going to hang up.''

"Yeah, okay; some millionaire could be trying to get through to offer Rosemary lots of bucks. Call me when you get a chance, will you? I want to hear everything. By the way, are you going to spend election evening there at the house, or are you coming home? I'd love to have company while I watch the returns. . . .''

The hint was so blatant it ended Erin's fading patience. She said, "Good-bye,'' and hung up without giving Fran a chance to reply. She couldn't have said why the call had left her feeling cross and on edge. She ought to be used to Fran by now.

That evening she ate alone and spent the evening watching television. The others were all out on campaign business, scattered across the state from Arlington to Charlottesville. Apparently she had not been needed. Rosemary's commercial had its first airing; though she meant to study it critically and impartially, Erin had a lump in her throat and tears in her eyes when it ended, even though she had learned enough about media techniques to understand how the effect had been produced. She picked up the book she was reading, on the running of a presidential campaign, but it failed to hold her attention; she didn't want to read about it, she wanted to do it. She knew she had a long way to go and a lot to learn, but she ached to be in on the action instead of being relegated to typing lists and washing dishes.

In that sullen mood of self-pity she went to bed. Voices and the sound of car doors slamming roused her; she pulled the blankets up over her head and went back to sleep. She did not hear Kay come up the stairs and enter her room. She heard nothing more till the birds woke her at dawn.

Down the stairs at a dead run, stumbling over the hem of her robe, catching herself with a desperate grab at the banister. Into the commons room and through the kitchen. No smell of coffee brewing, no comforting, calm presence . . . it was too early, the sun was barely over the horizon, Sarah wouldn't be there for another hour.

It seemed to take forever to turn the key and release the chain. Her fingers kept slipping. Out the door finally; there was frost on the ground, it burned like hot coals on her bare feet. They left dark prints across the whitened macadam of the stableyard. She pounded on the door with both fists and kept pounding till she heard a gruff, resentful voice grunt out a sleepy question. She would have answered it if she could, but when she opened her mouth no sounds came out. She beat on the door again.

It opened with an abruptness that sent her stumbling forward into Nick's arms. He was wearing only a pair of skimpy shorts, and she clung to him, grateful for the warmth of bone and muscle.

"Jesus, Erin! What happened?"

"Kay. She's dead. I just found her."

He made her sit down while he put on jeans and shirt and slipped his feet into sneakers. "Take deep breaths," he instructed. "Put your head down."

"It's all right. I'm all right now. I just can't . . . seem to catch . . . my breath."

"Are you sure?"

"About . . . Kay? Yes, I'm sure. I tried . . ."

"Okay. Let's go."

He didn't notice she was barefoot until she stepped on a sharp-edged pebble and cried out in pain. He picked her up, barely pausing, and carried her into the kitchen, where he deposited her in a chair.

"Stay here. You could make some coffee, if you feel up to it."

"Sure. That's a good idea."

The familiar domestic routine steadied her, as Nick had anticipated. He was back down before the liquid had finished dripping, his face visibly paler.

"She's dead, all right. Was that how you found her—lying on her back, with the covers down to her waist?"

"No. She was on her side, curled up—peaceful. I thought she was asleep. Then . . . I don't know what it was that alerted me. . . . Yes, I do. I couldn't hear her breathing. Usually I can hear her through the closed door. She snores. . . ."

"Yes, okay. So you turned her over—felt for a pulse?"

"I don't remember exactly what I did." Erin's brow wrinkled painfully. "Pulse, yes. I felt for a heartbeat. Then I tried mouth-to-mouth—"

"Jesus Christ, Erin! She was cold! Not ice-cold, but definitely chilly."

"I noticed that," Erin said dully. "That was when I lost my head and ran out of the house."

"Why didn't you wake Rosemary, or Joe?"

"I didn't know Joe was here. And I couldn't go to Rosemary, Nick—not at that unearthly hour, not just rush in and blurt it out." She pushed the tangled hair from her face and pressed her hands to her head. "I was looking for Sarah, I suppose. Someone warm and solid and unflappable. The rock in the storm. She wasn't here, so . . ."

"You mean I was your second choice?" Erin stared blankly at him, and Nick's feeble attempt at a smile never made it past his lips. "I should take that as a compliment. Let me think. I don't like to leave you alone—"

"I'm perfectly fine," Erin said.

"You're in shock, that's what you are." He filled a cup with coffee and poured in half the sugar bowl, waving aside Erin's protests. "Drink it. All of it. I'm going to wake Joe, and then one of us will have to break it to Rosemary. Hang on till I get back."

"No problem." Her hand was rock-steady as she reached

for the cup. Maybe I am in shock, she thought coolly. If so, I hope it lasts. This is no time to break down and blubber. We were wondering what would happen next. Well, now it's happened.

As the dreadful day wore on she could only marvel at the calm efficiency with which the others dealt with Kay's death. For Joe it was easy. Nothing mattered to him now except the election; his only concern was how the tragedy would affect Rosemary and her already overcrowded schedule. His attitude seemed horribly calloused to Erin, but when she said as much to Will, he shook his head.

"Joe isn't calloused, he's just honest. It may make you uncomfortable, but don't misjudge him. He didn't know Kay well, and he wasn't particularly fond of her. The pressure he's putting on Rosemary, to get on with her work, is the best possible thing for her. Don't worry, she can handle it. She's handled worse."

Later that morning Rosemary called her into her office. She was not alone. Standing beside the desk was a tall, raw-boned man with graying hair and a long, large-featured face. "This is Harry Blair, our local lawman," Rosemary said. "He wants to ask you a few questions."

She was pale but quite composed; the only trace of tears was the faint pinkness of her eyelids.

Blair's attitude was almost paternal. Erin told her story; when she started to explain why she had gone running out of the house, instead of notifying one of the occupants, he cut her off with a kindly, "Yes, I see. Perfectly natural thing to do. I don't suppose you happened to notice anything out of the way, anything unusual? Not that you'd be likely to, the way things were. . . ."

"*Was* there anything out of the way?" Erin asked.

Blair appeared a trifle disconcerted. Sweet little young ladies in a state of shock weren't supposed to ask leading questions. He ignored the question and asked one of his own. "Did you see the bottle of sleeping pills on the table by the bed?"

"No. I mean, I suppose it was there, I just didn't . . . Was that how she died? An overdose?"

"Suppose you just let me ask the questions, miss."

"You don't have to treat her like an idiot, Harry," Rosemary said with some asperity. ' Naturally she would wonder. Yes, Erin, that's the assumption. The bottle was almost full. Didn't you pick up a refill of that prescription last week?"

"It was Nick who picked it up, actually. I was going to, but the car—"

"Yes," Rosemary said quickly. "The point is that it was a refill. The original prescription was filled only the week before. I have explained that we can't be certain Kay took the medication as prescribed; if she didn't, there are fifteen or twenty of the capsules unaccounted for. Obviously you can't account for them. . . . Is there anything else you want to ask her, Harry?"

Blair's expression showed that he knew he was being manipulated, but he seemed more amused than resentful. "Just the usual things. Whether you noticed anything unusual in her behavior—signs of depression, confusion, anything abnormal?"

Rosemary's hands were folded on the desktop; her eyes were fixed on Erin. The message came across loud and clear. "I didn't know her that well," Erin said slowly. "I only met her a couple of weeks ago. She was annoyed because of her hand—not being able to do the things she normally did, it was frustrating for such an active person."

"Yes, we know about that. Well. I guess that's it, then. Thanks, Mrs. Marshall. I'm sorry about this. We'll make it as easy on you as we can."

"I appreciate that, Harry. If you want to talk to anyone else, ask Joe. He's in his office, I expect." Her gesture at Erin kept the latter in her chair; after the sheriff had left, Rosemary said, "I'm so sorry, Erin. I never imagined when I asked you to come here that you'd be faced with anything so dreadful. If there's anything I can do—"

"I'm the one who should be saying that," Erin broke in.

"You've already done a great deal and I expect you'll be

called on to do more. If you stay. If you choose to bow out—
for a few days, or forever—I won't blame you in the least.''

"I'll stay. Of course I'll stay.''

"Good.'' Rosemary's quick smile reshaped every feature,
warming her eyes, smoothing out the lines of weariness and
tension. It was the smile known and loved by millions of
voters; Erin suspected she could turn it on and off like a light
switch, but it had the same effect on her that it did on Rosemary's audiences.

"I was hoping you'd say that,'' Rosemary went on. "I just
want to tell you what has happened and what to expect. I
think you're like me—you'd rather know the worst than imagine things. There will be an autopsy. Depending on the results of the autopsy, there may or may not be an inquest. If
it is determined that Kay died of an overdose, the verdict will
almost certainly be accidental death.''

"I see.''

"Yes. You're a clever little thing, aren't you?'' Rosemary's
hands twisted. "I have one more thing to say. I'm going to
be candid with you, not only because you are intelligent
enough to figure it out for yourself but because I don't want
to leave you with any lingering doubts or feelings of regret.
I had known Kay for a long time. Our friendship was based
on shared experiences and memories and interests, rather than
emotional commitment, but it was very real. And yet her
death came as something of a relief. You look shocked. Please
don't. You were very tactful in your answer to Harry Blair,
but you must have noticed her memory lapses, and you, of
all people, have suffered from her increasingly short temper.
Sooner or later, it would have been necessary for me to replace Kay. She could not have accepted that. This is so much
kinder. To go out, painlessly and quickly, before your ambitions and hopes are shattered . . .'' Her reddened lids lowered and she bowed her head. "It's what I'd want for myself,''
she whispered.

Erin's eyes filled with tears, the first she had shed that day;
but even as she nodded in sympathetic agreement, some separate section of her mind told her that she had just witnessed

one of Rosemary's more impressive performances. Nick was absolutely right, she was getting better all the time.

* *

"THE INQUEST is Monday?" Erin exclaimed. "So soon?"

"That's what happens when you are a big shot, on your own turf," Nick said. "Everybody is cooperating. Get it over with, out of the way, so the important people won't be inconvenienced."

They were sitting on the tree trunk watching the sun set from Christie's favorite spot on the hill. Christie wasn't with them; she wouldn't get a chance to run that day, except to run herself ragged. Erin ought to have been in the office trying to help, but she had felt a desperate need to get away from the house. Nick had caught up with her along the path, scaring her half to death when she heard his pounding footsteps behind her.

Nick poked moodily at the ground with a stick he had picked up. Its rough point made little impression; the ground was baked hard. The stick cracked across, and Nick tossed it aside. "It's all wrong, Erin," he said. "Cover-up is the name of the game in politics, but this stinks. Joe is counting on a verdict of accidental death."

"The sleeping pills."

"Uh-huh."

"I don't believe it."

"Neither do I."

Nick shifted position. The log was certainly not the most comfortable of seats. "The police are thinking suicide," Erin said. "If the autopsy shows she had Alzheimer's or cancer, or some other horrible disease, that will confirm their theory. If it doesn't . . . well, everybody knows menopause is tough on these old ladies, they get funny ideas. So make it accidental death, spare the feelings of the survivors, don't dig around for dirt that might hurt Rosemary's campaign."

"Nasty, logical way you have of looking at things," Nick muttered. "Maybe she did kill herself. Maybe she was the arsonist."

"Menopause?" Erin suggested caustically.

"Blackmail, pure and simple. To remind Rosemary she knew the truth, and intended to hang on to her job."

"Then she got religion and repented? That would be a nice neat solution, wouldn't it? Criminal and judge in one; crime wave ended, punishment meted out."

"I'm afraid it's too neat," Nick admitted gloomily. "The other possibility is that she found out who was persecuting Rosemary, and the criminal silenced her."

"That would suggest that she confronted the suspect instead of going to Rosemary or the police. So it was someone she knew and liked?"

"Say rather someone she feared. That's the whole point about blackmail; the victim can't go to the police. So why should he kill her? It's usually the other way around."

"But we keep coming back to the same group of people," Erin argued. "It wouldn't have been difficult for any one of them to arrange for Kay to get an overdose."

"And it would have been almost impossible for anyone outside that group to have pumped the pills into her." Nick brooded. "Damn. That lets Laurence out. He was my favorite suspect."

"I don't like him either, but I can't think of any reason why he'd want to threaten or blackmail Rosemary. It all goes back to that fire in Richmond. Who else could have known about it?"

"Everybody and his kid brother," Nick said despondently. "We've been down that track before. However, I want you to know I'm finally getting my act together. I ran a few checks on some of our suspects today. Better late than never, right? If I hadn't sat on my butt dreaming dreams of glory, Kay might—"

"No, don't ever think that." Erin put a comforting arm around him. "It's unfair, untrue, and unproductive. If we had known what was going to happen, we'd all have behaved differently. But we didn't know. At least you were nice to her. She liked you."

"Mmmmmm." Nick returned the compliment physically and verbally, drawing her close before he said, "She liked you too."

"No, she didn't. And—and I really didn't like her very much. I wasn't as nice as I should have been."

"I expect everyone feels the same," Nick said gently. "You know something? I don't think Rosemary really liked her either. She's probably feeling guiltier than anyone."

"She has no reason to feel guilty. She put up with a lot more from Kay than most people would. Oh, Nick, what are we going to do?"

"How about a little canoodling? No, don't give me that reproachful look; as the man said, life goes on. The more love in it, the better."

She responded, not in words, but by raising her face to his. His kiss was warm and sweet; less than passionate and more than kind, both a fulfillment and a promise.

"Now, then," he said, "where were we?"

"Checking on suspects?"

"Right. I think we have to eliminate Joe. Not only does he have every reason to pray for victory, but he didn't know Rosemary until last winter, when he joined the campaign. I found no connection between them before that, except for casual encounters in the course of political business.

"Will she's known since college. Dated him a few times before she met the great Edward Marshall and was swept off her feet. He was married; got a divorce last year. Three kids. I couldn't find any evidence that he saw much, if anything, of Rosemary after she married Marshall. It's not likely that he would, you know."

"Not likely, but you can't be sure."

"True. I didn't have time for in-depth investigations. As for Laurence, he was Ed's friend originally, not Rosemary's. They met at Hah-vahd as undergraduates. We know Jeff is clean, but I looked him up anyway; he comes from Arizona, went to law school in LA, where he aced everything—law review, the works—and then went to work for the State's Attorney's office in Sacramento. He joined the campaign in April. Said he wanted to get into politics, and he liked Rosemary's style—"

"Isn't that an inadequate reason for giving up his job and

traveling clear across the country to work for a woman he'd never met?''

"No more inadequate than my reasons for giving up *my* job and scrounging scraps from Sarah to keep body and soul together. He may have met her casually, for all you know, and been swept off his feet. She has that effect on people. Where was I? Oh, yeah. Jeff's parents are both living, and he has two younger brothers.''

"Good work," Erin said. "How'd you find that out?''

"Personnel file. Same for Christie; mother's dead, father's married a second time, they live in Petersburg. Her birth date is May fourteenth.''

"That lets her out.''

"Right. Sarah—''

"Oh, Nick!''

"A sleuth has to keep an open mind. The woman who died in Richmond could have had a sister. If she did, it wasn't Sarah. Background is an open book. Same for Jackson. He's a native Washingtonian.''

"So where does that leave us?''

"Right back on square one," Nick said. "Any suggestions?''

"We can't take this to the police.''

"This tangled web of surmise and guesswork? No, dearie, we sure as hell can't. There's only one thing we can do. Confront Rosemary.''

"I didn't think you'd agree to do that.''

"Nothing else we can do without more time and a helluva lot more resources than either of us can command. But we've got to do something. Even if we're wrong, even if we end up looking like a pair of horses' behinds, we can't sit on our hands and wait for the next incident. If Kay's death was murder, we've got ourselves a whole new ball game.''

He jumped to his feet and began pacing up and down, his fists clenched. Erin got up too. "I agree. Completely. But we don't know how Kay died, not yet. Let's wait till after the autopsy.''

"I don't know if I can wait that long," Nick groaned. "Something else is going to happen, Erin. I can feel it.''

"Yes." A shiver ran through her. Nick stopped pacing and put his arm around her. "Cold?"

"No. Somebody walked over my grave."

"Don't say things like that!"

*   *

WHEN THEY NEARED the house Nick let out a grunt of disgust. "Damn, there's Laurence's car. I might have known that ghoul would be on the scene."

"How did he find out so quickly?"

"He has informants all over town. The word has gone out; I sent the obituary to the paper a couple of hours ago, and Christie called some people; Rosemary canceled her appointments for this afternoon, you know."

"I should know; I made several calls myself." Erin rubbed her forehead. She had had a dull headache all day, on which the aspirin she had taken had little effect. "I'm not functioning at peak efficiency."

"Me neither. Let's sneak in the back door. The mood I'm in right now, I don't think I can listen to Laurence ooze sympathy and advice."

"Rosemary doesn't seem to mind," Erin said thoughtfully. "And there are times—"

"Oh, for God's sake, not that again!"

"No, not that again. I was going to say that I have a feeling there's more to him than meets the eye, that his languid air is only a facade." She broke off with a laugh. "For instance . . ."

Laurence had just come out of the house. As usual, there were several cats waiting to sneak in; as soon as the screen door opened, a lean calico darted between his feet and he executed a complex, graceless stagger to avoid stepping on the animal. They heard his comment; it was profane but amused, and he paused to stroke one of the losers in the race. "Sorry, old chap, better luck next time."

It was too late for the guilty pair to retreat. Laurence caught sight of them and wove a tortuous path around the cats on the steps and the porch. "Hello, young Nick. I dropped by to discuss Sunday's show, but this is obviously not the time. Perhaps we can set up another appointment."

"I don't know," Nick began.

"Nor do I, as yet." Laurence took his gloves from his pocket and carefully drew them on. They were of fine morocco and fit like a second skin. His face was sober, with no trace of its habitual mockery. "Rosemary said the funeral will probably be on Tuesday. You'll let me know? I'll be there, of course."

"I'm very sorry," Erin said. "You were old friends, I know."

Laurence sighed. "Yes, I probably knew Kay as well as anyone—except Rosemary, of course. I believe . . . You were the one who found her, Erin? How dreadful for you."

"It was a shock, of course. But she looked very peaceful. I'm sure she didn't suffer."

"Thank you for telling me that." He smiled at her. "Take care of her, young Nick. She's a treasure."

He got in the car and drove away.

"That's a switch," Erin remarked. "He didn't think I was a treasure last week."

"Patronizing bastard," Nick muttered.

"He did seem to be genuinely distressed about Kay."

"Or putting on a good act. Why does he always have to call me young Nick?"

"Maybe he doesn't realize how it annoys you."

Nick made a rude noise through pursed lips. "Well, anyhow, things are back to normal," he said, as they approached the commons room and heard the voices within raised in strident argument. "You'd think Joe could keep off her back—now, of all times."

He opened the door and Joe's voice boomed out. "For once I agree with Laurence. Why the hell did you insist on an autopsy?"

Rosemary stood with her back to him. She was holding one of the knitting bags. "That's the proper procedure in a case of sudden death," she said.

"Yeah, but it wasn't . . . Doc White was perfectly willing to sign the death certificate. Heart failure."

Rosemary was dressed to go cut, in a black wool jersey dress with a wide lace collar. The full skirt swung out as she turned. "Jack White is a smug snob. He wants to put me in his debt by sparing me the embarrassment of an inquiry, and a lot of media attention. He thinks Kay had too much to drink, and that she overdosed on those wretched pills."

"So maybe she did. What's wrong with a kindly cover-up? Spare her, you, her family—"

"She had no family, only distant cousins. We—I was her family. That's why I owe her, at the least, the dignity of the truth." Rosemary's makeup was heavier than usual; it gave her face the smooth matte surface of a porcelain figurine. The glaze cracked momentarily, as she said, "Kay could not have taken an accidental overdose, Joe. Her sleeping pills were the mildest-possible prescription sedative. She'd have had to swallow every capsule in that bottle to get a fatal dose, and she hated taking pills, you know how she resisted it."

"Nembutal and alcohol—"

"She didn't drink that much. And she knew the danger of mixing drugs—who better than careful Kay? No, Joe. Either her heart gave out or she took those pills deliberately. One way or the other, I have to know."

"So you can wallow in guilt—one way or the other? For failing to notice she was ill, or depressed? Haven't you paid your dues to Kay, Rosemary? I don't give a damn how devoted she was to Ed Marshall, or how much she'd done for you, you stopped owing her a long time ago."

Rosemary's lips took on an ugly shape, but it was Will, watching from his corner, who spoke.

"Shut up, Joe. What's the point of arguing? We'll know tomorrow."

"That's right," Rosemary said "We'll know tomorrow. I must go now, or I'll be late. Jeff. . . ."

Erin hadn't seen him. Slouched in a chair by the window, he had been as motionless as a statue. He started violently when Rosemary spoke his name, and rose to his feet.

"Yes, right. I'm ready."

He picked up her coat and held it for her. Instead of slipping into it she put her hand on his cheek and forced him to look into her eyes. "My dear—you look exhausted. Joe can drive me, you stay here and rest."

"No, it's okay. If you can do it, I can. Don't be . . . don't coddle me, Rosemary."

"All right, if you say so. Come on, Joe."

They went out together. Rosemary took Jeff's arm; it was questionable as to who was supporting whom.

"So she's keeping her appointment," Erin said. "Just as if nothing had happened."

"This dinner was scheduled months ago," Will said mildly. "The governor will be there. He's a very popular man, and his active support means a lot to the campaign."

"You sound just like Joe," Erin muttered.

Will's gray eyes brightened, but not with amusement. "I take it that is not a compliment. Would you prefer Rosemary to lose the election, as a gesture of respect for her secretary?" Erin started to protest, but Will went on in his even, inexorable voice. "Kay was Ed's protégée and devotee. Rosemary inherited her along with a lot of other things, good and bad. Kay transferred her loyalty to Rosemary, and she has clung like a leech. Do you realize how tiring, how infuriating, that secondhand devotion can be? Always demanding perfection that can never be attained because nobody could possibly measure up to the standard of the great Edward Marshall? If Rosemary weren't the decent person she is, she'd have dumped Kay years ago. She doesn't deserve your jejune criticism."

He had risen to his feet and looked even taller than his real height.

"I'm sorry," Erin mumbled.

Will seemed to shrink inside his shabby gray cardigan. "My fault. I didn't mean to get so heated."

"All the same," Nick said, "Jeff seems a lot more upset than Rosemary."

"Yes," Will said. "He does, doesn't he?"

Chapter
Fifteen

IF THAT DAY had been mad, the next was sheer chaos. The obituary appeared in the morning *Post*, along with a short, factual story that described Kay as Rosemary's secretary and friend. Calls of genuine condolence and curiosity veiled as condolence started pouring in, and florists' vans beat a steady path to the house. Receiving one such offering—another of the twenty-dollar tasteful sympathy ensembles featured by "Flowers by Wire"—Christie was moved to plaintive protest. "The house is starting to smell like a funeral parlor. You know we'll have to acknowledge every single one of these damned bouquets."

"Who's it from?" Erin asked, watching Christie wrench the tasteful card from the flowers.

"A constituent, I suppose. Never heard of her." Christie tossed the card into the drawer in the hall table that had been designated as a temporary receptacle. "No address, of course, that wouldn't be tasteful. Her name is probably on file, one

of our constant correspondents. That'll be a nice little job for
someone—looking up all these names.''

"Do you want me to—"

"Not today, for God's sake. I need you on the phones.''

During her lunch break Erin walked to the gate to stretch
her legs and see what Sam thought of it all. He had been
pressed into service to screen callers, and she broke into a
broad grin when she saw his arrangements. There was no
doubt that Sam had taken his assignment seriously. He had
set himself up with a folding lawn chair and a matching table.
On the table was a thermos of coffee, a lunch pail, and a
clipboard. Leaning against the chair was a shotgun; and
pinned to Sam's jacket was an enormous "Rosemary Marshall" button.

"I came to ask if you wanted some coffee or a sandwich,''
she began.

"No, ma'am, I'm all set here, but I sure thank you for
thinking of it.'' He bounded to his feet, alert as a hunting
hound; a car had pulled up by the gate. "Can't you see the
sign?'' he shouted, making a megaphone of his withered
hands. "No admittance 'cept on business.''

There were two women in the car. The one on the passenger side put her head out the window. It was crowned with
pink curlers; a cheap rayon scarf failed to conceal these ornaments.

"That's a helluva nice way to greet people,'' she yelled
back. "We brought Rosemary some flowers. Came to tell her
we're sorry about her friend.''

"She ain't here.'' Sam limped to the gate. "I'll tell her.
Thank you,'' he added.

"I'll get them,'' Erin said, unhooking the gate. She took
the flowers—a brilliant if unmatched bunch of homegrown
chrysanthemums—and offered effusive thanks and explanations. The women received both amiably enough, but as they
left, the one in the curlers called, "Better get the grouchy old
nigger off the gate, honey, he's got no more manners than a
monkey.''

They were gone before Erin could think of a sufficiently
stinging reply. Flushed and furious, she hooked the gate after

her. She couldn't look at Sam; she was suffused with the guilt
decent people feel when faced with the indecency of others.
She dropped the gaudy chrysanthemums on the gravel and
stamped on them.

"You hadn't ought to do that," Sam said reprovingly.
"What if she seen you? She's a voter, you know."

"She's a horse's ass," Erin said.

"And you hadn't ought to use words like that, neither, you
been goin' around with that boy Nick too much." The old
man's face creased into a hundred wrinkles. "Felt good,
though, didn't it?"

"Felt great," Erin said. She planted her feet firmly on the
flowers.

"Well, okay this time, but you gotta learn to be polite no
matter how you feel," Sam said firmly. "That's what politics
is all about." He scratched his head and looked sheepish.
"Partly my own fault. She got on my nerves, was all; I seen
her around, heard her talk. . . . Then she turns up here with
them flowers she yanked outta her front yard, nothing better
to do than nose into other people's business, and calling Miss
Rosemary by her first name like she was a friend. I won't do
that again. You don't need to worry."

"I'm not worried. You're better at it than I am." Erin
grinned at him. "But don't you think the shotgun is a little
excessive?"

Sam grinned back. "It ain't loaded. But it sure is a powerful moral inducement."

Later that afternoon as she sat at her desk trying to find a
gracious way of ending a conversation with a caller who insisted on recounting every detail of every occasion on which
she had shaken Rosemary's hand, the outer door opened and
a man entered. Of medium height and lean, wiry build, he
was so astonishingly handsome, Erin stopped listening altogether and gaped. He was a stranger to her, and apparently
to Christie as well; the office manager bore down on him with
the obvious intention of evicting him. A low-voiced conversation ensued; then Christie shrugged helplessly and after hesitat-
ing for a moment let him into Kay's office. She returned to

her desk without comment, avoiding the curious stares of the others.

She didn't have to explain to Erin. The man's sleek cap of black hair and chiseled features didn't resemble even a conventional TV cop—producers have decided upon the tough, rugged, and homely stereotype—but there was something about him that shouted his profession aloud—the confidence of his carriage, the keen, watchful eyes, the way he walked.

Erin hung up on the caller. Her palms were damp; she wiped them on her skirt. For a wonder the phone didn't ring again the instant she put it down, and she got quickly to her feet. She had to find Nick.

He was in the commons room with Will. "The police are here," she announced breathlessly. "One policeman, anyway. Plainclothes."

"Is that so?" Will adjusted his glasses. "Well, well. How interesting."

"Sometimes your cool drives me crazy," Nick growled. "You act as if you expected this."

"I was prepared for such a contingency," Will replied sedately. "Weren't you?"

"I—uh—what contingency? Does this mean the autopsy was—"

Will didn't let him finish. "Let's get back to work, Nick. Philips will be along shortly, and he'll expect you to be ready for him."

"Mr. Laurence?" Erin exclaimed.

"He wants to discuss Sunday's show," Will said. "Nick, will you . . . Nick!" He nudged Nick, who was glaring off into space as if at some profoundly distasteful vision.

"What? Oh, hell, I can't concentrate on this, Will."

"We've covered most of it." Will nudged his papers into a neat stack and stood up. "I need to look up some figures. Give you time to get your wits together. Talk to him, Erin, knock some sense into him. Oh—by the way, a friend of yours called a while ago. I don't know how she got this number—"

"I do, and it wasn't from me," Erin said. "What did she want?"

"Nick talked to her. After that, at my suggestion, he took the phone off the hook." Will's eyes widened in a look of innocent surprise. "It made the most alarming noises for a while, but finally they stopped. I trust the instrument has not been permanently disabled. If you should wish to return the call—"

"Thanks, Will, but I've no intention of calling Fran. She just wants to get in on the action and she goes on and on, about . . . about . . ."

Will took her silence as an indication that she had finished a conversation in which he had minimal interest anyway; with a genteel nod, he ambled to the door and went out.

"She is a talker," Nick agreed. "Damn it, Erin, it looks as if we were right about Kay. It's funny, but you know I never quite believed our theory, even when—"

"Nick." She turned on him, caught him by the shoulders. "Nick, I just remembered. I know what it was Fran said that bugged me. Astrology. Signs. He's a Pisces, Nick, and that means—"

"Wait a minute." The emotion in her trembling voice and horrified expression made sense to him, even if her words did not. "We can't talk here, too many people around. Come outside."

The weather had turned gray and gloomy. Not a breath of wind stirred; the dismal sky sagged like a heavy blanket, trailing ragged clouds.

A rapturous chorus of barks heralded the arrival of the dogs; Nick picked up a stick and waved it threateningly at Tiny, who settled back onto his haunches and looked as if the idea of jumping up on people had never occurred to him. "Cut it out, guys. I'm not in the mood today."

The older dog was more sensitive. When they sat down on the bench he laid a graying head on Erin's lap and stared at her with melting, sympathetic eyes.

"Is it about Jeff?" Nick asked.

"Yes. Nick, where did you get those birth dates?"

"I told you. The personnel files."

"And where did the information on those files come from?"

"Why—from the people who filled out the application forms. You had to do one, didn't you? Name, address, educational and business experience . . ." Nick's jaw dropped. "Oh, shit. Oh my God. How could I have been so stupid?"

"I didn't think of it either. No one ever checked that information?"

"No, why should they? This isn't a security agency. Joe must have called Sacramento, he mentioned the raves he got from Jeff's boss. But he wouldn't ask about Jeff's birth date, any more than he'd question his height or his weight."

"There was no reason why he should," Erin agreed. "Or why we should think it odd that Jeff 'happened to let it slip' that his birthday was last week. But that's out of character, Nick; Jeff never talked about his family or his personal life. And then there was the fish. On his key chain," she added impatiently, as Nick stared at her in bewilderment. "I noticed it the first time he drove me out here. It was heavy silver, stylized, very handsome. Then it disappeared. Remember, Joe said something about Jeff losing his key chain, that was why he got him a new one for a birthday present. Jeff never mentioned it; and wouldn't you think he'd question people, ask whether they had seen it, if he had simply misplaced it? It looked expensive—a gift, maybe. But it was Fran rambling on about horoscopes that put the idea into my head. The fish is the astrological sign for Pisces. Depending on the system you follow, that's late February into March."

She didn't have to go on; she could tell by his stricken face that he remembered those fatal dates as well as she did. "Oh my God," he said hoarsely. "It all spells Merry Christmas, doesn't it? If he planned this from the start—if he came here looking for revenge—sure, he's a smart guy, he'd know the true date of his birthday would be a dead giveaway. It was perfectly safe for him to lie about it on that personnel file, nobody would think of questioning it or even notice it, until the incidents began. He'd be one of the first to be suspected by anyone who knew about the Richmond fire. A falsified record would probably dispel suspicion—it sure as hell dispelled ours. Then just to hammer the point home he mentioned his birthday was coming up. . . ."

"It's guesswork, though," Erin said. "No proof."

"No problem about that," Nick said. He dropped his head onto his hands. "One phone call is all we need."

"To California?"

"Right. The correct birth date is probably on his personnel file at the state offices; he wouldn't have any reason to lie about it at that point."

"We'd better do it, then. Before he comes back "

"Yeah," Nick said, not moving.

"Where is he?"

"Going the rounds with Rosemary and Joe. Coffee with the Friends of Virginia Wildlife lunch with the DAR, a strategy meeting at headquarters. . . . Geez. I hate this."

"Me too. Let's get it over with. Maybe we're wrong, Nick."

"A happy thought," Nick said gloomily.

They headed down the hall toward the offices. "No, not Kay's," Erin exclaimed. "The policeman is in there."

Nick stopped short. "Damn, I forgot about him. One disaster at a time is about all I can handle. Christ, Erin, he wouldn't be here unless the autopsy—"

"We'll cope with that when we're sure about Jeff. Come on." She tugged at him, seized with a fierce, sick impatience. It was like going to the dentist; you knew it would hurt, and you knew you had to do it, you just wanted to get it over with as soon as possible.

They went into Rosemary's office. Nick settled behind the desk and switched on the computer. "I hope I can remember. . . ." He pressed keys. "Yeah, here it is. Surveys, polls . . . personnel files."

Erin came around the desk and looked over his shoulder. "That's Jeff's?"

"Right. Jefferson Andrew Ross, male, age 31, born Prescott, Arizona, October 13, 1959."

"It looks so convincing, doesn't it?"

"That's the power of the printed word. Doesn't mean a damned thing. Let's see. Present employer, State's Attorney's Office, Sacramento, California, immediate superior . . . There's even a phone number. Okay, here goes "

His air of grim fortitude changed to annoyance as he was put through the conventional bureaucratic shuffle. "Oh, I want personnel? What a surprise. Switch me, will you, this is an out-of-state call. . . . Damn it, you gave me the wrong extension, operator, I want 367. . . . I know you can't give out information to unauthorized persons, lady, I'm calling from the office of Rosemary White Marshall, United States Congresswoman; what do you want, a security clearance? I'm not asking for his medical records, I just need a couple of vital statistics. Okay, I'll hold on."

Erin didn't have to hear the answer, she read it on Nick's face. "Thanks," he said slowly, and hung up.

"We were right?" she asked.

"You were right. It would be a pretty wild coincidence, wouldn't it, for two different men to have the same birth date?"

"Damn." After a moment she said reluctantly, "There's a convenient cop right down the hall."

The palely lit screen of the computer glared at them, with its damning evidence of deliberate misrepresentation. Nick slapped his hand down on the keyboard, and the square went dark. "No," he said. "Goddammit, I'm not going to turn the guy in without giving him a chance to defend himself. It could be a setup."

"Not very likely."

"Maybe not. I can see Jeff doing the other things—hell, I can even sympathize with him, if he really thinks Rosemary had a hand in the death of his family. But murder?"

"We're the only sickos who have considered murder," Erin muttered. "The autopsy might show Kay had taken a lethal dose of something, but there's nothing to prove it wasn't self-administered."

"Not yet, there isn't. There will be an investigation, count on it. And if anything funny turns up, and Jeff is known to have set the fires, he'll be in deep trouble."

"Okay, I'm with you. We talk to Jeff first."

"I talk to him. I may be a naive bleeding-heart sucker, but I'm not taking a chance with you."

"You're a naive bleeding heart and a male chauvinist to

boot. Don't you dare give me that 'women and children into the boats' crap!''

''For God's sake, don't yell!''

''I'm sorry.'' Erin clapped her hand to her mouth.

Nick got up. ''We'd better get out of here before someone wanders in. They're due back anytime now. We'll have to play it by ear—get Jeff off for a private conversation, find out what the autopsy showed.''

By mutual consent they avoided the offices and the commons room. It was impossible to think of working; Erin felt as if she were catching the flu; her face was hot and her stomach was queasy. Nick kept cracking his knuckles. They settled down on the porch steps, where they were immediately swarmed over by cats. Fortunately for their nerves they didn't have to wait long. A hazy swollen sun still hovered over the treetops when the Olds rolled along the drive and stopped in front of the house.

There were only two people in the car, both in the front seat. ''Rosemary and . . . who is it?'' Erin asked.

''Jeff. Joe must have stayed in town.''

Nick cracked another knuckle. Erin flinched and bit her lip. Not so much a visit to the dentist as pure stage fright. . . . She hoped Nick had some idea of how to introduce the subject, for her mind was a total blank.

Jeff got out of the car, gave them a curious look, and went around to help Rosemary out. She stood quite still for a few seconds, twisting her shoulders and her head as if her neck were stiff. Then a determinedly bright smile curved her lips and she started toward them.

''Taking a break?'' she asked. ''It must have been pure hell today.''

Nick got to his feet. ''The police are here,'' he blurted.

In the strange dull light, all the faces were shaded and sallow. Jeff's cheeks were a muddy grayish-brown; his color did not change, but his body jerked slightly, as if he had been struck by an invisible missile. Rosemary only nodded and went up the steps, automatically avoiding the cats.

Jeff turned toward the car.

''Where are you going?'' Nick asked.

."What's it to you?" The slam of the screen door as it closed behind Rosemary shot Nick forward as if propelled by a spring. Jeff spun around. "Get your hands off me!"

"Give me the car keys." Nick grabbed for them. Jeff caught his wrist; they stood locked in straining struggle, Nick's teeth bared in a snarl, Jeff's lips a tight line.

"Stop it." Erin ran toward them. "Don't, please don't. Jeff, you can't run away, that won't do any good. Nick, let him go."

"I'll let go if he will," Nick gasped.

They fell apart, both panting, not with exertion but with anger and tension.

"We know," Nick said. "Don't you get it? We know who you are. We haven't told anybody. I'm sorry I jumped you, I lost my head, I . . . Say something, damn it!"

Jeff leaned back against the fender. Every bone in his body slumped. "In a way, I'm glad," he said quietly. "I'm glad it's over."

* *

NICK SWITCHED ON the lights. His small cottage was almost as dark as night, the two narrow windows closely curtained. Jeff turned slowly, studying the room and its furnishings with the cool appraisal of a decorator trying to decide what should be done.

"What a dump," he said.

"A humble spot, but mine own." Nick indicated a shabby overstuffed chair, one of two that flanked the tiny, boarded-up fireplace. A couple of rickety tables, their tops stained with white rings, and a worn rag rug were the only other furniture. "Sit down."

"Sure you don't want to do a strip search?" Jeff asked pleasantly.

"Well, now that you mention it . . ." Nick advanced on him.

"Assume the position," Jeff muttered. Turning, he braced his hands on the mantel and spread his legs. Nick felt him over, from underarms to ankles; when he rose, his face was dull red.

"Sorry, I had to."

"Naturally. I'd do the same. Finished?" Jeff sat down and crossed his legs. He was much more at ease than either of his inquisitors, and as he contemplated their embarrassed faces he smiled faintly.

"How'd you find out?"

"That your name is really Raymond Wilson?"

Jeff's smile froze; Erin realized that until that moment he had not abandoned the forlorn hope that they were talking about something else. Then he shrugged. "I guess it doesn't matter now. I'm glad it's over, but I'm not sorry I did it. The only think I'm ashamed of is what I did to you, Erin. Until you turned up, I had confined my activities to a few anonymous letters. I was afraid to be more direct, because I knew I was the first person she'd suspect if anything happened right there in the house. I had to avoid suspicion at all costs, because I hadn't covered my tracks too well; the first serious investigation would show I had lied about a number of things. Then you appeared, like a sign from heaven—the obvious culprit. They couldn't prove anything, you were innocent— who knew that better than I—but it was a low-down trick all the same, and I regret—"

"Shut up!" Nick shouted. He clutched his head. "Damn it! You sit there chatting idly, like some high-class thief talking down to the dumb cops. . . . Why'd you do it? Why?"

"You know I'm Raymond Wilson and you ask me that?" Jeff said quietly.

"I know. It was horrible. But why Rosemary? She had nothing to do with it. It was an accident, a ghastly, tragic accident—"

"It was no accident," Jeff said.

Nick and Erin exchanged glances. Jeff saw the exchange, saw the sick look on Erin's face. "I'm sorry, Erin. If it's any consolation, I don't believe your father knew ahead of time what was planned. But he sure as hell knew or suspected afterward. That fire was set deliberately, for the insurance. And for another reason. Two birds with one stone. Such a convenient way of getting rid of all the excess baggage in a man's life."

He had them now, and he knew it; the faces that stared back at him were masks of horrified repugnance. His words stung like drops of acid. "I'm only sorry I couldn't do more. What sort of punishment would you inflict on a man who tried to burn his child and its mother alive?"

*   *

"No, THERE'S NO WAY I could be mistaken. I was ten years old—old enough to understand and ask questions, old enough to worry about what the hell was going to become of us. When you're poor and on the streets, you grow up fast.

"The man I thought was my father had been killed in an accident at work the year before. He was working construction, part-time; there was no pension and no insurance—and no compensation, they said he was drunk on the job. It was a lie. He didn't drink. He couldn't afford to.

"She was pregnant when it happened. She couldn't get a job, even if she had been able to find someone to take care of us. Cheap day care in those days wasn't just bad, it was nonexistent. Welfare? Oh, sure, it's such a munificent sum. All those welfare queens driving around in their Cadillacs. . . . Try to find some place to live that isn't infested with rats and roaches and perverts on what a benevolent society doles out to you.

"We struggled along for a while on the welfare and the little they had saved. I did odd jobs after school when I could get them. Everything came to a head one day in the summer. It had been so damned hot we were all sick with it, the baby was ailing, there'd been some bureaucratic foul-up about the welfare that month, and the landlord said we had to get out. That was the day Mary Sue came in, with her clothes torn, crying, because some man had pulled her into a doorway and tried to . . . She was six.

"It was that night she told me. My mother. She was at the end of her rope, there was nothing else she could do but turn to the man who'd gotten her pregnant—with me. She'd never asked him for a cent or a favor before, and all she wanted then was a place to stay where her kids wouldn't be raped or turned to drugs. He was rich, he owned property. Surely he could find some job for her. Maid, cook, scrubwoman, she didn't care, so long as it was honest work and we were safe. She wouldn't have asked for herself, but she'd lower herself for us.

"I tried to talk her out of it. I was sick with shame and rage. But two days later, when we got evicted, there wasn't much I could do; it was hot, and the baby was worse—we had to have someplace to go. We waited till after dark before we went to the place he'd told her about. 'Just till I can find a permanent home for you,' he'd said. 'Just for a few days.' She accepted his demand for secrecy; she'd never have betrayed him, even if he had refused to help. She pounded that into me—telling the truth could hurt him, and we weren't the kind who did low-down things like that.

"When we got to the place, one of the boards on the window was loose, just like he said it would be, and there was some furniture in an upstairs room. Just a couple of mattresses and a beat-up old table—and a broom and some rags. Wasn't that a cute touch? He wouldn't have the place cleaned up for us, but he knew her well enough to realize that damned broom was a symbol as well as a necessity to her.

"He'd left food, too, and a cooler with water and soft drinks, even some ice. The kids fell on those sandwiches like starving animals, they hadn't eaten all day. Neither had I. I can still taste that bologna sandwich. . . .

"I remember how she looked when she saw it. 'He's a good man,' she said. 'I told you, Raymond, he's a good man really. We'll be all right now.' "

He looked at Erin, whose face shone with the tears that slipped unchecked down her cheeks. "You don't want to hear the next part," he said. "I managed to get hold of Mary Sue and lead her out. The smoke was pretty bad; she fell down and I had to drag her most of the way. I thought the others were right behind me. When I got over coughing and being sick, and realized they were still inside . . . I tried to go back in, but the fire department had come by then, and they held me back."

Nick cleared his throat. "The paper—the newspaper—said the police found no evidence of arson."

"I heard one of the firemen say the building wouldn't have gone up so fast if it hadn't been torched," Jeff said calmly. "And there was one other thing. They said it started in the room under ours. Quite likely it did. It was an inferno when I saw it, on my way out. But it wasn't the only part of the building that was burning. There was another, separate fire on the stairs. The lowest flight. I pushed Mary Sue off the landing and jumped after her. If I'd been a minute later we wouldn't have made it."

Nick shook his head dazedly. "Jesus."

"It took me a long time to figure it out," Jeff went on in the same icy, dispassionate voice. "Years. It was several years before I could think about it or remember it. Sometimes I almost convinced myself it had never happened—that it was just a recurrent nightmare. Because afterward, everything was completely different. Like a new life—born again, right? There we were, Mary Sue and I, in a fancy hospital, with everybody treating us like paying patients; and after we got out, we went in different directions—Mary Sue to a family in Wyoming, me to Arizona. The Rosses were respectable, middle-class folks; he was manager of a hardware store, and she taught school. Two kids, both younger than I. At first I was in such a numbed state I didn't question what was happening. I had a room of my own, plenty to eat, clothes that fit, with no holes or patches—and a nice, kind mother-type who came in and held me at night when I woke up screaming. Mary Sue got on better. She was younger. I see her every now and then. She's married, with a couple of kids. I didn't tell her what I was planning. She doesn't know anything about . . . anything."

His voice was calm as ever, but when he talked of his sister his hands twisted and curled, with a horrible life of their own, tearing at each other like small animals. "I was in high school before I started asking questions. That's the rebel time, I suppose, the time when you question everything. God knows I had plenty to wonder about. Like where the money was coming from. A couple of years of psychiatric treatment costs a bundle. And there was my college fund, they kept talking about graduate school or med school as if there'd be no prob-

lem about paying for it. I finally asked her point-blank. She
didn't lie to me, I'll give her that. The money was part of the
deal—every month till I was twenty-one. She tried to tell me
they'd have taken me anyway, even without it, but I knew it
was a lie; I remembered enough to know what I must have
been like when they got me, a sullen, shivering, bed-wetting,
screaming idiot. I knew the money must be coming from
him, and I figured he must have something pretty heavy on
his conscience to lay out such a big sum. I remembered those
two separate fires—one of them cutting off our only means of
escape. And I knew what I had to do.

"That took more years. Getting a fancy education so I
could compete in whitey's world and find out what I needed
to know. I was in my second year of law school before I had
the expertise to trace it back, the complex pattern of inter-
locking companies that had been designed to conceal the real
ownership of that building. I figured it was your father, Erin,
who had handled the trust for me and Mary Sue, but I knew
he wasn't the one I was after. My daddy, the one who owned
the building, was a rich man, an important man. Some daddy,
huh? So I followed the trail and there it was in black and
white—his name, and hers right next to it.

"You can't imagine how I felt when I found out he was
dead. I was so disappointed I got stinking drunk. Then . . .
well, for a while I just let it lie. I probably wouldn't have
done anything if Rosemary had been . . . oh, you know, sick
or poor or miserable, or anything but what she is. But then
last year she announced for the Senate, and I saw her on some
television program, and she looked so young and successful
and everybody was bragging on her and saying maybe the
White House someday, and I thought of my mother, and how
she'd died, and how she'd looked like an old woman, what
with worry and hard work and all. She was twenty-seven
years old. Twenty-seven! And I couldn't—I couldn't . . ."

The even voice finally broke. He hid his face in his hands.
Erin started impulsively toward him, but Nick caught her and
held her back. He knew, as did she after a moment of thought,
that sympathy would have been an affront just then. Lines

from a poem she had once read came to her with stinging poignancy:

What voice can my invention find to say
So soft, precise, and scrupulous a word
You shall not take it for another sword?

Jeff lowered his hands. His eyes were dry, and his voice rose to a pitch of almost childish indignation when he spoke. "And you know what's really funny? I had decided to call it off. You probably won't believe me. If I caught a burglar red-handed, and he swore he had changed his mind and didn't intend to rob me, I'd fall down laughing. But it's true. The crowning irony was that it was the damned birthday party that did me in—the party I set up, in my infinite cleverness, to dispel suspicion. I hadn't been feeling too fond of myself anyway. Rosemary treated me so . . . ah, hell, I knew it was professional habit, she turns it on and off without even thinking about it, but it's awfully effective, you know? I started wondering whether maybe she didn't know about the fire. Maybe she was a victim of that swine too. She never once showed any sign of doubting me, but it seemed to me Kay was looking askance. She had been Marshall's confidential secretary and I felt sure she was in on the whole thing; at least she must have known about the trust, and about me. So I made a point of casually mentioning my birthday coming up, just in case it occurred to her to check up on l'il ole Raymond Wilson. And then she—Rosemary—that goddamn watch . . . I mean, of all the cornball, manipulative stunts. . . . And it worked, just the way she intended it should; I felt like a piece of shit. I had a couple of other things planned, but I couldn't . . ."

He got up and turned his back to them, his arm resting on the mantel, his head bowed on his arm.

"What do you mean, you couldn't?" Nick looked as forbidding as a Grand Inquisitor, but Erin knew he was fighting unwilling sympathy. "You did. I could almost overlook the other things, nobody was endangered by them; but the Mercedes was different. If Kay had been driving—"

"That wasn't me." Jeff did not raise his head. "There's no reason why you should believe that either, but it's true. If I hadn't already made up my mind to pack it up, that would have done it; it scared the hell out of me. I felt like Frankenstein, creating a monster and losing control of it. Only I didn't mean to . . . Leave me alone for a while, will you?"

Nick had to clear his throat before he spoke. "Yeah, all right. Look, Jeff, you stay here. If you try to run—"

"You've got the car keys," Jeff said, not turning.

"Oh, yeah. Okay. I'll just . . . We'll be back."

They tiptoed out, as from a sickroom. The sun was setting in a horror of dull flame; the crimson light made Nick's face look as if it had suffered a bad sunburn. They retreated to "their" bench before either spoke.

"Jesus," Nick said, wiping his brow. "That's the worst thing I've been through in a long time."

"It was awful, wasn't it?" Erin collapsed beside him.

"I can't decide whether I've just had my heartstrings lacerated by the most tragic story I've ever heard, or been conned by a consummate liar."

"Nick! You don't really believe he was lying!"

"No, I don't, but then I'm the biggest sucker on two feet. Hell, I cry over lost puppies. Everything he said about Rosemary applies to him, Erin. He's learned political tricks from the pros, and there are no bigger con men in the world."

"He meant every word he said," Erin insisted.

"Okay, so he meant it. That doesn't mean it's true. He's sick, Erin. Possibly psycho. Did you notice what he said about Kay—that she was getting suspicious? If he thought she was about to blow the whistle on him—"

"No. I don't believe it."

"I feel sorry for him too," Nick said gently. "One part of his story is certainly true, and it was horrible enough to turn anyone's brain. We'd better get back inside and find out what the cops are doing. Then we'll decide whether to tell Rosemary, or talk to Jeff again, or . . . Let's get away from this god-awful sunset. Your hair looks like it's on fire, and although it is astonishingly beautiful, the imagery doesn't exactly soothe me right now."

Nick's afflictions were only beginning. They arrived at the front of the house in time to see a car pull up and park by the steps with superb disregard for the convenience of others.

"Oh, God, it's Laurence again," Nick groaned. "I forgot he was coming. No use trying to duck, he's seen us."

Erin expected to hear a joking comment about their habit of playing hooky but the columnist was in no jesting mood.

"What a hellish evening," he said, contemplating the lurid sunset. "The sky looks like one of Turner's more frenetic efforts."

"Uh—yeah," Nick said. "Coming in?"

"Naturally. You hadn't forgotten our appointment? But then," Laurence added, as they climbed the steps, "I suppose you might be excused for doing so, you've had other problems on your minds."

"You don't know the half of it," Nick said under his breath.

Laurence was reputed to have the hearing of a bat, among other, even less attractive characteristics. "I do, though," he said. "I've seen situations that were a lot worse. This will blow over in time, don't worry."

As they entered the hall, a man rose from one of the chairs. He looked perfectly at ease, and Erin felt a flash of déjà vu that had nothing to do with her earlier sight of him. A memory older and less direct . . . That was it—a fifties film, colorized, of course—featuring one of the suave, sophisticated leading men who specialized in urbane comedies about the upper classes.

Nick stopped. "Who's that?" he hissed. "Not . . . he doesn't look like a cop."

"Ssssh."

Laurence showed no sign of surprise. He stepped forward with all the aplomb of the master of the house.

"Cardoza, isn't it? What is the D.C. criminal investigation department doing in the wilds of suburbia?"

"You've got a good memory, Mr. Laurence," was the smiling reply.

"You are a memorable individual," Laurence said. His eyes lingered on Cardoza's face just long enough to suggest that it was his good looks, not his professional talents, that made him so memorable.

"Let me see," Laurence went on. "It was five—no, six years ago we last met. The Martin case. Quite a remarkable series of events. You handled it admirably, as I recall. But you haven't answered my question. Aren't you out of your jurisdiction?"

"I'm not with the D.C.P.D.," Cardoza said. "I'm living in Leesburg now and working for the county sheriff's office."

"How delightful. You must find it a pleasant change."

"In some ways. If you'll excuse me, Mr. Laurence, I'd like to have a word with this young lady. You are Miss Erin Hartsock, aren't you?"

"Yes, I am."

Cardoza smiled at her. His teeth were as perfect as his other features, they all but shone with their own light. He was obviously trying to put her at ease. "The description was a good one. I won't take much of your time, Miss Hartsock, I know you people are pretty busy. Perhaps you wouldn't mind coming upstairs with me."

"Not without me," Nick said. He took Erin's arm. She glowered at him and tried to shake him off, to no avail.

"You must be Mr. McDermott," Cardoza said. "Certainly, come along if you like. I have a few questions for you too. Excuse us, Mr. Laurence."

The hint had no effect. Laurence followed them up the stairs and into Kay's room. "What's this all about, Cardoza?" he asked.

"I'm surprised you should have to ask, Mr. Laurence. The feeling around town is that you know everything before it happens."

Laurence leaned against the door and folded his arms. "It doesn't require clairvoyance to conjecture why you are here. What was the result of the autopsy?"

Cardoza looked him over from head to foot, in silence. "Come, come," Laurence said impatiently. "This child isn't going to answer any questions until you tell her what has happened."

"Just what I was going to say," Nick added.

Erin finally managed to detach herself from his grasp. "I would prefer to speak for myself, if you don't mind. Naturally I'm anxious to find out what is going on, but I'm chiefly interested in—in getting this over with. What is it you want to know, Mr. Cardoza?"

Cardoza's attractive smile seemed to be reserved for her. "A very sensible attitude, Miss Hartsock. I'd like you to try to remember yesterday morning. I'm sure it was a very shocking experience for you; no doubt your memory is somewhat blurred. But did you notice anything that struck you as unusual or unexpected?"

"Except for Kay being dead? No."

"Cardoza, I must insist," Laurence began.

"Oh, do be quiet, Mr. Laurence," Erin exclaimed. Laurence blinked. He looked, as Nick said later, almost human in his surprise.

"I think I know what you want," Erin said. "As Mr. Laurence has said, it doesn't take much intelligence to figure out what must have happened. If Kay had died of natural causes, you wouldn't be here. And you know about the sleeping pills; so you must be looking for something else. A bottle, or a container of some kind. I didn't see anything like that. I didn't see anything unusual."

"Oh, we found the container," Cardoza said calmly. "At least we found an empty bottle with a few grains of white powder in the bottom. The pharmacist's label had been torn off. It was in the medicine chest in the bathroom."

"White powder?" Nick repeated.

"Yes, the conventional, sinister white powder," Cardoza smiled. "It may turn out to be something as harmless as aspirin. We won't know until it has been analyzed."

"I never saw any unlabeled bottles," Erin said. "Not on her bedside table, anyway. We did share the bathroom, but I didn't put anything in the medicine chest; I can't remember ever opening it, in fact. I tried to be as unobtrusive as possible."

"The perfect guest. Was it you who cleaned the room after . . . afterward? I noticed the bed has been stripped, the wastebaskets emptied."

"No. It was one of the cleaning women, I think. I offered to do it, but I was needed elsewhere."

"I see. Well, I think that does it—for now. Thank you, Miss Hartsock."

"Aren't you going to ask me anything?" Nick demanded.

Cardoza's placid gaze rested on him. "No, Mr. McDermott, I've changed my mind. Is there something you want to tell me?"

"No. No, I guess not."

"Then I'll be going. Give my regards to Mrs. Marshall, will you please?" A sudden, unexpected grin lit his face. "Tell her she's got my vote."

Instead of following Cardoza downstairs, Laurence stayed with them. Not until they heard the distant sound of the front door closing did he speak.

"Where is Rosemary?"

"In her office, I suppose." It wasn't the question Erin had expected. "I'm sorry, Mr. Laurence, I shouldn't have spoken so rudely."

"I had it coming." The columnist smiled ruefully. "If people would slap me down more often I might not be so obnoxious. Look here, you two, developments have taken a nasty turn. I know Cardoza, he used to be one of the best homicide detectives in Washington."

"But he said he was working with the sheriff's office," Erin objected. "He didn't say anything about homicide."

"It's either homicide or suicide," Laurence replied curtly. "You displayed commendable acumen in your analysis, my dear. Cardoza wouldn't be looking for other drugs if Kay died from an overdose of medication she was known to have possessed. He let you off too easily. He didn't ask any of the obvious questions. So he'll be back. The next time, he'll be just as charming—that's one of his trademarks—and a lot more persistent. Sooner or later, he'll find out about the fires. Perhaps he's already made the connection; the incident in the graveyard was well publicized."

Nick had been fidgeting like a bored schoolboy, cracking his knuckles, shifting from one foot to the other. Erin knew why he was so nervous; she sympathized completely. But she wished he would control himself. He looked like a guilty felon. Laurence's reference to the fires was too much for him.

"With all respect, Mr. Laurence, I wish you'd get the hell out of here," he burst out. "All this intellectual speculation is a waste of time, and there's something—there are a lot of things I ought to be doing."

Laurence gave Nick a look that was almost affectionate. "I know you don't like me, Nick. Can't say I blame you. But with all respect to *you*, you are unaware of certain matters that make this situation very frightening and potentially dangerous. I'd like to take you wholly into my confidence. I would do so if I could; but is isn't my secret."

"Secret?" Nick repeated, his eyes widening.

"I have to talk to Rosemary."

Rosemary was nowhere to be found.

"I've no idea where she is," Christie insisted. Unlike the others in the office, who were visibly wilted after a long day, she appeared as fresh and well-groomed as ever. Her black eyes snapped as she responded to Laurence's insistent questions. "She left me in charge, told me to field questions and calls for the rest of the evening. If you think I can't handle it—"

"That was the farthest thing from my thoughts," Laurence's attempt at a smile produced only a grotesque grimace. "Rosemary is fortunate to have such a splendid deputy. I'm worried about her, that's all. This has been a ghastly experience for her."

"Yes." Christie's lips clamped together. She wasn't going to say anything that might appear in print.

Rosemary was not in her room, or in the commons room. The latter was unoccupied and dark until Nick turned on the lights. "Where the hell is everybody?" he asked.

"Good question." Laurence thought for a moment. Then he said crisply, "I'm not concerned about Will. I presume he's gone home; even a workaholic has to relax sometimes. Joe was in town this afternoon; he had a dinner appointment, so he's accounted for. Where is Jeff?"

Erin had expected the question and had believed she was braced for it, but Laurence shot the words at her like bullets, and the startling change in his manner had weakened her defenses. She had never seen him like this—curt, direct, all his irritating mannerisms in abeyance. Worst of all, he was afraid. She could feel his fear, like a cold, clammy aura.

She said, "I don't know," but her voice was breathy and unconvincing. Nick said nothing.

Laurence's eyes shifted from her to Nick and back again. "You do know something," he said. "What? Damn it, this is no time to play games. He's supposed to be here. Rosemary is supposed to be here. She's disappeared too. Do you see a possible connection?"

Nick's eyes fell before the older man's piercing look. "No."

He sounded as unconvincing, and unconvinced, as Erin had. They were amateurs at this game, both of them—a game of deception and duplicity, equivocation and downright lies. And Laurence was a master at his trade. Erin knew how his guests on "Firing Squad" must feel, pilloried and mercilessly stripped naked, down to the depths of their souls.

"No," Nick repeated. "She's gone off on one of her mysterious expeditions—"

"Ah." Laurence almost smiled. "You know about those, do you? You're a clever pair."

Nick flushed with chagrin. He had fallen for one of the oldest but most effective techniques of interrogation, admitting a lesser charge in his effort to deny one that was more serious.

"What else do you know?" Laurence demanded. "Come, come. Are you aware, for instance, that Jeff is your pyromaniac? Ah, I see you are. You two have a lot to learn if you intend to succeed at politics or poker. Your faces are as transparent as glass. Don't feel bad, you've done quite well for amateurs. Perhaps investigative reporting is your métier, Nick. All you need is a little more experience and the kind of network I've built up over the years."

He had them in full retreat now, reeling from one unexpected blow after the other, alternating firmness and flattery in the good-cop, bad-cop routine. Now his voice hardened.

"Jeff was to drive Rosemary home this afternoon. The car is here. Rosemary was here. Now she's gone. Where is Jeff?"

The facade, the mask, of indifference and cynicism were gone. His lean face was haggard, drawn not by fear but by pure desperation. "You don't trust me," he said. "There's no reason why you should, so it's up to me to convince you, even if, in order to do so, I must violate a trust I've held for more than twenty years, and dishonor the dead. Do you know who Jeff is?"

Their very failure to respond was an admission. If they had not known, the question would have produced curiosity and further questions instead of silence. By the time Erin realized this, it was too late. Laurence turned to her.

"The boy is out of his mind," he said earnestly. "Psychotic. If you recall, I suggested early on that the perpetrator of those tricks must be mentally disturbed. I blame myself, I ought to have acted earlier. I hoped to keep this business under wraps, get Jeff the help he needed without bringing criminal charges. The acts he had committed were, at worst, malicious mischief. I saw no sign of homicidal mania. I miscalculated. Badly. Fatally, in fact."

"Fatally," Nick repeated. "Are you accusing Jeff of . . . You mean Kay?"

"Kay would never have taken her own life. I talked to her the day she died, she was . . ." Laurence's eyelids fell. "It's too late for Kay. Rosemary is the one I'm concerned about now. We've got to find her. Or Jeff. If you know, or even suspect, where he may be, you must tell me."

The next seconds were the longest Erin had ever experienced. "He's right, Nick," she said finally. "We can't take the chance."

"He wouldn't hurt Rosemary," Nick said. "Oh, this is crazy! She's in no danger, she's gone haring off on one of her—" He broke off, paling, and Erin knew he was remembering what he had once said. If Rosemary knew who was playing the tricks on her, she would confront the perpetrator. And if she confronted Jeff, in his present state of mind . . .

"He said she was a victim too," Nick insisted. "It was Marshall he hated. Edward Marshall. His own father—"

"What?" Laurence turned on him like a tiger. "Ed? Jeff told you Ed was . . ."

"I'm sorry," Nick stood his ground, though Laurence loomed over him, fists clenched and face distorted. "I don't blame you for wanting to protect your friend. And Rosemary, if she didn't know . . ."

"Rosemary." The columnist passed a shaking hand over his face. "No. She knew nothing. She was a demure little housewife in those days, shy and insecure. Ed would never . . . Angels and ministers of grace defend us. This is worse than I feared. Give me a minute to think. . . ."

His control was incredible. It was no more than sixty seconds before his twisted features smoothed out. "So Jeff knows. Josie told him, I suppose."

"You knew her?" Nick asked.

"She was one of the maids at the Richmond house. I used to spend holidays with Ed when we were in college. Pretty little thing, with a very flirtatious manner. Ed used to joke with her, but I never imagined . . . Ah, well, there's no use trying to deceive you. He boasted about his conquest, as young men will. When I read about the fire, years later, I recognized the name—and I thought what a ghastly coincidence it was. So Jeff . . . No wonder the poor devil is demented. Nick. I have to talk to him. Maybe it's not too late. Maybe I can explain . . . Where is he?"

Nick was beyond resistance. The suggestion that Rosemary might be in danger had destroyed his last doubts. "He's at my place—the overseer's cabin. At least he was half an hour ago."

"Is the door locked?"

"No. Maybe I should have locked him in, but I didn't think—"

"It doesn't matter. You acted for the best. Let me talk to him. All we can do now is minimize the damage and the pain—especially to Rosemary. I think I see a way . . . Give me fifteen minutes alone with him."

He left the room, almost running. Nick took an uncertain step after him. "Why do I have the feeling I've made a horrible mistake?" he demanded.

"Probably because anything we do is going to end in disaster," Erin said dismally. "Shall we go after him?"

"He can take care of himself," Nick said. "Damn it, I still can't believe Jeff is a threat to anyone, much less Rosemary. Let's see if we can figure out where she might have gone."

Christie, now alone in the office, was in no mood for idle conversation. "What am I, the nursemaid?" she demanded. "I don't know *where* she's gone, or *if* she's gone. She could be in her room. I don't know where anybody is except you two, and I wish you were someplace else. I've got a heavy date tonight and a couple of things to finish before I can leave."

Chastened but no less alarmed, they retreated. A search of Rosemary's room revealed no message and no clue. They were about to leave when Nick stopped. "Wait a minute. Where's that god-awful wig?"

The wig was not in the closet or the dressing room. An empty hatbox, its lid askew, might have contained it. "That's it," Nick said, looking considerably more cheerful. "She's off on another escapade. I'm tempted to call Buzz Bennett and ask to speak to Miz Marylou."

"That's stupid," Erin said; she was far too worried to be tactful. "If Mrs. Bennett is at home we're right back where we started, and if she isn't, we haven't the slightest idea whether she's on her way to meet Rosemary or at the movies. Furthermore—"

"The pickup!" Nick slapped his forehead. "Why didn't I think of it before? If it's missing, we can stop worrying."

"That's not so stupid," Erin agreed. "Let's look."

The pickup truck was not in its usual place. A lighted window and the sound of the TV set made it clear Sam had not taken it. Nick sagged against the open garage door. "What a relief. I'd give a couple of my back teeth to know what the hell Rosemary is up to, but at least we know she's not having her throat cut by Jeff. I don't know why I let that louse Laurence con me—"

"Speaking of Laurence," Erin said. "He's been gone a lot longer than fifteen minutes."

"Maybe he's waiting for us in the commons room."

"We just came through that way. We'd have met him if he had been on his way back."

They turned, like puppets pulled by the same string, to stare at the door of Nick's cottage, only a few hundred feet away.

The curtains were drawn, as Nick had left them, but slits of yellow light showed at the sides. There was no other sign of life; and as they slowly approached the place they heard no sound whatever.

"I guess I ought to knock," Nick said, when they stood before the door.

He proceeded to do so. There was no answer. "Oh-oh," Nick said softly. The door was not locked. He threw it open.

"They're gone," he exclaimed. "Both of them. Unless . . ."

But the bathroom, the only closed-off cubicle in the one-room structure, was dark and deserted. "They must be at the house." Nick's voice was shrill. "We missed them somehow."

"No," Erin said. "Look at this."

She held out the piece of paper she had found on the table, weighted down by a book. Nick snatched it from her.

"Dear Nick [it read]. *Jeff has explained everything. We were all wrong about him. I've decided he should lie low for a while till we get this business straightened out. Better for you that you shouldn't know where he is, in case the police question you. I'll call you as soon as I get him settled. Don't worry, everything is going to be all right."*

They stared at one another for a moment. Nick let out a long, breathy sigh. "Things seem to be looking up," he said. "We don't know where Rosemary is, but we know where she's not—namely, and to wit, in the clutches of a homicidal maniac. Laurence has taken charge of the Jeff mess, and assures us all will be well. Maybe I misjudged the guy after all. Everything is hunky-dory, right?"

Erin didn't answer. "So why," Nick demanded, "are alarm bells jangling in my skull? You don't look too happy either."

"Those bells are deafening me. But I don't know why."

"We're in over our heads," Nick said. "I'm ready to scream for help, if that's okay with you."

"I'll join you. But who do we scream at? The cops?"

"I'm not quite ready to throw Jeff to the wolves yet. I want to talk to somebody with good sense and a clear head, who isn't as close to this as we are."

"Who, Joe?"

"Mr. Temper Tantrum? No, thanks. I was thinking of Will. Don't know why I didn't think of him before."

"Nobody thinks of Will," Erin said. "He works at being invisible. But until a few minutes ago we weren't sure he was innocent."

"We're sure now." Nick worried his lower lip. "Erin, did anything about that note strike you as odd?"

"Aside from the fact that it wasn't written in Laurence's pseudo-literary style—"

"That's it! I knew there was something, but I couldn't put my finger on it."

"He was in a hurry . . . concerned . . ."

"Yeah, maybe. I still want a consultation."

"But Will isn't here. What if he's on his way back to Charlottesville?"

"As it happens, Will is not in Charlottesville. He moved up here a few days ago, so he could be on the spot during the last days of the campaign. He's got a room at some hotel. . . . Damn, he told me the name, but I can't remember it. Wait a minute."

He grabbed the phone and punched a few numbers. When he spoke his voice was soft and wheedling. "Yes, ma'am, I sure hope you can. I'm looking for a hotel or a motel on fifty west, near Gilbert's Corners. Could be a Middleburg number, or maybe . . . Well, you see, ma'am, I had an accident a few years back, and both my eyes . . . Oh, thanks, ma'am, I sure would appreciate it. No, it wasn't a Ramada or a Sheraton. It had a name like . . . no . . . hey, right! That's it! May God bless you, ma'am, for your kind heart."

Erin pressed both hands over her mouth. She was afraid that if she started laughing she wouldn't be able to stop. "You ought to be ashamed," she hissed, as Nick dialed again.

He ignored her as she deserved. "Windy Hill Hotel? Yes, will you please connect me with Mr. William Gates? What? The hell you say! Listen, mister—"

He stared incredulously at the telephone.

"He hung up on me!"

"I don't blame him."

"Mr. Gates is not taking calls," Nick said, in savage mimicry of the clerk's refined tones. "Here, you call back and ask how to get there. He probably won't tell me."

Scenting a possible client, the clerk was happy to supply the information. "I didn't dare to ask for Will's room number," Erin began.

"That's okay, we'll find him." Nick towed her toward the door.

It should have taken longer than ten minutes to reach the motel. Nick's driving exceeded his best, or worst, effort in maniacal speed; either he had a sixth sense for police cars or their luck had turned, for they were not stopped. They almost missed the Windy Hill Hotel. Its small, discreet sign was half concealed by trees. Nick pulled a screeching turn and slammed on the brakes.

"Looks like a classier version of the Shady Lane Motel," he muttered as they cruised along the line of small cabins. The trees and shrubs that landscaped the grounds were losing their leaves, but they still provided a high degree of privacy for the occupants of the isolated buildings, which were designed to look like Swiss chalets. "Look for Will's car."

"I don't think I would . . . Is that it?"

"Yep." Nick glided to a stop beside the brown Ford. "He is at home, the bastard."

"That belligerent attitude won't get you any farther with Will than it did with the desk clerk. He deserves an evening off, he's probably reading or napping—"

"That's too damned bad." Nick slammed his door and strode purposefully to the cottage. A tiny porch enclosed the entrance; Nick began pounding on the door.

At first there was no reply. Nick continued the fusillade and finally a voice demanded he identify himself.

"It's me, Nick. Open up."

"I might have known." Will's voice was resigned but firm. "Get lost, Nick. I'm off duty and I intend to remain so."

"I've got to talk to you. We're in a real mess, Will. We need help."

"I know about the autopsy."

"No, you don't understand. That's the least of our problems. Let me in."

"No way, buddy. Whatever it is can wait till tomorrow."

"It can't wait," Nick bawled, rattling the door. "Rosemary has disappeared and Jeff's gone too, but it's worse than that, he's flipped his lid, gone crazy, and he's taken Laurence—"

"Stop bellowing," Will said sharply. "Wait a minute."

Nick pressed his ear to the door. After only a momentary hesitation Erin followed his example. Will must be watching television. She couldn't made out the words, but there were at least two voices, one higher in pitch than the other. . . .

The truth was beginning to dawn on her when the door opened, so suddenly that both eavesdroppers were caught in flagrante delicto. Nick had been too distracted to make the logical deduction from what he had heard; when he saw who it was, he literally staggered back.

Rosemary had let her hair down. It flowed loosely to her shoulders. She was wearing an astonishing negligee of chiffon and black lace and—as the light behind her made evident—nothing else.

Chapter
Sixteen

"WHAT'S THIS about Jeff?" Rosemary demanded.

Nick choked. "I—uh—I guess we'd better go."

Rosemary shaded her eyes. "Erin too? Come in, both of you." Nick didn't move. Rosemary poked him. "In, I said. Don't stand there gawking. What's happened to Jeff?"

The motel room had a certain charm, if your tastes ran to ruffles and chintz and heart-shaped ornaments. At least it was new and clean, and although the queen-sized bed was the most prominent piece of furniture, there were chairs and a table in an alcove. On the table stood a bottle of wine and two glasses, one half-full.

"Sit down," Rosemary ordered, pointing to the chairs. Nick dropped into one as if he had been shot. "Now talk. What about Jeff?"

"Listen," Nick began, cracking a knuckle. "I'm really sorry. I was looking for Will—"

"Oh, for goodness' sakes," Rosemary snapped. "You're a big boy, Nick, stop squirming. I don't advertise my extracurricular activities, but I'm not ashamed of them. Or of my feelings for Will.''

Will had retreated to the bed. Half-sitting, half-lying against plumped pillows, glasses askew on the tip of his nose, his lips were quivering with repressed laughter. ''Didn't you ever see a sex object before?'' he inquired.

A look passed between him and Rosemary, conveying such warmth and tenderness, such shared amusement and sheer delight in one another that Erin's self-consciousness vanished. If that was how it was for them, she was glad—and a little envious.

Then Will said briskly, ''Enough of this persiflage. Suppose you eschew journalistic hyperbole and try a straight narrative form, beginning at the beginning and continuing until you reach the end.''

Rosemary listened to the first part of Nick's story in silence. The soft tapping of her fingers on the tabletop was her only sign of impatience, and her face betrayed nothing. But when Nick explained—choking with embarrassment—about Jeff's discovery that Edward Marshall was his father, Rosemary sprang to her feet. ''That's impossible.''

''I'm sorry, Rosemary, I know it's hard,'' Nick began.

''Hard, my eye. It's impossible. Ed was . . . Never mind that, just take my word for it. Where did Jeff get this crazy idea?''

''His mother told him,'' Nick said. ''It couldn't have been a lie, or a delusion of Jeff's, Rosemary; there's too much confirmatory evidence. She said his father had agreed to help them. They were in desperate straits, or she never would have appealed to him. He had arranged for them to stay temporarily in that building, one he owned, until he could make better arrangements. That was the clue—the ownership of the building—that enabled Jeff to trace—''

''I get the picture,'' Rosemary broke in. Her pupils were so widely dilated, her eyes looked black. ''Enough of the orderly exposition, Nick. What was that about Jeff going off with Philips?''

Nick only got a few sentences out before she interrupted him again, even more dramatically. Her hand went to the neck of her robe and yanked. Erin had a flashing glimpse of bare skin before Rosemary dashed into the bathroom. "Go on," she yelled. "He left a note? Did he say where they were going?"

"No. He thought it would be better if we could tell the police we didn't—"

Rosemary emerged from the bathroom wearing jeans and buttoning her shirt.

Will was on his feet. "Better put on some shoes," he suggested, picking up his coat and shrugging into it.

Rosemary grabbed her sneakers but didn't stop to put them on. "Where?" she asked.

There might have been no one in the room but her and Will. "He wouldn't risk taking him to his apartment. They're probably still on the property. That would be the most logical—"

Rosemary flung the door open and ran out. Will paused in the doorway, car keys in his hand. "If you two want to join us, you'd better move," he said.

Will's headlights went on as they ran toward the car and piled into the backseat. Rosemary, in the passenger seat, bent over to slip on her shoes.

"Maybe I should drive," Nick suggested.

"Hang on," Will said.

Erin never forgot that drive. It exceeded anything she had ever gone through with Nick. Will didn't stop for signs or red lights; he banged on the horn and barreled through. Rosemary leaned forward, every muscle tense, as if she could add a few more miles per hour to the frantic pace. They were almost at the house before Nick got his breath back.

"We goofed, didn't we?"

"No, not at all," Will said. "Whoops—sorry; I'm afraid that turn was a little abrupt."

Erin got off Nick's lap. "Yes, we did. But I still don't understand what we did wrong. Is Mr. Laurence—is he in danger?"

Rosemary spoke. "Philips can take care of himself. No one better. It's Jeff I'm worried about. Can't you go any faster, Will?"

"We're almost there. Are the gates open, Nick?"

"Jesus, I hope so," Nick said devoutly, as Will made another slashing turn with no diminuation of speed.

They bounced along the driveway and came to a stop in front of the house. "The outbuildings first," Rosemary said, through clenched teeth. "We'll need a flashlight—"

"Glove compartment," Will said. Rosemary snatched the flashlight. They got out of the car, leaving the doors open and the headlights burning, as Will continued in the same unhurried voice. "Erin, get to a phone and call the police. Extreme emergency, missing person, possible hostage situation. We need all the personnel we can get. Nick—"

"What? What?" Nick danced up and down, too nervous to stand still.

"Wait a minute," Will said. "There's someone out there."

His hearing must have been abnormally acute. It was a few seconds before Erin heard footsteps—quick, heavy, uneven. Then a figure reeled into the glow of the headlights. He swayed to a stop and raised a hand to his head. "Rosemary?" he said uncertainly. "Rosemary, is it you?"

"It's me," Rosemary said. "Where's Jeff?"

"Out there." Laurence leaned weakly against the fender and gestured toward the dark belt of woodland. "He's gone crazy. He made me write a note and then he hit me over the head. . . . When I came to, I was tied to a tree. I managed to free myself. . . ." He held out his hands in mute witness and showed the reddened marks on his wrists. "I was afraid he had you too. Rosemary—"

She was gone, running as if pursued by demons.

"Stop her," Laurence cried. "Nick—Will—don't let her go after him. He has a gun!"

He turned as if to follow. Quickly as he moved, Will was quicker. He caught Laurence's arm. "Hold on a minute."

Laurence whirled, tried to free himself. "What the devil are you doing? She's gone after a—"

Will hit him. It was a classic right cross, precise and passionless as a diagram, but aimed with enough accuracy and force to topple Laurence backward onto the gravel. He lay motionless.

"No time for the police now," Will said, bending over the columnist's sprawled body. "I had intended to ask you to get another flashlight from the kitchen, Nick, but we haven't time for that either. Nor—I fear—will we need it."

The sky above the burning trees was a garish crimson. "We better hurry," Nick said, grim-faced. "What about him?"

Will straightened. "Leave him. I wouldn't have bothered decking him if I didn't have a prejudice against being shot in the back." Carefully he checked the safety on the automatic he had taken from Laurence before putting it in his coat pocket. "Straight down the path as far as we can safely go. I doubt Mr. Fastidious would venture into the underbrush, but if we haven't found them by then, we split up. You two stay together, go north. I'll go south."

Erin could only guess what it cost Will to speak so calmly and collectedly. It had required more patience than she had known she possessed to stand quietly awaiting orders instead of rushing off after Rosemary; but she was agonizingly aware of the fact that there was not the slightest room for error now, and no time to be wasted on false trails. A few seconds might mean the difference between life and death.

As soon as Will finished speaking, she ran as she had never run before, ably assisted by Nick, who pulled her along in a series of giant leaps; but Will had disappeared into the woods before they reached them. It was dark under the trees at first, but all too soon the glow of the fire brightened the path, and smoke began to sting their nostrils. When they caught up with Will he was hoisting himself to his feet; he had fallen heavily, his face and shirtfront were smudged with dirt, and blood trickled from his nose. "No, don't wait," he wheezed, as Nick went to help him. "They—they're up there. Listen."

They had gone a few feet farther before Erin heard Rosemary. She wasn't screaming, just yelling, steadily and wordlessly, in order to guide them. Erin could see the fire now—a solid curtain of flame—up ahead. Smoke coiled among the tree trunks like giant gray snakes.

Rosemary was on her knees beside Jeff, struggling with the knotted rope that held him bound to a tree. Her hair was smoldering, and she continued to shout, even after Nick dropped down beside her.

Erin slapped at the sparks in Rosemary's hair. She stopped yelling and looked up. "Where's Will?"

"Right here. Get out of the way, Nick." Will began sawing at the rope. Where he had gotten the knife Erin didn't know, but she wasn't surprised that he had one. Nothing Will did from that time on would ever surprise her.

The heat was so intense she felt like a piece of meat on the grill, but it never occurred to her to retreat. "He's unconscious." She forced the words past the smoke that clogged her throat. "Or is he—he isn't—"

Rosemary staggered to her feet. "No, he's breathing. Philips must have . . ." A fit of coughing interrupted her. "Hurry, Will."

"These damned Swiss Army knives aren't all . . . they're cracked up to be," was the reply. "Thank God for a southwest wind. If it had been blowing the other way—"

A dead pine went up like a Roman candle, showering them with sparks. Will straightened with a grunt of satisfaction, and Nick, who had been supporting Jeff's head, heaved the limp body over his shoulder. "Let's get the hell out of here."

As they fled down the path they heard the distant sound of sirens.

*   *

JOE HAD ARRIVED shortly after they entered the woods; seeing the flames, he had called the fire department. There wasn't much the fire fighters could do, or cared to do, other than contain the fire and prevent it from reaching the house and outbuildings. Thanks to the southwest wind Laurence had failed to take into consideration when he started the blaze, it would burn itself out on the far edge of the woods.

Aside from blisters, scorched skin, and minor smoke inhalation, the rescuers were uninjured. Jeff was still unconscious when they loaded him into the ambulance.

Rosemary had to be forcibly prevented from going to the hospital with him. It was not until Will dragged her into the house and put her in front of a mirror that she gave in. None of them was a specimen of sartorial elegance, but Rosemary was in worse shape than the rest; she had been closer to the fire for a longer time, and she wasn't wearing anything under the shirt that had been ripped half off her body by brambles.

After some cursory first aid they assembled in the commons room. Food and drink, especially the latter, were the first priority, far more important than appearance. Rosemary had gone upstairs to bathe and change. Joe, who had watched the proceedings in appalled silence, finally found his voice.

"If somebody doesn't tell me what this is all about, I'll have a heart attack!" he shouted.

"Have a drink," Will suggested.

"I have a drink. What I want is information."

Will cleared his throat professorially. His nose was swollen, his hair was scorched, and a blister was rising on his chin. "To begin at the beginning—"

"Not you," Joe said. "Him. No, her." His cigar moved from Nick to Erin. "I don't want a detailed piece of reasoned research and I don't want one of Nick's disorganized speeches. Erin?"

"It was Jeff," Erin said. "The pyromaniac. He's really Raymond Wilson."

"Who the hell is Raymond Wilson?"

Joe turned with obvious relief to Rosemary, who had just come in. She was wearing tailored slacks and a loose sweater, and she moved as if every muscle in her body ached, but she was smiling. "I just called the hospital. Concussion and smoke inhalation—but he's going to be all right."

"That's nice." Joe puffed savagely at his cigar. "I like the kid, whatever his name may be. Now, if you don't mind . . ."

Rosemary began with the long-past fire in Richmond. Joe's eyes bulged. "And your name was on those papers? Jesus, Rosemary! I asked you if there was anything—"

"It never entered my mind, Joe. Honestly. I had nothing to do with Ed's business affairs, I signed everything he put in front of me, like the young fool I was; and I had no idea there was anything sinister about that tragedy."

Erin glanced at Nick. They were sitting side by side on the

couch, but not touching; there was hardly an inch of skin on either of them that hadn't been scorched, scraped, or bruised.

"Some brilliant detectives we were," Nick mumbled.

Rosemary heard him. "I can't blame you for assuming I was involved, Nick. You don't realize—you can't possibly realize—how naive I was, and how different things were, even twenty years ago. 'Women's lib' was a dirty word to me and a lot of other docile idiots. I hadn't graduated from college when I married Ed; I didn't go back and finish my degree until several years later.

"It wasn't just a question of feeling inferior—I *was* inferior, in every measurable way—wealth, age, sophistication, education, family background. And in even more important ways that are not susceptible to measurement."

Her eyes met Erin's in a flash of empathy and understanding so eloquent they might both have spoken aloud. Erin knew she was the only one in the room who did fully understand, with her emotions as well as her intelligence—the only one who had been there herself.

Rosemary went on, "I knew one thing you did not know, Nick—that Philips was Ed's secret partner in that deal and in others. They had been friends since college; Philips's family had a lot more money than the Marshalls, but they were nouveau riche, not landed aristocrats. I think that was what attracted Philips to Ed; he's always been a first-class snob. I also assumed that was why Philips supported me—the old family name, plus a few sentimental memories. . . . I guess I'm still somewhat naive. He wanted my help; he did have political aspirations, he planned to run for Congress in two years. It wouldn't have done either of us any good if that story had been made public, but Philips stood to lose a lot more than I did. He could not have denied being involved; the funds for the trust must have come from him, Ed never had that kind of money."

"Doesn't sound like Laurence," Nick said cynically. "It would have been more in character for him to sneak into the hospital where the kids had been taken, and try to finish the job."

"For all we know, he may have tried," Erin said. "But I

think—I'd like to think—that they forced him to put up the money. Mr. Marshall and my father. If one or both of them suspected what he had done, but couldn't prove it, that was the only way they could make amends."

Rosemary's bloodshot eyes widened. "Is that what's been worrying you, Erin—that your father was involved? He handled the legal arrangements, yes, but I'm absolutely certain he was blameless. I wish I could be equally certain about Ed. He was in bad shape that year. Insomnia, nightmares . . ."

"To me that seems more indicative of innocence than guilt," Will said gently. "Put it out of your mind, Rosemary. If Ed had been hard up for money he might have gone along with the idea of burning the building for the insurance, but he would never have consented to the other thing. That was Philips. And I think Erin's point is well taken; there was no way Philips could have been indicted. He covered his tracks admirably. However, if the story had come out, the mere suspicion of arson would have wrecked his political hopes and perhaps his career. Not to mention the fact that he had an illegitimate black son."

Joe choked on his drink. "What? Son? Who—"

"It passed me right by," Nick said, slapping himself on the forehead. "Right through my thick skull. Jeff didn't know his father's name until he traced the records. All his mother told him was that his daddy owned that building. Laurence visited the house often when the girl worked for the Marshall family. He remembered her name—even knew her married name. He wouldn't be likely to, unless she had meant more to him than a pretty, flirtatious servant, twenty-three years dead."

"Laurence was . . . Jeff is . . ." Joe mumbled.

"Well, Rosemary is sure it wasn't Mr. Marshall," Nick said. "And she ought to know. Oh, damn—I mean—"

"Use your imagination, Nick," Rosemary said.

Nick's cheeks were crimson. "Anyway, the important thing—the charge we can prove—is that Laurence tried his damnedest to kill Jeff tonight. You remember, Erin, how dumbfounded he was when I told him Jeff believed Mr. Marshall was his father? He didn't know whether Josie Wilson had told her son about his true parentage; he still didn't know, even after he had identified Jeff as the Wilson boy. And then to find, after all those years, that young Wilson had got it all wrong. . . . I guess his fans didn't exaggerate his intelligence after all, it only took him a few seconds to see how he could use that mistaken belief to his advantage.''

"He was like a juggler trying to handle too many balls at once," Will said. "But he'd have gotten away with it, if he could have disposed of Jeff. We might have had our suspicions, but we couldn't have proved a thing. Not even arson.''

"No," Nick agreed. "Jeff was the only one who could have testified to that. Laurence fingered Jeff as the pyromaniac right away. His conscience—if I may use the word loosely—was a lot more sensitive than Rosemary's; he understood immediately what the fires meant. And he figured the pyromaniac wouldn't be so bitter unless he knew the Richmond fire was not an accident. It took him a while to confirm Jeff's identity—''

"Fingerprints!" Erin exclaimed. "Remember that anonymous letter, Nick, the one about there being no statute of limitations on murder? Laurence made off with it—''

"As I said, he was more sensitive to allegations of murder than Rosemary," Nick agreed. "I'm sure that was on his mind—testing the paper for fingerprints—but I doubt he got anything useful from it. Jeff would have been smart enough to wear gloves. Anyhow, all Laurence needed was the information we finally found—the respective birth dates.''

"He must have figured that out early on," Erin said. "And yet for a long time he behaved as if he suspected me.''

"He did more than suspect you," Nick said, looking self-conscious. "Ten to one it was Laurence who mugged you in the garden. Me and my brilliant ideas about dirty old men . . .''

"Nobody's perfect," Erin said consolingly. "I had hurt his sensitive feelings by talking back to him; maybe he just lost his temper.''

"Talking back to Philips would be sufficient grounds for mayhem in his book," Will said. "He may well have believed at first that you and Jeff were both potential blackmailers. Whether you were working together or independently, you were equally dangerous to him.''

"Later, he seemed to change his mind about me," Erin went on. "It may have been Kay who convinced him I was just as stupid and unwitting as I claimed to be. But he went right ahead and rigged the Mercedes. . . . It was Philips, wasn't it?''

"Yes," Nick said. "Jeff denied doing that, and I believe him. Laurence had the knowledge, he owned a similar model. I'm not entirely certain why he did it; it might have been pure bloody-mindedness, he didn't care who got hurt. But it may have been part of his plan to make Jeff look more dangerous than he really was, so that he would make an acceptable scapegoat for Kay's death.''

"Kay?" Joe repeated. "Death?''

"It must have been in the candy," Erin said. "He saw her the day she died. He let that slip, it was one of his few mistakes; but he covered it up nicely. She loved those little boxes of chocolates. Can't you see him giving them to her, with a pretty speech and a kiss on the cheek? She'd have eaten them that same night, there were only two in the box. I saw several empties in the wastebasket. I didn't give them a second thought, there were usually a few of them there. He must have slipped upstairs the next day and left that empty bottle in the medicine chest.''

"He didn't expect an autopsy," Nick added. "He was well aware of the doctor's reputation, and it never occurred to him that Rosemary would refuse to accept a convenient diagnosis of heart failure. When he found out she had demanded an autopsy he knew he had to act fast. I don't know what the coroner found—''

"Morphine," Rosemary said.

"He killed Kay?" Joe's glass was empty. He got up and went to the liquor cabinet.

"You're catching on," Will said encouragingly.

"But why, for God's sake?''

"She knew the whole story," Rosemary said. "She must have known. She was Ed's confidential secretary, and his acolyte. I knew something was bothering her, but she would never have told me; to Kay I was still Ed's dumb little wife and she was the keeper of the flame. She'd have told any lie, committed any crime, to keep his memory untarnished. But I think, toward the end, she was beginning to crack. Philips was afraid she would; and he knew if she broke down and told me the truth, I'd have insisted on a full investigation. He couldn't afford that. You see, she—she was fond of me. And of Jeff. Poor Kay . . .''

"Okay.'' Liquid sloshed musically as Joe filled his glass. He didn't bother adding ice cubes. "Okay. So the next question is, what are we going to do about this mess? Laurence wasn't here when I arrived, I suppose he's back home by now, wondering the same thing I am.''

Nick straightened. "You can't cover this up, Joe. No way. That son of a bitch committed six murders and was working on number seven!''

"Six?'' Erin repeated. "The three children and their mother, Kay . . .''

"And the anonymous wino in Richmond,'' Nick said. "The one the police blamed for starting the fire. What a neat setup that was. All Laurence had to do was supply the poor devil with a couple of bottles and a place where he could drink in peace. He'd wait till the guy passed out—maybe he tapped him on the head, or added something to the booze, to make sure he stayed out, before he set the blaze.''

Rosemary stood up and stretched. "Oh, it will all have to come out,'' she said calmly. "You'll have fun, won't you, Joe, trying to make me look like a heroine instead of a goat—or a criminal. It should be the challenge of your career.''

She started toward the door. "Where the hell are you going?'' Joe yelled.

"To the hospital. Will, you'll drive me?''

"Be there in a minute.''

"I'll get my coat.'' She vanished into the hall.

"I can't stand this,'' Joe groaned. "Is she kidding? She has to be kidding.''

"You know Rosemary,'' Will said. "However, I don't think the situation is quite clear. Seems to me Philips has only two choices, if he wants to avoid criminal prosecution and dis-

grace. He's not the type to go on the lam. It's such a hectic
life, lacking the adulation and public acclaim he craves. The
alternative . . .''

Joe's face brightened. ''You really think so?''

''What else would a pseudo-gentleman do? Hold off until
tomorrow, Joe. I have a feeling we'll learn something to our
advantage. And if he does his duty like a gent . . . well, the
word cover-up does come to mind. Good night, all.''

*   *

WILL WAS RIGHT. It made the morning news. Laurence had
been found by his manservant, slumped over his desk. He
had taken an overdose of morphine.

''Nice touch, that,'' Will said thoughtfully ''Poetic justice.
So typical of Philips. Nothing in his life . . .''

''Became him like the leaving it,'' Joe finished the quotation.
''Ain't it the truth. He was even thoughtful enough to leave a
suicide note, explaining about the deadly disease that was beginning to sap his manly strength and brilliant brain. There
won't be an autopsy, he spelled that out, and he has no friends
or family to demand one. I can't believe it. A god-awful mess
like that, and it looks as if we may be home free.''

''I see no point in being masochistic,'' Will agreed.
''Justice has been done. To come out with the truth now
would only injure the living. Jeff is going to be all right. You
should have seen his face when he opened his eyes and saw
Rosemary sitting there covered with blisters and holding his
hand.''

''Yeah, well, she'd better quit holding his hand and get
back to work,'' Joe grumbled ''Another swing through the
southwest—''

''Don't worry about the southwest,'' Will said with a peculiar smile. ''That's all taken care of.''

He went quietly away. Joe stared after him. ''What the hell
do you suppose he meant by that?''

*   *

THEY FOUND OUT on the last Friday before Election Day,
when Miz Marylou Bennett called a press conference and

announced to a group of flabbergasted reporters that she was
filing for divorce on grounds of adultery, infidelity, and physical cruelty. It was undoubtedly the high point of that and
many another campaign when, with the grace of Gypsy Rose
Lee and the dignity of Queen Victoria, Miz Marylou peeled
off the jacket she wore over a sleeveless, backless blouse, and
allowed the cameras to pan in on her bruises.

*   *

BENNETT CONCEDED shortly after the polls closed. "If he
weren't such an egotistical individual he would have with-
drawn Friday evening," Will remarked. "The exit polls must
have been devastating."

Jeff was already icing the champagne. The real celebration
would begin when Rosemary and Joe returned from their
rounds of the nearby campaign offices, where Rosemary
would join in the cheers and thank her devoted workers.

"Not that it mattered one spit in hell," Nick said. "Bennett shot himself in the foot."

He sounded uncommonly depressed for a man who had
just seen his career take a giant step forward. Erin made
sympathetic noises.

"Now, Nick, she could never have done it without you."

"Hey, you think my ego is on the line here? That's not it.
I know I did a good job. A damned good job!"

"What the hell is the matter with you then?" Erin demanded. "I was trying to be nice, but I'll be damned if I'll
put up with—"

Nick silenced her in a manner she found highly satisfac-
tory. They were sitting on the porch swing; the night was
clear and cold, and their backs were to the barren black
stumps on the hillside.

"Keep on doing that," Nick said after a while. "Slapping
me down when I get out of line."

"Don't worry, I will. I know why you're in such a bad
mood; and I must say, it does you no credit. You'll never
know for certain, Nick. Forget about it."

The rusty chains squeaked in soothing rhythm as the swing

moved back and forth. After a while Nick said, "Maybe he was gay."

"That wouldn't mean he was incapable of fathering a child."

"Impotent?"

"A man may be impotent with one woman and not with another. It comes and goes, I am told—"

"Sure, like hot flashes," Nick said disagreeably. "There's only one other possibility. She was certain, Erin. Absolutely certain."

"Nick, for heaven's sake—"

"Infertility can be cured. Even twenty years ago I suppose there were ways . . ."

"I'm sure there were."

"They only had the one child."

"Nick—"

"You don't suppose Will—"

"That does it." Erin jumped to her feet. "Your métier is investigative reporting, all right—for something like the *National Enquirer*."

Nick caught her hand and pulled her down beside him. "Come on, don't be so noble. People are not only the most interesting things in the world, but understanding how their minds work is the very essence of politics. Aren't you even a little curious?"

"Curious about Rosemary? Sure I am. What did one reporter call her—an enigma in ruffles and pink linen? But I honestly don't give a damn who fathered her child. She was in love with Will before she married Edward; if he lied to her about his inability to have kids, and Will was unmarried, and she was young and hurt and regretting her decision, and she and Will just happened to find themselves in one of those situations where they lost their heads . . . Who are you to judge them when you don't know the circumstances, or whether it ever happened? Now they've found each other again, after all those lonely years, and they aren't hurting a living soul by loving each other. It's nothing like those filthy affairs of Buzz Bennett's, if that's what you're thinking."

"I'm afraid to think around you," Nick said. "Not only

can you read my mind, you're too good at slapping me down.''

"I'm just happy they're together again. And I hope now Rosemary can come to terms with her feelings about her husband. Will said once that Rosemary had inherited a lot of things, both good and bad, from Edward Marshall. Surely one of the bad things is a sense of inferiority. Remember what she said the other night—'I *was* inferior, in every measurable way.' The look on her face when she said that . . .''

"You're a soap-opera sentimentalist.'' Nick put his arm around her and drew her closer. "She must have rid herself of that feeling long ago. She's made a brilliant success of her job—''

"A job she inherited from Edward. She's walked in his shadow all the way, Nick, and if that sounds like a soap opera, too bad, because it's true. This win is her win. Horrible as it is to say so, losing poor Kay has to help as well. Like having a hundred-pound weight lifted off your ego. But the most important thing is that she discovered Edward Marshall wasn't a faultless image of rectitude. Maybe now she can stop resenting him and accept him for what he was— flawed and human, good and bad, with a lot of dangerous weaknesses.''

Nick stirred restlessly. "I've been wondering about that so-called accident of Marshall's. Do you suppose he killed himself?''

"No, I think it's much more likely he was murdered by Philips Laurence.''

The chains squealed as Nick jumped and subsided. "Holy . . . I thought I had a lurid imagination! Or did I miss something?''

"Not really. But Laurence certainly had a strong motive for ridding himself of one of the people who knew the truth, especially if Congressman Marshall's conscience had been troubling him. I wouldn't put it past him.''

"You wouldn't put it past him,'' Nick repeated slowly. "Is this Nancy Drew I'm hearing, or the woman I allowed to assist me in a rational, reasoned criminal investigation?''

"I've no intention of helping you investigate Marshall's

death. Though I bet we could find out if we tried. Where
Laurence was that day, why Marshall was cleaning his
gun . . . But it isn't worth the effort. We've got more interesting things to do.''

She demonstrated. After a long, breathless interval Nick
said, ''I'm convinced.''

''No, you aren't. You're still depressed; I can tell. What's
the matter?''

''You can tell by the way I kiss that I'm—''

Erin made a sound of exasperation. '' 'Phlegmatic' is not
exactly the word for you, Nick. Are you sulking because
Rosemary didn't let you and Joe in on her little plot with Miz
Marylou?''

''No.'' Nick sighed. ''I'm depressed because if it hadn't
been for that slick trick, the voters of this enlightened democracy might have voted back into office one of the most
corrupt, cheating, cynical, incompetent, treacherous—''

''Wasn't it Churchill who said that democracy is a rotten
system, but it's the best there is?''

''First Nancy Drew, now Pollyanna,'' Nick grumbled. ''I
don't think those were his exact words.''

''Pick your own quotation, then! There are a lot of them,
mostly cynical. Politics is nothing but smoke and mirrors,
deception and image; power corrupts, particularly politicians. But politics isn't an exact science, Nick; it isn't perfect, or perfectable. How can it be, when its practitioners are
imperfect human beings? Life isn't perfect, either. So are you
going to kill yourself in a fit of childish pique because things
don't always work the way you want them to? I despise those
pious hypocrites who wrinkle their fastidious noses at the
dirty business of politics, and brag that they don't bother to
vote—''

''Hey, I didn't say—''

''If you don't like the way the world, or the political process, functions, then do something about it! You won't make
it perfect, but maybe you can make it a little better, if only
for a few people. That's what Rosemary is trying to do. Her
slick trick, as you term it, was a perfectly legitimate act; it
exposed a mean, vicious man to the public shame he de-

served, with the whole-hearted cooperation of his chief victim. It isn't in the same ballpark as the smears and insinuations and lies some politicians employ to discredit an opponent. There are some things Rosemary wouldn't stoop to, in order to win. I believe that; and if I ever stop believing it, if she shows signs of turning into a female version of Buzz Bennett, then, by God, I'll fight her tooth and nail!''

She broke off, breathless and a little embarrassed at her own passion. "Don't laugh at me, Nick," she said, in a small voice. "I guess that sounded corny and old-fashioned; but I meant every word."

"I'm not laughing," Nick took her hand. "I'm ashamed I didn't have the guts to say something along the same lines. It's a hell of a note—a hell of a world—when a person can't voice a belief in decency, in honor, in idealism, without expecting to be laughed at. . . . But, you know, it is hard to think of a quotation about politics that isn't cynical."

"Didn't someone once call politics the greatest and most honorable adventure?"

"That may be a slight exaggeration," Nick said cautiously. "But what the hell—it's something to work for. Something to occupy us when we're not canoodling."

Half amused, half reproachful, she would have replied; but before she could find the right words Nick found them for her—words she knew would endure as a commitment and a covenant between them.

"It is an adventure. Exciting, unpredictable, challenging, hazardous. But I'd rather think of it as a great and honorable endeavor. 'The energy, the faith, the devotion which we bring to this endeavor will light our country and all who serve it, and the glow from that fire can truly light the world.' ''

PETER
DISCIPLE—APOSTLE
MARTYR

PETER

DISCIPLE—APOSTLE—MARTYR

A Historical and Theological Study
by
OSCAR CULLMANN
Dr. Theol., D.D. (Edin.),
D.D. (Manchester)
Professor in Basel and Paris

Translated from the German by
FLOYD V. FILSON

Philadelphia
THE WESTMINSTER PRESS

The original edition
of this book was published in German under the title
PETRUS by Zwingli-Verlag, Zurich,
Switzerland

This edition
is published simultaneously in Great Britain and the
United States of America by the SCM Press Ltd.,
London, and The Westminster Press,
Philadelphia

First published in English
MCMLIII

PRINTED IN THE UNITED STATES OF AMERICA

To the
University of Manchester
And Especially
To its Theological Faculty
In Expression of Thanks
For the Conferring of the Degree of
Doctor of Divinity

"I believe in one holy catholic
and apostolic Church"

"You are 'Rock,' and on this Rock
I will build my Church"

"Built upon the foundation of
the Apostles and Prophets"

"I pray for those who believe
through the word of the Apostles"

TRANSLATOR'S PREFACE

PROFESSOR CULLMANN'S book on Peter deserves attentive reading by English-speaking Christians. We possess few thorough studies of Peter's career and position in the Church. Hundreds of lives of Jesus are available, and scores of lives of Paul, but there are few thorough presentations of the life and work of Peter, and none is up to date. This book therefore meets a definite need.

The usual discussion of Peter centres almost entirely on the question of his ecclesiastical office. Professor Cullmann gives a more balanced study; he includes also the significant role that Peter played in formulating the message of the Apostolic Church and in carrying out the missionary task of the first generation of Christians.

Recent excavations under St. Peter's Cathedral in Rome, and the explicit papal announcement that the burial place of Peter has been found, have caused increased attention to the subject of Peter's residence in Rome and his supposed martyrdom there. This book examines carefully the literary, liturgical, and archaeological evidence for the Roman residence and martyrdom of Peter.

No discussion of the work of Peter can ignore the claim that Peter was the first Pope, whose successors continue to hold the same ruling authority that he held. Professor Cullmann sketches the history of the interpretation of Matthew 16:17-19, which is the key passage on this subject. He then considers carefully the historical meaning of this passage, and goes on to state its theological significance for the Church today. His book is thus an important contribution to the ecumenical discussion of our time.

The author is constantly concerned to be fair to all sides. He is determined to go no further than the evidence permits. A few readers may wish that he had adopted a more polemic tone. Most of us, however, will be grateful for this calm and friendly spirit, and will find that it makes his argument the more compelling.

By reading the manuscript, offering suggestions, and answering

7

questions, Professor Cullmann has helped greatly in the preparation
of the English edition of his work. He has assured me that I have
understood his thought and rendered it faithfully. My hope is that I
have given it an effective English form, for the book has something
vital to say to students of the Bible, church history, theology, and
the ecumenical movement.

FLOYD V. FILSON

*McCormick Theological
Seminary, Chicago
January 15, 1953*

CONTENTS

FOREWORD

Before I decided that in order to pay a debt of thanks, as well as to express respect and friendly fellowship in a common task, I should dedicate this book to the University of Manchester and especially to its theological faculty, I had intended to dedicate it to my Roman Catholic friends, and particularly to the theologians among them. With them I sincerely feel myself united not only on the basis of general human esteem but also in questions of our Christian faith. However, I gave up this intention, because the final section of my work quite naturally will fail to win the approval of their Church, and so I feared that this dedication might in some way be misunderstood. I can assure them, nevertheless, that during the preparation of the final chapter I recalled many a conversation that I had had with them. I also kept in mind new objections that my discussions might evoke in them. Thus while writing that closing section I often found myself carrying on a silent discussion with them as absent members in a personal conversation.

My previous publications concerning Primitive Christian theological thought have found much genuine understanding even in Roman Catholic circles. Therefore I dare to hope and wish that my discussion of the very thing that separates us—for in the present investigation this comes quite frankly to expression, along with much that may win their assent—may do no harm, but may rather render a service to the conversation that Christian confessions have with one another.

This discussion must be continued in spite of the papal encyclical *Humani Generis*, and perhaps particularly as a result of it. If I am well informed, the admonitions of that document do not have in view those discussions with non-Roman Catholic Christians in which each side clearly represents its own standpoint. Indeed, we promote mutual and improved understanding only if we do not pass over in silence that which separates us. Where men, fully aware that they invoke the same name, make a sincere effort to listen to one another, they need not fear to speak also concerning the themes on which, as far as human eye can see, agreement is not possible. I often note, in discussions between representatives of the various confessions, that both parties take anxious pains to speak only concerning those questions regarding which there exists a common basis of discussion. The other questions are studiously avoided, even though as a rule the conversation necessarily reaches a point where it should move on to precisely those other questions for which the common basis is lacking. When this point it reached, one should go back to the reason for this lack of a common basis, not—let me repeat—to fight for one's position and not, indeed, with the illusory purpose of converting one's partner, but rather to listen to him. My purpose would not be furthered if certain things which I say were to be used as a polemic against the Roman Catholic Church. For I hold that in addition to the ecumenical achievements of recent decades it is precisely the simple discussion between Roman Catholic and Protestant theologians that is one of the encouraging events in the church history of our time.

It is in this spirit, and on the basis of the exegetical and historical principles which control the entire work, that I have written the latter part of this book. I hope that it will call forth numerous utterances, from both camps, concerning the fundamental questions over which Christendom is divided. In earlier times there was much discussion of them. Since then, however, men on both sides have become so accustomed to the fact that they do not agree in their point of departure that they often consider it unnecessary to speak about the matter at all—and what is worse, they neglect even to think about it. Apart from the fact that under these circumstances such discussions of individual questions or doctrines as have taken place in recent years are more or less futile, this procedure gives rise on both sides to prejudices and misunderstandings. Their removal should be our first aim, and indeed as much for reasons of scientific study as of faith. A resumption of the discussion concerning the primacy of Rome is also advisable because the arguments are no longer the same as they were in the sixteenth and seventeenth centuries.

In the present study I have purposely avoided raising the doctrinal question until the final chapter. This book as a whole is meant to be *a contribution to the science of history*, and in particular to that part which deals with the beginnings of the Christian faith and the Christian Church. If a librarian should be in doubt as to how to catalogue it, I should like to help him out of his perplexity at once. In spite of the sub-title and in spite of my personal interest in the theological question concerning Peter—an interest which I, even as a historian, make no attempt to conceal—this book belongs neither in the field of dogmatic theology nor in the literature of ecumenical debate nor even in the field of apologetics, but in that of the history of Primitive Christianity.

It is a historical study concerning the Apostle Peter that I here present.[1] But the history of Peter runs on without a break into the *evaluation* of this history which occurs in the continuing *historical* development. This evaluation, however, is likewise theological in nature, and the history of Peter has become the object of a dogmatic pronouncement by the Roman Catholic Church. Thus in a historical study which seeks to deal with Peter, the theological problem, on the one hand, is not to be avoided; yet this theological problem, on the other hand, can only be studied in the closest connection with the history.

May the faithful application of strictly historical methods, which I have taken care to use in dealing with this question, furnish a basis for the debate on the one hand between non-Christian and Christian historians, and on the other hand between Christian theologians of separate denominations who join in confessing One Catholic and Apostolic Church, but differ in the way they believe it is realized at the present time.

OSCAR CULLMANN

Easter, 1952

[1] This seemed to me the more necessary since we have but few scholarly works on Peter. Monographs on Paul are much more numerous. Recent *general* works on Peter include, on the Protestant side, F. Sieffert, *Realenzyklopädie für Theologie und Kirche*, 3rd ed., Article on "Peter," Vol. 15, pp. 190 ff.; F. J. Foakes-Jackson, *Peter, Prince of Apostles: A Study in the History and Tradition of Christianity*, 1927; W. Brandt, *Simon Petrus*, n.d. (popular in character); E. Fascher, *Realenzyklopädie des klassischen Alterthums*, Pauly-Wissowa, Article on "Peter," columns 1335 ff.; on the Roman Catholic side, C. Fouard, *S. Pierre et les premières années du christianisme*; L. Fillion, *Dictionnaire de la Bible*, Article on "S. Pierre"; A. Tricot, *Dictionnaire de Théologie catholique*, Article on "S. Pierre," 1935; M. Besson, *S. Pierre et les origines de la primauté romaine*, 1923 (beautifully illustrated); M. Meinertz, *Lexikon für Theologie und Kirche*, Article on "Petrus," 1936.

Part I

THE HISTORICAL
QUESTION

T HE SOURCES for our knowledge of Peter consist mainly of the writings of the New Testament. For the final period of his life we shall have to use both archaeological and liturgical evidence and texts of the Apostolic Fathers and the Church Fathers.

We can group the information we have concerning Peter under the following headings: (1) Peter the Disciple; (2) Peter the Apostle; (3) Peter the Martyr. In the section that deals with the Apostle we shall speak also of his theological views; in that dealing with the martyrdom we shall have to raise the radically important question concerning the stay of Peter in Rome.

Chapter One

PETER THE DISCIPLE

1. *Name, Origin, Call*

As sources concerning Peter the Disciple only the canonical Gospels are to be considered. The apocryphal gospels add only legendary material.

The fantastic attempt to deny the historical existence of Peter and to explain "the Christian Peter as the humanized form of the Persian Petros or Mithra" needs no refutation. It deserves mention only as a curiosity.[1]

We begin with the question as to the *name* of Peter; it is linked with the question of his role in the circle of the Twelve.

The original name of the apostle is Symeon or Simon. Symeon[2] is a Hebrew name much used among the Jews. We find this Semitic form used of Peter, however, only in Acts 15:14 and II Peter 1:1.[3] The Gospels use the Greek name Simon. This did not originate, as has been supposed, by rendering into Greek the Hebrew name. It is rather "native Greek"[4] and is already attested by Aristophanes. It is probable that the original Hebrew name Symeon was later replaced by the Greek name of similar sound. However, it does not seem to me at all impossible that Peter, like his brother Andrew, had been given a Greek name from the outset, especially since this is true of Philip, who according to John 1:44 comes from the same place, Bethsaida, and Hellenistic influence, moreover, is attested precisely for this region.[5] It is not impossible, therefore, that Peter, as was

---

[1] See A. Drews, *Die Petruslegende*, 1924. [2] שמעון.

[3] In Acts 15:14 this form is purposely used, since the speaker is James. In II Pet. 1:1 the reading "Simon," Σίμων (B) is almost certainly secondary. The latest scholar to oppose identifying Symeon (Acts 15:14) and Peter is E. Fuchs (*Zeitschrift für Theologie und Kirche*, 1951, p. 350).

[4] See F. Blass—A. Debrunner, *Grammatik des neutestamentlichen Griechisch*, 7th ed., 1943, Par. 53, 2, and Fick-Bechtel, *Die griechischen Personennamen*, 1894, pp. 30, 251. See also A. Deissmann, *Bibelstudien*, 1895, p. 184, note 1 (Eng. Tr., *Bible Studies*, 1901, p. 315, note 2).

[5] See below, p. 22.

customary in the Dispersion and as we probably must assume for Paul-Saul, had been given from the outset both the Hebrew name Symeon and the Greek name Simon of similar sound.

In addition to this name he has a descriptive title: *Kepha*. This is an Aramaic word and means "stone," "rock." Thus *Kepha* is not, as we might be inclined to believe, a proper name.[6] It is not a given name in ordinary use among the Jews, but is rather a common noun. In the New Testament we find this title at times in its Aramaic form, that is, merely *transcribed* in Greek letters; this is usually the case in Paul's letters (Gal. 1:18; 2:9; 2:11,[7] 14; I Cor. 1:12; 3:22; 9:5; 15:5). At times, however, it is *translated* into Greek: *Petros*. Paul writes *Petros* only once, in Galatians 2:7, 8,[8] perhaps because he here cites an official document, in the Greek translation of which the form *Petros* was used. The Gospels say at times *Simon*, at times *Petros*, at times *Simon Petros*.[9] The Syriac translations write *Simon Kepha*. Where in Greek environment the word is preserved in its aramaic spelling, it is supplied at the end with the Greek final -*s* in order to give it a Greek ending: *Kephas*. According to the Septuagint of Jeremiah 4:29 and Job 30:6, the preferable Greek translation would be *Petra*,[10]

---

[6] This is wrongly asserted by Th. Zahn, *Kommentar zum Neuen Testament, Das Evangelium des Matthäus*, 4th ed., 1922, p. 540; but he gives no example to support his view. M. J. Lagrange, in *L'Evangile selon S. Matthieu*, 5th ed., 1941, p. 324, also considers it possible.

[7] The completely unfounded idea that Gal. 2:11 is talking about another Cephas, who is entirely different from Peter and belongs to the Seventy disciples, appears in ancient times in Clement of Alexandria, *Hypotyposeis*, V (Eusebius, *Ecclesiastical History*, I, 12, 2), then in the lists of apostles (see Th. Schermann, *Propheten- und Apostellegenden nebst Jüngerkatalogen*, 1907, pp. 302 ff.), and in recent times in J. M. Robertson, *Die Evangelienmythen*, 1910 (German tr. of Part III of *Christianity and Mythology*, 1900), p.103, and D. W. Riddle, "The Cephas-Peter Problem and a Possible Solution" (*Journal of Biblical Literature*, 1940, pp. 169 ff.).

[8] In opposition to all the textual evidence A. Merx, *Die vier kanonischen Evangelien nach ihrem ältesten bekannten Text*, II, 1, *Das Evangelium Matthäus*, 1902, p. 161, regards "Peter" (Πέτρος) as secondary in these passages and assumes that in them too "Cephas" (Κηφᾶς) was the original reading.

[9] The Fourth Gospel prefers to say: Simon Peter.

[10] Elsewhere in the Septuagint πέτρα translates צור and סלע. See Hatch-Redpath, *A Concordance to the Septuagint and the other Greek Versions of the Old Testament*, 1897–1900. The Aramaic word כפא (Kepha) is translated by λίθος ("stone"), as A. Dell shows, in his article on "Matthäus 16:17–19" (*Zeitschrift für die Neutestamentliche Wissenschaft*, 1914, pp. 19 f.), by the evidence of the Jerusalem Gospel and the Sinaitic Syriac. Nevertheless, it remains true that *Kepha* in Aramaic means both "stone" and "rock." Therefore the results that A. Dell draws from the translation λίθος are to be rejected. See the following note.

which means "rock." Since, however, this word is feminine in Greek and has the feminine ending -a, the New Testament chooses for the translation a less usual Greek word which has the Greek masculine ending -os: *Petros* (John 1:42). There is no essential difference in meaning between *Petros* and *Petra*, for even if originally *Petra* designated live rock while *Petros* meant rather the detached stone, this distinction was not strictly observed.[11] The preference for the form *Petros* may have been due in part to the fact that in Aramaic there was a proper name *Petros*, which perhaps had the meaning "first-born."[12] This, however, is not certain.

In any event, the fact that the word *Kepha* was translated into Greek is significant. It confirms the fact that the word is not a proper name; proper names are not translated. The attempt has indeed been made to prove that even in pre-Christian times the name Peter existed as an abbreviation for the Latin Petronius and that it occurs in the Jewish author Josephus,[13] but the attempt at proof has failed.[14]

It is only because Peter has become for us today a familiar proper name that we are often tempted to forget that *Kepha* is a common noun. But this fact is important if we desire to judge rightly the bearing of the fact that Jesus gave Peter this title. It corresponds to Jewish custom to choose as titles words which somehow point to the promise in a particular situation and lay an obligation on their bearer. We know such examples from the Old Testament,[15] and in a similar way

---

11 In Homer, *Odyssey*, 243 ; Hesiod, *Theogony*, 675; and Wisdom 17:17 (LXX) πέτρα is used with the meaning "stone," "piece of rock." That the two words are interchangeable is said also by Galen, XII, 194. A. Dell, *op. cit.*, pp. 19 f., is probably wrong, therefore, in emphasizing that *Kepha* and *Petros* mean "stone" and not "rock."

12 J. Levy, *Neuhebräisch-chaldäisches Wörterbuch*, 1876 ff.; Dalman, *Aramäisch-neu-hebräisches Wörterbuch*, 2nd ed., 1922; Strack-Billerbeck *Kommentar zum Neuen Testament aus Talmud und Midrasch*, Vol. I, p. 530.

13 Josephus, *Antiquities*, 18, 6, 3. In reality what is involved here is a textual error for πρῶτος ("first").

14 The attempt has been made by A. Merx, *op. cit.*, pp. 160 ff. See also A. Meyer, *Jesu Muttersprache*, 1896, p. 51. It has been opposed by A. Dell, *op. cit.*, pp. 14 ff.: "The proper name Peter does not appear at all in pagan literature; it first appears in Tertullian." There was, on the contrary, as already mentioned (note 12), an Aramaic name פטרוס (Petros), which perhaps is to be connected with פטר (patar) "firstborn." The theory that the Greek *Petros* was first derived from it and gave occasion for a false retranslation *Kepha* into Aramaic is quite impossible, in view of the fact that in Paul's letters Cephas is already the usual designation and Peter clearly was only a later derivation from it.

15 Gen. 17:5 ff., 15; 32:28; Isa. 62:2; 65:15. See also on this point Justin, *Dialogue With Trypho*, 106, 3.

Jewish disciples also received from their Rabbi a title.[16] Jesus himself gave such a title not only to Peter but also to the Sons of Zebedee: *Boanerges*, which is explained in Mark 3:17 to mean "Sons of Thunder."[17] In order to understand what an impression the giving of a name to Peter must have made on him and on the other witnesses of this event, we would do well to translate the word *Kephas* not with the word Peter, which for us today is all too familiar and has become too rigidly fixed as a proper name, but with the English word "rock," and so call him Simon Rock.[18]

According to the unanimous witness of the Gospels, the giving of this name goes back to Jesus. It will not do to ascribe it to the fellow disciples, who supposedly gave him this name of honour only later, on the basis of the fact that he was the first who saw the risen Lord.[19] In saying this we have not yet said whether it was actually given to him in the situation described in Matthew, ch. 16. The agreement of the Evangelists concerning the basic fact is the more noteworthy in view of their absolute divergence about the circumstances in which the name was given. According to the basic passage, Matthew 16:18, with which we shall have to deal in detail, Jesus first gave Simon this title on the occasion when he likewise explained it more fully. This was at the moment when, according to Mark 8:27 ff., Peter uttered his famous confession of Jesus at Caesarea Philippi. There Jesus asks his disciples, "Who do men say that I am?"[20] The disciples report to him the various views current among the people. Thereupon Jesus asks, "And in your view, who am I?" Peter speaks up and says, "You are the Christ (Matthew adds: the Son of the Living God)." According to Matthew 16:17, Jesus answers, "Blessed are you, Simon son of Jonah! It was not a man but the Father in Heaven who gave you this revelation." Then he continues: "And I say to you, You are the Rock, and upon this Rock I will build my Church."

[16] See P. Fiebig, *Gleichnisreden Jesu*, 1912, pp. 53 ff.

[17] See on this point E. Preuschen, "Die Donnersöhne" (*ZNW*, 1917, pp. 141 ff.) and F. Schulthess, "*Zur Sprache der Evangelien*" (*ZNW*, 1922, pp. 243 ff.).

[18] H. Pernot, in his French translation of the Gospels (1943), rightly chooses the word *roc*, and it seems to me unjustified that this suggestion has been received with some scoffing.

[19] So K. G. Goetz, *Petrus als Gründer und Oberhaupt der Kirche und Schauer von Gesichten nach den altchristlichen Berichten und Legenden*, 1927, pp. 67 f. Further, E. Hirsch, *Frühgeschichte des Evangeliums*, II, 1941, pp. 306 ff.

[20] Instead of the pronoun "I" ($\mu\epsilon$), Matt. 16:13 writes "the Son of Man" ($\tau\grave{o}\nu$ $\upsilon\acute{i}\grave{o}\nu$ $\tau o\hat{\upsilon}$ $\mathring{a}\nu\theta\rho\acute{\omega}\pi o\upsilon$), according to the best textual witnesses, but since this reading awkwardly anticipates the answer, it is certainly secondary in comparison with Mark 8:27. See below, p. 175.

Thus in the same way that Peter gives to Jesus a name which later is regularly added to the name of Jesus, and finally becomes fixed as his proper name, "Christ" (in Hebrew "Messiah," that is, "Anointed One"), so, according to Matthew, Jesus gives to Peter a descriptive title: "Rock."

Did Jesus really give this title to Peter on the specific occasion indicated by this Gospel? We are justified in raising this question, for according to Mark 3:16 this event—without the addition of the explanation—took place upon another occasion, and John 1:42, moreover, places the giving of the name in still another setting. According to Mark 3:16 Jesus already called Peter "Rock" at the time of the call of the Twelve;[21] according to John 1:42 he did so even earlier, on the occasion of their first meeting in Judea, although Jesus here speaks in the future tense: "You *will be* called Cephas." From these variations, which one can harmonize if he is determined to do so,[22] we conclude that in the process of transmission the memory of the moment in which Jesus gave Peter the title had become lost; the same is true of the setting of many other stories in the Gospels.

We must keep this in mind when we come to the detailed exegesis of Matthew 16:16 ff. In itself the time when the name was given has no fundamental significance. What is important, however, is first of all *the fact* that according to the unanimous witness of the Gospels Mark, Matthew, and John, Jesus did give this name to Peter and, second, that according to a tradition handed down only by Matthew, Jesus *explained* this name on a special occasion by his purpose of founding his Church upon the Apostle whom he designated as the Rock.

*   *   *

We can derive from the Gospels the following additional *biographical notes.* According to Matthew 16:17, Peter is the son of Jonah—Aramaic *bar-yônâ*, which John 1:42 and 21:15 f. indicate is

---

[21] M. J. Lagrange, in agreement with A. Loisy, J. Knabenbauer, etc., maintains in *L'évangile selon St. Marc*, 6th ed., 1942, p. 65, that this is the original occasion: "The time chosen by Mark is probably that which best accords with the facts, since from then on Simon becomes the corner stone of the building begun by Jesus." From this moment Mark consistently avoids the name Simon, which up to this time he has regularly used. Only in ch. 14:37, in the Gethsemane scene, does Jesus say to him: "Simon, are you sleeping?" Perhaps Mark purposely avoids having Jesus address Simon in this situation as "Rock."

[22] See below, p. 177.

an abbreviation for John. Whether another explanation, which appeals to a Jewish lexicon, is correct must remain doubtful. According to it, the Aramaic *bar-yônâ* had no connection with the name John, but meant the same as "terrorist."[23] In that case Peter belonged to the party of the determined enemies of Rome, the so-called "Zealots," just as did Simon the "Zealot" (Luke 6:15; Acts 1:13[24]) and perhaps Judas Iscariot.[25]

According to John 1:44 Peter comes from Bethsaida ("fisherman's city"), which according to the view that is by far the most probable is to be sought on the eastern bank of the Jordan near the point where it empties into the Sea of Gennesaret.[26] Even if the place itself was Jewish, we must note, nevertheless, that it was located in Gentile surroundings. This is indicated, indeed, as John 1:44 and 12:21 suggest, by the Greek name of his brother Andrew and of Philip, who likewise came from Bethsaida, as well as by the name of Simon himself.[27] "Anyone brought up in Bethsaida would not only have understood Greek, but would also have been polished by intercourse with foreigners and have had some Greek culture."[28] Thus is explained the fact that according to John 12:21 the Greeks turn to Philip, the native of Bethsaida. If the information of the Gospel of John that Peter came from that place is true, this could be related to the fact that in the account of Acts, chs. 10 and 11, Peter champions a universalistic point of view and, as we shall see, is not too far removed from Paul in his theology. This does not prevent Acts 4:13 from characterizing him and his companion John as "uneducated."[29] He had not "studied" either by Jewish or by Greek standards.

Later we find that Peter has moved to Capernaum and settled

[23] So Robert Eisler, *Jesous basileus ou basileusas*, 1929 f., p. 67, who follows Eliezer ben Jehuda, *Thesaurus totius hebraitatis*. In favour of this view might be the fact that Jonah is not attested elsewhere as a shortened form of Johanan.

[24] The reading is Κανavaῖos in Mark 3:18; Matt. 10:4. This is not to be translated "Canaanite," but "Zealot," and the word merely transliterates the Aramaic word *qan'ānâ*.

[25] Iscariot would be derived from *sicarius* = "bandit." J. Wellhausen, *Das Evangelium Marci übersetzt und erklärt*, 1909, p. 23, mentions this interpretation, but does not consider it probable.

[26] See G. Dalman, *Orte und Wege Jesu*, 1919, pp. 158 ff. English translation, *Sacred Sites and Ways*, 1935, pp. 161 ff.

[27] See above, p. 17.   [28] G. Dalman, *op. cit.*, p. 163 (Eng. Tr., p. 165).

[29] ἀγράμματοί εἰσιν καὶ ἰδιῶται. F. J. Foakes-Jackson, *Peter, Prince of Apostles: A Study in the History and Tradition of Christianity*, 1927, p. 55, thinks that this judgment is to be ascribed to contempt for the Galilean accent.

(Mark 1:29 and parallels). It appears that Jesus often entered his home there, and perhaps actually lived with him for a short time (Matt. 8:14).

He was a fisherman by calling (Mark 1:16 and parallels: Luke 5:2 f.; John 21:3). He seems to carry on this work together with the two sons of Zebedee, who are described as "partners" (Luke 5:10).[30]

According to the testimony of the Synoptic Gospels (Mark 1:29 ff. and parallels) as well as of Paul (I Cor. 9:5), Peter was married. Later stories concerning his children[31] and the martyrdom of his wife, at which he supposedly was present,[32] are legendary.

The Johannine account (John 1:35 ff.) permits us to suppose that before he joined Jesus he, as well as his brother Andrew and the un-named disciple, had belonged to the inner or wider circle of the disciples of John the Baptist.[33]

2. His Position in the Circle of Disciples

We learn from the Synoptic Gospels that Peter actually occupies an unique position within the group of disciples. Together with the sons of Zebedee and his brother Andrew he belongs to the intimate circle of those who gathered about Jesus. According to Mark 1:16 and Matthew 4:18, he with Andrew is the first disciple whom Jesus calls. Mark 5:37 notes explicitly that Jesus permitted no one else to follow him into the house of the ruler of the synagogue except Peter and the sons of Zebedee. On other occasions also we find him to-gether with this pair of brothers (see Mark 9:2 and parallels; Mark 14:33 and parallels).

But even within this innermost circle it is almost always Peter who stands in the foreground. In the story of the miraculous catch of fish (Luke 5:1 ff.) he clearly plays the chief role, although at the very end the sons of Zebedee are included with him. According to Matthew 14:28, only Peter attempts to imitate his Master in walking on the sea. Almost always he appears as the spokesman for the

---

[30] κοινωνοί.

[31] Clement of Alexandria, Stromateis, III, 6, 52; concerning a daughter, see Actus Vercellenses.

[32] Eusebius, Eccles. Hist., III, 30, 2, who quotes Clement of Alexandria, Stromateis, VII, 11, 63; concerning Peter's wife, see further the Pseudo-Clementine Homily. XIII, 1, 11; Recognitions, VII, 25, 36; IX, 38.

[33] The hypothesis according to which "bar-Jonah" designates Peter as a "disciple of John the Baptist" cannot be proved.

Twelve. We have already seen that it is Peter who answers when Jesus directs a question to *all* the disciples (Mark 8:29 ff. and parallels). Correspondingly, the close of this Markan narrative (ch. 8:33) says that Jesus *looks upon all the disciples* as he speaks to Peter the stern word, "Depart from me, Satan. Your thinking is not under divine but under human control." The reproach is obviously directed equally to all the disciples, because Jesus knows that even the words which Peter has addressed to him to hold him back from his path of suffering reproduce the Satanic desire of all the Twelve. Thus here, too, Peter appears as the spokesman of all the disciples.

The same conclusion results from the transfiguration story, Mark 9:2 ff. Here, too, it is Peter who proposes to Jesus that they erect tents (Mark 9:5). The sons of Zebedee play on this occasion little more than the role of extras.

It is Peter who in various situations turns to Jesus with questions which all the disciples want answered: "Lord, how many times shall I forgive my brother who sins against me? As many as seven times?" (Matt. 18:21). "Lord, do you speak this parable to us or also to all?" (Luke 12:41). "Behold, we have left everything and followed you" (Mark 10:28 and parallels).

It also occurs that in one Gospel all the disciples ask the question, while in the parallel passage of the other Gospel it is only Peter who asks (Mark 7:17 compared with Matt. 15:15; Matt. 21:20 compared with Mark 11:21).

In Luke 22:8 Peter and John are directed by Jesus to prepare the Passover.—In Mark 14:29 Peter promises to be loyal to his Master.— Again, in Gethsemane, according to Mark 14:37 (Matt. 26:40), Jesus turns to Peter with the reproachful question whether he cannot watch one hour; but again the sons of Zebedee, who are likewise present, are included in the address.—According to Matthew 17:24 Peter is regarded by outsiders also as the special representative of the group of disciples. The people who collect the tax address their question to him.

The lists of the disciples (Mark 3:16; Matt. 10:2; Luke 6:14; Acts 1:13) do indeed vary in detail, but it is common to all of them that they give Peter the first place. The list in Matthew actually emphasizes the fact that he is the first (πρῶτος). Characteristic also is the expression "Peter and those with him,"[34] used to designate the group of disciples (Mark 1:36; Luke 9:32; 8:45 according to the best attested reading). Particularly striking is the word of the angel in

[34] Πέτρος καὶ οἱ σὺν αὐτῷ; Πέτρος καὶ οἱ μετ᾽ αὐτοῦ.

Mark 16:7: "Go and tell his disciples *and Peter* that (Jesus) goes before you to Galilee."

With respect to this unique position, therefore, there is no such difference as has often been asserted between Mark and the other two Synoptic Gospels. Precisely in the Gospel of Mark, of which it has been said that although written in Rome it knows no claim for the authority of Peter,[35] he appears as the spokesman among the disciples. An examination of the passages already listed is sufficient to convince one that in reality each of the three Synoptic Gospels emphasizes in its own independent way the pre-eminent position of Peter. Even though Mark lacks the saying of Matthew 16:17 ff. concerning the Church, yet his entire presentation leaves not the slightest doubt as to the special role that this Evangelist ascribes to Peter. To try to derive a tendency hostile to Peter from the fact that he does not keep silence about Peter's weaknesses is to misunderstand the significance of these items.[36] We have seen above[37] that at times all the disciples speak in one of the Synoptic Gospels, while only Peter speaks in the parallel passage of the other one. But we must notice that when this occurs it is not always the same Gospel that puts Peter in the foreground. Rather, we find that this emphasis upon this one disciple is found now in one and now in another of the Gospels. Thus in the Gospel of Mark (Mark 11:21) Peter takes the place of all the disciples, whereas in the parallel passage in Matthew (ch. 21:20) they ask the question concerning the withered fig tree.

Moreover, it will not do to make a basic distinction between Luke and Matthew in regard to their attitude to Peter, as though only Matthew had a special ecclesiastical interest in a permanent primacy for Peter.[38] Even if it is true that Matthew alone has the saying of

[35] H. Strathmann, "Die Stellung des Petrus in der Urkirche. Zur Frühgeschichte des Wortes an Petrus, Matt. 16, 17–19" (*Zeitschrift für Systematische Theologie*, 1943, pp. 223 ff.).

[36] Above all, we cannot speak of a hostility of Mark towards Peter, such as R. Bultmann assumes in "Die Frage nach dem messianischen Bewusstsein und das Petrusbekenntnis" (*ZNW*, 1919–20, p. 170). See M. Gogue, *L'Eglise primitive*, 1947, p. 191: "There is no trace of an anti-Petrine attitude in Mark."

[37] See p. 24.

[38] Thus H. Strathmann, *op. cit.*, judges each of the Gospels on the basis of its attitude to the claim of authority for Peter, according to the somewhat artificial scheme by which he assumes that it belongs to this or that Church: Mark—Rome—no interest in the Petrine claim; Luke and The Acts—Pauline missionary area—a primacy of Peter for only a limited time; Matthew—Antioch (see B. H. Streeter) — permanent primacy; John—Asia Minor—anti-Petrine and pro-Johannine tendency.

Matthew 16:17 ff., and also the story of Peter's walking on the sea (Matt. 14:28 ff.), as well as the designation "first" in Matthew 10:2, we must place on the other side the verses in which only Luke shows a positive interest in Peter; this is especially true in the story of the miraculous catch of fish (Luke 5:1 ff.). Furthermore, we must note particularly that in Luke's special material there is a parallel to the saying about the Rock in Matthew 16:18. It clearly gives to Peter for the future a unique function among his brothers: "Simon, Simon, behold, Satan has asked for you in order to sift you like wheat. But I have prayed for you that your faith may not fail, and when you have turned again (according to another reading: turn again and[39]) strengthen your brothers" (Luke 22:31). This saying's genuineness cannot be contested with the same arguments that are used against Matthew 16:17 ff., since it does not contain the word "church" (ἐκκλησία),[40] which many find objectionable on critical grounds. Hence it should be cited in this debate much oftener than it is. In this verse, too, Jesus says to Peter that he stands in a perilously close relation to Satan, but in this he is expressly linked with the other disciples: "Satan has asked (God) for you (plural) in order to sift you (plural)." We have seen[41] that this is also the silent assumption in Mark, ch. 8, and yet in both places Jesus directs the saying only to Peter, and particularly in giving the charge he speaks only to Peter: "Strengthen your brothers." Accordingly, it is impossible to discern in any of the Synoptic Gospels a bias for or against Peter.

Thus according to all three Synoptic Gospels Peter indubitably played the role of spokesman among the twelve disciples. Furthermore, according to the Gospels of Matthew and Luke Jesus appointed him specially to carry out later the mission of strengthening his brothers. So the knowledge of a special distinction given to Peter within the circle of disciples is common to the entire ancient tradition behind the Synoptic Gospels. This is clear even without taking into account the controversial passage Matthew 16:17 ff., which we shall discuss in detail in Part Two of this work. This unique position, which is attested not only in Matthew but also in Luke and Mark, cannot and must not be denied or even diminished in support of any confessional or critical tendency. We must add, however, that while in all these passages Peter is given prominence in the total group of

[39] E. Stauffer, "Zur Vor- und Frühgeschichte des Primatus Petri," *Zeitschrift für Kirchengeschichte*, 1943-44, p. 18, note 58, gives various reasons for preferring this reading.

[40] See below, pp. 164 f., 186 ff.   [41] See above, p. 24.

disciples, he always appears as their spokesman in "dialogue with Christ"; apart from this relation to Christ he never plays, as he does in the later literature, a leading role.[42]

A somewhat different picture emerges when we turn to *the Gospel of John*. Here the outstanding role of Peter, which is unchallenged in the Synoptic Gospels, becomes a problem, since for this Evangelist the mysterious unnamed "Beloved Disciple" of Jesus enters into a certain competition with Peter. Thus here, in a way different from the Synoptics, a contemporary interest of the author concerning the position of Peter may have influenced the presentation. However, it is noteworthy that this Gospel, which manifestly wishes to emphasize the particularly close relationship between Jesus and the "Beloved Disciple," nevertheless nowhere attempts to deny directly the special role of Peter within the group of disciples.[43] It only has the tendency to lessen this role, in so far as it seeks to show that beside the unique position of Peter there is the somewhat different special role of the "Beloved Disciple."[44] This is certainly connected with the receding of the entire group of the Twelve as such, a tendency which is characteristic of this Gospel's view of the disciples and to which as a rule not enough attention is given. That in spite of this manifest tendency the Fourth Gospel nevertheless accepts as a fact the pre-eminence of Peter appears to me to be a particularly strong proof that this fact was so well known in the Primitive Church that it could neither be directly denied nor passed over in silence, but only minimized.[45] It is only the exclusive nature of Peter's unique position that is opposed; in other respects the different character of the role of the two men is emphasized.

This appears in a particularly clear way in the Passion story, for example in ch. 13:24 on the occasion of the Last Supper, where Peter must turn to the Beloved Disciple, who is lying on the breast of the Lord, in order to learn a secret of Jesus. It appears again in ch. 18:15, where the Beloved Disciple enters with Jesus into the court of the high priest, while Peter remains outside before the gate. But particularly in the most decisive moment, at the foot of the cross, it is not Peter but the Beloved Disciple who is present, and he is

---

[42] This is rightly emphasized by J. L. Klink, *Het Petrustype in het Nieuwe Testament en de Oud-Christelike Letterjkunde*, Dissertation, Leyden, 1947.

[43] Peter also appears as spokesman for the other disciples in John 6:66 ff. and 13:36.

[44] The Gospel of the Hebrews goes much further in opposing the special position of Peter.

[45] This is also recognized explicitly by D. F. Strauss, *Das Leben Jesu. Für das deutsche Volk*, 1864, p. 423.

distinguished in a quite special way by the word here directed to him by the Crucified One.[46] Furthermore, the author tells how the Beloved Disciple comes first ($\pi\rho\hat{\omega}\tau os$, ch. 20:4) to the grave but does not enter, while Peter only comes after him but does go in. The Beloved Disciple enters the grave after Peter does, but on the other hand it is said only of this Beloved Disciple that he "believes" at once when he has "seen" (ch. 20:8).[47]

These facts throw light also upon ch. 1:41, where we find as the first disciples of Jesus two former disciples of the Baptist, an unnamed one and Andrew the brother of Peter. Thus here Peter is not the "first" disciple; he is not the $\pi\rho\hat{\omega}\tau os$. Nevertheless, *after* these two, whose meeting with Jesus serves rather as a kind of prelude, Peter is the first one who comes to Jesus. In fact, the writer speaks also in verses 41 of a "first" one, and this could refer to Peter. Nevertheless, the manuscripts here differ with regard to the ending of the word. Some read "the first one" in the nominative case ($\pi\rho\hat{\omega}\tau os$); Andrew is thereby designated as the first one, who as such finds his brother Peter. In this case it is emphasized that the honour of being "the first one" belongs to both former disciples of the Baptist, the unnamed one and Andrew. The other manuscripts read "the first one" in the accusative case ($\pi\rho\hat{\omega}\tau ov$). In this reading Peter receives the honourable rank of "the first one," yet only in so far as he is the first to be found and led to Jesus by his brother, the former disciple of the Baptist. This divergence of the manuscripts shows how it was recognized even in ancient times that the Fourth Evangelist was specially interested in this question; whether he himself wrote the nominative or the accusative case—and this is hard to decide—it remains a fact that thereby, exactly as in ch. 20, he intends to point to the remarkable relationship between Peter and that unnamed disciple, who is probably identical with the Beloved Disciple and who was a disciple of the Baptist when he first met Jesus. Here also, it seems, the evangelist did not intend to deny the pre-eminent position of Peter, but he did wish to show how the unnamed disciple is "first" in another respect, in the way he became Jesus' disciple.

This tendency is even clearer in view of the fact that here at the

---

[46] Ed. Meyer, "Sinn und Tendenz der Schlussszene am Kreuz im Johannesevangelium" (*Sitzungsbericht der preussischen Akademie der Wissenschaften*, 1924, p. 159), actually assumes that by the words directed to him and to the mother of Jesus the Beloved Disciple is so to speak accepted into the family of the Lord and adopted as his brother in the fullest sense.

[47] See O. Cullmann, "$\epsilon\hat{\iota}\delta\epsilon\nu$ $\kappa\alpha\hat{\iota}$ $\epsilon\pi\hat{\iota}\sigma\tau\epsilon\upsilon\sigma\epsilon\nu$," in the volume in honour of M. Goguel, *Aux Sources de la Tradition Chrétienne*, 1950, pp. 56 ff.

very beginning Andrew utters the confession of Jesus as the Messiah, while Peter comes to recognize this only later (ch. 6:66 ff.). Yet, as we must say on the other side, the Gospel of John expressly recognizes that Jesus gave to Peter the title of honour, "Rock," and as we have seen,[48] the Gospel puts this event at the very beginning (ch. 1:42). We must also say that it reports the decisive confession of Peter with an emphasis all its own (ch. 6:66 ff.).

Exactly the same double attitude toward the unique position of Peter is found again in the supplementary chapter 21, which thus in this respect agrees with chapters 1 to 20. On the one side, that position is explicitly recognized, while on the other side, it is reduced by being confronted with the unique position of the Beloved Disciple. Thus, at the beginning of the narrative here reported concerning the appearance of Jesus at the Sea of Galilee, Peter is named first in the series of disciples listed.[49] On the other hand, the Beloved Disciple is the first to recognize the Lord, but Peter again is the first to go to him. Thus this paralleling of the two unique positions marks this chapter also. It finds its climax in the conversation which, following the miracle, occurs between the Risen One and Peter. This account is characteristic of the way in which the author of this chapter, who, no matter who he is, belongs to the Johannine circle, has grasped the meaning of the entire Gospel of John; he shows this grasp by putting at the end precisely this conversation as a sort of crown or climax. In doing so, he probably has emphasized much too strongly this purpose which the Fourth Evangelist certainly had. But on the other hand, he has correctly understood the Evangelist's conception; in a quite analogous manner he sets the two disciples face to face and shows how the Risen One assigns a unique position to each one of them for the future, but gives each of them a different role.[50] Peter is installed in the office of shepherd;[51] to the Beloved Disciple, who

[48] See above, p. 21.

[49] According to E. Stauffer, op. cit., pp. 13 f., there lies at the basis of this narrative an early report, mentioned in I Cor. 15:5, concerning the appearance of Jesus to Peter alone. On this matter see below, p. 60.

[50] M. Goguel, L'Eglise primitive, 1947, p. 200, takes another view. He assumes that this dialogue serves to glorify Peter at the expense of the Beloved Disciple, and so stands in opposition to chs. 1-20.

[51] To dispute this, as K. G. Goetz, op. cit., p. 15, attempts to do, seems to me impossible. Goetz is no doubt correct when he writes that Peter is reinstated in the position of disciple that he had lost by the three-fold denial. At the same time, however, more is involved here than merely the confirmation of the call of a disciple. The fact that Jesus no longer lives on earth necessarily has as its result a new task for the disciple.

here only "follows" Peter, which in Johannine idiom[52] may also imply a spiritual attachment, it is promised that he will outlive Peter. In this context this promise quite probably signifies that he will have to fulfil a task which, though similar, is nevertheless, as in the entire Gospel, of a somewhat different kind.[53]

Thus the Gospel of John, precisely because, in distinction from the Synoptic Gospels, it has the tendency to emphasize the Beloved Disciple, indirectly confirms the result to which we were led by the investigation of the Synoptic passages concerning the disciple Peter: *Among the disciples of Jesus Peter, according to the united witness of the gospel tradition, occupies a peculiarly representative position.*

This does not mean, however, that during the lifetime of Jesus he possessed the role of *leader* in relation to his fellow-disciples. He is rather at all times their *spokesman*, their *representative* in good as in bad action. But he gives them no commissions in the name of Jesus, and the Master nowhere entrusts to him such a function for the period of his own earthly life. The three passages, Matthew 16:16 ff., Luke 22:31 f. and John 21:15 ff., in which he is charged with a special obligation towards his brothers, all refer to the future, to the time after the death of Jesus. Thus the gospel tradition knew how to

---

[52] See O. Cullmann, "Der johanneische Gebrauch doppeldeutiger Ausdrücke als Schlüssel zum Verständnis des vierten Evangeliums" (*Theologische Zeitschrift*, 1948, pp. 360 ff.).

[53] Thus R. Bultmann, *Das Johannesevangelium*, p. 547, writes that the authority of Peter here passes over to the Beloved Disciple. E. Stauffer, *op. cit.*, agrees with this, but adds that this involves the authority not only of the Evangelist, as Bultmann thinks, but also of the church leader John. This, however, confuses the difference between the two unique positions, a difference emphasized in the entire Fourth Gospel and also in this twenty-first chapter. The Roman Catholic scholar R. Graber, in *Petrus der Fels. Fragen um den Primat*, 1949, pp. 37 ff., considers the meaning of John, ch. 21, to be as follows: The question of Peter: "Lord, but what will happen to this man (the Beloved Disciple)" reckons with the possibility that the Beloved Disciple might be his "successor;" but the answer of Jesus, "If I will that he remain," is meant to reject explicitly this opinion of Peter, because others are destined to be his successors. This artificial explanation is much less justified than the hypothesis, well worth considering, of the first part of Graber's work (see below, pp. 38, 41); it merely aims to find a Scriptural witness to warrant the transfer of the apostolic succession of Peter to the Roman bishops. Moreover, the assertion of Graber (p. 39) that the Beloved Disciple was undoubtedly still living at the time of writing of John, ch. 21, is by no means proved by the argument that after his death it would have been nonsense to refute the idea that he would not die. Cannot one say, on the contrary, that precisely then it was necessary to show that the saying of Jesus concerning "remaining" was not proved false by the death of that disciple?

distinguish between the position of Peter before and after the death of Jesus.

In view of this fact, we must consider improbable the assertion some have made, that the pre-eminence of Peter in the circle of Jesus' disciples is merely a pre-dating of the position which he actually held only in the Primitive Church, after the death of Jesus. He is ascribed no leading position at all in relation to the group of the Twelve; on the contrary, he appears only as the most representative of the disciples. What all of them represent, do, and think, comes to particularly strong expression in his person.

One might indeed be tempted to go further and ask how this pre-eminence is to be *explained*. Is it due to the fact that by giving the name mentioned Jesus strengthened greatly Peter's consciousness of being a disciple? Or on the contrary, is it, together with the giving of the name, to be explained on psychological grounds by the character of Peter? The latter possibility has often been considered.[54] It takes its clue from the fact that during the lifetime of Jesus Peter did not show himself a "rock" at all; on the contrary, his human weakness was very striking. The scene at the Sea of Gennesaret gives a concrete illustration of Peter's character. He is impulsive and enthusiastic; in the first burst of enthusiasm, he does not hesitate to throw himself into the sea when Jesus calls him, but his courage soon fades and fear grips him. So, too, he is the first to confess loudly his loyalty to his Master, but he is the first one who will deny him in the hour of danger. And yet, so one assumes, precisely this character, with its notable contradictions, makes Peter appear as the disciple with special psychological fitness to be the "rock" among the other disciples. The exuberant enthusiasm, the fiery zeal of this disciple are said to be in fact the human qualities that are necessary to deserve such a title of honour. His instability and weakness are said to be only the dark side of these qualities.

Nevertheless, it is hardly possible to give a psychological basis for the unique position of Peter and for the giving to him of this name. Indeed, we should not ask at all why Jesus singled him out as "rock" instead of choosing another disciple.[55] According

---

[54] So especially by F. Sieffert in *Realenzyklopädie für Theologie und Kirche*, 3rd ed., Article on "Petrus," Vol. 15, p. 190.

[55] K. L. Schmidt, *Festschrift für A. Deissmann*, 1927, p. 301, rightly rejects this question as to the Why of the choice of Peter as the "rock." He observes that it can no more be answered than can the question why God chose the people of Israel.

to our sources, we can only confirm the fact of this distinction.

Probably, however, it is also a mistake to say that the representative position of the disciple Peter and the qualities mentioned were derived only from the giving of the name. We can hardly say that only by this act did he become conscious that in his person he represented, so to speak, the totality of the disciples, even during the earthly life of Jesus. Again we can only state *the fact*: Peter lets us see clearly everything that the call to discipleship involves in human weakness and privilege.

To the question whether his pre-eminence is to be explained by the giving of the name, or the giving of the name, on the contrary, by his actual pre-eminence, there probably is no simple answer. In reality what is involved is rather a reciprocal action. Jesus knows better than anyone else the qualities of Peter, both the good and the bad ones, and he takes account of them in his view of the work he intends his disciples to do. On the other hand, however, the special distinction given this disciple as a rock-man rests on the Master's act of sovereign decision, an act which may have strengthened Peter in the representative role that his nature had already given him.

For the period following the death of Jesus the question concerning the unique position of Peter presents itself in another way. The disciple becomes the apostle of the crucified and risen Lord. In this capacity his unique position necessarily takes on another character. Of this we must speak in the next chapter.

Chapter Two

PETER THE APOSTLE

ACCORDING to the sources at our disposal, the death and resurrection of Jesus creates for Peter a completely changed situation. This is true in two respects. In the first place, from this time on his unique role appears no longer merely as that of a representative; in view of the physical absence of the Lord, it naturally appears also in the leadership of the small community of disciples. The character and the time limit of this leadership, however, must still be more exactly determined. In the second place, this unique position now rests upon a specific commission, which must be defined on various sides.

We begin with the first point.

1. The Leadership of the Primitive Church

In *The Book of Acts* we clearly note that Peter takes a unique position in the Primitive Church in Jerusalem. Apart from the letters of Paul, of which we speak later, The Acts is our only source. We investigate first the data of the first twelve chapters.

It is Peter who in ch. 1:15 ff. prompts the choice of the twelfth disciple.[1] It at once becomes evident here that the fact of his being spokesman for the others signifies likewise that whatever may be his authorization, in every case he presides over the little group of believers.

He it is who explains to the assembled multitude the miracle of Pentecost (ch. 2:14). "He stands up with the Eleven," we are told, but he alone speaks. In verse 37 the witnesses present at the miracle address themselves, as the author puts it, "to Peter and the rest of the apostles."

In ch. 3 he performs the healing miracle on the lame man. In this

---

[1] P. Gaechter, "Die Wahl des Matthias (Apostelgeschichte 1, 15–16)" (*Zeitschrift für katholische Theologie*, 1949, pp. 318 ff.), traces the choice back to a special commission given by Jesus. See below, pp. 215 ff.

narrative John is named with Peter in a most remarkable manner. All the manuscripts mention him. But the way in which he is introduced and plays little more than the role of an extra could lead us to suppose that his name was added subsequently to that of Peter. Particularly noteworthy in this connection is verse 4: "Peter looked on the lame man, with John."[2] If the unnamed Beloved Disciple of the Fourth Gospel had at this time already been identified with John, one could ask whether the mention of John with Peter does not correspond to a tendency similar to that which we confirmed in the Gospel of John.[3] Concerning this point, however, we can say nothing certain. That John actually did occupy a certain authoritative position after Peter in the Primitive Church is made certain by Paul, who in Galatians 2:9 reckons him together with James and Cephas among the "pillars" of the Church.[4]

In the further development of the story it is Peter who defends the cause of the Gospel when the authorities take action against the apostles (chs. 4:8; 5:29). After the healing of the lame man it is Peter alone who speaks, although we are told in chapter 4:1: "While they were speaking . . ." and although John is again named with Peter in verse 13. In the latter case, however, the mention of his name again limps noticeably and looks like an addition. Thus it cannot be denied that according to this entire narrative Peter as a member of the Jerusalem church occupies the place of leader.

Particularly in the case of Ananias and Sapphira, however, he exercises church discipline in the congregation (ch. 5:1 ff.).[5] Here his authority is especially noticeable. However we may judge concerning the genuineness or spuriousness of Matt. 16:16 ff., and whatever may be the meaning of the words "bind" and "loose,"[6] in this narrative it is Peter who, as the earthly authority, holds court in the name of God, and according to verse 2 he does this publicly in the presence of the other apostles. The narrative concerning Simon the magician (ch. 8:18 ff.) also presupposes that Peter makes the decisions.

Furthermore, The Book of Acts emphasizes the faith of the people

---

[2] ἀτενίσας δὲ Πέτρος εἰς αὐτὸν σὺν τῷ Ἰωάννῃ.

[3] See above, pp. 27 ff.   [4] See below, pp. 42 ff.

[5] Ph.-H. Menoud, "La mort d'Ananias, et de Saphira (Actes 5, 1–11)," in *Aux sources de la tradition chrétienne. Mélanges offerts à M. Goguel*, 1950, pp. 146 ff., assumes that the intent of the entire section is to explain by their sin the fact of the death of the first members of the Church to die, Ananias and Sapphira.

[6] See below, pp. 204 f.

in the miraculous power of Peter in particular. They actually consider his "shadow" capable of effecting a healing (ch. 5:15). Although it is said also of the other apostles that miracles are done by their hands (ch. 5:12) and that they teach (chs. 2:42; 4:33), yet after the first chapters these same activities are carried on by Peter in a way which makes him appear, as he did in the days of Jesus, to be particularly representative. But this, in the changed situation after Jesus' death, can only mean that he thereby occupies a *leading* role in relation to the Church; he stands at its head.

This authority extends also to the missionary field in Samaria, which in the earliest days was dependent on Jerusalem. This land may be called the original field of the Christian mission. Its actual missionaries are the Christians who were driven from Jerusalem, most likely at the time of the martyrdom of Stephen; they probably represented a point of view similar to that of Stephen. In Acts 8:1 it is explicitly said that on that occasion the Twelve were *not* expelled.[7] Therefore we probably must seek the fugitives mainly among the Hellenists of the Church, and the Twelve appear to have taken an attitude different from that of those men; otherwise they could not have remained in Jerusalem. These church members driven from Jerusalem, accordingly, are mentioned as the first missionaries in Samaria (ch. 8:4), and among them only Philip is definitely named, although he probably shared this work with other Hellenistic fugitives whose names are not given. The missionary preaching of these men resulted in complete success: "Samaria has received the word of God" (ch. 8:14). It is so much the more astounding that the apostles who had remained in Jerusalem did not rest satisfied with this result, but later sent Peter and John to Samaria. The Book of Acts explains the necessity for this by saying that the Holy Spirit had not yet come upon the Samaritans (ch. 8:16), although, as previously said in verse 12, they had already believed and been baptized. So it was necessary that Peter and John subsequently lay hands upon those baptized, and only then did the converted Samaritans receive the Holy Spirit (ch. 8:17).[8] This clearly means that laying on of hands and giving of the Spirit were regarded as connected with the office of the Twelve; it shows that all missionary activity was at first considered completely dependent upon the Jerusalem

---

[7] πλὴν τῶν ἀποστόλων.

[8] See O. Cullmann, *Die Tauflehre des Neuen Testaments: Erwachsenen- und Kindertaufe (Abhandlungen zur Theologie des Alten und Neuen Testaments)*, 1948, pp. 7 f. (Eng. Tr., *Baptism in the New Testament*, 1950, pp. 11 f.).

church.[9] This fact is also of importance for the questions which arise when Paul's mission begins.

This dependence is here plainly presupposed. The presentation of The Book of Acts is merely allusive; nevertheless, it permits us to glimpse the state of affairs clearly enough. It gives the impression that those men driven from Jerusalem and now active as missionaries are to be put firmly in their subordinate position. I do not consider it improbable that the Fourth Evangelist opposes this view; when in connection with the mission in Samaria, he gives a saying of Jesus concerning "the others who have worked," while the apostles "have entered into their work" (John 4:38), he probably intends to put in the right light the work of those mostly unnamed missionaries to Samaria.

For our problem it is important that on this occasion also Peter was delegated by the Twelve in Jerusalem to go to Samaria. It is true that here again John accompanies him, but his individuality does not emerge at all in the story.

The special mention of the Hellenists in The Book of Acts— their special views as well as the particular lot which befell them— proves that even in the Primitive Church itself there were different tendencies. Peter and the Twelve as a whole appear to have taken a mediating position between the Judaizers and the Hellenists. Peter, therefore, was able to hold together the different elements.[10] As soon as James appears at the head of the Church, this situation will change.

Following the events in Samaria, Peter likewise appears in missionary activity in Lydda, Joppa, and Caesarea, where he performs several miracles and baptizes the Gentile Cornelius (Acts, chs. 9 and 10). This shows that there was a Jewish Christian mission not only among the Jews, but also among the Gentiles; and according to this narrative, Peter takes the first position also as a missionary to Gentiles and explicitly justifies this mission. The role that The Acts assigns to

---

9 P. Gaechter, "Jerusalem und Antiochia, ein Beitrag zur urkirchlichen Rechtsentwicklung" (*Zeitschrift für katholische Theologie*, 1948, pp. 1 ff.), rightly stresses the dependence of the missionary area on the Jerusalem church. The conclusions, however, which he draws for the cessation of the pre-eminence of this church from the fact that Peter, from a certain time on, left Jerusalem, cannot be defended. See below, p. 43, note 30; p. 44, note 31; p. 49, note 45. Ed. Schweizer, in *Geist und Gemeinde im N. T. und Heute* (now in press; to appear in *Theologische Existenz*), understands the connection with Jerusalem only in the sense of a connection in redemptive history.

10 See W. Grundmann, "Das Problem des hellenistischen Christentums innerhalb der Jerusalemer Urgemeinde" (*ZNW*, 1939, pp. 45 ff.).

Peter in the Primitive Church in Jerusalem has not been seriously questioned by scholars. As we shall see, the letters of Paul indirectly confirm it. But a definite objection to this picture has been raised as far as Peter's missionary activity is concerned. It has been held both in earlier as well as in quite recent times that this story, which traces the Gentile mission back to Peter, is entirely or partly the creation of the author of The Acts, who follows the tendency to make Peter parallel with Paul in every respect. Nevertheless, in the more recent studies, the fact that the Gentile Cornelius was converted by Peter is recognized,[11] even if it is claimed that the author's editorial activity, determined by theological interests, plays a more or less sizable role.[12]

After his imprisonment by Herod and his liberation, and in connection with these events, Peter leaves the Holy City, but the Book of Acts gives no information concerning the place to which he goes. The author here expresses himself in a somewhat mysterious manner: He went "to another place" (Acts 12:17).[13] The Roman Catholic exegetes—though not all of them—are accustomed to identify this "other place" with Rome.[14] Indeed, an argument recently urged

[11] See the historical kernel which W. Grundmann extracts in "Die Apostel zwischen Jerusalem und Antiochia" (*ZNW*, 1940, pp. 132 ff.). He rejects the chronology of The Book of Acts and transfers the story into the period of the events that occur after Acts, ch. 12, when Peter has already left Jerusalem.

[12] Among recent scholars M. Dibelius goes the furthest, in "Das Apostelkonzil" (*Theologische Literaturzeitung*, 1947, pp. 193 ff.); and also in "Die Bekehrung des Cornelius" (*Coniectanea Neotestamentica in honorem Antonii Fridrichsen*, 1948, pp. 50 ff.). He accepts as historical only the essential fact of the conversion of Cornelius. The entire treatment of the basic questions concerning the admission of Gentiles into the Church and table fellowship with Gentile Christians are to be ascribed, he says, to the author of The Acts and his special tendencies. J. R. Porter, on the contrary, in "The 'Apostolic Decree' and Paul's Second Visit to Jerusalem" (*Journal of Theological Studies*, 1946, pp. 169 ff.), assigns to the original narrative the treatment of the question of table fellowship of Jewish and Gentile Christians, but not that of the admission of uncircumcised persons into the Church; this, he says, was first added by the author of The Acts. See also R. Liechtenhan, *Die urchristliche Mission: Voraussetzungen, Motive und Methoden* (*Abhandlungen zur Theologie des Alten und Neuen Testaments*), 1946; he connects ch. 11:4–18 with 15:7–11.

[13] εἰς ἕτερον τόπον.

[14] J. Dupont, *Les problèmes du livre des Actes d'après les travaux récents*, 1950, p. 88: "If the apostle went to Rome at this time, one could explain the fact that Luke did not want to mention so early the city which was to represent the terminus of his story of the expansion of Christianity." J. Belser, *Die Apostelgeschichte*, 1905, p. 156, cites another argument; he refers to Ezek. 12:3: "remove from your place to another," where Babylon is meant. U. Holzmeister, on the contrary, in *Commentarius in epistolas Sanctorum Petri et Judae* (*Cursus Scriptorum*

anew[15] could speak in favour of this identification; I refer to the
parallel structure of the two parts of The Book of Acts. The first
part (chs. 1 to 12) closes with the imprisonment of Peter; the second
(chs. 13 to 28) with that of Paul. The second culminates in the arrival
of Paul at Rome (ch. 28:14);[16] so one could ask whether it is not the
journey of Peter to Rome that marks the climax of the first part: "he
departed to another place" (ch. 12:17). Nevertheless, the wording
does not permit the identification of the "other place" with Rome.
That the name of Rome was omitted for fear of the pagan authorities,
in order to keep secret the place where the head of the Church was
staying,[17] might indeed be a possible explanation. Nevertheless, it is
purely hypothetical, and would presuppose that The Book of Acts
was written during the lifetime of Peter. Again, it is possible that
Peter at this time went directly to Antioch, but the story does not say
so. It is true that Galatians 2:11 speaks of his presence in Antioch, but
concerning the time of his arrival in that city we learn nothing.[18] In
reality, that "other place" can be identified with any city of the
Roman Empire.[19] We must reckon with the possibility that even the
author himself of the Book of Acts had no definite place in mind.[20]
In that case, the statement would only mean that from this point on
Peter gives up his fixed residence in Jerusalem, and so also his position

Sanctorum), 1937, p. 62: "No argument proves that Peter left Palestine in the
year 42; how much more impossible it is to prove that he reached Rome as
early as that same year." C. Cecchelli, *Gli Apostoli a Roma*, 1938, p. 100: "Certainly it seems impossible to admit the presence of Peter in Rome before 63."

[15] R. Graber, *Petrus der Fels. Fragen um den Primat*, p. 21.

[16] See also J. Dupont, *op. cit.* above in note 14. R. Graber, *op. cit.*, p. 21, appeals to
A. Harnack, *Mission und Ausbreitung des Christentums*, 3rd ed., 1915, Vol. I,
pp. 95 f.

[17] This is the thesis of R. Graber, *Petrus der Fels*, pp. 16 ff.

[18] See below, pp. 52 f.

[19] S. G. F. Brandon, *The Fall of Jerusalem and the Christian Church*, 1951, pp. 211 f.,
225, 232, 242, assumes that Peter went to Alexandria. Matthew, who was connected with Alexandria, magnified Peter for this reason, while for the same
reason Luke, who plays Paul off against Alexandria, pushes Peter into the
background.

[20] Thus A. Fridrichsen, "Sprachliches und Stilistiches zum Neuen Testament"
(*Kungl. Human. Vetenskaps-Samfundet i Uppsala*, Aorsbok, 1943, pp. 28 ff.), assumes that it was a stereotyped manner of expression. D. F. Robinson, "Where
and When Did Peter Die?" (*Journal of Biblical Literature*, 1945, pp. 255 ff.), proposes a theory that is doubtful but worthy of mention: εἰς ἕτερον τόπον would
be identical with the "place of glory," that is, Peter died in Jerusalem at that
time, in the year 44; this, Robinson says, is the historical kernel which lies behind
the narrative of Acts 12:1-19.

in the church there; one aim, among others, was probably to escape
Jewish persecution. After this point Peter appears again in The Acts
only in ch. 15, at the so-called Apostolic Council, concerning which
we must speak later; then, strange to say, he vanishes completely
from the narrative. The above mentioned statement of Acts 12:17,
"he went to another place," thus plainly marks a transition in the
activity of Peter and also in his position in the Primitive Church.

But first we must ask how far *the letters of Paul* confirm the data
derived from the first twelve chapters of Acts concerning Peter's
function as head of the Primitive Church in Jerusalem. In so doing
we must note that the greater documentary value naturally belongs
to the letters of Paul; they are a direct and earlier source. Since they
nevertheless all belong to a later time than the events of Acts, chs. 1
to 12, we cannot expect to find in them many references to these
earliest events in the Primitive Church. For the most part, Paul mentions Peter in connection with events that occurred only in the later
period of Peter's life, events about which, except for the Apostolic
Council, the Book of Acts tells us so strikingly little. As a direct
parallel between Paul's presentation and that of The Book of Acts,
we thus have to consider only the Apostolic Council, and we shall
see what great problems result when we compare the two passages
here involved.

Yet the letter to the Galatians, in which Paul gives auto-bio-
graphical statements in support of the theological thesis he there
defends, does contain a short item which refers to that early period.
It confirms, indirectly at least, what we have learned from the first
chapters of The Acts concerning Peter's leading role in the Jerusalem
church. We hear in Galatians 1:18 ff. that during Paul's first visit to
Jerusalem, three years after his conversion, he desired to get acquainted with Cephas. It is true that according to this passage James
the brother of the Lord, who as we shall see will later succeed Peter
in the leadership of the church, is already in Jerusalem. However,
when Paul first comes to Jerusalem, James plainly does not yet occupy
an outstanding position. It seems likely that in his capacity as a
physical brother of Jesus he already is playing a certain role *beside*
Peter. For while Paul did not come to Jerusalem with the purpose
of meeting James, yet he is the only one whom Paul sees apart
from Peter. Obviously, even at this time, that is, three years after
Paul's conversion, it was already impossible for a Christian believer
to make a stay in Jerusalem without coming into contact with
James.

For the position of Peter, however, it is significant that Paul, who does not yet know him personally, undertakes the journey only on his account. Quite possibly a contributing factor may have been Paul's wish to receive from Peter personal memories of his life with Jesus. Other apostles in Jerusalem, however, could have given him such reminiscences. If he nevertheless wanted to become acquainted with Peter in particular, the reason probably was that Paul, like all converts, knew that this man then stood at the head of the Mother Church in Jerusalem. To be sure, the leadership of Peter did not have as yet the character of the later "monarchical" episcopate. The authority of his colleagues in the group of the Twelve, and probably that of James also, was too great to permit this. The role of the Twelve in Jerusalem must not be confused with that of the group of Elders who later stand at the side of the Bishop. Of that role we should probably be reminded by the added mention of John in the passages cited in The Acts. Only with this restriction can we speak of the episcopal office of Peter in Jerusalem.

The recognition of Peter's authority by Paul has the greater weight because it occurs in Galatians, in a letter, that is to say, written by Paul under special circumstances which prompted him to demonstrate in other respects his independence of the Jerusalem apostles. This independence, indeed, is clearly shown in the narrative of the conflict that broke out between Peter and Paul in Antioch (Gal. 2:11 ff.).

By the time Paul wrote his letter to the Galatians, the situation in Jerusalem had changed. Peter had long since left Jerusalem, and was now charged with the leadership of the Jewish Christian *mission*, while in Jerusalem itself James had become his successor.[21] It is therefore the more significant that Paul, in his account of that first journey to Jerusalem, nevertheless lets us see that at that time Peter still stood at the head of the Jerusalem church.

2. *The Mission in the Service of the Jewish Christian Primitive Church*

We have seen that according to Acts 8:14 Peter occasionally went, even in the first years of the Primitive Church, to the missionary district of Samaria. Thus gradually—above all by reason of the experiences which Acts, chs. 9 and 10, report that he had in Lydda,

21 F. M. Braun, *Neues Licht auf die Kirche*, 1946, p. 170, already speaks in this connection of "succession to apostles." But on this point see below, pp. 43 ff., 244 ff., 230.

Joppa, and Caesarea—he may have recognized that his real apostolic task, and probably also his spiritual gift, lay less in the leadership of the established Church than in missionary activity.[22] At any rate, it is quite remarkable that the apostle who later is regarded as the personification of organized church government in reality exercised such a function for only a short time at the beginning, and then exchanged it for missionary work. Peter is not the archetype of the church official but of the missionary.[23] The two functions—church administration and missionary work—were separated. These functions James and Peter divided among themselves. The division probably was not connected with any definite decision or act, as one might believe from later tradition, which says that the apostles, in obedience to a command of the Lord, left Jerusalem twelve years after the resurrection.[24] Although this is not completely excluded, the division was probably made rather by gradual and natural development. To this conclusion points the fact that while Peter is still the head of the Church, James already plays, as we have seen in Galatians 1:18 ff., a somewhat leading role *beside* him. According to Acts 12:17, when circumstances force Peter to be absent, James is already so to speak his substitute, for in verse 17 Peter says: "Tell this to James and to the brothers," just as it previously was said in Acts 2:37, in a way that corresponds to the existing situation: "Peter and the rest of the apostles." Certainly the final transfer of the leadership to James is connected with the imprisonment and liberation of Peter, as a result of which the latter had to leave Jerusalem.[25]

Accordingly, the vague statement of the similar passage Acts 12:17, "he went to another place," is intended simply to point out that after the liberation of Peter his final transfer to exclusively missionary

[22] According to W. Grundmann, "Die Apostel zwischen Jerusalem und Antiochia" (*ZNW*, 1940, pp. 129 ff.), Peter first went, after the events reported in Acts, ch. 12, to Joppa, Lydda, and Caesarea. Thus on this view The Book of Acts places this journey in the wrong chronological position.

[23] This fact is retained in the *Pseudo-Clementina;* no teacher is authorized without warrant from James (*Recognitions*, IV, 35); Peter is sent to Caesarea at the command of James to oppose Simon. There is thus no mention here of a transfer of the central leadership from Jerusalem to Rome. P. Gaechter, "Jerusalem und Antiochia" (*Zeitschrift für katholische Theologie*, 1948, pp. 1 ff.), does not take account of the actual role that James plays in Jerusalem.

[24] *Kerygma Petri*, according to Clement of Alexandria, *Stromateis*, VI, 5, 43. A. Harnack, *Geschichte der altchristlichen Literatur*, II, 1, 1897, p. 234, regards this tradition as very ancient.

[25] So rightly R. Graber, *Petrus der Fels*, p. 23: also W. Grundmann, "Die Apostel zwischen Jerusalem und Antiochia" (*ZNW*, 1940, p. 129).

activity took place. Preparation for the transfer had already been gradually made in the previous period.

In the later apocryphal Acts of Peter, probably the only point which we should preserve as the historical basis is the fact that in the second half of the exercise of his apostolic calling, Peter actually undertook extensive missionary journeys.

We also find this new function of Peter confirmed in the letters of Paul. In I Corinthians 9:5 he speaks of the fact that "the rest of the apostles, the brothers of the Lord, and Cephas take" their wives "with them" on their journeys. The comparison with Barnabas and Paul shows what is to be supplied: "on their missionary journeys."[26] Thus at a considerably earlier time Peter must already have begun to concentrate upon missionary work. Accordingly he, just like Paul and Barnabas, interrupted his missionary travels to go to Jerusalem for the so-called Apostolic Council.

At the time of this so-called Apostolic Council, as Paul presents it —that is, at the time when the two missionary districts, the Jewish Christian and the Gentile Christian, were separated on the basis of the friendly agreement of Galatians 2:1 ff.—the assumption of the leadership of the Church by James the brother of the Lord must already have been an accomplished fact. Already in this connection Paul indirectly ascribes to him the presiding role among the "pillars." According to the majority of the ancient manuscripts Paul here enumerates the "pillars" in the following order: James, Cephas, John. This could be mere accident. But in a text such as this one, in which the authority of the negotiating partners is not unimportant, the order does mean something. Indeed, the ancient copyists correctly sensed this. Hence arose the textual variants concerning this very point of order. The text designated by D places Peter before James in this list.[27] According to the principle that the "more difficult reading" is the more ancient, we must regard as secondary this variant attested by D. For we perceive that in later times one could take offence at this putting of James before Peter.[28]

[26] Thus we cannot speak of a transfer of the see from Jerusalem to Rome, as E. Stauffer, *op. cit.*, p. 32, suggests (see also P. Gaechter, in note 9 on p. 36). Paul is speaking of missionary journeys, which may have taken Peter in every direction, and so, of course, to Rome also. See below, pp. 77 ff.

[27] It might seem suspicious that D here, in agreement with verses 7 and 8, reads Πέτρος and not Κηφᾶς, as is customary in Paul. But P[46] also, which moreover correctly reads James in the first passage, reads Πέτρος.

[28] On the other hand, Codex Alexandrinus does not mention Peter at all. Perhaps an anti-Petrine tendency could be at work here.

At all events we conclude, from the order in which Galatians 2:9 lists the "pillars," that at the time of the incident reported it was no longer Peter but James who was the authoritative leader in Jerusalem.[29]

As far as the Jewish Christian missionary work dependent on Jerusalem is concerned, Peter stood at its head. For this reason Paul, in the same passage, Galatians 2:7 f., mentions only Peter as the organizer of the Jewish Christian mission, just as he regards himself as the organizer of the Gentile Christian mission: "(The leaders) saw that I had been entrusted with the gospel to the uncircumcised just as Peter had with that to the circumcised; for he who was at work in Peter to make him an apostle among the circumcised was also at work in me for the Gentiles."

Nevertheless, in this position as leader of the Jewish Christian mission Peter was dependent upon *Jerusalem*. This explains the fact that according to Galatians 2:12 he has to fear the "party of James" and must "dissemble" on their account.[30] In this fact, among others, lies the difference between his mission and that of Paul; he is a missionary in the closest dependence on Jerusalem, while Paul—by an understanding, it is true, with the Jerusalem "pillars"—has more independence as he carries out his preaching among the Gentiles.

The account in the letters of Paul informs us that there exists, in accord with the Jerusalem agreement of Galatians 2:9, a rather loose tie even between the Pauline mission to Gentiles and the Primitive Church of Jerusalem. This was the collection which Paul loyally made for Jerusalem in all the missionary churches that he founded. This collection for the Primitive Church was not only a humanitarian enterprise; it was conceived first of all as a manifestation of the unity of the Church, just as in Judaism the tax for the Jerusalem Temple represented the outward bond of unity for the entire company of Jewish believers dispersed throughout the Roman Empire.

---

[29] Against E. Fascher, in Pauly-Wissowa, column 1342. That James really was the authoritative leader of the entire Church is confirmed by the *Pseudo-Clementina*. See on this point H. J. Schoeps, *Theologie und Geschichte des Judenchristentums*, 1949, p. 125; *Aus frühchristlicher Zeit*, 1950, pp. 120 ff.; H. v. Campenhausen, *Zeitschrift für Kirchengeschichte*, 1950–51, p. 137. See further below, pp. 224 f., and the literature listed there in notes 18 to 22.

[30] P. Gaechter, *op. cit.*, p. 42 ff., who is concerned in his article that the role of Jerusalem should cease with the absence of Peter and pass over to Antioch, attempts to separate the party of James from James and minimize their role in Antioch. Peter, he says, yielded to them only "for the sake of desirable peace." This, however, conflicts with the fact that, as Paul explicitly writes, Peter *was afraid* ($\phi o\beta o\acute{\upsilon}\mu\epsilon\nu o\varsigma$) of the circumcision party. He has to fear these people!

The Pauline mission, which seems to have had its centre in Antioch, nevertheless remains subordinated, at least to the extent of this tie, to the leadership in Jerusalem.[31]

The bond created by the collection was the more necessary because now, as a result of the agreement reached at Jerusalem, there were two missionary organizations.[32] According to Galatians 2:9 this was the decision the apostles reached in Jerusalem: *Paul and his fellow workers were to go to the Gentiles, while the missionaries from Jerusalem went to the circumcised.* Thus there occurred even in Primitive Christianity a decisive church split, even though it took place in a peaceful way. In opposition to the later divisions, especially the great ones that go back to the sixteenth century Reformers, this first one, in spite of the complete and mutually recognized independence, nevertheless expressed the common bond in that joint task of the collection.[33] If conflicts nevertheless occurred at a later time, this was

---

[31] The reference which P. Gaechter himself gives, *op. cit.*, p. 44, to the collection and especially to Rom. 15:16 f. runs contrary to his attempt to minimize the important witness the collection gives against his thesis, according to which Jerusalem had ceased to be regarded as the metropolis.

[32] See on this point J.-L. Leuba, *L'institution et l'événement*, 1950, pp. 62 ff.

[33] If we look at the history of Christianity as a whole, it may be permissible, in view of the historical framework which is normative for the present work, to ask whether today also the Roman Catholic Church and the great Christian Council of Churches independent of Rome, frankly renouncing hope of agreement in matters of church polity and doctrine, should not seek to establish a similar tie in a shared task, which both sides would undertake with conscious surrender of any higher aim, simply as a sign of the fact that the two great separated Churches nevertheless invoke the name of the same Lord. For the unavoidable abstention of the Roman Catholic Church from all ecumenical conferences proves that as far as man can foresee, even though the effort to reach common convictions in central questions must never cease, there can no longer be a real union, at least in the points that cause that abstention. In proposing a common work which shall explicitly proclaim the unity, a proposal that perhaps even in this modest form is still utopian, we of course do not mean that the situation today is the same as it was at the time of the Apostolic Council. The gulf between the two separated Churches is unfortunately very much deeper. For here the division has not taken place in peace and "with a handshake," as it did in Jerusalem. Nevertheless, there too, in that Primitive Christian discussion concerning circumcision, what was involved was a doctrinal, *unbridged* difference, which concerned a *central point*, that is, the conception of grace. In this important respect, as the actual separation and the continued doctrinal discussions on this theme in the letters of Paul show, the discussion even on that occasion did not issue in a shared conviction. If nevertheless the decision to undertake separate labours was made *"with a handshake,"* this fact should give us food for thought even today.

because the separation could not be carried out in practice; the reason was that all of the local churches probably were already of *mixed* membership at the time of their origin. There naturally were no churches that were solely Gentile Christian, for in all the larger centres there were Jews; indeed, we know that Paul regularly addressed himself to them first of all. On the other hand, there were no churches that were solely Jewish Christian, for everywhere former pagans joined the existing Jewish Christian churches. This had not been taken into account in the separation decided upon in Jerusalem, and therefore conflict inevitably arose at once in Antioch.

Thus Jewish Christian missionaries could always build upon the fact that there were Jewish Christian members in the churches founded by Paul. They could use this fact to justify their interference in Pauline churches. Paul could have done the same thing in the churches that the Jewish Christian missionary organization had founded. In Romans 15:20, however, he explains explicitly that to him it was a matter of honour not to do so. This no doubt corresponded to the spirit of the Jerusalem agreement, even if the letter of it permitted an intervention in mixed congregations. Paul therefore always considered it an unjustified "intrusion" by the Jerusalem mission when their representatives intervened in the churches he had founded, probably with the argument that they were responsible for the Jewish Christian elements that such churches contained. Paul made but *one* exception; this was with regard to the church at Rome. Therefore he feels compelled to justify urgently this step; he appeals to his need of having in the capital city a working base for his further activity in the far West—Spain. More than elsewhere he fears that this step may cause conflicts to arise in Rome, and we shall see how justified these apprehensions were.[34]

The fact that the Jerusalem agreement did not take into account the unavoidably mixed composition of the churches has been insufficiently considered, it seems to me, in recent studies. Only this fact, however, makes intelligible the entire tragic debate whose echoes we hear in all the letters of Paul. We should emphasize here without delay that in this entire debate *Peter himself no doubt stood nearer to Paul* than did the other members of the Jerusalem mission.[35]

---

[34] The circumstances in which the martyrdom of Peter took place ("jealousy," I Clem., ch. 5) find explanation on this basis. See below, pp. 90 ff., 105 ff.

[35] J. L. Klink, *Het Petrustype in het Nieuwe Testament en de oudchristelijke Letterkunde*, 1947, actually assumes that Peter had to leave Jerusalem on account of his free attitude to the Gentile mission.

This emerges clearly from the way in which Paul speaks of him, and especially where he must blame him. Peter, of course, was bound by his position as the commissioned leader of the mission sent out from Jerusalem.

As far as the question about Peter is concerned, we must in any case be clear that from the time of the Apostolic Council there were two missionary organizations. On the one side was the one at whose head Peter stood. It depended directly on the Primitive Church at Jerusalem, which was now under the leadership of James. On the other side was the organization of Paul and Barnabas. It was independent of Jerusalem, and henceforth had with the Mother Church only the loose external connection provided by their joint work on the collection. We have seen that the Primitive Church in Jerusalem, even while Peter himself was still there, had claimed the right to exercise supervision over the mission in Samaria. Looked at in this light, the agreement of Galatians 2:9 meant that the Jerusalem group renounced in principle this claim of oversight with reference to the Pauline mission. *They henceforth acted as head only of the Jewish Christian mission carried out by Peter.*

This, however, means that in principle Paul was independent not only of the Mother Church in Jerusalem—towards which, however, he had the obligation of the collection—but especially of Peter. So we understand that when the conflict concerning table fellowship with converted Gentiles occurred at Antioch (Gal. 2:11 ff.), Peter does not appear in any sense as Paul's superior, but on the contrary *must accept a rebuke from him.* It may be that the Reformers, in their polemic against Rome, emphasized much too strongly the significance of this reprimand of Peter.[36] On the other hand, even the Church Fathers recognized its importance.[37] It may also be correct that Paul, in spite of this conflict, did not cease to designate Simon by

---

[36] See K. Holl, "Der Streit zwischen Petrus und Paulus zu Antiochien in seiner Bedeutung für Luthers innere Entwicklung" (*Gesammelte Aufsätze*, III, 1928, pp. 134 ff.).

[37] Chrysostom (Homily on Gal. 2:1; Migne, *P. G.*, LI, Col. 371 ff.) and Jerome (Epistles 86–97 and Commentary on Galatians) were so offended by this event that they used the highly artificial explanation that Peter and Paul staged the whole conflict as a trick to instruct the believers! Even Augustine (Epistles 8–19) protested against this interpretation. See J. A. Möhler, "Hieronymus und Augustinus im Streit über Gal. 2, 14" (*Gesammelte Aufsätze*, edited by J. Döllinger, 1839, pp. 1 ff.); Fr. Overbeck, *Die Auffassung des Streites des Paulus mit dem Petrus bei den Kirchenvätern*, 1877; A. M. Völlmecke, "Ein neuer Beitrag zur alten Kephasfrage" (*Jahrbuch von St. Gabriel*, 1925, pp. 69–104).

his title Cephas, Rock.[38] Nevertheless, this passage proves that from the time when each begins to exercise his parallel mission, no one can speak of a "primacy" of Peter in relation to Paul, and in Corinth Paul will no more permit a Cephas party than he will any other party whatever.[39] Was it perhaps with particular reference to this Cephas —"Rock"—party that Paul wrote I Corinthians 3:11, that no one can lay any other "foundation" except that one which is laid, Jesus Christ?

In estimating the important event of the Apostolic Conference and the separation of missionary areas made there, we have based the preceding discussions exclusively upon the information Paul gives in his letter to the Galatians. As already mentioned, however, Peter appears but once in The Book of Acts in the period following the events of ch. 12. It is the last time before he completely vanishes from the narrative. This appearance is in ch. 15, on the occasion of the Apostolic Council there described. We must inquire whether the role that Peter here plays agrees with what we have learned from the letters of Paul.

Before doing so, however, we must ask whether the meeting of the apostles recounted in Acts, ch. 15, is the same as the one in Galatians 2:1 ff. At the outset we note one fact: the answer to this much debated question does not have for our study of Peter the same fundamental importance which it naturally possesses in the endless discussions that occur in special studies, as well as in general presentations of the history of Primitive Christianity.

The question must nevertheless be raised. The detailed circumstances in the two accounts are so similar that the assumption almost forces itself upon us that both accounts must deal with the same event. If we make this assumption, undeniable differences appear between the presentation of Paul in Galatians 2:1 ff. and that of The Acts in ch. 15. These differences are hard to reconcile. It will suffice to mention here two points. According to Galatians 2:1, Paul went to Jerusalem by reason of a "revelation"; according to Acts 15:1 ff., on the contrary, he went by commission of the Church. Furthermore— and this is the most important difference—according to Galatians 2:6, no ritual requirements of any kind are imposed on Paul for his

[38] This is stressed by F. M. Braun, *op. cit.*, p. 84.
[39] Wilhelm Vischer, *Die evangelische Gemeindeordnung*, 1946, p. 18, writes on this very point: "By this teaching (that Peter should have a successor in his unique office) the papal Church enlarged the schism of the Corinthian Peter party into a yawning cleft in the foundation."

Gentile mission.[40] The fundamental question concerning the necessity of circumcision is not settled at all; the only decision is the already mentioned separation of missionary fields. The conference of Acts, ch. 15, on the contrary, ends with the passing of the so-called Apostolic Decree (ch. 15:19 f.); it requires of converted Gentiles the observation of a minimum number of regulations, chiefly of ritual character and having to do with meals.[41]

The difficulty that results from this last-named difference is further increased by the fact that in The Book of Acts itself this same "decree" is reported to Paul at a much later time, when he comes to Jerusalem for the last time (ch. 21:25). It is reported in a manner that does not at all presuppose he had previously known of it or actually taken part in deciding upon it. Moreover, it has been pointed out, especially in recent studies, that we really have to do with two quite different problems, which stand side by side in The Book of Acts without being clearly related to each other. On the one side is the question of the conversion of the Gentiles and so of the acceptance of uncircumcised men into the Church; on the other side is the question of table fellowship with them.

All these and other observations have long since stimulated the most varied attempts at a solution. We need not report here concerning them. I mention only the main types of explanation into which the most recent hypotheses can be divided.[42] According to one theory there is in the The Book of Acts absolutely no parallel to Galatians 2:1 ff. According to a second view, while the meeting of Galatians 2:1 ff. is reported in Acts, it is reported not in ch. 15, but in ch. 11:27; this passage tells of an earlier visit of Paul and Barnabas to Jerusalem, on the occasion of which they brought help to the Christian brothers who were suffering from famine. According to the third explanation, the event of Galatians 2:1 ff. is indeed identical with that of Acts, ch. 15, but on this view the differences must be explained either through a chronological inaccuracy of The Book of Acts, or by a conscious tendency of its author, or by the way he

[40] ἐμοὶ γὰρ . . . οὐδὲν προσανέθεντο ("for to me . . . they imparted nothing additional").

[41] H. Schlier, Der Brief an die Galater (Meyer's Kommentar, 10th ed.), 1949, ad. loc., seeks to solve the contradiction by emphasizing "to me" (ἐμοί): only on Paul personally was no further obligation placed.

[42] A good survey is given by Dom J. Dupont, Les Problèmes du livre des Actes d'après les travaux récents, 1950, pp. 51 ff., and also by W. G. Kümmel, "Das Urchristentum" (Theologische Rundschau, 1942, pp. 81 ff.; 1948, pp. 3 ff., 103 ff.; 1950, pp. 1 ff.).

combined various sources. We have mentioned here only the most important solutions; in reality there exist an innumerable mass of variations.[43] Indeed, it will hardly be possible to attain here to certainty, and we can proceed only by the use of hypothesis. The most probable one to me is still that one which sees in Galatians 2:1 ff. the same event reported in Acts, ch. 15; it furthermore considers correct its chronological location in Acts, ch. 15; but it transfers to a later time the passing of the Apostolic Decree, and assumes that the author of the Book of Acts erred in connecting the decree with his account of the Apostolic Council.[44]

This question is of interest to us only in its relation to our study of Peter. We must consider whether, on the assumption that in Acts, ch. 15, we have to do with the same event as in Galatians 2:1 ff., the role of Peter corresponds to that which he plays in the meeting Paul describes in Galatians 2:1 ff.

First of all, we note that Peter appears here in his capacity as missionary, and no longer as leader of the Church. This fits perfectly the picture we formed from the letter to the Galatians. In the narrative of The Book of Acts (ch. 15:7), Peter, it is true, stands up first to tell of his missionary experiences, before Paul and Barnabas begin to speak. But it is James, nevertheless, who plainly presides over the entire assembly, for he draws the conclusion from what has been heard and also formulates the "decree."[45] Even if the author of Acts was wrong in connecting this decree with this Council, he nevertheless clearly held that James then stood at the head of the Mother Church in Jerusalem, and this is the more important since in the earlier chapters of The Book of Acts this role always belongs to Peter.

We further note that in Acts, ch. 15, Peter speaks simply as the representative of the mission dependent on Jerusalem. This agrees

---

[43] Above all, in the third interpretation the event of Acts 11:27 ff. also is identified with that of Acts 15:1 ff., in which case, of course, the question arises whether the date of Acts 11:27 ff. or that of Acts 15:1 ff. is to be preferred.

[44] So on the whole, although again with various differences in chronology, H. Schlier, *Der Brief an die Galater*, 1949, pp. 66 ff.; M. Dibelius, "Das Apostelkonzil" (*Theologische Literaturzeitung*, 1947, pp. 193 ff.); M. Goguel, *La Naissance du Christianisme*, 1946, pp. 323 ff.; W. G. Kümmel (see especially *Theologische Rundschau*, 1950, pp. 27 f.). See also M. Dibelius—W. G. Kümmel, *Paulus* (Göschen), 1951, p. 118.

[45] James is thus not merely one of the "chief figures" of the Council, as P. Gaechter writes in "Jerusalem und Antiochia" (*Zeitschrift für katholische Theologie*, 1948, p. 41).

entirely with the assumption which earlier considerations have already forced upon us, that Peter as well as Paul and Barnabas *interrupted his missionary activity* to go to the Council at Jerusalem.

Among the missionaries present, it is true, he plays the leading role, since his task here is to represent the mission that reaches out from Jerusalem. In this respect the opening words of Peter in Acts 15:7 are characteristic: "Brothers, you know that in the early days God made choice among you[46] that by my mouth the Gentiles should hear the preaching of the Gospel and believe." This fits the situation perfectly. Peter, as we also learn from Galatians 2:14, in his innermost heart stood much nearer to Paul than to James in the whole question of table fellowship with Gentile Christians, and probably also in his general attitude toward the Law. In this conference, where the question at issue is the position on the problem of circumcision, he refers not to his experiences as apostle to the Jews but to the less frequent cases where he has converted Gentiles. He can also claim, in spite of the presence of Paul and Barnabas, that he has been elected to preach the gospel to the Gentiles. The right to do this *within the Jewish Christian mission* we must almost certainly concede to him, unless we banish entirely into the realm of legend the history of the conversion of Cornelius or, following the "Tübingen School," ascribe it to the author's tendency to obliterate the opposition between Jewish and Gentile Christians. We must recognize in it at least a historical kernel. Thus even before the decisive separation agreed on in Jerusalem, Peter belonged to another missionary organization than did the more independent apostle Paul.

Nevertheless, he represents a standpoint not far removed from that of Paul. To fail to take this sufficiently into account introduces great confusion into our conception of Primitive Christianity and leads to the formulation of unnecessary hypotheses. While Peter in administrative relations was dependent on the Jerusalem authorities, and for this reason has to "fear" the "party of James," nevertheless, in his relation to Gentile Christianity and the Law, he stands fundamentally much closer to Paul than to James.[47] It certainly contributed much

---

[46] According to Foakes-Jackson and Kirsopp Lake, *The Beginnings of Christianity*, *ad loc.*, we should translate: "that God has chosen us." (According to Torrey the Aramaic ב is the object.) See also II Esdras 19:7=Neh. 9:7: ἐξελέξω ἐν Ἀβραάμ: "Thou didst choose Abraham."

[47] The all too simple statement that Peter was nothing but a representative of the Jerusalem viewpoint is made under the influence of the "Tübingen school," whose influence still continues, for example, in H. Lietzmann, "Zwei Notizen zu Paulus" (*Sitzungsbericht der Berliner Akademie der Wissenschaften*, 1930, No. 8)

to the peaceful settlement of the conflict that Peter particularly, the missionary leader commissioned by Jerusalem, supported his colleagues Paul and Barnabas so powerfully at the Council.

That later at Antioch, contrary to his inner conviction, he "dissembled" due to fear (Gal. 2:11 ff.), may fit the psychological picture we get from the Synoptic Gospels—the picture of the impulsive disciple Peter, over-zealous in swearing loyalty to his Lord and yet denying him in the hour of danger. But on the other hand, it must be said in extenuation that as the missionary leader dependent on the Jerusalem church, he occupied in relation to the party of James *an infinitely more difficult position* than did the independent Paul. This conflict must have put Peter, the former and first head of the Church, in *a particularly painful dilemma*. Its difficulty we can only surmise, since we have no such extensive collection of letters from Peter as we have from Paul, and in addition, precisely by reason of his dependence on Jerusalem, he could scarcely speak so openly on this subject as Paul could.[48] We must keep this in mind in our interpretation of later events.

In any case, we dare not forget this aspect if we wish to form a correct picture of Peter the apostle. We must think of it particularly when we attempt to form a conception of Peter's apostolic travels, concerning which we know so little. Mediators always have a particularly difficult position, and Peter, as we have seen,[49] probably had to mediate between the Hellenists and the Judaisers from the very beginning of the Primitive Church.

With regard to the Apostolic Council, which falls in the first half of this activity, our conclusion is that the data of The Book of Acts

and also in his *Geschichte der alten Kirche* (Eng. Tr., *History of the Early Church*, 4 vols., 1937–51). See for the opposite view E. Hirsch, "Petrus und Paulus" (*ZNW*, 1930, p. 23). In ancient times this false picture was spread especially by the *Pseudo-Clementina*, and above all by the ancient source of the Preaching of Peter that they incorporated. See on this point H. J. Schoeps, *Theologie und Geschichte des Judenchristentums*, 1949, pp. 118 ff. I believe that especially in the conception of the atoning death of Jesus it was Peter in particular who stood very close to Paul. This is indicated by the fact that The Acts in the first chapters seems to have preserved the memory that Peter described Jesus as παῖς ("servant"), that is, as the Isaian Suffering Servant of God. See on this point below, pp. 66 ff.

[48] A recollection of this, however, could be preserved in I Clem., ch. 5, where it says that Peter "on account of unjustified jealousy had to suffer not one or two but manifold troubles." Is this not a reference to the way that Peter was *constantly* torn between the two positions? See below, p. 107.

[49] See above, p. 36.

concerning the position of Peter agree on the whole with the earlier observations which we made independently of Acts, ch. 15. This is true, no matter how we think in detail concerning other aspects of the relation between Galatians 2:1 ff. and The Book of Acts. In any case this very point confirms the assumption that the author of The Book of Acts placed the Apostolic Council (except for the decree) in its correct chronological location.

Concerning the entire second half of Peter's missionary activity we know, as has been said, practically nothing but the fact that it occurred. The introduction of I Peter (ch. 1:1) seems to presuppose that he did mission work in Asia Minor. Nothing definite concerning it is known. His name is chiefly connected, however, with three mission centres in particular: Antioch, Corinth, and Rome.

We have heard that at the time of the incident reported in Galatians 2:11 ff., Peter was at *Antioch*, where he had to submit to the rebuke by Paul. He may already have been there at an earlier time, but we have no certain information on this point. The Book of Acts only tells that those scattered as a result of the Stephen persecution came to Antioch (Acts 11:19). Since it is reported in ch. 8:1 that the apostles were not then dispersed with the others, the assumption that Peter founded the church at Antioch, while not explicitly excluded, is nevertheless hardly probable.[50] One could ask at the most whether Peter *subsequently* did not have to confirm the conversion of the Antioch Christians, and so indirectly confirm the foundation of that church, somewhat as he did in Samaria in the position he then held as head of the Primitive Church in Jerusalem. We possess no information, however, of any such role. In any case, the assertion that Peter founded the church at Antioch appears relatively early, in Origen, and then later in Eusebius, Chrysostom, and Jerome.[51] The church of Antioch can thus make a legitimate appeal to this rather ancient tradition. It must be emphasized that Antioch can thus raise in principle the same claim as Rome, since this Petrine tradition for Antioch is attested at least as well, if not better. We shall have to recall this in Part Two of this book, for this question is not without importance in reference to the exclusive claim that the Roman

[50] It is denied also by H. Katzenmayer, "Die Beziehungen des Petrus zur Urkirche von Jerusalem und Antiochien" (*Internationale kirchliche Zeitschrift*, 1945, pp. 116 ff.).

[51] Origen, *Homily on Luke*, VI, c (Migne, *P. G.*, XIII, Col. 1814 ff.); Eusebius, *Ecclesiastical History*, III, 36, 2 and 22; Chrysostom, *Homily on Ignatius* (Migne, *P. G.*, L, Col. 591); Jerome, on Gal. 2:1 (Migne, *P. L.*, XXVI, Col. 340); *De viribus illustribus*, 1 (Migne, *P. L.*, XXIII, Col. 637).

Bishop lays to Matthew 16:16 ff. Only from this point of view are we interested in the assertion that Peter founded the church at Antioch. As a historic fact, however, the claim cannot be supported.

We have already seen that it is arbitrary to identify the "other place" of Acts 12:17 with Antioch.[52] The only certain thing, accordingly, is that Peter made a stay in Antioch. He probably also maintained rather close relations with this church, as the incident of Galatians 2:11 ff. presupposes. Indeed, his position as leader of the Jewish Christian mission necessarily brought him into particularly close connection with this church, which by reason of its racial composition was the centre not only of the Gentile Christian but also of the Jewish Christian mission.

Did Peter visit *Corinth* during his missionary travels? Neither The Book of Acts nor Paul's Letters to Corinth say so, and in any case, The Book of Acts appears to know nothing of any participation by Peter in the *founding* of this church. Its narrative in ch. 18 speaks only of the conversion of the Corinthians through the preaching of Paul; it scarcely leaves room for a parallel activity of Peter. The statements of I Corinthians also exclude Peter's participation in the founding of the church. In I Corinthians 3:6 Paul writes: "I planted, Apollos watered, God gave the increase"; and in I Corinthians 4:15: "Even if you have countless masters in Christ, yet not many fathers. For in Christ Jesus *I*[53] became your father through the Gospel." Here Paul clearly considers himself the sole founder of this church.

In I Corinthians, however, there is support for the assertion often made that *later* Peter also came to Corinth and worked there as a missionary. In the first chapters of I Corinthians we are told of parties which were formed in Corinth, and ch. 1:12 mentions, in addition to a Paul party and an Apollos party and the uncertain "Christ party," a "Cephas party." Does not the existence of this Cephas party presuppose the presence and preaching of Peter at Corinth? The fact that this letter directed to the Corinthians makes special mention of the example of Cephas, who takes his wife with him in his missionary travel (I Cor. 9:5), could argue for this view; one could, if pressed for evidence, also cite the noteworthy fact that Paul, as he himself says (I Cor. 1:14 ff.), baptized only Gaius, Crispus, and Stephanas and his household. Could it be that he was of the opinion that to baptize with the Spirit was the business of the Twelve, as in Samaria (Acts 8:14 ff.)?[54]

On these brief indications, however, we can build at best only a

[52] See above, pp. 37 f. [53] ἐγώ. [54] See above, pp. 35 f.

hypothesis. The assertion that Peter was in Corinth has been made, as we have said, by the above named scholars. It has also found vigorous opponents.[55] In ancient times it first appears about the year 170, in the letter of Dionysius of Corinth to the Romans. Eusebius cites it: "By this exhortation you have united closely the tree of the Corinthians and that of the Romans—trees that were planted by Peter and Paul. For both (apostles) taught in the same way, in that they planted in our Corinth, and after they taught together in Italy they suffered martyrdom together."[56] The value of this testimony is lessened at once by the manifestly false assertion, refuted not only by The Book of Acts but also by Paul, that the church in Corinth was *founded* by Peter together with Paul.

Altogether apart from this assertion of Dionysius, however, we must take a stand concerning the deduction which draws from the existence of the Cephas party in Corinth the conclusion that Peter later made a stay in this city. This conclusion is in any event not convincing. For all Jewish Christian missionaries regarded Peter as the head of their mission; no doubt they took particular pleasure in setting him up against Paul as the "true apostle," and they probably appealed to his special relations with Jesus, as we can perceive indirectly in the letters of Paul. On this account Paul has to protest that he, too, has "seen Christ" (ch. 9:1). But Peter himself certainly did not belong to those against whom Paul turns with particular severity in his letters to the Corinthians. He is not one of those whom Paul elsewhere characterizes as "false brothers," who have followed him everywhere to discredit his person and above all his apostolic authority.[57]

[55] Among the defenders of the thesis that Peter made a stay in Corinth I name particularly Eduard Meyer, *Ursprung und Anfänge des Christentums*, Vol. III, pp. 441 (note 1), 498 ff.; A. Harnack, *Mission und Ausbreitung des Christentums in den ersten Jahrhunderten*, 3rd ed., 1915, p. 63, note 2; H. Lietzmann, "Die Reisen des Petrus" (*Sitzungsbericht der Berliner Akademie der Wissenschaften*, 1930, pp. 153 ff.); J. Zeiller, *L'Eglise primitive* (*Histoire de l'Eglise*, Vol. I, p. 227; Eng. Tr., *History of the Primitive Church*, Vol. I, 1942, p. 233); recently, H. Katzenmayer, "Das Todesjahr des Petrus" (*Internationale kirchliche Zeitschrift*, 1939, p. 85), and especially his article, "War Petrus in Korinth?" (*Internationale kirchliche Zeitschrift*, 1943, pp. 20 ff.). Among those who oppose this view should be named above all W. Bauer, *Rechtgläubigkeit und Ketzerei im ältesten Christentum*, 1934, p. 117; M. Goguel, "L'apôtre Pierre a-t-il joué un rôle personnel dans les crises de Grèce et de Galatie?" (*Revue d'Histoire et de Philosophie religieuses*, 1934, pp. 461 ff.); *La naissance du Christianisme*, 1946, pp. 335 ff.

[56] *Ecclesiastical History*, II, 25, 8.

[57] So rightly E. Hirsch, "Petrus und Paulus" (*ZNW*, 1930, pp. 63 ff.), in opposition to H. Lietzmann, *op. cit.*, in note 55 above. See also on this subject above, pp. 50 f.

In Galatians likewise the polemic of Paul does not have Peter in view. Here, too, there is no need to assume, as various historians have asserted, that Peter had been in Galatia. Nothing indicates that the incident at Antioch led to a breaking of the Jerusalem agreement and so to a break between Paul and Peter.[58] Peter himself, according to all that we have concluded concerning his attitude, is probably not directly responsible for the counter-mission of the "false brothers" who sought everywhere to sabotage the work of Paul. Presumably they took particular pleasure in appealing to the name of Peter, and probably represented in some way that he had sent them. But doubtless this was not so. It is sufficient, therefore, to assume that these people came into the Corinthian church that Paul had founded.

This, however, does not exclude the possibility that in the course of his journeys Peter once visited Corinth (and also Galatia). Since he stood at the head of the Jewish Christian mission, we certainly must reckon with this possibility. But it cannot be proved either from the existence of the Cephas party nor by any other indications.[59] The stay in Corinth, accordingly, can neither be definitely asserted nor denied, but it may be considered as possible.

We thus see that since our ancient sources give only extremely meagre reports, we can say nothing certain concerning this entire missionary activity of Peter. It is particularly significant that these sources, the Letters of Paul and The Book of Acts, are also completely silent concerning the stay of Peter in *Rome*, which later was universally accepted. This question, however, we shall consider in connection with the special chapter which we shall devote to Peter the Martyr.

Thus far, then, we have established that *the Apostle Peter, in the first period after the death of Jesus, leads the Primitive Church in Jerusalem; he then leaves Jerusalem, where the leadership passes over to James; and from then on, by commission of the Primitive Church and in dependence on it, he stands at the head of the Jewish Christian mission.*

---

[58] This is rightly emphasized by M. Goguel, against H. Lietzmann, *op. cit.*

[59] H. Katzenmayer, *"War Petrus in Corinth?"* (see above, note 55), uses among other things to support his argument I Clem., ch. 47, where it says that Apollos was approved by the apostles. It is claimed that he could have met Peter only in Corinth. Nevertheless, it is by no means established: 1. that Peter is here meant; 2. that he could have met Apollos only in Corinth.

3. *The Question of the Apostolic Commission*

It still remains to answer the question which we put at the opening of this chapter: does this apostolic activity of Peter—in its two successive expressions, the leadership of the Church and the missionary preaching—go back to a special commission which Peter received from Jesus?

We have seen that as far as the unique position of Peter *during the lifetime of Jesus* is concerned, we can no longer determine how far it has its basis in his peculiar character traits, and how far in the distinction Jesus gave him by bestowing on him the name "Rock." We have shown that both answers must be taken into account, and furthermore that at that time Peter's unique position did not yet take the form of setting him over the other disciples. For the period after the death of Jesus, however, where Peter for a time actually *led* the Jerusalem church, the question concerning his commission presents itself in another way.

The Primitive Church has the consciousness that everything which happens in it and to it belongs to the central redemptive action which is being fulfilled in Christ.; all these events are an integral part of the redemptive plan of God. Thus is explained the lofty apostolic consciousness of Paul, who does everything in the conviction that he is an instrument of the God-guided Christ Event. We are not so well informed concerning the consciousness of any other apostle, but in view of the fact that the first Christians always regarded themselves as the true people of God, we may assume without question that Peter also was conscious in his action of being specially commissioned by Christ.

Does this consciousness of Peter's also rest upon the experience of a special call, as we know it does in the life of Paul? Does not such an experience, in the Primitive Christian view, belong as a matter of course to the apostolic office?[60] If so, then with reference to Peter the further question arises: Did his actual call to be an apostle come through the *incarnate* Jesus, if it refers also to the time after his death? Or did it first come from the *risen* Christ? Or must we reckon with *both*?

The saying to Peter concerning the Church (Matt. 16:16 ff.) will be discussed in detail in Part Two of this book. It must be mentioned here merely in a preliminary way, in so far as it presents a basis for a

[60] See below, pp. 215 f., and the literature cited there; also, A. Fridrichsen, "The Apostle and his Message" (*Uppsala Universitets Arsskrift*, 1947).

commission from the historic Jesus which Peter must carry out after Jesus' death. The action of Peter in condemning Ananias and Sapphira (Acts 5:1 ff.) could be explained very well as the fulfilment of the promise there given.

Since, however, that passage is so vigorously disputed, we shall adduce it here, as we did in Chapter One, in a merely provisional manner. Here, as there, we must say that even if we make no use of this saying, the result remains on the whole the same; the less disputed commission of Jesus to Peter to "strengthen the brothers" (Luke 22:31 f.),[61] and furthermore, the undeniable fact that Jesus gave him the name "Rock" (even without the reason added in Matt. 16:17 ff.), are sufficient to trace the unique position of Peter as leader of the Jerusalem church back to a commission that the earthly Jesus gave.

Thus, even apart from Matthew 16:16 ff., we find it clearly possible that Peter's leading position in the Primitive Church rests upon the distinction or commission which Jesus gave to his disciple Peter even during his earthly life and which Peter has occasion to fulfil only after the Lord's death.

It has of course been asserted that the saying in Luke 22:31 f., as well as all the passages in the Synoptic Gospels which give Peter a place of distinction, were later creations of the Church; in this way, it is claimed, the Church later provided a legal authorization by the historical Jesus for the leading role that Peter had actually played in Jerusalem. But we have already seen that the distinction given Peter by the name Cephas can in no case be so explained. Altogether apart from the *confirmation* that Matthew 16:17 ff. gives, we have to do here with a fact which is not open to doubt.

More recent studies, on the other hand, do indeed assume a special commission, but transfer it into the period after the death of Jesus, when the *risen* Christ appears and gives a commission to Peter. This commission, it is claimed, the gospel tradition later transferred back into the life of Jesus. We shall have to return to this explanation with reference to its special bearing on Matthew 16:17 ff. For the time being, however, we must say of it that at least the giving of the name Cephas cannot thus be ascribed to the Primitive Church.[62]

We possess, it is true, trustworthy traditions which attest that the

---

[61] See above, pp. 26 f.

[62] K. Goetz, *op. cit.*, pp. 67 f., does indeed take even this final step; he considers it possible that the giving of the name is to be ascribed to the Primitive Church. See above, p. 20.

risen Christ gave to Peter a special distinction and a special commission. Here at any rate we stand upon solid ground, and although, as I am convinced, we must acknowledge that the historical Jesus had already given Peter a special distinction, so that the question does not confront us in the form of an unconditional alternative, nevertheless for the foundation of the apostolate of Peter a *greater and more direct significance* attaches to the commission from the *Risen* One. We recall that it was an important but not the exclusive[63] prerequisite of the call to apostleship that one had seen the *risen* Lord (I Cor. 9:1; Acts 1:22).[64] So a call to a special apostolic office by the *Risen* One appears almost a necessity, even if, as was doubtless true of Peter, a distinction had already been conferred by the earthly Jesus.

In view of the great significance which the appearance as such has for the call to apostleship, one can ask whether every appearance of the Risen One was not regarded in itself as a "call." In the case of Paul, at least, it is certain that the appearance of the Risen One, whom he sees on the way to Damascus, coincides with his call. As far as Peter is concerned, however, the two facts are reported separately; they are not combined in the sources we possess concerning the appearances of the Lord that he saw. We hear on the one hand, in I Corinthians 15:5 and in Luke 24:34, that Christ appeared to Peter; on the other hand, in John, ch. 21, we hear that on the occasion of an appearance at which, in addition to Peter, other disciples also are present, the special commission is given to him to "feed the sheep of Christ." It has indeed been asserted that these passages all deal with one and the same event. Before we decide concerning this hypothesis, we desire first to evaluate separately the fact reported in I Corinthians 15:5 and Luke 24:34, to see what it teaches as to the role of Peter in the Primitive Church.

First of all, it cannot be emphasized too strongly that according to I Corinthians 15:5 Peter is the *first* one to whom the Lord appeared.[65]

---

63 H. v. Campenhausen, "Der urchristliche Apostelbegriff" (*Studia theologica*, Lund, 1948, pp. 112 f.), rightly emphasizes how unsatisfactory is the recent custom which simply identifies apostle and witness to the resurrection. Sufficient to prove it unsatisfactory is the fact, clear from I Cor. 15:3 ff., that not all whom Paul enumerates as witnesses of the resurrection became apostles. (Note the more than five hundred brethren in I Cor. 15:6).

64 See K. H. Rengstorf, Article on ἀπόστολος ("apostle") in G. Kittel's *Theologisches Wörterbuch zum N.T.* See further on this question below, pp. 215 f.

65 F. Kattenbusch, "Die Vorzugstellung des Petrus und der Charakter der Urgemeinde zu Jerusalem" (*Festgabe für K. Müller*, 1922, pp. 328 ff.), and "Der Spruch über Petrus und die Kirche bei Matthäus" (*Studien und Kritiken*, 1922,

The risen Christ thereby put the seal, so to speak, upon the distinction which during his lifetime he had given Peter by naming him Cephas. The passage I Corinthians 15:5, which names Peter as the first witness of the resurrection, is perhaps the earliest Christian text that we possess; it is older than the letters of Paul and he explicitly quotes it as a citation from the earlier tradition transmitted to him.[66]

It is noteworthy that the Gospels do not tell of this appearance to Peter alone. Even Luke gives no account of it, although he briefly mentions the fact. In his Gospel the Eleven report to the returning Emmaus disciples: "the Lord has really arisen, and he has appeared to Simon" (Luke 24:34).

Was this appearance perhaps reported in the lost ending of Mark? The question forces itself upon us when we note that in two passages, and indeed in the last verses preserved for us, this Gospel makes special mention of Peter in connection with the journey to Galilee which Jesus announces is to occur after his resurrection.[67] In the former passage, Jesus says: "When I have risen I will go before you to Galilee" (Mark 14:28). It is Peter himself who in the following verse continues the conversation with a reference to this promise. In the other passage the young man at the grave who is clothed in white announces: "Say to his disciples *and to Peter* that he goes before you to Galilee" (Mark 16:7). In view of this one can indeed ask whether we must not postulate that a narrative concerning an appearance of Christ to Peter stood at the end of the Gospel of Mark.[68]

p. 130), wrongly denies this; he attempts to take the εἶτα ("then") in a non-chronological sense. For the enumeration in I Cor. 15:5, however, the order is obviously significant. Hence A. Harnack, "Die Verklärungsgeschichte Jesu," (*Sitzungsbericht der Preussischen Akademie der Wissenschaften*, 1922, p. 68); K. Goetz, *op. cit.*, pp. 4 ff.; and E. Stauffer, *op. cit.*, pp. 6 ff., have given proper attention to the fact that Peter is the first one who saw the Risen One. K. Goetz rightly points out, in opposition to F. Kattenbusch, that the words "last of all" in I Cor. 15:8 make it impossible to dispute the chronological element in the enumeration.

[66] According to our previous discussion it is in any case impossible to assert with E. Stauffer, *op. cit.*, p. 6, note 14, that "here speaks no partisan but rather an opponent of Peter." Neither the authors of the formula cited nor Paul, who cites it, can be called an opponent of Peter.

[67] The view championed by E. Lohmeyer, *Galiläa und Jerusalem*, 1936, that the appearance to Peter occurred in Jerusalem, is improbable both for this reason and on other grounds.

[68] So E. Stauffer, *op. cit.*, pp. 11 f. K. Goetz, *op. cit.*, p. 73, also considers this possibility. So does N. Huffman, "Emmaus Among the Resurrection Narratives" (*Journal of Biblical Literature*, 1945, pp. 205 ff.); to be sure, he rather arbitrarily seeks also to identify the unnamed disciple of the Emmaus story with

To assume this implies that the conclusion of Mark is lost and that
it contained the narrative of the appearance to Peter that I Corinthians 15:5 and Luke 24:34 mention. This naturally remains a hypothesis, but much speaks for its correctness. It is certainly noteworthy
that we possess no story concerning an event of such importance as
the first appearance of the Lord, especially since it concerned the very
disciple who shortly before had denied him. It may also justifiably
be asked whether that event has left in the texts *preserved* any other
traces, in addition to the two brief notices in I Corinthians and the
Gospel of Luke.

First of all, it is believed that we possess more than a trace, that we
actually possess an expansion of the actual narrative of that appearance, in the supplementary Chapter 21 of the Gospel of John.[69] It is
indeed striking how, in the second part of this story, Peter is pushed
into the foreground, but then, in the same way as in the corresponding passages of the preceding chapters, is put parallel to the Beloved
Disciple. The threefold assertion of love for his Lord and the three-
fold commission undoubtedly stand in intentional contrast to the
three-fold denial.[70] It may be that the miraculous catch of fish which
is reported in the first part of the story connects also with the story
of Peter's call in Mark 1:16 ff., and is intended to indicate the fulfilment of the promise there given concerning the "fishers of men." In
its present form the chapter certainly bears the "Johannine" stamp
in both its parts, and especially in the second one; it may be, however,
that a Marcan narrative concerning the appearance of Jesus to Peter
lies at the basis of the story.[71] Nevertheless, it must be conceded that
this assumption also is only a hypothesis, inasmuch as this entire

Peter and makes Luke responsible for the transfer of the scene to Jerusalem. On
the other hand, K. L. Schmidt, *Kanonische und apokryphe Evangelien und Apostelgeschichten*, 1944, p. 27; N. B. Stonehouse, *The Witness of Matthew and Mark to
Christ*, 1944, pp. 86 ff.; W. C. Allen, in *Journal of Theological Studies*, 1946,
pp. 46 ff.; 1947, pp. 201 ff., deny that the original conclusion of Mark has been
lost. They hold rather that the words "for they were afraid" (ἐφοβοῦντο γάρ)
are the intended conclusion of the Gospel.

[69] This was already the view of Arnold Meyer, *Die Auferstehung Jesu Christi*,
1905, p. 168.

[70] This interpretation, which had already been given by Ambrose and Augustine,
is rejected by M. Goguel, *L'Eglise primitive*, 1947, p. 192; *Jesus*, 1950, p. 390.
See on the other side J. Bernard, *A Critical and Exegetical Commentary on the
Gospel According to St. John*, 1928, Vol. II, p. 690.

[71] E. Stauffer, *op. cit.*, p. 16, actually writes that "The author of John, ch. 21, knew
and used the lost ending of Mark." See also A. Harnack, *Lukas der Arzt*, 1906
(Eng. Tr., *Luke the Physician*, 1907).

story, as it is preserved for us in the Gospel of John, deals neither with the first appearance nor with one supposed to have been granted to Peter alone. If, however, it should prove correct that the connection of the commission given to Peter with the words referring to the Beloved Disciple is due merely to the author of the supplementary chapter, then this hypothesis would have a greater degree of probability. This would be the more likely since later eastern sources also tell of an appearance of Christ to Peter connected with a special commission.[72]

We cannot here attain complete certainty. Nor can we do so with regard to the further assumption that the gospel tradition transferred the important event of Christ's appearance to Peter back into the earthly life of Jesus, so that this event now finds expression in the narrative of Luke 5:1 ff. concerning the miraculous catch of fish at the Sea of Gennesaret,[73] further in the narrative of Matthew 14:28 concerning the walking on the sea,[74] especially in the transfiguration story,[75] and finally—concerning this we shall have to speak further at a later point—in the saying to Peter concerning the Church in Matthew 16:17 f. and in the commission of Luke 22:32.[76]

Not without reason, moreover, have I Peter 1:3 and II Peter 1:16 ff. been connected with the vision seen by Peter.[77]

Even if all these hypotheses are correct, it still remains puzzling

---

[72] See below, p. 63, note 83.

[73] So J. Bernard, op. cit., p. 690, and E. Stauffer, op. cit., p. 17.

[74] H. Sasse, "Die erste Erscheinung des Auferstandenen" (Theologische Blätter, 1922, p. 59).

[75] Thus Wellhausen, Das Evangelium Marci, 1909, p. 71, already assumed, as did R. Bultmann, Geschichte der synoptischen Tradition, 2nd ed., 1931, p. 278, and K. Goetz, op. cit., pp. 76 ff., that the transfiguration story arose from the memory of a resurrection appearance. On the contrary, A. Harnack, "Die Verklärungsgeschichte Jesu, der Bericht des Paulus und die beiden Christusvisionen des Petrus" (Sitzungsbericht der Preussischen Akademie der Wissenschaften, 1922, pp. 76 ff.), and Ed. Meyer, Ursprung und Anfänge des Christentums, Vol. I, 1921, pp. 152 ff., hold that the transfiguration story is good tradition; they actually assume the opposite position, that this event from the earthly life of Jesus is the basis of the vision that Peter had after the Lord's death. E. Lohmeyer, "Die Verklärung Jesu nach dem Markusevangelium" (ZNW 1922, pp. 185 ff.), also disputes the derivation of the transfiguration story from a resurrection appearance; nevertheless, he does not consider the transfiguration historical, but holds that this narrative arose from Jewish conceptions.

[76] See E. Stauffer, op. cit., pp. 20 ff., 18 ff.; R. Bultmann, Theologie des Neuen Testaments, 1948, p. 46 (Eng. Tr., Theology of the New Testament, Vol. I, 1951, p. 45).

[77] Usually an allusion to the transfiguration story is seen here. K. Goetz, op. cit., p. 89, is probably correct in opposing this view.

that the memory of the appearance to Peter has been preserved only
in scattered traces. Hence an explanation has quite properly been
sought for this remarkable gap in our tradition. What interest may
have been present to push into the background this usually important
event? Some have thought of a conflict between adherents of James
and of Peter.[78] But this could hardly have occasioned the silence that
exists in the writings in which one expects a narrative concerning
this event. A more likely contributing factor could have been the
inner compulsion not to be content with *one* witness for so important a fact as an appearance of the Risen One, but to introduce two
or more (Deut. 19:15), so that the preference would be given to
appearances before more than one witness.[79] In this connection,
furthermore, one has recalled also the discussions between Jewish
and Gentile Christians, such as are attested for us from the beginning
of the second century and probably reach back into even earlier
times. We learn from the *Pseudo-Clementina* that in Jewish Christian
circles the apostolic rank of Paul was contested by pointing out that
it rests only upon a vision.[80] Thus in this Jewish Christian writing the
value of visions in general is denied by Peter himself.[81] If such considerations were already raised in the controversies between Paul and
the Judaizers, then we definitely must reckon with the possibility
that the Jewish Christian gospel tradition tended to prefer not to base
the authority of Peter upon a commission given only by the Risen
One. Connected with this could be the fact that the significance
which in the later life of Peter attached to the appearances in general,
and above all to that first appearance of Jesus, was curtailed. Recent
scholars, indeed, believe that they find in Peter a special capacity for
visions.[82]

---

[78] A. Harnack, *op. cit.*, p. 70.

[79] See Lyder Brun, *Die Auferstehung Christi*, 1925, p. 22; K. Goetz, *op. cit.*, p. 74.

[80] *Homilies* 17, 19. See O. Cullmann, *Le problème littéraire et historique du roman
pseudo-clémentin*, 1930, pp. 248 f. C. Holsten, *Die Messiasvision des Petrus und die
Genesis des petrinischen Evangeliums*, 1867, p. 120, already explained on this basis
the suppression of the report of Christ's appearance to Peter.

[81] *Recognitions*, II, 62. Peter here tells that at the Sea of Gennesaret he believed
in his spirit that he saw Jerusalem and Caesarea, and when he later came to
Caesarea, the reality did not correspond at all to what he had seen in vision.

[82] K. Goetz, *op. cit.*, pp. 98 ff., recalls in this connection Acts, chs. 10 and 11; 12:9;
in addition, he recalls the passage mentioned in the Pseudo-Clementine *Recognitions*, II, 62, and especially the Apocalypse of Peter, which likewise presupposes
that Peter was regarded as a "seer" in a special sense; he also recalls the famous
Quo-vadis story from the *Actus Vercellenses*, ch. 35. See also W. Grundmann,
"Die Apostel zwischen Jerusalem und Antiochia" (*ZNW*, 1940, p. 135).

However that may be, and in spite of its meagre emphasis in the Primitive Christian writings,[83] the unshakable fact remains that Peter was the first to see the Risen One. In the earliest period this certainly must have contributed greatly to his *authoritative position* in the Primitive Church.[84] For at that time there certainly existed no reason to belittle visions as a basis of apostolic authority. The enumeration of the appearances, which constitutes the content of the oldest Christian document preserved to us (I Cor. 15:3 ff.), proves on the contrary what a great value was ascribed to these events as an attestation of the resurrection. Thereby the witnesses themselves also received special distinction. It is clear that he to whom had been given the dignity of being the *first* witness of that mighty fact was regarded, just because of this chronological preferment, as the one especially commissioned by Christ to hand on this witness. Accordingly, even this first appearance of Jesus, which has sufficient documentary proof, would suffice to give the foundation for the authoritative position of Peter as the leader of the Church.[85] There is the additional point, however, as we have seen, that in John, ch. 21, we actually possess a tradition according to which Peter was explicitly commissioned by the Risen One to "feed his sheep." Whether this deals with the same event or not, the deeper meaning of the special commission to Peter in John, ch. 21, is in any case already implied in the fact of the appearance to Peter that I Corinthians 15:5 reports.

We still must consider the wording of the commission as it is formulated in John 21:16 ff.: "Feed my sheep." It has rightly been

[83] As attestations from *later* times should be named here: The Gospel of Peter, the Ethiopic Apocalypse of Peter, Pistis Sophia, the Syriac Treasure Cave (translation by C. Bezold, 1883, p. 71), and especially the mediaeval writing of the Arab Asch Shahrastani on "Religious Sects and Philosophical Schools" (*Die Religionsparteien und Philosophenschulen*, German translation by Th. Haarbrücker, I, 1850, pp. 360 f.). See on this subject F. Haase, *Apostel und Evangelisten in den orientalischen Ueberlieferungen*, 1922, pp. 208 ff.; further, K. Goetz, *op. cit.*, pp. 89 f.—According to A. Harnack, "Petrus im Urteil der Kirchenfeinde des Altertums" (*Festgabe für Karl Müller*, 1922, pp. 2 ff.), even Celsus knew of the appearance of Christ to Peter. He holds that Origen *Contra Celsum*, II, 55, refers to Peter.

[84] The importance of the first appearance of Christ for the Petrine question is also correctly understood by E. Seeberg, "Wer war Petrus?" (*Zeitschrift für Kirchengeschichte*, 1934, pp. 571 ff.). J. Klausner, *From Jesus to Paul*, translated from the Hebrew (1943), also emphasizes it strongly. In general, he ascribes to Peter the exclusive leading role in the origin of the Primitive Church.

[85] Therefore a special call separate from the appearance, such as is postulated by A. Fridrichsen, *op. cit.* (see above, p. 56, note 60), would not be absolutely necessary.

pointed out[86] that the Damascus Document discovered in 1910,[87] which in connection with the recent manuscript discoveries in Palestine takes on particular importance,[88] speaks of the leader of the fellowship as the "shepherd of the flock." His duty is to proclaim the word, explain the Scripture, and exercise community discipline (ch. 13:9).

The command to feed the sheep includes the two activities which we have shown to be the successive expressions of Peter's apostolate: leadership of the Primitive Church in Jerusalem and missionary preaching. We perceive from the conceptions which lie behind John, ch. 10, that not only the leadership of the Church but also the missionary work belongs to the office of shepherd. The linguistic usage, which there designates the Jews first of all as the "sheep," proves that both functions have primarily in view *the Jews*. In this sense Jesus speaks in the Synoptic Gospels of the "lost sheep of the house of Israel" (Matt. 10:6), to which he knows himself to be sent; this does not exclude but is in fact the foundation for his responsibility for the "other sheep" who do not belong to this flock (John 10:16).

We thus see that the commission given by the Risen One may be applied to the functions which the apostle Peter actually exercised successively in his relations with the Jewish Christian Primitive Church.

So we reach the conclusion that *his position probably rests in the first instance upon a commission from the risen Lord*; at the same time, however, the fact that the earthly Jesus gave him the special distinction of the name Cephas, and further the representative role of the former disciple of Jesus, helped to confer authority on him as leader of the Church and as missionary.

Even here, however, we must emphasize that in John, ch. 21, the commission to feed the sheep also has connected with it the prediction of the martyrdom of Peter. This, however, means that the commission to the Apostle Peter *has a time limitation*. That is, it is limited to *the period of the foundation of the Church*. We shall have

[86] E. Stauffer, *op. cit.*, pp. 4 ff.

[87] W. Staerk, *Die jüdische Gemeinde des neuen Bundes in Damaskus*, 1922; L. Rost, *Die Damaskusschrift*, 1933.

[88] From the almost endless literature on this subject I cite A. Dupont-Sommer, *Aperçus préliminaires sur les manuscrits de la Mer Morte*, 1950; P. Kahle, *Die hebräischen Handschriften aus der Höhle*, 1951; and the survey articles of W. Baumgartner, "Der Palästinische Handschriftenfund" (*Theologische Rundschau*, 1948–49, pp. 329 ff., and 1951, pp. 97 ff.), which are quite complete down to 1951.

to take this aspect into account in Part Two of the present book.[89]

4. The Theological Views of the Apostle

In view of the nature of the sources it would be a rash undertaking to try to present a "theology" of the apostle Peter. Even if one holds that the First Epistle of Peter was written by the apostle himself, the basis for this undertaking is too small. However, some very important points can be established with a relatively high degree of certainty.

More than once I have pointed to the fact that Peter was not far removed from Paul in theology.[90] Indeed, I should go even further and definitely assert that within the circle of the Twelve he is the one who in this respect *stands closest to Paul*.

We have already emphasized his *universalism*. In opposition to a widespread error, this is definitely attested, not only by The Book of Acts, which since the days of the Tübingen School scholars have regarded as tendential in this respect and therefore have wanted to discard as a proof, but also by Paul. Precisely in connection with the conflict at Antioch, Paul expressly recognizes that Peter in theory represents the same universal viewpoint that he himself holds. Indeed, he reproaches Peter at Antioch only because he has been untrue to his conviction out of fear of the people from James. It may even be true that his origin in the city of Bethsaida,[91] with its Hellenistic influences, had much to do with shaping this broad-minded attitude of Peter. But this attitude doubtless requires a deeper foundation.

Peter obviously learned from his Lord that the divine election of the Jewish people for a definite function does not mean that God's gracious working is limited exclusively to this one people. It was not in vain that Peter was an eye-witness. He understood Jesus' words concerning those who come from the East and the West to recline at table with Abraham, Isaac, and Jacob in the Kingdom of God (Matt. 8:11). He also understood the meaning of that scene with the centurion of Capernaum. Therefore later, in the Primitive Church at Jerusalem, he took a mediating attitude between the group of the

---

[89] See below, pp. 207 ff.
[90] See above, pp. 45, 49 f. On this subject, see E. Hirsch, "Petrus und Paulus" (*ZNW*, 1930, pp. 63 ff.).
[91] See above, p. 22.

Judaizers and that of the Hellenists, and he was able to hold the two sections together as long as he stood at the head.[92]

But his universalism seems to me to have a still deeper *theological* anchor. This was in the understanding he achieved that Christ's death was the atoning death. Perhaps he was the first one to grasp this after Jesus' resurrection. It is true that it has become common custom to regard the apostle Paul as the creator of the theology of the cross. Indeed, he did in a powerful way put his mighty spiritual gift of systematic thought at the service of the preaching of the cross, and Peter certainly never received the rabbinical training of a Paul. But I do not believe that Paul was the first one to understand the death of Jesus as an atoning death for the forgiveness of sins. On the contrary, I am inclined to ascribe to Peter this particular and fundamental insight. Although he was anything but a theologian, I think that here too he should be given the place of honour at the beginning of all Christian theology.

At this point we must keep in view the significance of the earliest Christology we possess, the explanation, namely, of the person and work of Jesus by the figure of the "Suffering Servant of God" prophesied by Second Isaiah. This explanation, in addition to the Son of Man Christology, certainly goes back to Jesus himself.

I believe, indeed, that this earliest Christological explanation can be shown to have the apostle Peter as its author.

The Book of Acts proves that in the earliest times of Primitive Christianity there existed an explanation of the person and work of Jesus which we may designate somewhat incorrectly as Christology of the "Servant of God," *ebed Yahweh*, in Greek *pais theou*; more correctly, we could call it "Paidology." We could even go further and assert that this is probably the earliest solution of the Christological question. The narrative concerning the conversion of the Ethiopian eunuch (ch. 8:26 ff.) is the chief evidence that Jesus was explicitly identified with this *ebed Yahweh* in the first century, and that the vivid memory was clearly preserved that Jesus himself so understood his divine mission.

Apart from this narrative, however, there are other passages in The

---

92 See on this point W. Grundmann, "Das Problem des hellenistischen Christentums innerhalb der Jerusalemer Urgemeinde" (*ZNW*, 1939, pp. 45 ff.), and "Die Apostel zwischen Jerusalem und Antiochia" (*ZNW*, 1940, pp. 110 ff.). W. Grundmann distinguishes, in partial dependence on E. Lohmeyer, *Galiläa und Jerusalem*, 1936, three groups in the Primitive Church: the Galilean, the Judaistic, and the Hellenistic.

Book of Acts which, while they do not all contain an actual quotation from the Book of Isaiah, are nevertheless of the greatest importance for our question. In them Jesus openly receives the very title
ebed Yahweh, "Servant of God," in the Greek rendering, *pais tou
theou*. In the Septuagint the latter phrase translates the expression
which Deutero-Isaiah uses for the Suffering Servant of God who
takes upon himself in a substitutionary way the sins of the people.
There are four passages of this kind; it is significant that all four occur
in the same section, in chs. 3 and 4, and that Jesus is called *pais tou
theou* in no other book of the New Testament. He first appears in this
capacity in Acts 3:13, where reference is made to Isaiah 52:13, then
in chapter 3:26, where we really have to do with a Christological
title. The expression here is Jesus—Pais, exactly as one will be accustomed later to say Jesus—Christ. Similarly one gets the clear impression in the next chapter, 4:27 and 4:30, that *pais* is used almost as a
fixed term; it is tending to become a proper name, just as occurred
in the case of the word Christ. This confirms the existence of a very
early Christology on the basis of which Jesus was called *ebed Yahweh*.
It will disappear in the following period, but its use must reach back
into the very earliest times.

It is probably no accident that of those four passages, the only ones
in the New Testament to designate Jesus as *pais*, *two stand in speeches
which are ascribed to the Apostle Peter* and two in a prayer spoken in
unison by the Jerusalem group of disciples when Peter is present.
The Book of Acts, which has twenty-eight chapters, uses this expression in no other passage. It is probably not too bold to conclude
from this fact that the author thus preserves the clear memory that it
was the apostle Peter who by preference designated Jesus as the "Suffering Servant of God."[93] This agrees with what we know of Peter.
According to Mark 8:32, he is the very one who at Caesarea Philippi
showed so little understanding of the necessity for Jesus to suffer.
He took Jesus aside to say to him: "This will not happen to you," so
that Jesus, who saw in him the same tempter who already had tried
once to turn him from his path, had to repulse him with the words:
"Away, Satan!" We understand that the same apostle who later,
according to I Corinthians 15:5, was the first to see the Risen One,

[93] For more detail on this, see O. Cullmann, "Jésus serviteur de Dieu" (*Le Dieu
vivant*, No. 16, 1950, pp. 19 ff.). There is a tendency toward this view in
W. Grundmann, *ZNW*, 1939, p. 53. According to R. Bultmann, *Theologie des
Neuen Testaments*, 1948, p. 51 (Eng. Tr., *Theology of the New Testament*, p. 50),
this passage suggests not the Suffering Servant but the Son of David (Acts 4:25).

thereafter in the light of the resurrection was also the *first* to preach the actual necessity of the suffering and the death of the Lord, concerning which during the lifetime of Jesus he wanted to know nothing. We understand the fact that he made the suffering and death of Jesus the very *centre* of his explanation of the earthly work of Jesus. The backward look to the denial likewise makes this easily intelligible, especially since as early as Luke 5:8 the story appears to presuppose a particular intensity in Peter's consciousness of sin.

In this connection it is interesting to recall the further fact that The First Epistle of Peter cites with emphasis the passages from the Book of Isaiah which refer to the *ebed Yahweh* (I Pet. 2:21 ff.). This observation remains of value for our study quite independently of the question whether this Epistle is genuine or not. For even if Peter did not write it, nevertheless the anonymous author who ascribed it to him was acquainted with the fact that Peter by preference applied to Jesus the conception of the Suffering Servant of God.

The Christology of the apostle Peter, if we may dare to use this expression, was quite probably dominated by the concept of the *ebed Yahweh*. If so, he who tried to turn Jesus from the way of suffering, and denied him at the decisive moment of the Passion story, was the first one who, after Easter, grasped the necessity of this offence. He could not express this conviction better than by using the designation *ebed Yahweh*; this was the more true since he must have known how great an importance Jesus himself had attached to the ideas connected with the phrase.

Thus of Peter's theological attitude we may say, though with some caution, that the rock apostle, who in Jerusalem was the leader of the first church and doubtless was the first to preach Christ there, was not merely the organizer with only practical interests, as we usually conceive him. Here too the picture of the Prince of the Church is incorrect. He certainly possesses a much greater significance in the foundation of Christian theology than we are accustomed to assume. If we had from him a large collection of letters, such as we have from Paul, it is certain that a different picture would result. It is true that he did not have the technical theological training of Paul, who studied with the Rabbis. But the great idea which Paul later worked out in systematic form very probably occurred first to the fisherman Peter.

This remains true although the same insight was revealed to Paul independently of Peter. For we must believe Paul when he writes in Galatians that he received his gospel neither from men nor through human mediation (Gal. 1:12). By the term gospel, Paul, in keeping with his whole theology, can only have meant its central point, the word of the cross.

Later times have often been unjust to Paul by putting him in the shadow of Peter. Theologically, however, scholars seem to me to be unjust to Peter when they put him entirely in the shadow of Paul, or regard him as Paul's antagonist devoid of understanding for the great Pauline insights.

Chapter Three

PETER THE MARTYR

1. *The Problem*

EVEN in our presentation of the missionary activity of Peter the fragmentary character of our sources drove us to inferences and hypotheses. Such measures are still more necessary when we undertake to determine definitely the circumstances of his death. It is noteworthy that the single ancient source from which we might expect information on this point, The Book of Acts, is as silent concerning the death of Peter as it is concerning that of Paul, and we have at our disposal no other ancient texts which report this event of such importance for the Primitive Church. We nevertheless must discuss the indirect witnesses from which conclusions concerning the martyrdom of Peter are drawn. The following sections must inquire whether or not these deductions are correct.

The question is the more important since it is closely connected with the problem of Peter's stay in Rome. The solution of this problem, in turn, is linked with the interpretation, so weighted with historical consequences, which the Roman Catholic Church still gives to the saying of Jesus in Matthew 16:17 ff. concerning the rock upon which the Church of Christ is to be built.

This explains also the violent emotion with which the whole discussion has been carried on ever since the stay of Peter in Rome was questioned, first by the Waldensians in the Middle Ages and in more recent times by Protestant scholars. All too often there slip into this debate, consciously or unconsciously, considerations of a confessional kind, which belong in the realm of Protestant-Catholic controversy. In opposition to such an attitude it must be emphasized at the outset that we are dealing here with a purely historical question, which can be handled only with the objective methods of scientific historical study. To proceed thus is the more important since the question whether the papal claim of power over the Christian Church is justified is much too complex for us to answer simply by solving the problem whether Peter ever made a stay in Rome. In reality the decision can only be reached by explaining Matthew 16:18 ff.

If indeed it could really be proved that Peter never set foot in Rome at all, as many have often asserted and still assert, then of course the papal claim could not be *historically* defended at all; it would have to rest content with a purely dogmatic justification,[1] which has often been declared sufficient from the Catholic standpoint.[2] Only in this respect is the theological and ecclesiastical question linked with the result of historical study. The opponents of the papal claim may always be greatly tempted to make the matter easy for themselves by thinking that perhaps in this radical way the entire problem can find a relatively quick solution. On the other hand, however, we must say that if scientific reasons indicate the correctness of the later tradition, which asserts that the apostle Peter made a stay in Rome, this alone, as we have noted, is still insufficient to furnish a foundation for the papal claim.

It is fortunate, therefore, that with the passage of time those confessional and polemic considerations have largely disappeared from scholarly discussion. In recent years it has actually been Protestant or confessionally independent scholars who have carried on the debate among themselves; in this debate some answer affirmatively the question whether Peter made a stay in Rome, while others deny it.[3] In the following pages we shall first sketch briefly the history of the problem, and then investigate whether it is possible to derive from the archaeological and literary witnesses to which appeal is made at least indirect indications of a Roman stay of our apostle.

2. History of the Debate Whether Peter Resided in Rome

The question was first raised in the Middle Ages by Christians for whom the Bible was the sole norm, the Waldensians. We can understand why it was they who did so. As we have seen, the New Testament nowhere tells us that Peter came to the chief city of the

---

[1] We may add that more or less cautious doubts have been expressed from time to time even by Roman Catholic scholars. Ellendorf goes the furthest in this sense, in *Ist Petrus in Rom und Bischof der römischen Kirche gewesen?*, 1941 (cited by F. Chr. Baur, *Paulus*, 2nd ed., 1867, Vol. II, p. 322; Eng. Tr., *Paul*, Vol. II, 1875, p. 296).

[2] See below, p. 232.

[3] For the earlier history of the problem I refer to K. Heussi, *War Petrus in Rom?*, 1936, pp. 8 ff., and F. Chr. Baur, *Paulus*, 1845, pp. 671 ff.; 2nd ed., 1867, Vol. II, pp. 316 ff. (Eng. Tr., *Paul*, Vol. II, 1875, pp. 291 ff.)

Empire and stayed there. For the Waldensians, the silence of the
Bible was quite decisive.[4] Later, in the year 1326, Marsilius of Padua,
in his *Defensor Pacis*, expresses cautious doubts as to whether Peter
was ever in Rome. He, too, appeals to the fact that from the sacred
Scriptures nothing can be proved concerning this. Perhaps—but
only perhaps— he did come to Rome and was bishop there; that
he held such a position can be asserted with certainty only for
Antioch.

For the next two hundred years we hear nothing of a real attack
upon the tradition. Not until 1519–1520 does an anonymous author
write an essay contending "that the apostle Peter was never in
Rome."[5] For him, too, as for the Waldensians, the chief argument
is the silence of the sacred Scripture. He is not content to express
doubts; like them, he goes on to direct denial. Sebastian Franck
echoes his thesis and his line of argument.[6] It might seem striking,
on the contrary, that the Reformers took no special interest in this
problem. In their fight against the Pope they did not build upon this
comfortable argument. This is the more noteworthy since they
plainly had at least a trace of doubt concerning the stay of Peter at
Rome.[7] Thus Luther writes: "There are some scholars who say that
Peter never came to Rome. And it is said to be difficult for the Pope
to defend himself against such scholars. I will not here be judge of the
question whether Peter was there or not. St. Paul alone was certainly
there, as Luke writes in The Book of Acts and Paul himself in his
letters; he can very well have instituted the Church and the bishops
at Rome."[8] He further reports that in Rome he saw and heard that
one did not know the graves of Peter and Paul.[9] But he adds: "And
the apostles St. Peter and St. Paul may then lie in Rome or not; that

---

[4] Concerning the opposition by the Waldensians see P. Moneta of Cremona
O. P., *Adversus Catharos et Waldenses*, V, 2, Rome, 1743, p. 411.

[5] His pseudonym is Ulricus Venelus Minhoniensis. See Melchior Goldast,
Monarchia S. Romani Imperii, Vol. III, 1613, where the tract is printed on
pp. 1–16.

[6] See H. Oncken, "Sebastian Franck als Historiker" (*Historische Zeitschrift*, 1899,
p. 412).

[7] In any case it is incorrect when J. Zeiller, *L'Eglise primitive* (*Histoire de l'Eglise*,
Vol. I, 1946 ed., p. 227; Eng. Tr., *History of the Primitive Church*, Vol. I, 1942,
p. 233) writes that the denial of the Roman residence of Peter arose in the
time of the Reformation, as a part of the Protestant polemic against the papal
primacy.

[8] M. Luther, *Wider das Papsttum vom Teufel gestiftet*, 1545 (Weimar edition, 54),
cited from E. Mülhaupt, *Luthers Evangelien-Auslegung*, 1947, Vol. II, p. 551.

[9] See below, p. 132.

makes no difference."[10] The Protestant church historian from the second half of the sixteenth century, Flacius Illyricus, writes somewhat cautiously in 1554 that it is "not absolutely certain" that Peter was in Rome,[11] while later in his great work, the Magdeburg *Centuries*, he speaks of the martyrdom of Peter and Paul in Rome.[12] A scientifically grounded challenge to the Roman tradition about Peter is offered only at the end of the seventeenth century, by the Reformed scholar Friedrich Spanheim.[13] His arguments are in part worthy of note even today. In spite of his critical spirit, however, the eighteenth century took no great interest in this problem. Gibbon, in his great *History of the Decline and Fall of the Roman Empire*,[14] does indeed question whether any of the disciples of Jesus became a martyr outside of Palestine. In the year 1804 the Göttingen scholar in ancient philology, J. G. Eichhorn, champions the view that the stay and martyrdom of Peter at Rome were not historical events, but were erroneously deduced from 1 Peter 5:13.[15] F. Schleiermacher, in his lectures concerning church history, numbers himself among those who "doubt the entire account of Peter's stay in Rome."[16] Likewise, W. M. de Wette, in his *Introduction to the New Testament*,[17] declares that the alleged fact, already improbable in itself, is a "saga." The majority of the Protestant theologians at the beginning of the nineteenth century, however, affirm the tradition of the Roman stay of Peter. Chief among them are the two great church historians A. Neander and J. Gieseler. The former describes the denial of the tradition as "hyper-criticism,"[18] the latter as an expression of "partisan polemic."[19] So much the more impressive was the attack

---

[10] He further writes in the same passage (Mülhaupt, p. 552): "They lie and invent hundreds and thousands of things about St. Peter himself, so that the idea has occurred to me that neither St. Peter nor St. Paul laid the first stone of the Church of Rome. Perhaps a disciple of the apostles came from Jerusalem or Antioch to Rome . . ."

[11] *Historia certaminum inter Romanos Episcopos etc., de primatu seu potestate papae bona fide ex authenticis monumentis collata*, p. 267.

[12] *Centuries*, I, Book II, pp. 28 and 527.

[13] *Dissertatio de ficta profectione Petri apostoli in urbem Romam deque non ura traditionis origine*. See *Works*, II, 1703, Col. 331 ff.

[14] *History of the Decline and Fall of the Roman Empire*, 1776 ff.

[15] *Einleitung in das neue Testament*, Vol. I, 1804, pp. 554 f. See also Vol. III, 1812, pp. 603 f.

[16] *Complete Works*, Section One, Vol. XI, edited by E. Bonnell, 1840, p. 69.

[17] *Einleitung in das N. T.*, p. 314.

[18] *Geschichte der christlichen Religion und Kirche*, Vol. I, 1826, p. 317.

[19] *Lehrbuch der Kirchengeschichte*, Vol. I, 2nd ed., 1827, p. 189.

which the Tübingen theologian F. Chr. Baur undertook against the tradition in 1831, in connection with his Hegel-inspired view of Primitive Christianity.[20] The ensuing discussion, however, was burdened by debate over this exaggeration of the opposition between Jewish Christianity and Gentile Christianity. The thesis of Baur, therefore, was almost universally rejected.

In the following period the denial of the Roman tradition about Peter was almost universally abandoned. A man like Ernest Renan assumed as a fact Peter's stay in Rome, and in the year 1897 it was the critical Protestant theologian and historian A. Harnack who wrote the notable sentence that the denial of the Roman stay of Peter is "an error which today is clear to every scholar who is not blind." So one had the impression that the tradition was finally confirmed. Harnack was of the opinion that "the martyr death of Peter at Rome was once contested by reason of tendentious Protestant prejudices, and then by reason of tendentious critical prejudices."[21] Although for most persons the question appeared settled, it was raised anew by the confessionally independent historian Ch. Guignebert in 1909, in his book on "The Primacy of Peter and the Coming of Peter to Rome."[22] He answered the question in the negative. In Germany C. Erbes and in Switzerland P. W. Schmiedel likewise opposed Harnack's conclusion.[23]

However, it seemed again that the last word had been spoken on the side of Harnack and the Roman Catholic tradition when Harnack's successor, the Protestant theologian H. Lietzmann, published in 1915 his important book, *Petrus und Paulus in Rom* (second ed., 1927). Lietzmann uses his archaeological and especially his wide liturgical knowledge to illuminate the question. He comes to the conclusion that the testimony from the year 170 concerning the graves

[20] "Die Christuspartei in der Korinthischen Gemeinde, der Gegensatz des petrinischen und paulinischen Christentums in der ältesten Kirche, der Apostel Petrus in Rom" (*Tübinger Zeitschrift für Theologie*, 1831, pp. 137 ff.). See also *Paulus, der Apostel Jesu Christi*, 1845, pp. 212 ff.

[21] *Die Chronologie der altchristlichen Literatur bis Eusebius*, Vol. I, 1897, p. 244, note 2.

[22] *La Primauté de Pierre et la venue de Pierre à Rome.*

[23] C. Erbes, "Petrus nicht in Rom, sondern in Jerusalem gestorben" (*Zeitschrift für Kirchengeschichte*, 1901, pp. 1 ff., 161 ff.). In his publications concerning the date of the death of the apostles Paul and Peter (*Texte und Untersuchungen*, 1899) and concerning the graves of the Apostles in Rome (*Zeitschrift für Kirchengeschichte*, 1924, pp. 38 ff.), Erbes is much more reserved in his judgment concerning the question of the Roman stay of Peter. P. W. Schmiedel's view is found in "War der Apostel Petrus in Rom?" (*Protestantische Monatshefte*, 1909, pp. 270 ff.); also in Th. K. Cheyne's *Encyclopaedia Biblica*, IV, pp. 459 ff.

of the two apostles at Rome must be correct. That is, the two apostles were actually buried in the two places in Rome which today are reverenced as their graves, Peter at the Vatican, Paul on the road to Ostia.

Nevertheless, this did not put an end to the dispute. It has been continued, chiefly among Protestant theologians, in connection with Lietzmann's book. In the year 1930 appeared my own essay concerning First Clement, ch. 5.[24] In it I conclude, from what we derive by inference from this text concerning the circumstances of the two martyrdoms of Peter and Paul, that Rome was the place of their martyrdom. E. Molland agreed with me,[25] and with the addition of some supplementary points A. Fridrichsen also accepted my interpretation.[26]

Lietzmann's conclusion, however, was opposed by Adolf Bauer, in the series of "Vienna Studies,"[27] by Ch. Guignebert,[28] and further by H. Dannenbauer.[29] The latter actually formulated the result of his investigation in these words: "Every little village in Palestine can claim with greater justification than can the imperial capital to be the place of Peter's death." To the opponents of the Lietzmann thesis belong further J. Haller[30] and E. T. Merrill,[31] while G. Krüger[32] championed the traditional thesis, chiefly on the basis of First Clement.

The chief arguments of the opponents of the tradition were gathered up in 1936 by Karl Heussi in the brochure he directed against Lietzmann, *War Petrus in Rom?* ("Was Peter Ever in Rome?"). This writing, which announced as its reliable result that "Peter never set foot in the city on the Tiber," aroused great interest. It called Lietzmann himself to the field of battle with a reply, "Peter:

---

[24] O. Cullmann, "Les causes de la mort de Pierre et de Paul d'après le témoignage de Clément Romain" (*Revue d'Histoire et de Philosophie Religieuses*, 1930, pp. 294 ff.).

[25] *Theologische Literaturzeitung*, 1937, columns 439 ff. There is also given here a good discussion of the controversy between Lietzmann and Heussi.

[26] "Propter invidiam. Note sur I. Clém. V" (*Eranos Rudbergianus*, 1946, pp. 161 ff.).

[27] "Die Legende von dem Martyrium des Petrus und Paulus in Rom" (*Zeitschrift für klassische Philologie*, 1916, pp. 270 ff.).

[28] "La sépulture de Pierre" (*Revue historique*, 1931, pp. 225 ff.).

[29] "Die römische Petruslegende" (*Historische Zeitschrift*, 1932, pp. 239 ff.); "Nochmals die römische Petruslegende" (*Historische Zeitschrift*, 1931, pp. 81 ff.).

[30] *Das Papsttum*, Vol. I, 2nd ed., 1950, pp. 1 ff., 472 ff. (polemic in a disagreeable and irritated tone).

[31] *Essays in Early Christian History*, 1924, pp. 267 ff.

[32] "Petrus in Rom" (*ZNW*, 1932, pp. 301 ff.).

Roman Martyr" (1936).[33] In the following years Heussi attempted again to defend his thesis that the assertion of the martyrdom of Peter at Rome is nothing but a legend.[34]

The war did not completely stop the discussion. Lietzmann, who died in 1942, took no further part. K. Heussi, however, has continued even into recent years to publish a series of articles which defend his position with vigour and with partly new arguments.[35] In 1942 M. Dibelius published an essay concerning "Rome and the Christians in the first century."[36] In it he too concerns himself chiefly with the most important indirect witness for the martyrdom of Peter, First Clement, ch. 5. He sides with Lietzmann, but seeks to explain the brevity of the notice chiefly by the literary character of the author.

In addition we should mention particularly the various studies which the Old Catholic scholar Katzenmayer published, during and after the war, in the *Internationale Kirchliche Zeitschrift*. In them he seeks in his own peculiar way to establish that both the Roman stay, which he assumes, and the death of Peter occurred long before the Neronian persecution, in the year 55.[37]

Since the end of the war the chief interest has focused on the excavations under the Church of St. Peter in Rome. Since, as we shall see, the results were kept an official secret much too long, while it

[33] "Petrus römischer Märtyrer" (*Sitzungsbericht der Berliner Akademie der Wissenschaften*, 1936, pp. 392 ff.).

[34] "War Petrus wirklich römischer Märtyrer?" (*Christliche Welt*, 1937, columns 161 ff.); *Neues zur Petrusfrage*, 1939. On the whole controversy between Heussi and Lietzmann, see also R. Draguet, *Revue d'Histoire ecclésiastique*, 1938, pp. 88 ff.

[35] *Deutsches Pfarrerblatt*, 1949, p. 82: "Das Grab des Petrus;" *ib.*, p. 301: "'Papst' Anenkletus I. und die Memoria Petri auf dem Vatikan;" *ib.*, p. 420: "Die Nachfolge des Petrus;" *ib.*, p. 501: "Der Stand der Frage nach dem römischen Aufenthalt des Petrus"; *Theologische Literaturzeitung*, 1952, pp. 67 ff.: "Gal. 2 und der Lebensausgang der jerusalemischen Urapostel."

[36] "Rom und die Christen im 1. Jahrhundert" (*Sitzungsbericht der Heidelberger Akademie der Wissenschaften, Philologisch-historische Klasse*, 1942.

[37] There appeared even before the war: "Zur Frage, ob Petrus in Rom war," 1938, pp. 129 ff.; "Das Todesjahr des Petrus," 1939, pp. 85 ff. We have already mentioned, p. 54, note 55, the essay, "War Petrus in Korinth?" (1943, pp. 20 ff.). See also "Die Schicksale des Petrus von seinem Aufenthalt in Korinth bis zu seinem Märtyrertod", 1944, pp. 145 ff.; "Die Beziehungen des Petrus zur Urkirche von Jerusalem und zu Antiochien," 1945, pp. 116 ff. In further articles in the same journal the author seeks to prove that a primacy of Rome or of its bishop is lacking until the end of the third century. Unfortunately, in the essays that are of interest to us in our study, the argument is often somewhat forced, and at times is built on arguments from silence.

was officially announced by the Pope that the grave of Peter had been found, the study of the literary sources has become somewhat hesitant in recent years. Scholars obviously desired to await the publication of the results of the excavations.[38]

The general tendency, even with regard to the literary witnesses, seems indeed to be moving in the direction of accepting the Roman stay of Peter. C. T. Craig expresses himself in favour of it in his presentation of Primitive Christianity.[39] So do H. von Campenhausen[40] and C. King.[41] M. Goguel, in his great book on the rise of Christianity,[42] reaches no decision, but rather inclines to strong scepticism toward the traditional theory.[43] As the latest study we mention the investigation by the Danish scholar, J. Munck, *Petrus und Paulus in der Offenbarung Johannis* ("Peter and Paul in the Book of Revelation," 1950); he makes the interesting attempt to find in Revelation 11:3–13 the earliest testimony to the martyr death of the two apostles at Rome.

3. The Literary Sources

What *sources* are to be considered in our study of the question of the Roman residence and martyrdom of Peter? The earliest Christian writings, the *letters of Paul*, contain no direct or indirect data whatever concerning a stay of Peter in Rome or concerning his death. At the time when Paul writes I Corinthians, Peter is making missionary journeys in company with his wife (I Cor. 9:5). That is all we hear in the letters of Paul concerning this period of Peter's life.

---

[38] On the Roman Catholic side, however, interest in I Clement, ch. 5, has continued: M. Schuler, "Klemens von Rom und Petrus in Rom" (*Trierer Theologische Studien*, I, 1941, pp. 94 ff.); L. Sanders, *L'hellénisme de S. Clément de Rome et le paulinisme*, 1943 (see below, pp. 93 f.); O. Perler, "Ignatius von Antiochien und die römische Christusgemeinde" (*Divus Thomas*, 1944, pp. 442 ff.); St. Schmutz, "Petrus war dennoch in Rom" (*Benediktinische Monatsschrift*, 1946, pp. 122 ff.); B. Altaner, "Neues zum Verständnis von I Clem. 5, 1–6, 2" (*Historisches Jahrbuch*, 1949, pp. 25 ff.).

[39] *The Beginning of Christianity*, 1943, p. 266.

[40] *Verkündigung und Forschung*, 1946–47, p. 230.

[41] "The Outlines of New Testament Chronology" (*Church Quarterly Review*, 1945, p. 149).

[42] *L'Eglise primitive*, 1947, pp. 203 ff. (a good presentation of the problem).

[43] A similar scepticism, although in its final result rather favourable to the acceptance of a late arrival of Peter in Rome and his martyrdom there, is represented by G. Miegge in his popularly written but quite instructive little writing, *Pietro a Roma* (n. d.).

From the mere fact of this silence we cannot infer that a Roman stay by Peter or his martyrdom there is excluded. The failure of the letters of Paul to report his *death* is no cause for wonder; we scarcely can assume that Peter died so long before Paul[44] that the latter could have spoken of it explicitly or by implication in a letter, even had he had occasion to do so. The situation is different with regard to the *stay* of Peter in Rome. There is, to be sure, no *a priori* necessity to claim that Paul must have spoken of this fact. Nevertheless, we possess from him a letter addressed to the Roman church itself, and although we must be cautious in using so-called arguments from silence, yet it must be said that if Peter were actually sojourning at the time in the church of the capital city, it would be astonishing for Paul not to refer to him at all in this letter, which greets by name numerous Roman Christians.[45]

The assertion that he purposely refrained from speaking of Peter, because the latter by his Judaizing preaching had worked in Rome in a way contrary to the teaching that Paul set forth in his letter to the Romans, shatters on the already established fact that Peter cannot be called a mere Judaizer; in reality, he stood much closer to the theology of Paul than to that of James.[46] The opposition that Romans expresses to Judaizing teachings no more presupposes a stay of Peter in Rome than does the anti-Judaizing polemic of the letters to Corinth or Galatia become intelligible only on the supposition of a personal stay of Peter in Corinth or in Galatia—although as far as

[44] K. Heussi, indeed, thinks that Peter died as early as the year 55. He holds that when Paul wrote Galatians, Peter was no longer alive (Gal. 2:6: "whoever they *were*"); *Theologische Literaturzeitung*, 1952, pp. 67 ff. H. Katzenmayer (see above, p. 76) also accepts the early date of 55 as the year of Peter's death.

[45] Even if ch. 16 should not belong to Romans, the silence concerning Peter in the other chapters would still be amazing. (T. W. Manson gives noteworthy new arguments—especially in the light of papyrus manuscript P[46], known since 1935—in favour of the old hypothesis that ch. 16 went to Ephesus; see his essay, "St. Paul's Letter to the Romans—and Others," in *Bulletin of the John Rylands Library*, 1948, pp. 3 ff.). Nor can this silence be explained by the hypothesis of Graber (see above, p. 38).

[46] H. Lietzmann, "Zwei Notizen zu Paulus" (*Sitzungsbericht der Berliner Akademie der Wissenschaften*, 1930, No. 8), has proposed the probably untenable thesis that Paul wrote Romans to oppose the Jewish Christian propaganda carried to Rome by Peter, and so to avert the danger that his gospel might find closed doors at the outset. E. Hirsch, "Petrus und Paulus" (*ZNW*, 1930, p. 63), makes extensive concessions to this thesis, but nevertheless reacts against Lietzmann's presentation, which would make of Peter a full-fledged Judaizer. In so doing Hirsch opposes at the same time Ed. Meyer's hypothesis, which sees Peter behind the false teachers in Galatia.

Corinth and Galatia are concerned we have not excluded the possibility that Peter at an earlier time made a stay in these regions.[47] In any case, we are forced to deny that Peter was present in the Roman church *at the time when Paul wrote Romans to them*; otherwise he could not possibly have been omitted from the list of the persons addressed in this letter.

It still does not follow, be it noted, that the tradition concerning the stay and martyrdom of Peter at Rome is therefore to be entirely rejected; the conclusion applies only to the time of writing of Paul's letter to Rome. Theoretically, Peter could have been in Rome prior to the sending of Paul's letter; he could then have left the capital city, and only later have returned there and suffered martyrdom. Nevertheless, this is not probable.[48] In any case, Paul's writing forces us in our study to the following conclusion: *at the time when Paul wrote his letter to Rome, Peter was not there*; if he came there at all, this can only have happened either before or, more likely after that time.

For any stay of Peter in Rome, however, Romans 15:20 comes indirectly into consideration. We have already seen[49] that Paul here excuses himself for coming to a church which he has not founded. Such a step he previously has avoided; he probably regarded this, in keeping with the spirit of the Jerusalem agreement, as irreconcilable with his apostolic honour. In view of this fact, and in connection with what we have concluded from Galatians 2:9, we probably are justified in concluding that the parallel Jewish Christian mission of the Jerusalem group regarded the Roman church as their field, since this church, which probably arose apart from the missionary programme, had an original membership of Jewish Christians.[50] Since the Jewish population of Rome was then large—it is estimated at 30,000 to 40,000[51]—such an original membership may certainly be assumed. This is especially convincing when we consider that when Paul writes his letter to Rome, the Jewish Christians are quite strongly represented in the Roman church along with the Gentile

[47] See above, p. 55.

[48] C. Cecchelli, *Gli apostoli a Roma*, 1938, p. 64, also declares this impossible.

[49] See above, p. 45.

[50] If the Jews from Rome who, according to Acts 2:10, were present at Pentecost in Jerusalem, brought the gospel to the capital city, this too points to Jewish Christian origin. So F. J. Foakes-Jackson, *Peter: Prince of Apostles*, 1927, p. 196.

[51] J. Juster, *Les Juifs dans l'empire romain*, 1914, pp. 209 f., actually speaks of 50,000 to 60,000.

Christians.[52] Of course, we dare not conclude with finality from this fact that Peter came to Rome or even founded that church. But we must ask whether in this case it is not probable that in his capacity as leader of the Jewish Christian Jerusalem-based mission, Peter himself did not at some time come to this church, founded as it was by Jewish Christians and still containing a strong Jewish Christian membership. Such a visit is especially likely since it was the capital city which was in question. If there was a Jewish Christian mission and if Peter was entrusted with it, then his coming to Rome, while not proved by these facts, is an assumption strongly suggested, especially if at a certain time traces of internal difficulties appear.[53]

Nothing more can be derived from the letters of Paul in either a positive or a negative sense.

*   *   *

If anywhere in our ancient sources, we should expect a report concerning the end of Peter's life in *The Book of Acts*. As a matter of fact, however, it does not contain even the slightest indirect allusion to a stay of this apostle in Rome. For as we have seen, it is arbitrary to understand the notice in ch. 12:17 as such an allusion.[54] It must be conceded at the outset that the silence of The Book of Acts constitutes a minus for the traditional view, inasmuch as thereby one of the earliest sources that could attest the tradition fails us. Nothing more, however, may be concluded from this silence; it is not permissible to go further and see in it any support for the attempt to prove impossible the fact that tradition asserts. To be sure, those whom we mentioned, in our survey of the history of the problem, as challengers of the stay of Peter at Rome take particular pleasure in citing this silence to establish their thesis.[55]

It is indeed striking that a "history of the apostles," in whose first part Peter plays so large a role, contains no word about the *end of his life*. Doubtless *this* notable fact calls for some explanation. As to the question, however, whether or not Peter was in Rome we can

[52] M. J. Lagrange, *Epître aux Romains*, pp. xxix f., even considers it the chief tendency of the letter to instruct the Gentile Christians concerning the role of Judaism in redemptive history and to warn them against any contempt for the Jewish Christians.

[53] See below, pp. 106 f.   [54] See above, pp. 37 ff.

[55] K. Heussi, to be sure, does not belong in this group. For he rightly admits (*War Petrus in Rom?*, pp. 17 ff.) that from the evidence in The Acts one cannot reach a certain conclusion.

draw no conclusion of any kind from this silence. For The Acts not only says nothing concerning the *Roman* stay of Peter we now are discussing; it is silent concerning his entire missionary activity, which by the evidence of I Corinthians 9:5 is an established fact, and also concerning his death.

There is the additional fact that nothing is reported concerning the martyr death of Paul, which nevertheless is not disputed. The Book of Acts ends abruptly with the mention of Paul's arrival at Rome and the remark that he remained there two years. In view of the detail with which the journeys of Paul are described in the closing chapters, this is much stranger than the silence concerning Peter. It calls even more urgently for an explanation. However, no matter what solutions have previously been given for the riddle of the abrupt ending of The Book of Acts, the different answers leave open the question as to whether or not Peter was in Rome.

These answers assume either that the author *knew nothing* concerning the unreported end of Paul's life—and probably also of Peter's— or that *he did not want to tell of it.* In the former case one must presuppose that he completed his book immediately after the close of the two years that followed Paul's arrival in Rome. In that case there would be the possibility—but only the possibility—that Peter reached Rome later and, like Paul, suffered martyrdom there.

The assumption, however, that the author completed his work exactly two years after the arrival of Paul in Rome is not probable. A long series of reasons that need not here be cited favour the view that the book was written only later, after the Neronian persecution and after the death of Peter and Paul. In this case we probably must assume that the author was as well informed concerning the end of Peter's life as concerning that of Paul. That he possessed no information about it is scarcely possible. There remains then only the explanation that he *chose* not to tell anything about it. The reason for this could be literary in character. Often, indeed, it actually is assumed that he chose to extend this book only to this point; he stopped with the arrival of Paul at Rome, whether he planned a third book[56] or not.[57] Or the reason was of theological character; on

---

[56] So Th. Zahn, *Einleitung in das Neue Testament*, 4th ed., 1924, pp. 16 ff., 861 f. (see Eng. Tr., *Introduction to the New Testament*, 2nd ed., 1917, Vol. III, pp. 57 ff.), and M. Goguel, *Introduction au Nouveau Testament*, Vol. III, 1922, *Le livre des Actes*, p. 340.

[57] W. Michaelis, *Einleitung in das Neue Testament*, 1946, p. 133, considers the possibility that the author could so limit his goal because his readers had been informed concerning the further course of events.

this view, to have told of these unreported events would in some way have been out of keeping with the theological aim of the book. These cases also permit no *a priori* conclusions either for or against the stay and martyrdom of Peter in Rome. For in principle both possibilities remain open: either that Peter after those two years (or possibly even earlier[58]) died in Rome as a martyr, or that after this time (possibly even earlier) he ended his life elsewhere.

Only if the further course of this investigation should prove that the very occurrence of the event in Rome gave the author a special theological reason for not mentioning the end of Peter's life—only then could his silence possibly be considered as indirect confirmation of the assumption that Peter suffered martyrdom in Rome. As a matter of fact, I shall at least propose such a hypothesis.[59] But this will be possible only by drawing upon other texts. For the time being we must say that The Book of Acts deserves mention in our study only to establish the fact that in its case one of our oldest sources fails to help us in the question as to Peter the Martyr.

Can we learn something positive from the letters that appear in the New Testament as *letters of Peter*? Whether they bear his name rightly or wrongly is of no importance for our present purpose; even if an unknown author put them under the authority of Peter, it is important to learn whether he knew that Peter was in Rome and whether accordingly he carried through the fiction of representing himself as present in Rome.

The Second Epistle of Peter contains no reference of any kind to Rome. It only refers to the martyrdom of Peter in ch. 1:14: "I know that the striking of my tent will come soon, as our Lord Jesus Christ has revealed to me." This writing, however, like the later apocryphal Petrine literature, does not require consideration here. This is primarily because, in the judgment of the great majority of scholars, it is the latest document included in the New Testament. It thus comes from a later period—at the earliest from the middle of the second century—when the tradition concerning the Roman stay of Peter begins to appear elsewhere as well. We are seeking here only the early witnesses.

Among them The First Epistle of Peter calls for mention. At the end of its final chapter stands a greeting. Concerning this greeting it

---

[58] *A priori*, indeed, it is not absolutely necessary to assume with regard to Peter the same reasons for silence that one does with reference to the death of Paul.

[59] See below, pp. 89 ff., 103 f.

is usually assumed that whether the writing is genuine or not, it presupposes the stay of Peter in Rome: "The fellow-elect (Church) in Babylon greets you, and so does Mark my son" (I Pet. 5:13).

Even this statement, to be sure, yields no absolute certainty. It seems to me far the most probable explanation that Babylon is a cryptic name for Rome. For if the author writes from Rome, his reason for substituting Babylon for Rome may very well have been similar to that which the author of the Apocalypse of John had. Either he wishes to avoid it out of fear of the Roman authorities, or more probably, he used the term Babylon because in his day that city, which with all that it meant for the people of Israel had been so important in Old Testament prophecy, had become a theological concept which could be applied especially well to Rome.[60]

We know indeed from ancient Christian literature how popular this typological use of geographical names was. We may think, for example, of Galatians 4:26, where the Church is called the "Jerusalem that is above," or of Hebrews 12:22, which speaks of the "heavenly Jerusalem." So for the author of I Peter "Babylon," in connection with the theological ideas that he held, may be a term meaning "exile," just as in ch. 2:11 (see also ch. 1:1) he has called the readers "aliens and sojourners." At the same time, however, it is also an expression of the capital city's power-linked corruption; this meaning connects with the Old Testament prophetic tradition, for example, Isaiah 43:14 and Jeremiah, chs. 50 and 51.[61] Since the greeting must have a definite city in mind, there could have been in the time of the writer no other place but Rome to which this figurative meaning of the ancient Babylon was applied.

The presupposition for this conclusion, of course, is that we do have here a figurative use of the word. This conclusion is rendered

---

[60] K. Heussi, *War Petrus in Rom?*, p. 38, does not see the reason for such a hide-and-seek game. But for the author of the Apocalypse of John it is clear that he was *unwilling* to name Rome. Moreover, the chapter that Heussi devotes to our passage is unsatisfactory; he discusses it only on the presupposition that I Clement, ch. 5, already proves with finality that Peter was not in Rome. It will not do, however, to interpret I Peter 5:13 on the basis of this conclusion, which we shall see is not at all assured, instead of considering the source in itself. On I Pet. 5:13, see further H. Windisch, *Die katholischen Briefe*, 3rd ed., 1951, revised by Herbert Preisker, p. 82; further, A. Schlatter, *Geschichte der ersten Christenheit*, 1926, pp. 299 ff., and B. W. Bacon, *Is Mark a Roman Gospel?*, 1919, pp. 23 ff. See also the article by G. Kuhn on "Babylon" in *Theologisches Wörterbuch zum Neuen Testament*, Vol. I, pp. 512 ff.

[61] This has been pointed out especially by E. G. Selwyn, *The First Epistle of St. Peter*, 1949, pp. 303 ff.

likely by the fact that such a use, with reference to Rome itself, is certainly attested in other writings. It occurs above all in the Apocalypse of John, where there can be no doubt that in chs. 14:8; 16:19; 17:5 ff.; 18:2 ff. Rome is meant by "Babylon." Perhaps the expression "Sodom and Egypt" in Revelation 11:8 is likewise a cryptic name for Rome.[62] We further find "Babylon" as a figurative designation for Rome in the pseudepigraphic late Jewish literature. It appears, for example in the Sibylline Oracles V, 159, where it is said: "The deep sea will burn, and so will Babylon itself and the land of Italy"; in the Apocalypse of Baruch 11:1; and in Fourth Esdras 3:1 ff., 28, 31.[63] Both in the Apocalypse of John and in the late Jewish texts, of course, we are dealing with writings which can hardly be earlier than our First Episle of Peter.[64] Nevertheless, they belong to approximately the same period.[65] In addition, the word "mystery," which in Revelation 17:5 refers to the saying concerning Babylon-Rome, appears to indicate that this covert manner of expression was already known to Christians.[66] For all these reasons, the interpretation that the word "Babylon" in I Peter 5:13 refers to Rome is doubtless the most natural, if we approach the passage without prejudice and without first taking into account the controversy concerning Peter's stay in Rome. Papias already explained the verse in this way.[67]

It must be said, however, that it is not completely certain that the

---

[62] So J. Munck, *Petrus und Paulus in der Offenbarung Johannis*, 1950, pp. 30 ff., in opposition to the majority of interpreters, who think they find in the expression a reference to Jerusalem.

[63] See on this point H. Fuchs, *Der geistige Widerstand gegen Rom*, 1938. The rabbinic passages are given in Strack-Billerbeck, *Kommentar zum Neuen Testament*, Vol. III, p. 816.

[64] E. G. Selwyn, *op. cit.*, pp. 243 and 303, believes that our passage contains the first witness to this usage of the word Babylon=Rome; he finds that usage in this passage.

[65] In the Church Fathers this use of the word Babylon is common; it occurs in Tertullian, *Adversus Judaeos*, 9; *Adversus Marcionem*, 3, 13, and is especially favoured by Origen and Augustine. See on this point H. Fuchs, *Der geistige Widerstand gegen Rom*, 1938, pp. 74 f., and B. Altaner, Article on "Babylon" in *Reallexikon für Antike und Christentum*, columns 1131 ff. It should also be mentioned that two minuscule manuscripts have replaced the word Babylon by Rome in their text. (See Th. Zahn, *Einleitung ins Neue Testament*, 3rd ed., Vol. II, pp. 17 ff.; cf. Eng. Tr., *Introduction to the New Testament*, 2nd ed., Vol. II, pp. 158 ff.).

[66] So E. G. Selwyn, *op. cit.*, p. 243.

[67] Eusebius, *Ecclesiastical History*, II, 15, 2. The explanation is frequently found in later times. See Jerome, *De viris illustribus*, 8.

expression *must* here be understood in a figurative way. We cannot fully exclude the possibility that the long famous ancient *Mesopotamian* city of Babylon was really meant. We know from Josephus[68] and from Philo[69] that this place was still inhabited in the New Testament period, although it had lost all importance, and according to another notice of Josephus that refers to the middle of the first century, the Jews had left the place to settle in the city Seleucia,[70] which in the meantime had come to outrank the ancient Babylon. So it has actually been assumed that on one of his missionary journeys Peter came to Babylon in Mesopotamia, or if not into the city itself, at least into the region of Babylonia, and wrote our letter[71] from there. One cannot exclude this possibility. Nevertheless, it is not probable, and it is not supported by the later Christian tradition, which knows nothing of a missionary work of Peter in these regions. To them it brings only the apostle Thomas. To this we must add the fact that the Babylonian Talmud attests the presence of Christians in this region only from the third century on.

The assumption that the author who ascribed the letter to Peter knew nothing definite concerning the places where the apostle worked, and therefore chose the nebulous distant Babylon,[72] finds no support in fact. It is improbable also because of the explicit mention of Mark.

Theoretically still another Babylon might be considered. This is the military camp in *Egypt*, near the modern Cairo. It is mentioned by Strabo[73] and Josephus.[74] One can scarcely accept, however, the misguided idea that I Peter 5:13 refers to this rather obscure Babylon. The only possible support for this view is the fact that the apocryphal Gospel of Peter and the Apocalypse of Peter are of Egyptian origin.

The other cities which have been proposed, Jerusalem[75] or even Joppa,[76] have still less claim to serious consideration. It is impossible

---

[68] *Antiquities*, XV, 2, 2.   [69] *Legatio ad Caium*, 232, p. 587.

[70] Josephus, *Antiquities*, XVIII, 9, 8. See on this point Th. Zahn, *Einleitung ins N. T.*, Vol. II, 2nd ed., 1900, pp. 17 ff. (Eng. Tr. of 3rd ed. see note 65 above); and H. Windisch, *Die katholischen Briefe* (*Handbuch zum Neuen Testament*, herausgegeben von G. Bornkamm), 3rd ed., revised by H. Preisker, 1951, p. 82.

[71] A. Schlatter, *Geschichte der ersten Christenheit*, 1926, p. 299, and others; in earlier times, Erasmus. It is often argued that the rather friendly attitude of the letter towards the State speaks against the identification of Rome and Babylon. (See J. Haller, *Das Papsttum*, Vol. I, 1951, p. 477.)

[72] K. Heussi, *op. cit.*, p. 38, note 6.

[73] XVII, 30, p. 807.   [74] II, 15, 1.

[75] A. Harnack, *Chronologie der altchristlichen Literatur bis Eusebius*, 1897, p. 459.

[76] Syncellus ad a. m. 5540 (ed. Bonn 627), probably in view of Acts 9:36 ff.

to explain how they could have been designated by the name "Babylon." The passage in Revelation 11:8, concerning the city which "spiritually is called Sodom and Egypt," has been cited as an analogy at least for Jerusalem. But as we have already mentioned, this verse cannot be taken as a certain reference to Jerusalem; it possibly refers to Rome.[77] It is pure fantasy to assume, on the basis that Clement of Alexandria declares The Second Epistle of John to have been addressed to a certain Babylonia, that the reference here is to a highly esteemed lady named Babylonia, who belonged to a church in Asia Minor.[78]

We thus reach the conclusion that First Peter, whether genuine or not, quite probably means by its place reference "Babylon" the city of Rome. It thereby presupposes a stay of Peter in Rome, although another interpretation of this reference is not entirely excluded.

Another passage from the same First Episle of Peter (ch. 5:1) is still to be mentioned. However, it deals only with the other question, whether Peter died as a martyr. The author here speaks of himself as a "witness of the sufferings of Christ and a partaker of the glory soon to be revealed." This expression also is not unequivocal. Yet it probably justifies us in assuming that the author, whether Peter or someone else, refers to a sharing in Christ's sufferings, including his death. For the witness here mentioned probably refers not only to something once seen and now proclaimed, but in keeping with the demonstrably early usage of the Greek word, refers to a witness in act.[79]

In the same connection we still must mention, of the New Testament books that should be considered in our study, *The Gospel of John*. Of especial importance is ch. 21:18 ff.: "As long as you were

---

[77] See J. Munck, *op. cit.*, pp. 30 ff.

[78] This proposal comes from K. Heussi, *op. cit.*, p. 39, note 6, but he himself puts a question mark after it.

[79] So also R. Knopf, *Die Briefe Petri und Judä*, 1912, p. 188; H. Windisch—H. Preisker, *Die katholischen Briefe*, 3rd ed., 1951, p. 79; also K. Heussi himself: *War Petrus in Rom?*, p. 31, note 21; likewise H. Lietzmann, "Petrus römischer Märtyrer" (*Sitzungsbericht der Berliner Akademie der Wissenschaften*, 1936, p. 399). The expression is referred only to the apostolic office, on the contrary, by F. Hauck, *Das Neue Testament Deutsch*, Vol. III, 1930, p. 203, and C. Bigg, *The Epistles of St. Peter and St. Jude*, 2nd ed., 1910, p. 186. H. Strathmann, in G. Kittel's *Theologisches Wörterbuch zum N. T.*, Vol. IV, p. 499, admits a "sharing in Christ's sufferings," but rejects here the technical martyrological meaning. On the entire question see O. Michel, *Prophet und Märtyrer*, 1932; H. v. Campenhausen, *Die Idee des Martyriums in der alten Kirche*, 1936; H. W. Surkau, *Martyrien in judischer und frühchristlicher Zeit*, 1938; E. Günther, *Martys*, 1941.

young, you girded yourself and went wherever you chose; but when you have become old, you will stretch out your hands, and another will gird you and carry you where you do not want to go." It is almost universally recognized that these words are intended as a prediction of the martyrdom of Peter, even if there should lie behind them a proverb which simply says: The young go where they choose, the old must permit themselves to be carried.[80] When the following verse says that these words indicate by what kind of death Peter "is to glorify God," it is beyond doubt that this "glorifying" can only mean his martyrdom. Perhaps John 13:36 ff. also belongs here.

It is not entirely certain whether the "stretching out of the hands" in John 21:18 is intended to indicate a special manner of execution, by crucifixion.[81] The Greek expression makes this quite likely.[82] Concerning the place of martyrdom the prediction contains no precise information. Even if ch. 21 was only added later to the Gospel of John, we still are dealing with a text that is relatively early. We thus have two rather early witnesses to the essential fact of the martyrdom of Peter: certainly John 21:18, and possibly I Peter 5:1, to which about the middle of the second century II Peter 1:14 is added. This evidence, it is true, does not prove the "historicity" of this manner of Peter's death, but it renders it probable.[83] For the question whether Peter was in Rome this preliminary question, whether he died as a martyr at all, is not unimportant. For in ancient

[80] So R. Bultmann, *Das Evangelium des Johannes*, 2nd ed., 1950, p. 552.

[81] This is rejected by R. Bultmann, *op. cit.*, p. 552. See on the contrary already in Tertullian, *Scorpiace* 15: "Peter is girded by another when he is fastened to the cross."

[82] ἐκτείνειν ("stretch out"). See on this point W. Bauer, *Das Johannesevangelium* (*Handbuch zum Neuen Testament*), 3rd ed., 1933, p. 238. He points out that in assuming this the order of stretching out the hands and being girded is not reversed (as R. Bultmann says, *op. cit., ad loc.*), since "the criminal had to carry the cross to the place of execution with arms spread out and chained to it."

[83] K. Heussi raises the question whether Peter died as a martyr at all. The manner, however, in which he seeks to minimize the testimony of John 21:18 ff. is not convincing; he claims that this tradition, which he concedes the author must have found already in existence, deals with the transfer of Paul's martyr death to his rival Peter (*War Petrus in Rom?*, p. 30, note 21; *Neues zur Petrusfrage*, 1939, p. 24; see on this point more recently, "Der Stand der Frage nach dem römischen Aufenthalt des Petrus," in *Deutsches Pfarrerblatt*, 1949, p. 503). R. Bultmann, *op. cit.*, p. 553, writes in opposition to this view that if, on the one side, one cannot establish by this prediction the historicity of the martyrdom, yet on the other side one cannot prove that verses 18 f. have the aim of establishing the legend.

times it was hardly customary to hand down accounts of the martyr-doms with no indication of place.[84] Thus we must at least assume that those who, in the texts mentioned, show that they know the tradition of Peter's martyrdom knew also the place, even though in this passage they had no occasion to name it. This fact will call for consideration in forming a judgment concerning First Clement, ch. 5.

As the last New Testament text which we need to discuss in con-nection with our problem we now may add *Revelation* 11:3 ff. The hypothesis has recently been proposed that the Apostles Peter and Paul are meant here by the "two witnesses," who, after they have given their witness, are attacked, overcome, and killed by the "beast from the abyss." In the same passage it is said that the corpses of the two witnesses continue to lie upon the street of the "great city," where earlier their Lord had been crucified. For "three and a half days" men of all peoples see them lying there and refuse to permit their burial. These two witnesses have so troubled the inhabitants of the earth that the latter, out of joy over their death, now send presents to one another. The spirit of life from God re-enters the two dead men; a voice resounds from heaven: "Come up here," and they ascend to heaven in a cloud.

These witnesses, who previously were always interpreted to be Moses and Elijah, could in fact be Peter and Paul.[85] If this hypo-thesis is correct, we probably would have here the oldest tradition concerning the two martyrdoms. The "great city" in this case would have to be Rome.[86] We would have to assume that the two apostles,

---

[84] This is rightly stressed by H. Lietzmann, *Petrus und Paulus in Rom*, 2nd ed., 1927, pp. 235 f.

[85] This hypothesis, first expressed by the Jesuit, Juan de Mariana, *Scholia in Vetus et Novum Testamentum*, Madrid, 1619, pp. 1100 f., has now been given a scholarly foundation by Johannes Munck in his recently published monograph, *Petrus und Paulus in der Offenbarung Johannis*, 1950. This thesis is also presented, inde-pendently of J. Munck, by the Roman Catholic exegete, R. P. Boismard, *L'Apocalypse* (*La Sainte Bible*, Jérusalem), 1950, pp. 21 f., 53 f.; in doing so, however, he tries to find in the resurrection and ascension of the two witnesses a symbol of their "triumph with God" or even of their "resurrection in the person of their successors."

[86] See above, p. 84, on "Sodom and Egypt." In that case the words "where earlier their Lord was crucified" are hard to interpret. J. Munck, *op. cit.*, pp. 34 ff., knows no other escape here except either to consider the words as an interpola-tion or to understand them not in a geographical but in a figurative sense, which then might possibly be applied to Rome. R. B. Boismard, *op. cit.* above in note 85, considers the words an interpolation inspired by Matt. 23:37. The manuscript evidence, however, does not justify striking out the words concerned.

even if they did not do missionary work at the same time, did suffer martyrdom there *simultaneously*, and that contrary to later accounts, they were not buried, but their corpses continued to lie on the public street in Rome. In addition this tradition would tell of the ascension of these two martyrs, such as possibly is attested for Paul in The Acts of Paul.

The only possible time for these events would be the Neronian persecution. This is especially true since other features of the Apocalypse of John continue to find their best explanation as references to Nero.

Although much favours the correctness of this new hypothesis concerning this passage, we nevertheless cannot regard it as a *certain* basis for assuming that Peter was martyred at Rome. The cryptic manner of speech of the Apocalypse inevitably makes uncertain every interpretation in terms of contemporary history. In our passage, for one thing, the names of the "two witnesses" are not given; moreover, the designation "apostle" is lacking, although it is correct that elsewhere in the New Testament the apostles are called "witnesses" in crucial passages;[87] furthermore, the name of the "great city" where the Lord was crucified is not given, and the explanation that it means Rome does not appear immediately convincing, but actually offers difficulties. The passage permits other interpretations. Thus here also only a *possibility* remains. If, however, we could identify more clearly, on the basis of another text, an early tradition of the stay and martyrdom of Peter in Rome, then this interpretation also, which in itself is possible, would acquire greater value as a testimony.

Up to this point, however, we have nowhere found a solid foundation. The New Testament attests only the fact of the martyrdom of Peter. As far as the place is concerned, even the interpretation of I Peter 5:13 has offered us thus far only a great probability, and the silence of Romans permitted us to conclude only that at a specific time Peter certainly was not in Rome.

*　　*　　*

We still have two texts which contain brief references to Peter and Paul and *in point of time* at least still belong in the New Testament sphere: the First Epistle of Clement, which probably dates from the end of the first century, and the Letter of Ignatius of Antioch to the

[87] See J. Munck, *op. cit.*, pp. 17 f.

Romans, from the beginning of the second century. Of these two *First Clement* is by far the more important for our question; it is rightly regarded as the decisive literary witness, by both the defenders and the opponents of the tradition concerning the Roman stay of Peter. We therefore shall make a more detailed study of it. For if a relatively great probability is anywhere attainable for one view or the other, it must be in the fifth chapter of this writing.

The Epistle quite probably dates as early as the end of the first century. It has even been said that it is the document of ancient Christianity which can be dated with the greatest certainty; and it is usual to give the year 96 as the date of its composition.[88]

I too consider this important text the most solid basis for a solution of our question. As we approach the study of it, we must emphasize at the outset a twofold necessity. On the one hand, we must read the decisive section without any prejudice; on the other hand—and this seems to me of crucial importance—we must not tear it out of the context in which it stands, as is continually done, but must explain it strictly in that setting. Hence before we speak of the section which directly interests us, I first of all sum up the content of the immediately preceding chapters.

Ch. 5, which we must study in greater detail, stands in a larger context which embraces chs. 3 to 6. Over the entire section we could place as a heading: *Concerning the Results of Jealousy*. The theme is formulated at the end of the third chapter, where, with a citation from Wisdom 2:24, the author defines jealousy as follows: "*The unrighteous and godless jealousy through which death entered into the world.*" Ch. 9:1 speaks again of strife and of the jealousy "which leads to death."

The writing undertakes to prove by examples that jealousy among brothers brings harmful results. The examples cited form two groups of seven.[89] The former contains examples from earlier times, and

---

[88] A. Harnack, *Chronologie*, Vol. I, p. 255: "between 93 and 95." Recently Ch. Eggenberger, *Die Quellen der politischen Ethik des 1. Klemensbriefes*, 1951, has thought it necessary to bring the date down into the beginning of the reign of Hadrian. This dating is connected with the much too one-sided perspective in which he regards the entire writing as an "apology for the court." Everything that is said concerning conditions in Corinth, he says, is fiction! With other reasons A. Loisy, *La Naissance du Christianisme*, 1933, p. 33, also transfers the writing to the years 130–135.

[89] See R. Knopf, *Die Lehre der Zwölf Apostel; die zwei Klemensbriefe (Handbuch zum Neuen Testament, Ergänzungsband)*, 1923, pp. 48 ff.

stands in ch. 4. They are taken from the Old Testament: 1. Cain and Abel. 2. Jacob and Esau. 3. Joseph and his brothers. 4. Moses and the Jew who reproaches him for having killed the Egyptian. 5. Moses and Aaron and Miriam. 6. Moses and Dathan and Abiram. 7. David (the Philistines) and Saul.

The second group comprises the examples from the *immediate* past. It too contains seven members, and it stands in chs. 5 and 6. Here, then, we come to the much-disputed passage which, on account of its importance, I give in full in translation:

Chapter 5: "But now, to leave the examples from ancient times, let us come to the contestants of the most recent past. Let us take the noble examples of our own generation. On account of jealousy and envy the greatest and most righteous *pillars* were persecuted and contended unto death. Let us set before our eyes our excellent apostles:[90] *Peter*, who because of unrighteous jealousy had to bear not one or two but many torments, and so, after he had given his witness, went to the place of glory which was due him. On account of jealousy and strife *Paul* displayed the prize of endurance. Seven times he was chained; he was exiled; he was stoned; he became a herald both in the east and in the west; and so he received for his faith glorious fame. After he had taught the whole world righteousness, had reached the furthest boundary of the west, and had given witness before the authorities, he thus was freed from the world and went to the holy place, as the greatest example of endurance."—Chapter 6: "To these men, who have lived a holy life, was joined a great *multitude of elect ones*, who on account of jealousy suffered many kinds of outrage and tortures and so became most glorious examples *among us*. On account of jealousy *women* were persecuted; as Danaids and Dircae they suffered fearful and horrible ill-treatment, and so they reached the goal of their steadfast course of faith and received a glorious prize—

[90] The literal translation here, depending on whether one refers "our" to "apostles" or to "eyes," would be either "let us set before *our* eyes the excellent apostles" or "let us set before the eyes *our* excellent apostles." P. Monceaux, "L'apostolat de Saint Pierre à Rome, à propos d'un livre récent (*Revue d'Histoire et de Littérature religieuses*, 1910, pp. 225 f.), holds that only the translation "our excellent apostles" is possible; and he thinks that this expression should be understood in the sense of "the apostles who have preached in Rome and Corinth." But in ch. 44:1 the expression "our apostles" designates the apostles in general. M. Dibelius, "Rom und die Christen im ersten Jahrhundert" (*Sitzungsbericht der Heidelberger Akademie der Wissenschaften*, 1942, p. 20), interprets ἀγαθοί ("good," "excellent") in the sense of *fortes*, "valiant." See examples for this in B. Altaner, "Neues zum Verästndnis von 1. Klem. 5, 1–6, 2" (*Historisches Jahrbuch*, 1949, p. 25).

they, the physically weak ones. Jealousy has estranged *wives* from their husbands and perverted the saying of our father Adam: 'This is now bone of my bone and flesh of my flesh.' Jealousy and strife have destroyed *great cities* and uprooted great peoples."

This is thus the only early text that speaks explicitly of the death of Peter, and it should be said at the outset that we do not learn much from it. We therefore must see whether and how far it is permitted to derive more from the context.

Here again seven victims of jealousy are assembled:[91] 1. The pillars. 2. Peter. 3. Paul. 4. The great multitude of the elect. 5. The martyred women. 6. The separated spouses. 7. The destroyed cities. Of these seven examples the first, sixth, and seventh are described in quite general terms; they do not permit us to think of particular concrete events. The last two evidently are intended only to complete the number of seven. In our interpretation we must take into account the deliberately artificial arrangement of this section,[92] and we must note the difficulty which Clement inevitably encountered in finding for the relatively short period of the most recent (that is, the Christian) past the number of examples that would correspond with the group taken from the Old Testament. So perhaps in the first example also we should not think of particular names when—probably in dependence on Galatians 2:9—the passage speaks of the "pillars." The author seems to think here in a general way of apostles and leading men of the Primitive Church who have suffered martyrdom. In

[91] So rightly R. Knopf, *Handbuch zum Neuen Testament, Ergänzungsband*, 1923, p. 49.

[92] Even for this reason we must reject the new thesis which K. Heussi strangely continues to advance in his second reply to H. Lietzmann, *Neues zur Petrusfrage*, 1939. His thesis is that the passage concerning Peter, in paragraphs 3 and 4, can be a later *insertion*. But in this way the entire carefully constructed pattern of Clement would be destroyed. Apart from that fact, this thesis, which he proposed to supplement his original view, witnesses that he feels some uncertainty concerning his own arguments as presented in his earlier writing, *War Petrus in Rom?*, 1936. In the main chapter of that book he actually sought to show that in this passage Clement reports the vague and empty generalities that he knows about Peter, and that μαρτυρήσας ("having borne witness") does not refer to the martyr death. In his writing of 1939 he writes astonishingly that if the paragraph concerning Peter is an insertion, then μαρτυρήσας, in correspondence with the μαρτυρήσας that refers to Paul, would still be understood in the sense of a martyr death! But he further explains: Anyone who cannot accept the thesis of interpolation should hold to those other results which his earlier study of the passage brought to light! Here one gets the painful impression that *at any price* it *must* be proved that the letter of Clement cannot be used as a proof of the martyr death of Peter in Rome.

any case the "conflict unto death" means martyrdom.[93] Probably the author includes Peter and Paul among these men, but in order to obtain the number seven he probably first, before he speaks of each of them separately, names them together with the others who are collectively described as pillars. These two cases, especially that of Paul, seemed to him particularly fitted to prove the thesis he seeks to establish, that envy and jealousy lead to ruin. For we wish to establish without delay this fact: we owe the mention of Peter and Paul entirely to the circumstance that the author, in order to give greater emphasis to his warning to the Corinthian church against envy and strife, used examples from the history of the Primitive Church, and chose exactly seven for the sake of symmetry.

Unfortunately he expresses himself very briefly in the lines that deal with Peter. The thing particularly regrettable from our standpoint is that the point in which we are especially interested, the place where Peter suffered the many torments, is not named at all. Thus even this single early text which finally gives us a certain reference to the death of Peter seems to fail us. Indeed, it is not even clearly said that the apostle died as a martyr. The text in its actual form only says that sometime and somewhere Peter had to endure many torments, that he "bore witness," and that he then attained to the place of glory.

If one reads these statements apart from the context in which they occur, then indeed, in company with those who contest the Roman stay of Peter, one must deny that the passage gives any information of any kind concerning a Roman martyrdom or even concerning any martyrdom whatever. The sentences regarding Peter theoretically permit the interpretation that in his life he had to suffer manifold trials, that (through preaching) he bore witness, and that then, somewhere and at some time, he died a natural death and finally, as the reward of his endurance, was taken up to the place of glory.

---

[93] The remark of K. Heussi, in *War Petrus in Rom?*, p. 25, is indeed correct: in ch. 4:9 it is said of Joseph that he was persecuted "unto death" ($\mu\acute{\epsilon}\chi\rho\iota$ $\theta\alpha\nu\acute{\alpha}\tau\sigma\upsilon$), and yet he escaped with his life. Consequently, according to Heussi, neither is the "struggle unto death" in ch. 5:2 to be interpreted of the martyr death. But in connection with $\acute{\alpha}\theta\lambda\acute{\epsilon}\omega$ ("struggle," "contend") the words $\acute{\epsilon}\omega\varsigma$ $\vartheta\alpha\nu\acute{\alpha}\tau\sigma\upsilon$ ("unto death") are probably not merely rhetorical emotion as they are in the example of Joseph. In the latter example, moreover, the author makes clear that a real death is not in mind. For he expressly adds, "unto slavery." The preceding emotional "unto death" he put here only in view of the main thesis expressed in ch. 3:4 (9:1).

It has been correctly pointed out that the author cites the series of Old Testament examples, beginning with Cain and Abel, in chronological order. Hence it has been considered necessary to conclude from this fact that Peter died before Paul suffered martyrdom. The fact that the author reports so little concerning Peter, while he says much more about Paul, is said to be explained by the fact that he knows nothing more about Peter than the very vague facts mentioned above.[94]

With reference to the martyr death itself (apart from the question of where it occurred), we must first of all recall that this death, as we have seen, is attested about the time of the writing of First Clement, at least in John 21:18, and perhaps also in I Peter 5:1. Could it be then that Clement knew nothing of such a death? This is indeed improbable.

Furthermore, the context shows that the two items concerning Peter and Paul are constructed in a quite similar way, even if it is true that the one concerning Peter is much shorter. Now it is universally conceded that in any event the notice concerning Paul speaks of his martyr death.[95] But if in that account the expression "bear witness" is, to say the least, closely connected with the words, "and so he went to the holy place," then it cannot properly be understood otherwise when it is similarly said of Peter: "and so, after he bore witness, he

---

[94] This is *grosso modo* the thesis developed by K. Heussi, *War Petrus in Rom?* H. Dannenbauer, "Die römische Petruslegende" (*Historische Zeitschrift*, 1932, pp. 246 f.), also asserts that I Clement is completely ignorant concerning the fate of Peter. He explains this ignorance by the fact that the Neronian persecution completely destroyed the Roman church and broke the chain of all living Christian tradition. For the contrary view, see G. Krüger, "Petrus in Rom" (*ZNW*, 1932, pp. 303 f.). That Clement had no definite knowledge at all concerning Peter is asserted also by Ch. Guignebert, *op. cit.*, p. 275, and K. Holl, *Gesammelte Aufsätze*, Vol. II, 1928, p. 65, note 1. The latter, however, assumes that Peter came to Rome, though only after the death of Paul, and then was there but a short time; he explains in this way the fact that precisely in Rome the church had as few memories of Peter as I Clement, ch. 5, shows us they did (*Gesammelte Aufsätze*, Vol. II, 1928, p. 67). Accordingly, it is quite remarkable when one reads the following in J. Haller, *Das Papsttum*, Vol. I, p. 476: " . . . who knows how many have protested in silence (against the acceptance by modern scholarship of a Roman stay of Peter), without raising their voice! I know concerning the most learned and acute church historian of the last fifty years, Karl Holl, that he did not share the 'prevailing view.' "

[95] K. Heussi also assumes this, though here too he still does not understand μαρτυρήσας ("having borne witness") as a reference to martyrdom (*War Petrus in Rom?*, p. 25).

went to the place of glory that was due him."[96] In addition, we must also take into account the elsewhere attested usage in stories of martyrdom, in which the Greek word *doxa* refers to glory. The word *martyrein* for "bear witness" is at least already on the way to becoming the technical term for witness by martyrdom.[97]

Not as proof but as confirmation we may also recall that according to the theme stated at the end of ch. 3, it is death that is portrayed as the result of jealousy.[98] To be sure, in most examples of the first group the trial does not lead to death, but doubtless the writer's special concern is with the cases which ended in this way. That is why the first example of the entire section, the story of Cain and Abel, is treated with disproportionately large detail.[99]

If we thus must assume with the greatest probability that Clement here refers to the martyr death of Peter, then—we must repeat—he himself at least knew also the place of the martyrdom, since it is not customary to hand down narratives of martyrdoms without any indication of place.[1] In our passage Clement does not need to mention it, since he can assume that it is known; moreover, he is not giving a report about martyrs but an example of the results of envy and strife.[2]

[96] This testimony probably does not resume the preceding "suffering of manifold torments," but cites the μαρτυρεῖν ("bear witness") as a further point; for οὕτω ("so," "thus") is best referred to ἐπορεύθη ("went"), just as οὕτως in the notice concerning Paul belongs to ἀπηλλάγη ("was freed"). So H. von Campenhausen, *Die Idee des Martyriums in der alten Kirche*, 1936, p. 54, who shows that what is involved is a "martyrological" way of speaking, which here is applied to Peter and to Paul, and in Eusebius, *Ecclesiastical History*, II, 23, is used of James. So also H. Lietzmann, *Petrus römischer Martyrer*, 1936. This is in opposition to Heussi, *op. cit.*, p. 24, note 12.

[97] So J. B. Lightfoot, *The Apostolic Fathers*, I, 1-2, 2nd ed., 1890, *ad loc.* R. Knopf, *Handbuch zum Neuen Testament, Ergänzungsband*, 1923, p. 51, also interprets μαρτυρήσας ("having borne witness") in the sense of martyr death. So do H. Delehaye, *Sanctus, Essai sur le culte des Saints dans l'antiquité*, 1927, p. 79, and H. v. Campenhausen, *op. cit.*, p. 54. On the contrary, E. Günther, *Martys, Geschichte eines Wortes*, 1941, pp. 117 ff., rejects the meaning "be a martyr," and H. Strathmann, in G. Kittel's *Theologisches Wörterbuch zum N. T.*, Vol. IV, p. 511, is very hesitant. L. Sanders, *L'hellénisme de S. Clément de Rome et le paulinisme*, 1943, pp. 21 f., wishes to give the word the same meaning it has in Epictetus.

[98] See above, p. 90.

[99] This is rightly emphasized by R. Knopf, *Handbuch zum Neuen Testament, Ergänzungsband*, 1923, p. 49.

[1] So H. Lietzmann, *Petrus und Paulus in Rom*, 2nd ed., 1927, pp. 235 f. See above, pp. 87 f.

[2] B. Altaner, "Neues zum Verständnis von 1. Klem. 5, 1-6, 2" (*Historisches Jahrbuch*, 1941, p. 25), shows that ch. 9 of the Epistle of Polycarp uses I Clem.,

There is the further fact that examples one, three, and four, and probably also the disputed fifth one,[3] speak of Christians who have suffered death as martyrs. The fourth example is reasonably clear in this respect; the great multitude of the elect here mentioned are, as is *universally recognized*, the Christians who suffered the martyr death under Nero, for we know nothing of any other persecution of a "great multitude"[4] in this period apart from that which Nero instigated. Concerning it, the narrative of Tacitus, *Annals*, XV, 44, speaks exactly as does Clement of a *multitudo ingens*, a "great multitude."

But the notice concerning this fourth example contains still another item that is very important for our study: "they became a glorious example *among us*."[5] Since Clement writes from Rome, we thus possess, at least for this group of martyrs, the information concerning the place. It is Rome. This confirms the conclusion that we are here dealing with the martyrs of the Neronian persecution.[6] However, the champions of the Roman tradition about Peter are often much too hasty in drawing from this place reference of the fourth example a conclusion concerning the preceding examples, in which, as we have seen, nothing is said concerning the place. If the examples of the second group are actually to be separated from one another and placed, like those of the first group, in a strictly chronological series, then we have so much the less right to say without further evidence that the words "among us" refer also to Peter and Paul. This is particularly true if the "pillars" of the first example likewise did not all "suffer persecution and contend unto death" in Rome.

---

ch. 5, almost word for word, and he seeks to show that Polycarp understood the passage to mean that Paul, Ignatius, Zosimus, and "other apostles" suffered martyrdom in Rome.

3 One usually thinks of cruelties, especially executions, in the form of mythological presentations (Tertullian, *Apology*, 15). That would correspond also to the *ludibria* attested for the Neronian persecution in Tacitus, *Annals*, XV, 44. Another explanation: L. van Liempt, Handelingen van het veertiende nederlandsche Philologen-Congres te Amsterdam, 1931, pp. 37 f., whom M. Dibelius follows (*op. cit.*, p. 24), says that the martyr women are here only *named* after the mythical heroines, to express the greatness of their sufferings, not the manner of their punishment: "They are true Dircae and Danaids." The most recent, interesting conjecture is by A. Dain, in *Recherches de Science religieuse*, 1951–52, pp. 353 ff.: there is here a scribal error for *neanides paidiskai* ("slave maidens").

4 πολὺ πλῆθος.   5 ἐν ἡμῖν.

6 This is recognized also by K. Heussi, *op. cit.*, although on p. 21, note 9, he does not intend to exclude the possibility that ἐν ἡμῖν means "in the midst of us Christians."

We dare not be too hasty in adding the words "in Rome" to the verb in the statement, "they (the great multitude) were joined[7] to these men (Peter and Paul)," as though there were any necessity to ask at what place they were joined to them. The assembling here mentioned is not necessarily meant in a geographical sense. Nor is it meant in the sense in which the challengers of the Roman tradition are accustomed to interpret it: "at the place of glory." Rather, the question as to the "where" should not be asked at all.[8] The intent of the verb "they were joined to them" is probably to add to the other examples as a simple *fact* the example of the great multitude; it is a further illustration, from the quite recent past, of Christian martyrdoms suffered as a result of jealousy.

Precisely on the basis of this factual connection, however, we must ask whether in examples two to five we are not dealing with the same outward circumstances. If so, the division into four particular cases could again be connected with the fact that the author was determined to attain the number of seven for this second group also. Indeed, we have seen that he added examples six and seven only for this reason. But if that is true, we must consider the possibility that the sequence of examples two to five need not be understood as a chronological succession.[9]

The possibility thus exists of assigning all four examples to the Neronian persecution in Rome. It is indeed correct that the expression "nearest to us" in ch. 5:1[10] is given a temporal sense only to distinguish the second group from the first; this conclusion is also indicated by the phrase "our generation," which stands in the following sentence. But the fact that, at least in the fourth example, Clement uses the words "among us" proves that he is concerned to give in the second group examples that are particularly close to him also in place.

We have no right, however, to extend the words "among us" to the notice concerning Peter, unless it can be proved that other really

---

[7] συνηθροίσθη.

[8] Against K. Heussi, *op. cit.*, p. 22; but also against M. Dibelius, *Rom und die Christen im ersten Jahrhundert*, 1942, p. 23. The latter in connection with his thesis that Clement here follows the pattern that popular philosophy draws from athletic contests and wishes to give examples of Christian "endurance" and Christian "athletic prowess," writes: "the place where the two groups meet is rather the imaginary arena in which the contests of the Christian 'athletes' occur."

[9] In that case the argument mentioned above on p. 96 collapses.

[10] ἔγγιστα.

important features connect examples two to four (and perhaps also five) so closely together that we must assume that all three or four occurred at the same time and at the same place.

Here again we must recall the aim that this entire enumeration serves. What is common to all these examples of both groups, the Old Testament as well as the Christian ones? Each of them, with deliberate monotony, is introduced by the words "on account of jealousy," or "on account of jealousy and envy," or "on account of jealousy and strife." The citation of each example contains at least one of these words. The connecting link between all these very different cases is therefore this: jealousy, envy, and strife have always caused disaster. At times it is suffered by the righteous, that is, by the victims; at times by the guilty, that is, the authors of envy, jealousy and strife—as is the case in examples five and six of the first group.

This context should be given more careful attention not only in the general interpretation, but also in the explanation of details. Special emphasis has recently been laid on the idea that Clement is strongly influenced by *Hellenism* and is concerned to apply to the Bible and to the history of the beginnings of the Church the literary artistry and concepts of the Cynic-Stoic philosophy.[11] This is undoubtedly correct. But it will not do to see in this attempt, so to speak, the main aim of the discussions in our section, as though Clement intended to offer here a moralistic and philosophical discussion concerning endurance, and clothed it in the favourite Cynic and Stoic illustration of the contest in athletic games. No doubt Clement borrows illustrations from this pattern to describe the afflictions of the apostles. But it constitutes a misunderstanding of his purpose when it is said that he here desires to show the exemplary character of the endurance of the apostles. The central theme of the section is not endurance but envy, jealousy, strife.

Thus the brevity of the statement concerning Peter, as compared with the much more detailed report concerning Paul, could be con-

---

11 M. Dibelius, "Rom und die Christen im ersten Jahrhundert" (*Sitzungsbericht der Heidelberger Akademie der Wissenschaften, Philologisch-historische Klasse*, 1942), has shown this in a thorough study. See above, p. 76, note 36, and p. 97, note 8 (even before him E. Dubowy, *Klemens von Rom* . . . 1914). Still more comprehensive is the work written independently of M. Dibelius by the Roman Catholic theologian L. Sanders, *L'héllenisme de S. Clément de Rome et le paulinisme*, 1943. On the illustration of the contest, much used in popular philosophy, see also P. Wendland, *Die urchristlichen Literaturformen*, 1912, p. 357, note.

nected with the fact that *in this respect* the example of Peter had less to offer than that of Paul.[12]

Perhaps, however, the above mentioned central theme may actually permit us to draw indirect conclusions as to the unnamed place of the events. Clement is characterizing the vice which is causing such devastating results in the previously so exemplary church of Corinth that he is addressing. It is the vice which has caused such bad results in the earlier Biblical period as well as in the quite recent Christian past. The word or rather the words that he uses to describe it do not mean simply in a general way, "hate of the world for the children of God."[13] This is the meaning some have given, in an attempt to escape the only possible conclusion that results from our text when it says that Peter and Paul suffered on account of jealousy and strife. The three synonymous Greek words mean jealousy, envy, strife. The word that we have translated jealousy[14] appears sixteen times in our section; the one that we have translated envy,[15] four times; the one that we have translated strife,[16] three times.

It is of course correct that the first-named word, that is, the one most often used here, means primarily "zeal" in a good sense, and

---

[12] M. Dibelius, *op. cit.*, p. 28, explains this brevity from the fact that Clement did not wish to speak more in detail of the martyr death of the two for political reasons; he did not wish to present the Roman state as the opponent of the Christian athlete. Rather, in connection with his philosophical scheme of Christian athletic activity, he preferred to limit himself to the πόνοι ("torments," "troubles") and ἔργα ("works"). Concerning that subject, there was much more to tell of Paul than of Peter, who probably came to Rome only for execution, perhaps, like Ignatius, as a prisoner.

[13] So L. Sanders, *op. cit.*, p. 5, note 1, and J. Munck, *op. cit.*, pp. 58 ff., both of whom think they must therefore oppose the thesis that I defended in "Les causes de la mort de Pierre et de Paul d'après le témoignage de Clément Romain (*Revue d'Histoire et de Philosophie religieuses*, 1930, pp. 294 ff.). R. Knopf, *Handbuch zum Neuen Testament, Ergänzungsband*, p. 47, in his comment on ch. 3:2, quite correctly defines ζῆλος as "jealousy of the esteem, position, advantages of the other." With this, however, does not agree the fact that on p. 50 he writes of "hate, envy, and jealousy of the world against the children of God." P. Meinhold, "Geschehen und Deutung im 1. Clemensbrief" (*Zeitschrift für Kirchengeschichte*, 1939, p. 90) correctly states that "ζῆλος ('jealousy') and ἔρις ('strife') are used by Clement in a sense similar to that in which they are used by Paul in Rom. 13:13; I Cor. 3:3; II Cor. 12:20; Gal. 5:20. For Clement as well as for Paul they signify those moral weaknesses of *ill will* and *envy* which proceed from the dominance of the passions over the man who is no longer led by the Spirit." Meinhold, however, does not draw from this the consequences for the explanation of I Clement, ch. 5.

[14] ζῆλος.   [15] φθόνος.   [16] ἔρις.

so understood it actually appears as a divine quality.[17] But the very change of meaning from the good to the bad quality shows that the vice which finally is characterized by this word is primarily not simply hate in a general sense, but rather jealousy that has sprung from zeal (*aus Eifer entstandene Eifer-Sucht*).[18] To be sure, the word can also take on the more general meaning of "hate." But the fact that the three words are here grouped together shows that what is here to be thrown into the foreground is precisely that which is common to all three, and this is not simply hate but specifically envy and jealousy.[19]

I cannot understand how one can even suggest that the word here means hate in the general sense; this entire section is introduced by Clement only because it is this particular vice of jealousy that threatens to corrupt the whole church to which he writes. He says this quite plainly in the introduction of the Letter, in the three opening chapters which immediately precede our section. In them he does not speak of "hate in general," but of jealousy, envy, and strife, which have arisen among the members of the Christian church at Corinth (ch. 3:2, 4). It is for this reason, and only for this reason, that Clement speaks in the following chapters of this vice "through which death entered into the world," as he says with an allusion to the envy of the devil at the very beginning of the world (chs. 3:4 and 9:1).[20]

[17] See A. Stumpff in Kittel's *Theologisches Wörterbuch*, Vol. II, pp. 879 f.

[18] Chr. Eggenberger, *Die Quellen der politischen Ethik des 1. Clem.*, 1951, p. 36, thinks here of "Zealots." Similarly, but with better arguments, Bo Reicke, *Diakonie, Festfreude und Zelos in Verbindung mit der altchristlichen Agapenfeier*, 1951, pp. 373 ff.

[19] The example that J. Munck, *op. cit.*, pp. 60 f. cites from I Clem. 45:4 would be no counterproof sufficient to outweigh the weighty majority of clear examples where ζῆλος means "jealousy" in chs. 3 and 4, even if ch. 45:4 were an exception that had in mind only the hate of the world. But, as he himself concedes, jealousy is certainly present in one of the two examples cited in ch. 45:4 ff.; also in the case of the three men in the fiery furnace it is not to be forgotten that the starting point is a denunciation by some Chaldeans against certain Jews who had been entrusted by Nebuchadnezzar with the administration of the province Babylon (Dan. 3:12).

[20] J. Munck, *op. cit.*, p. 60, note 84, concedes that in this quotation from Wisdom 2:24 the devil is intended; in doing so, he refers to B. Noack, *Satanas und Soteria*, 1948, pp. 43 f. But that which is involved in this passage is *envy*, and *death* as its result; it is not the fact of the hate of the "powers hostile to God." There at the beginning envy appears in its clear original form as the power of the devil hostile to God. But it is the special characteristic of this devilish vice that since its entrance into the world it has been at work *among brothers*. This belongs to the very nature of "jealousy," "envy," and "strife." This is seen in the Corinthian church, and this is what Clement wishes to prove by his examples, at the head of which he puts in detailed form the one of Cain and Abel.

It is further clear that in the Old Testament examples the author, following his explicit aim, deals with envy and jealousy among *brothers*. According to the passage of Wisdom 2:24 cited in ch. 3:4, it is admittedly the power hostile to God, the death-dealing devil, who is here at work. But among brothers! It is for this reason that the classic example of Cain and Abel, with which the entire series is introduced, takes so disproportionate an amount of space. It is the example that is especially typical. Only one among the Old Testament examples could be considered an exception it is that of David and the Philistines. But it is connected with the example of David and Saul; it is only mentioned with reference to that example, and for the very purpose of emphasizing that Saul belongs to the same people that David does. Hence Clement writes, "On account of jealousy David not only had to endure envy from foreigners, but he also was persecuted by Saul, the King of Israel." The emphasis rests upon the latter fact.

The other examples are quite clear in this respect: the jealousy of Cain for his *brother* Abel; of Esau for his *brother* Jacob; of the sons of Jacob for their younger *brother*. The fourth example is particularly interesting. Here the author explicitly stresses the fact that Moses had to flee from Pharaoh on account of the jealousy of one of *his own people*.[21] The two remaining examples from the earlier period also have this point in common with the others.

The examples of the second group, with the exception of that of Paul, are not known from other sources, or are too little known to serve to support or undermine this result Only the quite generally stated example of the married partners readily confirms the previous conclusion. But even with regard to the others, we must assume from the start that Clement chose these particular Christian examples so that they not only harmonize with the Old Testament ones but are convincing for the readers in view of the *aim of the writer*. What meaning would it have in this letter simply to adduce in so general a way examples that illustrate persecutions of Christians and show their endurance? The thing needed here is rather to prove to the Corinthian Christians, divided by jealousy and envy, where these vices lead. We therefore must expect that in this second group also the author is speaking of jealousy among members of *one and the same fellowship*.

From this fact, however, there results an important conclusion for the examples which are here of particular interest to us. When

21 ὁμόφυλος.

Clement, in this very passage, writes that Peter had to suffer "on account of unrighteous jealousy," and Paul "on account of jealousy and strife," and the great multitude of the elect "on account of jealousy," this in the context of our letter can only mean that they were victims of jealousy from persons who counted themselves members of the Christian Church. In saying this we naturally do not mean that they were martyred or perhaps murdered by other Christians, but that the magistrates were encouraged by the attitude of some members of the Christian Church, and perhaps by the fact that they turned informers, to take action against others. In just the same way Moses, in one example of the first group, had to flee from the Egyptian King because of the jealousy of a fellow-countryman.

We are, of course, unable to say anything more definite concerning the nature of this jealousy. It should be remembered, however, that even the examples of the first group would be in part *quite unintelligible if we did not have the Old Testament.* In any case, however, the discussion must deal with the jealousy and envy of other Christians and not, for example, with that of the magistrates. The latter really had no reason at that time to be envious or jealous of the Christians, but they might well have had reasons for taking action against Christians.[22]

We have seen that statements are made concerning the life and the death of Peter as well as Paul. It has indeed been asserted that the mention of jealousy refers only to the life and not to the death of the two apostles.[23] In the notice concerning Peter, however, the words "on account of jealousy," which stand at the beginning of the relative clause, must be connected grammatically not only with the first part, "he endured many torments," but also with the second part, " he went to the place of glory." Since this second part of the sentence marks so to speak the climax, we must assume that the words "on account of jealousy" are to be connected also and particularly with this second part, and we have seen that the "entrance into the place of glory" obviously presupposes his death. But in that case Peter attained martyrdom "on account of jealousy." Moreover, in the statement concerning Paul, the words "on account of jealousy and strife" are so placed that they clearly have in view the end. They look to the time when Paul receives the victor's prize, even if the subsequently mentioned sufferings, troubles, and glorious deeds

22 The Jews cannot be meant here as authors of jealousy, for in the time of Clement they were no longer regarded as belonging to the same fellowship.
23 J. Munck, *op. cit.,* pp. 61 ff.

which precede his death are connected with the crowning with the victor's prize and form its presupposition. Grammatically, no doubt, this description is no longer dependent on the words "on account of jealousy and strife," and since the characterization of Paul's activity here has a greater rhetorical and factual detail, it is possible that we should not ask how far each individual event is conditioned by jealousy. However, it should certainly be emphasized that in II Corinthians 11:26, in the enumeration of his afflictions, Paul names in particular the "dangers among false brothers!"[24] Apart from this fact, it should also be recalled that Clement, in keeping with the theme announced for the section in ch. 3:4, must necessarily be interested particularly in those cases that have "led to *death*" (ch. 9:1).

We find a confirmation of this interpretation of our passage in ch. 47, which refers directly to the aim of the writing. Here are mentioned the quarrels which have broken out in the Corinthian church and threaten not only its unity but its very existence. The author reminds the disunited church members that in their own church at Corinth there had once been dissension. He recalls that Paul at that time warned them against divisions, when some had declared that they belonged to the party that used his own name, others that they belonged to that of Cephas, and others that they belonged to that of Apollos. Clement ends this exhortation with the following decisive words, which are really a commentary on ch. 5 and prove that one cannot possibly interpret it in any other way than we have done: "The news (of your present quarrels) has reached not only us but also *persons of different faith*, so that your folly causes the name of the Lord to be blasphemed and *brings you yourselves into danger*" (that is, at the hands of those of different faith).

We now understand still better why Clement, the Roman Bishop, reminds the divided Corinthians how, not long before, jealousy and strife among Christians had led to the suffering of martyrdom by the greatest apostles and by a great multitude of elect ones. The situation is the same, in so far as the danger of death threatens from *those outside the Church*, while the occasion for their intervention is given by the jealousy of *Christian brothers*. That, according to ch. 4:10, was exactly the situation of Moses and his fellow countryman in relation to the king of Egypt.

In all of these cases Clement is content to mention, without giving detailed circumstances, the mere fact of the jealousy; it is the thing

[24] κίνδυνοι ἐν ψευδαδέλφοις.

with which he is concerned. He could omit details because he could assume that the facts were known. The death of the two apostles, indeed, cannot be dated much more than thirty years before the writing of First Clement. So he can limit himself to references, just as in giving the Old Testament examples he could assume that the detailed circumstances were known in part from the Bible.

It is of course probable that not much was said of the particularly painful circumstances that contributed to those martyrdoms. The Christians who had caused the death of other Christians did not offer an edifying example for others. Moreover, it is possible that the abrupt ending of The Book of Acts may be explained in this way.[25] Did the author, who wishes to show the working of the Holy Spirit in the Church of Christ, perhaps have scruples about speaking of this grievous and momentous jealousy? However that may be, Clement on the contrary had every reason for mentioning it in *his* writing, in order to show what danger threatens the most valuable members of a church at the hands of pagan persecutors, if the church is divided by jealousy.

I find a further confirmation of the correctness of this explanation of our text by comparing the statement of Clement concerning jealousy with what we read on the same subject in the letters of Paul. This comparison will then lead us straight back to our main problem, the question as to the place. Thus far we have learned from the letter of Clement only that Peter, like Paul and others, fell victim to non-Christian persecutors as a result of disunity caused by jealousy. We now ask: *in what place*, according to the sources at our disposal, could *such events* have occurred? Where, in the time of Peter and Paul, did there exist in a local church jealousy which could lead to persecution and the death of martyrs?

We possess a letter of Paul in which the apostle explicitly writes that envy and strife reign in the church where he is at the time of writing; he further says that he is there as a prisoner. This is found in Philippians 1:15–17: "There are some people here who preach Christ out of *envy and strife*. Others do it out of good will. Some proclaim Christ out of love, for they know that I lie here (in prison) for the defence of the Gospel. Others, however, do it because of *a quarrelsome spirit*, not out of pure motives; they wish to *bring affliction upon me in my imprisonment*." It is startling that we find here in a letter of Paul, written from a place where the apostle is held prisoner, almost the same words that occur in I Clement, ch. 5: envy, strife.[26]

25 See above, pp. 80 ff.   26 φθόνος, ἔρις, ἐριθεία.

The place of writing of Philippians is of course uncertain, since it is not definitely named in the letter. Independently of our problem I, like many scholars, have long assumed that it must refer to the imprisonment in Rome.[27] We have seen that the great multitude of elect ones who are mentioned in I Clement 6:1 as having suffered martyrdom on account of jealousy must *certainly* be sought in Rome; "among us" proves that. Furthermore, we shall see in particular that *Romans* contains features which point to friction between the Jewish Christian and Gentile Christian sections of the Roman church. Without reasoning in a "vicious circle," we thus may combine these data and conclude that only concerning the *Roman* church do we know (1) that jealousy ruled in it (I Clem. 6:1); (2) that Paul seems to have feared difficulties in it due to the fact that its membership included both Jewish and Gentile Christians (Rom. 15:20); (3) that Paul spent a time in it as a prisoner of the Roman Empire and during his imprisonment had to expect "affliction"[28] from other members of the church (Phil. 1:15 f.).

We here should recall the vigorous tone which Paul uses in this same Epistle to the Philippians against the Jewish Christians, who are probably to be sought in the circles of those whom he designates in Galatians 2:4 as "false brothers." In Philippians 3:2 he actually goes so far as to call them "dogs." These people, who have caused him difficulties everywhere on his journeys, he accordingly encountered also in Rome. *Peter* certainly did not belong to their number. We have seen that he, on the contrary, always stood closer to Paul, and it would be an error to believe that after the episode in Antioch a break occurred between Peter and Paul.[29] According to I Clement, ch. 5, it is rather to be assumed that Peter himself had to suffer at the hands of those people.

[27] So among others A. Jülicher—E. Fascher, *Einleitung ins N.T.*, 7th ed., 1931, pp. 120 f.; K. Holl, *Gesammelte Aufsätze*, Vol. II, p. 67. The necessity of assigning the letter to the doubtful imprisonment at Ephesus, as do P. Feine—Behm, *Einleitung in das N. T.*, 1936, pp. 174 ff., W. Michaelis, *Einleitung ins N. T.*, 1946, pp. 205 ff., and recently also P. Benoit, *La S. Bible* (Jerusalem), *Les Epîtres de S. Paul. Aux Philippiens*, 1949, pp. 11 f., and others, I have never really seen, even if it is true that the mention of the "praetorium" and of the people "of the house of Caesar" does not *necessarily* refer to Rome. The distance between Rome and Philippi I do not feel to be a difficulty. In content the letter fits much better at the end of the life of Paul.

[28] θλίψιν (Phil. 1:17).

[29] This is rightly challenged also by M. Dibelius—W. G. Kümmel, *Paulus* (Göschen), 1951, p. 124.

We recall that in the preceding chapter[30] we concluded on other grounds that Peter, as a delegated representative of the Jerusalem church, found himself by reason of his free attitude toward the Law *in an even more difficult situation than Paul* (Gal. 2:11 ff.). In view of this fact, one could very well say that the *"varied* troubles" caused by jealousy (I Clem. 5:4) refer to such difficulties with the Jerusalem leaders who commissioned him and with their over-zealous helpers.[31]

That such conflicts already existed in Rome before Paul arrived there is indicated above all by Paul's *letter to Rome.* Paul must have heard of such things. Only so can we explain the way he opposes Judaism in this letter, which he addresses to a church he has not yet visited. We mentioned above [32] how concerned he is in ch. 15:20 ff. to excuse himself for making an exception this time and coming to a church that he has not founded. We have seen further the reason why this troubles his conscience so much; he thereby is untrue to a principle whose observance he has considered a "point of honour," because it seems to him to correspond to the spirit of the Jerusalem agreement (Gal. 2:9). The emphasis with which he speaks of this in ch. 15 proves that he does not go without some anxiety to this church which probably was founded and then cared for by the Jewish Christian group. If he already had to contend, in the churches which he had brought into being, against the opposition of the Jerusalem mission, how much more in this church, where he may be treated from the outset as an intruder. That entire section in ch. 15 clearly betrays anxiety. It is possible that this anxiety presupposes in Paul special knowledge of the situation in Rome, which plainly is controlled by the Jewish Christians. This explains the unusually long and careful description of himself in the opening verses, and also the special content of the letter.[33]

The events in Rome show only too well how justified was Paul's fear.[34] The conflicts there became acute. Even Peter, who as the

---

[30] See above, p. 51.
[31] That these difficulties had already begun for Peter at an earlier time is rightly emphasized by W. Grundmann, "Die Apostel zwischen Jerusalem und Antiochien" (*ZNW*, 1940, p. 128).
[32] See above, p. 45.
[33] We have seen above that one cannot conclude from this fact with H. Lietzmann, *Sitzungsbericht der Berliner Akademie der Wissenschaften*, 1930, that Peter came to Rome and agitated against Paul. See p. 78. On this subject see E. Hirsch, "Petrus und Paulus" (*ZNW*, 1930, pp. 63 ff.).
[34] C. Cecchelli, *Gli Apostoli a Roma*, 1938, p. 101, has actually proposed the hypothesis that Paul, on account of conditions in Rome, asked Peter to come

responsible organizer of the Jewish Christian mission had come at this time to the capital city, perhaps for the very purpose of removing internal difficulties, was apparently singled out for attack and was deserted by some of his own group. This was doubtless the result of the very conciliatory standpoint that he took. As the official leader of the Jerusalem mission he no doubt had everywhere, as we have mentioned, a difficult position. But now he was made the object of unusually strong hostility by the extremists of the Jewish Christian party.

After the writing of Philippians, therefore, the conflicts, which seem to have become more acute after Paul's arrival at Rome, may finally have degenerated into open attacks, and things may even have gone so far that during the time of persecution those people did not shrink from pointing out to the magistrates the leading men, when summoned to do so. This furthermore may find a confirmation in the pagan source which tells of Nero's action against the Christians; in Tacitus, *Annals*, XV, 44, we read: "The (Christians) first seized who made a confession were convicted, and then upon their evidence a great multitude . . ."[35] It has been said that such informing during a persecution, when the hearing is accompanied by torture, is nothing abnormal.[36] Nevertheless, Tacitus makes it a special point to mention this fact. Naturally we cannot prove, but can only suppose, that the zealous ones were really to be sought among those "first seized." In any case, this would correspond completely with the saying of Jesus preserved in Matthew 24:10: "They will deliver up one another."

It could also be that the attention of the Empire was turned to the apostles by some other way than by direct report. This much, however, is certain: *according to the opinion of Clement* it happened as a

to the capital city. The fact that Peter was so to speak responsible for the Jewish Christian part of the Church could indeed argue for this hypothesis. Moreover, C. Cecchelli also assumes a betrayal of the two apostles by a "new Judas." See *op. cit.*, p. 96.

[35] *Igitur primo conrepti qui fatebantur, deinde, indicio eorum, multitudo ingens* . . . On recent interpretation of this text see H. Fuchs, "Tacitus über die Christen," (*Vigiliae christianae*, 1950, pp. 65 ff.), and A. Kurfess, "Tacitus über die Christen" (*Vigiliae christianae*, 1951, pp. 148 f.). According to Chr. Eggenberger, *Die Quellen der politischen Ethik des 1. Klem.*, 1951, pp. 127 f., Clement would be dependent on Tacitus at this point.

[36] J. Munck, *op. cit.*, p. 63.—He further writes that from this passage it follows that the persecution was already going on. That is correct. But I do not understand how this is supposed to argue against my interpretation. After all, it is not necessary to assume that Peter and Paul had been seized at the very beginning.

result of the jealousy which separated the members of a church from one another; and since such an assertion, which runs contrary to all later tendencies, could not possibly have been invented, the opinion that Clement here expresses must have corresponded with the reality.

Theoretically, of course, the possibility remains open that what took place in Rome could also happen elsewhere, that therefore disputes in the Church could become the external occasion for executions of other Christians by the Empire, so that we would not have to assume as a certainty that the martyrdom of Peter occurred in the same place as did that of Paul and the great multitude. But this is improbable, and in any case the fact remains that the existence of such jealousy is attested only for Rome, where it is attested by I Clement 6:1, almost certainly by Paul's letter to Philippi, and indirectly also by the letter to the Romans. Therefore the indication of place in ch. 6:1, "among us," that is, in the church of Bishop Clement of Rome, quite probably refers to all the Christian martyrdoms mentioned by the author and caused by jealousy.

It is likely, moreover, that by way of warning for the disunited Corinthians Clement recalled, in addition to the parties which at an earlier time had split their church (ch. 47), precisely such Christian examples of jealousy and division as he could report from his own Roman church.

Furthermore, it has been suggested that in Mark 15:10 the Evangelist added the remark, "Pilate knew that the high priests had delivered Jesus up *out of envy*,"[37] under the special influence of the events in Rome; Mark indeed wrote his Gospel in Rome, and so was a witness of those events.[38]

Finally, a further trace of these unhappy events appears to have been preserved in the *later legends* of the Acts of Peter. When we there hear that Peter was executed because he induced prominent Roman ladies to leave their husbands, the element of jealousy may constitute at least the historical kernel of this legend.[39]

Still more striking, however, are two passages of the Acts of Paul.[40] They reproduce legends in which Paul expressly appears as

[37] διὰ φθόνον.
[38] This thesis has been defended, in conjunction with my article (see above, p. 75), by A. Fridrichsen, "Propter invidiam, Note sur 1. Clém. Rom. V" (*Eranos Rudbergianus*, 1946, pp. 161 ff.).
[39] *Actus Vercellenses*, 33 ff.
[40] I owe this reference to my colleague Erik Peterson. See *ΠΡΑΞΕΙΣ ΠΑΥΛΟΥ. Acta Pauli nach dem Papyrus der Hamburger Bibliothek*, edited by C. Schmidt, 1936.

the victim of jealousy. First, in Ephesus, it is said that a certain Diophantos, whose wife was a disciple of Paul and was with him day and night, became jealous and occasioned his battle with wild beasts.[41] It is further told[42] that in Corinth a Spirit-filled man predicted to Paul that he would depart from this world in Rome as a victim of jealousy.[43] Here, no doubt, statements of Paul (I Cor. 15:32) are combined with I Clement, ch. 5. In any case both the Acts of Peter and the Acts of Paul have correctly preserved from I Clement, ch. 5, the fact that the death of the two apostles had been occasioned by jealousy, although they could only conceive this jealousy in the primitive form of the jealousy of a pagan husband with regard to his Christian wife. The idea of jealousy among church members, of a "danger among false brethren" (II Cor. 11:26), was far from their minds; such a thought contradicted their entire outlook.

We reach the following conclusion. From the investigation of I Clement we conclude, not with absolute certainty but yet with the highest probability, that Peter suffered martyrdom at Rome about the time of the Neronian persecution, while divisions existed in the church there. Peter and Paul, therefore, became martyrs at about the same time, not necessarily on the same day, but probably in the same period of persecution, which may have covered a more or less extended period.[44] Concerning Peter, First Clement does not permit us to say whether he also carried on a real activity in Rome as a missionary or church leader. Just as little can we learn from this text when he came to Rome.[45] The quarrels of which we hear render likely the assumption that this happened shortly before the persecution, and specifically in connection with his responsibility for the Jewish Christian part of the Church.

We now come to the last of the early literary witnesses, the *Letter of Ignatius of Antioch to the Romans*. At the beginning of the second

---

[41] Page 2, line 8 of the Papyrus.   [42] Page 6, line 27 of the Papyrus.

[43] ζηλωθέντα ἐξελθεῖν.

[44] A greater separation in time, such as K. Holl, for example, assumes in *Gesammelte Aufsätze*, Vol. II, 1928, p. 67, note, is naturally not excluded.

[45] J. Munck, *op. cit.*, assumes that they both came thither as condemned men. That both suffered martyrdom *together* he believes it necessary to conclude from the fact that only the common death can have caused the ancient tradition to name the two apostles together, although they had worked quite separately; indeed, all the later apocryphal Acts, apart from the Acts of Peter and Paul, which dates only from the fifth century, also tell of them separately. He finds the common martyrdom confirmed also in Rev. 11:3.

century this martyr, a prisoner condemned to execution in the Circus at Rome, writes while en route to the Christian church of that city, which soon will witness his martyrdom.

In ch. 4:3 of this writing we read: "Not like Peter and Paul do I give you commands.[46] They (were) apostles, I am a condemned man; they were free, I am even till now a slave; but when I suffer, I shall become Jesus Christ's freeman, and I shall arise in him as a free man." This is what Ignatius writes to the Roman church. It is to be noted that he recalls to the mind of this particular church the examples of Peter and Paul.

To be sure, not a word is said to indicate that the two apostles were in Rome. The sentence could be taken simply to mean that Ignatius wished to say: "I do not command you *as if* I were Peter and Paul." The parallel passages in the letter of Ignatius to the Ephesians (ch. 3:1) and to the Trallians (ch. 3:3) could support such an interpretation. There Ignatius actually does write in very general terms: "I do not command you as though I were somebody," "not as an apostle."[47] Nevertheless, it is noteworthy that precisely in his letter to the *Romans* he is not content with such a general way of expressing himself, but refers to Peter and Paul *by name*. In no case can it be said that the combined mention of Peter and Paul would *necessarily* force itself upon a writer as soon as he sought for apostles to name. This might be true in a later time, but not in the time of Ignatius. One cannot evade the question: How could it happen at that time that Ignatius named the two together? After all, these two apostles, apart from their meetings in Jerusalem and their conflict in Antioch, nowhere worked together. Indeed, according to the Jerusalem agreement of Galatians 2:9, they headed two separate missionary organizations.[48]

The most plausible answer seems to me to be the reference to their common martyrdom in Rome, especially since it can be shown that in another passage (ch. 3:1) Ignatius refers to First Clement.[49] Thus the combined mention of the two in our writing is also best explained by saying that Ignatius cites by name to the Romans those

---

[46] οὐχ ὡς Πέτρος καὶ Παῦλος διατάσσομαι ὑμῖν.

[47] K. Heussi rightly points to these parallels in *War Petrus in Rom?*, pp. 40 ff.

[48] J. Munck, following W. Bauer, *Rechtgläubigkeit und Ketzerei*, 1934, p. 116, rightly puts this question. In any case, the answer of H. Dannenbauer, "Die Römische Petruslegende" (*Historische Zeitschrift*, 1932, p. 258), that the two apostles had been together in Antioch, is insufficient.

[49] O. Perler, "Ignatius von Antiochien und die römische Christengemeinde" (*Divus Thomas*, 1944, pp. 442 f.), has demonstrated this.

apostles who were with them as martyrs, just as he himself is now coming to them as a martyr. Even if he here emphasizes the difference between them and himself, yet this negative comparison has meaning only if the writer is conscious that he nevertheless has something in common with them. This is not the apostolic office, but probably the martyrdom in Rome. In the parallel passage in the Letter to the Trallians (ch. 3:3) Ignatius gives no names of apostles, precisely because in relation to this church, which no apostle has visited, there is no occasion to do so. In his letter, on the other hand, to the Ephesians, whom *Paul* had visited, he mentions the name of this apostle, even if in a quite different context (ch. 12:2).

It must be admitted, of course, that even these texts of Ignatius do not give us absolute certainty. However, we again must conclude that Ignatius in all probability knew of a Roman martyrdom of Peter and Paul.

Does this passage also permit the conclusion that the two apostles were active in Rome prior to their martyrdom? The expression "give commands"[50] appears to make this likely. It has, indeed, been said that this word simply refers to the instructions of Paul's letter to Rome. In that case, however, Peter would then be wrongly linked with Paul. It therefore could be that Ignatius here refers to a missionary and ecclesiastical activity of the two apostles. The connection, however, in which Ignatius here speaks of "giving commands" makes this unlikely. The chapter at whose end stands the sentence that interests us contains in its first part the famous summons to the Roman Christians not to intervene with the imperial authorities on behalf of Ignatius, since he does not want to be deprived of martyrdom. The mention of the commands of Peter and Paul, therefore, stands in a context in which Ignatius is speaking of his martyrdom and of the attitude of the Roman church towards this martyrdom. Ignatius himself is compelled at the beginning of this chapter to "give a command" regarding this.[51] So the most natural explanation probably is that the giving of commands by Peter and Paul also was connected with their own martyrdoms. If so, this mention contains no indication concerning a longer preaching activity of the two apostles, although on the other hand it does not exclude such preaching. It is sufficient, then, to assume that before their death the two apostles had an opportunity to give instructions to the Roman church with reference to their martyrdom.

[50] διατάσσεσθαι.
[51] Ch. 4:1: ἐντέλλομαι; this means that he gives a command "to all churches."

With some reservations we can add as a further indirect witness from the first century a passage from the apocryphal writing, the *Ascension of Isaiah*,[52] of which it has been said that it is the first and earliest document that attests the martyrdom of Peter in Rome. The passage in question is ch. 4:2 f., where we read the following prediction: ". . . then will arise Beliar, the great prince, the king of this world, who has ruled it since its origin; and he will descend from his firmament in human form, king of wickedness, murderer of his mother, who himself is king of this world; and he will persecute the plant which the twelve apostles of the Beloved shall have planted; one of the Twelve will be delivered into his hands." It seems beyond doubt that Nero is here meant by Beliar, who descends in human form and murders his mother. Less clear is the mention of the "one of the Twelve" who is delivered into his hands. As apostles who were victims of Nero, Peter and Paul are to be considered.[53] Paul, however, cannot be meant here, for according to ch. 3:17 the author uses the phrase "the Twelve" in the narrower sense.[54] In that case this passage probably refers to Peter. The statement is of course vague, and the mention of the "delivering up" stands in need of further definition.[55] Above all, the indication of the place is also lacking. Nevertheless, the passage speaks of an apostle who fell into Nero's hands, and so we probably can think only of Rome. The difficulty, however, lies in the dating of the Christian apocalypse, chs. 3:13 to 4:19, to which this passage belongs. While some think it was written in the lifetime of Nero,[56] others wish to put it later, in the third century.[57] Even if the decision for a date about 100 is the most probable,[58] we cannot reach a certain conclusion. Nevertheless, this witness should not be simply ignored, as has often happened in recent discussions.

★   ★   ★

[52] See R. H. Charles, *The Ascension of Isaiah*, 1900; E. Tisserant, *Ascension d'Isaïe*, 1909; J. Flemming—H. Duensing, *Die Himmelfahrt des Jesaja*, in E. Hennecke, *Neutestamentliche Apokryphen*, 2nd ed., 1924, pp. 303 ff.
[53] According to E. Zeller, *Zeitschrift für wissenschaftliche Theologie*, 1896, pp. 558 ff., what is involved is the exile of the apostle John.
[54] E. Tisserant, *op. cit.*, p. 117, rightly points to this fact.
[55] For this reason A. Harnack, *Geschichte der altchristlichen Literatur, Die Chronologie*, Vol. I, 1897, p. 715, denies that this passage speaks of the martyrdom of Peter.
[56] C. Clemen, "Die Himmelfahrt des Jesaja, ein ältestes Zeugnis für das römische Martyrium des Petrus" (*Zeitschrift für wissenschaftliche Theologie*, 1896, pp. 388 ff.).
[57] A. Harnack, *op. cit.*, pp. 578 f.
[58] So R. H. Charles, *op. cit.*, and E. Tisserant, *op. cit.*, p. 60.

We have reached the end of our study of the early literary documents[59] and can now sum up the results:

Prior to the second half of the second century no document asserts explicitly the stay and martyrdom of Peter in Rome. Nevertheless, we have established: 1. As far as the *fact of the martyr death* of Peter is concerned, we possess an ancient tradition concerning it, John 21:18 ff., and this seems presupposed also in other texts. 2. As far as the *stay of Peter in Rome* is concerned, this is excluded for the time at which Paul writes his letter to the Romans. The founding of the Roman church by Peter can neither be proved nor regarded as probable. Since, however, according to Romans 15:20, it was the work of Jewish Christians, there exists a cogent reason for saying that he came to the capital city as the responsible leader of the Jewish Christian mission. The First Epistle of Peter probably presupposes in ch. 5:13 that at some time Peter was in Rome. As far as his *activity* in the Roman church is concerned, no early text compels us to contest it. But on the other hand, neither is it explicitly mentioned by a single text of the ancient period, and in any case it is difficult, for reasons of chronology, to include a very long activity. Of an episcopal office of Peter nothing is ever said. In the form in which this office is first asserted in the fourth century,[60] it is historically impossible. From everything that we know concerning the situation within the Roman church from Paul's letters to Rome and Philippi and from First Clement, his activity, like that of Paul, may be connected with the relations between the Jewish Christian and Gentile Christian parts of the Church. 3. As far as the *martyr death of Peter in Rome* is concerned, we have concerning it two texts that must be regarded as indirect witnesses: I Clement, ch. 5, and Ignatius, Romans 4:3. Neither of them says explicitly that Peter had been in Rome. In both cases,

[59] J. Zeiller, *L'Eglise primitive* (*Histoire de l'Eglise*, 1946 ed., p. 229; Eng. Tr., *History of the Primitive Church*, Vol. I, 1942, p. 235), adds as a further witness from the first half of the second century that of Papias; as reported by Eusebius, *Ecclesiastical History*, III, 39, 15, he tells that Mark wrote his Gospel in accord with the sermons of Peter. But that the Gospel was written in Rome ("composé à Rome") and that the sermons of Peter were preached in that city ("en cette ville"), as J. Zeiller asserts, this text of Papias does not say at all!

[60] *Catalogus Liberianus* (year 354): "After the resurrection of Christ the blessed Peter received the episcopal office . . . for twenty-five years, one month, and eight days he was (bishop) in the time of Tiberius Caesar, Gaius, Claudius, and Nero, from the consulate of Minucius and Longinus to that of Nerinus and Verus."—That would be from 30 to 55. All these statements stand in such flagrant contradiction to The Acts and the letters of Paul that it is unnecessary even to discuss them.

however, and particularly in First Clement, which presupposes in the Church definite circumstances that fit only Rome, we can establish a great probability. It is sufficient to let us *include the martyrdom of Peter in Rome in our final historical picture of the early Church, as a fact which is relatively though not absolutely assured.* We accept it, however, with the self-evident caution that we have to use concerning many other facts of antiquity that are universally accepted as historical. Were we to demand for all facts of ancient history a greater degree of probability, we should have to strike from our history books a large proportion of their contents.

The argument from silence cannot be used as a counterproof against the martyr death of Peter at Rome, especially since the reason for that silence can be explained from the special circumstances of the martyrdom, as we can deduce them from I Clement, ch. 5. Furthermore, from the later silence of the Roman Bishop Anicetus, in the first Passover debate about the middle of the second century, we cannot conclude that at that time nothing was known as yet of a stay of Peter in Rome. In that controversy Polycarp, the Bishop of Smyrna, appeals to John and other apostles with whom he has associated to support the way of celebrating the Passover festival which he defends, while Anicetus only recalls the usage of those who were "the most ancient ones before him," and says not a word concerning Peter.[61] This, however, could at the most be cited as evidence that Anicetus knew nothing of a leading activity of Peter in Rome; in no case can it be cited to show lack of knowledge concerning his martyrdom.[62]

If it were not imperative to handle with caution all arguments from silence, one could reverse the argument. To support the indications we possess of a martyrdom in Rome one could cite the fact that the entire early Christian literature is *completely* silent concerning the death of Peter. We do not have even the slightest trace that points to any *other* place which could be considered as the scene of his death. In favour of Rome there are at least important even if indirect hints, which there are good grounds for so interpreting. Their value as proof, moreover, is increased precisely by their indirect and merely

---

[61] Eusebius, *Ecclesiastical History*, V, 24, 16.

[62] Apart from that fact, Anicetus also could not boast, as Polycarp could, of direct relations with the apostles. M. Goguel, *L'Eglise primitive*, 1947, p. 213, explains the failure of Anicetus to appeal to the apostles by the consciousness of the Roman church that the Easter festival had been introduced only a short time before, and so did not reach back into the apostolic age.

allusive character. It is a further important point that in the second and third centuries, when certain churches were in rivalry with the one in Rome, it never occurred to a single one of them to contest the claim of Rome that it was the scene of the martyrdom of Peter. Indeed, even more can be said; precisely in the east, as is clear from the Pseudo-Clementine writings and the Petrine legends, above all those that deal with Peter's conflict with Simon the magician, the tradition of the Roman residence of Peter had a particularly strong hold.

In the second half of the second century the Roman tradition about Peter begins to be explicitly attested. It can scarcely be proved that this is to be explained as a defence against Marcion, who recognized only Paul as a true apostle.[63] It is sufficient rather to take account of the universal effort, which appears in this period, to prove the apostolic origin of the churches. It will not do, however, to ascribe to such tendencies the *invention* of Peter's stay and martyrdom at Rome; their function can be limited to the emphasizing and development of traditions that already existed independently of them.

On the other hand, the chief value for historical study of these *late* texts, which now in increasing number assert that Peter was in Rome and became a martyr there, concerns only the history of dogma; they attest the *development* of the tradition. In theory the possibility cannot be excluded that perhaps here and there the basis of the tradition is a good earlier source which we no longer possess. Yet even if this is so, we must be fundamentally sceptical toward these later texts, when we see how in this very period the development of Christian legend flourishes and how it seeks to fill out the gaps in the New Testament narrative. Where in addition contradictions between these texts and the early sources appear, their trustworthiness must be challenged from the start. With this reserve, however, it is interesting to get acquainted with at least the earliest of these witnesses, those of the second and third centuries.

*   *   *

First of all, however, we must note the silence of a Christian writer who lived in Rome. This is *Justin Martyr*, from whom we possess extensive writings that date from the middle of the second century.

---

[63] So K. Heussi, *op. cit.*, p. 56, according to whom Peter's stay and death in Rome were first invented to meet the necessities of this anti-Marcionite struggle.

Neither in his Apologies nor in the Dialogue with Trypho is Peter's Roman residence mentioned. This is the more striking in view of the fact that he speaks three times of Simon the magician, who in this period was regarded as the great opponent of Peter.

Among the later texts the chief one is the letter, already mentioned, from the Corinthian Bishop *Dionysius* to the Romans. Its date is about the year 170. Eusebius has preserved some fragments of it for us.[64] We have already spoken of it in connection with the question concerning the stay of Peter in Corinth.[65] Dionysius takes pains to prove the common bond between the two churches of Rome and Corinth. He recalls first the letter of Clement, which, he says, was regularly read in Corinth, and which bound the two churches together. For example, Peter and Paul had "planted" the church of Corinth and had taught there; in like manner, both had taught together in Italy as well, and had borne witness at the same time. We have already seen[66] that at least *one* historical error occurs here: the assertion that Peter together with Paul *founded* the church of Corinth. This is excluded by I Corinthians 3:6 and 4:15. In addition, Dionysius here asserts that they had taught *together* [67] in Italy, which certainly refers to Rome. This *joint* preaching activity is not indeed impossible in view of the early texts, but the statement scarcely goes back to early tradition.

Toward the end of the second century *Irenaeus* writes,[68] chiefly in connection with a description of gospel origins that goes back to Papias, that Peter and Paul had preached in Rome and founded the church, and he repeats this assertion when he speaks of the Roman church as the "very ancient and universally known church founded and organized by Peter and Paul." Here, too, occurs at least *one* error: the Roman church in any case was not *founded* by Paul. That is entirely clear from his letter to the Romans. This at once calls in question the historical trustworthiness of the statement. Concerning the martyr death of Peter in Rome, be it noted, nothing is said here. But from this fact no negative conclusion can be drawn,

---

[64] Eusebius, *Ecclesiastical History*, II, 25, 8.

[65] See above, p. 54.   [66] See above, p. 54.

[67] It is impossible to defend the assertion that ὁμόσε ("to the same place," "together") only indicates that they went to the same place, Italy, but not at the same time. For ὁμόσε here as often stands for ὁμοῦ ("together"). See Blass-Debrunner, *Grammatik des neutestamentlichen Griechisch*, 7th ed., 1943, Part II, Supplement, Par. 103, p. 19. See also W. Bauer, *Griechisch-deutsches, Wörterbuch*, ὁμόσε.

[68] *Adversus Haereses*, III, 1-3.

for neither is anything said here concerning the martyr death of Paul.[69]

In contrast to this, *Tertullian*[70] at about the same time congratulates the Roman church because the apostles "have spread their teaching" in it "with their shed blood," because in it Peter has suffered a martyrdom "like the death of the Lord," and Paul in the manner of John the Baptist has attained the "palm of martyrdom." When, however, he adds at the same time the legend that the apostle John was dipped in boiling oil at Rome and yet survived uninjured, the value of his statements concerning Peter and Paul is thereby lessened. We must speak later of a further text of Tertullian[71] which probably refers to the *grave* of Peter.

Clement of Alexandria reports[72] that Peter wrote his first letter in Rome and "used a cryptic word in designating the city of Rome by the name Babylon." This is a notice which at the most need be considered in the history of the interpretation of I Peter 5:13.

The statement of *Origen*[73] that Peter was crucified in Rome with his head downward scarcely has historical value, even if the crucifixion as such appears to be attested in John 21:18 f.[74]

The statement of the Roman Presbyter *Gaius*, however, deserves greater respect. Not as though the fact of the stay and martyrdom of Peter in Rome could be based upon it. It dates only from the beginning of the third century. The importance of this account, which comes from Rome itself, consists rather in the fact that here the Roman tradition about Peter is given a definite topographical support, which can serve as a clue in the archaeological search for Peter's grave.

Gaius is here opposing the Montanist Proclus, who in his polemic had appealed to the fact that the church of Hierapolis in Asia Minor possesses the graves of Philip and his daughters.[75] Gaius writes the following words:[76] "But I can show the trophies[77] of the apostles,

---

[69] This is rightly stressed by M. Goguel, *L'Eglise primitive*, 1947, p. 216, in opposition to Ch. Guignebert, "La sépulture de Pierre" (*Revue historique*, 1931, pp. 225 ff.).

[70] *De praescriptione haereticorum*, 36; *Scorpiace*, 15; *Adversus Marcionem*, IV, 5.

[71] See below, p. 121.   [72] Eusebius, *Ecclesiastical History*, II, 15, 2.

[73] *Idem*, III, 1, 2.

[74] In Christian typology the phrase ἔκτασις τῶν χειρῶν ("stretching out of the hands") refers to the crucifixion. Tertullian, *Scorpiace*, 15, already refers the ζώσει ("he will gird") of John 21:18 to the binding to the cross.

[75] Eusebius, *Ecclesiastical History*, III, 31, 4.

[76] *Idem*, II, 25, 7.   [77] τρόπαια.

for if you go to the Vatican Hill or to the highway to Ostia, you will find the trophies of those who have founded this church."

We need not stop to consider the statement concerning the joint *founding* of the Roman church by the two apostles; this statement, in spite of its historical inaccuracy, had become by this time a fixed tradition. It is important, however, to know that in the time of Gaius the places which were connected with the martyrdoms of Peter and Paul were definitely located.

Whether the word "trophies" here means graves is disputed. The Greek word can also mean simply "victory memorials" and need not always designate a definite object. It can be meant quite generally as a place which recalls a victory or an event interpreted as a victory,[78] and in the ancient Christian view martyrdom belongs to this category. The narrower meaning of "burial place," however, is also clearly attested.[79] Thus there are two possibilities. The two places designated as "trophies" were regarded either as the burial places of the apostles[80] or as the places where they had been executed.[81]

It is clear in any case that Eusebius understood the word in the sense of "burial places." For he introduces the quotation from Gaius with the remark that Gaius, who is speaking against Proclus, speaks of the places "in which were buried the sacred bodies of the apostles named (Peter and Paul)."[82] Furthermore, the mention of the places by Gaius is probably to be considered parallel to the appeal that his Montanist opponent Proclus makes to the graves of Philip and his daughters in Asia Minor, although Eusebius reports this latter point in another part of his book.[83] If the two are parallel, the assumption is still more likely that in the opinion of Gaius the "trophies" of Peter and Paul meant their graves.

---

[78] See F. Lammert, Article on τρόπαιον in Pauly-Wissowa, *Reallexikon der klassischen Altertumswissenschaft.*

[79] See P. Monceaux, "Enquête sur l'épigraphie chrétienne d'Afrique" (*Mémoires présentés à l'Academie des Inscriptions et Belles-Lettres*, Vol. 88, 1910, p. 260.

[80] So H. Lietzmann, *Petrus und Paulus in Rom*, p. 210, and also K. Heussi, *War Petrus in Rom?*, p. 64. Likewise, H. Delehaye, *Les origines du cult des martyrs*, 1933, p. 264.

[81] So C. Erbes, "Das Alter der Gräber und Kirchen des Paulus und Petrus in Rom" (*Zeitschrift für Kirchengeschichte*, 1885, pp. 1 ff.); *Die Todestage der Apostel Paulus und Petrus und ihre römischen Denkmäler*, 1899; "Die geschichtlichen Verhältnisse der Apostelgräber in Rom" (*ZKG*, 1924, pp. 38 ff.). Likewise Ch. Guignebert, *La primauté de Pierre et la venue de Pierre à Rome*, 1919, pp. 305 ff. See also Th. Klausner, *Jahrbuch für Liturgiewissenschaft*, 1924, p. 296.

[82] Eusebius, *Ecclesiastical History*, II, 25, 6.

[83] Ch. Guignebert, *op. cit.*, believes for this reason that this reference must be denied.

Thus the only certain fact is that about the year 200 there were shown in Rome the places with which was connected the memory of the martyrdoms of Peter and Paul. For it is inconceivable that Gaius only invented these locations to serve the needs of his anti-Montanist polemic. The tradition which designated these two places *must therefore have existed before he wrote*.

This still does not prove, however, that the tradition is true as far as the *graves* are concerned. For in any event almost a century and a half lies between the death of the apostles and this earliest testimony as to the place where it occurred. In favour of its correctness it has been argued, as we shall see, that if the tradition were only a later invention, these places would not have been invented in such great geographical distance from one another as are the Vatican Hill and the highway to Ostia. It has further been argued that in this case the burials would have been located not in pagan cemeteries but rather, in accordance with a later tendency, in Christian catacombs.[84] This argument certainly deserves serious consideration. On the other hand, it still is not completely decisive, for as has already been remarked, the tendency to join the two apostles is not common in the ancient apocryphal literature.[85]

Should the word "trophies" refer to *graves*, the following argument can be made against the correctness of the tradition that Gaius attests concerning their location. It is hard to conceive that the surviving Roman Christians could have recognized the bodies of the apostles among the many corpses, largely charred as they probably were by fire, and could then have taken them away and have honoured Peter with a grave in the very garden of Nero. This is hardly conceivable if we are dealing with the Neronian persecution, in which we must assume that the remains were thrown into the Tiber.[86] We should also emphasize that in the first century *not the slightest trace of a cult of martyr relics* can be found. The first testimony to that we find only about A.D. 150, in the Martyrdom of Polycarp.[87] In view of the *expectation of the end of the world* in the immediate future, a concern for relics clearly constitutes an anachronism in thinking of the sixth decade of the first century, especially in those terrible days of persecution under Nero. We shall return to this point

[84] So H. Lietzmann, *Petrus und Paulus in Rom*, pp. 246 ff.

[85] See above, p. 109, note 45; p. 110.

[86] See K. Holl, *Gesammelte Aufsätze*, Vol. II, p. 65, note 1.

[87] According to H. Grégoire's latest thesis (see below, p. 150, note 70), the year is 177

when we speak of the archaeological results. Finally, should the most recent hypothesis be correct, according to which "the two witnesses" of Revelation 11:3 ff. are to be identified with the two apostles Peter and Paul, then their bodies were not buried at first and the rise of the tradition of their direct rapture to Heaven would exclude any knowledge of the place of their burial.[88]

In case the "trophies" mentioned by Gaius, however, are not the ancient burial places, there still remains the possibility that the two places were the *places of execution*, which then without further evidence were later regarded, perhaps even by the time of Gaius, as the burial places. On the other hand, it can be assumed that the executed persons, if buried at all, were buried at the place of their execution, or at any rate in the immediate neighbourhood. This being so, the graves would then be at least approximately located, though not precisely identified—this was not possible or even attempted in the earliest period.

We must return to this text of Gaius when we speak of the results of the excavations under the Church of St. Peter. At present our chief task is to evaluate the significance of this literary witness as such. Although it dates only from the beginning of the third century, yet greater importance attaches to it than to the previously discussed witnesses of equal antiquity. It is true that a purely topographical tradition is not free from the influence of partisan interests. This is especially clear since, as we know also from the Letter of Polycrates,[89] the possession of graves was regarded at this time as a guarantee of the genuineness of a tradition, and so led also to the making of "deposition lists." Yet such a tradition naturally offers a greater guarantee of correctness than does a tradition concerning the events themselves.

The attempt has been made to explain this locating of the graves as a later deduction from the narrative of Tacitus. It locates the place of martyrdom of the persecuted Christians[90] in the gardens and the Circus of Nero, which according to the latest excavations were located not, as one had believed, under the present Cathedral of Peter, but probably quite close to it.[91] It is doubtful, however, whether that sort of scholarly reflection, resting upon the study of pagan sources, could conceivably have been at work at that time in the origin of a Christian tradition about where things happened. Apart from this fact, this assumption in any case does not apply to the "trophy" of

[88] See above, pp. 88 f.   [89] Eusebius, *Ecclesiastical History*, V, 24, 2 ff.
[90] See below, p. 142.
[91] So K. Heussi, *War Petrus in Rom?*, p. 66, and M. Goguel, *L'Eglise primitive*, p. 214.

Paul on the highway to Ostia, and if one does not come to our text with the *a priori* presupposition that Peter was not in Rome, it is hard to see why the traditional statement that Gaius attests concerning the place of execution or the grave of Peter deserves less credence than does the tradition concerning that of Paul.

Nevertheless, the only certain conclusion that we can retain from the text of Gaius is that about the year 200 not only was it universally accepted in Rome that the martyrdom of Peter and Paul occurred in this city, but Christians also *pointed out there the places which were regarded as the places of their execution or perhaps even as their graves.*

In this connection should be mentioned the well-known text of *Tertullian,* which according to the most probable assumption was directed against the Roman Bishop *Callistus,* and specifically against the edict he had issued. According to this edict, and contrary to the early practice of the Church, penance should be granted also for sins of unchastity.[92] On this occasion Tertullian turns against what seems to him the arrogant presumption of this Bishop, who refers to himself, and so to "every church that is near Peter" (*ad omnem ecclesiam Petri propinquam*), the saying of Jesus to Peter concerning binding and loosing, when in fact this saying was directed to Peter alone. In recent study these quoted words have been explained, and probably correctly, in the sense of a purely local nearness, that is, "at the grave of Peter." [93] According to this interpretation, Tertullian reproaches Callistus because he refers Matthew 16:18 to himself, with the argument that he is Bishop of a church that has the grave of Peter near it. In this case we find the view attested here that from the grave of Peter, so to speak, the power to loose and bind which had been given to Peter actually streams forth in physical manner and passes over to the Bishop of the church in whose district the grave is located.

[92] *De Pudicitia,* 21. The passage of interest to us is as follows: "I now inquire into your opinion, (to see) from what source you usurp this right to 'the Church.' If, because the Lord has said to Peter, 'Upon this rock I will build my Church,' 'To thee have I given the keys of the Kingdom of Heaven,' or 'Whatsoever thou shalt have bound or loosed in earth, shall be bound or loosed in heaven,' you therefore presume that the power of binding and loosing has derived to you, that is, to every church near to Peter, what sort of man are you, subverting and wholly changing the manifest intention of the Lord, conferring (as that intention did) this (gift) personally upon Peter?" See *The Ante-Nicene Fathers,* Vol. IV, 1890, p. 99.)

[93] W. Köhler, "Omnis ecclesia Petri propinqua" (*Sitzungsbericht der Heidelberger Akademie der Wissenschaften, Philosophisch-historische Klasse,* 1933). H. Koch. *Cathedra Petri,* 1930, pp. 5 ff., takes a different view.

If this explanation is correct, it is here presupposed at the beginning of the third century that Peter was buried at the place of execution or near it. This does not necessarily mean that one possessed relics or that the "trophy" was connected with an actual grave. But the tradition concerning the place of execution also included a statement concerning the place of burial, in so far as it was the custom for executed persons to be buried in the neighbourhood. Whether one knew the *exact* place of burial thus remains doubtful, even if we accept the above interpretation.

Among the later literary witnesses we should mention further the statement of *Macarius Magnus* (III, 22), since it goes back to *Porphyrius*, the Neo-Platonic foe of the Christians. In this passage, evidently with the malicious purpose of setting the great promises to Peter in contrast with his actual insignificant work, it is reported that Peter was "crucified after he had shepherded the sheep for only a few months." Although this information dates no earlier than the end of the third century, it still has greater value than the witnesses from the second century, since it goes back to an enemy of the Christians and contradicts the Christian tendencies that aim rather to glorify Peter and so seek to extend as much as possible his Roman activity.[94]

In this text Porphyrius, the foe of the Christians, alludes to the command of the Risen One in John 21:16 f. and wishes to show that the "feeding of the sheep" there promised was not very extensive, since it only lasted so short a time. To be sure, he does not mention Rome. But in this passage no other place need be considered. This results at once from the simple consideration that Porphyrius, in speaking of the brief "feeding of the sheep," can only have thought of the same place at which occurred the crucifixion mentioned in the same sentence; the "few months" would not cover the entire preceding missionary activity of Peter in the rest of the Empire. But we know, on the other hand, that in the time of Porphyrius the tradition concerning the martyrdom of Peter in Rome was already so widespread that he certainly must have said so if he had thought of any other place but Rome.[95] Thus we probably can conclude from this

[94] A. Harnack, "Porphyrius gegen die Christen" (*Abhandlungen der Berliner Akademie der Wissenschaften*, 1916); *Mission und Ausbreitung des Christentums in den ersten drei Jahrhunderten*, 1924, Vol. I, p. 63, note 2, rightly ascribes to this notice the highest value as a source. The older assumption of Carl Schmidt, *Die alten Petrusakten*, 1903, pp. 167 ff., that it was taken only from the *Acts of Peter*, would indeed if correct lessen this value, but his theory is incapable of proof.

[95] I should like to argue this against H. Dannenbauer, "Die römische Petruslegende" (*Historische Zeitschrift*, 1932, p. 243), and K. Heussi, *War Petrus, in Rom?*, p. 61.

text that Peter came to Rome only a short time before his martyr death.

Thus of the later witnesses discussed in this section which assert, beginning with the second half of the second century, the Roman stay and martyrdom of Peter, at least the statement of Gaius, the text of Tertullian against the edict of Callistus, and also the declaration of Porphyrius, must be considered as sources for our study in spite of their later date. They deserve attention in so far as two of them reproduce for the period about the year 200 an exact topographical tradition concerning the places of execution or the graves of the apostles in Rome, while the other one is evidence that Peter worked in Rome but a very short period before he suffered martyrdom.

4. The Liturgical Sources

We still have to study the *liturgical sources* and then examine the results of the excavations. The two are closely connected with one another. The liturgical texts, on the one hand, contain statements concerning the date and place of the martyrdoms or of the martyr festivals, and so can serve as a clue for archaeological investigation; the excavations, on the other hand, can confirm these statements or even show their lack of historical value.

It might be expected that our study could finally gain from such a comparison of liturgical history and archaeology the fully certain result to which none of the previously discussed sources has led us. So one has always approached these studies with great hopes.[96]

The most relevant liturgical texts we find in the calendar prepared for Rome. Furius Dionysius Filocalus, the later secretary of Pope Damasus, issued it in the year 354, probably making use of the episcopal archives.[97] He here unites three collections: 1. the *Depositio Episcoporum*, which contains the days of death and burial of the Roman Bishops from Lucius (†254) to Sylvester (†335). 2. The *Depositio Martyrum*, a list of the festivals for the martyrs and of the

---

[96] H. Lietzmann built his epoch-making work, *Petrus und Paulus in Rom*, entirely upon the connection between the history of liturgy and the study of archaeology.

[97] See Th. Mommsen, *Monumenta Germaniæ historica. Auctores antiquissimi* 9, 1892, pp. 15 ff. L. Duchesne, *Le liber Pontificalis I*, 1886, pp. 10 f. C. Kirch, *Encheiridion fontium historiae ecclesiasticae antiquae*, 1923, p. 331. See also H. Lietzmann, *Die drei ältesten Martyrologien (Kleine Texte)*, 3rd ed., 1921, pp. 2 ff. H. Achelis, "Die Martyrologien, ihre Geschichte und ihr Wert" (*Abhandlungen der Gesellschaft der Wissenschaften in Göttingen, Philologisch-historische Klasse*, New Series, III, 3, 1900, pp. 6 ff.).

fixed festivals of the church year. 3. The *Catalogus Liberianus*, a detailed list of popes from Peter to Liberius (352–366), with notes concerning the duration and the special events of their pontificate; from this list there then arose later, in the sixth century, the *Liber Pontificalis*.

Two statements of the *Depositio Martyrum* concern us here. (The already mentioned statement[98] which the *Catalogus Liberianus* contains concerning his twenty-five-year ministry as bishop is completely worthless.)

One of the statements refers to February 22 and is as follows:

> *VIII cal. Martias natale Petri de cathedra.*

The other refers to June 29 and is as follows:

> *III cal. Jul. Petri in catacumbas et Pauli*
> *Ostense, Tusco et Basso consulibus* (= 258).

We need not pause very long on the former statement. In its present form it is a charge to observe the "anniversary of Peter's entrance upon office," for that is probably what we should understand by *natale de cathedra*. The hypothesis according to which a pagan festival of *cara cognitio* or also *caristia*, in which the Romans held meals at the graves of their dead, is here simply transferred to Peter, is probably correct. Since this festival was also designated by the Greek word *cathedra* ("chair," "seat"), either on account of the custom of sitting at table or of reserving a seat for the deceased, it thus is explained how it was connected particularly with the supposed "episcopal see" of Peter.[99]

It could also be that before June 29 was regarded as the day of the death of the two apostles, February 22 was originally considered, in view of the meaning of the ancient *caristia* celebration, as the *day of their death*.[1]

We need not concern ourselves with the fact that in the so-called Jerome *Martyrologium*, in addition to February 22, there further

---

[98] See above, p. 113.

[99] H. Usener, *Das Weihnachtsfest*, 1911, p. 274; Fedor Schneider, "Ueber Calendae Januariae und Martiae im Mittelalter" (*Archiv für Religionswissenschaft*, 1920–21, pp. 386 ff.); H. Lietzmann, *op. cit.*, pp. 19 ff.; L. Duchesne, *Origines du culte*, 5th ed., 1925, p. 294; Ch. Guignebert, "La sépulture de Pierre" (*Revue historique*, 1931, pp. 225 ff.). Against the connection with the pagan *Caristia* see especially P. Batiffol, *Cathedra Petri*, 1938, pp. 123 ff.

[1] So C. Erbes, *Die Todestage der Apostel Paulus und Petrus*, 1899, p. 44, and M. Goguel, *L'Eglise primitive*, p. 225.

appears as *cathedra Petri* January 18, which corresponds to an ancient Celtic festival. Indeed, February 22 appears as the festival of Peter's episcopal office in Antioch, January 18 of that in Rome. What we have here is a later harmonization of two competing dates for the same festival.[2]

From the statements concerning the festival of Peter's entrance upon office we thus obtain neither directly nor indirectly any addition to our knowledge concerning the activity of Peter.

More important is the already cited notice of the *Depositio Martyrum* for June 29: "Peter in the catacombs, Paul on the Highway to Ostia, in the consulship of Tuscus and Bassus." Its content stands in direct connection with the archaeological work and discussions, for it mentions the catacombs and the highway to Ostia. According to it, the celebration for Peter was held only in the catacombs (not on the Vatican Hill), and that for Paul on the highway to Ostia. The fixing of the date by naming the consulate of Tuscus and Bassus, however, is at first sight obscure. This consulate falls in the year 258, and what we expect is the indication of the year that the apostles died. To identify one of the two consuls, Bassus, with the consul of the same name under Nero is purely hypothetical.[3] But the notice cited from the *Depositio Martyrum* has been compared with a similar one for the same day, June 29, which stands in the late Bern manuscript (eight century) of the *Jerome Martyrologium*. For this day it runs as follows:

> *III. cal. Jul. Romae, via Aurelia, natale sanctorum Petri et Pauli apostolorum, Petri in Vaticano, Pauli vero in via Ostensi, utrumque in Catacumbas, passi sub Nerone, Basso et Tusco consulibus.*
> That is, "June 29, on the Aurelian Way, martyr festival of the holy apostles Peter and Paul, of Peter on the Vatican Hill, of Paul on the Highway to Ostia, both in the catacombs, suffered under Nero, in the consulate of Bassus and Tuscus"=258.

---

[2] By rigorous reasoning H. Lietzmann, *op. cit.*, pp. 29 ff., reached this conclusion.

[3] So P. Monceaux, "L'apostolat de S. Pierre à Rome à propos d'un livre récent" (*Revue d'Histoire et de Littérature religieuses*, 1910, pp. 216 ff.), who expands the text as follows: *passi sub Nerone Basso (et Crasso consulibus; translati in Catacumbas Basso) et Tusco consulibus*, that is, "suffered under Nero in the consulship of Bassus (and Crassus; transferred to the catacombs in the consulship of Bassus) and Tuscus." Dom H. Quentin also, in "Tusco et Basso consulibus" (*Resi conti della Pontificia Accademia de archeologia*, 1926–27, pp. 145–147), traces the mention of the two consuls back to a copyist's error.

Thus here the burial place of Peter on the Vatican Hill is also mentioned.

This notice, which thus connects the martyrdom of Peter with the Vatican Hill and that of Paul with the Highway to Ostia, but then mentions also the catacombs, appears more complete than the one cited above from the *Depositio Martyrum*, whose statement connects Peter and the catacombs on the one hand, and on the other hand Paul and the Highway to Ostia. However, as it stands it too yields no clear meaning. For on the one hand it says that the apostles suffered martyrdom under Nero, while on the other hand the consuls Bassus and Tuscus are named. The consulate of these two, however, is dated, as we have said in the year 258. Therefore it has been proposed to alter the text by striking out the words *via Aurelia* and *passi sub Nerone* and changing *utrumque* into *utriusque*.[4] The following text then results:

> "June 29th: Martyr festival of the holy apostles Peter and Paul, of Peter on the Vatican Hill, of Paul on the Highway to Ostia; of both together in the catacombs. In the consulate of Bassus and Tuscus."[5]

This text presupposes that in the year 258 the memory of *both* apostles was celebrated in the catacombs, and it is now customary to interpret this in the sense that the relics were later *transferred to the catacombs*, and *to this transfer the date of 258 would refer*. The place in question would be the so-called Saint Sebastian Catacomb on the Appian Way, where, as we shall see, the excavations have brought to light a cult room in which, according to the inscriptions it contains, memorial meals, so-called *refrigeria*, were held in the fourth century. In this way it would be explained how the remembrance of Peter was celebrated at two places at the same time, that is, on the Vatican Hill and in the catacombs: His bones were first buried on the Vatican Hill, then in the year 258 were transferred to the catacombs, and finally in the fourth century were brought back to the Basilica that Constantine built on the Vatican Hill at the original place of burial.

Since the persecution of the Christians under Valerian took place in the year 258, the transfer would be explained either by the fear of the Christians that the relics of the apostles might be dishonoured,

---

[4] So L. Duchesne, *Liber Pontificalis* I, pp. civ ff., and H. Lietzmann, *op. cit.*, pp. 110 ff.

[5] Similarly J. P. Kirsch, *Der stadtrömische christliche Festkalendar*, 1924.

or—on account of an imperial ban—by the impossibility of assembling for the memorial festivals at the graves located in pagan cemeteries.[6]

Such a transfer, furthermore, could be supported by a whole series of more or less legendary later traditions concerning the graves. In themselves they have scarcely any historical value; nevertheless, they are to be considered in so far as almost all of them, though indeed in different ways, reckon with a removal of the graves occasioned by definite events.[7] Apart from Prudentius (fifth century), who transfers the two graves together into the "marshland of the Tiber," and the *Acts* of Pseudo-Linus (sixth century),[8] who names as the place the Naumachia, the material in question is chiefly the *Martyrdom of Peter and Paul* (fifth century). It speaks of the attempt—frustrated by an earthquake—which pious eastern Christians made to steal the sacred relics of the two apostles and take them back to the east. This had as its result that the bodies were buried where the Orientals, when they fled, had left them lying; there they remained until a year and seven months later, when they were transferred back to their original place.[9] According to the *Life* of Pope Cornelius (251–253), which stands in the *Liber Pontificalis*, a certain Lucina, with the consent of the Pope, brought the bodies out of the catacombs and buried Paul near the place of his execution, while Peter was

[6] See H. Lietzmann, "The Tomb of the Apostles ad Catacumbas" (*Harvard Theological Review*, 1923, p. 157). As a result of his book on *Petrus und Paulus in Rom* the theory of the *Translatio* (the transfer of the bodies) has been widely accepted. It had already been defended by L. Duchesne, *Liber Pontificalis*, 1886, pp. civ ff., and "La memoria apostolorum de la Via Appia" (*Atti della Pontificia Accademia Romana di Archeologia*, I, 1, 1923, pp. 1 ff.). It is also supported by J. P. Kirsch, "Die neu entdeckte memoria Apostolorum an der Via Appa bei Rom" (*Jahresbericht der Görresgesellschaft*, 1921, p. 27; "Die 'memoria Apostolorum' an der Appischen Strasse zu Rom und die liturgische Festfeier des 29 Juni" (*Jahrbuch für Liturgiewissenschaft*, 1923, pp. 33 ff. See below, p. 129, note 15, for the names of those who oppose this theory.

[7] See Ch. Guignebert, *La sépulture de Pierre*, and M. Goguel, *L'Eglise primitive*, pp. 222 ff.

[8] A. Lipsius, *Die apokryphen Apostelgeschichten und Apostellegenden*, 1883–1890, Vol. II, p. 113.

[9] This story is found in another form in the *Passio* (the story of the suffering) of the Syrian martyr Sharbil (W. Cureton, *Ancient Syriac Documents*, 1864, pp. 61 ff.). Lipsius, *op. cit.*, Vol. II, p. 312, and C. Erbes, "Die Gräber und Kirchen Pauli und Petri in Rom" (*Zeitschrift für Kirchengeschichte*, 1885, pp. 31 ff.), have proved that the origin of this story is to be sought in a misunderstanding of the Damasus inscription in the Saint Sebastian Catacomb, where it is said that the Orient *sent* the apostles. See below, p. 134.

buried by Cornelius on the Vatican Hill in the Temple of Apollo.[10]

Possibly the sole historical kernel in these late traditions is just the memory of a transfer. However, we cannot simply accept this transfer as an assured fact, for in its generally accepted form there is no ancient text that actually mentions it for the year 258. Rather, we are dealing here only with a *hypothesis*; moreover, it rests upon the correction of the text of the Jerome *Martyrologium*, and this correction has not been thoroughly substantiated.[11]

The only solid fact is that the memory of Peter was celebrated on the Appian Way, and as we shall find confirmed by the result of excavations, so was that of Paul. In earlier times the opinion attested by the *Liber Pontificalis*, I, 67, was widely held, that the apostles were buried together here *from the beginning* and only later were transferred to separate graves. In more recent times this view still found occasional defence;[12] it was then almost universally abandoned, but seems again to be receiving at least some consideration in connection with the completely unsolved riddles which the latest excavations under the Cathedral of St. Peter present.[13] The date 258 proves, however, that the entire notice in the *Depositio* and the *Martyrologium* refers to the time not of burial but of another event, which must be connected with the memory of Peter (and Paul).

Nevertheless, this event need not be the transfer of the bones from their original graves to the Appian Way. Due to the authority of Lietzmann, this assumption has become almost a dogma among scholars today, and in St. Sebastian it is presented as fact by the monks who lead conducted tours. But apart from the fact that it is

[10] Duchesne, *Liber Pontificalis*, I, p. 150. C. Erbes, "Die geschichtlichen Verhältnisse der Apostelgräber" (*ZKG*, 1924, pp. 72 f.), believes that he finds a historical nucleus in the notice regarding Paul.

[11] The later Bern text of the Jerome *Martyrologium* from the eighth century perhaps does not deserve unqualified trust, since we could have here a subsequent attempt at explanation by a copyist, who did not know what to make of the date of the *Depositio Martyrum* (June 29, 258). In any case, the year 258 is not necessarily to be connected with the catacombs.

[12] P. Styger, *Die römischen Katakomben*, 1933, p. 350 f.; *Römische Märtyrergrüfte*, 1935, I, pp. 15 ff. F. Tolotti, "Ricerche intorno alla Memoria Apostolorum" (*Rivista Archeologia Cristiana*, 1946, pp. 7 ff.).

[13] See the report by A. Ferrua concerning the latest excavations: "A la recherche du tombeau de S. Pierre" (*Etudes*, 1952, pp. 35 ff.). A. Ferrua here recalls this ancient tradition in a very involved sentence; in an article that appeared at about the same time, "La Storia del sepolcro di san Pietro" (*La civiltà cattolica*, 1952, pp. 15 ff.), he merely explains that this theory has been given up by scholars.

not really supported by a single text, there is the added fact that other considerations make the assumption of a transfer very difficult *if not impossible*. According to the Roman legislation for the protection of graves, it was a crime punishable by death to remove from the grave the remains of a deceased person. Any infraction of this law by the Christians, moreover, would have been extremely dangerous at the time of Valerian's persecution of the Christians, since Christian meetings at cemeteries were then forbidden and these places therefore were probably closely watched to enforce the ban. Furthermore, it recently has been correctly pointed out that the transfer to the Appian Way in particular is quite improbable; it was one of the busiest streets, and a few hundred yards away, at the tomb of Caecilia Metella, there was an imperial police station.[14] In addition, it is impossible to see how the Christians could have feared injury to the graves, since such a thing was contrary to Roman feelings, and moreover the cult of relics was not yet so developed at that time that the Christians would need to reckon with imperial action against the graves of martyrs. In reality that persecution was directed against the leaders of the church. For these reasons a line of scholars for many years back have completely refused to believe in a transfer of the remains of the two apostles.[15]

[14] I owe this reference to the article by Alfons Maria Schneider, "Die Memoria Apostolorum an der Via Appia" (*Nachrichten der Akademie der Wissenschaften in Göttingen, Philologisch-Historische Klasse*, 1951, p. 5). I was able to see this article while it was still in process of publication.

[15] So J. Wilpert, "Domus Petri" (*Römische Quartalschrift*, 1912, p. 121); G. La Piana, "The Tombs of Peter and Paul ad Catacumbas" (*Harvard Theological Review*, 1921, pp. 81 ff.); C. Erbes in *Zeitschrift für Kirchengeschichte*, 1924, p. 38; especially H. Delehaye, "Hagiographie et archéologie romaines, II, Le Sanctuaire des apôtres sur la voie Appienne" (*Analecta Bollandiana*, 1927, pp. 297 ff.), and *Les origines du culte des martyrs*, 2nd ed., 1933, pp. 264 f. A. von Gerkan, in the report he adds to the second edition of H. Lietzmann's *Petrus und Paulus in Rom*, pp. 248 ff., also takes a sceptical attitude towards the acceptance of the *Translatio*. Recently E. Schäfer, "Das Petrusgrab" (*Evangelische Theologie*, 1951, pp. 477 f.), has spoken definitely against it. He argues chiefly that no reason existed for a transfer, since Valerian's prohibition against entering Christian cemeteries dates not from the year 258 but from 257. Moreover, the grave of Peter was located not in a Christian cemetery at all, but in a pagan once; fear that the grave would be violated would have been groundless, since indeed nothing is known of violations of Christian graves in times of persecution. Most recently, A. M. Schneider, *op. cit.*; see the preceding note. For further orientation on this entire question see also: H. Leclercq, Article on "St. Pierre" in *Dictionnaire d'archéologie chrétienne et de liturgie*, 1939, columns 822 ff., and L. Hertling—E. Kirschbaum, *Die römischen Katakomben und ihre Märtyrer*, 1950, pp. 102 ff.

This transfer is the more questionable since the excavations under the Basilica of St. Sebastian, of which we still must speak, also prove only that a *cult* of the apostles was practised at that place; they do not prove that the relics were to be found there.

But why, then, was this specific day June 29, 258, connected with this cult? As far as this day is concerned, we should consider first of all the insufficiently noticed fact that June 29 was celebrated as the day of the foundation of Rome by Quirinus Romulus. To the festival for the founder of the city corresponded the festival for the founder of the Church.[16] We may note further that it was also the day on which was deposed the rival pope Novatian, who died about this time. This fact, in connection with other observations, could incite us to propose interesting hypotheses, but we omit them here since there is still much to clarify.[17] For the time being, the following explanation gives the most light. We have seen that the naming of the year 258 cannot refer to the original graves of the apostles, and probably also cannot refer to the more than doubtful transfer of the bones. It is rather concerned only with the rise of a cult dedicated to the apostles. Whether the cult arose at the same time at the three places named—the Vatican Hill, the Highway to Ostia, and the Appian Way—or at first only at the two former places, or only on the Appian Way, cannot be determined from the liturgical sources. Only excavations could throw further light on this point. The need of a cult veneration and of a cult place appeared just at that time, about the middle of the third century, and so at the time when a catacomb for the Roman bishops was laid out, the Callistus Catacomb. So it is intelligible that especially at that time Christians desired to honour the memory of the two apostles who had long been regarded as the founders of the church. In this connection it is very interesting that they still *desired to distinguish clearly the founders from the bishops;*

16 See C. Erbes, *Die Todestage der Apostel Paulus und Petrus und ihre römischen Denkmäler*, 1899, pp. 39 f.: "The festival for the founder of the city of Rome was best suited for the festive celebration of the founder or founders of the Roman Church." Pope Leo the Great, in Sermon 82 on June 29th, points out: "The apostles founded the city better than did those who built the walls and sullied them by fratricide."

17 *Martyrologium Hieronymianum*, in the text on June 29 as contained in the entire textual tradition. See H. Delehaye—H. Quentin, *Acta Sanctorum Novembris*, Vol. I, 1931, p. 342. Concerning the grave of Novatian, found in 1932, and its historical connections, see L. C. Mohlberg, "Osservazioni storico-critiche sulla Iscrizione tombale de Novaziano" (*Ephemerides liturgicae*, 1937, pp. 242 ff.).

they did not choose for the founders simply the Bishop's Vault. Moreover, the same veneration was still paid to Paul that was given to Peter. The theory of the exclusive episcopal office of the Prince of Apostles thus did not yet exist, or at least had not yet fully triumphed.

The two notices cited from the *Depositio Martyrum* concerning June 29 refer to the cult veneration. But if that is true, we can leave as it is the far earlier notice of the two, that is, the brief one; we do not need to change its text.[18] We then understand why Peter is mentioned here only in connection with the catacombs, and why he alone is mentioned. At the time when the Roman calendar originated, that is, in the year 354, the Basilica which Constantine had begun to build for Peter at the place of the Vatican "trophy" was not yet complete.[19] So for a time the only cult site at which Peter was venerated was still the place in the catacombs, while in the case of Paul the Basilica of St. Paul Outside the Walls, which was much smaller and therefore required less time for completion, was already dedicated to the cult.[20]

On the basis of the liturgical sources, therefore, we can only say the following: The remembrance of Peter in Rome was attached to different places, to the Vatican Hill and to the catacombs. June 29 is not the day of the death of the two apostles.[21] It has a connection—probably by association with the memorial day of the founder of the city of Rome—with a Christian celebration of the year 258. This year became decisive for the origin of the cult dedicated to the two apostles. According to the usual thesis, indeed, this was because at that time the transfer of the bones to the Appian Way took place. But according to the more probable view, it was because the memory of the apostles was first venerated without such a transfer, and perhaps without the physical presence of the remains.

The liturgical sources, taken by themselves, thus yield little help in solving our problem. Indeed, in view of the disharmony in the liturgical tradition, which connects the Vatican Hill on the one hand and the catacombs on the other with the memory of Peter, the problem has long since become greatly complicated. This fact has

[18] See above, p. 125.   [19] See below, p. 140.

[20] This convincing line of argument is used by E. Kirschbaum, "Petri in Catacumbas" (*Miscellanea liturgica in honorem L. Cuniberti Mohlberg*, 1948, pp. 221 ff.).

[21] So also P. Batiffol, *Cathedra Petri*, 1938, p 174: "The festival of the two apostles will be celebrated the same day, June 29, not because this date is the anniversary of their martyrdom, but because it is the anniversary of the institution of a joint observance in their honour."

created among scholars as well as among churchmen an embarrassment, which becomes noticeable today as soon as anyone speaks of
this double tradition. This may also explain the fact that even in the
fifteenth and sixteenth centuries there obviously was no certainty
concerning the place of burial of the apostles. This is clear from the
following rarely noted *passage in Luther*:[22] "But this I can cheerfully
say, because I have seen it and heard it at Rome, that at Rome they
do not know where the bodies of St. Peter and St. Paul lie and
whether they lie there. The pope and cardinals know quite well that
they do not know these things."

5. The Excavations

Do the results of the excavations carry us further? It corresponds
fully to the statements of the literary and liturgical sources if a burial
took place at two places: on the Vatican Hill, under the present
cathedral of St. Peter, and on the Appian Way, in the catacombs
under the present Basilica of St. Sebastian. A third task still awaits
fulfilment by archaeological investigation; systematic excavations
should also be carried out under the Church of St. Paul Outside the
Walls. It is true that various archaeological observations have already
been made there, following the fire of the year 1823 and in connection with the rebuilding. But a systematic archaeological examination of the place has not been made in recent times.[23]

We speak first of the excavations which were undertaken in 1915
on the Appian Way, in the catacombs under the Basilica of St.
Sebastian.[24] In earlier times this basilica was called the "Basilica of

[22] M. Luther, *Wider das Papsttum vom Teufel gestiftet*, 1545 (Weimar edition, 54),
cited from E. Mülhaupt, *Luthers Evangelien-Auslegung*, Vol. II, p. 551.

[23] Concerning the grave of Paul see C. Cecchelli, "La Tomba de S. Paolo"
(*Capitolium*, 1950, pp. 115 ff.).—Excavations under Saint Paul's would be
especially instructive, inasmuch as less mediaeval plundering would be expected
here than under the Basilica of Peter.

[24] See on that point the already mentioned fifty page report by A. von Gerkan,
published in the second edition of H. Lietzmann, *Petrus und Paulus in Rom*, 1927,
pp. 248 ff. See also J. P. Kirsch, "Das neuentdeckte Denkmal der Apostel Petrus
und Paulus 'in Catacumbas' an der Appischen Strasse in Rom" (*Römische
Quartalschrift*, 1916–1922, pp. 5 ff.); G. Mancini—O. Marucchi, "Scavi sotto la
basilica de S. Sebastiano sulla Appia antica" (*Notizie degli Scavi*, 1923); R.
Chéramy, *Saint-Sébastien-hors-les-murs*, 1925; A. Prandi, "La memoria Apostolorum in Catacumbas" (*Romana sotterranea Cristiana*, 2, 1936); Alfons Maria
Schneider, "Die Memoria Apostolorum an der Via Appia" (*Nachrichten der
Akademie der Wissenschaften in Göttingen, Philologisch-historische Klasse*, 1951,
pp. 1 ff.).

the Apostles"; only later did it serve as the grave of Saint Sebastian, from whom it then received its present name.[25]

According to the *Liber Pontificalis*, Pope Damasus erected a church there, at the place "where the bodies of the holy Apostles Peter and Paul had rested." They had lain there under the *platonia* (*platoma*, marble slab). The excavations, however, have not confirmed this assertion. They have shown, however, that in the first century there was at this place a Roman villa, columbaria, and graves. More important for our question was the discovery of a *triclia*, that is, a cult room; according to the inscriptions, which invoke Peter and Paul,[26] it served for the veneration of the two apostles.

It can be shown that this room can hardly have originated before A.D. 300. Its inner arrangement, with stone benches encircling the room, as well as some of the inscriptions, permit us to see that here were celebrated so-called *refrigeria*, meals for the dead, in honour of Peter and Paul. We read, for example, in one of the graffiti: "For Peter and Paul I, Tomius Caelius, have held a *refrigerium*."[27] The meal eaten in honour of the apostles was naturally considered a meritorious work. This abuse appears to have been especially widespread after the triumph of the Church in the fourth century. It continued the pagan religious meals; since these could not be uprooted, they were given a Christian framework in the Church by being connected with the martyr cult. Augustine later denounced the abuses to which this bad custom gave occasion.[28] In his time such meals had already been banned for several decades, but they continued to be celebrated in secret.

It cannot be disputed that such "meals for the dead" presuppose in theory the presence of the relics of the martyrs venerated. This has been made the chief support for the assertion that the apostles were

[25] See on that point F. W. Deichmann, *Frühchristliche Kirchen in Rom*, 1948, pp. 22 f.

[26] 191 graffiti have been discovered, 33 of them in Greek. They are in part written in low Latin and invoke the intercession of the apostles; for example, *Paule et Petre petite pro Victore* ("Paul and Peter, pray for Victor"). We certainly have here a popular cult. It is conceivable that the pilgrims who came to Rome from abroad stopped here on the Appian Way before their entrance into the city. See concerning the graffiti: E. Diehl, *Inscriptiones latinae christianae veteres*, 1924; H. Lietzmann, *op. cit.*, pp. 163 ff. A. M. Schneider, *Refrigeria nach literarischen Quellen und Inschriften*, 1928; P. Styger, *Die römischen Katakomben*, 1933, pp. 341 ff.

[27] *Petro et Paulo Tomius Caelius refrigerium feci XIV kal. Apriles.*

[28] Augustine, Epistle XXIX *ad Aurelium*.

actually buried for a time in the catacombs.[29] But in view of the fact that the Church prohibited these *refrigeria*, it is possible that in exceptional cases *refrigeria* were held in spite of the absence of relics.[30]

That the cult in memory of the apostles could arise here, even if their bones were not present, becomes explicable from an inscription which has been found near the crypt of the Basilica of St. Sebastian. It is a thirteenth century copy of an inscription that goes back to Damasus. Its text is probably to be translated as follows:[31] "Whoever you may be who searches for the names of Peter and Paul, you should know that here the holy ones once dwelt. The Orient has sent us the disciples—that we concede without argument; but on account of the merit of the (shed) blood—for indeed they have followed Christ beyond the stars and have reached the heavenly bosom and the kingdom of the pious—Rome has the greater right to claim them as its citizens. Damasus desires to sing this to your praise, ye new stars."

The statement concerning the "dwelling" of Peter and Paul is usually explained to mean that their remains once rested in St. Sebastian.[32] To be sure, there are other possible interpretations of this word. One could think, for example, of a tradition according to which the apostles had actually lived here during their lifetime. With this would agree the fact that this place was in a Jewish quarter.[33] One could even assume that the inscription had in mind a cult presence of the two apostles. It is of course doubtful whether Damasus, when in the fourth century he used the word "dwelling," thought only of a cult presence. But in any case the most natural

---

[29] For H. Lietzmann this is one of the decisive arguments that favour acceptance of the theory of the transfer of the bones in the year 258 ("The Tomb of the Apostles ad Catacumbas," *Harvard Theological Review*, 1923, pp. 147 ff.).

[30] So G. La Piana, "The Tombs of Peter and Paul ad Catacumbas" (*Harvard Theological Review*, 1921, pp. 81 ff.).

[31] *His habitasse prius sanctos cognoscere debes, nomina quisque Petri pariter Paulique requiris. Discipulos Oriens misit, quod sponte fatemur. Sanguinis ob meritum—Christumque per astra secuti aetherios petiere sinus regnaque piorum—Roma suos potius meruit defendere cives. Haec Damasus vestras referat, nova sidera, laudes.*

[32] See above, p. 133.

[33] According to Juvenal, Satire III, 12 ff., the sacred grove of Egeria is leased to the Jews. See G. La Piana, "Foreign Groups in Rome during the First Centuries of the Empire" (*Harvard Theological Review*, 1927, pp. 341 ff.; further, J. B. Frey, "Les communautés juives à Rome aux premiers temps de l'Eglise" (*Recherches de Science religieuse*, pp. 275 ff.). Actual dwelling here was first assumed by J. Wilpert, *Römische Quartalschrift*, 1912, pp. 117 ff.

thing is to explain the origin of the cult on the Appian Way in the
third century not by the presence of relics, but by the need of ven-
erating the memory of the two founders of the Roman church at a
place where such veneration was possible, even if the bones were not
there. This view is the more probable since we can point out in St.
Sebastian, though not indeed in the *triclia*, possible traces of a double
cenotaph, that is, a fictitious grave, such as one often set up in ancient
times when one wished to celebrate the memory of a deceased person
at a place other than the site of the actual grave. The choice of the
Appian Way as a cult site can be explained by the fact that in the
immediate vicinity the Callistus Catacomb had been laid out, from
the time of Pontianus (A.D. 235), for the burial of the Roman
bishops; Christians wished to assemble in the vicinity of the later
bishops for the cult veneration of the founding apostles.

Without the use of hypothesis we cannot hope to explain the fact
that there was in the catacombs a common memorial place for the
two apostles, which still served this purpose even when Christians
definitely fixed the location of the graves not here, but on the Vatican
Hill and on the Highway to Ostia. Quite improbable is the supposition that in the catacombs we have the *original* grave of the apostles.[34]
Another hypothesis is that in the third century the remains were
transferred to the catacombs for a limited time. As we have seen, this
hypothesis, in spite of its wide popularity, which it owes chiefly to
Lietzmann's book, offers so many difficulties that the current tendency to give it up is doubtless justified.[35] It is theoretically possible
to assume that in the third century Christians sought out relics of the
apostles that up to then they had not possessed, and so in the year 258
there occurred the so-called discovery, *inventio*, of the (genuine or
spurious) remains, objects such as we find were held to be martyr
relics in the fourth and fifth centuries.[36] This, however, is nothing
more than an unproved and unprovable possibility.

Thus concerning the place at the Sebastian catacombs we conclude
that even if one did not have the bones at this place, there arose here
in the third century a cult in honour of the two apostles.[37] Did this

[34] See above, p. 128.   [35] See above, p. 129.

[36] See H. Achelis, *Die Martyrologien, ihre Geschichte und ihr Wert*, 1900, pp. 74 ff.;
E. Schäfer, *Die Epigramme des Papstes Damasus I. als Quelle für die Geschichte der
Heiligenverehrung*, 1932, pp. 101 ff.; also "Das Petrusgrab" (*Evangelische Theo-
logie*, 1950, pp. 474 f.).

[37] Alfons Maria Schneider, *op. cit.* (see p. 129, note 14), pp. 1 ff., does not believe
that this happened as early as the year 258; rather, in this year arose the cult on
the Vatican Hill and the Highway to Ostia.

happen because at the site of the "trophies" of Peter and Paul on the Vatican Hill and on the Highway to Ostia, which *as places* certainly had been venerated in earlier times, assemblies for worship became difficult since they were located in pagan cemeteries? Or was it, on the contrary, one of the schismatic churches of the third century which first of all created the cult site on the Appian Way, before the great Church took it over at the beginning of the fourth century? In favour of the second possibility weighty reasons have recently been presented.[38]

*   *   *

Even before the rise of a *cult* of the apostles the *memorial places* for the apostles already existed on the Vatican Hill and on the Highway to Ostia. For even before the year 258, probably for more than half a century before, efforts were being made to possess the relics or at least the burial places of the apostles. In the east, this need had made itself felt much earlier than in Rome, where, as we shall see, there was no interest at all in relics or burial places, not even in those of the great martyrs of Rome, prior to the end of the second century.[39] In the Martyrdom of Polycarp we hear for the first time of a cult of relics, devoted to the memory of the great Bishop of Smyrna. Towards the end of the second century Polycrates, the Bishop of Ephesus, writes to the Roman Bishop Victor concerning the Easter celebration. In this connection he appeals explicitly to the fact that "in Asia great stars, who will arise on the last day when Christ returns, have found their resting place,"[40] and he enumerates them. The more the time receded when Christians could still see on the basis of living tradition the connection of a church with apostles, so much the greater need did the east feel of proving apostolicity in another way, namely by the possession of apostolic burial places. We have every reason to assume that this tendency arose in the east, where, in the debates over the claims of Rome, which were presented with ever increasing vigour, this argument was not overlooked.

In order not to leave this claim to fame to the eastern churches alone, there arose in Rome at the very end of the second century the effort to make a similar appeal to the possession of apostolic "trophies." To this effort we owe that statement of Gaius concerning

---

[38] See A. M. Schneider, *op. cit.*   [39] See below, pp. 150 f.
[40] Eusebius, *Ecclesiastical History*, III, 31, 3.

the "trophies" on the Vatican Hill and on the Highway to Ostia; it comes from precisely this time. With this also agrees quite well the view that we have found attested for this same period, according to a likely interpretation, in the text of Tertullian.[41] It declares that from the grave of the apostle Peter the power committed to Peter streams forth upon the Roman Bishop. Hence there was created—again about that same time—a burial place for the Roman bishops.

We thus establish the fact that the church in Rome, in the decades that immediately precede the origin of the cult of the apostles in the year 258, also became interested in possessing apostolic "trophies." But just for this reason it is improbable that Christians would have transferred these trophies away from the Vatican Hill and the Highway to Ostia, after having appealed to them, as the Gaius reference proves, for a period of limited duration. Those places remained unmolested. If an additional cult centre was also created on the Appian Way, those ancient "victory sites" retained their power to attest and prove the apostolicity of the church. But what now is the situation with reference to these "trophies," in particular the "trophy" of Peter on the Vatican Hill?

*   *   *

We thus come to the actual question concerning the *excavations* under the Church of St. Peter. Quite recently, in the year 1939, work highly important for archaeology was here undertaken. In an unusually clear manner it gives us information concerning the nature of the terrain lying under the present Church of St. Peter and the use made of it in ancient Christian times. If archaeology is in any position to throw light upon the question concerning Peter, it could be expected that it would do so here, and many probably cherished the hope that here, at one stroke, a final solution would be found for the much debated historical question whether Peter died in Rome as a martyr.

It was not the first time that excavations had been made there. As early as the year 1615, when the present *Confessio* of the Cathedral of St. Peter was built, and especially in 1626, when the foundations were laid under the dome for the four spiral bronze pillars of the Bernini Canopy, discoveries were made concerning the secrets concealed underneath. It was discovered that the place at which one locates the grave of Peter contains exclusively pagan graves and

[41] See above, pp. 121 f.

burial chambers. They date from the years 150 to 300, and are at different depths, of which several more were later found. The seventeenth century reports of these first diggings have been carefully studied in recent times.[42] But only the systematic work of 1939 has finally clarified the topography under the Church of St. Peter. They also have put an end to erroneous earlier assumptions that rested on false reports. Although they were undertaken in a way that excluded broad participation by scholars, their results, thanks to a series of articles by competent writers, were made known as early as the years 1941–1950,[43] except for the archaeological details concerning a simple ancient monument located under the present altar, and three ancient graves found close by, which probably date from the first century. In a radio broadcast in the year 1942 Pope Pius XII referred quite briefly to this monument, and identified it with that "trophy" of Peter which Gaius mentioned.

In his Christmas message on December 23, 1950, he definitely asserted that "the grave of the Prince of Apostles has been found." At the same time he conceded in all honesty that the remains of human bones found in the region of the grave cannot be identified with certainty as the mortal remains of the apostle.

Now at last the categorical assertion that the grave itself has been found can be tested by the archaeologists. A year later, at the Christmas season of 1951, appeared the long announced official publication concerning this part of the excavation. It had been impatiently awaited by the scholarly world, and appeared after a remarkable delay.[44] The impatience was the more intelligible since, except for the excavation leaders appointed by the Vatican, almost no archaeologist was permitted to see that place under the altar, while the

---

[42] See H. Lietzmann, *Petrus und Paulus in Rom*, 1927, pp. 191 ff.

[43] From the unusually numerous and steadily increasing reports we select the following: C. Respighi, "La tomba apostolica del Vaticano" (*Rivista di Archeologia Cristiana*, 1942, pp. 5 ff.); E. Josi, *Gli scavi nelle sacre Grotte Vaticano: Il Vaticano nel 1944*, pp. 189 ff.; *Idem*, *Le Sacre Grotte: Vaticano*, edited by G. Fallani and M. Escobar, 1946; E. Kirschbaum, "Die Ausgrabungen unter der Petruskirche in Rom" (*Stimmen der Zeit*, 1949, pp. 292 ff.); *Idem*, "Gli scavi sotto la basilica di S. Pietro" (*Gregorianum*, 1948, pp. 544 ff.); L. Lemerle, "Les fouilles de St-Pierre de Rome" (*La Nouvelle Clio*, 1950, pp. 393 ff.); E. Schäfer, "Das Petrusgrab" (*Evangelische Theologie*, 1951, p. 459).

[44] B. M. Apollonj-Ghetti, A. Ferrua, E. Kirschbaum, E. Josi (Foreword by L. Kaas), *Esplorazioni sotto la Confessione de S. Pietro in Vaticano*, 2 Vols. (one volume of text and one of illustrations), 1951 (cited hereafter as *Espl. Vat.*, 1951). As the title says, this work deals only with the result, kept secret up to this time, of the excavations under the altar; it does not deal with the rest of the cemetery.

remaining part of the excavations was already accessible, at least to scholars. It is to be expected and hoped that now numerous archaeologists of all faiths will form their independent judgment, not only by means of the elaborately presented publication, splendidly illustrated in a second volume,[45] but on the spot and at the site itself. It is certain that in view of the result of the excavations, which as we shall see permits quite different interpretations, a vigorous discussion will develop.[46] Without anticipating this discussion, which must deal first of all with the technical side of the question, it is already possible, on the basis of the information that the publication contains, for us to take a provisional position; it permits us to decide whether these most recent excavations are capable of solving the question concerning the Roman stay of Peter in one way or another. Even here, however, I note explicitly that even if this question should be answered in the negative, this does not mean at all that Peter was never in Rome. *The question concerning the grave of Peter and the question concerning his stay in Rome are to be kept strictly separate.*

Let us now begin with that part of the new excavations concerning which a rather detailed documentation has already been published. We must first recall that under the present Church of St. Peter was the ancient basilica which Constantine erected in the fourth century in honour of Peter. It was completely torn down at the building of the present Church of St. Peter, which was begun in the year 1506 and completed about 150 years later. Unfortunately there is no ancient text which tells of its origin. However, we possess an early description of its form from Canon Tiberius Alfaranus of the sixteenth century;[47] we also possess ancient engravings. Various extensive studies have been carried on recently to sift this material.[48]

[45] Unfortunately the plans contained in it do not have a uniform scale, and cross-sections of the strata are lacking; this makes use of the work difficult.

[46] Up to the present time (beginning of February, 1952), important statements have appeared only from the Roman Catholic side. Apart from purely journalistic reports, two articles particularly deserve mention here. Both come from one of the leaders, A. Ferrua: "La Storia del sepolcro di san Pietro" (La Civiltà cattolica, 1952, pp. 15 ff.), and "A la recherche du tombeau de S. Pierre" (*Etudes*, 1952, pp. 35 ff.). It is noteworthy that his results diverge *in essentials* from those of the official publication which he shared in issuing (see below, pp. 147 f.). Differences in nuance exist also between the two above-named articles.

[47] Tiberius Alfaranus, "De Basilicae Vaticanae antiquissima et nova structura" (*Studi e testi*, 1914).

[48] H. Grisar, "Die alte Petruskirche zu Rom und ihre frühesten Ansichten" (*Römische Quartalschrift*, 1895, pp. 237 ff.).

It appears that this building was begun under Constantine about the year 333;[49] it probably was completed under Constantius.[50] It lay about three metres under the level of the present church, and so upon the level of the present grottoes of the Vatican, in which many popes, even in recent times, have been buried.

The excavations undertaken several years ago had at first no scientific purpose whatever. They were intended simply to enlarge these grottoes and at the same time to lower their floor level about eighty centimetres. This had become necessary in connection with the burial of Pope Pius XI, who died in 1939. He had left behind the direction that his remains should rest in the grottoes of the Vatican. During the work Roman walls were laid bare, and this gave occasion for a systematic uncovering of the terrain situated beneath the grottoes.

The chief thing that the workmen encountered was an unusually thick wall of considerable size. It was believed at first that this could be identified with the wall of the Circus of Nero, since, according to

[49] Of the older datings, the most favoured fixed upon the year 324 (Lietzmann, Nicolosi, Marucchi). More recent ones have preferred the year 325 (Th. Klausner, "Vom Heroon zur Märtyrerbasilika," *Kriegsvorträge der Universität Bonn*, 62, p. 22), and Fr. W. Deichmann, *Frühchristliche Kirchen in Rom*, 1948) or the year 326 (H. von Schoenbeck, *Beiträge zur Religionspolitik des Maxentius und Constantin*, Supplementary volume to *Clio*, 1939, p. 89). In opposition to these views, a promising hypothesis has been proposed, in connection with the latest excavations under the Church of St. Peter, by W. Seston, "Hypothèse sur la date de la Basilique constantinienne de Saint-Pierre de Rome" (*Cahiers archéologiques*, 1946, pp. 153 ff.). This theory is that the law which Constans promulgated on March 28, 349, allows us to fix the beginning of the construction under Constantine in the year 333. That law fixes the amount of the punishments for all who have removed parts of tombs, and the act is made retroactive to the year 333. We shall see that Constantine was compelled to dig up an entire necropolis in order to erect the basilica for Peter. It is intelligible that this act, which Constantine was forced to take in his capacity as *Pontifex Maximus*, gave occasion for more and more violations of graves, which were justified by appeal to what Constantine had done. This hypothesis could find confirmation in the fact that precisely in the year 333 paganism quite obviously recedes in Constantine's region. See A. Piganiol, *L'empereur Constantin*, 1932, p. 185. This suggestion is confirmed especially by the latest excavations; the graffiti at the *Tropaion* show the monogram (see below, p. 145).

[50] See the inscription on the apse in Diehl, *Inscriptiones latinae veteres*, No. 1753.— If the assumption is correct (see above, p. 131), according to which at the time of the composition of the *Depositio Martyrum* the basilica for Paul was completed, but that of Peter was not yet dedicated to the cult, the completion of the latter must have taken place after 354. See E. Kirschbaum, "Petri in Catacumbas" (*Miscellanea Liturgica in honorem L. C. Mohlberg*, 1948, pp. 221 ff.).

a misleading report from the beginning of the seventeenth century,[51] the southern walls of the Basilica of Constantine stood upon the northern walls of the Circus of Nero, so that the Church of St. Peter would be situated over the Circus. As early as 1895 a futile effort was made to find traces of the Circus. Now for the first time, however, it has become clear what was the real purpose of this thick Roman wall, which had evidently been seen when the present church was being built in the sixteenth and seventeenth centuries. It did not belong to the Circus of Nero; it simply served to make level the sloping hillside under the present church, in order to serve as a substructure for the Basilica of Constantine. The result was that the emperor erected his church directly above this slope. The summit of the hill lies north of the church, approximately where the Vatican buildings stand today. The hill slopes away in two directions: in a gradual slope toward the east, and so in the direction from the altar to the entrance of the church, to the Piazza of St. Peter and on to the Tiber; and in a much steeper abrupt drop to the south, and so on the left side of the present basilica when viewed from the Piazza of St. Peter.

It was on this steep slope that Constantine erected his Basilica of Peter. The terrain was thus extremely unfavourable; in order to level it off, it was necessary to erect, on the south, high walls, which at the deepest point of the valley reach a height of thirteen metres. On the north, the surface of the hill had to be partly removed, and it required great quantities of soil to make a level size. These extensive labours could have been avoided if the church had been built either above on the hill top or below in the valley. We therefore must assume that there was *a special reason* for building it right over the steep slope, and this reason can only be that in the time of Constantine it was not simply the Vatican Hill in general but rather this very slope, and probably a particular spot on this slope, that was regarded as the place where Peter was executed or buried.

This is further confirmed by another difficulty that the builders had to accept and overcome when they built the church at this place. The most important discovery that came to light in the course of these excavations is an entire cemetery, situated on this very slope. It consists of two rows of well preserved mausoleums, separated by a narrow passageway.

[51] Giacomo Grimaldi, *Codex Ambros. A. 178*, edited by Ch. Huelsen (*Miscellanea*, 1910, pp. 257 ff.). *Cod. Barb. lat. 2732, 2733,* Bibl. Vat. H. Lietzmann, *op. cit.*, pp. 311 ff.

Thus while previously one knew only of separate graves under the Church of St. Peter, there has been discovered here an extensive necropolis. The graves date from the second and third centuries after Christ, with the exception of some that are located in the western portion, under the present *Confessio*. They can be dated at the end of the first century, but not before the year 70. The two rows run along the slope, about eight metres under the present church, in the direction of the longitudinal axis of the church; indeed, they are so situated that they run slightly uphill towards the west, and so to the place beneath the altar.

The fact that Constantine had to destroy this entire site, in which actual works of art were found, shows anew that there must have been a special reason for him to build the church right at this point. This is especially clear since destruction of cemeteries was regarded in antiquity as especially serious, and he doubtless could permit himself to do this only in his capacity as *Pontifex Maximus*.[52]

How distant the cemetery was from the famous Via Cornelia, on which the grave of Peter is supposed to have been situated,[53] cannot be said with certainty, since no trace of this street has been found where it has been customary to look for it, on the longitudinal axis of the church. Probably it ran to the north, and so above the northern row of graves; the mausoleums of this row are in most cases provided with steps which lead up the hill, so that in addition to the lower entrance on the south they had also an entrance from the upper slope of the hill. It is possible therefore that the Via Cornelia passed by on that side.

We have already mentioned that the Circus of Nero, contrary to the earlier view, was not situated under the Church of St. Peter. But it doubtless was in the vicinity. For in the mausoleum of a certain C. Popilius Heracla, located on the extreme east, an inscription mentions the wish of this deceased pagan that he may rest on the Vatican Hill at the Circus, *in vaticano ad circum*.[54]

Those buried in the cemetery belonged to the most varied pagan cults. Some few Christians of this period also were buried in these pagan mausoleums with their relatives of other faiths, and a complete Christian mausoleum, adorned with Christian mosaic motifs and

---

[52] See W. Seston, *op. cit.*, p. 156.

[53] H. Lietzmann, *Petrus und Paulus in Rom*, 1927, pp. 178 f.

[54] That the Circus lay on the Vatican Hill is attested by Tacitus, *Annals*, XIV, 4, and *Historia Augusta*, Elagabalus, 23, and further by Pliny, *Natural History*, XXXVI, 11, 74.

dating from the third or the beginning of the fourth century, is found among the pagan graves. It is of the greatest importance for the beginnings of Christian art.[55] For our question, the important thing in this connection is that this room is found in this vicinity, that is, only a few metres east of the *Confessio*. Did the Christian who had this mausoleum built at this place wish to be buried as near as possible to the place which was held to be the place where the apostle Peter was buried or executed? In this period, indeed, the tendency was already widespread to have oneself buried by the graves of the martyrs. It is a striking fact, however, that the Christian inscriptions of the graves of the Vatican cemetery do not mention the name of Peter.[56]

But what is the truth about the grave of Peter itself? Is it really true, as the Pope explicitly announced in his Christmas message of December 23, 1950, that a grave has been found in which Peter had been buried? We have seen that at the time of Constantine there must have existed a fixed tradition that located the site of the "trophy," whatever the latter was, at the place where the altar was erected in the Basilica of Constantine. Otherwise, we could not explain the choice of so unsuitable a terrain and especially of a cemetery.

We take the following information from the official publication that has recently appeared. First of all, those conducting the excavations were forced to conclude that the sixth century statement of the *Liber Pontificalis*, I, 176, according to which Constantine surrounded the entire grave of Peter with huge bronze slabs and erected over it a *Confessio* with a golden cross, belongs in the realm of legend. The excavations, at any rate, failed to bring to light anything of that sort; but above all, no traces were discovered to suggest the possibility that such an adornment was present.

In the area under the altar, on the contrary, traces were found of a columnar monument. It may be reconstructed (see p. 144), although but little of its original form is preserved. Its west wall is formed by the middle part of a strong wall, more than seven metres long and about two and a half metres high; it runs from north to south. To this wall a multiple purpose is ascribed. On the one hand, the so-called *Memoria* is supported by it; on the other hand, it is intended to support a stairway that leads up the hill and is built parallel to it on the back side, that is, on the west. Under these steps ran a small

[55] H. Speier, "Die neuen Ausgrabungen unter der Petruskirche in Rom" (in R. Herbig, *Vermächtnis der antiken Kunst*, 1950, pp. 199 ff.).
[56] W. Seston, *op. cit.*, p. 155, emphasizes this point.

Reconstruction of the Monument
Located under the Church of St. Peter

It should be explicitly noted that we have here only a conjectural reconstruction on the basis of data from the Vatican. Only little of the monument can still be seen, and for all details we are thus far reduced to suppositions. See *Espl. Vat.*, 1951, I, Plate G (where there is also given an attempted reconstruction of the upper storey), and A. Ferrua, *La Civiltà Cattolica*, 1952, p. 25, Fig. 3.

water channel covered over with bricks. On the front side, that is, on the east of the wall, is found a shallow niche 72 centimetres wide and about 1.40 metres high. On both sides of the niche the wall is painted red. About 74 centimetres in front of the niche two pillars were erected. These support a slab of travertine, which serves as a kind of roof and is fitted into the wall. Above this slab is found a wider and deeper niche—a sort of second storey. It, however, can no longer be exactly reconstructed. Since several bricks of the channel bear the stamp of Marcus Aurelius Caesar, this small monument can be dated in the second half of the second century, *if it actually was built at the same time as the channel*. This would agree well with the statement in which Gaius reports that he can show the "trophy" of Peter on the Vatican Hill. In this connection, to be sure, we must not forget that this text *by itself* does not permit us to decide whether the "trophy" is the place only of the martyrdom, or of a grave, or even merely of a memorial.[57] Since Constantine obviously oriented his entire basilica with reference to this place, it may be assumed with some probability, from the conclusions reached above concerning the unsuitable terrain, that we really are dealing with that "trophy" of Gaius.[58] This presupposes, of course, that the channel and the monument can both be dated in the same year (*Espl. Vat.*, 1951, I, pp. 103 f.).

Later, towards the end of the third century, a gray wall was erected on the north side of the monument. This occurred in connection with the extension of the cemetery and the building of numerous mausoleums in the vicinity. On the ancient red west wall, but especially upon the later north wall just mentioned, a large number of pilgrim inscriptions have been written. They date from a relatively late period, give the name of Christ in the form of the monogram, and express the wish that the deceased may "live in Christ."[59] It is remarkable that the name of Peter is never found, whereas in the graffiti on the Appian Way Peter and Paul are invoked. This fact

[57] This is not sufficiently taken into account in *present-day* discussion. The excavations can perhaps settle that controversial question, but may not *start* from it, as though the text of Gaius *in itself* rendered certain one or the other interpretation of the word *tropaion*.

[58] The report of the *Liber Pontificalis*, according to which Pope Anicletus had already erected a *Memoria* for Peter in the first century, has thus finally been proved false. K. Heussi, " 'Papst' Anencletus I. und die Memoria auf dem Vatikan" (*Deutsches Pfarrerblatt*, 1949, pp. 301 ff.), has already emphasized that this statement cannot be trusted.

[59] *Victor cum sui (s), Gaudentia vibatis in Christo. Paulina vivas, Nicasi vibas in Christo*, etc. (*Espl. Vat.*, 1951, I, p. 129; II, Plate LVII, a, b; LVIII, a, b).

does not really make it insuperably difficult to identify the edifice with the "trophy" of Peter that Gaius mentioned; nevertheless, it is astonishing, especially since, as already noted, even the Christian inscriptions of the later mausoleums never refer to Peter. These graffiti, in any case, should be studied much more carefully than appears to have been the case thus far. Whether they date before or after Constantine seems to me to be very important; it could even influence the dating of the monument itself.

Provisionally, however—though not at all with certainty—we may assert, for the reasons given, that the "trophy" of Gaius appears to have been found. If this is true, it is the single positive result of the excavations as far as they concern Peter; the result is thus a confirmation of the literary testimony of Gaius, which, however, takes us back only to the end of the second century. Even apart from the meaning of the word "trophy," however, there was no reason to doubt the correctness of his testimony. Previously, to be sure, it was disputed whether by the word "trophy" Gaius understood only the place of execution or a monument or a grave. If the identification of the "trophy" with the columnar monument should finally prove correct, then by "trophy" we should understand not only a place but also a building found there; even if not the grave, it is a memorial monument. It must further be assumed, then, that a similar monument is located under the Church of St. Paul; this, however, must be confirmed by excavation.

What was *under* this "trophy" of Peter, however, and whether in particular it concealed a real grave, is another question. It is not answered even by the identification of the "trophy," although reports in newspapers and illustrated magazines flatly assert that it has been. It is true that before the niche is a cavity 80 centimetres wide and 80 centimetres long; it was covered with a thick slab. Is this square place, which H. Grisar saw more than fifty years ago, to be called "the grave of Peter"? The dimensions could lead one at first to suppose that at a *later* time his relics had been brought here. I really cannot understand how anyone can speak without qualification of a "discovered grave of Peter," since in any case *no remains of a grave survive*. The most that one could say would be that one may *conjecture* the earlier existence of a normal grave at a deeper level, *if that grave was really crossed over later by the red wall* (*Espl. Vat.*, I, p. 139).

But what are the reasons cited to support this assumption? Around the empty square space are found a row of graves in the ground.

Three of them lie rather deep, and two of them date from a very ancient period. The one in which was buried a small boy, whose skeleton is present, was crossed over and damaged in the building of the red wall. The other is situated at the same depth, and is covered with a seal which bears the stamp of Vespasian, and so was used at the earliest in the year 70. We thus see that none of these graves surrounding the spot reaches back into the Neronian period, although they still belong to the first century. Accordingly it is not proved that in Nero's time this place was already used as a burial ground. Nevertheless, the great depth of these graves is pointed out, as is the further fact that burials in the earth took place only here. One points also to the striking poverty of these graves; to the fact that the orientation of the threshold before the niche differs from that of the wall; and to the remains of a wall which could have served to protect the side wall of the supposed grave. All these indications, so it is said, prove that even in the first century Christians had themselves buried here around the grave of Peter. But are they really Christian graves?

In the extension of the niche beneath the ground some bones were admittedly found (*Espl. Vat.*, 1951, I, p. 121, Fig. 87). But it cannot occur to anyone to wish to found a proof on this fact; the Pope himself, as already mentioned, has candidly conceded this. For it is not astonishing that bones are found in a plot containing graves. On the other hand, attention has been called to the fact that later, in the time of Constantine, a small marble box, 77 centimetres long and 30 centimetres in breadth and depth, was embedded in the graffiti-covered north wall. This box was discovered in the excavations. It contains an unidentifiable mass of earth and all sorts of remains. The assertion that at a certain time it was emptied, but once had contained bones of the apostle, is a hypothesis that cannot be demonstrated. Constantine, according to this assertion, had the bones placed in the box as far as they were still preserved.[60] In that case, it becomes necessary to assume that they had then been brought from some other place, and specifically, in accordance with the theory of the transfer, from the Appian Way.[61] Thus would be explained the fact that the grave assumed to lie under the memorial structure contains neither skeleton nor urn. This latter fact, on the other hand, has been explained by

[60] A. Ferrua, "A la recherche du tombeau de S. Pierre" (*Etudes*, 1952, pp. 44 f.). There is an exact description in *Espl. Vat.*, 1951; see Vol. I, p. 162; Vol. II, Plate LVII, b.

[61] A. Ferrua, *op. cit.*, p. 45.

saying that the grave was plundered in later centuries, and especially by the Saracens in the year 846.[62] According to the most recent hypothesis, one would have to assume that this small casket placed in the wall was also plundered. Or must we suppose that the place had already been destroyed by the elephants which, according to Aelius Lampridius (ch. 22), Elagabalus brought to the Vatican Hill?

Even Roman Catholic scholars probably had little expectation that one would find genuine relics of Peter, although the pious Roman Catholic from the common people, who like many others has believed for centuries that he kneels above the bones of the Prince of Apostles in the present Church of St. Peter, was able to cherish this illusory hope. From the scientific point of view it can only be asked whether at the time of Constantine Peter's bones were still really there. Concerning that we know absolutely nothing.[63]

He who reads without prejudice the report of the most recent excavations must concede that if one assumes that the bones of Peter had rested under the monument discovered, the entire archaeological question concerning the grave of Peter becomes only more complicated than it already was. Prompt witness of this is the fact that one of the leaders of the excavations, in an essay published soon after the appearance of the official report, discusses the assumption—with the most extreme caution, to be sure, and only as a query—that the bones had already been transferred once from the Appian Way to the Vatican Hill. (On account of the small dimensions of the square cavity before the wall, he says), there forces itself upon one the memory of the ancient tradition according to which Peter, after his martyrdom, was first buried not here, but on the Appian Way together with Paul.[64] He thus suggests the old thesis that has been rather generally rejected.[65] Be that as it may, the author goes on to say that in the second half of the second century the relics of Peter were deposited on the Vatican Hill in a small urn. There they supposedly remained until 258, when they were (again) transferred to

---

[62] *Ann. Bertiniani ann. 846.*—The graves of the apostles were spared by the Goths in the year 410 and by the Vandals in 455.

[63] According to C. Cecchelli, "La Tomba di S. Paolo" (*Capitolium*, 1950, p. 122), the heads of the apostles had already been brought to the Lateran by Constantine. However, other defenders of the genuineness of these relics date their transfer at a much later time.

[64] A. Ferrua, *op. cit.* (*Etudes*, 1952, p. 43). But in the above mentioned article in *La Civiltà cattolica*, p. 17, he seems rather to approve the rejection of this theory.

[65] See above, p. 128. In other points the articles of Ferrua, especially the one in *Etudes*, are more reserved than the official publication.

the Appian Way, and finally, under Constantine, were brought back a second time.

This complicated hypothesis shows clearly what difficulties result when one assumes that the bones of Peter had rested at the place so constituted as the recently published report describes.

On the assumption that Peter had been buried here, the most recent excavations raise more new questions than they answer old ones. Did the wall painted red really *cross over* the supposed "grave of Peter" as well as that of the boy? *Is such a site of the "trophy" conceivable?"* Is it certain that *Christians* lay in the surrounding graves? Does not a libation tube which was found argue rather for pagans?

We have seen how difficult it is to hold the theory that the bodies were transferred to the Appian Way about the year 258. Even more difficult is the theory of an original burial on the Appian Way.

At the moment I ask only the question whether everything is not explained much more simply if we assume that perhaps the pillar monument was the "trophy" of Gaius, but was so regarded at first only in the sense of a memorial monument erected at the place of the martyrdom. With this idea, to be sure, the thought of the grave may have been connected very early, even if one had no relics. For somewhere on the Vatican Hill—possibly in a common grave—the victims of the Neronian persecution will have been buried. Is it not possible that in the cavity under the "trophy" we are dealing only with a *cenotaph*, in much the same way, perhaps, as we must assume there was one on the Appian Way?[66] In that case the three memorial sites, on the Vatican Hill, on the Highway to Ostia, and on the Appian Way, were all three not burial places but memorial or cult sites, at which Christians celebrated the memory of the apostles, since they did not possess a real grave. The fact that in addition to the separate cult sites there also arose the common one on the Appian Way *could* be explained, as said, by the fact that in the pagan cemeteries on the Vatican Hill and on the Highway to Ostia assemblies were hindered and the need was felt of holding a celebration for both apostles at *one* place. Or it *could* even be that at first one of the schismatic churches of the third century had honoured here the memory of the apostles. In such a case we might be driven to think of the Novatian group, who likewise appealed to the primacy of Peter; this suggests itself especially since the liturgical sources possibly

[66] For the designation *sepulchrum* for cenotaph, see Tacitus, *Annals*, II, 83.

point in this direction.[67] The memorial site would then have been taken over by the great Church at a later time.

These, we grant, are only hypotheses; but without hypotheses we can reach no conclusions in this question. They seem to me, however, to do more justice to the archaeological evidence, in so far as they take into account only such objects as have actually been found.[68]

In order to prove that the bones of Peter really rested in the supposed grave under the present dome, we would need more certain indications than have been produced by the most recent excavations. Indeed, we actually must say that in this case particularly convincing and absolutely irrefutable arguments would have to be presented, since *the reasons which speak* a priori *against the possibility that Christians buried Peter in the neighbourhood of Nero's garden are almost overwhelming.* How could the Christians undertake an interment here in the terrible days of the Neronian persecution?[69] Did any possibility exist of distinguishing the body of Peter from the others? Is it not to be assumed that the bones of those executed, in case their ashes were not scattered on the Tiber, were thrown into a common grave?

Furthermore, how can Christians in Rome have had any interest in *relics* in the first century? In the time of Nero the Christians expected the world to end soon. In any case, we do not have even the slightest trace of a cult of relics before the martyrdom of Polycarp, and so at the earliest the middle of the second century, and then we still are not dealing with Rome but with Smyrna.[70] In *Rome* no one

---

[67] See above, p. 130.

[68] The failure, moreover, of the graffiti and the Christian inscriptions of the cemetery to mention the name of Peter could perhaps find an explanation in this way. For it is indeed striking that in the graffiti of the Appian Way Peter and Paul are invoked, while here they are not. The Memorial on the Vatican Hill was different from that on the Appian Way in that it did not serve merely for the cult of the apostle; the Vatican Hill was also known from times past as the place of execution of *other* victims of the Neronian persecution. May not the form the inscriptions took have been affected by the memory that Peter was here executed with many other Christians, and in any case was buried near them? No doubt the remembrance of Peter may have dominated over that of the nameless multitude, but it is at least possible that Christians thought also of these others and perhaps for this reason did not mention the name of Peter. Nevertheless, I do not wish to assert that the failure to name the apostle can be explained only in this way.

[69] So rightly K. Heussi, "Das Grab des Petrus" (*Deutsches Pfarrerblatt*, 1949, pp. 82 ff.).

[70] According to the most recent theory (H. Grégoire, "La véritable date du martyre de S. Polycarpe, 23 févr. 177," in *Analecta Bollandiana*, 1951, pp. 1 ff.; *Les persécutions dans l'empire romain*, 1951, pp. 28, 106 f.), the martyrdom of Polycarp should be dated later, in the year 177.

took an interest in the graves of the martyrs in the first two centuries. Indeed, prior to the third century there was no interest whatever in the graves; even the graves of the Bishops of Rome exist only from the beginning of the third century, and then in the Catacombs of Callistus.[71] If prior to this time emphasis was already placed in Rome on the possession of the mortal remains of martyrs and bishops, how then does it happen that we hear nothing of a grave either of Ignatius of Antioch, whose desire to be *completely* consumed by the wild beasts (Rom. 4:2) can scarcely have been fulfilled,[72] or of the martyr bishop Telesphorus, or of Justin, who nevertheless suffered the martyr death in Rome and were highly honoured there?[73]

In reality this interest first arose in Rome about the time when Gaius wrote to Proclus, when Callistus appealed to the nearness of Peter's grave, and when Bishop Fabian created in the Catacomb of Callistus a resting place for the bishops. This, then, occurred in the first half of the third century. It occurred in connection with the necessity of proving the apostolicity of the Roman tradition, after this tendency had arisen somewhat earlier in the east.[74]

This, however, concerns only the question of the grave. Regarding the location of the *places of execution*, the question stands otherwise. It is clear without further argument that the memory of the place of execution long continued, especially when it concerned victims of the terrible Neronian persecution. Even this memory would perhaps have been lost in the course of time, if in the third century there had not been an interest in finding the very graves of Peter and Paul, who had long been regarded as the founders of the church. Naturally one looked for them where the *execution* was located by the tradition, which still remained alive and for a part of the Neronian victims was fixed in writing by Tacitus.[75] Now at this time, that is, in the *third Christian century*, a pagan cemetery had existed at this place or in its vicinity for at least a hundred years. This

---

[71] See above, p. 135.

[72] The fact that in the fourth century (Chrysostom, *Homily on the Martyr St. Ignatius*, Migne, P. G., Vol. 50, pp. 587 ff., and Jerome, *De viribus illustribus*, Migne, P. L., Vol. 23, pp. 632 ff.) we hear that his remains were brought to Antioch only proves that in a time when the cult of relics was flourishing the question as to the remains of Ignatius was raised.

[73] This point, which seems to me decisive, is rightly stressed also by E. Schäfer, "Das Petrusgrab" (*Evangelische Theologie*, 1951, pp. 472 f.).

[74] It is not by chance that the lists of the bishops of Rome, the *Depositio Martyrum*, and the *Depositio Episcoporum*, begin in the first half of the third century.

[75] *Annals*, XV, 44.

we know from the latest excavations. Thus there was so much the more occasion to *connect the place of execution and the later cemetery as the place of burial.*

The same development is probably to be assumed for the tradition as to Paul's grave, which also was located in a pagan cemetery, situated in the direction of the place of execution at the Three Fountains. For St. Paul's Church also is situated in the area of a pagan necropolis. Paul as a Roman citizen probably was not executed at the same place as Peter and the other victims.

We come accordingly to the following result, which can also be regarded as the conclusion of this entire section concerning Peter the Martyr: The archaeological investigations do not permit us to answer in either a negative or an affirmative way the question as to the stay of Peter in Rome. The grave of Peter cannot be identified. The real proofs for the martyrdom of Peter in Rome must still be derived from the indirect literary witnesses, and from them we have reached the conclusion that probably Peter actually was in Rome and suffered execution under Nero. The excavations speak in favour of the report that *the execution of Peter took place in the Vatican district.*

*   *   *

In summary of our entire historical section, to the end of which we now have come, we must say that during the life time of Peter he held a pre-eminent position among the disciples; that after Christ's death he presided over the church at Jerusalem in the first years; that he then became the leader of the Jewish Christian mission; that in this capacity, at a time which cannot be more closely determined but probably occurred at the end of his life, he came to Rome and there, after a very short work, died as a martyr under Nero.

We must keep in mind these historical results as we now turn to the theological question of the primacy of Peter and his significance for the later Church.

Part II

THE EXEGETICAL
AND THEOLOGICAL
QUESTION

THE PROBLEM

WE SHALL start here with the exegesis of the saying of Jesus in Matthew 16:17 ff.: "You are Rock, and upon this Rock I will build my Church. . . ." In a first chapter we deliberately limit ourselves to the *strictly exegetical question*: What place do these words occupy in the framework of the Synoptic tradition? Are they really genuine words of Jesus or were they only ascribed to him by the Church? In the former case, what did Jesus intend to say by them? In that connection a special problem results from the fact that in the Greek the statement of Matthew 16:18 refers to the future: I *will* build my Church. Moreover, the imperative in the two parallel sayings most closely related to ours, the command in Luke 22:31 f.: "Strengthen your brothers," and the commission of the Risen One in John 21:16: "Feed my lambs," refer to the time after the death of Jesus. Does this mean to say that in the promise of Matthew 16:18 Jesus reckons with centuries, with the Church of *all* generations? Or does it mean that he has in mind only the Church which was then to be built in the Apostolic Age, that is, in the life-time of Peter after Christ's death? This question also is first of all a purely exegetical and historical one.

After answering this question, however, we must examine in a second *doctrinal and theological chapter* the question whether, even if the exegesis should conclude that Jesus thought only of the time of Peter, there is a legitimate possibility of extending that promise and that commission beyond the period of the foundation that Jesus had in view and applying it to the entire period of the later Church down to the present day.

Here in this quite concrete application arises the problem of the New Testament conception of time, which I have discussed elsewhere.[1] Is the period when the foundation was laid normative for the later period, in such a way that it represents the permanent unique foundation upon which the entire later structure rests once for all? Or is it normative in the sense that what happened at the beginning

---

[1] O. Cullmann, *Christus und die Zeit. Die urchristliche Zeit- und Geschichteauffassung*, 2nd ed., 1948 (Eng. Tr., *Christ and Time*, 1950).

is continually repeated in an analogous way during the entire period of the Church, so that the promises and commissions which Jesus gave for the period of the apostolic foundation should be handed on, without hesitation or change, as commissions valid for Christians who live in later years?

I note in advance that we must not make the matter all too easy for ourselves by answering too hastily with a clear-cut Yes or No. For in reality the problem is too complex to permit a solution in this simple manner. It is impossible for us to say in advance, in a generalizing way, that everything which Jesus said may be referred only to his time and the time of his immediate disciples, and so can have no validity for later generations. But on the other hand, it is also much too simple when it is declared that everything which Jesus said to an apostle concerning the Church can only be understood as said also to a whole chain of bishops, who can be designated as successors of *this specific apostle*. An application to the future is conceivable which respects the historical uniqueness of the situation in which the Church was founded. In reality, therefore, the problem presents itself in the following way: *How is the unique element to be marked off from that which is constantly repeated?*

This means, however, that we must raise the fundamental question concerning the essential difference between the apostolic office and the office of bishop. Can the uniqueness and unrepeatable quality which belong to the apostolic office in the New Testament be reconciled with an extension of a specifically apostolic commission to later bishops? Here, too, we propose to be on our guard against thinking that the question is already solved in advance.

In conclusion, however, we have to discuss also the very important problem whether it is justified for a saying addressed to an apostle to be *geographically* limited to bishops of a *particular* city. In other words, can that utterance be extended chronologically on the one hand, while at the same time it is limited in its spatial application? Is it actually to be held that the principle of a succession tied to one bishop's see is the only possible view? Or is this view legitimate at all? From the viewpoint of exegesis this question would scarcely be asked if the Roman Catholic Church did not proclaim as a dogma that Peter as the Prince of Apostles handed on his succession to the chain of *Roman* bishops. Can *such* a dogmatic extension of the saying of Jesus be reconciled with the results of exegesis and with what we know of the history of Primitive Christianity? Can that saying of Jesus legitimately be limited to the future bishops of a particular city, when the Scripture says not a word on this point, and does not even consider it necessary to mention the stay of the apostle in this city, and when in addition the historical tradition concerning a Roman episcopal office of Peter is of such a character as we have shown it to be?

To what extent, finally, does the actual *historical role* that the Roman church and its bishops played in the second and third centuries justify the Bishop of Rome in making a theological and indeed exclusive claim to the saying that Jesus addressed to Peter? Is it legitimate to give such absolute validity to a situation which only appears during the course of ancient church history, but is neither present nor hinted at when the apostles are founding the Church? In other words, the Roman church does not play a leading role at all during the lifetime of the apostles. At the earliest it begins to play such a role in Christendom at the turn from the first to the second century. Even then this role has no theological foundation. Is it possible to derive from the fact of this later role the standard that in all subsequent times, even down to the end of the period of the Church, only the bishop of this city may stand at the head of the entire Church? Is it permissible to take this position and then interpret the saying of Jesus to intend the limitation just described, as though there were no other possible way of applying it to the present?

As a marginal issue, the purely theological question may also arise whether the appeal to a *dogma* is sufficient here. In this case of the primacy of the Roman bishop, it is not just any dogma that is involved, but the one that *gives the basis of the claim of the Roman Catholic Church* that it alone is justified in proclaiming any dogmas whatever.

These questions are intended to state the problem and to show how the theological problem is connected with the exegetical one.

Usually the only possible fulfilment of the saying to Peter that is even considered is the Roman Catholic one. With a certain unquestioning confidence that the issue is self-evident, some give an affirmative and some a negative answer. We, however, shall study whether exegesis does not lead to another solution, so that the apostle Peter actually has for the Church of all times a "fundamental" importance in the etymological sense, but in a way that corresponds with the meaning and purpose of that saying as well as with the basic New Testament view.

Chapter One

THE EXEGETICAL QUESTION:
THE MEANING OF
MATTHEW 16:17-19

THE INTERPRETATION of Matthew 16:17 ff., like the discussion of the historical question concerning the stay of Peter in Rome, has been blurred all too often by confessional prejudices. Just as it is not permissible, in dealing with the question whether Peter was in Rome, to solve it in one way or the other on the basis of one's attitude toward the papacy, even so the discussion of the question as to what Christ meant by his words to Peter concerning the Church must not be burdened in advance by one's judgment regarding the later papal claim. As in the former question, so also here one must react against the conscious or unconscious popular view—as though, for example, one who recognizes the genuineness of that saying somehow makes a concession to this papal claim, or as though one who challenges its genuineness deals a particularly effective blow to this claim to power.

The history of interpretation which we prefix to the study of our passage teaches us that the confessional standpoint has quite often coloured the exegesis, and that usually the result is fixed in advance and then subsequently read into the text.

1. *The History of the Leading Interpretations*

We lack a detailed history of the way in which our section has been interpreted throughout the centuries, from the ancient Church Fathers down to our own day. Such a work would be of the greatest value not only for exegetes but also for the historians of doctrine and of the Church. To be sure, we find, in the older commentaries and also in books on church history, references to the interpretations that the Church Fathers and the Reformers gave. There is lacking, however, a complete and connected presentation of the patristic interpretations of the saying. Only with reference to more recent study are we in a substantially more favourable situation; in recent commentaries, and also in articles in journals, the various contributions that the last fifty years have made to the understanding of our text have already become in part the subject of systematic survey.[1]

We cannot pretend to give here even an approximately complete survey of the history of the exegesis of Matthew 16:17 f. Of the older explanations I shall mention only those which are particularly typical. I shall speak somewhat more in detail of the more recent ones, but at first will report only their conclusions. In our interpretation of the text we shall come back to individual arguments of earlier exegetes.

The first attempts at explanation are still free from the ecclesiastical and political tendency to use the saying for or against the claim of the Roman Bishop. Only at the beginning of the third century, in the west, does this interest in the saying of Jesus become prominent.

In the first two centuries we find very few traces of any use of Matthew 16:17 ff. The first certain evidence of such a use occurs in *Justin's Dialogue* (100,4; 106,3),[2] and further in the *Pseudo-Clementina*. *Origen* starts from his distinction between letter and spirit in order to explain that the letter directs this saying concerning the Rock to Peter, while the Spirit has in mind everyone who becomes such as Peter was.[3]

When we come to the explanation of *Tertullian* mentioned above,[4] we already find ourselves in the area of exegesis influenced by ecclesiastical politics. In his struggle against the author of that edict concerning the extension of penance, whom we may identify with the

---

[1] See J. R. Geiselmann, *Der petrinische Primat* (*Mt. 16, 17*), *seine neueste Bekämpfung und Rechtfertigung*, 1927, and especially K. L. Schmidt, Article on ἐκκλησία in G. Kittel's *Theologisches Wörterbuch zum N. T.* (this article has now appeared also separately in English translation under the title, *The Church*, 1950, in the series, *Bible Key Words* From Gerhard Kittel's *Theologisches Wörterbuch zum N. T.*). On the latest literature see R. Bultmann, "Die Frage nach der Echtheit von Mt. 16, 17-19" (*Theologische Blätter*, 1941, pp. 265 ff.), and A. Oepke, "Der Herrenspruch über die Kirche: Mt. 16, 17-19 in der neuesten Forschung" (*Studia Theologica*, Lund, 1948-1950, pp. 110 ff.).

[2] See E. Massaux, *Influence de L'Evangile de S. Matthieu sur la littérature chrétienne avant S. Irénée*, 1950. The possibility of use he accepts for Ignatius and the Odes of Solomon.

[3] Origen on Matt. 16:18: "For rock means every disciple of Christ."

[4] *De pudicitia*, 21. See above, p. 121.

highest probability as the Roman Bishop Callistus,[5] he explicitly rejects the interpretation that "the power to bind and loose has passed on to this bishop, that is, to the entire Church that is near to Peter."[6] This, he says, would "twist the obvious purpose of the Lord, who committed this to Peter *personally*."[7] And Tertullian proceeds: "What does all that have to do with the Church, and particularly with you, psychic one? According to the person of Peter this authority belongs to spiritual men . . ." From this we probably may conclude that Callistus (217–222) had already referred Matthew 16:17 to himself,[8] perhaps indeed with special appeal to Peter's grave.[9]

5 The expressions *pontifex maximus* and *episcopus episcoporum*, which Tertullian uses in the same passage to designate the author of the edict, which he calls an *edictum peremptorium*, are best suited, even though they are ironical, to Callistus, whom Hippolytus also reproaches in his *Philosophoumena* for his lax exercise of penance. This in any case is more natural than it is to follow P. Galtier ("Le véritable édit de Calliste," *Revue d'Histoire ecclésiastique*, 1927, pp. 465 ff.; "Ecclesia Petri propinqua, A propos de Tertullien et de Calliste," *Revue d'Histoire ecclésiastique*, 1928, pp. 40 ff.; *L'Eglise et la rémission des péchés aux premiers siècles*, 1932, pp. 139 ff.) in ascribing the edict to a Carthaginian bishop Agrippinus (see also G. Bardy, "L'édit d'Agrippinus," *Revue des Sciences religieuses*, 1924, pp. 1 ff.). The great majority of scholars identify the bishop addressed with Callistus; so P. Batiffol, *L'Eglise naissante et le Catholicisme*, 1927, p. 350; *Cathedra Petri*, 1938, pp. 175 ff.; H. Koch, *Kallist und Tertullian*, 1920; *Cathedra Petri*, 1930, p. 6; E. Caspar, *Geschichte des Papsttums von den Anfängen bis zur Höhe der Weltherrschaft*, Vol. I, 1930, p. 26, and especially A. Harnack, "Ecclesia Petri propinqua" (*Sitzungsbericht der Berliner Akademie der Wissenschaften*, 1927). M. Goguel, *L'Eglise primitive*, 1947, holds on the contrary that the theory of P. Galtier is possible, but he does not make a definite decision.

6 On the expression *ad omnem ecclesiam Petri propinquam* see above, p. 121, the hypothesis of W. Köhler, "Omnis ecclesia Petri propinqua, Versuch einer religionsgeschichtlichen Deutung" (*Sitzungsbericht der Heidelberg Akademie der Wissenschaften*, 1937–38). Harnack's proposal (*op. cit.* in the preceding note) to take *omnem* as a scribal error for *romanam* is purely hypothetical, and is rejected even by most Roman Catholic scholars. See Batiffol, *Cathedra Petri*, 1938, p. 178. Contrariwise K. Adam, "Neue Untersuchungen über den Ursprung der kirchlichen Primatslehre" (*Tübinger Theologische Quartalschrift*, 1928, pp. 169 ff.).

7 For the text of this passage see above, p. 121, note 92.

8 A different view is taken by K. Heussi, "Die Nachfolge des Petrus" (*Deutsches Pfarrerblatt*, 1949, pp. 420 f.). According to him Callistus appealed to Matt., ch. 16, only to prove the right of *all* bishops to forgive sins.

9 According to E. Caspar, "Primatus Petri" (*Zeitschrift der Savigny-Stiftung für Rechtsgeschichte*, 1927, pp. 253 ff.), Callistus did not appeal to Matt. 16:17 ff. Tertullian first did so, to oppose Callistus; but he did not suspect what spirits he was conjuring up. In this way, much as Cyprian later did without intending to do so, he gave the Roman episcopal see the weapons with which it would henceforth defend its primacy. Against this theory M. Goguel, *L'Eglise primitive*,

Tertullian completely rejects that application of the saying to later bishops, and indeed not only to those of Rome but to bishops generally.

In doing so he stands in opposition to Cyprian; the latter also is unwilling to see any ground for the primacy of the Roman Bishop over the remaining bishops derived from the saying of Jesus, but he does consider that the whole body of bishops is addressed in Peter. When Jesus says only to Peter that he is the Rock, he thereby points simply to the necessity of the unity of the Church.[10] Cyprian developed his view, which he already had championed at an earlier time, mainly in connection with his dispute with the Bishop Stephan (254–257).[11] The latter, therefore, evidently appealed, as Callistus did, to Matthew 16:17 ff.; he as Bishop of Rome proposed to derive from it his primacy over the entire Church. Firmilian, Bishop of Caesarea in Cappadocia, in a letter to Cyprian, opposes this interpretation of Stephan in which the Roman Bishop claims that he is entitled by succession to the *cathedra* of Peter.[12]

These explanations are burdened with tendencies drawn from ecclesiastical politics. For a time, the saying of Jesus to Peter plays scarcely any role in grounding the papal claim. Then, from the beginning of the Middle Ages, it is regularly used by the popes, as

1947, pp. 195 f., makes the point that on this view it would be remarkable that this effect of the argument of Tertullian and Cyprian does not show itself until so much later.

[10] *De catholicae ecclesiae unitate*, cap. 4–5; *Epistolae* 33, 59, 73, 75, 76, 81, etc. Concerning Cyprian's exegesis, see J. Chapman, *Revue Bénedictine*, 1902–3; *ib.*, 1910; and K. Adam, "Cyprians Kommentar zu Mtth. 16, 18–19 in dogmengeschichtlicher Beleuchtung" (*Tübinger Theologische Quartalschrift*, 1912); H. Koch, *Cyprian und der römische Primat*, 1910; *Cyprianische Untersuchung*, 1926; especially *Cathedra Petri*, 1930.

[11] By using all of the writings of Cyprian a unified interpretation of the saying to Peter can be made, in so far as he always recognizes the primacy of Peter as a sign of unity, but on the other hand always refuses to derive from it for the later Bishops of Rome a pre-eminent position over the other bishops, who are all successors of Peter. However, it is not quite clear how he connects with this view the "pre-eminence" (*principalitas*) he recognizes for Rome (*Epistola* 59, 14). P. Batiffol, *Cathedra Petri*, 1938, emphasizes in all parts of his book this idea, that according to Cyprian Rome is "the chief church, whence the sacerdotal unity has arisen" (*ecclesia principalis, unde unitas sacerdotalis exorta est*). (See on this point H. Koch, *Cyprian und der römische Primat*, 1910; *Cathedra Petri*, 1930.) If *principalis* were really to be thus understood, that Jesus with the words "you are Peter" founded *this* church, then Cyprian's exposition could scarcely be regarded as *entirely* consistent and unified.

[12] In connection with Cyprian, *Epistola* 75, 17.

II

though no other understanding of it were possible. Yet it is note-worthy that the outstanding ancient commentators who concerned themselves with Matthew 16:17 ff. without discussing questions directly related to church politics considered other possibilities of interpretation. Thus *Chrysostom* explains that the rock on which Christ will build his Church means the faith of confession.[13] Accord-ing to *Augustine*, Jesus meant by the rock not Peter but himself, an explanation which Luther will follow.[14] In his *Retractationes*[15] Augustine writes that earlier, under the influence of Ambrose, he referred the word "rock" to Simon. However, he goes on, it does not say, "You are the rock," but "you are Peter"; the rock is men-tioned only in the following sentence, and there it seems best to refer the word to Christ. He leaves the decision to his readers. A similar embarrassment is to be observed in other writers, for example *Cyril of Alexandria.* We thus see that the exegesis that the Reformers gave —though, as we shall see, it is questionable—was not first invented for their struggle against the papacy; it rests upon an older patristic tradition.

We mentioned earlier the striking fact that the Reformers at-tached little significance to the question whether Peter was in Rome or not, even though Luther had doubts about the matter. We find among them rather an intensive concern with the saying of Jesus in Matthew 16:17 ff., and their specific interest is in polemic against the Pope. *Luther*, on the one hand, like Augustine, interprets the rock to mean Christ himself: "Thus this rock is the Son of God, Jesus Christ himself and no one else."[16] From this basis he establishes the connection with Peter; he emphasizes that the word directed to Peter has in view (not his person but) only his faith in Jesus the Rock: "You are . . . the rock man, for you have recognized the true man who is the true Rock, and you have named him as the Scripture names him, that is, Christ."[17] "Not upon the rock . . . of the Roman Church is the Church founded, as some decrees explain it, but upon the faith which Peter confessed for the entire Church."[18] *Calvin*

---

[13] See J. Chapman, *Early Papacy*, pp. 72 ff.

[14] Augustine, *Sermons* 76, 147, 149, 232, 245, 270, 295.

[15] I, 21, 1.

[16] *Wider Das Papsttum vom Teufel gestiftet* (Weimar edition, 54; E. Mülhaupt, *Luthers Evangelien-Auslegung*, Vol. 2, pp. 545 f.).

[17] *Ib.*, Mülhaupt, p. 548.

[18] "Resolution Lutheriana super propositione XIII de potestate papae 1519" (Weimar edition, 2; E. Mülhaupt, *op. cit.*, Vol. 2, p. 525). Further passages in Mülhaupt, *op. cit.*, Vol. 2.

argues quite similarly: the words which the Roman Catholic teaching refers to the person of a man were in reality spoken only of Peter's faith in Christ. Hence the designation "rock" is addressed both to Simon and to the other believers. The bond of faith in Christ is the basis on which the Church grows.[19] Likewise for *Zwingli* Peter is only the type of him who believes in Christ as the sole Rock.[20] It is only a variation of all these interpretations when Melanchthon refers the saying to preaching and the preaching office.[21] Thus in the final analysis all the Reformers agree that Peter was named "Rock" by Jesus not as a person but only as a believer. The true Rock of the Church, they hold, is Jesus Christ.

We pass over the following centuries and come to recent times. We speak first of two typical interpretations which are rather closely connected with the Reformation view, but seek to give it a more solid exegetical basis. First of all, there is the interpretation of *Th. Zahn*. Like the Reformers, he emphasizes the faith of Peter, but on the other hand he also takes account of the fact that Peter was the *first* confessor and so occupies a special position in the foundation of the Church.[22] The commentary of *Strack-Billerbeck* connects more closely with the Reformers. It starts from the assumption that the Greek text was a mistranslation from an Aramaic original text. The correct English translation of the original would be as follows: "I say to you, yes to you, Peter: On this rock I will build my Church."[23] The word "rock" in this passage, therefore, would not mean Peter. Jesus did not say: "You are the rock," but rather: I say to you, Peter," etc. When he then proceeds: "On this rock I will build my Church," he speaks of his own Messianic dignity, his own divine sonship, in which men must believe.

Toward the end of the nineteenth and at the beginning of the twentieth century, however, another interpretation dominated in Protestant scholarship. The saying, it was held, was not spoken by

---

[19] See Calvin, *Commentaire, ad loc.*
[20] Among other places, his sermon on providence (Zwingli, *Hauptschriften*, Vol. II, p. 195); "Concerning the True and the False Religion" (Zwingli, *Hauptschriften*, Vol. 9, pp. 158 ff.).
[21] *De potestate et principatu Papae.*
[22] See Th. Zahn, *Das Evangelium des Matthäus*, 4th ed., 1922, *ad loc.*
[23] *Kommentar zum N. T. aus Talmud und Midrasch*, Vol. I, pp. 732 ff. Jesus, on this view, said: גם אני אמר לך אתה פטרוס. The translator by mistake understood אתה as the subject of a new sentence, when it was only the repeating of the second person singular pronoun already contained in לך. This is also the view of G. Gloege, *Reich Gottes und Kirche*, 1929, pp. 274 f.

Jesus at all. It was ascribed to him later, and this was done at a time and place where one had an interest in glorifying Peter. Even today the discussion of our passage often revolves around this question of "genuineness" or "spuriousness." Can this saying have been spoken by Jesus, or was it only created by the Church after his death? This question, as already noted, should be independent of that concerning the justification of the papal claim. As a matter of fact, even today the battle lines are not so drawn in this matter that the genuineness is recognized only by Roman Catholic scholars, while Protestant scholars contest it. Rather the discussion on this issue—as on the question of Peter's stay in Rome—takes place among Protestant exegetes themselves. Indeed, even in the area of Protestant exegesis it is not true that only the exegetes who rightly or wrongly are called "conservative" defend the genuineness of the saying, while the interpreters who rightly or wrongly are given the liberal label oppose it. On this point we should recall above all that even such radical critics as *D. F. Strauss* and *F. Ch. Baur* regarded the genuineness as quite obvious.

It was New Testament scholars, and above all *H. J. Holtzmann*, who toward the end of the nineteenth century first denied vigorously that Jesus uttered the saying; he could not possibly have so spoken, because he had no intention of founding a Church. The passage, on this view, appears to have received its present form only in the second century. The church consciousness which comes to expression in it is already basically Catholic in character. Indeed, Holtzmann actually goes so far as to explain that we here have to do with a first stirring of the Roman self-consciousness.[24] The entire course of critical study at the beginning of the twentieth century is then dominated by this conception, and it would take too long to cite here the names of all those who regard the saying as irreconcilable with the teaching of Jesus. The chief reason for denying that Jesus said it is always said to be the mention of the "Church." How can Jesus have spoken of the Church? After all, he preached only the Kingdom of God. It was only after his death that something quite different, that is, the Church, appeared. According to the famous word of A. Loisy: "Jesus announced the Kingdom of God, but what appeared was the Church."[25] It was to justify subsequently this unexpected development that this saying was ascribed to Jesus. So we hear from

[24] *Handkommentar*, I, *ad loc.*
[25] *L'Evangile et l'Eglise*, 1902, p. 111. See also *Les évangiles synoptiques*, 1908.

Johannes Weiss and *E. Klostermann* to *M. Dibelius, B. S. Easton, M. Goguel*, and many other representatives of New Testament scholarship, and from historians of this generation,[26] that the saying cannot come from Jesus. The only exception, apart from such conservative scholars as *Th. Zahn*[27] and *A. Schlatter*,[28] is *A. Schweitzer*, who recognizes the genuineness of Matthew 16:18; he takes his starting point, it is true, from the same contrast between an earthly Church and the Kingdom of God, but identifies the Church here with the Kingdom of God and interprets the passage in a purely eschatological way.[29] Among opponents of the genuineness, the representatives of the school of comparative religion, for example, *A. Dell*,[30] *H. Gressmann*, and *R. Reitzenstein*, attempt to explain the statement of Matthew 16:17 ff. not only from the tendency to legitimitize the later Church, but also from motifs found in comparative religion.

A. Harnack takes a somewhat less radical attitude. To be sure, he too holds that Jesus cannot have spoken the promise with reference to the Church. This saying rather was coined at a later time, and probably in Rome, as it strove for the primacy. But in contrast to his predecessors Harnack denies to Jesus, in the entire section, only this one sentence concerning the Church; the remaining parts of the utterance addressed to Peter he regards as genuine. With these words Jesus assured Peter of immortality: "You are Peter, and death will not conquer you." This is how the words concerning the gates of hell are to be understood. Jesus said nothing to Peter, however, concerning the building of the Church. This part was rather inserted later into the original promise.[31] Since Harnack did not intend to put forth his explanation as a mere conjecture, he attempted to determine an original text in which those words concerning the Church, and only those words, had actually been lacking. This text, he held, was the Diatessaron of Tatian. This latter assertion,

---

26 See also J. Grill, *Der Primat des Petrus*, 1904 p. 79; J. Schnitzer, *Hat Jesus das Papsttum gestiftet?*, 1910, p. 82; F. Heiler, *Der Katholizismus. Seine Idee und seine Erscheinung*, 1923, pp. 39 ff.

27 See above, p. 163.

28 *Der Evangelist Matthäus*, 1929.

29 *Geschichte der Leben-Jesu-Forschung*, 4th ed., 1926, p. 416 (cf. Eng. Tr., *The Quest of the Historical Jesus*, 2nd ed., 1911, p. 369, note).

30 *ZNW*, 1914, pp. 1 ff. See above, p. 19.

31 "Der Spruch über Petrus als den Felsen der Kirche" (*Sitzungsbericht der Berliner Akademie der Wissenschaften*, 1918, pp. 637 ff.)

however, was refuted from the Roman Catholic side as early as 1922.[32]

We thus have seen that it is mainly the mention of the Church that has caused scholars to declare the passage spurious. So also it is precisely on this point that a change of opinion occurred in the period between the two world wars; the attempt was made to prove that in reality Jesus could very well have spoken of a Church, on the condition that in this connection one does not think of the Church in the modern sense, but of what the Aramaic equivalent meant to a Jew of that time. Here it is chiefly two scholars who must be named: *F. Kattenbusch*, who in his work on the place of origin of the Church proposes the thesis that the Son of Man idea leads to that of a "People of the Saints";[33] and then *K. L. Schmidt*, who in two decisive articles[34] seeks to determine the Aramaic expression which lies behind the Greek word for Church, and on this basis shows that the word fits perfectly as an utterance of Jesus, since it refers to the idea of the People of God, the remnant or the separate synagogue.

In this way the chief argument against genuineness seemed to be removed. At the same time, interesting studies by *J. Jeremias*[35] emphasized by other arguments the Semitic character of the word and its roots in Jewish conceptions of the cosmic rock. Hence there now occurred a swing back to an extensive agreement among Protestant exegetes in favour of accepting the genuineness. It finds expression, for example, in the book of *O. Linton* concerning "The Problem of the Primitive Church in Recent Study."[36] The late Roman Catholic New Testament scholar from Fribourg, *F. M. Braun*, O.P., in his exceedingly instructive book, "New Light on the Church," also con-

---

[32] See especially S. Euringer, "Der locus classicus des Primates (Mt. 16, 18) und der Diatessarontext des heiligen Ephraim" (*Festgabe für A. Ehrhard*, 1922, pp. 141 ff.); also, A. Kneller, *Innsbrucker Zeitschrift für katholische Theologie*, 1920, pp. 147 ff.; J. Sickenberger, "Eine neue Deutung der Primatstelle (Matt. 16, 18)" (*Théologique Revue*, 1920, pp. 1 ff.); and against A. Harnack also Ed. Meyer, *Ursprung und Anfänge des Christentums*, Vol. I, p. 112.

[33] *Festgabe für A. Harnack*, 1921, pp. 143 ff. The collective meaning of the Son of Man concept is also emphasized by T. W. Manson, *The Teaching of Jesus*, 1931, p. 211, and R. Newton Flew, *Jesus and his Church*, 1938. See also H. Odeberg, *The Fourth Gospel*, 1929, pp. 39 f.; N. A. Dahl, *Das Volk Gottes*, 1941, p. 90.

[34] "Das Kirchenproblem im Urchristentum" (*Theologische Blätter*, 1927, columns 293 ff.); "Die Kirche des Urchristentums" (*Festgabe für Ad. Deissmann*, 1927, p. 259). See also especially *Theologisches Wörterbuch zum N. T.*, Vol. III, Article on ἐκκλησία, 1936 (English translation, *The Church*; see note 1 of this chapter).

[35] *Golgotha*, 1926, pp. 68 ff.; *Angelos*, 1926, p. 109.

[36] *Das Problem der Urkirche in der neueren Forschung*, 1932.

firms this new consensus among Protestant scholars.[37] So it might seem that the question as to genuineness has finally been settled along this line.

In the year 1941, however a reaction again occurred. It came from R. *Bultmann*, in connection with my remark in my monograph on "The Kingship of Christ and the Church."[38] I had said that the challenge to the genuineness of Matthew 16:17 ff. cannot be justified on scholarly grounds. In a rather long essay in *Theologischen Blätter*,[39] Bultmann seeks to undermine this statement; he defends anew the assertion of spuriousness that he had championed earlier. He seeks to refute F. Kattenbusch and K. L. Schmidt; he points to the absence of the word "Church" in the teaching of Jesus, and above all tries to demonstrate that Jesus spoke only of a Kingdom to come in the future, not of a Church that is now being realized. In so doing, he, like his earlier predecessors, believes that in the last analysis he must think in terms of a modern understanding of the word "Church." Even Bultmann, however, had already conceded in previous studies that the saying must have been coined and ascribed to Jesus at a very early time, since its character is entirely Semitic and so it comes from the period of debates concerning the law in Palestine.

Thus the question was raised anew by R. Bultmann. In the subsequent debate *W. G. Kümmel* took a prominent role with his much discussed essay on "The Church Concept and the Consciousness of History in the Primitive Church and in the Mind of Jesus."[40] He likewise comes to the conclusion that the saying was not uttered by Jesus but was only ascribed to him later by the Church. His arguments, however, are essentially different from the earlier ones. His starting point is that in Primitive Christianity, as with Jesus, there was a tension between the eschatological future and the present, but that the tension was solved in a different way in each case. In the case

---

[37] *Neues Licht auf die Kirche*, 1946 (German translation of *Aspects Nouveaux du problème de l'Eglise*, 1942, enlarged and revised by the author). On p. 8; Braun names as representatives of this consensus: F. Kattenbusch, K. L. Schmid-, H. D. Wendland, G. Gloege, W. Michaelis, J. Schniewind, F. Leenhardt, R. Otto, A. Fridrichsen, R. Newton Flew, O. Cullmann. The list could easily be extended, for example by those whom Braun often cites: O. Linton, J. Jeremias, etc.

[38] *Königsherrschaft Christi und Kirche*, 1941, p. 22.

[39] "Die Frage nach der Echtheit von Matth. XVI, 17–19" (*Theologische Blätter*, 1941, pp. 265 ff.).

[40] *Kirchenbegriff und Geschichtsbewusstsein in der Urgemeinde und bei Jesus (Symbolae Biblicae Upsalienses)*, 1943. Even earlier W. G. Kümmel had opposed the genuineness, in *Die Eschatologie der Evangelien*, 1936, p. 16.

of Primitive Christianity, the Church was regarded as the already present fulfilment; for Jesus, on the contrary, the already present fulfilment was connected only with his person. The two solutions, according to Kümmel, could not have stood side by side in the mind of Jesus.

Others have challenged the genuineness with still other arguments. For example, *Emanuel Hirsch* does so after the manner of the older critics and without considering the recent statement of the problem.[41] *J. Haller* completely rejects the recent studies and discards the saying without offering any real exegetical foundation.[42] *H. Strathmann*[43] regards the saying, in connection with his somewhat schematic geographical division of the roles of the evangelists, as the creation of the church at Antioch.[44] *E. Stauffer* takes a special position; while he regards the utterance as a saying of the Lord, he assigns it not to the Incarnate Jesus, but to the Risen One, who spoke the words on the occasion of his first appearance, which was granted to Peter.[45]

N. A. Dahl[46] and *O. Michel*[47] do not deny the genuineness categorically, but take an extremely cautious attitude. *R. Liechtenhan*, on the contrary, while he carries on a debate with R. Bultmann and continues the ideas of Kümmel, nevertheless uses these ideas in a different way. He represents the view that Jesus' eschatological expectation concerning the future included the foundation of his Church; towards the setting and form of the saying, however, he takes a critical attitude.[48] Especially does the last major work, which comes from *A. Oepke*,[49] offer anew a full defence of the genuineness. In doing so, it emphasizes mainly the idea of the People of God, an

---

[41] *Frühgeschichte des Evangeliums*, II, 1941, pp. 306 ff.

[42] *Das Papsttum*, 2nd ed., 1951, pp. 4 f., 473 f. The saying, he contends, could only have originated after the year 70, when events proved that the temple rock had no permanence. This unexpected conclusion J. Haller draws from the above mentioned work of J. Jeremias.

[43] "Die Stellung des Petrus in der Urkirche. Zur Frühgeschichte des Wortes an Petrus Mt. 16, 17–19" (*Zeitschrift für systematische Theologie*, 1943, pp. 223 ff.).

[44] See above, p. 25, note 35.

[45] "Zur Vor- und Frühgeschichte des Primatus Petri" (*ZKG*, 1943–44, pp. 1 ff.

[46] *Das Volk Gottes. Eine Untersuchung zum Kirchenbewusstsein des Urchristentums*, 1941, p. 165.

[47] *Das Zeugnis des Neuen Testaments von der Gemeinde*, 1941, pp. 9 f., 22 f.

[48] *Die urchristliche Mission*, 1946 (*Abhandlungen zur Theologie des Alten und Neuen Testaments*).

[49] "Der Herrnspruch über die Kirche, Mt. 16, 17–19, in der neuesten Forschung" (*Studia Theologica*, 1948–50, pp. 110 ff.).

idea solidly rooted in Jewish conceptions; on the other hand, by showing the rhythm in which these verses are constructed, it seeks to ascribe the saying to the Logia Source and at the same time to show its organic attachment to the narrative framework as it appears also in Mark.

Thus at the present time the question is once more in flux, and we can scarcely speak any longer of a consensus of opinion. A statistical study of the position that thirty-four modern authors take on this question has shown that they divide into two approximately equal groups.[50]

Up to this point we have mentioned only Protestant scholars. The genuineness of the saying naturally cannot be challenged by Roman Catholic exegetes. In general, the modern Roman Catholic commentators limit themselves to offering a searching detailed exegesis. It is noteworthy that we find very little concerning the point which one would gladly find discussed by precisely these scholars—concerning the question, that is, whether and how it accords with the purpose of Jesus to refer these words to bishops as successors, whether and how, indeed, the promise of Jesus contains any idea whatever of a succession. *F. M. Braun*, in debate with K. L. Schmidt in the above mentioned work,[51] is the only one who ever takes up the question. He does not, indeed, discuss it in an exegetical way; this the scope of his book scarcely permitted. In the Roman Catholic *commentaries* the presence of the idea of succession is for the most part not examined; it is rather presupposed as an undiscussed fact. And yet this should be proved, for it certainly is not at all self-evident, and he who reads the saying without prejudice will never by himself get the idea that Jesus here speaks—in a sort of prophetic way—to successors of Peter. The Roman Catholic exegetes really owe a more thorough explanation on this point than one usually reads in their commentaries.

I choose as examples two recent Roman Catholic commentaries which have dealt with the Gospel of Matthew. They are by P. Dausch and M. J. Lagrange. In *Dausch*[52] we read but a single sentence concerning the specific question that here interests us: "since, according to the second half of verse 18, the Church founded upon Peter is to be unshakable in its stability and in its duration, and since it is almost universally conceded that Peter came to Rome and died

---

[50] See A. Oepke, *op. cit.*, p. 111, note 1.
[51] See above, pp. 166 f.
[52] *Kommentar zum Matthäusevangelium*, 1936, *ad. loc.*

there, the primacy is already assured on this basis alone." *F. M. Lagrange*, however, deals with this question somewhat more in detail.[53] After an intensive criticism of Harnack, he mentions the objection of the "Anglicans" that the passage speaks only of Peter, not of any possible successors. Why this objection is ascribed only to the Anglicans is not clear. In reality we are dealing here with a question which Protestants of all denominations have raised long since and repeatedly in opposition to the Roman Catholic presupposition. Lagrange replies that in this saying Jesus did not limit the duration of the Church. As long as there is a Church, it will have the same foundation, even if the head and the members change. There thus exists, he claims, a "successive unity" in the leadership of the Church. Jesus will see to it that in order to provide the foundation for the Church there will be at all times shepherds of the quality of Peter, that is, of the same faith. History proves that this has been the case, and this confirms the trustworthiness of the Lord's saying.[54] Concerning this retreat from exegesis to later history, which we find almost universally among Roman Catholic scholars,[55] we shall speak in the closing chapter. For in any case it can be considered only as a confirmation and not as a justification of the exegesis.

2. *The Narrative Framework of Matthew 16:17–19*

We now undertake, on the basis of a careful examination of the text, to explain the verses under discussion. First of all we must give close attention to the context in which they stand. This very context raises questions, especially since Mark and Luke have the same narrative framework, but without the crucial verses which here concern us. These momentous words concerning the rock on which Jesus will build his Church thus stand in but one of our four Gospels, the Gospel of Matthew. For many this fact still constitutes what we may call the first external occasion for challenging the genuineness. This argument, however, should certainly be discarded. The fact that a saying belongs to the so-called special material of Matthew is no justification at all for even raising the question of genuineness. How many pearls we would have to discard as spurious from Jesus'

[53] *Evangile selon S. Matthieu*, 5th ed., 1941, *ad loc.*

[54] J. Sickenberger also omits any discussion of successors in his explanation of Matt. 16:17 ff. in *Biblische Zeitfragen*, 1929, pp. 16 ff.

[55] See for example K. Pieper, *Jesus und die Kirche*, 1932, and K. Adam, *Wesen des Katholizismus*, 1934.

Sermon on the Mount—to name only this one example—if we were to let ourselves be guided by this principle![56]

The point has been made that the historical framework, which is found also in Mark and Luke though without these verses, is interrupted by this section in Matthew in a rather unfortunate way. We therefore propose to begin by studying this argument. Do the verses fit the narrative framework or not? On this point one thing must be noted in advance; even if it should prove true that the section with which we are concerned breaks the narrative framework, or in chronological respects is actually irreconcilable with it, we still could not draw from that fact the conclusion that the words are spurious, that is, that they were not spoken by Jesus. This conclusion would rather warrant only the preliminary conclusion that a unit of tradition, handed down separately, has been inserted here by Matthew in a setting in which it did not originally belong.

First, however, we must look more closely at this historical framework. It deals with the famous confession of Jesus by Peter at Caesarea Philippi, and we propose to read this narrative in the form in which it stands in the Gospel of Mark. On the whole, Matthew gives it, apart from variations in detail, in the same form that Mark has; only he introduces in this framework the promises of Jesus to Peter.

While the story of Peter's confession of Jesus is common to all three Synoptics, it is probably presented most vividly and in most effective simplicity in Mark. Precisely in this Gospel, moreover, it has a quite central position. One is inclined to trace the story back to a direct participant, that is, to the chief participant, to Peter himself, in case the notice of Papias is correct, according to which the evangelist Mark was the interpreter of Peter, and in his Gospel reported the stories from the life of Jesus which Peter cited in his sermons as illustrative examples.[57] In any case, Matthew and Luke, in the parallel passages, do not possess the same freshness as does Mark, in whose Gospel a certain animation marks this entire narrative. This animation permits us in a way to share in the excitement of those who were present at the event itself.

[56] It therefore seems to me unnecessary to follow the explanation that Eusebius gives in his *Demonstratio evangelica*, 3, 5. He explains the silence of the Gospel of Mark, which goes back to Peter, by the humility and modesty of the apostle. This is the interpretation given by Roman Catholic exegetes such as P. Dausch, *Kirche und Papsttum—eine Stiftung Jesu*, 1911.

[57] Eusebius, *Ecclesiastical History*, III, 39, 15 f.

Mark is conscious of the fact that in this moment something of special importance must have happened. Even the beginning of the conversation must have been an impressive moment. Previously Jesus had commanded silence and had done everything to prevent any discussion of his Messianic calling from arising. Now on his own initiative, though in the narrow circle of disciples, he starts a conversation concerning this question to which previously he had carefully avoided making so much as the merest allusion. Now he is the very one who asks: "Who do the people say that I am?" Then he asks further—and here we note how both the questioner and the persons questioned are inwardly moved—"And you, who do you say that I am?" Then comes the answer of Peter, which again in its modest brevity embodies the emotion of the disciple: "You are the Christ." Matthew, who has a slight tendency to edifying liturgical paraphrase, may well have weakened somewhat the effect of this answer when he gave it the fuller form: "You are the Christ, the Son of the Living God." This expansion appears rather a weakening of the Marcan text, even if we must be somewhat cautious in making such judgments, which rest upon subjective impressions. The Lucan text also was not content here with the simple wording of Peter's answer as we read it in Mark. It says: "The Christ of God." In contrast, the simple words: "You are the Messiah," are more powerful in their simplicity and sound more original. What the demon-possessed man had already said to Jesus in Capernaum: "Jesus the Messiah," this we now hear from the mouth of the disciple who is the representative and spokesman of the others. In the name of all he utters the great word that up to this time no disciple had dared to speak in the presence of Jesus. Among themselves the disciples may have discussed it when Jesus was absent, and the confession of Peter will have rested upon their firm conviction.[58]

They knew that they were not mere disciples of a rabbi, as were all other disciples. They were certain that their teacher was more than a rabbi, and they had the proud consciousness, which emerges in other passages, that they formed the following of the Messiah. One speaks a great deal of the self-consciousness of Jesus. We could also speak of the self-consciousness of the disciples.

According to Mark, Jesus at first answers nothing in response to this confession, and this is very significant. The disciples still do not

[58] W. Michaelis, *Das Evangelium nach Matthäus (Prophezei)*, Part II, 1949, p. 339, assumes on the contrary that Peter previously had suspected nothing of this kind; Jesus' words presuppose a sudden disclosure.

know in what way he conceives this Messianic calling. Jesus says neither Yes nor No. He simply commands the disciples not to tell this to anyone, that is, not to tell anyone that he is the Christ. Only when he shall suffer will the people recognize in him the Messiah. The disciples, however, must now be the first ones to be taught in what sense he is the Messiah. This instruction follows in verses 31 f. It is attached to the commandment to say nothing to anyone concerning his Messianic calling, and it likewise explains this command. This is *the entirely natural continuation of the narrative*. In view of the importance of the occasion the passion prediction necessarily followed here, and it explains all the commands to be silent. This prediction and the protest of Peter by no means form a new narrative. Neither are they a sort of epilogue. Rather, they give *the point of the entire event at Caesarea Philippi*.[59] Now that the word "Messiah" has been uttered, and Jesus has not rejected this title but also has not accepted it, he must inform the disciples of the restricted sense in which alone he applies the word to himself: Messiah—yes, but in a quite different way from what you think; Messiah, but as a suffering, rejected, executed one. Mark adds that Jesus now spoke openly—he "said everything."[60]

And then follows—not at all a new narrative or an appendix but—

---

[59] This must be emphasized in opposition to R. Bultmann, "Die Frage nach dem messianischen Bewusstsein Jesu und das Petrus-Bekenntnis" (*ZNW*, 1919–20, pp. 165 ff.), and *Geschichte der synoptischen Tradition*, 2nd ed., *ad. loc.*, whose view is that the Marcan narrative of the event at Caesarea Philippi closes with the command of silence (in this point, but only in this point, he agrees with K. L. Schmidt, *Der Rahmen der Geschichte Jesu*, 1919, pp. 217 ff.). He then further asserts that the report in Mark is a torso; the original narrative, which to be sure was only created by the Church, demands the continuation that we read in Matthew. Mark shortened the account here due to his "anti-Petrine" attitude (see on this point above, p. 25), and so robbed the story of its conclusion. Quite similar, though with acceptance of the genuineness of the Matthean narrative, is the judgment of W. Michaelis, *Das Evangelium nach Matthäus*, Part I , p. 339. A. Schlatter, *Der Evangelist Matthäus*, 1929, *ad loc.*, actually goes so far as to explain the Marcan omission of Jesus' words of Matt. 16:17–19 as an effort to make a belated connection of the passion prediction with the confession of Peter. In reality the final verses offer the key to the understanding not only of what happened at Caesarea Philippi but also of the so-called "messianic secret." Hence the central position of our section in the Synoptic Gospels. Only in Matthew do the verses which contain the passion prediction and the protest of Peter seem a sort of afterpiece, more or less separated from the preceding narrative by the words ἀπὸ τότε ("from that time"). This very fact speaks in favour of the originality of the Marcan narrative.

[60] παρρησία ("freely," "openly," "plainly").

the *real point* of the story, in which the protest of Peter proves that even the innermost group of disciples had not grasped the real meaning that the Messianic calling had for Jesus. Peter, too, shared completely the diabolical conception of the Messianic calling, as the devil had represented it in person in the temptation story, when he offered to Jesus the kingdoms of the world. The idea of a suffering Messiah was entirely foreign to Peter, and *according to Mark it was entirely foreign to him when he uttered that confession, "You are the Messiah."* This fact must be emphasized, that even when he spoke that confession, according to Mark, he still had not grasped *its essential meaning.* And even now he does not grasp it. He reacts against this idea of the suffering of the Messiah, and so great is his astonishment and his emotion that he dares to "rebuke" Jesus. Nowhere else do we hear that a disciple did this. But this shows how great the astonishment of Peter must have been; it was so much the greater since Jesus has finally for once spoken with his disciples concerning his Messianic calling and evoked the confession of his Messianic role. Peter's position as a disciple, indeed, will also be affected if Jesus is a suffering Messiah; in that case he, like the others, is the disciple of a suffering and rejected Messiah, and for them, too, everything is quite different from what they have conceived it to be.

Jesus, however, turns around, and Mark now notes very acutely that in the words he addresses to Peter, he also has in view the other disciples, for what he says applies also to them. Jesus knows that they, too, share that false conception of his Messianic role and consequently of their discipleship. The example of the sons of Zebedee, for example, proves that.

And then Jesus utters the unusually strong words: "Depart from me, Satan!"[61] Thus he uses the word that he had hurled at the devil himself at the time of the temptation (Matt. 4:10). The devil is now making use of Jesus' own disciple, Peter; that is his greatest trick. Nevertheless, Jesus recognizes it, and here too Mark portrays with special vividness how he accompanies this harsh word to Peter with the simultaneous look at the other disciples. He who tries to force upon Jesus another Messianic task than the one he has received from God, he who thereby seeks to turn him from this task he has received from God, is a tool of Satan!

---

61 We may leave undiscussed the question whether ὕπαγε ὀπίσω μου is to be understood literally, that is, (depart) "after me," in the sense of a summons to follow him as a disciple. I do not believe that it has a meaning essentially different from the simple ὕπαγε ("depart") in Matt. 4:10.

The originality of this Marcan narrative, in comparison with the parallels in Luke and Matthew, appears not only in its unclouded clearness, which really is striking, but also in various points of detail. Thus this entire story does not play in Matthew the dominating role that it has in Mark. In Matthew, that is, the disciples have already at an earlier time confessed before Jesus his majesty, at the time of the walking upon the sea (Matt. 14:33). Matthew thereby reduces in advance the importance of the story here reported.[62] In Mark its unique significance rests upon the very fact that here for the *first* time the disciples speak with Jesus with regard to what he is in their eyes.

Here it is seen that the arrangement of material, which of course is due to the evangelists, can become important in giving significance to the individual narrative. It is, so to say, a commentary on the part of the evangelist. So for the understanding of this narrative concerning Peter's confession, it makes a difference whether or not there already appears at some earlier point in the story a narrative in which the disciples confess the Messianic role of Jesus. Matthew, by introducing the disciples' saying: "You are the Son of God," in a chapter that *precedes* this sixteenth chapter of his work, has really robbed this event of its unique significance. Mark, on the contrary, has plainly preserved the memory of the fact that in order to understand this event it is essential to realize that what happened here had not yet happened at any previous time. Therefore in his arrangement of material he saw to it that in his Gospel no narrative preceded in which the disciples had already made a confession of Jesus as the Messiah.

Details within the narrative itself also seem to point to the conclusion that Matthew had a shallower grasp than Mark of the bearing of the event. For example, Matthew formulates the opening question of Jesus in a way that already anticipates the answer: "Who do the people say that *the Son of Man* is?" In Mark this is put in a form that is certainly more original, "Who do the people say that *I* am?"[63]

By this, we do not mean to say in any *a priori* way that verses 17–

[62] W. Michaelis, *Das Evangelium nach Matthäus* (*Prophezei*), p. 338, seeks to minimize the significance of this fact by writing that at this point Matthew was conscious that he was anticipating.

[63] Too far-fetched is the explanation of R. Graber, *Petrus der Fels*, 1949, p. 31. He takes the contrary position and gives Matthew the preference here. He holds that Mark and Luke here replaced the expression "Son of Man" by the first person singular, because the mention of the Son of Man, which points to Daniel and alludes to the people of God who will defeat the world powers, seemed to them too dangerous in this passage.

19, which concern us and are found only in Matthew, are a later creation of the Primitive Church. Nevertheless, the point just made must also be considered when we now put the question that was our chief objective in making a closer examination of this narrative framework: Does Jesus' saying to Peter, which only in Matthew follows Peter's confession of Jesus, fit harmoniously into *this framework*? Do these verses 17–19 really belong to this event, and were they spoken on this occasion, or on the contrary did they originally belong in another context and were they first inserted in this passage by Matthew? Even in the latter case, as we have said, they may be fully genuine, that is, spoken by Jesus but on another occasion.

We must consider, at least theoretically, the second possibility, that it was Matthew who inserted into the framework of the Marcan narrative these words of Jesus to Peter. This necessity is made clear by the entire manner in which the evangelists, and Matthew in particular, have arranged the material transmitted to them by the oral or already written tradition. It is the lasting merit of the works on "Form Criticism" to have proved that the oral gospel tradition, like all oral tradition, contained only single units, without any chronological or geographical connections between them. The work of the evangelists, who assembled these single units of the tradition, consists in the fact that they combined them each in his own way. Thus they are not only collectors but also arrangers. In this connection it can be shown that each one proceeded to arrange the material in his own way, and it is particularly instructive to compare Matthew and Luke in this regard. Matthew in grouping his material follows a plan based on considerations of content and theology; that is, he connects with one another the stories which seem to him to belong together in their theological significance: miracle stories, sayings concerning the Law (Sermon on the Mount), sayings concerning John the Baptist (Matt., ch. 11), parables (Matt., ch. 13), sayings against the Pharisees (Matt., ch. 23), etc. It is of no primary concern to Matthew whether he thereby preserves the chronological sequence; from the start he has written his Gospel from this other point of view. The evangelist Luke, on the contrary, strives, as he himself says in his prologue, to report the events in their chronological sequence.

Hence it is not only justified but actually imperative to ask first not whether the words are genuine, that is, spoken by Jesus, but whether Matthew, who alone includes them, has put them in their chronological setting, or whether here too he has simply connected this section with Peter's confession of Jesus because *in its content* it seemed to him to fit here. In the latter case, to Peter's confession of Jesus as the Messiah there corresponds, so to speak, a confession of Jesus to Peter as the rock of his Church.

First of all, we must recall that in Matthew the giving of the name Cephas—Rock seems first to occur at this point. In Mark, on the contrary, Jesus, as we have seen,[64] gives this name to Simon at an earlier time, when he forms the group of the Twelve (ch. 3:16); and in the Gospel of John he actually gives it at the very first meeting (ch. 1:42). One may say, of course, that in Matthew 16:17 Peter does not *receive* this name for the first time, but that here it is only *explained* to him, after being given to him at an earlier time.[65] In that case there would be no direct chronological conflict between Mark and John. It is noteworthy, however, that Matthew has not reported the giving of the name on any earlier occasion. He thus appears to be of the opinion that this did not take place until the moment when Jesus also explained the name by telling of his purpose to build his Church upon this rock.[66] Then we should assume that although it was accepted as unquestioned fact that Jesus gave to Peter the title Cephas, there was no definitely fixed tradition concerning the time at which he did this.[67] So if Matthew really identified the giving and the explanation of the name, it might be so much the more natural for him to seek for these verses, which he found in the tradition, a place where they seemed to him to fit in view of their content; this was the principle he followed in arranging material.

But however that may be, Matthew by his very act of grouping material according to its content created a chronological connection: the utterance of Jesus, in the light of this context, appears in this Gospel as an *answer* to Peter's confession of Jesus, and it receives in this way a particular meaning. In Mark and Luke, however, the

[64] See above, p. 21.

[65] This is stressed especially by Th. Zahn, *Das Evangelium des Matthäus*, 4th ed., 1922, *ad loc.* He points to the fact that the Matthew passage lacks the formula customary in *giving* names (Gen. 17:5, 15; 32:28; Matt. 1:21, 25; 2:23; Luke 1:13, 31, 59–63; 2:21).

[66] W. Michaelis, *op. cit.*, pp. 340 f., is also of the opinion that Matthew here intends to tell of the *giving* of the name. He thinks that John 1:42 and Mark 3:16 are intended only as a reference to this later time.

[67] See M. J. Lagrange, *L'Evangile selon S. Matthieu*, 5th ed., 1941, p. 324: "the tradition of the change of name was attested by all, but there was less certainty concerning the occasion." See also Lagrange's judgment concerning the originality of the setting that Mark presupposes for the giving of the name. See above, p. 21, note 21.

narrative of the confession of Peter does not lead to that answer of
Jesus. On the contrary, Jesus is silent about it and commands silence.
Hence we must ask whether Matthew, when he gave this sequence
of content and chronology to the unit of tradition that he alone
transmits, did not connect two originally separate groups of sayings,
of which the one does not really fit as an echo or answer to the other.

We have seen, in fact, that in the narrative framework Peter plays
the role of one who does not understand the Messianic role of Jesus.
He rather shares that very conception of the Messiah which Jesus
regards as a temptation from Satan. To be sure, he utters the words:
"You are the Messiah." But the continuation of this story makes
clear how abysmally deep is the misunderstanding that separates
Peter from Jesus even here. Indeed, we must actually say that the
entire story leads on to this continuation; *this is its point*: "Depart
from me, Satan!" We have seen that the parallel to the temptation
story is clear. In both cases the devil seeks to persuade Jesus to fulfil
a Messianic role radically different from the one with which he
knows he is entrusted.

Thus the conclusion of the narrative framework shows that he
who spoke those words: "You are the Christ," was a tool of Satan,
not indeed in uttering the confession of the Messiah but rather *in his
conception of these words*. This time Satan comes to Jesus in the person
of Peter. Therefore Jesus says to his disciple: "You are not thinking
of the things of God but of the things of men."

When one considers the meaning of this narrative framework, it
becomes difficult indeed *a priori* to assume that *in this very context*
Jesus said to Peter: "You are inspired by the Father in Heaven; he
has given you a special revelation." But this is what we read in
verse 17. This certainly does not fit well with what we have just
established to be the intent in the narrative of Peter's confession.
Precisely at this point the quite vivid portrayal of Mark seems to be
interrupted and also twisted, if it is followed by the saying of Jesus
concerning Peter the rock. For the fact that in the narrative of Mark
Jesus at first says nothing at all in reply to this confession of Peter, and
so does not take any position with regard to it, corresponds completely to the attitude he maintains towards the title of Messiah in
the entire Synoptic tradition; he always manifests a notable *reserve*
toward this title, without explicitly rejecting it.[68] One can trace this

[68] Jean Héring, *Le Royaume de Dieu et sa venue*, 1937, pp. 111 ff., goes further in
saying that he rejected the title. The irreconcilability of Matt. 16:17 ff. with the
narrative framework of Mark 8:27 ff. he also emphasizes strongly (p. 127, note 2).

in the hearing before the High Priest. He knows that the title of Messiah, used without qualification and addition, can give rise to grave misunderstandings. Thus the silence of Jesus, as Mark presupposes it in our passage, can scarcely be explained as an accidental or deliberate omission of a saying of Jesus; it rather has theological significance.[69]

I therefore consider it exegetically probable that Matthew found in an ancient oral tradition the words with which Jesus explains the title Cephas; in accord with his constant method of arranging material he sought for this separately transmitted unit of tradition a place that was fitting *from the point of view of its content*; he thought that he had found it in the story of the confession of Peter at Caesarea Philippi. It may have been chiefly the correspondence of the statement of Peter: "You are the Christ," with the statement "You are Peter," that led him to insert verses 17–19 in this place. We shall discover later (p. 182 f.) further reasons for the insertion at this point.

A further trace of the fact that originally these words did not stand in this context could be found in the fact that in verse 17 the object is lacking. It does not say in that verse: "*This* (namely, that I am the Christ) has been revealed to you not by flesh and blood but by my heavenly Father." The demonstrative pronoun "this," which we usually add in the translation, is lacking in the Greek text. In the original tradition also some object certainly must have stood here; it cannot have been lacking even in a separate unit of tradition. However, one can ask whether the fact that it is lacking in Matthew is not to be explained by saying that the unit originally had another introduction. This part of the saying of Jesus, which in content belongs to Matthew 11:27, could actually have been placed at this point by the Evangelist to connect it with the narrative framework.

The very reverse has been asserted—that verses 17–19, as far as geographical location is concerned, stand in a setting entirely suitable to them.[70] Indeed, it has actually been asserted that the Marcan

---

[69] This is in opposition to Héring, *op. cit.*, p. 125, who takes account of this possibility. Mark, he says, already interpreted the silence in the sense of an unqualified acceptance of the Messianic title; I on the contrary believe that Mark correctly understood the meaning of this silence, that is, he also regarded it not directly as a sharp rejection, such as J. Héring ascribes to Jesus, but as an attitude of *reserve*. This reserve is in full harmony with the "Back, Satan"; nevertheless, there exists in our narrative a heightening, which leads from this silence to that climax.

[70] On the geographical question, see O. Immisch, "Matthäus 16, 18" (*ZNW*, 1916, pp. 18 ff.).

narrative is a torso in its present form, that is, without the verses that Matthew alone contains. It is said to require just such an answer as the explanation of Jesus which we read in Matthew. Since Jesus himself evoked the Messianic confession of his disciples, the narrative cannot have ended with the mere command not to tell about it. Matthew 16:17 ff. would thus present the original and natural conclusion.[71] This view, however, overlooks the fact that the conclusion of the Marcan narrative is *not* the command to keep silent. It is rather those words of Jesus to Peter: "Depart from me, Satan!"—and they are also taken over by Matthew. The attempt has also been made to show that the answer of Jesus has been constructed in exact parallelism to Peter's confession. Just as in that confession it says: "You are the Christ," so here: "You are Peter." But as we have already said, it could very well be that it was just this rather formal analogy that led Matthew to combine the two units. Of course it is not excluded that even at an earlier stage of the tradition the two groups of sayings were united as they are in Matthew; but this is not probable.

On the basis of what has been said, however, we must at least take into account the strong possibility that the disputed verses did not belong originally in the context in which Matthew has put them. This opinion says nothing concerning genuineness or spuriousness.

If the event of Caesarea Philippi is not really the original framework of these traditional words, then the question arises whether, if we provisionally assume their genuineness, it still is possible to discern their setting. The most favoured theory in this case is that while the saying was indeed spoken by Jesus, it was spoken not by the Incarnate Jesus, but rather by *the Risen One*, on the occasion of an appearance to Peter alone. On this view, the entire incident was transferred back into the life of the Incarnate One at a later time.[72] Many things favour this possibility. It really is striking that the very first and so possibly the most important appearance of Jesus, that is, the one to Peter, is nowhere narrated in the New Testament. And yet it is clearly presupposed—for example, in the oldest text that we possess, in the earliest summary of the Christian faith, in I Corinthians 15:5. We have seen that in this passage the appearance to Peter stands first in a chronological enumeration of those who have seen

---

71 So R. Bultmann, W. Michaelis, A. Schlatter (see above, p. 173, note 59), and also Th. Zahn, *ad loc.*

72 So chiefly E. Stauffer, "Zur Vor- und Frühgeschichte des Primatus Petri" (*ZKG*, 1943-44, pp. 1 ff.); R. Bultmann, *Theologie des Neuen Testaments*, 1948, p. 46 (Eng. Tr., *Theology of the N. T.*, I, p. 45). See above, p. 61.

the risen Lord. Furthermore, we have found in Luke 24:34 the mention of the fact that the Lord appeared to Simon; indeed, the way in which it is mentioned shows that here too we must be dealing with the first of the appearances. We have noted that the significance of this fact for the position of Peter in the Primitive Church simply cannot be overestimated, and we have also attempted to find an explanation of the fact that no narrative account of this most important of all appearances has been preserved.[73]

A trace of such a narrative could indeed exist in ch. 21 of the Gospel of John. To be sure, we have here an appearance before *several* disciples in Galilee. But the dialogue that begins in verse 13 takes place essentially between the Risen One and Peter. The beloved disciple comes in, so to speak, quite incidentally. Therefore it may justifiably be asked whether, although the missing narrative of this appearance of Jesus to Peter alone is not reproduced, it is not at least utilized. For the dialogue refers in its first part only to the relationship between Christ and Peter, and to the commission which is given to Peter. We have spoken of the hypothesis that the lost conclusion of Mark lies behind this passage.[74]

Was it not this narrative, taken up into John, ch. 21, which Matthew found in a somewhat different version, transferred back into the life of the Incarnate One, and so connected with Peter's confession of Jesus at Caesarea Philippi? The very content of the dialogue between Jesus and Peter in John 21:15 ff. might favour this hypothesis. It deals indeed with the same question as Matthew 16:17 ff.; that which in Matthew is a promise appears here in the imperative, as a commission of the Risen One to Peter: "Feed my lambs."

It must be conceded that this hypothesis is attractive. At the least, we may reckon with the possibility that it is correct. Yet after all it is only a hypothesis. For we possess no conclusion of Mark which narrates the appearance to Peter alone, and John, ch. 21, does not say that its account deals with such an appearance.[75]

On the other hand, it is improbable to me that Jesus never *during his lifetime* explained the title "Rock." For it is quite certain that it was during his lifetime that he gave the title to Peter. It is true that "Sons of Thunder," the title of the sons of Zebedee, is also nowhere explained. But that may be connected with the fact that the gospel tradition naturally had less interest in them. In reality, Jesus must have explained their title also. On this ground I cannot

[73] See above, pp. 61 f.   [74] See above, pp. 59 f.   [75] See above, pp. 60 f.

agree with the above mentioned hypothesis without further evidence.

But must we not consider another occasion *within* the lifetime of Jesus when the explanation of the title could have been given? It has been supposed that there might have been a situation *similar* to that of Caesarea Philippi.[76] At that time, however, Jesus did not speak of his suffering; rather, the simple confession of his divine sonship stood in the foreground, so that verse 17 was entirely in place. One could think, for example, of John 6:66; this hypothesis has actually been proposed,[77] and its possibility must be recognized.

In this case, however, we are not restricted to a pure hypothesis. Rather, we have in one of the Synoptic Gospels a parallel text that contains the commission to Peter to strengthen his brothers, and gives it in another setting, namely that of the Last Supper. This is Luke 22:31 ff., a passage already often mentioned. It presents an exact parallel to Matthew 16:17 ff., not indeed in its literal wording, but in its meaning. It is embedded in the prediction of Peter's denial: "Simon, Simon, Behold, Satan has asked for you in order to sift you in the sieve like wheat. But I have prayed for you that your faith may not waver, and do you, when you have turned, strengthen your brothers." Peter then said to him: "Lord, with you I am ready to go even to prison and death." Jesus replied: "I tell you, Peter, the cock will not crow today until you have denied me three times."

This dialogue thus contains three things: (1) The vow of Peter that he will go with his Lord to prison and to death. (2) The prediction of Peter's denial. (3) The command of Jesus to Peter to strengthen his brothers after his conversion.

Was not this the true context also of our saying in Matthew 16:17 ff.?[78] If so, we could easily understand how Matthew could hit upon the idea of connecting it with Peter's confession at Caesarea Philippi. There, too, the chief thing reported is a confession of Peter, even though it is of another kind than in this passage, where it has taken the form of a declaration that he is ready to stand courageously for his Lord. On this view Matthew could have had a further reason for introducing the saying in the place where we now read it. Simon, together with the other disciples, is here brought into connection

---

[76] So K. L. Schmidt, "Die Kirche des Urchristentums" (*Festgabe für Ad. Deissmann*, 1927, p. 283).

[77] So Bernhard Weiss (*Meyer's Kommentar*, 10th ed., 1910), *ad loc*.

[78] A similar yet somewhat different position is taken by R. Liechtenhan, *op. cit.*, pp. 9 ff.

with *Satan*, and this occurs specifically with reference to the suffering of Christ, which is indirectly in view also in the prediction of the denial. Was this, perhaps, also a contributing factor in the choice of the scene of Caesarea Philippi, where Peter is addressed at the end as Satan? We cannot of course assert this with certainty.

I am inclined to presuppose that the framework of the Passion story as Luke gives it was the setting also for the saying reproduced by Matthew. My reason is that ch. 21 of the Gospel of John, which in many respects appears to be a still more direct parallel to Matthew 16:17 ff. ("feed my sheep"), seems consciously to refer to a tradition according to which there occurred during the lifetime of Jesus a scene such as Luke 22:31–34 portrays. The dialogue between the Risen One and Peter, in John 21:15 ff., presents a direct replica of that dialogue in Luke 22:31–34 between the Incarnate One and Peter, and probably can only be understood in the light of the latter passage.[79] It is striking that we find here exactly the same connection between vow, prediction, and command that we have in Luke 22:31–34, except that in John these words correspond to the post-resurrection situation. For the first time since the prediction of the denial Peter again stands before his Lord, but now he stands before the Risen One. In place of the three-fold denial by Peter comes now his three-fold assurance: "Yes, Lord, you know that I love you." To the vow of Peter that he will go with the Lord to prison and to death corresponds the prophecy of the martyrdom. In place of the command to strengthen his brothers there comes here the command to feed the sheep of Christ.

Some scholars, as we have seen above, assume that the basis for Matthew 16:17 ff. was a resurrection appearance to Peter, which has been used in John 21:15 ff.[80] On the basis of the inner and formal relationship between Matthew 16:17 ff., Luke 22:31 ff., and John 21:15 ff., I also assume a relationship between John 21:15 ff. and Matthew 16:17 ff. But I do so in the reverse sense; John 21:15 ff. attests a knowledge of a narrative from the passion story of the Incarnate One; according to this narrative Jesus, after the Last Supper, on the evening before the crucifixion, and on the occasion of Peter's assurance that he will follow his Lord to death, predicts the denial,

---

[79] This is contested by M. Goguel in *L'Eglise naissante*, 1947, p. 192, and *Jésus*, 1950, p. 390 (see above, p. 60), probably in connection with his unconvincing thesis that the denial of Jesus by Peter is unhistorical ("Did Peter Deny his Lord? A Conjecture," *Harvard Theological Review*, 1932, pp. 1 ff.).

[80] See above, p. 181.

but at the same time predicts also Peter's conversion and the found-ing of his flock on Peter as the rock. This connection is present in Luke 22:31–34. The wording of the Lucan passage, to be sure, does not agree with that of Matthew 16:17 ff.; this is the only weak point in the theory here proposed. But as far as the wording is concerned, Matthew may very well have had at his disposal here a special tradition which originally belonged in the same framework as the words of Luke 22:31 ff. The Synoptic tradition offers examples enough of this. The author of John 21:15 ff., who shows a know-ledge of this connection, seems to have known this special tradition of Matthew. For the picture of "the sheep that Peter is to feed" im-plies that of the "flock," and this concept, as we shall see, is closely related to the one of the "Church" of Matthew 16:18.[81]

We thus reach the conclusion that the saying in Matthew 16:17 ff. probably belongs to the Passion story; it was originally transmitted in connection with the prediction of Peter's denial, but was placed by Matthew in another setting. We shall see later[82] that the im-mediate nearness of the death of Jesus, and above all the connection with the Last Supper, make the saying concerning the "Church" particularly intelligible. We are dealing here with an exegetical probability, to the acceptance of which I am led by the undeniable difficulty that results for exegesis from the insertion of Matthew 16:17 ff. into the framework of the narrative of Peter's confession at Caesarea Philippi. This is not without significance for determining the meaning in detail of the verses in question. Nevertheless, I note expressly that *the interpretation as a whole that is given in what follows does not stand or fall with the acceptance of this theory concerning the original setting.*

3. Genuineness and Meaning of the Saying

We must first test whether the reasons that have been urged against the genuineness are valid. The assumption of earlier opponents of the genuineness, that the verses were lacking originally even in Matthew and were inserted into the text only later under the influence of Roman claims, we can leave undiscussed.[83] It is refuted by the

81 See below, p. 197.
82 See below, p. 190. The theological relation to the Passion is emphasized very strongly, though to be sure on the basis of the narrative framework, by Karl Barth, *Kirchliche Dogmatik*, II, 2, 1942, pp. 482 ff.
83 K. L. Schmidt, *Die Kirche des Urchristentums*, p. 281, rightly calls it "too clumsy to be taken seriously."

textual tradition and the history of the use of these words. So today the thesis of spuriousness is still defended only in the form that Matthew has reproduced here a saying that was not uttered by Jesus but created by the Church. In that case, however, it must be demanded at the start that the defenders of this thesis make clear the circumstances and reasons that led the Church to create such a saying as early as the days before Matthew was written.

This demand is the more urgent since the great antiquity and the Palestinian origin of the section may today be considered beyond question. This is shown by the quite Semitic linguistic character of this section. On this point, in fact, almost all scholars are united, whether they accept or reject the genuineness.[84] We have observed that even Bultmann, who is particularly emphatic in denying that Jesus spoke these words, has always claimed that the Palestinian church must have created the saying. Above all it is emphasized here, and probably correctly, that the saying could hardly have arisen first in the Greek Dispersion, because in the Greek, and so in the gospel text as we have it, the word play here plainly intended is not contained at all. Only in the German translation is it restored: "You are rock (Fels), and upon this rock (Felsen) I will build my Church." In Greek Simon's title reads *Petros*, with the masculine ending. We have seen that the name *Kepha* was reproduced in Greek by *Petros*. But Jesus says that he will build his Church upon this *Petra*. The words that should correspond do not really correspond here. In the Aramaic, however, we have both times the same word *Kepha*: "You are *Kepha* and upon this *Kepha* I will build my Church." Thus here the name and the thing are exactly identical. Therefore we must assume that the saying was originally coined in Aramaic.[85]

The Semitic character is confirmed by various other observations: the designation of the father of Peter as *bar-yônâ*;[86] the expression "flesh and blood" for "men";[87] the word pair "bind and loose";[88] then also the strophic rhythm—three strophes of three lines each—which is found similarly in other sayings of Jesus, for example,

---

[84] So also A. Harnack, "Der Spruch über Petrus als den Felsen der Kirche: Mtth. XVI, 17 f." (*Sitzungsbericht der Berliner Akademie der Wissenschaften*, 1918, pp. 637 ff.).

[85] M. Goguel, *L'Eglise naissante*, 1947, p. 189, note 4, finds this argument indecisive, since in a play on words the correspondence need not be complete.

[86] See above, p. 22, on the thesis of R. Eisler in *Jesous basileus ou basileusas*, p. 67.

[87] In the N. T. in I Cor. 15:50; Gal. 1:16; Eph. 6:12; Heb. 2:14. Frequent in Jewish literature (Sirach 14:18), but not yet in the O. T.

[88] אסר and שרא. See below, pp. 204 ff.

Matthew 11:7–9 and 11:25–30;[89] and further the illustration of the rock as foundation, to which there is an exact parallel in the rabbinical literature, where Abraham is mentioned as the rock of the world.[90]

The fact that only the Palestinian Matthew gives the saying also points to the Palestinian origin of the tradition.[91] Still another consideration can be cited to show that the tradition is very early. The story would scarcely have been handed on at a time when Peter no longer stood at the head of the Jerusalem church and James was already the leader there. The saying must thus have been transmitted at a time when Peter was still in Jerusalem.[92] The very early character of the tradition, which is vouched for by the Palestinian character of the verses, naturally does not prove beyond question that the utterance must come from Jesus, but it nevertheless is an important *presupposition* for that conclusion.

We have seen that the *chief objection* to its genuineness concerns the mention of the "*Church*." Jesus, it is said, cannot have spoken of the Church, since he proclaimed only the coming Kingdom of God.

The first thing to note, in reply to this claim, is that it is correct that the word for "Church" (*ekklesia*) occurs in the Gospels only *one* other time. This, too, is in the Gospel of Matthew, ch. 18:17: "If (the brother who has sinned) does not listen to you, tell it to the Church." The genuineness of this passage also is vigorously disputed; in addition, the meaning here is not the same.

---

[89] See J. Jeremias, *Angelos*, 1926, pp. 107 ff., and especially A. Oepke, *op. cit.*, pp. 150f.

[90] See the rabbinical explanation of Isaiah, ch. 53, in Strack-Billerbeck, *Kommentar zum N. T. aus Talmud und Midrasch*, Vol. I, p. 733; J. Jeremias, *Golgotha*, p. 73: "When God looked upon Abraham, who was to appear, he said: Behold, I have found a rock on which I can build and base the world. Therefore he called Abraham a rock."

[91] H. Strathmann, "Die Stellung des Petrus in der Urkirche" (*Zeitschrift für systematische Theologie*, 1943, pp. 255 ff.; see above p. 25), in connection with his view of the geographical origin of each Gospel, assigns this saying to the Antiochene tradition. In opposition to this, W. Michaelis, *op. cit.*, p. 353, makes the point that in Antioch Greek was spoken.

[92] W. Michaelis, *Das Evangelium nach Matthäus*, p. 350, actually thinks that the reason Luke did not include this saying was that it found its fulfilment only in the earliest period. Others, however, are of the opinion that it was precisely later Palestinian disputes between Peter and James (relatives of Jesus) that could have given occasion to the creation of the saying. (So K. Goetz; R. Bultmann thinks of debates in Palestine over the Law; M. Goguel of discussions that took place after 70). But we know too little of such disputes to explain on this basis the origin of the saying. According to J. Jeremias, the early character of the saying is clear also from the fact that we find such early traces of its use, in the N. T. itself: Gal. 1:16–18 and 2:9.

These statistics concerning the use of the word, however, cannot be decisive. The issue in question is rather whether not only the word but also the thing that the word designates is lacking. That is how we must put the question. In this connection it has justly been recalled[93] how striking it is that in the entire letter of Paul to Rome the word "cross" does not occur a single time, although the letter treats of the atoning death of Christ from beginning to end. It has further been pointed out that in the Gospel of John also the Greek word for Church (*ekklesia*) is nowhere found, and yet it cannot be doubted that this Gospel speaks of the Church; indeed, the peculiar character of this Gospel consists precisely in the fact that it connects the historical Jesus with the Church.[94]

The problem lies elsewhere. First of all we must be on our guard against falling into the mistake of most exegetes, who think that they must oppose the genuineness of the utterance because it mentions the "Church." They assume it to be self-evident that the word for "Church" can only designate an organized Church in the later sense. Then they seek to show that Jesus cannot have held this anachronistic view of the Church. Such a procedure, however, must be rejected.

We first must emphasize that the Greek word for Church, *ekklesia, does not designate anything like a Christian creation*, but belongs to the Jewish sphere.[95] We still find the word in this original meaning in the New Testament, in Acts 7:38: "It is this (Moses) who was in the *ekklesia* in the wilderness with the angel ..." In this passage *ekklesia* means the people of Israel whom Moses led through the wilderness. In the Greek translation of the Old Testament, the Septuagint, *ekklesia* occurs about a hundred times, and in these cases it usually translates the Hebrew *qahal*, which, when connected with the genitive *Yahweh*, "of God," always designates the people of Israel with a reference to redemptive history. There is a series of still other Hebrew and Aramaic words that can be rendered in Greek

[93] See A. Oepke, *op. cit.*, p. 114.

[94] See O. Cullmann, *Urchristentum und Gottesdienst* (Eng. Tr., *Early Christian Worship*, 1953, pp. 38 ff. (cf. *Les sacrements dans l'Evangile johannique*, 1951, pp. 9 ff.). On the question of the Church in the Gospel of John, see also E. Gaugler, "Die Bedeutung der Kirche in den johanneischen Schriften" (*Internationale kirchliche Zeitschrift*, 1924, pp. 97 ff.).

[95] See L. Rost, *Die Vorstufen von Kirche und Synagoge im Alten Testament*, 1938; further, O. Michel, *Das Zeugnis des Neuen Testaments von der Gemeinde*, 1941, pp. 5 ff.; J. Y. Campbell, *Journal of Theological Studies*, pp. 130 ff.

by *ekklesia*.[96] All of these expressions, of which some can also be translated into Greek by *synagoge*, refer to Israel as the people of God; one of them (*kenishta*) can also mean "separate synagogue."

We must start from the meaning "people of God" when we ask the question whether or not Jesus can have spoken of the Church. Let us then put in place of the all too modern word "Church" the expression "people of God": "on this rock I will build my people of God." In this sense Jesus did not have to create anew the concept used. It already existed; indeed, it was *quite common* in Jewish thinking. Every Jew was certain that he was a member of this *ekklesia*. As soon as a group within late Judaism became conscious that the role of the people of God, to which Israel as a whole had proved disloyal, was being realized in them and through them, the concept of the *ekklesia* in its Semitic form necessarily moved into the foreground. This was especially true in the Jewish "congregation of the New Covenant," which has become so well known through the recent discoveries near the Dead Sea.[97] The ancient prophetic idea of the "remnant" of Israel (Isa. 7:3; 10:21) leads directly to such a revitalization of the people of God consciousness in small separate communities.

[96] Hebrew equivalents: *qahal, Edhah, ṣibbur, kᵉneseth;* Aramaic: *qahᵃla, ṣibbura,* and most frequently *kᵉnishta.* On all lexicographical questions it is sufficient to refer to K. L. Schmidt's basic article on ἐκκλησία in G. Kittel's *Theologisches Wörterbuch;* it carries further the older but helpfully orienting compilation of H. Cremer, in H. Cremer-Kögel, *Biblisch-theologisches Wörterbuch des neutestamentlichen Griechischen,* 11th ed., 1923. There is much in favour of *kᵉnishta* as the basic word (K. L. Schmidt). Whether however it is to be preferred because it likewise designates the building I would assert with less confidence, since indeed the figure of the building is included in the general idea of the people of God, and so is also implied by the phrase *qehal Yahweh.* (See on this point Ph. Vielhauer, *Oikodome, das Bild vom Bau in der christlichen Literatur vom Neuen Testament bis Clemens Alexandrinus,* 1939.) I would prefer, with M. J. Lagrange, *Commentaire, ad loc.,* to leave open the question as to which Aramaic word should be considered most likely. Indeed, it is not of basic importance, for the important thing is that all of these words belong to the thought world of the people of God. Lagrange considers both *qahᵃla* and *kᵉnishta* as possible Aramaic equivalents, Zahn *kᵉnishta,* Bultmann and Michaelis *qahᵃla.* Schlatter points to the Hebrew words *qahal* and *edhah.*

[97] Examples taken from the earlier discovery (see L. Rost, *Die Damaskusschrift,* in *Kleine Texte,* 1938): *edhah* in vii, 20; x, 4, 8; xiii, 13; *qahal* in vii, 17; xi, 22 (S. Schechter's edition). See also O. Michel, *Das Zeugnis des Neuen Testaments von der Gemeinde,* 1941, pp. 17 ff. With regard to the new discovery see among others K. G. Kuhn, "Die in Palästina gefundenen hebräischen Texte und das Neue Testament" (*Zeitschrift für Theologie und Kirche,* 1950, pp. 194 ff.). See above, p. 64.

Above all, the Jewish Messianic expectation includes the conception of a Messianic community and is inconceivable without it.[98] Here we should recall the Son of Man designation; in the Book of Daniel (ch. 7:9–28) it refers to "the people of the saints," and on the basis of the idea of representation is applied to a single personality. But an eschatological community is the essential possession also of the Messiah of the official Jewish hope.

In so far as we, in agreement with the entire gospel tradition, ascribe to Jesus the Messianic consciousness in any form whatsoever, we should have to assume, even if we had no text on the subject, that his thinking included the idea of the eschatological people of God that belonged to him. If he considered himself to be the Danielic Son of Man (Mark 14:62 and parallels), he also knew that according to Daniel 7:18, 27 the Son of Man represents the "people of the saints."[99] The concept of representation, which is indispensable for the understanding of the Old Testament redemptive history, is fundamental for Jesus' knowledge of his own redemptive work. When he speaks of the people of God that he is founding he certainly thinks of the "remnant of Israel," which will represent this people in its entirety and about which the Gentiles will be gathered.[1]

Compared with the ancient Jewish idea of the people of God, the new feature which Jesus brought is that this *ekklesia*, this people of God, is reconstituted in view of the end. It is reconstituted on the basis of what he conceives to be his special Messianic deed, the suffering of the Servant of God. In the creation of this new people of God built upon this basis consists his specific work on earth.

In this *Jewish* sense there is an "ecclesiology" even in the thinking of Jesus, and it is solidly anchored in his "Christology." Therefore we can understand it when a scholar such as Bultmann, who denies that Jesus had any Messianic consciousness, also challenges the

---

[98] Enoch 38:1; 53:6; 62:8; 83:8; 84:5.

[99] To have centred attention on this idea is the lasting merit of F. Kattenbusch, "Der Quellort der Kirchenidee" (*Festgabe für Harnack*, 1921, pp. 142 ff.). T. W. Manson and R. Newton Flew hold the same idea; see above, p. 166, note 33.

[1] K. L. Schmidt and F. Kattenbusch also assume that the "remnant," the "separate congregation," represents Israel in its entirety. For this reason I consider unjustified the criticism that Oepke, *op. cit.*, pp. 114 ff., 140, who here agrees with R. Bultmann, makes against K. L. Schmidt and F. Kattenbusch. The idea of a Pharisaic separation is not at all essential to the idea of the remnant; the former only presents the danger to which the latter *can* lead. The fact that the group of Jesus comprises precisely the *lost* sheep excludes all Pharisaism. See below, p. 190.

genuineness of the word concerning the *ekklesia*. He who, on the contrary, is of the opinion that Jesus regarded himself as the Messiah, even if in the special sense of the Son of Man and the Suffering Servant of God—and this today includes the great majority of exegetes—should refrain even on this basis from rejecting too quickly the genuineness of Matthew 16:17 ff.; as Messiah Jesus must have had in view a community.[2]

Connected with this special way in which Jesus conceived his Messianic work is the fact that the people of God is no longer simply identical with the Jewish nation. Even the prophetic idea of the remnant and the preaching of John the Baptist had already purified the conception of the people of God in this sense. Jesus knew himself to be sent to the "lost sheep of the house of Israel" (Matt. 10:6; 15:24), but this very limitation to the *lost* sheep finally breaks through every national restriction and likewise excludes every Pharisaic-sectarian separation. It is true that the redemptive road to the founding of the people of God goes by way of Israel. But the very reduction to this fellowship within Israel creates the presupposition for the realization of the people of God that is to include all mankind.

The Messianic reconstitution of the people of God aims at the "new covenant," which Jesus announces and likewise establishes *at the Last Supper*, on the evening before his death. Covenant and people of God belong together.[3] If my theory is correct that Jesus gave the promise of Matthew 16:17 ff. in the setting indicated by Luke 22:31 f., and so in connection with the Last Supper and the words spoken there, then *in this context* the prediction of the building of the *ekklesia* stands out in unusually bold relief. The connecting of the new building with Jesus' Messianic work of suffering unto death then becomes particularly clear. But it also is clear on other grounds.

Jesus speaks of his *ekklesia*. To me this does not seem, as has been claimed, irreconcilable with the fact that in Judaism the concept involved was the people *of God*, the *qehal Yahweh*, the *ekklesia* of the Lord (Num. 16:3; Deut. 7:6). It is possible, in fact, for the Messiah-

---

2 See P. Volz, *Die Eschatologie der jüdischen Gemeinde im neutestamentlichen Zeitalter*, 1934, p. 49. This is very strongly stressed also by F. J. Leenhardt, *Etudes sur l'Eglise dans le Nouveau Testament*, 1940, p. 16. See also O. Linton, *Das Problem der Urkirche in der neuern Forschung*, 1932, p. 148: "The Messiah is not a private person. Essential to his rule is a Church."

3 See L. Rost, *Die Vorstufen von Kirche und Synagoge im Alten Testament*, 1938, pp. 18 ff. On the Church and the Last Supper see F. Kattenbusch, *op. cit.*

Son of Man to speak of *his ekklesia*.[4] In this capacity he also can say that he will "build" this people. There is no contradiction here with the fact that this building is the work of God.[5]

If one reads the words of Matthew 16:17 in the light of this essentially Jewish idea and takes account of the fact that in the time of Jesus *qahal—ekklesia* was a quite common concept, firmly rooted in Jewish thinking, one really cannot on *that basis* deny the genuineness of the saying. I therefore maintain my statement, which Bultmann took as the starting point of his recent denial of this genuineness; I hold that there is no scientific justification for this denial. For sound scientific method requires that we explain the concepts first of all according to the sense that they have in the environment to which the writing belongs whose text is to be explained. It is not right to start from a later concept of the *ekklesia* and then conclude that it cannot possibly be ascribed to Jesus. It must first of all be asked whether there is not an *ekklesia* concept that corresponds to the Jewish thinking whose categories Jesus took over.

Furthermore, it can be shown that this very image of the *rock* is connected in Judaism with the idea of the community. Reference has properly been made to the conception of the holy rock. But we can discern a still more precise context if we recall that in the *Book of Daniel*, which Jesus must have known, the Son of Man concept, so central for him, is connected with the conception of the Messianic "people of the saints," which brings to an end the world empires. In the same Book of Daniel (ch. 2:34 f., 44 f.) we read of a block of stone which is *interpreted to mean an empire* that will shatter all empires.[6] This block of stone separates from the mountain, smashes the statute of Nebuchadnezzar, and then grows into a great mountain, which fills the entire world. Already in Judaism this stone had been referred to the Messiah.[7] Still more important for our study, however, is the fact that the saying of Jesus in Luke 20:17 f. certainly has in mind this passage of Daniel: "What means this saying of Scripture: The stone which the builders rejected has become the cornerstone? He who falls on this stone will be shattered; on whomsoever

---

[4] Matt. 13:41 speaks of the "Kingdom of the Son of Man."

[5] The difficulty seen here by K. L. Schmidt, *Die Kirche des Urchristentums*, p. 288, I do not feel. Yet E. Klostermann, *Das Matthäusevangelium*, p. 140, also finds it objectionable that Jesus says "my" Church.

[6] To have shown these connections is the merit of Joachim Jeremias; see his book, *Golgotha*, pp. 77 ff.

[7] Strack-Billerbeck, *Kommentar zum N. T. aus Talmud und Midrasch*, Vol. I, p. 877.

it falls, it crushes him."[8]—In the designation of Abraham as the rock
we have already found a Jewish preparation for the view that Jesus,
and later the apostles,[9] become the rock, the foundation.[10]

Moreover, the image of the *building* of a community is fully intelligible from the Jewish manner of thinking and expression.[11] The
Old Testament speaks of the *House* of Israel (Num. 12:7; Ruth 4:11;
Amos 9:11; etc.) Jesus also uses this expression in Matthew 10:6 and
15:24. Therefore the illustration, in its application to the Church, is
quite common with the writers of the New Testament books, particularly in I Timothy 3:15, which speaks of the house of God, which
is the *ekklesia* of the living God, and further in I Peter 2:5 (the
spiritual house), Ephesians 2:22, Hebrews 3:2 ff.; 10:21. We must
further recall that the idea of "edifying"[12] is common in application
to the fellowship (Amos 9:11 f.; in the New Testament particularly
Acts 9:31). Paul also uses it, originally not in the specific individual-
istic and pietistic sense, but in the meaning that the illustration contains of the building up of the Church.[13] Of especial importance for
our question, however, is the fact that Jesus himself, as we shall see,[14]
speaks in another saying concerning the fellowship founded by him;
he here uses the analogous illustration of the *temple* that he will
rebuild.

* * *

In our passage it is presupposed that the people of God will be
formed while the present age still lasts. The future "I will build"
could perhaps mislead us to identify its realization with that of the
purely future Kingdom of God which comes at the end. But what
follows, the saying concerning "binding and loosing," and par-

---

[8] The verb λικμᾶν is explained only by Dan. 2:34 f., 44 f. R. Graber, *Petrus der
Fels*, 1948, p. 29, shows that the relation to the Daniel passage is much closer
when seen from Matthew 21:42 ff. than it is from the parallel Lucan passage,
from which J. Jeremias starts. This, however, is the case only if vs. 44, which
is lacking in good textual witnesses, is original. The discussions of R. Graber are
perhaps particularly fitted to prove this originality. R. Bohren, *Das Problem der
Kirchenzucht im Neuen Testament*, 1952, pp. 32 ff., believes that he sees another
connection, which however has in view only the prophet. This is Jer. 1:18 f.:
"I make you today an iron pillar and a bronze wall . . . they will fight against
you, but will not overcome you."

[9] See below, pp. 216 f.   [10] See above, p. 186.

[11] For all details I refer to the careful study of Ph. Vielhauer, *Oikodome, das Bild
vom Bau in der christlichen Literatur vom N. T. bis Clemens Alexandrinus*, 1939.

[12] οἰκοδομεῖν.   [13] I Cor. 8:1–10; Rom. 14:19; 15:2, 20.

[14] See below, pp. 198 f.

ticularly the contrast between earth and heaven, shows that Jesus means a people that already appears in this age.

This very fact, however, leads many to deny that Jesus spoke this saying. Is it possible that Jesus, who certainly announced the Kingdom which comes at the end, actually expected the realization of the people of God *in this present age*? In the last analysis this problem of time stands in the background of the entire debate. In considering it, we wish to distinguish from one another the following limited questions: 1. Did Jesus lay the foundation of a Messianic fellowship even in his life-time? 2. Did he expect that even after his death this age would still continue, and that then especially this fellowship would be built up, before the end would come?

As we begin to consider the first question, we should note at the outset that it is given a false perspective if it is placed in the form of an alternative: present *or* future Messianic community. The Jewish idea of the people of God—*qahal*—*ekklesia* cannot be forced into this alternative. Rather it includes both present and future. Particularly, however, it must be considered that for Jesus, in view of his Messianic selfconsciousness, present and future, promise and fulfilment, even if distinguished, nevertheless do not represent opposites; on the contrary, in his person the fulfilment has already been anticipated. Particularly in reference to the Messianic community we must not say: present *or* future, promise *or* fulfilment.

Perhaps the quite one-sided view of Albert Schweitzer is responsible for the fact that many are still unable to see the problem except in the form of an either-or alternative. Before Schweitzer the scholars, in their presentation of the teaching of Jesus, were all too quick to push eschatology into the background or completely discard it. They described it by using the slogan: "a concession conditioned by contemporary Jewish ideas." Thus they held that the essential thing in it was only the relation to the contemporary situation. For this reason the reaction of Albert Schweitzer was entirely necessary. But it in turn succumbed again to the temptation to survey the entire teaching of Jesus in a false time perspective; it presented his teaching as though Jesus expected everything from the future. In reality it is the very tension between "already fulfilled" and "not yet fulfilled" that is characteristic of the New Testament conception of time.[15] This conception, indeed, runs through the entire New Testament; it already marks the attitude of Jesus in the Synoptic

[15] See O. Cullmann, *Christus und die Zeit*, 1948, pp. 72 ff. (Eng. Tr., *Christ and Time*, 1950, pp. 84 ff.).

Gospels.[16] Even in Jesus' own preaching the Kingdom of God is on the one hand still not present, for it comes only at the end; and yet in the presence of Jesus it has already broken in: "If I cast out demons by the Spirit of God, then the Kingdom has already come to you" (Matt. 12:28). "Tell John what you hear and see: the blind see again, the lame walk, lepers are cleansed, the deaf hear, the dead rise, and to the poor the good news is preached" (Matt. 11:4 f.).

Thus there can be no doubt that Jesus himself reckons with such an anticipation of the Kingdom of God; in him the decision has already occurred, even if the completion is expected only in the final time. It would curtail the preaching of Jesus to accept as valid only the one or the other aspect. He who regards as decisive only the sayings concerning the future should ask himself what it is then that really distinguishes Jesus at all from other prophets. Promise was uttered by all prophets, even promise for a near future. But the new thing with Jesus is the very fact that even now there is a fulfilment.

It is doubtless universally conceded that after the death of Jesus, in *Primitive Christianity* and for *Paul*, this tension between present and future, promise and fulfilment, really exists. But in Primitive Christianity this does not mean, as the adherents of Albert Schweitzer in particular assert, a reinterpretation or falling away from the position of Jesus, who had spoken only of the future; rather, this tension is *already present for him*. There does exist on this point a certain difference between Jesus and the Primitive Church; Jesus is conscious that the fulfilment is present *in his person*, while the Primitive Church sees the fulfilment *in the Church*. But there is no conflict here at all. Rather, the fulfilment in the person of Jesus leads directly to the fulfilment in the Church, and the fulfilment in the Church points back in turn to the fulfilment in the person of Jesus.[17] Therefore it is not merely possible that Jesus also sees the people of God already beginning to be constituted in his day; we would almost have to postulate this even if we had no clear texts to prove it.

A direct contradiction between the future Kingdom of God and

---

[16] See W. G. Kümmel, *Verheissung und Erfüllung* (*Abhandlungen zur Theologie des Alten und Neuen Testaments*, 1945).

[17] This must be given unqualified emphasis in opposition to W. G. Kümmel's much esteemed essay, *Kirchenbegriff und Geschichtsbewusstsein in der Urgemeinde und bei Jesus*, 1943 (see above, pp. 167 f.). The point to note is that he sees here an irreconcilable parallelism of two related forms of the historical consciousness, and draws from this the conclusion that Matt. 16:17 ff. is spurious. The conclusions which W. G. Kümmel here draws seem to me in reality to contradict his own premises.

the already realized people of God is only a construction built on the basis of modern thinking. For Jesus the two aspects certainly do not coincide, but they do not form opposites, as we are inclined to believe on the basis of a modern thought pattern. The higher concept that even in Judaism unites both aspects, present and future, is this very idea of the "people of God." It is used here equally with reference to its present and its future realization, and as soon as the conviction is present that the end has already been anticipated, even if the completion is still to come, the distinction practically loses its importance.

Thus the foundation of the earthly people of God dates back in the time of the Incarnate One, even if it is really "built up" only after his death. Jesus created the foundation for this people of God even in his lifetime. In order to prove this by texts, we again must refuse to be misled into regarding as decisive only the occurrence of the word *ekklesia*. We must investigate whether the thing is not actually present in passages where the word is lacking. In this connection particular reference has properly been made to the forming of the group of the Twelve. The attempt has indeed been made to deny that Jesus did this and to transfer its origin into the later time of the Primitive Church.[18] But there really exists no necessity for doing this, and what is more, it is quite impossible to see how this group could have arisen as late as the time of the Primitive Church; on the contrary, it was necessary rather to take pains to re-establish it after the defection of Judas. But what could the establishing of this group mean if not the founding of the people of God which is to prepare for the Kingdom of God? The reference to the Jewish idea of the people of God is here quite plainly present. The number Twelve, indeed, must be connected with the number of the twelve tribes of Israel.

The most important thing, however, is not merely the *choice* of the twelve disciples; it is above all the *mission* they received from Jesus, that is, the role that he gives to this fellowship. It cannot be sufficiently emphasized that the command he gives in sending them forth refers to the identical *Messianic* functions that *Jesus himself* fulfils in his role of the "Coming One." Here it is confirmed that even in the present age the Messiah needs for his preparatory work a

18 So, following many others, R. Bultmann, "Die Frage nach der Echtheit . . ." (*Theologische Blätter*, 1941). On the contrary, the significance of the Twelve as a preliminary stage of the Church is emphasized with special force by G. Gloege, *Reich Gottes und Kirche im N. T.*, 1929, and also by H. D. Wendland, *Die Eschatologie des Reiches Gottes bei Jesus*, 1931.

community, and that the group of the Twelve represents at least the start of the future Messianic *ekklesia*. We have seen that in his answer to the Baptist Jesus cites these facts as a sign that with his coming *the time of redemption has already broken in*: "the blind see, the lame walk, lepers are cleansed, the dead rise, to the poor the good news is preached." In a strikingly parallel manner Jesus commands his disciples when he sends them forth: "Go to the lost sheep of the house of Israel and proclaim that the Kingdom of Heaven has come near . . . heal the sick, raise the dead, cleanse the lepers, cast out demons" (Matt. 11:4 f.; 10:7 f.). The analogy between this command and the answer to the Baptist deserves further consideration. For here it becomes clear that for Jesus not only his own coming but *also the existence and the work of the group of disciples is already the fulfilment and inbreaking of the time of redemption*. The same deeds that he himself does they also are to accomplish, as proof that the prophecy has already been fulfilled in him.[19] Thus the forming and the sending forth of the group of disciples is quite closely connected with his Messianic conviction. When he also says, on the other hand, that they will not have completed visiting the cities of Israel before the Son of Man comes (Matt. 10:23)—a saying which moreover permits various interpretations[20]—it still remains true that the work of the group of disciples is a Messianic work, and that thus, even in the lifetime of Jesus, the fulfilment does not occur only in his person; rather, in these men the people of God has already begun to be realized.[21] We should understand in this way the saying concerning the fishers of men (Mark 1:17 and parallels) and that concerning the work in the harvest (Matt. 9:37 f.); and the parable of the fishnet (Matt. 13:47 ff.) confirms the provisional and yet anticipatory character of the catch of fish.

Where such things happen as Jesus enumerates in his answer to the Baptist (Matt. 11:4 f.), the question whether the Kingdom of God is future or present loses all point.[22] The anticipation of the Kingdom

---

[19] It is connected with this, as H. Riesenfeld points out in *Ämbetet i Nya Testamentet*, n. d., pp. 17 ff., that the metaphors with which Jesus' functions are described are transferred to the apostles.

[20] See O. Cullmann, *Le retour du Christ, Espérance de l'Eglise selon le Nouveau Testament*, 1943, pp. 23 f.

[21] This should be stressed against A. Loisy, *L'Evangiles Synoptiques*, p. 9, with whom R. Bultmann, *op. cit.*, column 275, allies himself when he writes that the fact that Jesus gathered disciples has nothing to do with the Church.

[22] Wherever the Kingdom of God is *a living reality*, this is the case. Think of Blumhardt.

of God thus occurs here even in the lifetime of Jesus; the foundation of the people of God is laid, even if it also remains true that the real building is only carried out after the death of Jesus, on the basis of the new covenant. This *ekklesia* that is "built" after the death of Jesus will be an anticipation of the Kingdom of God, but the group of disciples in the lifetime of Jesus is on its part an anticipation of that *ekklesia*.

Jesus regards the narrower and the wider group of disciples as a fellowship with a particular task. As such it already represents a realization. This is clear also from other passages; it appears, for example, when he speaks of his true family (Mark 3:33 ff. and parallels), and especially when he addresses the disciples as a "flock," as he does in Luke 12:32: "Fear not, little flock, for it has pleased your Father to give you the Kingdom;" and further in Matthew 26:31: "I will smite the shepherd and the sheep of the flock will be scattered." With this agrees also the already mentioned "lost sheep of the house of Israel" (see also Matt. 9:36). We know from the Damascus Document that also in the Jewish "community of the New Covenant," which has now become better known, the concept of the shepherd was common, and that the *ekklesia* concept is in reality expressed by this image.[23] In the remaining writings of the New Testament the designations flock, shepherd, sheep, and feeding almost always refer to the Church. We should think here above all of the Gospel of John: John 10:1 ff.; 21:16 ff., but also of I Corinthians 9:7 and Acts 20:28.[24]

*   *   *

The fellowship that Jesus founded even in his lifetime does of course point to the *future*. Only after his death will it develop, will it be "built up" in the real sense. We have seen that the Messianic consciousness must lead to the founding of the Church. For Jesus, however, this consciousness involves the necessity of his death. Therefore his death is the real starting point of the new people of God. The establishing of the Lord's Supper[25] can only mean that the new fellowship is founded by his death. But here the question arises whether for Jesus the time immediately after his death is the time of the complete fulfilment or whether, before the end comes, the time

---

[23] See above, pp. 63 f., 188.

[24] R. Bultmann, *op. cit.*, column 268, denies that in the Synoptic passages the idea of a group is present; in the Gospel of John, he claims, the words have a quite different meaning.

[25] See above, p. 190.

of anticipation begun by his earthly work will still continue for a while, and continue as the period of the Church. Matthew 16:17 ff. implies this second assumption. Before we deal with the question whether this agrees with the general expectation of Jesus as we are able to deduce it from the Synoptic Gospels, we still must study a very important utterance of Jesus. It seems to me to be an exact parallel to Matthew 16:17 ff., and it also refers to the time after the death of Jesus. I refer to the saying that Jesus spoke concerning the *temple* and that obviously played a decisive role in his so-called trial.[26] To be sure, it was—at least according to Mark 14:57 f.— false witnesses who accused Jesus of having said: "I will destroy this temple made by hands and in three days build up another not made by hands." Later also, however, at the cross, a similar saying is ascribed to him by the passers-by. Moreover, it is possible to explain wherein the *false* witness probably consisted, if we take into account another saying of Jesus, which stands in Mark 13:2. A disciple there says to Jesus: "Behold what great stones and what great buildings!" Jesus answers him: "There will not remain one stone upon the other which will not be destroyed." He thus clearly predicts here the destruction of the temple. It therefore is probably true that what Jesus really said was worded in the way that the Gospel of John (ch. 2:19) actually puts it into his mouth on the occasion of the cleansing of the temple: "*Destroy* this temple, and in three days I will build it up." The falsified feature in this saying, accordingly, as it is ascribed to the false witnesses in Mark, would be only the change of person in the first half of the sentence. Jesus would not have said: "*I* will destroy," but "the temple will be destroyed." In the second half of the sentence, on the contrary, the first person seems quite in place: "I will rebuild it."

[26] M. Goguel, *Jésus*, 2nd ed., 1950, pp. 330 ff. (Eng. Tr., *The Life of Jesus*, 1933, pp. 507 ff.), speaks in support of the genuineness of this saying, but does not connect it with Matt. 16:17 ff. (He relates it, on the contrary, to the parable of the vinedressers; extension to the Gentiles.) As arguments in favour of genuineness he points out that the prediction of the destruction of the Temple cannot be a prophecy "*ex eventu*," since indeed the temple was destroyed in 70 by fire, not by earthquake, as the saying of Jesus presupposes ("there will not remain one stone upon another"); he further cites the fact that to Stephen also a similar saying is ascribed (Acts 6:10 ff.). M. Goguel assumes that Judas informed the Jewish magistrates of this utterance of Jesus. A high estimate of the saying about the temple and its significance for Primitive Christian thinking is found in Marcel Simon, "Retour du Christ et reconstruction du Temple dans le pensée Chrétienne primitive" (*Aux sources de la tradition chrétienne, Mélanges M. Goguel*, 1950, pp. 249 ff.).

Only in the Gospel of Mark do we read "another not made by hands," after it has been said previously of the temple at Jerusalem that it "was made by hands." But whether this precision is original or not—there is no real reason why it should not be so—in any case Jesus had in view a fellowship when he announced that he would again erect the destroyed temple. We have already seen, indeed, that it was already common in Jewish terminology to apply to the people the image of the building. In the New Testament area this usage is quite common; the Church is the temple or the "spiritual house," as it is called in First Peter (ch. 2:5 ff.).[27] It is possible that the author of the Gospel of John, when he went on to apply the saying about the temple to the body of Christ, likewise thought of the Church.[28]

In any case, however, it must be assumed, in keeping with the Synoptic tradition, that Jesus proclaimed the building of a temple not made by human hands. By this he can only have meant the new people of God that he intended to found.[29] For our study this saying about the temple is the more important since here, exactly as in Matthew 16:18, the illustration of the building occurs. *We thus have here a direct parallel to the saying concerning the ekklesia*, and if it plays so small a role in discussions of our question, this results only from the fact that scholars let themselves be misled by statistics of word usage, and so no longer pay attention to the essential idea.

★   ★   ★

By his saying concerning the temple, as well as by the words of institution of the Lord's Supper, Jesus announces a new fellowship for the time *after his death*. With this agrees the fact that in Matthew 16:17 ff. he speaks in the future tense: "I *will* build my *ekklesia*." We have seen that according to this saying this future must still fall in this age, since otherwise the contrast between heaven and earth would have no meaning. This very fact, however, gives occasion for the final objection which is raised against the genuineness of the passage. It is claimed that if Jesus spoke of a future realization of the people of God, to follow after his death, he can only have meant its final realization in the Kingdom of God. Those other promises, such

---

[27] See above, p. 192.

[28] See O. Cullmann, *Urchristentum und Gottesdienst* (Eng. Tr., *Early Christian Worship*, pp. 71 ff.

[29] Concerning the Jewish Messiah and the rebuilding of the temple see Enoch 90:28 ff. On this point see J. Engnell, *Studies in Divine Kingship*, 1943; E. G. Kraeling, "The Real Religion of Ancient Israel" (*Journal of Biblical Literature*, 1928, p. 138). H. Riesenfeld, *Jésus transfiguré*, 1947, p. 59.

as the saying concerning the temple, must in such a case be understood to mean that with the death of Jesus the consummation of the Kingdom of God already occurs. Since, however, in Matthew 16:17 ff. the *ekklesia* is already realized in the present age, it is alleged that there exists here a contradiction, and therefore this saying cannot come from Jesus.[30]

The question thus arises: Did Jesus then expect any intermediate period between his death or resurrection and his return? If it is really true, as Albert Schweitzer asserts, that Jesus expected the Kingdom of God to come at the moment of his death, then indeed there would no longer be any place for a period of the Church. The people of God would pass over directly into the final Kingdom of God. We cannot discuss this problem in its full extent, and I mention only a few outstanding points. First of all, we have no text which really supports Schweitzer's hypothesis. For Jesus his own death undoubtedly constitutes the central event in the redemptive process that leads to the Kingdom of God. But he sees the tension between present and future; it is already present in his lifetime, and he knows that by his death it is not yet removed.[31]

It is sufficient to recall the necessity of the *Gentile mission*, which Jesus often emphasized and which must be carried out only after his death, before the coming of the end (Mark 14:62). That will be the specific task of the little flock in the period after his death and before the end; it is to build up the people of God in such a way that the Gentiles find acceptance in it. What Jesus has already revealed as proclamation, the inclusion of the Gentiles in the people of God, is to become reality after his death. Therefore the redemptive history must still continue for a period after his death, because the command given at the sending forth of the disciples is not yet fully carried out; it can only be fully carried out when Jesus has died and arisen.[32] The establishing of the new covenant at *the Last Supper* probably pre-

---

[30] So R. Bultmann, "Die Frage nach der Echtheit von Mtth. 16, 17–19," *Theologische Blätter*, 1941.

[31] See on this point W. Michaelis, *Der Herr verzieht nicht die Verheissung*, 1942; W. G. Kümmel, *Verheissung und Erfüllung*, 1945, pp. 38 ff.; O. Cullmann, *Christus und die Zeit*, pp. 131 f. (Eng. Tr., *Christ and Time*, pp. 149 f.).

[32] E. Peterson, in his highly regarded essay, "Die Kirche," 1929 (now printed in the collection, *Theologische Traktate*, 1951), is right when he sees in this the real essence of the Church. So also O. Cullmann, *Christus und die Zeit*, 2nd ed., 1948, pp. 138 ff. (Eng. Tr., *Christ and Time*, pp. 157 f.); in this matter I stress strongly the retention of the eschatology, while in the view of E. Peterson it is, so to speak, dissolved in the Church.

supposes, even if the explicit command to repeat the rite should not be original, a continuation of the Messianic time of preparation that has begun in the earthly work of Jesus.

Moreover, the promise of Mark 14:28, whose genuineness usually is not contested, is probably only correctly understood by assuming that in it Jesus did not consider that his death was identical with the consummation: "but after I have risen I will go before you into Galilee." Here belong further the sayings concerning fasting (Mark 2:18 ff.): "When the bridegroom is taken from them, then they may fast." Also in his answer to the high priest (Mark 14:62 and parallels), Jesus distinguishes between the moment when the Son of Man will sit at the right hand of God and the one when he will come again on the clouds of Heaven. To be sure, Jesus scarcely reckons with a duration of millenniums, but he does assume that there will be a rather brief period of time between his resurrection and return. That, however, does not concern us in our study.[33] The important thing here is that he anticipates after his death also some period within which the Kingdom of God is prepared, and if it has already been anticipated, it is nevertheless not yet completed. In this period of time falls the building of the *ekklesia* of which Jesus speaks in Matthew 16:17 ff.

*   *   *

Now that we have thus established from every angle that Jesus spoke of a building of the new people of God, and have seen in what sense he did so, we still have to explain the further sayings connected with this subject. The question as to who is meant by the rock we postpone until we have discussed the remaining points, since it will lead us directly to the doctrinal question.

In the saying we first hear that the gates of Hades will not prevail against this *ekklesia* which Jesus will build upon the rock. By Hades is meant the realm of the dead[34]—and not chiefly the realm of sin and damnation.[35] This is the truth in the thesis according to which

---

33 See O. Cullmann, "Das wahre, durch das Ausbleiben der Parusie gestellte Problem" (*Theologische Zeitschrift*, 1947, pp. 177 ff.).

34 So also E. Klostermann, *Das Matthäusevangelium, ad loc.*, and A. Schlatter, *Der Evangelist Matthäus, ad loc.*

35 R. Bohren, *Das Problem der Kirchenzucht im Neuen Testament*, 1952, pp. 63 f., assumes rather that from the gates of hell stream forth spirit hosts who fight to prevent the building of the Church. W. Vischer, *Die evangelische Gemeindeordnung*, 1946, sees both united. So does M. Meinertz, *Theologie des Neuen Testaments*, Vol. I, 1950, p. 75. On the entire subject see especially W. Bieder, *Die Vorstellung von der Höllenfahrt Jesu Christi*, 1949, pp. 43 ff.

this passage speaks of the triumph that the resurrection brings over death.[36] Whether a translation error for "porter" is present here may remain undiscussed.[37] It is possible. Nevertheless, the image of the gates of the realm of the dead is already found in Israelite and Jewish writings: Isaiah 38:10; Psalms 9:13; 107:18; Job 38:17[38]; Wisdom of Solomon 16:13; III Maccabees 5:51; Psalm of Solomon 16:2. The idea is that the gates of the realm of the dead, which close behind all men, will no more be opened, that the realm of the dead will no more permit its dead to escape. Matthew 16:18 states, probably with the same figure and in dependence on it, that before the attack of the Church the gates which otherwise stand firm against every attempt, however strong, to storm them, lose their previously unconquerable power; before the Church they must open. If this is the case, the *ekklesia* is here thought of as the attacker. One could indeed seek also to regard the gates as the attackers.[39] When we think that the *ekklesia* is conceived in this illustration as a building, this might seem almost likely. But the question whether the *ekklesia* or the world of the dead is thought of as the attacker can hardly be answered with certainty.[40]

It is clear, on the contrary, that according to this saying *the ekklesia is included in the function of Jesus*, which consists of his victory over

[36] A. Harnack, "Der Spruch über Petrus als den Felsen der Kirche, Matth. XVI, 17 f." (*Sitzungsbericht der Berliner Akademie der Wissenschaften*, 1918, pp. 637 ff.), deletes the saying concerning the Church. He prefers to see here only a prediction of the resurrection of *Peter*; he replaces αὐτῆς ("it") by σου ("you"). (See above, p. 165.) This, however, is impossible, because the explanation of the name Peter requires the figure of the building. (So rightly M. J. Lagrange, commentary on Matthew, p. 324.) Whether αὐτῆς ("it") is to be connected with ἐκκλησία ("church") or with πέτρα ("rock") was already considered by the Church Fathers (Origen); πέτρα is too far removed, and on the basis of content also ἐκκλησία must be the word meant here. (See M. J. Lagrange, commentary on Matthew, p. 327.)

[37] R. Eppel, *Aux sources de la tradition chrétienne, Mélanges offerts à M. Goguel*, pp. 71 ff., holds that πύλαι ("gates") would represent שַׁעֲרֵי, while πυλωροί ("gatekeepers," "porters") would represent שֹׁעֲרֵי (reference to Job 38:17, LXX). In another way Ed. Bruston, *Les promesses de Jésus à l'apôtre Pierre*, 1945, pp. 10 ff., assumes here a translation error for "assaults of the abyss."

[38] The LXX, to be sure, reads πυλωροί ("gatekeepers," "porters") here. See the preceding note.

[39] R. Eppel, *op. cit.*, p. 72, appeals to J. Dutlin, "The Gates of Hades" (*Expository Times*, 1916, pp. 401 ff.), in pointing out that the verb κατισχύω ("prevail") fits an attack rather than a defence.

[40] For the conception of the gates as the attacking force, see Th. Zahn, commentary on Matthew, p. 542, and M. J. Lagrange, commentary on Matthew, p. 326.

death by his death and resurrection. The task that was given to the disciples during Jesus' lifetime as a Messianic function,[41] the conflict with death, whether in the form of healings of the sick or raisings of the dead (Matt. 10:7 f.), is here promised to the entire *ekklesia*. The foundation that is laid in Peter thus has to support a building that means victory over death. It is predicted that the *ekklesia* founded upon Peter as the rock will indeed exist in the time when death still rules, and so will exist in the present age,[42] but it will nevertheless share already in the resurrection power that marks the Kingdom of God. We shall remind ourselves, when we discuss and reach a conclusion concerning the essential nature of an apostle, that in the New Testament the apostles are first of all witnesses of the resurrection who are entrusted with a commission.

The illustration of the building, and likewise that of the door, give occasion to use that of the *keys* of the Kingdom of God. Mention has just been made of the gates of Hades; now the doors of the Kingdom of Heaven are in mind. Just as Hades is the realm of the dead, so the Kingdom of Heaven is that of life in the resurrection. This illustration of the keys seems to have been common. In Revelation 1:18 it is said of the Son of Man that he has the keys of death and of Hades, manifestly in order to open them for those imprisoned within. In Revelation 3:7 it is said, with a reference to Isaiah 22:22, that the Holy One has the "keys of David," with which he irrevocably opens and closes (see also Rev. 21:25). In Matthew 16:19 it is presupposed that Christ is the master of the house, who has the keys to the Kingdom of Heaven, with which to open to those who come in. Just as in Isaiah 22:22 the Lord lays the keys of the house of David on the shoulders of his servant Eliakim, so Jesus commits to Peter the keys of his house, the Kingdom of Heaven, and thereby installs him as administrator of the house.[43] There exists a relation between the house of the *ekklesia*—whose building was mentioned just before, and whose foundation is Peter—and the heavenly house whose keys he receives. The connecting element here too is the idea of the people of God.

Here again Peter is connected with the resurrection. The so-called

---

[41] See above, pp. 195 f.

[42] This confirms the view that it is not simply the coming Kingdom of God that is meant here.

[43] On the illustration of the steward of the household see Mark 13:34; Luke 12:42; 16:1 ff.; I Cor. 4:1; I Pet. 4:10. Th. Zahn, *Das Evangelium nach Matthäus, ad loc.*, is hardly right when he thinks here not of admission but only of authority over secret chambers.

power of the keys makes him, so to speak, the human instrument of the resurrection. He is to lead the people of God into the resurrection Kingdom. That is the task which he will have to carry out on earth after the death and resurrection of Jesus. In this connection we must think of that other saying of Jesus which rests upon the very same illustration; it is his saying to the Pharisees: "you close the door to the Kingdom of Heaven" (Matt. 23:13). The Pharisees might indeed boast that they on the contrary open the door to the Kingdom of Heaven. But it is not they, it is rather the called rock, Peter, who has this office. As in Matthew 23.13, in the saying against the Pharisees, so here too may be in mind the *mission* that Peter will carry out by his preaching, and by which he will open access to the Kingdom of Heaven, while the Pharisees "rush over sea and land to make a single proselyte, and when he has become one, they make of him a son of Hell who is twice as bad as they are" (Matt. 23:15).[44] It is characteristic that in Matthew this utterance follows right after the one on the opening of the Kingdom of Heaven, and this justifies us when we also connect with the apostolic mission the giving of the "keys of the Kingdom of Heaven" in Matthew 16:19.

Just as this saying concerning the keys of the Kingdom of Heaven connects directly with the one that deals with the "building" of the *ekklesia* and with the gates of the realm of the dead, so also the words concerning "binding" and "loosing" must be understood in connection with what precedes. This must be considered first of all in regard to the way the expressions "on earth" and "in heaven" correspond. These expressions are to be understood first of all not in a spatial but in a temporal sense. What Peter does for the *ekklesia* is effective for the coming Kingdom of Heaven. Here again it is seen how close is the connection between the Messianic present and the future, between the already realized fulfilment and the consummation still to come.

What do the expressions "bind" and "loose" signify? According to Rabbinical usage[45] two explanations are equally possible: "prohibit" and "permit," that is, "establish rules";[46] or "put under the

---

[44] The connection with Matthew, ch. 23, has been pointed out by J. Schniewind, *Das Evangelium nach Matthäus* (*Das N. T. Deutsch*), 1927, *ad loc.*, and also by W. Vischer, *Die evangelische Gemeindeordnung*, 1946, pp. 24 f.

[45] אסר and שרא.

[46] So G. Dalman, *Worte Jesu*, I, p. 175 (Eng. Tr., *The Words of Jesus*, 1909, p. 214); E. Klostermann, *Das Matthäusevangelium*, *ad loc.*; likewise Th. Zahn, *Das Evangelium nach Matthäu..*, *ad loc.* (he denies any connection with John 20:23); and W. Michaelis, commen..ry on Matthew, *ad loc.*

ban" and "acquit."[47] Since for Jesus entrance into the Kingdom of
Heaven is closely connected with forgiveness of sins (Matt. 18:18
and John 20:23), the latter meaning is doubtless chiefly in mind here,
but without excluding the other, which is equally well attested by
Rabbinical texts.[48] Indeed, the power to teach and to discipline cannot be sharply separated. Peter thus receives a share in the authority
of Christ to forgive sins. To the functions that had been committed
to the disciples even in the lifetime of Jesus, the same ones, as we have
seen,[49] that Jesus himself exercises (Matt. 11:4 ff.; 10:7 f.), there is
now added this highest office of forgiving sins, an office that Christ
alone controls but commits also to Peter with a view to establishing
the earthly people of God. In case the binding is meant to refer also
to the demonic powers, there would be a further connection with
the preceding illustration.[50]

I recall at this point that this promise is given not only to Peter,
but in almost the same words to the other disciples as well: "Truly
I tell you, all that you shall bind on earth will be bound in heaven,
and all that you shall loose on earth will be loosed in heaven"
(Matt. 18:18); "If you forgive the sins of any, they will be forgiven;
if you retain the sins of any, they will be retained" (John 20:23). This
is important for the question as to the character of the pre-eminence
with which Peter is certainly distinguished here. The "binding" and
"loosing" he shares with the other disciples. This corresponds completely with what we have established in the historical section, in our
chapter concerning the disciple Peter and his position among the
Twelve. He is to be sure the first among them, but nevertheless is
their representative in all things; he always speaks in the name of the
others, and people turn to him in order to speak at the same time to
all the disciples. This unique position comes to expression also in the
fact that the promise of the effectiveness of his "binding" and
"loosing" is given not only to him but also to the other disciples,
but it is given to him in a special way, and only for him is it connected with the announcement that upon him as the rock the *ekklesia*
is to be built. This corresponds with the historical fact which, as we
have established, occurred after the death of Jesus; Peter, in the

[47] So A. Schlatter, *Der Evangelist Matthäus, ad loc.;* J. Schniewind, *Das Evangelium
nach Matthäus, ad loc.;* Ed. Schweizer, *Gemeinde nach dem N. T.,* 1949, p. 13.
[48] See Strack-Billerbeck, *op. cit.,* Vol. I, p. 738, on Matthew, *ad loc.*
[49] See above, pp. 195 f.
[50] So R. Bohren, *Das Problem der Kirchenzucht im Neuen Testament,* 1952, pp. 52 ff.,
who agrees with F. Heiler, *Urkirche und Ostkirche,* 1937, p 59. With a somewhat
different turn, A. Dell, *op. cit.* (ZNW, 1914, pp. 38 ff.).

earliest period, stands at the head of the Primitive Church in Jerusalem, but soon gives up this position to act in dependence on James in organizing the Jewish Christian missionary work; this work he does in company with other disciples, but as its leader.

*   *   *

This, however, leads us to the final exegetical question we must ask; it will also form the transition to the discussion of the doctrinal problem: Whom does Jesus mean when he says that upon the rock the new people of God will be built? The question could seem superfluous were it not that the really self-evident reference to the person of Peter has been contested, and often is still contested, from the Protestant as well as from the Catholic side.

The solution of the Reformers, that the rock is only the faith of Peter,[51] does not satisfy. In the first place, this explanation stands or falls with the very questionable connection of the words with the narrative framework, and we have seen that precisely in this story there is little concern with the faith of Peter, which here is anything but exemplary. But in addition to this, the text offers no real support for this interpretation. Rather, the parallelism of the two statements: "you are rock, and upon this rock I will build . . ." shows that the second rock refers to nothing different from the first one.[52] This is more clearly expressed in the Aramaic, where the same word *kepha* occurs both times, than it is in the Greek. The explanation that Jesus did not say at all: "You are Peter," but: "I say to you, yes to you, Peter,"[53] is purely hypothetical, in spite of the fact that it refers back to the Aramaic. There may indeed be some truth in the view that in the last analysis the rock means Christ himself (as in Matt. 21:42). But that is not what is said here; this passage says that Jesus' role as rock is transferred to a disciple.[54] So there remains only the one possibility, that by this saying Jesus actually meant the person whom he characterized by the name "rock." Indeed, if the saying

[51] See above, pp. 162 f.

[52] For this reason we must also pronounce unsatisfactory the thesis that G. Gander represents in his article "*ΠΕΤΡΟΣ-ΠΕΤΡΑ*" (*Revue de Théologie et de Philosophie*, 1941, pp. 5 f.). He holds that *Kepha*, in Syriac *Kipha*, is a name of both persons and things, so that it refers to Peter only in the first but not in the second part of the sentence.

[53] Strack-Billerbeck, *op. cit.*, see above, p. 163.

[54] H. Riesenfeld, *Ämbetet i Nya Testamentet*, n. d., pp. 17 ff., shows how the metaphors which designate Jesus' own functions are transferred to the apostles.

were referred to the faith of Peter, one could no longer directly discern the connection with the giving of the name, and the saying certainly intends to point to this and even to explain it. The giving of the name, which is an established fact even apart from Matthew 16:17 ff., deals with the person of Peter, and not merely with his faith, just as the person of the sons of Zebedee is in view when Jesus gives them the title "Sons of Thunder."

For this reason all Protestant interpretations that seek in one way or another to explain away the reference to Peter seem to me unsatisfactory. No, the fact remains that when Jesus says that he will build his *ekklesia* upon this rock, he really means the person of Simon. Upon this disciple, who in the lifetime of Jesus possessed the specific advantages and the specific weaknesses of which the Gospels speak, upon him who was then their spokesman, their representative in good as well as in bad, and in this sense was the rock of the group of disciples—upon him is to be founded the Church, which after the death of Jesus will continue his work upon earth.

The Roman Catholic exegesis must be regarded as correct when it rejects those other attempts at explanation.[55] On its part, however, it proceeds in an even more arbitrary way when it tries to find in this text a reference to "successors." He who proceeds without prejudice, on the basis of exegesis and only on this basis, cannot seriously conclude that Jesus here had in mind successors of Peter; this was not his meaning when he said to Peter that he was the rock on which was to be built the fellowship of the people of God that leads to the Kingdom of God. We shall speak later concerning the doctrinal problem; we shall ask whether it cannot be said subsequently, in the light of church history, that the saying may be referred to certain successors. But at first we propose to keep this question clearly separate from the exegetical one, as all serious exegetes, including Roman Catholic ones, are accustomed to do when they deal with other Biblical passages.

On exegetical grounds we must say that the passage does not contain a single word concerning successors of Peter. It speaks on the one hand of *Peter* and on the other hand of the *Church*. Of these two words one, the *ekklesia*, refers to a fellowship which is to be built in the future, without any time limit being given. The other word,

<hr>

[55] M. Meinertz, *Theologie des Neuen Testaments*, Vol. I, 1950, p. 74, does indeed make one concession to the Protestant interpretation when he writes, "the confession (that Peter makes) in faith is the presupposition." But naturally he nevertheless considers that it is the *person* of the confessing one that is addressed.

Peter, refers to a human person, whose earthly activity will necessarily be limited by his death. Accordingly it could be said that a single human person, who will die at a certain time, cannot be the foundation of a fellowship which is to continue for an indefinite period.

It is true that the duration of the Church is not limited in Jesus' words. However, neither is it *explicitly* extended to the period after the death of Peter, and this also must be noted in a saying addressed to the historical Peter. The question of duration is not considered at all; it is left open. In no case, however, is it justified to proceed as Roman Catholic scholars usually do. Since the period of building is not limited, they conclude too hastily that in the entire promise to Peter Jesus must have spoken also of the period after Peter's death, and therefore successors of Peter must also be addressed here.[56] *Peter's feeding of the lambs in John 21:16 ff. is certainly limited by his martyrdom!* So the statement "I will build my *ekklesia*" need not be extended beyond the lifetime of Peter. It could be that at the moment when he gave a promise to Peter in particular, Jesus limited himself to speaking concerning the initial building immediately after his resurrection; this need not mean that he thought the building would be completed in the lifetime of Peter.

But if we nevertheless assume that in *this first statement* Jesus thought of a period embracing many generations,[57] this does not mean at all that the rock—Cephas—Peter mentioned in this sentence includes also successors of Peter. In this sentence it is *only the work of*

---

56 Even in so thorough and cautious an exegete as F. M. Braun, *Neues Licht auf die Kirche,* 1946, we read on p. 165: "Since . . . the apostles appear endowed with special and complete authority and since the operation of the Church, which is to continue to the fulfilment of the times, extends over an intermediate period of indeterminate duration, it would only be consistent, even apart from other considerations, if the 'new consensus' (see above, pp. 166 f.) would concede that the succession corresponds to Jesus' intention and that the apostles, after exercising their power for some years, transferred to others their authority as church leaders." In opposition to K. L. Schmidt, whom F. M. Braun cites on the same page, I prefer to avoid playing off a "prophetic succession" against the "apostolic succession." That an apostolic succession is directly or indirectly present in *other* passages of the New Testament, but in a sense still to be defined (see below, pp. 219 f.), I freely recognize. But I deny the more emphatically that Jesus spoke of such a succession in Matt. 16:17 ff. W. Michaelis, *Das Evangelium nach Matthäus,* p. 354, actually makes an argument for genuineness out of the failure to mention the succession; had the saying been invented later, the succession would have been mentioned.

57 W. Michaelis, *op. cit.,* p. 346, believes it necessary to conclude from the illustration of the "building" that Jesus must have "had in mind a longer development."

building which belongs to an unlimited future, *not the laying of the foundation of the rock* on which is built In the future Jesus will build upon a foundation which is laid in the time of his earthly career and in the time and person of the historical apostle Peter. We shall see[58] that in the entire New Testament the illustration of the foundation, which indeed is identical in meaning with that of the rock, always designates the unique apostolic function, which is chronologically possible only at the beginning of the building; see Ephesians 2:20; Romans 15:20; I Corinthians 3:10; Galatians 2:9; Revelation 21:14, 19. In Matthew 16:18 Peter is addressed in his unrepeatable apostolic capacity.

Everything that is said of Peter in this entire promise really concerns the Peter who then lived, even if the period of building that continues after Peter is explicitly in mind. The content of *the next sentence*, the giving to Peter of the keys, the power to bind and loose, also refers to the future. In this case, however, the reference is not to an unlimited future, but to the life of Peter following the death *of Jesus*. Here Jesus certainly speaks no longer of building during an unlimited period; he speaks rather of the specific rock itself, the apostolic foundation—represented by Peter—of the Church that is to be built. The preceding saying concerning building, which is not limited as to time, gives no exegetical justification for assuming an unlimited duration of time for the entrusting with the keys, the binding and loosing, which is given explicitly to Peter, the rock of the building. Whether and in what way these words directed to Peter may also be legitimately applied *subsequently* to the *later* Church we shall not discuss until the final chapter. On exegetical grounds it must be said that we have no right to see successors addressed in Peter. That would have to be indicated in some way. Wherever Jesus speaks elsewhere of the functions his disciples are to exercise, he plainly means only the disciples themselves and not their successors. And if in the first sentence, which deals with the building, Jesus really includes the period after Peter, this means only that the *unique* mission as rock which the historical Peter fulfils *in the redemptive history* is of such a character that its unique effectiveness continues even beyond his death, so that the historical Peter—and not any successors—is and remains the foundation even in this unlimited further building. When the Johannine Christ, in the high priestly prayer (John 17:20), speaks concerning the coming generations who

---

[58] See below, pp. 217 f., and H. Riesenfeld, *Ämbetet i Nya Testamentet*, n. c., pp. 17 ff.

will believe "through the word of the apostles," he does not speak also of successors to the apostles. He speaks of the *apostles themselves*, of what their once-given preaching signifies for the future Church.

That successors are not addressed is clear also from the Lucan parallel to Matthew 16:17 ff. We have seen that in that passage the command to strengthen the brothers is quite closely connected with the prediction of the denial. Peter must first be converted. Here it is certainly clear that in this section, which implicitly speaks of the future Church, Jesus did not include in his outlook any successors. What is said here is directed only to the historical Peter who denied Jesus.

To be sure, the sentence concerning the keys, concerning loosing and binding, speaks of functions of the historical Peter that continue in the Church. They refer to church leadership, and this indeed must continue to exist. That, however, does not mean that in this saying in Matthew 16:17 ff. Jesus is speaking of the leadership that *later* leaders will give. On the contrary, all that is said here deals with the leadership of him who, according to the preceding sentence, has also the unique mission, absolutely decisive for the Church and not to be repeated, of being the *rock*, of presiding as apostle over the Church immediately after the death and resurrection of Jesus.

As soon as any saying Jesus spoke to the disciples refers to a continued effect of the deeds of the apostles, the Roman Catholic exegetes speak of *successors*. It must be said with all emphasis, however, that continued effect need not mean continued effect *in* "*successors*."

In what he says Jesus certainly does not exclude the activity of other church leaders in later times. But in this *saying concerning the foundation* he does not speak of them; he speaks of Peter. Concerning men who are installed as leaders by apostles the New Testament actually does speak elsewhere, and we shall mention the passages later.[59] Here, however, in what Jesus says to Peter in Matthew 16:17 ff., nothing of the sort is said.

It therefore will not do to argue in the following way: The time of building that Jesus mentions in the first sentence is not limited. But the historical Peter will die. Consequently he cannot be the rock of a Church that continues to exist after him. Therefore Jesus must have successors in mind along with Peter.

It is also impossible to start from the second sentence to give an

[59] See below, pp. 219 ff.

exegetical defence for the reference to successors and so to say something like the following: The power of the keys, and further the binding and loosing, which are entrusted to Peter, must be exercised also in the Church later built by Jesus. Consequently, together with Peter, successors also must be addressed who will carry out this binding and loosing and administer the keys. This also is too hasty a conclusion. Jesus will build not upon the keys, nor upon the binding and loosing, but *upon the apostle Peter*, to whom Jesus *at that time* committed the keys and the binding and loosing.

It must again be explicitly noted that the exegetical conclusion, that this passage speaks only of Peter, still says nothing concerning the possible application of the saying. It may be proper, however, for us to indicate a crucial point which stands *on the border line of exegetical study*. The Roman Catholic position concludes, from the continuance of the Church and from the continued necessity of church leadership, that successors are included in the person of the rock addressed, Peter. This conclusion appears to me connected with a failure to grasp the basic attitude of all New Testament thought. In opposition to Hellenism, it is characteristic of the thinking of Jesus as of all Biblical thinking that *what continues has its roots in the once-for-all unique event*. A historically unique event is the redemptive event; that is, it definitely cannot be repeated but is the *foundation* of a continuing situation whose ongoing life derives from this never-to-be-repeated event. This paradox lies at the basis of Jesus' sayings about the future, and finds a classic expression in the illustration of the rock and the *subsequent* building. In this sense we must also regard all the apostolic action, including the loosing and binding promised to Peter, as *the basic event*. It belongs to what happened once for all; it belongs, one may say, to the incarnation of Christ.[60]

But in saying this we have already stepped outside the field of exegesis. Our exegetical study has led us to the following result: The saying in Matthew 16:17 ff. is genuine. It was spoken by Jesus, not at Caesarea Philippi, but in another setting, possibly that of the passion story. Jesus promises Peter that he will build upon him the earthly people of God that will lead to the Kingdom of God; he promises that in this people Peter will have the leadership, both in missionary work and in organization. His immediate thought, just

---

[60] To use the illustration I gave in *Christus und die Zeit* (Eng. Tr. *Christ and Time*): the Apostolic Age belongs to the midpoint, to the *centre*, by which as norm we must measure everything else that occurs in the redemptive process on the time line.

as in John 21:16 ff., probably deals only with the time of Peter. But even if he explicitly had in view the period following Peter's death as the time of the building of the Church, what is said of Peter as the Rock refers only to him, the historical apostle; he represents once for all the earthly foundation, the beginning who supports the whole structure of the *ekklesia* that is to be built in the future.

Chapter Two

THE DOCTRINAL AND THEOLOGICAL QUESTION: THE APPLICATION OF MATTHEW 16:17 ff. TO THE LATER CHURCH

W E NOW LEAVE the exegetical standpoint and ask the doctrinal question. We connect the exegetical result with our knowledge both of the actual course of the history of the Christian Church and of the fact that there still exists today a Christian Church. On this basis we ask: Are we justified in going further? In the light of these facts can we attribute to the saying a significance that is at least a legitimate *extension* of the promise of Jesus? Roman Catholic theologians, indeed, are accustomed to concede explicitly that the Roman primacy cannot be based upon the exegesis of Matthew 16:17 ff. alone. They grant that this is possible only when this passage is connected with later history.

At the outset we must make a basic statement. It is our right and duty to apply to later generations and to our situation even those sayings of Jesus which deal directly with a unique situation and with specific persons of his time. This, of course is no longer exegesis in the strict sense; but it may be called application of the exegesis. Preachers do this, and no one thinks of reproaching them with the *a priori* charge that in so doing they are untrue to the text. What Jesus says concerning prayer and almsgiving, for example, in the Sermon on the Mount is of course directed to the disciples who lived in his time; no one, however, will consider it unjustified or contrary to the mind of Jesus to apply his teachings on these subjects to all later Christians. Nevertheless, it must be added that this application must really extend in a straight line the basic idea contained in the saying. That is, it must agree with the exegesis and be grounded in the total witness of the New Testament.[1]

When, as is the case in Matthew 16:17 ff., the saying of Jesus does not have a content addressed simply to the wider circle of disciples, as are, for example, the instructions of the Sermon on the Mount, but refers rather to *quite specific functions*, then in the application the special character of these functions must be respected. This must be done in a two-fold way: on the one hand, the significance of the saying for the present may not be seen in the *repetition* of a function, if this is *basically* unique; and on the other hand, the application may not be arbitrarily *restricted*.

With regard to the former point, a role that Jesus promises to an apostle may not be transferred to men of later times, if it belongs to the very *meaning and nature* of the designated function that it can only be exercised by such men as have lived with the Incarnate One *during the earthly life of Jesus*. Indeed, this limitation in time must be taken into account even when—and indeed precisely when—the saying of Jesus in question assigns to this function a lasting significance for the later Church even down to the present time. We shall have to ask whether this is not the case for at least *one* aspect of the saying in Matthew 16:17 ff.

With regard to the latter point, a promise of Jesus may not be limited to a certain category of later Christians, for example, one strictly limited to one episcopal see, if the function in question is one that can and must be taken over by men of the post-apostolic period down to the present time, but according to Jesus' saying is neither explicitly nor by suggestion limited to one place or to be determined according to a particular *principle of succession*. We have to ask whether that sort of narrowing can be justified by the role in church history that the Christian church of one city has played and still plays for the entire Church.

Both of the viewpoints just named must be considered in the application of Matthew 16:17 ff. For we have seen that two things are promised to Peter: 1. He is the rock for the coming Church that is being built. 2. He holds the leadership in the Church whose building is begun. To this corresponds the fact that Peter plays in Primitive Christianity a double role: the unique one as apostle, and the one that is continued in the Church, as leader of the Church. Although the two promises are closely connected with one another, yet for

[1] Here a synthetic combination of the theological views of the various writings of the New Testament is both justified and essential.

their *application* they must be treated separately. This is because the previously posed question, whether too wide an extension or too narrow a limitation is being made, presents itself differently for each of them.

1. *The Laying of the Foundation of the Church*

Even in the course of the exegesis we established the fact that the laying of the foundation is to be understood in the temporal sense. As we now go beyond exegesis, we first must say that this saying, as far as it concerns the rock on which the structure is to be built, is directed to an apostle, not to a bishop. At the moment when Peter receives the promise of being the rock of the coming Church, he is addressed as one of the Twelve. According to the united witness of the New Testament, however, the apostolic office, particularly that of the Twelve, is a unique office not to be repeated. In the post-apostolic period there must always be church leaders, bishops, and missionaries in the Church of Christ, but never again can there be apostles. In the next paragraph we shall speak of the fact that often in the earliest period an apostle himself can be a community leader, at least for a certain time; indeed, Peter himself as apostle led the Primitive Church until he dedicated himself entirely to the mission. But even this will never exist again: there will never again be bishops who, like Peter, lead churches as *apostles*. The functions of leading and doing missionary work do indeed continue; they must continue in the Church. But the function of leading and doing missionary work as an apostle cannot continue. The saying concerning building the Church on Peter as the rock, however, designates an apostle as the basis of the Church that is to be built. When, as in the case of Peter, we are dealing with a church head and missionary who is likewise an apostle, the apostolic concept is necessarily the dominant concept.

We here must ask what the nature of the apostolic office is in the New Testament.[2] The apostle is given a special commission by Jesus as the Incarnate One or when he appeared after his resurrection; so, according to the rule in late Judaism, he is like Jesus himself, and is

[2] See K. H. Rengstorf, Article on ἀπόστολος in G. Kittel's *Theologisches Wörterbuch zum N. T.*, Vol. I, 1933, pp. 397 ff., and the essay by H. von Campenhausen cited above, p. 58, note 63. Further: Ed. Schweizer, *Das Leben des Herrn in der Gemeinde und ihren Diensten*, 1946, pp. 69 ff.; *Gemeinde nach dem N. T.*; and T. W. Manson, *The Church's Ministry*, 1948, pp. 31 ff.

bound to give accounting to him. Upon the fulfilment of his commission, he returns it to Jesus and cannot hand it on to another.

During Jesus' lifetime the content of the commission is the fulfilment of the Messianic function that Jesus himself fulfilled, the function of preaching and healing the sick.[3] Since after the death of Christ the preaching is first of all witness to the resurrection of Christ, the apostle from then on must be a personal "witness of the resurrection of Christ" (Acts 1:22).

The necessity for an apostle to be a witness of the resurrection is clear from I Corinthians 9:1. In that passage Paul has to defend his apostolic office. He does it by pointing to the fact that he also, like the other apostles, has seen the Risen One. In Acts 10:41 Peter says: "Christ appeared to us who after his resurrection ate and drank with him." Thus after the death of Jesus there were more apostles than the Twelve. This follows clearly from the enumeration in I Corinthians 15:5 ff., which speaks on the one hand of the Twelve, and on the other hand of *all the apostles.*

But the "having seen" must always be connected with a commission.[4] Concerning Paul we know this (Gal. 1:16). The Eleven also receive such a commission from the Risen One (Matt. 28:19), and so does Peter in particular (John 21:16 ff.). In the case of the Twelve, however, a further special condition must be fulfilled: they must in addition have lived with the historical incarnate Jesus. That is clearly said in Acts 1:21, where the substitute for Judas is chosen. The conditions that he must fulfil to belong to the circle of the Twelve are there clearly given: first of all, he, like all apostles, must be a "witness of the resurrection of Christ"; in the second place, he must have "gone in and out" with Jesus during his lifetime. In other words, the Twelve have the additional function of guaranteeing the continuity between the risen and the historical Jesus. Therein consists their unique function. They twice receive the apostolic commission, first from the Incarnate One, then from the Risen One. Among them Peter is the most important. Only at that time could one be an eyewitness of the historical Jesus, an eyewitness of the resurrection. *There never will be such a witness again.* Upon one of these eyewitnesses Christ intends to build his Church.

From the men of his time Jesus chose those who were to be his

---

3 In the lifetime of Jesus there are the smaller group of the Twelve and the larger one of the Seventy (Luke 10:1 ff.)

4 See A. Fridrichsen, "The Apostle and his Message" (*Uppsala Universitete Arsskrift,* 1947). See above, pp. 56, 63.

witnesses, and among them Peter, to whose witnessing he attached a particular value. We shall see that Peter, precisely on the basis of the *apostolic concept* just established, is actually the first among the apostles. It must be said at once, however, that according to the united testimony of the New Testament he shares this "fundamental" function with the other apostles. Thus in Ephesians 2:20, where exactly *the same illustration of the building* is used as in Matthew 16:18, Paul writes that the Church "is built upon the foundation of the apostles and prophets." So also Revelation 21:14 speaks of the "twelve foundations of the walls of the Holy City, on which the twelve names of the twelve apostles of the lamb are written," and with the same illustration Paul mentions the "pillars" in Galatians 2:9.[5]

From this it follows that the first Christians actually considered the apostles as such to be the foundation of the Church. Hence also, in the light of the total conception of the New Testament, which we have to consider in this doctrinal section, it is not at all arbitrary when in Matthew 16:17 ff. we see Peter addressed in his *apostolic capacity* and hence emphasize so strongly the apostolic concept. In any case, the illustration of the building in Ephesians 2:20 and Revelation 21:14 is connected with the apostolic function, and this is important. So also in Romans 15:20 the illustration of the foundation occurs to Paul: "that I may not build upon another foundation." (See also I Corinthians 3:10.) Perhaps the New Testament passages named actually refer to Jesus' saying concerning the rock in Matthew 16:17 ff. In that case we might say that we have here the oldest commentary on it.

In I Corinthians 3:11; 10:4; Matthew 21:42; and I Peter 2:4 ff. it is said that Jesus himself is the foundation stone or corner stone. This is doubtless the silent presupposition in all the other passages. But this does not prevent the apostles from being the foundation composed of human instruments of God and resting in turn upon Christ; nor does it prevent Peter from having the prominent role among them and for the Church of all later time.

Just as in Ephesians 2:20 and in Romans 15:20 the foundation is to be understood in a chronological way, so also in Matthew 16:17 ff. In Ephesians 2:20 and Romans 15:20, as well as in Revelation 21:14, it nevertheless is impossible, even as a later application, to think of successors of the apostles. Indeed, a recent study has actually proved

---

[5] James, although not belonging to the Twelve, very probably was regarded as an apostle. See below, p. 230, note 31.

that in contrast to other New Testament metaphors that were transferred from Jesus to the apostles and from them to the later offices,
the illustration of the Rock, of the foundation, is used solely for the
apostles. In this fact the uniqueness and unrepeatable character of the
apostolate comes clearly to expression.[6]

In the foundation that *all* the apostles form Peter is the specially
visible rock. Here again our earlier historical conclusion is confirmed;
he does indeed share his dignity with the other disciples, but within
the group he is particularly representative. Precisely in connection
with the concept of the apostle as the specially commissioned witness
of the resurrection it is also confirmed that Peter, with the other
apostles, forms the foundation and yet at the same time constitutes
the rock within this foundation. Peter, that is to say, was the *first* who
saw the Risen One on Easter. Probably he also received then confirmation of the apostolic commission,[7] and this is the more important since he was the one who had denied Jesus. He accordingly
is the apostle *par excellence*. In this essential relation as the outstanding
one, he is in a particular way what all the other apostles are. It is
interesting to note that here too his position as leader within the
apostolic circle rests upon a chronological distinction; *he is the first
one who saw the Risen One*, and according to John 21:15 ff. the special
apostolic commission given him by the Incarnate One is renewed by
the Risen One. We recall that Matthew, in his list of the apostles,
gives to Peter the title of honour, "first." Thus this also is a part of
the essential role of the apostle Peter. He is particularly qualified to
hand on the news that Jesus, who lived and died on earth, died and
rose for the salvation of the world.

Thus the events immediately after the death of Jesus confirmed the
saying concerning the rock, and if one seeks in the happenings of this
period a *confirmation and illumination of Jesus' saying*, he should seek
it in the fact that Peter is the first witness of the resurrection, and that
his apostolic commission is renewed by the Risen One. This is closely
connected with the result of the exegetical interpretation of the statement: "the gates of the realm of the dead will not overpower the
Church."[8] In the light of the Easter events this interpretation, con-

---

[6] See H. Riesenfeld, *Ämbetet i Nya Testamentet*, n. d., pp. 17 ff.

[7] So especially if the hypothesis is correct that a report concerning the first appearance of Jesus to Peter, such as perhaps was given in the lost ending of Mark, is
used in John 21:15 ff. See above, pp. 59 ff., 180 ff.

[8] See above, p. 202, note 36. Only in this form may we recognize a grain of truth
in the interpretation of A. Harnack—rejected above—that the promise of Peter's
resurrection is here given him.

nected with the promise that the Church is founded on Peter as the rock, receives a particularly strong confirmation in the fact that it is he who is the most important witness of the resurrection of Christ. We have seen that it is not the faith of Peter that is meant by the rock, as the Reformers taught, but rather his person. We now add that it is his person in so far as he had been chosen by the incarnate Christ and in so far as the Risen One appeared to him first of all.

Thus it is absolutely irreconcilable with the New Testament concept of apostleship when a saying on the founding of the Church that was addressed to an apostle is simply referred to future bishops. Elders and bishops certainly do take the place of the apostles, and one may call them successors, even if this expression opens the way to misunderstandings. But in any case it must not be forgotten for a moment that they occupy a completely different position, and they must not be regarded as successors in the sense of "continuers of the apostolic function." They are successors in the chronological sense, but not in their nature. *Their function follows that of the apostles, but as a fundamentally different one.*[9]

So we hear indeed in the New Testament that apostles installed church officers. Paul and Barnabas appointed elders in the cities of Lystra, Iconium, and Antioch (Acts 14:23); moreover, Paul, in his farewell to the elders of Ephesus, commits to them the "flock," especially in anticipation of false teachers (Acts 20:17 ff.). Tendencies towards a so-called "apostolic succession"—if we choose to use this ambiguous expression—are thus actually to be found in the New Testament,[10] but with the explicit reservation that this succession, as far as it concerns the essence of the apostolate, is not to be understood in the sense of a continuation. The apostles give over to those

---

[9] Against the Roman Catholic theologian M. Meinertz, *Die Theologie des Neuen Testaments*, Vol. I, 1950, p. 79: ". . . thus the apostolate requires a continuing present."

[10] This is quite strongly stressed by W. Mundle, "Das Apostelbild der Apostelgeschichte" (*ZNW*, 1928, pp. 36 ff.), an article to which Erik Peterson attaches special importance. See E. Peterson, *Theologische Traktate*, 1951, p. 296 (letter to A. Harnack) and p. 411 ("Die Kirche"). On the question of apostolic succession see also K. H. Rengstorf, "Das Wort Gottes und die apostolische Sukzession" (*Die Kirche Jesu Christi und das Wort Gottes*, edited by W. Zoellner and W. Stählin, 1937, pp. 187 ff.); A. M. Ramsey, "The Word of God and Apostolic Succession" (*Lutherische Kirche in Bewegung, Für Fr. Ulmer zum 60. Geburtstag*, 1937, pp. 179 ff.). See Ed. Schweizer, *op. cit.*, pp. 75 ff.; T. W. Manson, *op. cit.* (note 2 of this section), pp. 52, 54. The Anglican standpoint is represented by K. E. Kirk, *The Apostolic Ministry*, 1946 (especially the essay by G. Dix, "The Ministry in the Early Church").

men the leadership, *but not their own apostolic office*. For they knew quite well that they could not hand this on at all, since it could only be given by Jesus himself directly and *without mediation* (Gal. 1:12 ff.!). Therefore they did not install any "apostles" as successors in leadership, but rather "bishops" and "elders." In what way the latter in turn are to follow one another, the New Testament does not say at all, and since the authority of the bishop may not be identified with that of the apostle, the above named New Testament passages that speak of the installing of local church leaders by the apostles permit no deductions as to how bishops are to follow bishops in the future.[11] In the high-priestly prayer the Johannine Christ speaks of what will follow the apostles. After the petition for the apostles he goes on to speak of those who "believe through the word" (of the apostles; John 17:20). Thus the apostles are followed by the entire Church of the believers. Accordingly the Church has the power of control over the episcopal office, and it is to exercise it as the Holy Spirit guides it (Acts 20:28).

Foundation and building may not be interchanged. Elders and bishops are only *watchmen* who are to see to it that further building is really done on the foundation of the apostles; they are not themselves the foundation. A confusion of foundation and building is present, however, when one appeals to the fact that the apostles installed elders and bishops in order to claim for a bishop Jesus' saying to the rock apostle. Although Roman Catholic theology itself emphasizes very strongly the uniqueness of the apostolic office, it devaluates that office in this decisive point of the application of Matthew 16:17 ff. There will be no more men who, like Peter, have eaten and drunk with Jesus the Incarnate One, have seen his suffering and his death, and to whom, after the denial, Jesus has appeared as the Risen One three days after his death. Later we shall speak also of the fact that there also will be no more men who, like Peter, are leaders of the *first* Church of Christ, the original church at Jerusalem.

Therefore, in the light also of *the total New Testament witness concerning the apostolic office*, and in the light of *the events of the Primitive Church*, that part of the promise of Jesus that speaks of building on the rock Peter may receive subsequent interpretation and application

---

11 This does not intend to say that the Scripture condemns the principle of succession. It does not express itself as to the How of determining the succession of bishops. Only this is certain, that the Holy Spirit operative in the Church is to be at work in the process. So rightly K. H. Rengstorf in p. 202 of the essay cited in the preceding note.

to the later Church only in such a way that this later Church rests once for all and in every generation upon the foundation that was laid *once*; it was laid, that is, at the beginning, at the midpoint of the times, in the time of revelation, when Christ lived on earth, died, and rose.

And now we ask further: But how can the foundation, understood in this chronological way, continue to play this role for the Church of all later times? How can every generation understand that for the Church Peter—and this really means Peter, not pretended successors—is "actually" Peter in the etymological sense? How can the Church today still be founded upon the historical person of the apostle Peter?

This is only possible if this very temporal uniqueness of the foundation formed by the apostles is respected, that is, if the historically unique effect of their person and their work continues to exist in our present as a concrete gift from the time of revelation. This unique gift, which constitutes the continuance of the apostles in the period of the Church, is the Apostolic Scripture. It is not confessional prejudice, but simply the Primitive Christian apostolic concept, that leads me to affirm this. Here in these writings we today, in the midst of the twentieth century, meet the person of the apostles, the person of the first among the apostles, Peter; in this way they continue to support, he continues to support, the structure of the Church. In the only New Testament text that explicitly speaks of the relation of the apostles to the Church that follows them—I refer to the already mentioned section of the high priestly prayer in John 17:20—the further working of the apostles is connected not with the succession principle but rather with the *word of the apostles*: "those who believe through their word."

Without apostles we would have no New Testament, no knowledge at all of Jesus the Risen One. Everything that we know of him we owe to them. And this—we repeat—is true of Peter in a special way. Papias tells that the Gospel of Mark was written according to the sermons of the apostle Peter, and so rests upon his testimony. If this report is correct, then it is also historical to say that the oral tradition lying behind the written Gospels goes back in the first instance to the apostle Peter, especially if we, in agreement with recent study, regard the Gospel of Mark as the oldest Gospel.

When we read the Gospels, we are thus in contact with the person of the apostles and the rock apostle. We today are no longer in the situation to hear for ourselves the eye witnesses of the historical life of Jesus and of his resurrection. We can no longer go to Jerusalem, as Paul did, to "make the acquaintance of Peter" (Gal. 1:18). Nor shall we meet the eyewitness Peter in any other city. But he does remain for us the rock, the foundation; he remains such in the Gospels and in a derived way in the Book of Acts and the letters, which rest entirely upon the first apostolic witness. Here the historical apostolic foundation of the revelation, on which Christ in every generation builds his Church anew, takes concrete form for us also, and *yet retains its unique and never repeated form*. Here the apostles continue to live, and so all Christian Churches, not only the Roman Catholic Church, should write upon their church buildings: "You are Peter, upon this Rock I will build my Church." "Built upon the foundation of the apostles and prophets." "I pray for those who believe through the word of the apostles." Every Christian Church should be *"ecclesia catholica et apostolica,"* a catholic and apostolic Church. A Church that is not apostolic is no longer a Christian Church. But it is perverse to wish to be content, for example, with the apostle Paul, as often happens in Protestant churches. It has become the custom to connect the apostle Peter only with the Roman Catholic Church, and the apostle Paul with the Protestant Church.[12] In reality every Church needs also the apostle Peter, because he as "first" among the twelve apostles has to guarantee the continuity with the incarnate Jesus.[13]

The application of the saying concerning the rock to the later period can thus be made in this sense, in full agreement with the exegesis, but also with the history of the beginnings of the Church.

The question that is asked from the Roman Catholic side is: Who guarantees in the present the scriptural link that leads back to the apostles? This question is justified in itself. But it may not be answered *on the basis of the saying concerning the rock*, on the basis of Matthew 16:17 ff., which is a "foundation saying"; for the rock is and remains the once-for-all foundation. To be sure, there must be guarantors, watchmen, shepherds, interpreters in the Church. But they are quite false to this their role if they refer to themselves the saying concerning the rock. They are indispensable materials of which Christ makes use in the further building of his Church. Their

---

[12] This is the usual and particularly favoured procedure at ecumenical conferences. In such a connection the eastern churches hold to the apostle John as their Patron.

[13] I wish to make this reservation also in regard to the book of J. L. Leuba, *L'Institution et l'evénement*, 1950, which otherwise offers a good historical basis for interdenominational conversations.

specific task is to take care that this rock remains unshaken in the place where Christ has put it, and that it remains just as he has put it. Thus watchmen, shepherds, bishops are instruments of the promise Jesus made to build his Church on Peter.[14]

2. *The Leadership of the Church*

It is a frequent error of Protestant theologians that they do not sufficiently consider in their theological application the continuation of the saying, in which Jesus clearly speaks of the leadership of the Church. Even if the power of the keys concerns primarily the missionary leadership,[15] yet the power to bind and loose, in both of its possible meanings,[16] definitely presupposes church leadership.

We have said already that the leadership of the Church by Peter is also *apostolic* leadership, and so belongs to the never to be repeated Rock role, the laying of the foundation. For we dare not forget that the *entire* promise is dominated by the saying about the rock; it indeed, in connection with the giving of the name, forms the point of departure. But on the other hand, we have pointed out many times that in contrast to the office of the apostle, that of the leader in the Church continues. Thus we here must pay attention to two things: on the one hand, to the non-transferable character of the leadership of the Primitive Church by Peter; on the other hand, to the fact that there must also be leadership later in the Church, so

[14] Richard Baumann, *Des Petrus Bekenntnis und Schlüssel*, 1950, in general formulates the problems correctly, but solves them too quickly along the lines of Roman Catholic teaching. In doing so he is concerned to base his argument entirely on the Scripture. On p. 49 he formulates the following objection against the conception according to which the Church of all time builds *further* on the foundation laid *once*, that is, at the beginning, so that in this building one "layer" or "story" rises on the other to the end of time. He says that in this case "that which is present in the first layer at the first Pentecost would be something unfinished, scarcely begun"; and that is "no house and no temple." This argument, however, is incorrect to this extent, that here the word "unfinished" is understood in the sense of "qualitatively uncompleted." It is not the case, however, that further building takes place because the building without the upper stories would be incomplete and would represent nothing finished. It is "unfinished" before the end of time simply in the chronological sense. A qualitative judgment is never included when reference is made to the end, to the fulfilment of the times. The building is already a complete whole in the lowest storey of the church structure; the number of storeys has only chronological significance. The foundation remains the same; it is so firm that it bears the uppermost storeys as well as the lowest ones.

[15] See above, pp. 203 f.   [16] See above, pp. 204 f.

that Peter is in a certain respect the archetype and example for all future church leadership.[17]

Since we are dealing here with application, it is permitted and required that we connect Matthew 16:17 ff. with what we have learned from The Acts and the Letters concerning the actual role that Peter played in the Primitive Church. When we read the promise of Jesus in the light of the history of the Apostolic Age, it must be said that it was fulfilled in the sense that Peter actually is the head of the Primitive Church. As we have seen, he stands at the head of the Primitive Church of Jerusalem, though to be sure only in the very earliest time. For James will soon take over the leadership in Jerusalem. Nevertheless, Peter retains for all time the unique greatness and dignity of having been *in the first days of the Church of Jesus Christ* the leader of the Primitive Church and thereby of the entire Church of that time. This must stand first of all as a fixed fact in the redemptive history at the beginning. In agreement with this is the result of the exegesis of Matthew 16:17 ff., according to which Jesus, when he promises to Peter the power of the keys, of binding and loosing, thinks of the lifetime of Peter. What Peter will do belongs to the period of revelation, to the time of the apostles, and so to the foundation. For this reason, his exercise of the power of the keys, the power to bind and loose, is so important.

Only the original Church was led by this apostle, and he led it only in its earliest period. For as soon as the foundation for this leadership is laid, Peter will give it up. Another, James, will take it over in Jerusalem, while Peter will concentrate entirely on his missionary work and will do so, indeed, in a *subordinate role under James*.

This later subordination of Peter under James is a fact important in every respect. It confirms first of all that the leadership of the Church by Peter also has its significance for us chiefly as a *starting point*. James is the actual head of the Church from the moment that Peter dedicates himself completely to missionary work. The memory of that fact was steadily retained in the whole of Jewish Christianity, which took an interest in the ancient traditions. According to Hegesippus, "The brother of the Lord, James, takes over the leader-

17 Ph. Menoud, *L'Eglise et les ministères selon le Nouveau Testament*, 1949, pp. 25 ff., rightly distinguishes between the unique never to be repeated witnessing office of the apostle and his functions that continue to be exercised in the Church. On this see Ed. Schweizer, *Geist und Gemeinde im N. T. und heute* (*Theologische Existenz heute; in press*).

ship of the Church with the apostles."[18] Particularly important is the fact that the *Pseudo-Clementina*, which are friendly to Peter, clearly subordinate Peter to James.[19] Peter has to "give an accounting" to James, "the bishop of the holy Church." To him Peter sends his public addresses,[20] and Clement calls him "Bishop of Bishops," "leader of the holy church of the Hebrews and of the churches *founded everywhere* by God's providence."[21] Clement traces Peter's commission to him back to a commission that James gave to Peter.[22] These late reports thus agree with what we can learn concerning James from the letters of Paul and Book of Acts.[23]

It will not do, however, to make some such objection as that Peter went to Rome just at that time in order to *"transfer"* the primacy from Jerusalem to that place. In reality Peter does not leave Jerusalem in order to transfer the primacy elsewhere; he leaves rather to spread the gospel. But the significant thing, as said, is that in relation to the new leadership at Jerusalem he does not continue in some superior position, as though James were only his substitute, or were only Bishop of the church at Jerusalem, already sunk to the position of a local church. He rather subordinates himself to the authority of James as the central government. In a time, therefore, *when Jerusalem continues to hold the leading position* and all other churches—even those founded by Paul, as the collection shows—still look to Jerusalem, Peter himself is dependent on the new leadership in Jerusalem; in Antioch he has to "fear the people who come from James" (Gal. 2:12)!

---

[18] Eusebius, *Ecclesiastical History*, II, 23, 4. According to Eusebius, *Eccles. Hist.*, II, 23, 1, he receives it "from the Apostles."

[19] See C. Schmidt, *Studien zu den Pseudo-Clementinen*, 1929, pp. 108 ff., 322 ff. O. Cullmann, *Le problème littéraire et historique du roman pseudo-clémentin*, 1930, pp. 250 ff. H. J. Schoeps, *Theologie und Geschichte des Judenchristentums*, 1949, pp. 122 ff.

[20] *Recognitions*, I, 17; *Homilies*, I, 20; *Epistle of Peter* 1.

[21] *Epistle of Clement.* [22] *Recognitions*, I, 17; *Homily*, I, 20.

[23] According to Clement of Alexandria, who likewise stresses particularly Peter's special position among the disciples (*Quis dives salvetur*, ch. 21), Peter, James, and John, after the ascension of Jesus, renounced the pre-eminent position and chose James the Just as the Bishop of Jerusalem. (*Hypotyposes*, in Eusebius, *Eccles. Hist.*, II, 1, 3. See Jerome, *De viribus illustribus*, ch. 2.) Here, however, the fact is obscured that Peter had the leadership in the *earliest* period. So also among recent scholars we find the opinion represented that James had the highest leadership *from the beginning* (see H. Koch, *Cathedri Petri*, 1930, pp. 171 ff.). But to say that is to transfer back into the earliest period a situation that only emerged after some time. Correctly H. v. Campenhausen, *ZKG*, 1951–52, pp. 135 f.

One certainly must not exaggerate the importance of the clash between Peter and Paul at Antioch.[24] Nevertheless, it clearly proves something else that seems to me much more important than the rebuke that Paul gave Peter. It proves that *in relation to James*, whose representatives he fears, Peter does not take a leading role. Therefore one cannot speak of a transfer of the leadership by Peter to another place.

The Roman Catholic tradition asserts that Peter was *bishop also in Antioch*.[25] But Galatians 2:12 proves that even if this is correct, he does not in any case lead the entire Church from this centre. It thus proves that he did not transfer the leadership from Jerusalem to Antioch and then from Antioch to Rome. He exercised leadership over the entire Church only at the beginning of the Jerusalem church and thereby at the beginning of the whole Church. Then he carries out the missionary phase of his apostolic office, and does so in the service of the Jewish Christian church of Jerusalem, whose leadership is in other hands.

As far then as the church leadership by Peter is concerned, we must take seriously the fact that the rock apostle led the *entire* Church only at *one* time. That was when, in the days immediately after Christ's resurrection and in the days of the giving of the Spirit to the Mother Church in Jerusalem, he stood at its head and exercised the work of binding and loosing, the memory of which the narrative about Ananias and Sapphira has preserved (Acts 5:1 ff.). When, therefore, the history of the Primitive Church is invoked to give present significance to the primacy of Peter in relation to leadership over the entire Church, this can happen only in the following way: The Church of today recognizes the redemptive plan of God in the fact that at its initial stage—this really was true at its initial stage—stands the apostle to whom Jesus gave the name "Rock," and to whom he announced that on him he would build the Church.

*   *   *

But in addition to the honoured place in redemptive history that our present Church should give to Peter as the first and indeed the apostolic head of the Church, one may take a further step in applying to the later period Jesus' promise to Peter. We have seen that there must be leadership in the Church, even after the apostolic period when the foundation is laid and down to the present day. In this

24 See above, pp. 46 f.   25 See above, pp. 52 f., and below, p. 33.

respect the leadership of the first head of the Church may be example and pattern, but nothing more than this. The leader or leaders of the future Church are given an example in the leadership that is committed to Peter. But Peter himself cannot so to speak arise in every new generation. Never again will the *kepha*, the rock, himself exercise the leadership. But all leadership of the later Church built upon the apostle should know that the keys are given to it and that it has the task of binding and loosing.

It is a fact that in the beginning a single person stood at the head of the Church as a "rock" among the ' pillars." But it is not necessary to conclude from this that also in all later times a single person must stand at the head of the entire Church. The entire Church is no longer identical, as it was in the first days, with one local church.

The question as to what principle is to determine the leadership of the whole in the following period cannot be answered on the basis of an almost automatically operating mechanism. With a certain blindness to the problems involved, the Roman Catholic Church regards it as self-evident that no other principle can here be considered except that of succession tied to a specific local church. It claims as decisive—in connection with its view that Matthew 16:17 ff. has in mind successors—first, the fact that Peter was bishop of a specific church, that is, Rome, and second, that this very church has actually "led" in the history of the Church.

If, in accord with all that has been said, the leadership of the Church by Peter is to be considered only as a pattern, this means that such an exclusive application to the Roman bishops is really impossible from the start. If in what follows we nevertheless examine the different arguments with which this limitation is defended, we do so only to show that on the one hand the arguments lack any foundation in the history of the historical Peter, and on the other hand that they cannot stand theologically without this foundation.

We first of all must return to the principle of apostolic succession, of which we already have spoken in connection with Peter's role as the rock. In doing so, we now have to focus particularly on the relation of the succession principle to Rome as the seat of the *leadership of the entire Church*. We have seen[26] that the idea of succession in its later form cannot be derived from Matthew 16:17 ff., even if we add to it the New Testament passages that speak of the appointment of local church heads by the apostles. Completely lacking in Matthew 16:17 ff., however, is any reference to the idea that a

[26] See above, pp. 207 ff., 219 f.

specific local church would have to carry the succession in the leader-ship of the *entire Church*. This, to be sure, is admitted by the defenders of the Roman claim to primacy, and they never support their argu-ment upon this saying alone, without adding those other theological considerations of which we shall speak later. But we still must ask here whether, even if one does not hold the Scripture alone to be authoritative, it is not at least noteworthy that in the entire apostolic record, that is, the entire New Testament, not a single passage so much as mentions the name of Rome *in connection with Peter*, and therefore it is not only in Matthew 16:17 ff. that reference to the limitation to a particular local church is completely lacking. This latter fact should cause serious thought when this very saying of Matthew 16:17 ff. is limited to the Bishops of Rome and when this saying, whatever the decisive additional arguments may be, is always regarded as at least the starting-point for the proof that is supposed to justify a development of such tremendous scope.

From the historical point of view, as we have seen, we can indeed explain the *silence* of the entire New Testament concerning any relation of Peter to Rome. *Theologically*, however, we hardly can do so *if* this relation is to justify the exclusive claim that the Roman Bishops make to this saying of Jesus.[27] In our historical study we have concluded, on the basis of all sorts of indirect arguments, that Peter very probably came to Rome at the end of his life and there became a martyr. But does this suffice as the starting-point for an assertion that takes so uniquely important a theological role in the picture of redemptive history, the assertion, that is, that only *this* church that is linked with the chain of Roman bishops may appeal to Peter and that it is the only "catholic and apostolic Church"? In particular, should not the silence of the Scripture concerning Peter's episcopal office in Rome stimulate us to consider whether it is really true that for all time to come the Church is to be led by this episcopal see?

We now go on, however, beyond the Scriptural witness. What is the truth in general concerning the presupposition, assumed with-out any discussion, that the leadership of the entire Church in the post-apostolic period is to be determined from one and the same

[27] M. Meinertz, *Theologie des Neuen Testaments*, Vol. I, 1950, p. 79, concedes: "With regard to the succession to Peter, there naturally is still no supporting proof for that in the New Testament." My opposition to this statement is directly against the word "naturally." For this does not seem to me at all natural, if salvation is really to depend on this succession.

episcopal see by the chain of succession of the occupants of this see? Of certain *individual churches* we can say that by instituting local church heads [28] the apostles, in their unique capacity as apostles, thus created the first bishops of these churches. This, to be sure, says nothing at all as to who after them is to choose the subsequent bishops.[29]

The apostle Peter, on the other hand, never established a bishop as the leader of the *entire Church*, and above all he himself never gave distinction to any Church *except Jerusalem* as the seat of his own leadership of the entire Church. *For even if, after his leadership of the Jerusalem church, he temporarily as apostolic missionary was the leader of still other churches, yet so much at least is definite, that when he was there he was only the leader of those single churches, and in no case leader of the entire Church. Peter was the leader of the entire Church only at Jerusalem.*

Thus if *one* church wished to claim a special position in this respect and if the geographical principle as such were not completely arbitrary, it could only be the church of Jerusalem. In the New Testament this is the only church of which we hear that Peter stood at its head. Of other episcopates of Peter we know nothing certain. Concerning Antioch, indeed, as we shall see—and we shall return to this point—there is a tradition, first appearing in the course of the second century, according to which Peter was its bishop. The assertion that he was Bishop of Rome we first find at a much later time. From the second half of the second century we do possess texts that mention the apostolic *foundation* of Rome, and at this time, which is indeed rather late, this foundation is traced back to *Peter and Paul*, an assertion that cannot be supported historically.[30] Even here, however, nothing is said as yet of an episcopal office of Peter. But even if Peter did occupy in Rome an episcopal position, this could hold good at the most for the *local* church in Rome, for it is a fixed fact that at that time, in the sixth decade of the first century, Rome still played no leading role in the Church at large, and Peter did not rule the entire Church from Rome. In our present discussion, however, we are concerned with the question as to how the succession was determined, and this concerns the leadership of the *Church at large*. In that

[28] See above, pp. 219 f.

[29] Ed. Schweizer, *Das Leben des Herrn in der Gemeinde und ihren Diensten*, 1946, pp. 75 f., emphasizes here that even this installation by the apostles in the Pastoral Epistles did not take place without the presence of the congregation, and in *Geist und Gemeinde im N. T. und heute* (in press) he stresses that in I Tim. 1:18 the installation occurs only after "preceding prophetic instruction."

[30] See above, pp. 116 f., 45, 79 f.

connection we only wish to show, in an anticipatory way, that not only in the Scriptures, but also *in the history of Primitive Christianity, there is no trace at all* that the succession to Peter in the leadership at large was to be determined by the fact that he was bishop in this or that city. In the life of Peter there is no starting-point for a *chain of succession* in the leadership of the Church at large.

The fact that Peter most probably suffered his martyrdom in Rome cannot give to this church the dignity that belongs solely to the Mother Church in Jerusalem, the dignity of having once represented the entire Church and of having been led as such by the apostle Peter *in the apostolic period of revelation.*

But even Jerusalem naturally is not to be considered as permanent bearer of succession in the universal leadership of the Church. The authority of James, moreover, is not derived from Peter but from his direct relations to Jesus. He probably was regarded as an apostle who was instituted as such by Jesus himself. This is the view of Paul,[31] and the later tradition also was still able to report that he was appointed bishop by Jesus himself.[32] A chain of succession in the leadership of the *entire Church*, going back to Peter and to Matthew 16:17 ff., thus does not exist. Concerning Clement of Rome, who is so eagerly designated as the Roman Pope appointed by Peter, it cannot be proved from reliable sources either that he received his office from Peter or that he was the leader of the Church at large; to exhort a divided sister church to harmony in a letter is not enough to establish one as the pope. Peter at the beginning led the entire Church in Jerusalem. But which bishop after him is to play the leading role in each case cannot be decided by the principle of a succession determined according to the location of the bishop's seat. There is no succession that leads from Jerusalem to another city. This must be stated as a basic proposition.

---

[31] This conclusion, moreover, seems to follow from the fact that Paul reckons him among the "pillars" (Gal. 2:9), and especially from Gal. 1:19 (ἕτερον δὲ τῶν ἀποστόλων οὐκ εἶδον εἰ μὴ Ἰάκωβον: "but other of the Apostles I did not see except Peter"). H. Koch, however, in "Zur Jakobus-frage, Gal. 1, 19" (*ZNW*, 1934, pp. 264 ff.), thinks he can explain the passage otherwise: Paul saw no other apostle but Cephas, but did indeed see James. He is regarded as an apostle also by K. Holl, "Der Kirchenbegriff des Paulus, in seinem Verhältnis zu dem der Urgemeinde" (*Gesammelte Aufsätze*, Vol. II, p. 49); H. v. Campenhausen, *ZKG*, 1950-51, p. 137.

[32] According to the Pseudo-Clementine Epistle of Peter to James, V, and *Recognitions*, I, 43, James was installed by the Lord; so also according to Epiphanius, *Heresies*, 78, 7, and Chrysostom, in *Homily on First Corinthians*, 38, 5.

Moreover, there are other churches besides Jerusalem and Rome,[33] above all *Antioch*, which regard Peter as their first bishop. We have seen[34] that the tradition of the episcopate at Antioch is exceedingly hard to defend on historical grounds, even if the letters of Ignatius suggest the assumption that the monarchical episcopate developed relatively early at Antioch. It must nevertheless be emphasized that this tradition is much older and better attested than is that of the Roman episcopate. In the time of Peter the Roman church had no more significance, and perhaps even less, than did the one at Antioch. They were both local churches, and as such they were led by Peter, if the traditions in question are correct.

If one were determined to maintain the completely arbitrary principle according to which Peter's episcopal office in a church could aid in giving to its later bishops the exclusive claim to Matthew 16:17 ff., then on this basis Antioch could establish a greater claim to the primacy than Rome. Nevertheless, we have already mentioned and shall again speak of the fact that according to the judgment of most Roman Catholic theologians, even the episcopate of Peter is by no means sufficient of itself. Just as little does the interpretation of Matthew 16:18 suffice. Rather, to both arguments there must be added as the decisive criterion of the primacy the effective role that a church has played and plays in the further history. Since, however, the episcopate of the apostle and the relation of Jerusalem to Rome are regularly cited as arguments in connection with the history of Peter, we had to examine this question on all sides. We come to the conclusion: There is no basis whatever in any ancient text for the assertion that Rome inherited the legal succession from Jerusalem. Even if Antioch should be inserted as an intermediate stage, such a theory would not be any better supported. *For Peter ruled the Church at large in that period neither from Antioch nor from Rome, but only in Jerusalem and for a short time.* The history of Primitive Christianity gives no warrant of any kind for the assumption that Peter came to Rome to transfer the primacy to that place.

There are some well-known Roman Catholic theologians who, in view of the lack of any basis for such an assertion, do not make the primacy of Rome depend at all on the *stay of Peter in Rome*. Indeed, they believe that in their theological statement they can actually in

---

[33] The Pseudo-Clementine *Homily* 3, 53, presupposes that there is in Caesarea a *Cathedra Petri* (an episcopal "chair of Peter").

[34] See above, pp. 52 f.

principle forgo this basis, since it is only *the fact* that the Bishops of
Rome are successors of Peter—not the How—that is decisive, and
since the transfer of the succession to Peter to the Bishops of Rome
is even conceivable without Peter himself having been in the city
of this later episcopal see.[35] This view completely surrenders the
appeal to the history of the historical Peter. However, the Roman
Catholic teaching seems not completely consistent on this point, and
one can ask whether this surrender can really be reconciled with the
wording of the Vatican pronouncement.[36]

But in any case it is true that the stay of Peter in Rome has never
been the only decisive argument for the primacy of Rome. All
Roman Catholic theologians argue rather that later, from the beginning of the second century on, *Rome effectively played an outstanding
and leading role in the Christendom of that time.* One thus can say, they
contend, that the historical *development of church history* proves that
after the destruction of Jerusalem the primacy passed from Jerusalem
to Rome.

To this, however, it must be replied that from the effective historical role which a church plays in *post-apostolic times* no divine right
can be derived for *all* time if, as we have just established, this role
lacks any connection with the Apostolic Age. It will not do to appeal to

---

[35] See R. Graber, *Petrus der Fels,* 1949, p. 37, and Ch. Journet, *L'Eglise du verbe
incarné,* 1941, pp. 522 ff. R. Graber cites Dunin-Borkowski, "Die Kirche als
Stiftung Jesu" (*Religion, Christentum und Kirche,* 1923, pp. 45 f.): "It is a widespread error that the Catholic apologetic must necessarily make the papacy, as
the continuation of the rule of Peter, dependent on the stay of the Prince of
Apostles in Rome and on his episcopal office there. This is not the case. Certainly
one can give such a proof, but it is by no means necessary. . . . As soon as it . . .
is established that Christ not merely fixed the primacy of Saint Peter but spoke
of this primacy as a lasting institution, there is lacking only the proof that the
Roman bishops alone claimed the special rights of the Rock man." Further,
L. Kösters, *War Petrus in Rom?,* 1938, pp. 50 f.: "It would be entirely conceivable
that Peter had appointed the chief of the Roman Church as his successor in
the primacy received from Christ, even if he himself had never been in
Rome."

[36] *Vaticanum,* fourth session, July 18, 1870, ch. 2: . . . *qui* (Peter) *ad hoc usque tempus
et semper in suis successoribus episcopis sanctae Romanae Sedis, ab ipso fundatae eiusque
consecratae sanguine, vivit et praesidet et iudicium exercet* ("who even unto this time
and always lives and governs and exercises judgment in his successors, the bishops
of the holy Roman see, *which was founded by him and consecrated by his blood*").
From the significance, moreover, which is attached in Roman circles to the discovery of the grave of Peter, it seems proved that the opinion held by those
named in the preceding footnote and by many eminent Roman Catholic
theologians is not generally shared.

tradition as a source of revelation to justify this flight into later history; the sole justification for the Roman Catholic tradition rests on this very assertion of the primacy of Rome. It simply is not true that every development in church history is to be accepted without question as legitimate tradition. And one cannot prove the *foundation* of the Roman tradition by use of this tradition itself. The problem is to show that the tradition of the primacy of Rome, on which all remaining Roman Catholic tradition depends, is valid.

The flight into later history could only assure the permanent primacy to a certain episcopal see if, in the first place, Matthew 16:17 ff. justified us in seeking successors in the sense of a tie with one church, and if, secondly, the line could be drawn backwards from the later effectively exercised primacy of one church to the apostolic period and so to the historical Peter. *Neither of these things, however, is true.* That being the case, the effective role that the Roman Church has played and now plays does not prove that it has to exercise *the same* primacy that Peter exercised in Jerusalem after it was promised to him by Jesus.

The Roman church, it is true, gradually attained a pre-eminent position in the course of the second and third centuries. No historian or theologian will dispute this. The question, however, is whether the primacy promised to Peter in Matthew 16:17 ff. and actually exercised by him in Jerusalem in the beginning is therefore to be transferred exclusively to the Bishops of the Roman church. That a church occupies a pre-eminent position still does not prove that it stands in such a relation to Matthew 16:17 ff. as to give it a divine right for all time to come. The secular historian, indeed, explains that pre-eminent position by the purely "immanent" consideration that Rome was the chief city of the Roman Empire, so that the Christian church located there naturally and necessarily attained a special dignity. This reason certainly did play a strongly contributory role. In addition, the theologian will discover factors within the Church, grounded in the situation of that time, and with Ignatius of Antioch he may recognize that the Roman church of that time has also a "pre-eminence in love."[37] But even if we wish to speak here of a divinely intended *development* in the history of the Church of Christ, it does not follow from this that this historical role is a sign that it is a divinely intended *norm* for the leadership of the Church of all time. For we say once more: Matthew 16:17 ff. does not say a word as to how the succession to Peter in the leadership of the

[37] Ignatius, *To the Romans* 1:1: προκαθημένη τῆς ἀγάπης.

Church at large is to be determined. It is arbitrary to take into account *a priori* only this *one* possibility that one church, which—not in the apostolic period of revelation, but later—stands out among the other churches, must *for ever* furnish the successor of Peter. The fact that the bishops of this church in later times *make the claim* that they alone are intended in the promise of Jesus in Matthew 16:17 ff. cannot prove the legitimacy of this claim.

Moreover, *until the beginning of the third century* it never occurred to a single Bishop of Rome to refer the saying in Matthew 16:17 ff. to himself in the sense of the leadership of the entire Church. It was probably Callistus (217–222), though according to others it was actually Stephanus (254–257),[38] who first applied to himself the words "You are Peter," and this did not pass without contradiction. Tertullian protests that he intends to refer the saying only to the person of Peter and not to the bishops at all; Cyprian, on the contrary, refers it to *all* later bishops and not to the Bishop of Rome alone.[39] The appeal that the Roman Bishops made to Matthew 16:17 ff., moreover, fell far short of general acceptance even in the third century, and only much later does the exclusive reference to Rome become a self-evident axiom.

Irenaeus, to be sure, speaks even in the second century of the oft cited "more powerful and pre-eminent position of Rome" (*potentior principalitas*).[40] To support this, however, he does not appeal to Matthew 16:17 ff.[41] Rather, in accordance with the tradition principle of the rabbis and the philosophical schools, which Hegesippus, following the Gnostics, seems to have naturalized in the ancient Church,[42] he points to the particularly well-preserved apostolic tradition; this is connected only with the *foundation* of the Roman church, and indeed by both Peter *and* Paul; it is not connected with the primacy of Peter.

Moreover, the entire controversy as to whether in Rome appeal was first made to Matthew 16:17 ff. at a somewhat earlier or later

---

[38] So, for example, recently also K. Heussi. See above, p. 160, note 8.

[39] See E. Caspar, *Geschichte des Papsttums von den Anfängen bis zur Höhe der Weltherrschaft*, Vol. I, 1938. On this subject, see above, pp. 160 f.

[40] *Against Heresies*, III, 3, 2.

[41] P. Batiffol, "Cathedra Petri" (*Etudes d'Histoire ancienne*, 1938, p. 14), thinks that in the word *principalitas*, which is to be understood chronologically, the "You are Peter" is implied. His interpretation, however, does not seem to me to be sufficiently grounded.

[42] H. von Campenhausen, *Lehrerreihen und Bischofreihen im 2. Jahrhundert. In Memoriam Ernst Lohmeyer*, 1951, pp. 240 ff.

time does not have for our question as much significance as is attached to it.[43] In any case, more than one hundred years passed before the primacy of Rome was connected with the promise of Jesus to Peter. The fact that, in a time when the Roman church already had a certain consciousness of pre-eminence, it still did not justify its consciousness by reference to Matthew 16:17 ff., should certainly cause one to think. There is, indeed, a chain of succession of Roman bishops, which may have its value for the Roman church. *There is no chain of succession of leaders of the Church at large*, even though the local Roman chain was later made for this purpose. In the period after James there is a great gap. In the hortatory writing of Clement which is called the First Epistle of Clement, a bishop speaks in a brotherly way to a sister church, just as also happened elsewhere without any conclusion being drawn that such an act justifies a claim to primacy.

It is arguing in a circle, a *petitio principii*, to assert that since on the one hand the promise of Jesus to Peter exists, and on the other hand the fact exists that Rome exercised a primacy from a relatively early date, we therefore must conclude that this primacy rests on that promise, in such a way that it is the norm for all time. That this relation exists between Matthew 16:17 ff. and the pre-eminent position that Rome later occupied is precisely the thing it is necessary to prove.

In answer to these and other objections the Roman Catholic theologians are accustomed to point out that the promise to Peter had to become *visible* in history, since the Church is a visible Church and continues on earth the work of Christ. The idea of the continuation of the work of Christ in the visible earthly Church I affirm, since I find it especially in the entire Gospel of John as a central declaration. Therefore, as far as I am concerned—I do not speak here at all in the name of official "Protestant theology"—it is not true that on this point the common basis for discussion is lacking. It should be sufficiently clear from my previous writings that I really take seriously the fact that the present in which we stand, the period of the Church, belongs in the redemptive history; this history, to be sure, must continually find its norm in the apostolic period of revelation as the central point of time. The promise of Jesus to Peter was visibly fulfilled in Jerusalem in the days following the resurrection. But from this it does not result that the Roman claim to be henceforth the only

[43] It was chiefly A. Harnack, P. Batiffol, H. Koch, and E. Caspar who took part in this controversy.

legitimate visible Church is justified on the ground that Rome actually occupied a pre-eminent position from a certain time on. It should not be disputed that this pre-eminent position has some significance for the development of the gospel line of redemptive history in the period of the Church. But this position does not necessarily rest upon the promise of Jesus to Peter, in the sense that therefore for all time to come only the occupant of this episcopal see can be the leader of the true Church; such a conclusion does not follow from faith in the visibility of the Church in which Christ continues his work.

There have been and there are today, outside of the Roman Church, visible churches in other centres also, and it would be arguing again in a circle to reply that such a church is not a real church because it does not stand in succession to Peter. From Matthew 16:17 ff. and the rest of the New Testament come other criteria, in addition to the narrow criterion connected with an episcopal see, which permit us to recognize that Church *which Christ builds upon Peter the Rock*. We cannot discuss here the entire involved question of the criterion of the Church and of tradition.[44] But it should be emphasized that it is arbitrary to assert that Christ built his Church upon Peter only at the place where, at a certain date, this or that church was the leader of Christendom.

Developments of the *post-apostolic* period of church history, important as they may be for the development of redemptive history in the period of the Church, cannot give a permanent and exclusively *normative* position to any of those leading places. For one thing, the intent of Jesus leaves us no possibility of understanding Matthew 16:17 ff. in the sense of a succession determined by an episcopal see. Moreover, the history of Peter knows nothing of a transfer of the ruling seat (*cathedra*) of the Church at large from Jerusalem to another city. In the apostolic period Rome was not the centre of the Church at large. There at the midpoint of the times, the point decisive for the Christian, no hint is anywhere given that the Roman or any other bishop's seat is in the future to be the permanent centre of the Church at large. In addition to Rome there were, in the post-apostolic period as previously, other centres of the visible Church; there are now other centres and there probably will be still others, whether their name is Antioch, Corinth or Ephesus, Alexandria or Constantinople, Wittenberg, Canterbury or Geneva, Stockholm or Amsterdam.

The actual power that these centres have exercised or now exercise

44 I hope to do this in another place.

proves nothing as to the legality of any claim they may make that they *alone* stand in succession to the first leader, Peter, whom Christ established over the Church at large. Even the fact that only one of these outstanding places has asserted and now asserts such a claim proves nothing.

The decision as to who at each time is to stand at the head of the entire Church cannot be made from the standpoint of an episcopal see fixed once for all. The apostolic quality, the connection with Peter, can be preserved in another way. Neither from Scripture nor from the history of the ancient Church can a divine right for the primacy of Rome be derived.

For this reason even the Roman Catholic Church appeals to a dogmatic utterance according to which the Bishops of Rome are the sole successors of Peter.[45] We do not need to return again to the question how far this utterance lacks basis either in Scripture or in the most ancient tradition. We should, however, ask this question: Is it not another and final begging of the question, *a petitio principii*, when this very assertion, which is so notably basic for the Roman claim, is founded only upon later dogmas? For the exclusive claim to *proclaim dogmas through the possession of sole apostolic authority* is nevertheless dependent on this very dogma of the legal succession to Peter. What is involved here is not just another dogma; it is that dogma that is meant to justify completely the exclusive right of the Roman Catholic Church to promulgate dogmas. In such a situation, can every other basis be lacking, above all the witness of Scripture, which Rome does not mention at all in connection with Peter? Can ancient tradition also be lacking? It knows nothing of a government of the Church at large from Rome by Peter, and also knows nothing of a transfer of his succession to the Roman Bishops.

We reach the following conclusion of these doctrinal and theological discussions:

In so far as Peter is the rock, he is such in the temporal sense of laying the foundation as an apostle. In every generation Christ intends to build his Church on the foundation of the apostles, and among them Peter is the most important.

In so far as he is the leader of the Primitive Church in Jerusalem, this also has chiefly temporal significance, and in this respect his bearing

---

[45] See the sentence from the *Vaticanum* cited above in note 36. The most thorough presentation of the Roman Catholic doctrine seems to me to be offered by the already mentioned work of Ch. Journet, *L'Eglise du verbe incarné*, 1941. See, especially, pp. 522 ff.

for the redemptive history of all later time consists in the fact that he held the leadership of the original Church.

If we wish to derive further from the saying that after Peter also there must be in the Church a universal leadership that administers the keys, the power to bind and loose, this cannot take place in the sense of a limitation to the future occupants of one episcopal see. This principle of succession cannot be justified either from Scripture or from the history of the ancient Church. In reality the leadership of the Church at large is not to be determined by succession in the sense of a link with one episcopal see. The significance of individual churches for the Church at large comes and goes. But the rock, the foundation for all churches of all times, remains the historical Peter. At that time he was especially chosen by Jesus from among the Twelve; he was given special distinction as a witness of Jesus' life and death and as the first witness of his resurrection. On him Christ, who is himself the cornerstone, will keep building his Church as long as there is such a Church on earth.

INDEX OF
AUTHORS CITED

239

INDEX OF
BIBLICAL PASSAGES